Purity

ALSO BY JONATHAN FRANZEN

NOVELS

Freedom
The Corrections
Strong Motion
The Twenty-Seventh City

NONFICTION

Farther Away
The Discomfort Zone
How to Be Alone

TRANSLATION

The Kraus Project (Karl Kraus)
Spring Awakening (Frank Wedekind)

Purity

Jonathan Franzen

PICADOR   FARRAR, STRAUS AND GIROUX   NEW YORK

NOTE: If you purchased this book without a cover you should be aware that this book is stolen property. It was reported as "unsold and destroyed" to the publisher, and neither the author nor the publisher has received any payment for this "stripped book."

This is a work of fiction. All of the characters, organizations, and events portrayed in this novel are either products of the author's imagination or are used fictitiously.

PURITY. Copyright © 2015 by Jonathan Franzen. All rights reserved. Printed in the United States of America. For information, address Picador, 175 Fifth Avenue, New York, N.Y. 10010.

picadorusa.com • picadorbookroom.tumblr.com
twitter.com/picadorusa • facebook.com/picadorusa

Picador® is a U.S. registered trademark and is used by Farrar, Straus and Giroux under license from Pan Books Limited.

For book club information, please visit facebook.com/picadorbookclub or e-mail marketing@picadorusa.com.

Design by Abby Kagan

The Library of Congress has catalogued the Farrar, Straus and Giroux edition as follows:

Franzen, Jonathan.
    Purity : a novel / Jonathan Franzen. — First edition.
        p. cm.
    ISBN 978-0-374023921-3 (hardcover) — ISBN 978-0-374-71074-3 (e-book)
    I. Title.
    PS3556.R352 P87 2015
    813'.54—dc23   2015010131

Picador International Mass Market ISBN 978-1-250-11618-5

Our books may be purchased in bulk for promotional, educational, or business use. Please contact your local bookseller or the Macmillan Corporate and Premium Sales Department at 1-800-221-7945, extension 5442, or by e-mail at MacmillanSpecialMarkets@macmillan.com.

First published by Farrar, Straus and Giroux

First Picador International Mass Market Edition: August 2016

10 9 8 7 6 5 4 3 2 1

for Elisabeth Robinson

. . . Die stets das Böse will und stets das Gute schafft

Purity
in Oakland

Oh pussycat, I'm so glad to hear your voice," the girl's mother said on the telephone. "My body is betraying me again. Sometimes I think my life is nothing but one long process of bodily betrayal."

"Isn't that everybody's life?" the girl, Pip, said. She'd taken to calling her mother midway through her lunch break at Renewable Solutions. It brought her some relief from the feeling that she wasn't suited for her job, that she had a job that nobody could be suited for, or that she was a person unsuited for any kind of job; and then, after twenty minutes, she could honestly say that she needed to get back to work.

"My left eyelid is drooping," her mother explained. "It's like there's a weight on it that's pulling it down, like a tiny fisherman's sinker or something."

"Right now?"

"Off and on. I'm wondering if it might be Bell's palsy."

"Whatever Bell's palsy is, I'm sure you don't have it."

"If you don't even know what it is, pussycat, how can you be so sure?"

"I don't know—because you didn't have Graves' disease? Hyperthyroidism? Melanoma?"

It wasn't as if Pip felt good about making fun of her mother. But their dealings were all tainted by *moral hazard*, a useful phrase she'd learned in college economics.

She was like a bank too big in her mother's economy to fail, an employee too indispensable to be fired for bad attitude. Some of her friends in Oakland also had problematic parents, but they still managed to speak to them daily without undue weirdnesses transpiring, because even the most problematic of them had resources that consisted of more than just their single offspring. Pip was it, as far as her own mother was concerned.

"Well, I don't think I can go to work today," her mother said. "My Endeavor is the only thing that makes that job survivable, and I can't connect with the Endeavor when there's an invisible *fisherman's sinker* pulling on my eyelid."

"Mom, you can't call in sick again. It's not even July. What if you get the actual flu or something?"

"And meanwhile everybody's wondering what this old woman with half her face drooping onto her shoulder is doing bagging their groceries. You have no idea how I envy you your cubicle. The invisibility of it."

"Let's not romanticize the cubicle," Pip said.

"This is the terrible thing about bodies. They're so *visible*, so *visible*."

Pip's mother, though chronically depressed, wasn't crazy. She'd managed to hold on to her checkout-clerk job at the New Leaf Community Market in Felton for more than ten years, and as soon as Pip relinquished her own way of thinking and submitted to her mother's she could track what she was saying perfectly well. The only decoration on the gray segments of her cubicle was a bumper sticker, AT LEAST THE WAR ON THE ENVIRONMENT IS GOING WELL. Her colleagues' cubicles were covered with photos and clippings, but Pip herself understood the attraction of invisibility. Also, she expected to be fired any month now, so why settle in.

"Have you given any thought to how you want to not-celebrate your not-birthday?" she asked her mother.

"Frankly, I'd like to stay in bed all day with the covers over my head. I don't need a not-birthday to remind me I'm getting older. My eyelid is doing a very good job of that already."

"Why don't I make you a cake and I'll come down and we can eat it. You sound sort of more depressed than usual."

"I'm not depressed when I see you."

"Ha, too bad I'm not available in pill form. Could you handle a cake made with stevia?"

"I don't know. Stevia does something funny to the chemistry of my mouth. There's no fooling a taste bud, in my experience."

"Sugar has an aftertaste, too," Pip said, although she knew that argument was futile.

"Sugar has a *sour* aftertaste that the taste bud has no problem with, because it's built to report sourness without dwelling on it. The taste bud doesn't have to spend five hours registering strangeness, strangeness! Which was what happened to me the one time I drank a stevia drink."

"But I'm saying the sourness does linger."

"There's something very wrong when a taste bud is still reporting strangeness five hours after you had a sweetened drink. Do you know that if you smoke crystal meth even once, your entire brain chemistry is altered for the rest of your life? That's what stevia tastes like to me."

"I'm not sitting here puffing on a meth stem, if that's what you're trying to say."

"I'm saying I don't need a cake."

"No, I'll find a different kind of cake. I'm sorry I suggested a kind that's *poison* to you."

"I didn't say it was poison. It's simply that stevia does something funny—"

"To your mouth chemistry, yeah."

"Pussycat, I'll eat whatever kind of cake you bring me, refined sugar won't kill me, I didn't mean to upset you. Sweetheart, please."

No phone call was complete before each had made the other wretched. The problem, as Pip saw it—the essence of the handicap she lived with; the presumable cause of her inability to be effective at anything—was that she loved her mother. Pitied her; suffered with her; warmed to the sound of her voice; felt an unsettling kind of nonsexual attraction to her body; was solicitous even of her mouth chemistry; wished her greater happiness; hated upsetting her; found her dear. This was the massive block of granite at the center of her life, the source of all the anger and sarcasm that she directed not only at her mother but, more and more self-defeatingly of late, at less appropriate objects. When Pip got angry, it wasn't really at her mother but at the granite block.

She'd been eight or nine when it occurred to her to ask why her birthday was the only one celebrated in their little cabin, in the redwoods outside Felton. Her mother had replied that she didn't have a birthday; the only one that mattered to her was Pip's. But Pip had pestered her until she agreed to celebrate the summer solstice with a cake that they would call not-birthday. This had then raised the question of her mother's age, which she'd refused to divulge, saying only, with a smile suitable to the posing of a koan, "I'm old enough to be your mother."

"No, but how old are you *really*?"

"Look at my hands," her mother had said. "If you practice, you can learn to tell a woman's age by her hands."

And so—for the first time, it seemed—Pip had looked at her mother's hands. The skin on the back of them wasn't pink and opaque like her own skin. It was as if the bones and veins were working their way to the surface; as if the

skin were water receding to expose shapes at the bottom
of a harbor. Although her hair was thick and very long,
there were dry-looking strands of gray in it, and the skin
at the base of her throat was like a peach a day past ripe.
That night, Pip lay awake in bed and worried that her
mother might die soon. It was her first premonition of the
granite block.

She'd since come fervently to wish that her mother had
a man in her life, or really just one other person of any
description, to love her. Potential candidates over the years
had included their next-door neighbor Linda, who was
likewise a single mom and likewise a student of Sanskrit,
and the New Leaf butcher, Ernie, who was likewise a
vegan, and the pediatrician Vanessa Tong, whose powerful crush on Pip's mother had taken the form of trying to
interest her in birdwatching, and the mountain-bearded
handyman Sonny, for whom no maintenance job was too
small to occasion a discourse on ancient Pueblo ways of
being. All these good-hearted San Lorenzo Valley types
had glimpsed in Pip's mother what Pip herself, in her early
teens, had seen and felt proud of: an ineffable sort of greatness. You didn't have to write to be a poet, you didn't have
to create things to be an artist. Her mother's spiritual
Endeavor was itself a kind of art—an art of invisibility.
There was never a television in their cabin and no computer before Pip turned twelve; her mother's main source
of news was the *Santa Cruz Sentinel*, which she read for
the small daily pleasure of being appalled by the world.
In itself, this was not so uncommon in the Valley. The
trouble was that Pip's mother herself exuded a shy belief in her greatness, or at least carried herself as if she'd
once been great, back in a pre-Pip past that she categori-
cally refused to talk about. She wasn't so much offended
as mortified that their neighbor Linda could compare her
frog-catching, mouth-breathing son, Damian, to her own

singular and perfect Pip. She imagined that the butcher would be permanently shattered if she told him that he smelled to her like meat, even after a shower; she made herself miserable dodging Vanessa Tong's invitations rather than just admit she was afraid of birds; and whenever Sonny's high-clearance pickup rolled into their driveway she made Pip go to the door while she fled out the back way and into the redwoods. What gave her the luxury of being impossibly choosy was Pip. Over and over, she'd made it clear: Pip was the only person who passed muster, the only person *she* loved.

This all became a source of searing embarrassment, of course, when Pip hit adolescence. And by then she was too busy hating and punishing her mother to clock the damage that her mother's unworldliness was doing to her own life prospects. Nobody was there to tell her that it might not be the best idea, if she wanted to set about doing good in the world, to graduate from college with $130,000 in student debt. Nobody had warned her that the figure to pay attention to when she was being interviewed by Igor, the head of consumer outreach at Renewable Solutions, was not the "thirty or forty thousand dollars" in commissions that he foresaw her earning in her very first year but the $21,000 base salary he was offering, or that a salesman as persuasive as Igor might also be skilled at selling shit jobs to unsuspecting twenty-one-year-olds.

"About the weekend," Pip said in a hard voice. "I have to warn you that I want to talk about something you don't like to talk about."

Her mother gave a little laugh intended to be winsome, to signal defenselessness. "There's only one thing I don't like to talk about with you."

"Well, and that is exactly the thing I want to talk about. So just be warned."

Her mother said nothing to this. Down in Felton, the

fog would have burned off by now, the fog that her mother was daily sorry to see go, because it revealed a bright world to which she preferred not to belong. She practiced her Endeavor best in the safety of gray morning. Now there would be sunlight, greened and goldened by filtration through the redwoods' tiny needles, summer heat stealing through the sleeping porch's screened windows and over the bed that Pip had claimed as a privacy-craving teenager, relegating her mother to a cot in the main room until she left for college and her mother took it back. She was probably on the bed practicing her Endeavor right now. If so, she wouldn't speak again until spoken to; she would be all breathing.

"This isn't personal," Pip said. "I'm not going anywhere. But I need money, and you don't have any, and I don't have any, and there's only one place I can think to get it. There's only one person who even theoretically *owes* me. So we're going to talk about it."

"Pussycat," her mother said sadly, "you know I won't do that. I'm sorry you need money, but this isn't a matter of what I like or don't like. It's a matter of can or can't. And I can't, so we'll have to think of something else for you."

Pip frowned. Every so often, she felt the need to strain against the circumstantial straitjacket in which she'd found herself two years earlier, to see if there might be a little new give in its sleeves. And, every time, she found it exactly as tight as before. Still $130,000 in debt, still her mother's sole comfort. It was kind of remarkable how instantly and totally she'd been trapped the minute her four years of college freedom ended; it would have depressed her, had she been able to afford being depressed.

"OK, I'm going to hang up now," she said into the phone. "You get yourself ready for work. Your eye's probably just bothering you because you're not sleeping enough. It happens to me sometimes when I don't sleep."

"Really?" her mother said eagerly. "You get this, too?"

Although Pip knew that it would prolong the call, and possibly entail extending the discussion to genetically heritable diseases, and certainly require copious fibbing on her part, she decided that her mother was better off thinking about insomnia than about Bell's palsy, if only because, as Pip had been pointing out to her for years, to no avail, there were actual medications she could take for her insomnia. But the result was that when Igor stuck his head in Pip's cubicle, at 1:22, she was still on the phone.

"Mom, sorry, gotta go right now, good-bye," she said, and hung up.

Igor was Gazing at her. He was a blond Russian, strokably bearded, unfairly handsome, and to Pip the only conceivable reason he hadn't fired her was that he enjoyed thinking about fucking her, and yet she was sure that, if it ever came to that, she would end up humiliated in no time flat, because he was not only handsome but rather handsomely paid, while she was a girl with nothing but problems. She was sure that he must know this, too.

"I'm *sorry*," she said to him. "I'm sorry I went seven minutes over. My mom had a medical issue." She thought about this. "Actually, cancel that, I'm not sorry. What are the chances of me getting a positive response in any given seven-minute period?"

"Did I look censorious?" Igor said, batting his eyelashes.

"Well, why are you sticking your head in? Why are you staring at me?"

"I thought you might like to play Twenty Questions."

"I think not."

"You try to guess what I want from you, and I'll confine my answers to an innocuous yes or no. Let the record show: only yeses, only nos."

"Do you want to get sued for sexual harassment?"

Igor laughed, delighted with himself. "That's a no! Now you have nineteen questions."

"I'm not kidding about the lawsuit. I have a law-school friend who says it's enough that you create an atmosphere."

"That's not a question."

"How can I explain to you how not funny to me this is?"

"Yes–no questions only, please."

"Jesus Christ. Go away."

"Would you rather talk about your May performance?"

"Go away! I'm getting on the phone right now."

When Igor was gone, she brought up her call sheet on her computer, glanced at it with distaste, and minimized it again. In four of the twenty-two months she'd worked for Renewable Solutions, she'd succeeded in being only next-to-last, not last, on the whiteboard where her and her associates' "outreach points" were tallied. Perhaps not coincidentally, four out of twenty-two was roughly the frequency with which she looked in a mirror and saw someone pretty, rather than someone who, if it had been anybody but her, might have been considered pretty but, because it was her, wasn't. She'd definitely inherited some of her mother's body issues, but she at least had the hard evidence of her experience with boys to back her up. Many were quite attracted to her, few ended up not thinking there'd been some error. Igor had been trying to puzzle it out for two years now. He was forever studying her the way she studied herself in the mirror: "She seemed good-looking yesterday, and yet . . ."

From somewhere, in college, Pip had gotten the idea—her mind was like a balloon with static cling, attracting random ideas as they floated by—that the height of civilization was to spend Sunday morning reading an actual paper copy of the Sunday *New York Times* at a café. This had become her weekly ritual, and, in truth, wherever the idea had come from, her Sunday mornings were when she felt most civilized. No matter how late she'd been out drinking, she bought the *Times* at 8 a.m., took it to Peet's Coffee, ordered a scone and a double cappuccino, claimed her favorite table in the corner, and happily forgot herself for a few hours.

The previous winter, at Peet's, she'd become aware of a nice-looking, skinny boy who had the same Sunday ritual. Within a few weeks, instead of reading the news, she was thinking about how she looked to the boy while reading, and whether to raise her eyes and catch him looking, until finally it was clear that she would either have to find a new café or talk to him. The next time she caught his eye, she attempted an invitational head-tilt that felt so creaky and studied that she was shocked by how instantly it worked. The boy came right over and boldly proposed that, since they were both there at the same time every week, they could start sharing a paper and save a tree.

"What if we both want the same section?" Pip said with some hostility.

"You were here before I was," the boy said, "so you could have first choice." He went on to complain that his parents, in College Station, Texas, had the wasteful practice of buying two copies of the Sunday *Times*, to avoid squabbling over sections.

Pip, like a dog that knows only its name and five simple words in human language, heard only that the boy came from a normal two-parent family with money to burn. "But this is kind of my one time entirely for myself all week," she said.

"I'm sorry," the boy said, backing away. "It just looked like you wanted to say something."

Pip didn't know how not to be hostile to boys her own age who were interested in her. Part of it was that the only person in the world she trusted was her mother. From her experiences in high school and college, she'd already learned that the nicer the boy was, the more painful it would be for both of them when he discovered that she was much more of a mess than her own niceness had led him to believe. What she hadn't yet learned was how not to want somebody to be nice to her. The not-nice boys were particularly adept at sensing this and exploiting it. Thus neither the nice ones nor the not-nice ones could be trusted, and she was, moreover, not very good at telling the two apart until she was in bed with them.

"Maybe we could have coffee some other time," she said to the boy. "Some not-Sunday morning."

"Sure," he said uncertainly.

"Because now that we've actually spoken, we don't have to keep looking at each other. We can just read our separate papers, like your parents."

"My name's Jason, by the way."

"I'm Pip. And now that we know each other's names, we especially don't have to keep looking at each other. I can think, oh, that's just Jason, and you can think, oh, that's just Pip."

He laughed. It turned out that he had a degree in math from Stanford and was living the math major's dream, working for a foundation that promoted American numeracy while trying to write a textbook that he hoped would revolutionize the teaching of statistics. After two dates, she liked him enough to think she'd better sleep with him before he or she got hurt. If she waited too long, Jason would learn that she was a mess of debts and duties, and would run for his life. Or she would have to tell him that her deeper affections were engaged with an older guy who not only didn't believe in money—as in U.S. currency; as in the mere possession of it—but also had a wife.

So as not to be totally undisclosive, she told Jason about the after-hours volunteer "work" that she was doing on nuclear disarmament, a subject he seemed to know so much more about than she did, despite its being *her* "work," not his, that she became slightly hostile. Fortunately, he was a great talker, an enthusiast for Philip K. Dick, for *Breaking Bad*, for sea otters and mountain lions, for mathematics applied to daily life, and especially for his geometrical method of statistics pedagogy, which he explained so well she almost understood it. The third time she saw him, at a noodle joint where she was forced to pretend not to be hungry because her latest Renewable Solutions paycheck hadn't cleared yet, she found herself at a crossroads: either risk friendship or retreat to the safety of casual sex.

Outside the restaurant, in light fog, in the Sunday-evening quiet of Telegraph Avenue, she put the moves on Jason and he responded avidly. She could feel her stomach growling as she pressed it into his; she hoped he couldn't hear it.

"Do you want to go to your house?" she murmured in his ear.

Jason said no, regrettably, he had a sister visiting.

At the word *sister*, Pip's heart constricted with hostility. Having no siblings of her own, she couldn't help resenting the demands and potential supportiveness of other people's; their nuclear-family normalcy, their inherited wealth of closeness.

"We can go to my house," she said, somewhat crossly. And she was so absorbed in resenting Jason's sister for displacing her from his bedroom (and, by extension, from his heart, although she didn't particularly want a place in it), so vexed by her circumstances as she and Jason walked hand in hand down Telegraph Avenue, that they'd reached the door of her house before she remembered that they couldn't go there.

"Oh," she said. "Oh. Could you wait outside for a second while I deal with something?"

"Um, sure," Jason said.

She gave him a grateful kiss, and they proceeded to neck and grind for ten minutes on her doorstep, Pip burying herself in the pleasure of being touched by a clean and highly competent boy, until a distinctly audible growl from her stomach brought her out of it.

"One second, OK?" she said.

"Are you *hungry*?"

"No! Or actually suddenly maybe yes, slightly. I wasn't at the restaurant, though."

She eased her key into the lock and went inside. In the living room, her schizophrenic housemate, Dreyfuss, was watching a basketball game with her disabled housemate, Ramón, on a scavenged TV set whose digital converter a third housemate, Stephen, the one she was more or less in love with, had obtained by sidewalk barter. Dreyfuss's body, bloated by the medications that he'd to date been good about taking, filled a low, scavenged armchair.

"Pip, Pip," Ramón cried out, "Pip, what are you doing now, you said you might help me with my vocabbleree, you wanna help me with it now?"

Pip put a finger to her lips, and Ramón clapped his hands over his mouth.

"That's right," said Dreyfuss quietly. "She doesn't want anyone to know she's here. And why might that be? Could it be because the German spies are in the kitchen? I use the word *spies* loosely, of course, though perhaps not entirely inappropriately, given the fact that there are some thirty-five members of the Oakland Nuclear Disarmament Study Group, of which Pip and Stephen are by no means the least dispensable, and yet the house that the

Germans have chosen to favor with their all too typically German earnestness and nosiness, for nearly a week now, is ours. A curious fact, worth considering."

"Dreyfuss," Pip hissed, moving closer to him to avoid raising her voice.

Dreyfuss placidly knit his fat fingers on his belly and continued speaking to Ramón, who never tired of listening to him. "Could it be that Pip wants to avoid talking to the German spies? Perhaps especially tonight? When she's brought home a young gentleman with whom she's been osculating on the front porch for some fifteen minutes now?"

"*You're* the spy," Pip whispered furiously. "I hate your spying."

"She hates it when I observe things that no intelligent person could fail to notice," Dreyfuss explained to Ramón. "To observe what's in plain sight is not to spy, Ramón. And perhaps the Germans, too, are doing no more than that. What constitutes a spy, however, is *motive*, and there, Pip—" He turned to her. "There I would advise you to ask yourself what these nosy, earnest Germans are doing in our house."

"You didn't stop taking your meds, did you?" Pip whispered.

"*Osculate*, Ramón. There's a fine vocabulary word for you."

"Whassit mean?"

"Why, it means to *neck*. To *lock lips*. To *pluck up kisses by their roots*."

"Pip, you gonna help me with my vocabbleree?"

"I believe she has other plans tonight, my friend."

"Sweetie, no, not now," Pip whispered to Ramón, and then, to Dreyfuss, "The Germans are here because we invited them, because we had room. But you're right, I need you not to tell them I'm here."

"What do you think, Ramón?" Dreyfuss said. "Should we help her? She's not helping you with your vocabulary."

"Oh, for Christ's sake. Help him yourself. You're the one with the huge vocabulary."

Dreyfuss turned again to Pip and looked at her steadily, his eyes all intellect, no affect. It was as if his meds suppressed his condition well enough to keep him from butchering people in the street with a broadsword but not quite enough to banish it from his eyes. Stephen had assured Pip that Dreyfuss looked at everyone the same way, but she persisted in thinking that, if he ever stopped taking his meds, she would be the person he went after with a broadsword or whatever, the person in whom he would pinpoint the trouble in the world, the conspiracy against him; and, what's more, she believed that he was seeing something true about her falseness.

"These Germans and their spying are distasteful to me," Dreyfuss said to her. "Their first thought when they walk into a house is how to take it over."

"They're peace activists, Dreyfuss. They stopped trying to be world conquerors, like, seventy years ago."

"I want you and Stephen to make them go away."

"OK! We will! Later. Tomorrow."

"We don't like the Germans, do we, Ramón?"

"We like it when it's jus' the five of us, like famlee," Ramón said.

"Well . . . not a family. Not exactly. No. We each have our own families, don't we, Pip?"

Dreyfuss looked into her eyes again, significantly, knowingly, with no human warmth—or was it maybe simply no trace of desire? Maybe every man would look at her this heartlessly if sex were entirely subtracted? She went over to Ramón and put her hands on his fat, sloping shoulders. "Ramón, sweetie, I'm busy tonight," she said. "But I'll be home all night tomorrow. OK?"

"OK," he said, completely trusting her.

She hurried back to the front door and let in Jason, who was blowing on his cupped fingers. As they passed by the living room, Ramón again clapped his hands to his mouth, miming his commitment to secrecy, while Dreyfuss imperturbably watched basketball. There were so many things for Jason to see in the house and so few that Pip cared for him to see, and Dreyfuss and Ramón each had a smell, Dreyfuss's yeasty, Ramón's uriney, that she was used to but visitors weren't. She climbed the stairs rapidly on tiptoe, hoping that Jason would get the idea to hurry and be quiet. From behind a closed door on the second floor came the familiar cadences of Stephen and his wife finding fault with each other.

In her little bedroom, on the third floor, she led Jason to her mattress without turning any lights on, because she didn't want him to see how poor she was. She was horribly poor but her sheets were clean; she was rich in cleanliness. When she'd moved into the room, a year earlier, she'd scrubbed every inch of floor and windowsill, using a spray bottle of disinfectant cleaner, and when mice had come to visit her she'd learned from Stephen that stuffing steel wool into every conceivable ingress point would keep them out, and then she'd cleaned the floors again. But now, after tugging Jason's T-shirt up over his bony shoulders and letting him undress her and engaging in various pleasurable preliminaries, only to recall that her only condoms were in the toiletries bag that she'd left in the first-floor bathroom before going out, because the Germans had occupied her regular bathroom, her cleanliness became another handicap. She gave Jason's cleanly circumcised erection a peck with her lips, murmured, "Sorry, one second, I'll be right back," and grabbed a robe that she didn't get fully arranged and knotted until she was halfway down the last flight of stairs and realized she'd neglected to explain where she was going.

"Fuck," she said, pausing on the stairs. Nothing about Jason had suggested wild promiscuity, and she possessed a still-valid morning-after prescription, and she was feeling, at that moment, as if sex were the only thing in her life that she was reasonably effective at; but she had to try to keep her body clean. Self-pity seeped into her, a conviction that for no one but her was sex so logistically ungainly, a tasty fish with so many small bones. Behind her, behind the marital bedroom door, Stephen's wife was raising her voice on the subject of moral vanity.

"I'll take my chances with moral vanity," Stephen interrupted, "when the alternative is signing on with a divine plan that immiserates four billion people."

"That is the essence of moral vanity!" the wife crowed.

Stephen's voice triggered in Pip a longing deeper than any she felt for Jason, and she quickly concluded that she herself wasn't guilty of moral vanity—was more like a case of moral low self-esteem, since the man she really wanted was not the one she was intent on fucking now. She tiptoed down to the ground floor and past the piles of scavenged building supplies in the hallway. In the kitchen, the German woman, Annagret, was speaking German. Pip darted into the bathroom, stuffed a three-strip of condoms into the pocket of her robe, peeked out of the door again, and pulled her head back quickly: Annagret was now standing in the kitchen doorway.

Annagret was a dark-eyed beauty and had a pleasing voice, confounding Pip's preconceptions about the ugliness of German and the blue eyes of its speakers. She and her boyfriend, Martin, were vacationing in various American slums, ostensibly to raise awareness of their international squatters' rights organization, and to forge connections with the American antinuke movement, but primarily, it seemed, to take pictures of each other in front of optimistic ghetto murals. The previous Tuesday evening, at a communal dinner that Pip had attended unavoidably, because it was her night to cook, Stephen's wife had picked a fight with Annagret on the subject of Israel's nuclear arms program. Stephen's wife was one of those women who held another woman's beauty against her (the fact that she held nothing against Pip, but tried to be maternal to her instead, confirmed Pip's nongrandiose assessment of her own looks), and Annagret's effortless loveliness, more accentuated than marred by her savage haircut and her severally pierced eyebrows, had upset Stephen's wife so much that she began saying blatantly untrue things about Israel. Since it happened that Israel's nuclear arms program was the one disarmament subject that Pip was well versed in, having recently prepared a report on it for the study group, and since she was also sorely jealous of Stephen's wife, she'd cut loose with an eloquent five-minute summary of the evidence for Israeli nuclear capability.

Ridiculously, this had fascinated Annagret. Pronouncing herself "super impressed" with Pip, she led her away from the others and into the living room, where they sat on the sofa and had a long girl talk. There was something irresistible about Annagret's attentions, and when she began to talk about the famous Internet outlaw Andreas Wolf, whom it turned out she knew personally, and to say that Pip was exactly the kind of young person that Wolf's Sunlight Project was in need of, and to insist that Pip leave her terrible exploitative job and apply for one of the paid internships that the Sunlight Project was now offering, and to say that very probably, to win one of these internships, all she had to do was submit to a formal "questionnaire" that Annagret herself could administer before she left town, Pip had felt so flattered—so *wanted*—that she promised to do the questionnaire. She'd been drinking jug wine steadily for four hours.

The next morning, sober, she'd regretted her promise. Andreas Wolf and his Project were currently conducting business out of South America, owing to various European and American warrants for his arrest on hacking and spying charges, and there was obviously no way that Pip was leaving her mother and moving to South America. Also, although Wolf was a hero to some of her friends and she was moderately intrigued by Wolf's idea that secrecy was oppression and transparency freedom, she wasn't a politically committed person; she mostly just tagged along with Stephen, dabbling in commitment in the same fitful way she dabbled in physical fitness. Also, the Sunlight Project, and the fervor with which Annagret had spoken of it, seemed possibly cultish. Also, as she was certain would become instantly clear when she did the questionnaire, she was nowhere near as smart and well-informed as her five-minute speech on Israel had made her seem. And so she'd been avoiding the Germans until this morning, when, on her way out to share the Sunday *Times* with Jason, she'd found a note from Annagret whose tone was so injured that she'd left a note of her own outside Annagret's door, promising to talk to her tonight.

Now, as her stomach continued to register emptiness, she waited for some change in the stream of spoken German to indicate that Annagret was no longer in the kitchen doorway. Twice, like a dog overhearing human speech, Pip was pretty sure that she heard her own name in the stream. If she'd been thinking straight, she would have marched into the kitchen, announced that she had a boy over and couldn't do the questionnaire, and gone upstairs. But she was starving, and sex was becoming more of an abstract task.

Finally she heard footsteps, the scrape of a kitchen chair. She bolted from the bathroom but snagged the hem of her robe on something. A nail in a piece of scavenged wood. As she danced out of the way of falling lumber, Annagret's voice came up the hall behind her.

"Pip? Pip, I'm looking for you since three days ago!"

Pip turned around to see Annagret advancing.

"Hi, yeah, sorry," she said, hastily restacking the lumber. "I can't right now. I've got . . . How about tomorrow?"

"No," Annagret said, smiling, "come now. Come, come, like you promised."

"Um." Pip's mind was not prioritizing well. The kitchen, where the Germans were, was also where cornflakes and milk were. Maybe it wouldn't be so terrible if she ate something before returning to Jason? Might she not be more effective, more responsive and energetic, if she could have some cornflakes first? "Let me just run upstairs for one second," she said. "One second, OK? I promise I'll be right back."

"No, come, come. Come now. It takes only a few minutes, ten minutes. You'll see, it's fun, it's only a form we have to follow. Come. We're waiting the whole evening for you. You'll come do it now, ja?"

Beautiful Annagret beckoned to her. Pip could see what Dreyfuss meant about the Germans; and yet there was relief in taking orders from someone. Plus, she'd already been downstairs for so long that it would be unpleasant to go up and beg Jason for further patience, and her life was already so fraught with unpleasantnesses that she'd adopted the strategy of delaying encounters with them as long as possible, even when the delay made it likely that they would be even more unpleasant when she did encounter them.

"Dear Pip," Annagret said, stroking Pip's hair when she was seated at the kitchen table and eating a large bowl of cornflakes and not greatly in the mood to have her hair touched. "Thank you for doing this for me."

"Let's just get through it quickly, OK?"

"Yes, you'll see. It's only a form we have to follow. You remind me so much of myself when I was at your age and needed a purpose in my life."

Pip didn't care for the sound of this. "OK," she said. "I'm sorry to ask, but is the Sunlight Project a cult?"

"Cult?" Martin, all stubble and Palestinian kaffiyeh, laughed from the end of the table. "Cult of personality, maybe."

"*Ist doch Quatsch, du*," Annagret said with some heat. "*Also wirklich.*"

"Sorry, what?" Pip said.

"I said it's really bullshit, what he's saying. The Project is the opposite of cult. It's about honesty, truth, transparency, freedom. The governments with a cult of personality are the ones who hate it."

"But the Project has a very cher*iss*metic leader," Martin said.

"Charismatic?" Pip said.

"Charismatic. I made it sound like *arissmetic*. Andreas Wolf is very charismatic." Martin laughed again. "This could nearly be in a textbook for vocabulary. How to use the word *charismatic* in a sentence. 'Andreas Wolf is very charismatic.' Then the sentence makes immediate sense, you know right away what the word means. He is the definition of the word itself."

Martin seemed to be needling Annagret and Annagret not liking it; and Pip saw, or thought she saw, that Annagret had slept with Andreas Wolf at some point in the past. She was at least ten years older than Pip, maybe fifteen. From a semitransparent plastic folder, a European-looking office supply, she took some pages slightly longer and narrower than American pages.

"So are you like a recruiter?" Pip asked. "You travel with the questionnaire?"

"Yes, I have authority," Annagret said. "Or not authority, we reject authority. I'm one of the people who do this for the group."

"Is that why you're here in the States? Is this a recruiting trip?"

"Annagret is a *multitasker*," Martin said with a smile somehow both admiring and needling.

Annagret told him to leave her and Pip alone, and he went off in the direction of the living room, apparently still serenely unaware that Dreyfuss didn't like having him around. Pip took the opportunity to pour herself a second bowl of cereal; she was at least putting a check mark in the nourishment box.

"Martin and I have a good relationship, except for his jealousy," Annagret explained.

"Jealousy of what?" Pip said, eating. "Andreas Wolf?"

Annagret shook her head. "I was very close with Andreas, for a long time, but that's some years before I knew Martin."

"So you were really young."

"Martin is jealous of my female friends. Nothing more threatens a German man, even a good man, than women being close friends with each other behind his back. It really upsets him, like it's something wrong with how the world is supposed to be. Like we're going to find out all his secrets and take away his power, or not need him anymore. Do you have this problem, too?"

"I'm afraid I tend to be the jealous party."

"Well, this is why Martin is jealous of the Internet, because this is how I primarily communicate with my friends. I have so many friends I haven't even met—real friends. Email, social media, forums. I know Martin sometimes watches pornography, we don't have secrets from each other, and if he didn't watch it he probably would be the only man in Germany who didn't—I think Internet pornography was designed for German men, because they like to be alone and control things and have fantasies of power. But he says he only watches it because I have so many female Internet friends."

"Which of course may just be porn for women," Pip said.

"No. You only think that because you're young and maybe don't need friendship so much."

"So do you ever think about just going with girls instead?"

"It's pretty terrible right now in Germany with men and women," Annagret said, which somehow amounted to a no.

"I guess I was just trying to say that the Internet is good at satisfying needs from a distance. Male or female."

"But women's need for friendship is genuinely satisfied on the Internet, it's not a fantasy. And because Andreas understands the power of the Internet, how much it can mean for women, Martin is jealous of him also—because of *that*, not because I was close with Andreas in the past."

"Right. But if Andreas is the charismatic leader, then he's the guy with the power, which to me makes it sound like he's just like all the other men, in your opinion."

Annagret shook her head. "The fantastic thing about Andreas is he knows the Internet is the greatest truth device ever. And what does it tell us? That everything in the society actually revolves about women, not men. The men are all looking at pictures of women, and the women are all communicating with other women."

"I think you're forgetting about gay sex and pet videos," Pip said. "But maybe we can do the questionnaire now?

I've kind of got a boy upstairs waiting for me, which is why I'm kind of just wearing a bathrobe with nothing underneath it, in case you were wondering."

"Right now? Upstairs?" Annagret was alarmed.

"I thought it was just going to be a quick questionnaire."

"He can't come back another night?"

"Really trying to avoid that if I can."

"So go tell him you only need a few minutes, ten minutes, with a girlfriend. Then you don't have to be the jealous one for a change."

Here Annagret winked at her, which seemed a real feat to Pip, who was no good at winking, winks being the opposite of sarcasm.

"I think you'd better take me while you've got me," she said.

Annagret assured her that there were no right or wrong answers to the questionnaire, which Pip felt couldn't possibly be true, since why bother giving it if there were no wrong answers? But Annagret's beauty was reassuring. Facing her across the table, Pip had the sense that she was being interviewed for the job of being Annagret.

"*Which of the following is the best superpower to have?*" Annagret read. "*Flying, invisibility, reading people's minds, or making time stop for everyone except you.*"

"Reading people's minds," Pip said.

"That's a good answer, even though there are no right answers."

Annagret's smile was warm enough to bathe in. Pip was still mourning the loss of college, where she'd been effective at taking tests.

"*Please explain your choice,*" Annagret read.

"Because I don't trust people," Pip said. "Even my mom, who I do trust, has things she doesn't tell me, really important things, and it would be nice to have a way to find them out without her having to tell me. I'd know the stuff I need to know, but she'd still be OK. And then, with everyone else, literally everyone, I can never be sure of what they're thinking about me, and I don't seem to be very good at guessing what it is. So, it'd be nice to be able to just dip inside their heads, just for like two seconds, and make sure everything's OK—just be sure that they're not thinking some horrible thought about me that I have no clue about—and then I could trust them. I wouldn't abuse it or anything. It's just so hard not to ever trust people. It makes me have to work so hard to figure out what they want from me. It gets to be so *tiring*."

"Oh, Pip, we hardly have to do the rest. What you're saying is fantastic."

"Truly?" Pip smiled sadly. "You see, even here, though, I'm wondering why you're saying that. Maybe you're just trying to get me to keep doing the questionnaire. For that matter, I'm also wondering why you care so much about my doing it."

"You can trust me. It's only because I'm impressed with you."

"You see, but that doesn't even make any sense, because I'm actually not very impressive. I don't know all that much about nuclear weapons, I just happened to know about Israel. I don't trust you at all. I don't trust you. I don't trust people." Pip's face was growing hot. "I should really go upstairs now. I'm feeling bad about leaving my friend there."

This ought to have been Annagret's cue to let her go, or at least to apologize for keeping her, but Annagret (maybe this was a German thing?) seemed not very good at taking cues. "We have to follow the form," she said. "It's only a form, but we have to follow it." She patted Pip's hand and then stroked it. "We'll go fast."

Pip wondered why Annagret kept touching her.

"Your friends are disappearing. They don't respond to texts or Facebook or phone. You talk to their employers, who say they haven't been to work. You talk to their parents, who say they're very worried. You go to the police, who tell you they've investigated and say your friends are OK but living in different cities now. After a while, every single friend of yours is gone. What do you do then? Do you wait until you disappear yourself, so you can find out what happened to your friends? Do you try to investigate? Do you run away?"

"It's just my friends who are disappearing?" Pip said. "The streets are still full of people my age who aren't my friends?"

"Yes."

"Honestly, I think I'd go see a psychiatrist if this happened to me."

"But the psychiatrist talks to the police herself and finds out that everything you said is true."

"Well, then, at least I'd have one friend—the psychiatrist."

"But then the psychiatrist herself disappears."

"This is a totally paranoid scenario. That is like something out of Dreyfuss's head."

"You wait, investigate, or run away?"

"Or kill myself. How about kill myself?"

"There are no wrong answers."

"I'd probably go live with my mom. I wouldn't let her out of my sight. And if she somehow disappeared anyway, I'd probably kill myself, since by then it would be obvious that having any connection to me wasn't good for a person's health."

Annagret smiled again. "Excellent."

"What?"

"You're doing very, very well, Pip." She reached across the table and put her hands, her hot hands, on Pip's cheeks.

"Saying I'd kill myself is the right answer?"

Annagret took her hands away. "There are no wrong answers."

"That sort of makes it harder to feel good about doing well."

"*Which of the following have you ever done without permission: break into someone's email account, read things on someone's smartphone, search someone's computer, read someone's diary, go through someone's private papers, listen to a private conversation when someone's phone accidentally dials you, obtain information about someone on false pretenses, put your ear to a wall or door to listen to a conversation, and the like.*"

Pip frowned. "Am I allowed to skip a question?"

"You can trust me." Annagret touched her hand yet again. "It's better that you answer."

Pip hesitated and then confessed: "I've been through every scrap of paper my mother owns. If she had a diary, I would have read it, but she doesn't. If she had an email account, I would have broken into it. I've gone online and searched every database I can think of. I don't feel good about it, but she won't tell me who my father is, she won't tell me where I was born, she won't even tell me what her real name is. She says she's doing it for my protection, but I think the danger is only in her head."

"These are things you need to know," Annagret said gravely.

"Yes."

"You have a right to know them."

"Yes."

"Do you understand that these are things the Sunlight Project can help you find out?"

Pip's heart began to race, in part because this had not, in fact, occurred to her before, and the prospect was frightening, but mainly because she sensed that a real seduction was kicking into gear now, a seduction to which all of Annagret's touchings had merely been a prelude. She took her hand away and hugged herself nervously.

"I thought the Project was about corporate and national security secrets."

"Yes, of course. But the Project has many resources."

"So I could just, like, write to them and ask for the information?"

Annagret shook her head. "It isn't a private detection agency."

"But if I actually went and did an internship."

"Yes, of course."

"Well, that's interesting."

"Something to think about, ja?"

"Ja-ah," Pip said.

"*You're traveling in a foreign country*," Annagret read, "*and one night the police come to your hotel room and arrest you as a spy, even though you haven't been spying. They take you to the police station. They say that you may make one call that they will listen to both sides of. They warn you that anyone you call will also be under suspicion of spying. Whom do you call?*"

"Stephen," Pip said.

There was a flicker of disappointment in Annagret's face. "This Stephen? The Stephen here?"

"Yes, what's wrong with that?"

"Forgive me, but I thought you would say your mother. You've mentioned her in every other answer so far. She's the only person you trust."

"But that's only trust in a deep way," Pip said. "She'd go insane with worry, and she doesn't know anything about how the world works, and so she wouldn't know who to call to help me. Stephen would know exactly who to call."

"To me he seems a bit weak."

"What?"

"He seems weak. He's married to that angry, controlly person."

"Yes, I know, his marriage is unfortunate—believe me, I know."

"You have feelings for him!" Annagret said with dismay.

"Yes, I do, so what?"

"Well, you didn't tell me. We're telling each other everything, on the sofa, and you didn't tell me this."

"You didn't tell me you used to sleep with Andreas Wolf!"

"Andreas is a public person. I have to be careful. And that's many years ago now."

"You talk about him like you'd do it again in a heartbeat."

"Pip, please," Annagret said, seizing her hands. "Let's not fight. I didn't know you had feelings for Stephen. I'm sorry."

But the wound the word *weak* had inflicted was hurting Pip more now, not less, and she was aghast to realize how much personal data she'd already surrendered to a woman so confident of her beauty that she could fill her face with metal and chop her hair (so it looked) with lawn clippers. Pip, who had no grounds for such confidence, snatched her hands away and stood up and noisily dropped her cereal bowl in the sink. "I'm going upstairs now—"

"No, we still have six questions—"

"Because I'm obviously not going to South America, and I don't trust you one bit, not the tiniest bit, and so why don't you and your masturbating boyfriend go down to L.A. and squat in somebody else's house and give your questionnaire to somebody who's into somebody stronger than Stephen. I don't want you in our house anymore, and neither does anybody else. If you had any respect for me, you would have seen I didn't even want to be here now."

"Pip, please, wait, I'm really, really sorry." Annagret did seem genuinely distressed. "We don't have to do any more questions—"

"I thought it was a form we had to follow. Had to, had to. God, I'm stupid."

"No, you're really smart. I think you're fantastic. I think only maybe your life revolves too much about men, a little bit, right now."

Pip stared in amazement at this fresh insult.

"Maybe you want a female friend who's something older but used to be so much like you."

"You were never like me," Pip said.

"No, I was. Sit down, please, ja? Talk with me."

Annagret's voice was so silky and commanding, and her insult had cast such humiliating light on Jason's presence in Pip's bedroom, that Pip almost obeyed her and sat down. But when she was gripped by her distrust of people it became physically unbearable to stay with them. She fled down the hallway, hearing the scrape of a chair behind her, the sound of her name being called.

On the second-floor landing, she paused to seethe. Stephen was weak? She thought about men too much? *That is so nice. That really makes me feel good about myself.*

Behind Stephen's door, the marital fighting had stopped. Pip very quietly moved closer to it, away from the sound of basketball downstairs, and listened. Before long, there came a creak of a bedspring, and then an unmistakable whimpering sigh, and she understood that Annagret was right, that Stephen *was* weak, he *was* weak; and yet there was nothing wrong with a husband and a wife having sex. Hearing it and picturing it and being excluded from it filled Pip with a desolation that she had only one means of assuaging.

She took the rest of the stairs two at a time, as if shaving five seconds off her ascent could make up for half an hour's absence. Outside her door, she composed her face into an expression of sheepish apology. It was a face she'd used a thousand times on her mother, to reliably good effect. She opened the door and peeked in, wearing the look.

The lights were on and Jason was in his clothes again, sitting on the edge of the bed, texting intently.

"Psst," Pip said. "Are you horribly mad at me?"

He shook his head. "It's just I told my sister I'd be home by eleven."

The word *sister* dispelled much of the apology from Pip's face, but Jason wasn't looking at her anyway. She went in and sat down by him and touched him. "It's not eleven yet, is it?"

"It's eleven twenty."

She put her head on his shoulder and her hands around his arm. She could feel his muscles working as he texted. "I'm sorry," she said. "I can't explain what happened. I mean, I can, but I don't want to."

"You don't have to explain. I kind of knew it anyway."

"Knew what?"

"Nothing. Never mind."

"No, what, though? What did you know?"

He stopped texting and stared at the floor. "It's not like I'm so normal myself. But relatively speaking—"

"I want to make normal love with you. Can't we still do that? Even just for half an hour? You can tell your sister you'll be home a little late."

"Listen. Pip." He frowned. "Is that your real name, by the way?"

"It's what I call myself."

"Somehow it doesn't seem like I'm talking to *you* when I use it. I don't know . . . 'Pip.' 'Pip.' It doesn't sound . . . I don't know . . ."

The last traces of apology drained from her face, and she took her hands away from him. She knew she had to resist an outburst, but she couldn't resist it. The best she could do was keep her voice low.

"OK," she said. "So you don't like my name. What else don't you like about me?"

"Oh, come on. You're the one who left me up here for an hour. More than an hour."

"Right. While your sister was waiting for you."

Speaking the word *sister* again was like tossing a match into an oven full of unlit gas, the ready-to-combust anger that she walked around with every day; there was a kind of *whoosh* inside her head.

"Seriously," she said, heart pounding, "you might as well tell me everything you don't like about me, since we're obviously never going to fuck, since I'm not normal enough, although what's so abnormal about me I could use a little help in understanding."

"Hey, come on," Jason said. "I could have just left."

The note of self-righteousness in his voice set fire to a larger and more diffuse pool of the gas, a combustible political substance that had seeped into her from her mother and then from certain college professors and certain grossout movies and now also from Annagret, a sense of the unfairness of what one professor had called the *anisotropy* of gendered relationships, wherein boys could camouflage their objectifying desires with the language of feelings while girls played the boys' game of sex at their own risk, dupes if they objectified and victims if they didn't.

"You didn't seem to mind me when your dick was in my mouth," she said.

"I didn't put it there," he said. "And it wasn't there long."

"No, because I had to go downstairs and get a condom so you could stick it inside me."

"Wow. So this is all me now?"

Through a haze of flame, or hot blood, Pip's eyes fell on Jason's handheld device.

"Hey!" he cried.

She jumped up and ran to the far side of the room with his device.

"Hey, you can't do that," he shouted, pursuing her.

"Yes I can!"

"No, you can't, it's not fair. Hey—hey—you can't do that!"

She wedged herself underneath the child's writing desk that was her only piece of furniture and faced the wall, bracing her leg on a desk leg. Jason tried to pull her out by the belt of her robe, but he couldn't dislodge her and was apparently unwilling to get more violent than this. "What kind of freak are you?" he said. "What are you doing?"

Pip touched the device's screen with shaking fingers.

> Let's meet at sfmoma at 4.

"Fuck, fuck, fuck," Jason said, pacing behind her. "What are you doing?"

She pawed the screen and found the next thread.

> Coitus interruptus maximus! 62 min and counting!!

> She hot at least?

> Nice face fantastic body.

Define fantastic. Tits?

8+

Worth the wait I say.

U can have her # if u
have a taste for weird.

68 min!

She slumped to one side, put the device on the floor, and gave it a push in Jason's direction. Her anger had burned off as quickly as it had ignited, leaving ashen grief behind.

"It's only the way some of my friends talk," Jason said. "It doesn't mean anything."

"Please go away," she said in a small voice.

"Let's start over. Can we just, like, reboot? I'm really sorry."

He put a hand on her shoulder, and she recoiled. He took the hand away.

"OK, look, let's talk tomorrow, though, OK?" he said. "This was obviously the wrong night for both of us."

"Just go away now, please."

Renewable Solutions didn't make or build or even install things. Instead, depending on the regulatory weather (not *climate* but *weather*, for it changed seasonally and sometimes seemingly hourly), it "bundled," it "brokered," it "captured," it "surveyed," it "client-provided." In theory, this was all very worthy. America put too much carbon into the atmosphere, renewable energy could help with that, federal and state governments were forever devising new tax inducements, the utilities were indifferent-to-moderately-enthusiastic about greening their image, a gratifyingly non-negligible percentage of California households and businesses were willing to pay a premium for cleaner electricity, and this premium, multiplied by many thousands and added to the money flowing from Washington and Sacramento, minus the money that went to the companies that actually made or installed stuff, was enough to pay fifteen salaries at Renewable Solutions and placate its venture-capitalist backers. The buzzwords at the company were also good: *collective*, *community*, *cooperative*. And Pip wanted to do good, if only for lack of better ambitions. From her mother she'd learned the importance of leading a morally purposeful life, and from college she'd learned to feel worried and guilty about the country's unsustainable consumption patterns. Her problem at Renewable Solutions was that she could never quite figure out what she was selling, even when she was finding people to buy it, and no sooner had she finally begun to figure it out than she was asked to sell something else.

At first, and in hindsight least confusingly, she'd sold power-purchase agreements to small and midsize businesses, until a new state regulation put an end to the outrageous little cut that Renewable Solutions took of those. Then it was signing up households in *potential* renewable energy districts; each household earned Renewable Solutions a bounty paid by some shadowy third party or parties that had created an allegedly lucrative futures market. Then it was giving residents of progressive municipalities a "survey" to measure their level of interest in having their taxes raised or their municipal budgets rejiggered to switch over to renewables; when Pip pointed out to Igor that ordinary citizens had no realistic basis for answering the "survey" questions, Igor said that she must not, under any circumstances, admit this to the respondents, because positive responses had cash value not only for the companies that made stuff but also for the shadowy third parties with their futures market. Pip was on the verge of quitting her job when the cash value of the responses went down and she was shifted to solar renewable energy certificates. This had lasted six relatively pleasant weeks before a flaw in the business model was detected. Since April, she'd been attempting to sign up South Bay subdivisions for waste-energy micro-collectives.

Her associates in consumer outreach were flogging the same crap, of course. The reason they outperformed her was that they accepted each new "product" without trying to understand it. They got behind the new pitch wholeheartedly, even when it was risible and/or made no sense, and then, if a prospective customer had trouble understanding the "product," they didn't vocally agree that it sure was difficult to understand, didn't make a good-faith effort to explain the complicated reasoning behind it, but simply kept hammering on the written pitch. And clearly this was the path to success, and it was all a double disillusionment to Pip, who not only felt actively punished for using her brain but was presented every month with fresh evidence that Bay Area consumers on average responded better to a rote and semi-nonsensical pitch than to a well-meaning saleswoman trying to help them understand the offer. Only when she was allowed to work on direct-mail and social-media outreach did her talents seem less wasted; having grown up with no television, she had good language skills.

Today being a Monday, she was telephonically harassing the many 65+s who didn't use social media and hadn't responded to the company's direct-mail bombardment of a Santa Clara County development called Rancho Ancho. Micro-collectives only worked if you got near-total community buy-in, and a community organizer couldn't be dispatched before a fifty percent response rate was achieved; nor could Pip earn any "outreach points," no matter how much work she'd done.

She put on her headset and forced herself to look at her call sheet again and cursed the self she'd been an hour earlier, before lunch, because this earlier self had cherry-picked the sheet, leaving the names GUTTENSCHWERDER, ALOYSIUS and BUTCAVAGE, DENNIS for after lunch. Pip hated the hard names, because mispronouncing them immediately alienated the consumer, but she gamely clicked Dial. A man at the Butcavage residence answered with a gruff hello.

"Hiiiiii," she said in a sultry drawl into which she'd learned to inject a note of apology, of shared social discomfort. "This is Pip Tyler, with Renewable Solutions, and I'm following up on a mailing we sent you a few weeks ago. Is this Mr. Butcavage?"

"Boocavazh," the man corrected gruffly.

"So sorry, Mr. Boocavazh."

"What's this about?"

"It's about lowering your electric bill, helping the planet, and getting your fair share of state and federal energy tax credits," Pip said, although in truth the electric-bill savings were hypothetical, waste energy was environmentally controversial, and she wouldn't have been making this call if Renewable Solutions and its partners had any intention of giving consumers a large share of the tax benefits.

"Not interested," Mr. Butcavage said.

"Well, you know," Pip said, "quite a few of your neighbors have expressed strong interest in forming a collective. You might do a little asking around and see what they're thinking."

"I don't talk to my neighbors."

"Well, no, of course, I'm not saying you have to if you

don't want to. But the reason they're interested is that your community has a chance to work together for cleaner, cheaper energy and real tax savings."

One of Igor's precepts was that any call in which the words *cleaner*, *cheaper*, and *tax savings* could be repeated at least five times would result in a positive response.

"What is it you're selling?" Mr. Butcavage said a mite less gruffly.

"Oh, this is not a sales call," Pip lied. "We're trying to organize community support for a thing called waste energy. It's a cleaner, cheaper, tax-saving way to solve two of your community's biggest problems at once. I'm talking about high energy costs and solid-waste disposal. We can help you burn your garbage at clean, high temperatures and feed the electricity directly into the grid, at a potentially significant cost savings for you and real benefit to the planet. Can I tell you a little bit more about how it works?"

"What's your angle?" Mr. Butcavage said.

"I beg your pardon?"

"Somebody's paying you to call me when I'm trying to take a nap. What's in it for them?"

"Well, basically we're facilitators. You and your neighbors probably don't have the time or the expertise to organize a waste-energy micro-collective on your own, and so you're missing out on cleaner, cheaper electricity and certain tax advantages. We and our partners have the experience and the know-how to set you up for greater energy independence."

"Yeah, but who pays you?"

"Well, as you may know, there's an enormous amount of state and federal money available for renewable-energy initiatives. We take a share of that, to cover our costs, and pass the rest of the savings on to your community."

"In other words, they tax me to pay for these initiatives, and *maybe* I get some of it back."

"That's an interesting point," Pip said. "But it's actually a little more complicated. In many cases, you're not paying any direct tax to fund the initiatives. But you *do*, potentially, reap the tax benefits, and you get cleaner, cheaper energy, too."

"Burning my garbage."

"Yes, the new technology for that is really incredible. Super clean, super economical." Was there any way to say *tax savings* again? Pip had never ceased to dread, in these calls, what Igor called the pressure point, but she now seemed to have reached it with Mr. Butcavage. She took a breath and said: "It sounds like this might be something you're interested in learning more about?"

Mr. Butcavage muttered something, possibly "burn my own garbage," and hung up on her.

"Yeah, bite me," she said to the dead line. Then she felt bad about it. Not only had Mr. Butcavage's questions been reasonable, he also had an unfortunate name and no friends in his neighborhood. He was probably a lonely person like her mother, and Pip felt helplessly compassionate toward anyone who reminded her of her mother.

Because her mother didn't drive, and because she didn't need a photo ID in a small community like Felton, and because the farthest she ever went from Felton was downtown Santa Cruz, her only official identification was her Social Security card, which bore the name Penelope Tyler (no middle name). To get this card, using a name she'd assumed as an adult, she would have had to present either a forged birth certificate or the original copy of her real birth certificate along with legal documentation of her name change. Pip's repeated fine-toothed combings of her mother's possessions had turned up no documents like these, nor any safe-deposit key, which led her to conclude that her mother had either destroyed the documents or buried them in the ground as soon as she had a new Social

Security number. Somewhere, some county courthouse may have had a public record of her name change, but the United States contained a lot of counties, few of them put their records online, and Pip wouldn't even have known what time zone to start looking in. She'd entered every conceivable combination of keywords into every commercial search engine and ended up with nothing but an acute appreciation of the limitations of search engines.

When Pip was very young, vague stories had satisfied her, but by the time she was eleven her questions had grown so insistent that her mother agreed to tell her the "full" story. Once upon a time, she said, she'd had a different name and a different life, in a state that wasn't California, and she'd married a man who—as she discovered only after Pip was born—had a propensity to violence. He abused her physically, but he was very cunning about inflicting pain without leaving serious marks on her, and he was even more abusive psychologically. Soon she became a total hostage to his abuse, and she might have stayed married until he murdered her if he hadn't been so enraged by Pip's crying, as a baby, that she feared for Pip's safety as well. She tried running away from him with Pip, but he tracked them down and abused her psychologically and brought them home again. He had powerful friends in their community, she couldn't prove that he abused her, and she knew that even if she divorced him he would still get partial custody of Pip. And she couldn't allow that. She'd married a dangerous person and could live with her own mistake, but she couldn't put Pip at risk. And so, one night, while her husband was away on business, she packed a suitcase and boarded a bus and took Pip to a battered-wives shelter in a different state. The women at the shelter helped her assume a new identity and get a new, fake birth certificate for Pip. Then she boarded a bus again and took refuge in the Santa Cruz Mountains, where a person could be whoever she said she was.

"I did it to protect you," she'd told Pip. "And now that I've told you the story, you have to protect yourself and never tell anyone else. I know your father. I know how enraged he must have been that I stood up for myself and took you from him. And I know that if he ever found out where you are, he would come and take you from me."

Pip at eleven was profoundly credulous. Her mother had a long, thin scar on her forehead which came out when she blushed, and her front teeth had a gap between them and didn't match the color of her other teeth. Pip was so sure that her father had smashed her mother's face, and felt so sorry for her, that she didn't even ask her if he had. For a while, she was too afraid of him to sleep alone at night. In her mother's bed, with stifling hugs, her mother assured her that she was completely safe as long as she never told anyone her secret, and Pip's credulity was so complete, her fear so real, that she kept the secret until well into her rebellious teen years. Then she told two friends, swearing both to secrecy, and in college she told more friends.

One of them, Ella, a homeschooled girl from Marin, reacted with a funny look. "That is so weird," Ella said. "I feel like I've heard that exact story before. There's a writer in Marin who wrote a whole memoir with basically that story."

The writer was Candida Lawrence (also an assumed name, according to Ella), and when Pip tracked down a copy of her memoir she saw that it had been published years before her mother had told her the "full" story. Lawrence's story wasn't identical, but it was similar enough to propel Pip home to Felton in a cold rage of suspicion and accusation. And here was the really weird thing: when she laid into her mother, she could feel herself being abusive like her absent father, and her mother crumpled up like the abused and emotionally hostage-taken person she'd portrayed herself as being in her marriage, and so, in the very act of attacking the full story, Pip was somehow confirming its essential plausibility. Her mother sobbed revoltingly and begged Pip for kindness, ran sobbing to a bookcase and pulled a copy of Lawrence's memoir from a shelf of more self-helpy titles where Pip would never have noticed it. She thrust the book at Pip like a kind of sacrificial offering and said it had been an enormous comfort to her over the years, she'd read it three times and read other books of Lawrence's too, they made her feel less alone in the life she'd chosen, to know that at least one woman had gone through a similar trial and come out strong and whole. "The story I told you is *true*," she cried. "I don't know how to tell you a truer story and still keep you safe."

"What are you saying," Pip said with abusive calm and coldness. "That there is a truer story but it wouldn't keep me 'safe'?"

"No! You're twisting my words, I told the truth and you have to believe me. You're all I have in the world!" At home, after work, her mother let her hair escape its plaits into a fluffy gray mass, which now shook as she stood and keened and gasped like a very large child having a meltdown.

"For the record," Pip said with even more lethal calm, "had you or hadn't you read Lawrence's book when you told me your story?"

"Oh! Oh! Oh! I'm trying to keep you safe!"

"For the record, Mom: are you lying about this, too?"

"Oh! Oh!"

Her mother's hands waved spastically around her head, as if preparing to catch the pieces of it when it exploded. Pip felt a distinct urge to slap her in the face, and then to inflict pain in cunning, invisible ways. "Well, it's not working," she said. "I'm not safe. You have failed to keep me safe." And she grabbed her knapsack and walked out the door, walked down their steep, narrow lane toward Lompico Road, beneath the stoically stationary redwoods. Behind her she could hear her mother crying "Pussycat" piteously. Their neighbors may have thought a pet had gone missing.

She had no interest in "getting to know" her father, she already had her hands full with her mother, but it seemed to her that he should give her money. Her $130,000 in student debt was far less than he'd saved by not raising her and not sending her to college. Of course, he might not see why he should pay anything now for a child whom she hadn't enjoyed the "use" of, and who wasn't offering him any future "use," either. But given her mother's hysteria and hypochondria, Pip could imagine him as a basically decent person in whom her mother had brought out the worst, and who was now peaceably married to someone else, and who might feel relieved and grateful to know that his long-lost daughter was alive; grateful enough to take out his checkbook. If she had to, she was even willing to offer modest concessions, the occasional email or phone call, the annual Christmas card, a Facebook friendship. At twenty-three, she was well beyond reach of his custody; she had little to lose and much to gain. All she needed was his name and date of birth. But her mother defended this information as if it were a vital organ that Pip was trying to rip out of her.

When her long, dispiriting afternoon of Rancho Ancho calls finally came to an end, at 6 p.m., Pip saved her call sheets, strapped on her knapsack and bike helmet, and tried to sneak past Igor's office without being accosted.

"Pip, a word with you, please," came Igor's voice.

She shuffled back so he could see her from his desk. His Gaze glanced down past her breasts, which at this point might as well have had giant eights stenciled on them, and settled on her legs. She would have sworn they were like an unfinished sudoku to Igor. He wore exactly that frown of preoccupied problem-solving.

"What," she said.

He looked up at her face. "Where are we with Rancho Ancho?"

"I got some good responses. We're at, like, thirty-seven percent right now."

He nodded his head from side to side, Russian style, noncommittal. "Let me ask you. Do you enjoy working here?"

"Are you asking me if I'd prefer to be fired?"

"We're thinking of restructuring," he said. "There may be an opportunity for you to use other skills."

"Good Lord. 'Other skills'? You really are creating an atmosphere."

"It will be two years, I think, on August first. You're a smart girl. How long do we give the experiment in outreach?"

"It's not my decision, is it?"

He waggled his head again. "Do you have ambitions? Do you have plans?"

"You know, if you hadn't done that Twenty Questions thing to me, it would be easier to take the question seriously."

He made a tsking sound with his tongue. "So angry."

"Or tired. How about just tired? Can I go now?"

"I don't know why, but I like you," he said. "I'd like to see you succeed."

She didn't stick around to hear more. Out in the lobby, her three female outreach associates were putting on running shoes for their Monday after-work female-bonding jogging thing. They were in their thirties and forties, with husbands and in two cases children, and it required no superpowers to divine what they thought of Pip: she was the complainer, the underperformer, the entitled Young Person, the fresh-skinned magnet for Igor's Gaze, the morally hazardous exploiter of Igor's indulgence, the person with no baby pictures in her cubicle. Pip concurred in much of this assessment—probably none of them could have been as rude to Igor as she was and not been fired—and yet she was hurt that they'd never invited her to go jogging with them.

"How was your day, Pip?" one of them asked her.

"I don't know." She tried to think of something uncomplaining to say. "Do any of you happen to have a good recipe for a vegan cake with whole-grain flour and not too much sugar?"

The women stared at her.

"I know: right?" she said.

"That's kind of like asking how to throw a good party with no booze, desserts, or dancing," another of them said.

"Is *butter* vegan?" the third said.

"No, it's animal," the first said.

"But ghee. Isn't ghee just fat with no milk solids?"

"Animal fat, animal fat."

"OK, thank you," Pip said. "Have a good run."

As she descended the stairs to the bike rack, she was pretty sure she could hear them laughing at her. Wasn't asking for a recipe supposed to be good coin of the feminine realm? In truth, though, she had a dwindling supply of friends her own age, too. She was still valued in larger groups, for the relative bitterness of her sarcasm, but when it came to one-on-one friendships she had trouble interesting herself in the tweets and postings and endless pictures of the happy girls, none of whom could fathom why she lived in a squatter house, and she wasn't bitter enough for the unhappy girls, the self-destructive ones, the ones with aggressive tattoos and bad parents. She could feel herself starting down the road to being a friendless person like her mother, and Annagret had been right: it made her too interested in the Y-chromosomal. Certainly her four months of abstinence since the incident with Jason had been dreary.

Outside, the weather was unpleasantly perfect. She felt so beaten-down that she poked along the Mandela Parkway in first gear, going no faster than the jammed traffic above her on the freeway. Across the bay, the sun was still well up in the sky over San Francisco, not dimmed but made gentler by a hint of high ocean mist. Like her mother, Pip was coming to prefer drizzle and heavy fog, for their absence of reproach. As she pedaled up through the sketchy blocks of Thirty-Fourth Street, she shifted into higher gears and avoided eye contact with the drug sellers.

The house where she lived had once belonged to Dreyfuss, who had drawn the down payment from an inheritance with which he'd also opened a used-book store off Piedmont Avenue, following his mother's suicide. His house had mirrored the condition of his mind, for a long time fairly orderly, then more eccentrically cluttered with things like vintage jukeboxes, and finally filled floor to ceiling with papers for his "research" and foodstuffs for a coming "siege." His bookstore, which people had enjoyed visiting for the experience of talking to someone smarter than themselves (because nobody was smarter than Dreyfuss; he had a photographic memory and could solve high-level chess and logic problems in his head), became a place of putrescent smells and paranoia. He snarled at his customers when he rang up their purchases, and then he started shouting at anybody who walked in the door, and then he took to hurling books at them, which led to visits from the police, which led to an assault, which led to his being involuntarily committed. By the time he was released, on a new cocktail of meds, he'd lost the store, its stock had been liquidated to cover unpaid rent and real or trumped-up damages, and his house was in foreclosure.

Dreyfuss had moved back into the house anyway. He spent his days writing ten-page letters to his bank and its agents and various governmental agencies. In the space of six months, he threatened four different lawsuits and managed to force the bank into a stalemate; it helped that the house was in terrible repair. But apart from his disability payments Dreyfuss had no money, and so he allied himself with the Occupy movement, befriended Stephen, and agreed to share the house with other squatters in exchange for food and upkeep and utilities. At the height of Occupy, the place was a zoo of transients and troublemakers. Eventually, though, Stephen's wife had imposed some order on it. They kept one room for short-term squatters and gave two others to Ramón and his brother, Eduardo, who'd come along with Stephen and his wife from the Catholic Worker house where they'd been living.

Pip had met Stephen at the Disarmament Study Group a few months before Eduardo was struck and killed by a laundry truck. These months were a happy time for her, because she had the distinct impression that Stephen and his wife were estranged. Pip had been instantly attracted to Stephen's intensity, to his extreme-fighter physique and his little-boy mop of hair, and she sensed that other girls in the study group felt the same way. But she was the one bold enough to invite him out for an after-meeting coffee (to be paid for by her, since he didn't believe in money). Given how warmly he said yes, it seemed not unreasonable to assume that they were having a sort-of first date.

Over subsequent coffees, she told him about her undergraduate phobia of nuclear weapons, her wish to do good in the world, and her fear that the study group was as useless as Renewable Solutions. Stephen told her how he'd married his college sweetheart, and how they'd spent their twenties in Catholic Worker houses, living under a vow of poverty, doing the whole Dorothy Day thing, uniting radical politics and religion, and how their paths had then diverged, the wife becoming more religious and less political and Stephen the opposite, the wife opening a bank account and going to work at a group home for the disabled, while Stephen devoted himself to organizing for Occupy and living cash-free. Even though he'd lost his faith and left the Church, his years at the Worker had given him an almost female emotional directness, an exciting propensity for cutting to the heart of things, which Pip had never encountered in a man before, let alone in a man so street-tough. In an access of trust, she spilled out more personal stuff, including the fact that she paid an unsustainably high rent for a share with college friends, and Stephen listened to her so intensely that when he offered her Eduardo's room for zero rent, soon after Eduardo was killed, she took it to mean she had a chance with him.

When she went to the house for her tour and interview, she discovered that Stephen and his wife were not so estranged as not to be still sharing a bed. Also, Stephen hadn't bothered to show up that night; maybe he'd known that the bed situation would be a shocker for Pip? She felt that he'd misled her about the status of his marriage. And yet: Why had he misled her? Wasn't this, in itself, grounds for hope? The wife, Marie, was a red-faced blonde in her late thirties. She conducted the interview while Dreyfuss sat sphinxlike in a corner and Ramón wept about his brother. And either Marie was vain enough not to perceive a threat in Pip, or her Catholic charity was so true-believing that she was genuinely moved by her financial plight. She took to Pip with a mothering kindness which was then and remained ever after a reproach to the stomach-churning jealousy Pip felt toward her.

Except for this jealousy, and for the creepiness of Dreyfuss, which was itself offset by the pleasure of watching his mind work, she'd been happy in the house. The most consistent proof of her human worth was the care she gave Ramón. She'd learned, soon after moving in, that Stephen and Marie had legally adopted him a year before Eduardo's death, so that Eduardo could develop his own life. Although Ramón was no more than a year or two younger than Stephen and Marie, he was now their *son*, which would have seemed utterly insane to Pip had she not so quickly come to love him herself. Helping him with his vocabulary, learning to play the basic video games that he was capable of, on a console that she'd bought for the house as a Christmas present, with money she didn't really have, and making him heavily buttered popcorn, and watching his favorite cartoons with him, she understood the attraction of Christian charity. She might even have tried churchgoing if Stephen hadn't come to hate the Church for its venality and its crimes against women and the planet. Through the marital bedroom door, she heard Marie throwing Stephen's own love of Ramón in his face, shouting at him that he'd let his head poison his heart against the Gospel, that his heart was obviously still full of the Word, that the example of Christ was right there in his loving-kindness to their adopted son.

Even though she never went to church, Pip had been losing her college friends one by one, after texting them one too many times that she couldn't hang with them because she'd promised to play a game with Ramón or take him to a thrift store to buy sneakers. This hampered social planning, but the real problem, she suspected, was that her friends had begun to write her off as a squatter-house weirdo. She was now down to three friends with whom she drank on Saturdays and stayed in textual touch while carefully withholding information; because she really was kind of a squatter-house weirdo. Unlike Stephen and Marie, who came from good middle-class Catholic families, she'd barely even lowered her station in going from her mother's little cabin to Thirty-Third Street, and her student debt was functionally a vow of poverty. She felt more effective at doing her house chores and helping Ramón than at anything else in her life. And yet, to answer Igor's question, she *did* have an ambition, if not a plan for achieving it. Her ambition was not to end up like her mother. And so the fact that she was effective at being a squatter didn't give her much satisfaction; it filled her, more often, with dread.

As she rounded the corner onto Thirty-Third Street, she saw Stephen sitting on their front steps, wearing his little-boy clothes, his secondhand Keds and secondhand seersucker shirt, its short sleeves strained by his large biceps. The subtle evening mist was making shafts of the golden light beneath the nearby freeway viaducts. Stephen's head was bowed.

"Hello, hello," Pip said cheerily, as she dismounted.

Stephen raised his head and looked at her with reddened eyes. His face was wet.

"What is it?" she said.

"It's over," he said.

"What's over? What happened?" She let her bike fall to the ground. "Did Dreyfuss lose the house? What happened?"

He smiled wanly. "No, Dreyfuss did not lose the house. Are you kidding? I lost my marriage. Marie's gone. She's moved out."

His face twisted, and cold fear surged outward from Pip's center; but when it passed below her waist it became a terrible warmth. How well aware the body was of what it wanted. How quickly it gleaned the news it could use. She took off her helmet and sat down on the stoop.

"Oh, Stephen, I'm so sorry," she said. Until this moment, their only hugs had been of hello and good-bye, but her limbs were suddenly so shaky that she had to put her hands on his shoulders, as if to keep her arms from falling off. "This is so sudden."

He snuffled a bit. "You didn't see it coming?"

"No, no, no."

"That's right," he said bitterly, "because how can she remarry? That was always my ace in the hole."

Pip squeezed him and rubbed his biceps, and there was nothing wrong with this; he needed a comforting friend. But his muscles were testosterone-hardened and warm. And the great impediment was *gone, moved out, gone.*

"You guys have been fighting so much, though," she suggested. "Almost every night, for months."

"Not so much lately," he said. "I actually thought things were getting better. But that was only because . . ."

He put his face in his hands again.

"Is there somebody else?" Pip said. "Somebody she . . ."

He rocked in a kind of whole-body nod.

"Oh, God. That's terrible. That's terrible, Stephen." She pressed her face into his shoulder. "Tell me what I can do for you," she whispered into the seersucker of his shirt.

"There is one thing," he said.

"Tell me," she said, nuzzling the seersucker.

"You can talk to Ramón."

This brought her out of the unreality of what was happening; made her aware that she had her face in somebody's shirt. She took her arms away and said, "Shit."

"Exactly."

"What's going to happen to him?"

"She's got it all figured out," Stephen said. "She's got the entire rest of her life plotted out like some corporate master plan. She gets custody and I get visitation, as if that was the point of adopting him—visitation. She's been . . ." He took a deep breath. "She's involved with the director of the home."

"Oh, Jesus. Perfect."

"Who is apparently friends with the archbishop, who can get the marriage annulled for her. Perfect, right? They're going to put Ramón in the home and try to give him voc ed, and then she can pop out three quick babies in her spare time. That's the plan, right? And what judge is not going to give full custody to the mother with a full-time paying job at a place for people like Ramón? That's the plan. And you would not believe how righteous she is about every bit of it."

"I can sort of believe it," Pip ventured to say.

"And I love the righteousness," Stephen said, his voice trembling. "She *is* righteous. She really does burn with moral purpose. I just didn't want to have three babies."

Well, thank God for that, Pip thought.

"So Ramón's still here?" she said.

"She and Vincent are coming back for him in the morning. Apparently they've had the thing planned for weeks now—they were just waiting for a bed to open up." Stephen shook his head. "I thought Ramón was going to be what saved us. To have a son we both loved, so it wouldn't matter if we disagreed about everything else."

"Well," Pip said with some hostility, owing to the obvious persistence of Marie's hold on him, "you're not the first couple whose relationship having a child didn't save. I was probably a child like that myself in fact."

Stephen turned to her and said, "You're a good friend."

She took his hand and wove her fingers into his and tried to calibrate the pressure of her squeeze. "I am your good friend," she agreed. But now that his hand was in direct contact with hers, her body was making clear, with thudding heart and shallow breath, that it expected to have his hands all over it in a matter of days, possibly hours. It was like a big dog straining on the leash of her intelligence. She allowed herself to bump his hand once on her thigh, where she most wanted him to place it at this moment, and then released it. "What did you say to Ramón?"

"I can't face him. I've been out here since she left."

"He's just been sitting in there without your saying anything to him?"

"She only left like half an hour ago. He's going to be upset if he sees me crying. I thought you could sort of prepare him, and then I could talk to him reasonably."

Pip here recalled Annagret's fateful word *weak*; but it didn't make her want Stephen any less. It made her want to forget about Ramón and stay out here and keep touching, because being weak might mean being unable to resist.

"Will you talk to me, too, later on?" she said. "Just me? I really need to talk to you."

"Of course. This doesn't change anything, we'll still have the house. Dreyfuss is a bulldog. Don't worry about that."

Although it was obvious to Pip's body that, in fact, everything had changed, her intelligence could forgive Stephen for being unable to see this so soon after being dumped by his wife of fifteen years. Heart still thudding, she stood up and took her bike inside. Dreyfuss was sitting by himself in the living room, dwarfing a scavenged six-legged office chair and mousing at the house computer.

"Where's Ramón?" Pip said.

"In his room."

"I guess I don't even have to ask you if you know what's going on."

"I don't meddle in family affairs," Dreyfuss said coolly.

Like a six-legged spider, he rotated his bulk in Pip's direction. "I have, however, been checking facts. The St. Agnes Home is a fully state-accredited and well-reviewed thirty-six-bed facility, opened in 1984. The director, Vincent Olivieri, is a forty-seven-year-old widower with three sons in their late teens and early twenties; he holds an MSW from San Francisco State. Archbishop Evans has visited the home on at least two occasions. Would you care to see a picture of Evans and Olivieri on the front steps of the home?"

"Dreyfuss, do you *feel* anything about this?"

He looked at Pip steadily. "I feel that Ramón will be getting more than adequate care. I will miss his friendly presence but not his video games or his very limited conversational range. It may take some time, but Marie will likely be able to get her marriage annulled—I've identified several precedents in the archdiocese. I confess to some concern about house finances in the absence of her paychecks. Stephen tells me we need a new roof. As much as you seem to enjoy helping him with house maintenance, I have trouble imagining the two of you in a roofing capacity."

By Dreyfuss standards this was a very feeling speech. Pip went up to Ramón's room and found him lying on his tangled bedsheets, his face to a wall covered with Bay Area sports posters. The combination of his strong smell and the smiling star athletes was so poignant that her eyes filled.

"Ramón, sweetie?"

"Hi Pip," he said, not moving at all.

She sat down on his bed and touched his fat arm. "Stephen said you wanted to see me. Do you want to turn around and see me?"

"I want us to be famlee," he said, not moving.

"We're still family," she said. "None of us is going anywhere."

"I'm going somewhere. Marie said. I'm going to the home where she works. It's a different famlee but I like our famlee. Don' you like our famlee, Pip?"

"I do like it, very much."

"Marie can go but I wanna stay with you an' Stephen an' Drayfuss, just like before."

"But we'll all still see you, and now you can make some new friends, too."

"I don' wan' new frens. I wan' my old frens, just like before."

"You like Marie, though. And she'll be there every day, you'll never be alone. It'll be sort of the same and sort of new—it'll be nice."

She sounded to herself just like she did when she was lying on the phone at work.

"Marie don' do things with me like you an' Stephen an' Drayfuss do," Ramón said. "She's too busy. I don' see why I have to go with her an' not stay here."

"Well, she takes care of you in a different way. She earns money, and we all benefit from that. She loves you just as much Stephen does, and anyway she's your mother now. A person has to stay with their mother."

"But I like it here, like famlee. Wha's gonna happen to us, Pip?"

She was already imagining what would happen to them: how much more time she'd have alone with Stephen. The best part of living here, even more than discovering her capacity for charity, had been that she got to be around him every day. Having grown up with a mother so unworldly that she couldn't even hang a picture on a wall, because it would have entailed buying a hammer to drive the nail, Pip had arrived on Thirty-Third Street with a hunger to learn practical skills. And Stephen had taught her these skills. He'd shown her how to spackle, how to caulk, how to operate a power saw, how to glaze a window, how to rewire a scavenged lamp, how to take apart her bicycle, and he'd been so patient with her, so generous, that she (or at least her body) had had a feeling of being groomed to be a worthier mate for him than Marie, whose domestic skills were strictly of the kitchen. He took her dumpster-diving, demonstrating how to jump right in and toss things around, digging for the good stuff, and sometimes she even did this by herself now, when she saw a promising dumpster, and exulted with him when she brought home something usable. It was a thing they had together. She could be more like him than Marie was, and thus, in time, more liked. This promise made the ache of her desire more bearable.

By the time she and Ramón had had a good cry together, and he'd refused to go downstairs with her, insisting that he wasn't hungry, two of Stephen's young friends from Occupy had arrived with quarts of low-end beer. She found the three of them sitting at the kitchen table, talking not about Marie but about wage/price-feedback loops. She preheated the oven for the frozen pizzas that were Dreyfuss's contribution to communal cooking, and it occurred to her that she would probably get stuck with more cooking now that Marie was gone. She considered the problem of communal labor while Stephen and his friends, Garth and Erik, imagined a labor utopia. Their theory was that the technology-driven gains in productivity and the resulting loss of manufacturing jobs would inevitably result in better wealth distribution, including generous payments to most of the population for doing nothing, when Capital realized that it could not afford to pauperize the consumers who bought its robot-made products. Unemployed consumers would acquire an economic value equivalent to their lost value as actual laborers, and could join forces with the people still working in the service industry, thereby creating a new coalition of labor and the permanently unemployed, whose overwhelming size would compel social change.

"I have a question, though," Pip said as she tore up the head of romaine lettuce that Dreyfuss considered a salad in itself. "If one person is getting paid forty thousand dollars a year to be a consumer, and another person is getting forty thousand to change bedpans in a nursing home, isn't the person changing bedpans going to kind of resent the person doing nothing?"

"The service worker would have to be paid more," Garth said.

"A *lot* more," Pip said.

"In a fair world," Erik said, "those nursing-home workers would be the ones driving the Mercedeses."

"Yeah, but even then," Pip said, "I'd rather just ride a bike and not have to change bedpans."

"Yeah, but if you wanted a Mercedes and changing bedpans was the way to get it?"

"No, Pip's right," Stephen said, which gave her a modest thrill. "The way you'd have to do it is make labor compulsory but then keep lowering the retirement age, so you'd always have full employment for everybody under thirty-two, or thirty-five, or whatever, and full unemployment for everybody over that age."

"Kind of sucks to be young in that world," Pip said. "Not that it doesn't already suck in this world."

"I'd be up for it," Garth said, "if I knew that starting at thirty-five I'd have the rest of my life to myself."

"And then, if you could get the retirement age down to thirty-two," Stephen said, "you could make it illegal to have kids before you retire. That would help with the population problem."

"Yeah," Garth said, "but when the population goes down, the retirement age necessarily goes up, because you still need service workers."

Pip took her phone out onto the back porch. She'd listened to a lot of these utopian discussions, and it was somehow comforting that Stephen and his friends could never quite work all the kinks out of their plan; that the world was as obstinately unfixable as her life was. While the light faded in the west, she replied, dutifully, to some texts from her remaining friends and then dutifully left a message for her mother, expressing hope that her eyelid was better. Her own body was still under the impression that something big was about to happen to it. Her heart went *dunk, dunk, dunk* as she watched the sky above the freeway turn from orange to indigo.

Dreyfuss was serving pizza when she went back inside, and the talk had turned to Andreas Wolf, the famous bringer of sunlight. She poured herself a large glass of beer.

"Was it a leak, or did they hack in?" Erik said.

"They never say," Garth said. "It could be that somebody just leaked them the passwords or the keys. That's part of Wolf's M.O.—protect the source."

"He's making people forget there ever was a Julian."

"At least Julian still blows him out of the water as a coder. Wolf's hackers are all hired guns. He couldn't even hack an Xbox by himself."

"But Wiki was dirty—people died because of Wiki. Wolf is still reasonably pure. In fact, that's his whole brand now: purity."

The word *purity* made Pip shudder.

"This definitely helps us," Stephen said. "There's a bunch of East Bay properties in the document dump. This is exactly the kind of shit we've been trying to document from the outside. We need to reach out to all the East Bay homeowners in the leak and get them on our side, do a rally with them or something."

Pip turned to Dreyfuss for an explanation. He ate with

such pleasureless speed that food just disappeared from his plate without his seeming to touch it. "The Sunlight Project," he said, "released thirty thousand internal emails from its undisclosed tropical location on Saturday night. Most of the emails are from the Bank of Relentless Pursuit, which is, interestingly, as you know, my own bank. Although my own case is nowhere mentioned in the emails, I believe it falls short of pathological to imagine that the German spies might have tried to do us a favor, having nosed out the identity of my bank. In any event, the emails are highly damning. Relentless Pursuit is still engaged in a pattern of misrepresentation, deceit, bullying, stonewalling, and the attempted theft of equity from homeowners in temporary distress. In toto, it casts a devastatingly unflattering light on the federal government's settlement with the banks."

"The Germans weren't spying, Dreyfuss," Stephen said. "I told Annagret about your bank."

"What?" Pip said sharply. "When?"

"When what?"

"When did you tell Annagret? Are you guys still in touch?"

"Of course we are."

She searched Stephen's beer-flushed face for evidence of guilt. She didn't see any, but her jealousy discounted this and moved right on to imagining that, with Marie out of the picture, Annagret would dump her boyfriend and move to Oakland and take Stephen and drive Pip out of the house.

"It's an amazing leak," Stephen said to her. "It's all there—how to work out a re-fi with the homeowner and then go nonresponsive, and then 'lose' the paperwork, and initiate foreclosure proceedings. They even name the numbers. Anybody with more than two consecutive missed or partial payments and seventy-five thousand in net equity gets the treatment. And quite a bit of it is right here in the East Bay. It's an incredible gift to us. I'm pretty sure Annagret made it happen."

Too agitated to eat, Pip drank down her beer and poured more. In the past four months, she'd received at least twenty emails from Annagret, all of which she'd marked as Read without reading. She wasn't much of a Facebook user, in part because she felt bludgeoned by happier people's photographs and in part because personal social-media use was frowned upon at work, but in order to keep using it at all she'd had to reject Annagret's overture of friendship, so as not to be bombarded with messages there as well. Her memory of Annagret was tangled up with the memory of Jason, and it made her feel strangely dirty, as if she'd been not robed but fully naked when she did the questionnaire and had then inflicted her dirtiness on Jason; as if she'd had some very wrong sort of personal intercourse with Annagret, the sort a person had bad dreams about. And now it was connected with the word *purity*, which to her was the most shameful word in the language, because it was her given name. It made her ashamed of her own driver's license, the PURITY TYLER beside her sullen head shot, and made filling out any application a small torture. The name had accomplished the opposite of what her mother had intended by giving it to her. As if to escape the weight of it, she'd made herself a dirty girl in high school, and she was still a dirty girl, desiring someone's husband . . . She kept drinking beer until she felt dulled enough to excuse herself and take some pizza to Ramón.

"I'm not hungry," he said, his face to the wall.

"Sweetie, you have to eat something."

"I'm not hungry. Where's Stephen?"

"He has friends over. He'll be up soon."

"I wanna stay here with you an' Stephen an' Drayfuss."

Pip bit her lip and went back down to the kitchen.

"You guys need to go now," she said to Garth and Erik. "Stephen needs to talk to Ramón."

"I'll go up soon," he said.

The plain fear in his face made her angry. "He's your *son*," she said. "He's not going to eat until you talk to him."

"All right," he said with a little-boy irritation that he normally directed at Marie.

Pip watched him go and wondered if she and he were going to skip right over the bliss part to the bitchy-relationship part. Having broken up the party, she sat and finished off the beer. She could feel an outburst coming on, and she knew she ought to go to bed, but her heart was beating too hard. Eventually her desire and anger and jealousy and distrust coalesced into a single beery grievance: Stephen had forgotten that he'd promised to have a private talk with her tonight. He stayed in touch with Annagret but he *abandoned* Pip. She heard his bedroom door close upstairs, and while she waited to hear it open again she silently repeated her grievance, rewording and rewording it, trying to strengthen it to bear the weight of her feeling of abandonment; but it couldn't bear the weight. She went upstairs anyway and knocked on Stephen's door.

He was sitting on the marital bed reading a book with a red title, something political.

"You're reading a *book*?" she said.

"It's better than thinking about things I have no control over."

She shut the door and sat down on a corner of the bed. "A person wouldn't have guessed anything unusual had even happened today, the way you were talking with Garth and Erik."

"What are they going to do about it? I still have my work. I still have my friends."

"And me. You still have me."

Stephen looked aside nervously. "Yeah."

"Did you forget you'd said you'd talk to me?"

"Yeah, I did. I'm sorry."

She tried to deepen and slow her breathing.

"What?" he said.

"You know what."

"No, I don't know what."

"You promised you were going to talk to me."

"I'm sorry. I forgot."

Her grievance was as puny and useless as she'd feared. There was no point in airing it a third time.

"What's going to happen to us?" she said.

"You and me?" He closed his book. "Nothing. We'll find a couple of new housemates, preferably female, so you don't have to be the only one."

"So nothing changes. Everything the same."

"Why would anything change?"

She paused, listening to her heart. "You know, a year ago, when we were having those coffees, I had the impression that you liked me."

"I do like you. A lot."

"But you made it sound like you were hardly even married."

He smiled. "Yeah, well, it turns out I was right about that."

"No, but *back then*," she said. "*Back then* you made it sound that way. Why did you do that to me?"

"I didn't do anything to you. We were having coffee."

She looked at him beseechingly, searching his eyes, asking them if he really was so clueless or was just pretending to be clueless for some cruel reason. It killed her that she couldn't figure out what he was thinking. Her breaths came harder, followed by tears. Not sad tears—upset tears, accusing tears.

"What is it?" he said.

She kept looking into his eyes, and finally he seemed to get it.

"Oh, no," he said. "No, no, no. No, no, no."

"Why not."

"Pip, come on. No."

"How could you not see," she said with a gasp, "how much I want you?"

"No, no, no."

"I thought we were just *waiting*. And now it's happened. It finally happened."

"God, Pip, no."

"Don't you like me?"

"Of course I like you. But not like that. Truly, I'm sorry, not like that. I'm old enough to be your father."

"Oh, come on! It's fifteen years! It's nothing!"

Stephen looked at the window and then at the door, as if weighing escape options.

"Are you telling me you never felt anything?" she said. "It was all in my head?"

"You must have misinterpreted."

"What?"

"I never wanted to have kids," he said. "That's the whole issue with Marie and me, I didn't want babies. I kept telling her, 'What do we need babies for? We have Ramón, we have Pip. We can still be good parents.' And that's what you are to me. Like a daughter."

She stared at him. "That's my role? To be like *Ramón* for you? Would you be even happier if I *stank*? I *have* a parent! I don't need another parent!"

"Well, actually, it kind of seemed like you did," Stephen said. "Like a father was exactly what you needed. And I can still do it. You can still stay here."

"Are you out of your mind? Stay here? Like this?"

She stood up and looked around wildly. It was better

to be angry than to be hurt; maybe even better than being loved and held by him, because maybe anger was what she'd been feeling toward him all along, anger disguised as wanting.

In a kind of anarchy of involition, she found herself pulling off her sweater, and then taking off her bra, and then dropping to her knees on the bed and pushing herself at Stephen, abusing him with her nakedness. "*Do I look like a daughter?* Is that what I look like to you?"

He cowered with his hands over his face. "Stop it."

"Look at me."

"I'm not going to look at you. You're the one who's out of your mind."

"Fuck you! Fuck you, fuck you, fuck you, fuck you. Are you too fucking weak to even look at me?" Where were these words coming from? What hidden place? Already a riptide of remorse was swirling around her knees, and already she knew it would be worse than all of her previous remorses combined, and yet there was nothing to be done but see it through, and do what her body wanted, which was to collapse on Stephen. She rubbed her bare chest against his seersucker shirt, pulled his hands from his face and let her hair fall around it; and she could see that she'd really done it this time. He looked terrified.

"Just be sure, OK?" she said. "Be sure that's all I am to you."

"I can't believe you're doing this to me. Four hours after she left the house."

"Oh, so four days would make a difference? Or four months? Four years?" She lowered her face toward his. "Touch me!"

She tried to guide his hands, but he was very strong and pushed her off him easily. He scrambled away from the bed and retreated to the door.

"You know," he said, breathing hard, "I don't really believe in therapy, but I'm thinking you could use it."

"As if I could afford it."

"Seriously, Pip. This is totally fucked up. Are you even thinking about what I'm feeling?"

"Last I checked, you were reading—" She picked up his book. "Gramsci."

"If you're pulling shit like this with other people, people who aren't looking out for you, you're not doing yourself any favors. I don't like what it says about your impulse control."

"I know. I'm abnormal. It's like the refrain of my life."

"No, you're great. You're wonderful, I mean it. But still—seriously."

"Are you in love with her?" Pip said.

He turned back from the door. "What?"

"Annagret. Is that what this is about? You're in love with her?"

"Oh, Pip." His look of pity and concern was so pure that it almost overcame her distrust; she almost believed she had no reason to be jealous. "She's in Düsseldorf," he said. "I hardly even know her."

"Riiiiight. But you're in touch with her."

"Try to listen to yourself. Try to see what you're doing."

"I'm not hearing a no."

"For God's sake."

"Please tell me I'm wrong. Just say I'm wrong."

"The person I want is Marie. Don't you understand that?"

Pip squeezed her eyes shut, trying to understand it while also refusing to. "But Marie's with someone else now," she said. "And you're in touch with Annagret. You don't even know you're in love with her yet, but I think you are. Or you will be soon. She's the right age for you, right?"

"I've got to get some air. And you need to leave my room."

"Just show me," she said. "Come show me I'm wrong. Just hold my hand for a second. Please. I won't believe you otherwise."

"Then you're going to have to not believe me."

She drew herself into a ball. "I knew it," she whispered. The pain of jealousy was delicious in comparison to the thought that she was simply being crazy. But the thought was getting stronger.

"I'm heading out," Stephen said.

And he left her lying on his bed.

TUESDAY

She texted in sick to work, pleading stomach sickness, which wasn't totally a lie. Around ten o'clock Marie came knocking on her door, asking her to say good-bye to Ramón, but the slightest movement of Pip's body reminded her of what she'd done the night before. When Marie came upstairs a second time and ventured to open her door and look in on her, Pip could barely put any voice into the words *go away.*

"Are you all right?" Marie said.

"Please go away. Please shut the door."

She heard Marie approaching her and kneeling. "I wanted to say good-bye," she said.

Pip kept her eyes shut and said nothing, and the words that Marie then poured down on her were devoid of sense, were just blow after blow on her brain, a torment to be endured until it stopped. When it finally did stop, it was followed by the worse torment of Marie stroking her shoulder. "Won't you talk to me at all?" she said.

"Please, please, please, go away," Pip managed to say.

Marie's reluctant departure was yet another nearly unendurable torment, and the sound of the door closing didn't end it. Nothing could end it. Pip couldn't leave her bed, let alone leave her room, let alone go outside, where the strong sunlight of another hideously perfect day might honestly have caused her to die of shame. She had half a bar of dark chocolate in her room, and this was all she ate all day, taking one bite and then lying completely still to recover from the reminder that she had a physical self—"so *visible*, so *visible*," as her mother had said. Even to cry would have been a reminder, and so she didn't cry. She did think that at least nightfall might bring some relief, but it didn't. The only thing that changed was that she was able to sob at her loss of Stephen, off and on, for many hours.

WEDNESDAY

Thirst and hunger woke her up at dawn. With her senses sharpened by the need for stealth, she quickly changed her clothes and packed her knapsack and crept downstairs to the kitchen. Her one imperative was not to encounter Stephen, ideally for the rest of her life, and even though he wasn't an early riser she didn't slow down to eat anything but simply grabbed some food at random and stuffed it into her knapsack. Then she drank three glasses of water and made a stop in the bathroom. When she came out, Dreyfuss was standing in the front hallway, wearing his nighttime sweatclothes.

"Feeling better, I see," he said.

"Yeah, I had a stomach thing yesterday."

"I thought Wednesdays were one of your late days. And yet here you are at six fifteen."

"Right, I have to make up for yesterday."

Even the most transparent lies didn't unsettle Dreyfuss. They merely gave his brain more to process, briefly slowing it down. "Am I correct in assuming that you'll be moving out now, too?"

"Probably, yeah."

"Why."

"You obviously know why, since you assumed it, and so why are you asking me? You obviously know everything that happens in this house."

He considered this affectlessly. "It may interest you to know that I've read through Stephen's email and social-media correspondence with the German woman. It's entirely innocent, if somewhat tediously ideological. I'd hate to think of losing your intelligent company over a matter as small as that."

"Wow," Pip said. "I was about to say I was going to sort of miss you, and now you tell me that not only do you eavesdrop, you read our email."

"Just Stephen's," Dreyfuss said. "We share the computer, and he never logs out. I believe this constitutes 'plain sight,' in legal parlance."

"Well, for your information, Annagret is the least of my worries now."

"Interestingly, many of her messages to Stephen concern you. She's evidently very distressed that you don't want to be friends with her. I find your position eminently reasonable, perhaps even strongly advisable. Yes: advisable. But you might care to know that as far as the German woman is concerned, you are the person of interest in this house. Not our Stephen. Nor, it goes without saying, Ramón or Marie. Nor even, if I examine the facts with rigorous logic, I myself."

Pip was putting on her bike helmet. "OK, great," she said. "Good to know."

"There was something not right about those Germans."

At an anonymous Starbuck's on Piedmont Avenue, while consuming scones and a latte, she wrote and then agonized over and finally found the courage to send an email to Stephen, who had no text capability, since phone plans cost money. That Dreyfuss would read the email didn't much matter to her; it was like knowing that a dog or a computer "knew" things about her.

> I apologize for what I did. Please tell me when you won't be home this week, so I can get my stuff.

Sending this message made her loss more real, and she attempted to fantasize about how things might have gone in his bedroom if he'd been unable to resist her, but her imagination instead kept summoning up what had actually happened; and weeping in a public café was a bad idea.

Two tables over, a white-bearded chai-drinker type was looking at her. When she surprised him by looking back, his eyes dropped down guiltily to his tablet device. Why hadn't Stephen looked at her like this? Was that so much to ask?

It seemed like a father was exactly what you needed: of all of Stephen's cruelties in the bedroom, this had been the worst. And yet there was clearly something wrong with her, and clearly the more appropriate object of her anger was her missing father. She narrowed her eyes and stared at the chai drinker. When he looked at her again, she gave him a phony grimace, a mean smile, to which he responded with a courtly nod and then angled his body away from her.

She texted her friend Samantha and asked if she could crash with her. Of her remaining friends, Samantha was the most self-involved and thus the least likely to ask embarrassing questions. Samantha was also a cook, with equipment in her kitchen, and Pip hadn't forgotten that she owed her mother a not-birthday cake on Friday.

She still had three hours to kill before her late work-day started. This would have been a low-risk time to leave a message for her mother, since her mother was always too deep in her Endeavor in the early morning to pick up the phone, but Pip couldn't do it. She watched the people lining up for pastries and coffee drinks, nice racially diverse Oakland people freshly showered and able to afford a daily bought breakfast. Oh, to have a job you liked, a mate you trusted, a child who loved you, a purpose in life. And it occurred to her that a purpose in life was what Annagret had offered her. Annagret had wanted her. Annagret had wanted *her*. She was ashamed to recall how crazily she'd latched on to the idea that there was anything between Annagret and Stephen. It must have been the beer she'd drunk.

She picked up her device and assembled all the emails that Annagret had sent her in the past four months. The earliest was headed please forgive me. As she read the message, savoring its pleading tone and its compliments to her intelligence and character, Pip found herself obeying the subject header and forgiving Annagret, with an alacrity that was perhaps itself a bit crazy. And yet maybe not so crazy, because Annagret not only liked her but had been *right*—right about Stephen, about men, about everything. And had not given up on her; had sent her twenty emails, the most recent just a week ago. Nobody else in her life would have been that persistent.

She opened a message headed wonderful news, from two months ago.

Dearest Pip, I know you must be still angry with me and maybe not even reading my emails, but I must tell you some very good news: You are APPROVED for an internship with the Sunlight Project! I hope you will take advantage of this superfun and awarding opportunity.

I'm still thinking all the time of what you said about the private information you wanted—well this is your chance for that. TSP will pay your room and meals in the most interesting part of the world, in addition a small monthly stipendium, and often it can lend assistance with money for your air travel. You can read the attached letter and factsheet for more details. I only want you to know that I gave you the HIGHEST recommendation with every sincerity. And it looks like Andreas and the others still trust my determinations! ;) I'm very excited for you and hope you will consider. I'm only sorry, if you go, I won't be there with you. But maybe, if you're still angry with me, this will make you more interested to go? ;) With hugs, Annagret
PS: here is Andreas's email: ahw@sonnenlicht.org You can write to him personally with questions.

Reading this, Pip felt obscurely disappointed. It was like a questionnaire with no wrong answers: if an internship was this easy to get, how much could it be worth? And no sooner had she started to change her mind about Annagret than Annagret tried to fob her off on yet another man, albeit a rather famous and cher*iss*metic man. Peevishly, and without stopping to think, she put a fingertip on Wolf's email address and fired off a message to him:

Dear Andreas Wolf, what's your deal? A person named Annagret who I hardly know tells me I can be a paid intern with your project. Is this like a sex opportunity for you, or what? Do you guys have a keg of Kool-Aid? The whole thing frankly sounds deeply creepy to me. I don't care very much about the work you're doing down there, in the jungle or whatever, but Annagret doesn't seem to think it even matters if I do. Which really makes me wonder.
Yours, Pip Tyler, Oakland, California, USA

As soon as she hit the Send button, she had a spasm of remorse; her interval between action and remorse was diminishing so rapidly that soon she might be all remorse, unable to act at all; which might not be such a bad thing.

By way of penance, she opened a search engine and did some belated research on Wolf and his project. Given the multitude of haters on the Internet, it was impressive how few hostile comments about Wolf she was able to find if she disregarded the carpings of die-hard Julian Assange defenders and the statements of governments and corporations with an obvious self-interest in calling Wolf a criminal. Otherwise, in terms of universal admiration, he was right up there with Aung San Suu Kyi and Bruce Springsteen; a search of his name plus the word *purity* yielded a quarter million matches.

Wolf's motto, and his project's battle cry, was *Sunlight is the best disinfectant*. Born in East Germany in 1960, he'd distinguished himself in the 1980s as a daring and sensational critic of the Communist regime. After the Berlin Wall came down, he'd led the crusade to preserve the enormous East German secret-police archives and open them to the public; here again he was hated only by former police informants whose post-reunification reputations had been tarnished by the exposure of their pasts to sunlight. Wolf had founded the Sunlight Project in 2000, focusing first on assorted German malfeasances but soon broadening his scope to social injustice and toxic secrets worldwide. Several hundred thousand Web images showed him to be a very good-looking man, but he'd apparently never married or had children. He'd fled prosecution in Germany in 2006 and Europe generally in 2010, receiving asylum first in Belize and more recently in Bolivia, whose populist president, Evo Morales, was a fan. The only thing Wolf kept secret was the identity of his major financial backers (thereby prompting a terabyte or two of

heated online chatter about his "inconsistency"), and the
only even vaguely unseemly thing about him was the intensity of his rivalry with Assange. Wolf had tauntingly
denigrated Assange's methods and personal life, while
Assange had contented himself with pretending that Wolf
did not exist. Wolf liked to contrast WikiLeaks—in his
words, "a neutral and unfiltered platform"—with the work
of his more "purpose-driven" Sunlight Project, and to
make a moral distinction between his *benign and openly
admitted motive* in protecting his backers' privacy and the
malignant concealed motives of the parties whose secrets
he exposed.

Pip was struck by how many of the exposures had to do
with the oppression of women: not just big issues like
rape as a war crime and wage inequalities as a deliberate
policy but stuff as small as the luridly sexist emails of a
bank manager in Tennessee. Rare was the interview or
press release in which Wolf's militant feminism went un-
mentioned. She understood better how Annagret could
prefer the company of women and still admire Wolf.

The high seriousness and sheer volume of the online
information about Wolf deepened her remorse about the
email she'd sent him. He: authentic risk-taking hero and
friend of presidents. She: snarky little twerp. Not until she
was about to leave for work could she bring herself to
check for new messages. And here they were already,
Stephen and Wolf, one after the other.

> Apology accepted, incident on its way to being
> forgotten. There's no reason for you to move out. You're a
> great housemate, and we'll have Ramon three evenings a
> week—Marie and I worked it out yesterday. S.

A drawback of email was that you could only delete it once:
couldn't crumple it up, fling it to the floor, stomp on it, rip it

to shreds, and burn it. Was there anything crueler, from the person who'd rejected you, than compassionate forbearance? Her anger momentarily chased away her remorse and shame. She *wanted* the "incident" to be remembered! She wanted his complete attention! She fired back:

> With all this forgetting, I guess you forgot my question too: when will you not be home?

Despite having got up four hours early, she was now on the verge of being late to work, but while her blood was up and her remorse was at bay she went ahead and read Wolf's message.

> Dear Pip Tyler,
>
> Your email is LOL—I could use many more like it. And of course you have questions, we would be disappointed if you didn't. But, no, I am not a white-slaver, and our beverage of choice here is bottled beer. Also, we have more outstanding hackers and lawyers and theorists than I know what to do with. What we *frankly* (your funny word) never have enough of is laypeople of high intelligence and independent character who can help us to see the world as it is, and help the world to see us as we are. I have known and trusted Annagret for many years and never heard her more enthusiastic about an applicant. We would be delighted if you come and visit our operation. If you don't like us, you can enjoy our beautiful surroundings as a vacation and then go home. But I think you'll like us. Our dirty little secret is that we're having lots of fun down here. Send me more questions, the more LOL the better.
>
> Yours,
> Andreas

After everything she'd been reading about Wolf, she couldn't believe she'd gotten such a long email from him, and so quickly. She reread it twice before getting on her bike and heading downhill, propelled by gravity and by the thrill of imagining that she really was an extraordinary person, and that this was the true reason her life was such a mess, and that Annagret had been the first to recognize it, and that even if Wolf turned out to be the world's cleverest debaucher and Annagret his sexually traumatized procuress, and even if she, Pip, fell victim to Wolf herself, she would still be getting her revenge on Stephen; because, whatever else Wolf was, he wasn't *weak*.

She still had five minutes to kill when she reached the office. She stopped in the bike room and typed out the reply she'd been composing in her head.

Dear Mr. Wolf, Thank you for the nice note and suspiciously speedy response. If I were trying to lure an innocent young person to Bolivia for purposes of sex slavery and/or cultish subservience, I would have written the exact same note. In fact . . . come to think of it . . . how do I know the note wasn't written by a cultishly subservient sex-slave assistant of yours? Somebody of high intelligence and formerly independent character? We have a verification problem here! Yours, Pip T.

Hoping this would make him LOL again, she went upstairs to her cubicle. Beside her computer was a sticky note from one of her outreach colleagues (*Found this—*☺ *Janet*) and a printout of a recipe: "White Whole Wheat Cake with Vegan Cream Cheese Frosting and Olallie-berries." She dropped into her chair with a heavy sigh. As if she didn't have enough to feel bad about already, she had to regret thinking ill of her colleagues.

On the plus side, she seemed to have begun a flirtatious

correspondence with somebody world-famous. She'd always considered herself immune to celebrity—had even, to some extent, resented it, for reasons hazily akin to her resentment of people with siblings. Her feeling was: *what makes you so much worthier of attention than me?* When a college friend of hers had landed a Hollywood job and started bragging about the famous actors he was meeting, she'd quietly severed communications with him. But now she saw that what mattered about celebrity was that other people were *not* immune to it: that they might be impressed with her connection to it, and that this might give her somewhat more than the zero power she currently felt she had. In a pleasantly seduced frame of mind, she waded back into her Rancho Ancho call sheet and deliberately refrained from checking her device, so as to prolong the anticipation.

At her dinner break she found Wolf's reply.

I am seeing why Annagret likes you. My note would have reached you even faster if it hadn't had to travel through four times the usual number of servers. Nowadays there is really only one habit of highly effective people: Don't fall behind with email. Unfortunately, for security reasons, I can't offer to video chat with you. More important, our Project needs risktakers with good judgement. You will have to judge for yourself the risk of trusting my emails. You may of course use every available internet tool to help you judge, and I can assure you, if you jump, we are here to catch you with open arms. But it is finally yours to decide whether to believe me. A.

She noted with pleasure that he'd already dispensed with a salutation, and she did the same intimate thing in her reply.

But trust goes both ways, right? Shouldn't you also have to trust *me*? Maybe we should each tell the other some

little thing we're ashamed of. I'll even go first. My real
name is Purity. I'm so ashamed of it I always hold on
tight to my wallet when I take it out with friends, because
sometimes people grab wallets to make fun of people's
driver's license pictures, and my name is on the license.

How about that, Mr. Purity? Now it's your turn.

Too giddy with temerity to eat, she marched down the hall
to Igor's office. He was packing his briefcase, his day
already done. He frowned when he saw her.

"Yeah, I know," she said. "I haven't washed my hair in
three days."

"Your stomach's better? You're not contagious?"

She plopped herself down in a guest chair. "So listen.
Igor. Your twenty questions."

"Let's forget that," he said quickly.

"The thing you wanted from me, that I was supposed
to guess. What was it?"

"Pip, I'm sorry. I'm taking my sons to the A's game.
This is not a good time."

"I was just kidding about the lawsuit."

"Are you really feeling all right? You don't seem like
yourself."

"Are you going to answer the question?"

Igor's look of fear was reminiscent of Stephen's two
nights earlier. "If you need more time off, you can take
it. Take the rest of the week if you want."

"Actually, I'm thinking of taking the rest of my life
off."

"It was a stupid joke, the twenty questions. I apologize.
But my sons are waiting for me."

Sons: even worse than siblings!

"Your sons can wait five minutes," she said.

"We'll talk first thing in the morning."

"You said you liked me, although you don't know why. You said you wanted to see me succeed."

"Both things completely true."

"But you can't take five minutes to tell me why I shouldn't quit?"

"I can take the whole morning, tomorrow. But right now—"

"Right now you don't have time to flirt."

Igor sighed, looked at his watch, and sat down in the other guest chair. "Don't quit tonight," he said.

"I think I'm going to quit tonight."

"Is it the flirting? I don't have to do that. I thought you enjoyed it."

Pip frowned. "So there wasn't actually anything you wanted from me."

"No, just fun. Just teasing around. You're so funny when you're hostile." He seemed pleased with his explanation, pleased with his own good nature, not to mention his good looks. "You could have California's Most Hostile Employee of the Year Award."

"So it was never going to be anything but flirting."

"Of course not. I'm happily married, this is an office, there are rules."

"So in other words I'm nothing to you except your worst employee."

"We can talk about a new position for you in the morning."

She saw that all she'd done by confronting him was ruin the long-running game with him, the game that had made her work here halfway bearable. Earlier in the day, she'd thought she couldn't feel more alone than she already did, but now she saw that she could.

"This is going to sound crazy," she said, with a catch in her throat. "But could you possibly ask your wife to go to the game tonight? Could you possibly take me to dinner and give me some advice?"

"Ordinarily, yes. But my wife has other plans. I'm already late. Why don't you go home and come back in the morning?"

She shook her head. "I really, really, really need a friend right now."

"I'm so sorry. But I can't help you."

"Clearly."

"I don't know what happened to you, but maybe you should go home and see your mother for a few days. Come back on Monday and we'll talk."

Igor's phone rang, and while he took the call she sat with her head bowed, envying the wife to whom he was apologizing for being late. When he was finished, she could feel him hesitating behind her shoulder, as if weighing whether to lay a hand on it. He apparently decided against it.

When he was gone, she returned to her cubicle and typed out a letter of resignation. She checked her texts and emails, but there was nothing from either Stephen or Andreas Wolf, and so she dialed her mother's number and left a message, telling her that she was coming to Felton a day early.

THURSDAY

The Oakland bus station was a mile-and-a-half walk from her friend Samantha's apartment. By the time Pip got there, wearing her knapsack and carrying, in a roller-skate box that she'd borrowed from Samantha, the vegan olallieberry cake that she'd spent the morning making, she needed to pee. The door to the ladies' room was blocked, however, by a cornrowed girl her own age, an addict and/

or prostitute and/or crazy person, who shook her head emphatically when Pip tried to get past her.

"Can't I quickly pee?"

"You just gonna have to wait."

"Like, how long, though?"

"Long as it takes."

"Takes for what? I won't look at anything. I just want to pee."

"What's in the box?" the girl demanded. "Those skates?"

Pip boarded the Santa Cruz bus with a full bladder. It went without saying that the bathroom at the back was out of order. Apparently it was not enough that her entire life was in crisis: all the way to San Jose, if not to Santa Cruz, she would have to worry about wetting herself.

Control pee, she told herself. *Control-P.* As a teenager, when she was living in Felton and going to school in Santa Cruz, all her friends had owned Apple computers, but the laptop her mother had bought her was a cheap, generic PC from OfficeMax, and what she'd typed on it, when she needed to print, was Control-P. Printing, like peeing, was evidently a thing you *needed* to do. "I need to print," the people at Renewable Solutions were always saying. This exact, strange phrase: *I need to print. Need to P. Need to control pee . . .* The thought struck her as good; she prided herself on having thoughts like this; and yet it went around in circles without leading anywhere. At the end of the day (people at Renewable Solutions were always saying "at the end of the day"), she still needed to pee.

When the freeway momentarily rose out of the industrial East Bay bottomlands in which it wallowed, she could see fog piling up behind the mountains across the bay. There would be fog over the hill tonight, and she hoped that if she had to wet her pants she could wait and do it under its merciful cover. To get her mind off her bladder, she stuffed her ears with Aretha Franklin—at least she could finally stop trying to like Stephen's hard-core boy rock—and reread her latest exchanges with Andreas Wolf.

He'd emailed back to her the night before, while she was knocked out with Samantha's Ativan on Samantha's couch.

> The secret of your name is safe with me. But you know public figures must be especially careful. Imagine the state of distrust in which I move through the world. Revealing anything shameful to anyone, I run the risk of exposure, censure, mockery. Everyone should be told this about fame before they start pursuing it: you will never trust anyone again. You will be a kind of damned person, not only because you can't trust anyone but, still worse, you must always be considering how important you are, how newsworthy, and this divides you from yourself and poisons your soul. It sucks to be well-known, Pip. And yet everyone wants to be well-known, it's what the whole world is made of now, this wanting to be well-known.

> If I told you, when I was seven years old my mother showed me her genitals, what would you do with this information?

Reading this message in the morning, and immediately doubting that Wolf had actually entrusted her with a shameful secret, she'd searched *andreas wolf mother genitals seven years old* and found only seven quality matches, all random. Among them was "72 Interesting Facts About Adolf Hitler." She wrote back:

> I would say holy shit and keep it to myself. Because I think you might be overdoing the self-pitying famous-person thing. Maybe you've forgotten how it sucks to have

nobody be interested in you and not have any power.
People will believe you if you expose my secret. But if
I expose yours, they'll just say I fabricated your email for
some sick reason, because I'm a girl. We girls are
supposed to at least have these amazing sexual powers,
but in my recent experience this is just a lie told by men to
make them feel better about having ALL the power.

Afternoons in Bolivia must have been Wolf's time for
emailing, because his reply came back quickly, the security of umpteen extra servers notwithstanding.

I'm sorry that I sounded self-pitying—I was trying to sound
tragic!

It's true I'm male and have some power, but I never asked
to be born male. Maybe being male is like being born a
predator, and maybe the only right thing for the predator to
do, if it sympathizes with smaller animals and won't accept
that it was born to kill them, is to betray its nature and
starve to death. But maybe it's like something else—like
being born with more money than others. Then the right
thing to do becomes a more interesting social question.

I hope you'll come down and join us. You might find out
you have more kinds of power than you think you do.

This reply discouraged her. Already the agreeable flirtation was slipping into German abstraction. While the cake
layers were baking, she replied:

Mr. Appropriately Named Wolf!

No doubt due to my psychology, the messed-up state of
which many people in my life can now attest to, I'm feeling

more like the smaller animal that accepts its nature and just wants to be eaten. All I can picture about your Project is lots of better-adjusted people happily realizing their potential. Unless you have a spare $130000 lying around, so I can pay off my student loans, and unless you feel like writing to my (single, isolated, depressed) mother and convincing her to do without me indefinitely, I'm afraid I won't be finding out about these amazing other powers of mine.

Sincerely, Pip

The email had stunk of self-pity, but she'd sent it anyway, and then mentally replayed her latest rejections by men while she frosted the cake with puttylike vegan icing and packed her knapsack for the trip to Felton.

Because of heavy traffic, the bus didn't stop long enough in San Jose for her to get off. Bladder ache radiated throughout her abdomen as the bus proceeded up Route 17 and over the Santa Cruz Mountains. Around Scotts Valley, the dear fog appeared, and suddenly the season was different, the hour less determinate. Most evenings in June, a great paw of Pacific fog reached into Santa Cruz, over the wooden roller coaster, along the stagnant San Lorenzo, up through the wide streets where surfers lived, and into the redwoods on the hills. By morning the ocean's outward breath condensed in dew so heavy that it ran in gutters. And this was one Santa Cruz, this ghostly gray late-rising place. When the ocean inhaled again, midmorning, it left behind the other Santa Cruz, the optimistic one, the sunny one; but the great paw lurked offshore all day. Toward sunset, like a depression following euphoria, it rolled back in and muted human sound, closed down vistas, made everything very local, and seemed to amplify the barking of the sea lions on the underpinnings of the pier. You could hear them from miles away, their *arp, arp, arp* a homing call to family members still out diving in the fog.

By the time the bus pulled off Front Street and into the station, the streetlights had come on, tricked by atmospherics. Pip hobbled to the station's ladies' room and into an unoccupied stall, dropped her knapsack on the dirty floor, put the cake box on top of it, and yanked down her jeans. While various muscles were unclenching, her device beeped with an incoming message.

The internship lasts three months, with an option for renewal. Your stipend should cover your loan payments. And maybe it would do your mother good to be without you a little while.

I'm sorry you're feeling bad and powerless. Sometimes a change of scene can help with that.

I have often wondered what the prey is feeling when it is captured. Often it seems to become completely still in the predator's jaws, as if it feels no pain. As if nature, at the very end, shows mercy for it.

She was scrutinizing the last paragraph, trying to discern a veiled threat or promise in it, when her knapsack made a small comment, a kind of dry sigh. It was slumping under the weight of the cake box. Before she could stem the flow of her pee and lunge for the box, it fell to the floor and opened itself, dumping the cake facedown onto tiles smeared with condensed fog and cigarette ash and the droppings and boot residues of girl buskers and panhandlers. Some olallieberries went rolling.

"Oh, that is so nice of you," she said to the ruined cake. "That is so special of you."

Weeping at her ineffectiveness, she conveyed the uncontaminated chunks of cake into the box and then worked for so long to wipe the icing from the floor with paper towels, as if it were smeary albino shit, as if anybody but her actually cared about cleanliness, that she nearly missed the bus to Felton.

A fellow rider, a dirty girl with blond dreads, turned around and asked her, "You going up to 'Pico?"

"Just to the bottom of the road," Pip said.

"I'd never been up there till three months ago," the girl said. "There's nothing else quite like it! There's two boys there that let me sleep on their couch if I have sex with them. I don't mind that at all. Everything's different in 'Pico. Do you ever go up there?"

It happened that Pip had lost her virginity in Lompico. Maybe there really was nothing else quite like it.

"It sounds like you've got a good thing going," she said politely.

"'Pico's the best," the girl agreed. "They have to truck in their water on this property, because of the elevation. They don't have to deal with the suburban scum, which is great. They give me food and everything. There's nothing else quite like it!"

The girl seemed perfectly contented with her life, while to Pip it seemed to be raining ashes in the bus. She forced a smile and put in her earbuds.

Felton was still fog-free, the air at the bus stop still scented with sunbaked redwood litter, but the sun had dropped behind a ridge, and Pip's childhood bird friends, the brown towhees and the spotted ones, were hopping on the shadowed lane as she walked up it. As soon as she could see the cabin, its door flew open and her mother

came running out to meet her, crying "Oh, oh!" She wore
an expression of love so naked it seemed to Pip almost
obscene. And yet, as always, Pip couldn't help returning
her mother's hug. The body that her mother was at odds
with felt precious to her. Its warmth, its softness; its mor-
tality. It had a faint but distinctive skin smell that took Pip
back to the many years when she and her mother had
shared a bed. She would have liked to bury her face in
her mother's chest and stand there and take comfort, but
she rarely came home without finding her mother in the
middle of some thought that she was bursting to express.

"I just had the nicest conversation about you with
Sonya Dawson at the store," her mother said. "She was remembering how sweet you were to all the kindergarteners
when you were in third grade. Do you remember that? She
said she still has the Christmas cards you made her twins. I'd
completely forgotten you made cards for *all* the kindergarteners. Sonya said, that whole year, whenever anybody
asked the twins what their favorite anything was, they
answered 'Pip!' Their favorite dessert—'Pip!' Their favorite color—'Pip!' You were their favorite everything! Such
a loving little girl, so good to the smaller kids. Do you
remember Sonya's twins?"

"Vaguely," Pip said, walking toward the cabin.

"They adored you. Revered you. The entire kindergarten did. I was so proud when Sonya reminded me."

"How unfortunate that I couldn't remain eight years
old."

"Everyone always said you were a special girl," her
mother said, pursuing her. "All the teachers said so. Even
the other parents said so. There was just some kind of
special magic loving-kindness about you. It makes me so
happy to remember."

Inside the cabin, Pip set down her things and promptly
began to cry.

"Pussycat?" her mother said, greatly alarmed.

"I ruined your cake!" Pip said, sobbing like an eight-year-old.

"Oh that doesn't matter at all." Her mother enveloped her and rocked her, drawing her face to her breastbone, holding her tight. "I'm so happy that you're here."

"I spent all day making it," Pip choked out. "And then I dropped it on the dirty floor at the bus station. It fell on the floor, Mom. I'm so sorry. I got everything so dirty. I'm sorry, I'm sorry, I'm sorry."

Her mother shushed her, kissed her head, and squeezed her until she'd expelled some of her misery, in the form of tears and snot, and began to feel as if she'd ceded an important advantage by breaking down. She extricated herself and went to the bathroom to clean up.

On the shelves were the faded flannel sheets that she'd slept on as a girl. On the rack was the same tired bath towel that her mother had used for twenty years. The concrete floor of the tiny shower had long ago lost its paint to her mother's scrubbing. When Pip saw that her mother had lit two candles by the sink for her, as for a romantic date or religious ceremony, she nearly fell apart again.

"I got the smoky lentils and the kale salad you like so much," her mother said, hovering near the door. "I forgot to ask if you were still eating meat, so I didn't get you a pork chop."

"It's hard to live in a communal house and not eat meat," Pip said. "Although I'm no longer living in a communal house."

While she opened the bottle of wine she'd bought for her exclusive use, and while her mother spread out the bounty of her New Leaf employee discount, Pip gave a mostly fictitious account of her reasons for leaving the Thirty-Third Street house. Her mother seemed to believe every word of it. Pip proceeded to attack the bottle while her mother reported on her eyelid (not spasming but still feeling as if it might spasm again at any moment), the latest workplace incursions on her privacy, the latest abrasions of her sensitivities by New Leaf shoppers, and the moral dilemma posed by the 3 a.m. crowing of her next-door neighbor's rooster. Pip had imagined that she might hide out at the cabin for a week, to recover and to plan her next move, but despite her supposed centrality to her mother's life she was feeling as if her mother's miniature universe of obsession and grievance was sufficient unto itself. As if there was, actually, no place in her life for Pip now.

"So, I also quit my job," she said when they'd eaten dinner and the wine was nearly gone.

"Good for you," her mother said. "That job never sounded worthy of your talents."

"Mom, I have no talents. I have useless intelligence. And no money. And now no place to live."

"You can always live with me."

"Let's try to be realistic."

"You can have the sleeping porch back. You love the sleeping porch."

Pip poured the last of the wine into her glass. Moral hazard allowed her to simply ignore her mother when she felt like it. "So here's what I'm thinking," she said. "Two possibilities. One, you help me find my other parent, so I can try to get some money out of him. The other is I'm thinking of going to South America for a while. If you want me to stay around here, you have to help me find the missing parent."

Her mother's posture, fortified by her Endeavor, was as beautifully vertical as Pip's was crappy and slouched. A faraway look was coming over her, almost a different kind of face altogether, a younger face. It could only be,

Pip thought, the face of the person she'd once been, before she was a mother.

Looking into the now-dark window by the table, her mother said: "Not even for you will I do that."

"OK, so I guess I'm going to South America."

"South America . . ."

"Mom, I don't want to go. I want to stay closer to you. But you have to help me out here."

"You see!" her mother cried, still with her faraway look, as if she were seeing more than just her own reflection in the window. "He's doing it to me even now! He's trying to take you from me! And I will not let that happen!"

"This is fairly crazy talk, Mom. I'm twenty-three years old. If you saw where I've been living, you'd know I know how to take care of myself."

Finally her mother turned to her. "What's in South America?"

"This thing," Pip said with some reluctance, as if confessing to an impure thought or action. "This kind of interesting thing. It's called the Sunlight Project. They give paid internships and teach you all these skills."

Her mother frowned. "The illegal leak thing?"

"What do *you* know about it."

"I do read the newspaper, pussycat. This is the group that the sex criminal started."

"No, you see?" Pip said. "You see? You're thinking of WikiLeaks. You don't know anything about the Project. You live in the mountains and you don't know anything."

For a moment her mother seemed to doubt herself. But then, emphatically: "Not Assange. Somebody else. Andreas."

"OK, I'm sorry. You do know something."

"But he's the same as the other one, or worse."

"No, Mom, actually not. They're completely different."

At this, her mother closed her eyes, sat up even straighter, and began to do her breathing. It always happened when she got too upset, and it put Pip in a bind, because she didn't like to disturb her but also didn't want to spend an hour waiting for her to resurface.

"I'm sure that's very calming for you," she said. "But I'm still sitting here, and you're not dealing with me."

Her mother just breathed.

"Do you want to at least tell me what really happened with my dad?"

"I told you," her mother murmured, her eyes still shut.

"No, you lied. And you want to know something else? Andreas Wolf can help me find him."

Her mother's eyes sprang open.

"So you can either tell me," Pip said, "or I can go to South America and find out for myself."

"Purity, listen to me. I know I'm a difficult person, but you have to believe me: if you go to South America and do that, it will kill me."

"Why? Lots of people my age travel. Why can't you trust that I'll come back? Can't you see how much I love you?"

Her mother shook her head. "This is my worst nightmare. And now Andreas Wolf. This is a *nightmare*, a *nightmare*."

"What do you know about Andreas?"

"I know that he is not a good person."

"How? How do you know that? I just spent half a day researching him, and he's the opposite of a bad person. I have emails from him! I can show you."

"Oh my God," her mother said, shaking her head.

"What? Oh my God what?"

"Has it occurred to you why a person like that is emailing you?"

"They have a paid internship program. You have to take a test, and I passed it. They do amazing work, and they actually *want* me. He's been sending me all these personal emails even though he's incredibly busy and famous."

"It could be some assistant who's writing to you. Isn't that the thing about emails? You never know who's writing them."

"No, this is definitely him."

"But think about it, Purity. Why do they want you?"

"You're the one who's been telling me I'm so special for twenty-three years."

"Why does a man with bad morals pay a beautiful young woman to come to South America?"

"Mother, I'm not beautiful. I'm also not stupid. That's why I researched him and wrote to him."

"But pussycat, the Bay Area is full of people who could want you. Appropriate people. Kind people."

"Well, it's safe to say I haven't been meeting them."

Her mother took hold of Pip's hands and searched her face. "Did something happen to you? Tell me what happened to you."

The maternal hands suddenly seemed like grasping claws to Pip, and her mother like a stranger. She pulled her own hands away. "Nothing happened to me!"

"Dearheart, you can tell me."

"I wouldn't tell you if you were the last person on earth. You don't tell me *anything*."

"I tell you everything."

"Nothing that matters."

Her mother fell back in her seat and looked at the empty window again. "No, you're right," she said. "I don't. I have my reasons, but I don't."

"Well, so then leave me alone. You don't have any rights with me."

"I have the right to love you more than anything in this world."

"No you don't!" Pip cried. "No you don't! No you don't! No you don't!"

The Republic
of Bad Taste

The church on Siegfeldstraße was open to anyone who embarrassed the Republic, and Andreas Wolf was so much of an embarrassment that he actually resided there, in the basement of the rectory, but unlike the others—the true Christian believers, the friends of the Earth, the misfits who believed in human rights or didn't want to fight in World War III—he was no less an embarrassment to himself.

For Andreas the most achievedly totalitarian thing about the Republic was its ridiculousness. It was true that people who tried to cross the death strip were unridiculously shot, but to him this was more like an oddity of geometry, a discontinuity between Eastern flatness and Western three-dimensionality that you had to assume to make the math work. As long as you avoided the border, the worst that could happen was that you'd be spied on and picked up and interrogated, do prison time and have your life wrecked. However inconvenient this might be for the individual, it was leavened by the silliness of the larger apparatus—the risible language of "class enemy" and "counterrevolutionary elements," the absurd devotion to evidentiary protocol. The authorities would never just dictate your confession or denunciation and force or forge your signature. There had to be photos and recordings, scrupulously referenced dossiers, invocations of democratically enacted laws. The Republic was heartbreakingly *German* in its striving to be logically consistent and do things right. It was like the most earnest of little boys, trying to impress and outdo its Soviet father. It was even loath to falsify election returns. And mostly out of fear, but maybe also out of pity for the little boy, who believed in socialism the way children in the West believed in a flying *Christkind* who lit the candles on the Christmas tree and left presents underneath it, the people all went to the polls and voted for the Party. By the 1980s, it was obvious that life was better in the West—better cars, better television, better chances—but the border was closed and the people indulged the little boy's illusions as if recalling, not unfondly, their own illusions from the Republic's early years. Even the dissidents spoke the language of reform, not overthrow. Everyday life was merely constrained, not tragically terrible (Olympic bronze was the *Berliner Zeitung*'s idea of calamity). And so Andreas, whose embarrassment it was to be the megalomaniacal antithesis of a dictatorship too ridiculous to be worthy of megalomania, kept his distance from the other misfits hiding in the church's skirts. They disappointed him aesthetically, they offended his sense of specialness, and they wouldn't have trusted him anyway. He performed his Siegfeldstraße ironies privately.

Alongside the broad irony of being an atheist dependent on a church was the finer irony of earning his keep as a counselor of at-risk youth. Had any East German child ever been more privileged and less at risk than he? Yet here he was, in the basement of the rectory, in group sessions and private meetings, counseling teenagers on how to overcome promiscuity and alcohol dependency and domestic dysfunction and assume more productive positions in a society he despised. And he was good at what he did—good at getting kids back into school, finding them jobs in the gray economy, connecting them with trustworthy government caseworkers—and so he was himself, ironically, a productive member of that society.

His own fall from privilege served as his credential with the kids. Their problem was that they took things too seriously (self-destructive behavior was itself a form of self-importance), and his message to them was always, in effect, "Look at me. My father's on the Central Committee and I'm living in a church basement, but do you ever see me serious?" The message was effective, but it shouldn't have been, because, in truth, he was scarcely less privileged for living in a church basement. He'd severed all contact with his parents, but in return for this favor they protected him. He'd never even been arrested, the way any of his at-risk charges would have been if they'd pulled the shit he'd pulled at their age. But they couldn't help liking him and responding to him, because he spoke the truth, and they were too hungry to hear the truth to care how privileged he was to speak it plainly. He was a risk the state seemed willing to run, a misleading beacon of honesty to confused and troubled adolescents, for whom the intensity of his appeal then became a different sort of risk. The girls practically lined up outside his office door to drop their pants for him, and if they could plausibly claim to be sixteen he helped them with their buttons. This, too, of course, was ironic. He rendered a valuable service for the state, coaxing antisocial elements back into the fold, speaking the truth while enjoining them to be careful about doing it themselves, and was paid for his service in teen pussy.

His unspoken agreement with the state had been in place for so long—for more than six years—that he assumed he was safe. Nevertheless, he continued to take the precaution of avoiding friendships with men. He could tell, for one thing, that the other men around the church envied his way with the youngsters and therefore disapproved of it. Avoiding men also made actuarial sense, since there were probably ten male informers for every female. (The actuarial odds further argued for preferring females in their teens, because the spy runners were too sexist to expect much of a schoolgirl.) The biggest drawback of men, though, was that he couldn't have sex with them; couldn't cement that deep complicity.

Although his appetite for girls seemed boundless, he prided himself on never knowingly having slept with anyone below the age of consent or anyone who'd been sexually abused. He was skilled at identifying the latter, sometimes by the fecal or septic imagery they used to describe themselves, sometimes merely by a certain telltale way they giggled, and over the years his instincts had led to successful prosecutions. When a girl who'd been abused came on to him, he didn't walk away, he ran away; he had a phobia of associating himself with predation. The sort of things that predators did—groping in crowds, lurking near playgrounds, forcing themselves on nieces, enticing with candy or trinkets—made him murderously angry. He took only girls who were more or less of sound mind and freely wanted him.

If his scruples still left an apparent residuum of sickness—a worry about what it meant that he felt compelled to repeat the same pattern with girl after girl, or that he not only never tired of it but seemed to want it only more, or that he preferred having his mouth between legs to having it near a face—he chalked it up to the sickness of the country he lived in. The Republic had defined him, he continued to exist entirely in relation to it, and apparently one of the roles it demanded he play was *Assibräuteaufreißer*. It wasn't he, after all, who'd made all men and any woman over twenty untrustable. Plus, he came from privilege; he was the exiled blond prince of Karl-Marx-Allee.

Living in the basement of a rectory, eating bad food out of cans, he felt entitled to the one small luxury that his vestigial privileges afforded. Lacking a bank account, he kept a mental coitus ledger and regularly checked it, making sure that he remembered not only first and last names but the exact order in which he'd had them.

His tally stood at fifty-two, late in the winter of 1987, when he made a mistake. The problem was that number fifty-three, a small redhead, Petra, momentarily residing with her unemployable father in a cold-water Prenzlauer Berg squat, was, like her father, extremely religious. Interestingly, this in no way dampened her hots for Andreas (nor his for her), but it did mean that she considered sex in a church disrespectful to God. He tried to relieve her of this superstition but succeeded only in making her very agitated about the state of his soul, and he saw that he risked losing her altogether if he failed to keep his soul in play. Once he'd set his mind on sealing a deal, he could think of nothing else, and since he had no close friend whose flat he could borrow and no money for a hotel room, and since the weather on the crucial night was well below freezing, the only way he could think to gain access to Petra's pants (which now seemed to him more absolutely imperative than any previous access to anyone else's, even though Petra was somewhat loopy and not particularly bright) was to board the S-Bahn with her and take her out to his parents' dacha on the Müggelsee. His parents rarely used it in the winter and never during the work week.

By rights, Andreas ought to have grown up in Hessenwinkel or even Wandlitz, the enclave where the Party leadership had its villas, but his mother had insisted on living closer to the city center, on Karl-Marx-Allee, in a high-floor flat with big windows and a balcony. Andreas suspected that her real objection to the suburbs was bourgeois-intellectual—that she found the furnishings and conversations out there unbearably *spießig*, dowdy, philistine—but she was no more capable of uttering this truth than any other, and so she claimed to be pathologically prone to carsickness, hence unable to commute by car to her important job at the university. Because Andreas's father was indispensable to the Republic, nobody minded that he lived in town or that his wife, again on grounds of carsickness, had selected the Müggelsee as the site of the dacha where they went for weekends in the warmer months. As Andreas came to see it, his mother was not unlike a suicide bomber, forever carrying the threat of crazy behavior fully armed and ready to detonate, and so his father acceded to her wishes as much as possible, asking only that she help him maintain the necessary lies. This was never a problem for her.

The dacha, walkable from the train station, was set on a large plot of piney land sloping gently to the lake shore. By feel, in the dark, Andreas located the key hanging from the customary eave. When he went inside with Petra and turned on a light, he was disoriented to find the living room outfitted with the faux-Danish furniture of his childhood in the city. He hadn't been out to the dacha since the end of his homeless period, six years earlier. His mother had apparently redecorated the city flat in the meantime.

"Whose house is this?" Petra said, impressed with the amenities.

"Never mind that."

There was zero danger of her finding a photograph of him. (Sooner a portrait of Trotsky.) From the tower of beer crates he took two half liters and gave one to Petra. The topmost *Neues Deutschland* on the outgoing stack was from a Sunday more than three weeks earlier. Imagining his parents alone here on a winter Sunday, childless, their conversation infrequent and scarcely audible, in that older-couple way, he felt his heart veer dangerously close to sympathy. He didn't regret having made their later years barren—they had no one but themselves to blame for that—but he'd loved them so much, as a child, that the sight of their old furniture saddened him. They were still human beings, still getting old.

He turned on the electric furnace and led Petra down the hall to the room that had once been his. The quick cure for nostalgia would be to bury his face in her pussy; he'd already touched it, through her pants, while they were making out on the train. But she said she wanted to take a bath.

"You don't have to on my account."

"It's been four days."

He didn't want to deal with a damp bath towel; it would have to be dried and folded before they left. But it was important to put the girl and her desires first.

"It's fine," he assured her pleasantly. "Take a bath."

He sat down with his beer on his old bed and heard her lock the bathroom door behind her. In the weeks that followed, the click of this lock became the seed of his paranoia: why would she have locked the door when he was the only other person in the house? It was improbable for eight different reasons that she could have known or been involved in what was coming. But why else lock the door, if not to protect herself against it?

Then again, maybe it was just his bad luck that she was immobilized in the bathtub with the water still running, her splashing and the flow in the pipes loud enough to have covered the sound of an approaching vehicle and footsteps, when he heard a pounding on the front door and then a barking: "*Volkspolizei!*"

The water in the pipes abruptly stopped. Andreas thought about making a run for it, but he was trapped by the fact that Petra was in the tub. Reluctantly, he heaved himself off the bed and went and opened the front door. Two *VoPos* were backlit by the flashers and headlights of their cruiser.

"Yes?" he said.

"Identification, please."

"What's this about?"

"Your identification, please."

If the policemen had had tails, they wouldn't have been wagging; if they'd had pointed ears, they would have been flattened back. The senior officer frowned at Andreas's little blue book and handed it to the junior, who carried it back toward the cruiser.

"Do you have permission to be here?"

"In a certain sense."

"Are you alone?"

"As you find me." Andreas beckoned politely. "Would you care to come in?"

"I'll need to use the telephone."

"Of course."

The officer entered circumspectly. Andreas guessed that he was more wary of the house's owners than of any armed thugs who might be lurking in it.

"This is my parents' place," he explained.

"We're acquainted with the undersecretary. We're not acquainted with you. No one has permission to be in this house tonight."

"I've been here for fifteen minutes. Your vigilance is commendable."

"We saw the lights."

"Really highly commendable."

From the bathroom came a single plink of falling water; in hindsight, Andreas would find it noteworthy that the officer had shown no interest in the bathroom. The man simply paged through a shabby black notebook, found a number, and dialed it on the undersecretary's telephone. In the moment, Andreas's main feeling was a wish that the police would go away and let him get on with eating little Petra. Everything else was so unfortunate that he didn't want to think about it.

"Mr. Undersecretary?" The officer identified himself and tersely reported the presence of an intruder who claimed to be a relative. Then he said "Yes" several times.

"Tell him I'd like to speak to him," Andreas said.

The officer made a silencing gesture.

"I want to talk to him."

"Of course, right away," the officer said to the undersecretary.

Andreas tried to grab the receiver. The officer shoved him in the chest and knocked him to the floor.

"No, he's trying to take the phone . . . That's right . . . Yes, of course. I'll tell him . . . Understood, Mr. Undersecretary." The officer hung up the phone and looked down at Andreas. "You're to leave immediately and never come back."

"Got it."

"If you ever come back, there will be consequences. The undersecretary wanted to make sure you understand that."

"He's not really my father," Andreas said. "We just happen to have the same last name."

"Me personally?" the officer said. "I hope you come back, and I hope I'm on duty when you do."

The younger officer returned and handed Andreas's ID to the senior, who examined it with his lip curled. Then he flipped it into Andreas's face. "Lock the door behind you, asshole."

When the police were gone, he knocked on the bathroom door and told Petra to turn off the light and wait for him. He turned off the other lights and went out into the night, heading toward the train station. At the first bend in the lane, he saw the cruiser parked and dark and gave the officers a little wave. At the next bend, he ducked behind some pine trees to wait until the cruiser drove away. The evening had been damaging, and he wasn't about to waste it. But when he was finally able to creep back into the dacha and found Petra cowering on his boyhood bed, mewling with fear of the police, he was too angry about his humiliation to care about her pleasure. He ordered her to do this and do that, in the dark, and it ended with her weeping and saying she hated him—a feeling he entirely reciprocated. He never saw her again.

Three weeks later, the German Christian Youth Conference invited him to speak in West Berlin. He presumed (though you could never know for sure; that was the beauty of it) that the conference had been thoroughly infiltrated by his cousin once removed, the spymaster Markus Wolf, because the invitation came forwarded from the Foreign Ministry with a notice to pick up a visa that had already been granted. It was laughably obvious that if he crossed the border he wouldn't be allowed to reenter the country. Equally obvious was that the invitation was a warning from his father, a punishment for his indiscretion at the dacha.

Everyone else in the country wanted permission to travel even more than they wanted cars. The bait of attending some miserable three-day trade conference in Copenhagen was enough to entice the ordinary citizen to rat out colleagues, siblings, friends. Andreas felt singular in every way, but in none more than his disdain for travel. How the royal Danish poisoner and his lying queen had wanted their son out of the castle! He felt himself to be the rose and fair expectancy of the state, its product and its antic antithesis, and so his first responsibility was to not budge from Berlin. He needed his so-called parents to know that he was still there on Siegfeldstraße, knowing what he knew about them.

But it was lonely to be singular, and loneliness bred paranoia, and he soon reached the point of imagining that Petra had set him up, the whole rigmarole about sex in churches and the need for a bath a ruse to lure him into violating his tacit agreement with his parents. Now every time another at-risk girl appeared at his office door with that familiar burning look in her eyes, he remembered how uncharacteristically selfish he'd been with Petra, and how humiliated he'd been by the police, and instead of obliging the girl he teased her and drove her away. He wondered if he'd been lying to himself about girls forever—if the hatred he'd felt for number fifty-three was not only real but retroactively applicable to numbers one through fifty-two. If, far from indulging in irony at the state's expense, he'd been seduced by the state at his point of least resistance.

He spent the following spring and summer depressed, and therefore all the more preoccupied with sex, but since he suddenly distrusted both himself and the girls, he denied himself the relief of it. He curtailed his individual conferences and ceased trolling the *Jugendklubs* for at-risk kids. Though he was jeopardizing the best job an East German in his position could hope to find, he lay on his bed all day and read British novels, detective and otherwise, forbidden and otherwise. (Having been force-fed Steinbeck and Dreiser and Dos Passos by his mother, he had little interest in American writing. Even the best Americans were annoyingly naïve. Life in the U.K. sucked more, in a good way.) Eventually he determined that what had depressed him was his childhood bed, the bed itself, in the Müggelsee house, and the feeling that he'd never left it: that the more he rebelled against his parents and the more he made his life a reproach to theirs, the more deeply he rooted himself in the same childish relation to them. But it was one thing to identify the source of his depression, quite another to do anything about it.

He was seven months celibate on the October afternoon when the church's young "vicar" came to see him about the girl in the sanctuary. The vicar wore all the vestments of renegade-church cliché—full beard, check; faded jean jacket, check; mod copper crucifix, check—but was usefully insecure in the face of Andreas's superior street experience.

"I first noticed her two weeks ago," he said, sitting down on the floor. He seemed to have read in some book that sitting on the floor established rapport and conveyed Christlike humility. "Sometimes she stays in the sanctuary for an hour, sometimes until midnight. Not praying, just doing her homework. I finally asked if we could help her. She looked scared and said she was sorry—she'd thought she was allowed to be here. I told her the church is always open to anyone in need. I wanted to start a conversation, but all she wanted was to hear that she wasn't breaking any rules."

"So?"

"Well, you are the youth counselor."

"The sanctuary isn't exactly on my beat."

"It's understandable that you're burned out. We haven't minded your taking some time for yourself."

"I appreciate it."

"I'm concerned about the girl, though. I talked to her again yesterday and asked if she was in trouble—my fear is that she's been abused. She speaks so softly it's hard to understand her, but she seemed to be saying that the authorities are already aware of her, and so she can't go to them. Apparently she's here because she has nowhere else to go."

"Aren't we all."

"She might say more to you than to me."

"How old is she?"

"Young. Fifteen, sixteen. Also extraordinarily pretty."

Underage, abused, and pretty. Andreas sighed.

"You'll need to come out of your room at some point," the vicar suggested.

When Andreas went up to the sanctuary and saw the girl in the next-to-rear pew, he immediately experienced her beauty as an unwelcome complication, a specificity that distracted him from the universal female body part that had interested him for so long. She was dark-haired and dark-eyed, unrebelliously dressed, and was sitting with a Free German Youth erectness of posture, a text-book open on her lap. She looked like a good girl, the sort he never saw in the basement. She didn't raise her head as he approached.

"Will you talk to me?" he said.

She shook her head.

"You talked to the vicar."

"Only for a minute," she murmured.

"OK. Why don't I sit down behind you, where you don't have to see me. And then, if you—"

"Please don't do that."

"All right. I'll stay in sight." He took the pew in front of her. "I'm Andreas. I'm a counselor here. Will you tell me your name?"

She shook her head.

"Are you here to pray?"

She smirked. "Is there a God?"

"No, of course not. Where would you get an idea like that?"

"Somebody built this church."

"Somebody was thinking wishfully. It makes no sense to me."

She raised her head, as if he'd slightly interested her. "Aren't you afraid of getting in trouble?"

"With who? The minister? God's only a word he uses against the state. Nothing in this country exists except in reference to the state."

"You shouldn't say things like that."

"I'm only saying what the state itself says."

He looked down at her legs, which were of a piece with the rest of her.

"Are you very afraid of getting in trouble?" he said.

She shook her head.

"Afraid of getting someone else in trouble, then. Is that it?"

"I come here because this is nowhere. It's nice to be nowhere for a while."

"Nowhere is more nowhere than this place, I agree."

She smiled faintly.

"When you look in the mirror," he said, "what do you see? Someone pretty?"

"I don't look in mirrors."

"What would you see if you did?"

"Nothing good."

"Something bad? Something harmful?"

She shrugged.

"Why didn't you want me to sit down behind you?"

"I like to see who I'm talking to."

"So we *are* talking. You were only pretending that you weren't going to talk to me. You were being self-dramatizing—playing games."

Sudden honest confrontation was part of his bag of counseling tricks. That he was sick of these tricks didn't mean they didn't still work.

"I already know I'm bad," the girl said. "You don't have to explain it to me."

"But it must be hard for you that people don't know how bad you are. They simply don't believe a girl so pretty can be so bad inside. It must be hard for you to respect people."

"I have friends."

"So did I when I was your age. But it doesn't help, does it? It's actually worse that people like me. They think I'm funny, they think I'm attractive. Only I know how bad I am inside. I'm extremely bad and extremely important. In fact, I'm the most important person in the country."

It was encouraging to see her sneer like an adolescent. "You're not important."

"Oh, but I am. You just don't know it. But you do know what it's like to be important, don't you. You're very important yourself. Everyone pays attention to you, everyone wants to be near you because you're beautiful, and then you harm them. You have to go hide in a church to be nowhere, to give the world a rest from you."

"I wish you'd leave me alone."

"Who are you harming? Just say it."

The girl lowered her head.

"You can tell me," he said. "I'm an old harmer myself."

She shivered a little and knit her fingers together on her lap. From outside, the rumble of a truck and the sharp clank of a bad gearbox entered the sanctuary and lingered in the air, which smelled of charred candle wick and tarnished brass. The wooden cross on the wall behind the pulpit seemed to Andreas a once magical object that had lost its mojo through overuse both for and against the state; had been dragged down to the level of sordid accommodation and dreary dissidence. The sanctuary was the very least relevant part of the church; he felt sorry for it.

"My *mother*," the girl murmured. The hatred in her voice was hard to square with the notion that she cared that she was doing harm. Andreas knew enough about abuse to guess what this meant.

"Where's your father?" he asked gently.

"Dead."

"And your mother remarried."

She nodded.

"Is she not at home?"

"She's a night nurse at the hospital."

He winced; he got the picture.

"You're safe here," he said. "This really is nowhere. There's no one you can hurt here. It's all right if you tell me your name. It doesn't matter."

"I'm Annagret," the girl said.

Their initial conversation was analogous, in its swiftness and directness, to his seductions, but in spirit it was just the opposite. Annagret's beauty was so striking, so far outside the norm, that it seemed like a direct affront to the Republic of Bad Taste. It shouldn't have existed, it upset the orderly universe at whose center he'd always placed himself; it frightened him. He was twenty-seven years old, and (unless you counted his mother when he was little) he'd never been in love, because he had yet to meet—had stopped even trying to imagine—a girl who was worth it. But here one was.

He saw her again on each of the following three evenings. He felt bad about looking forward to it just because she was so pretty, but there was nothing he could do about that. On the second night, to deepen her trust in him, he made a point of telling her that he'd slept with dozens of girls at the church. "It was a kind of addiction," he said, "but I had strict limits. I need you to believe that you personally are way outside all of them."

This was the truth but also, deep down, a total lie, and Annagret called him on it. "Everyone thinks they have strict limits," she said, "until they cross them."

"Let me be the person who proves to you that some limits really are strict."

"People say this church is a hangout for people with no morality. I didn't see how that could be true—after all, it's a church. But now you're telling me it *is* true."

"I'm sorry to be the one to disillusion you."

"There's something wrong with this country."

"I couldn't agree more."

"The Judo Club was bad enough. But to hear it's in the church . . ."

Annagret had an older sister, Tanja, who'd excelled at judo as an *Oberschule* student. Both sisters were university-tracked, by virtue of their test scores and their class credentials, but Tanja was boy crazy and overdid the sports thing and ended up working as a secretary after her *Abitur,* spending all her free time either dancing at clubs or training and coaching at the sports center. Annagret was seven years younger and not as athletic as her sister, but they were a judo family and she joined the local club when she was twelve.

A regular at the sports center was a handsome older guy, Horst, who owned a large motorcycle. He was maybe thirty and was apparently married only to his bike. He came to the center mostly to maintain his impressive buffness— Annagret initially thought there was something conceited about the way he smiled at her—but he also played hand-ball and liked to watch the advanced judo students spar-ring, and by and by Tanja managed to score a date with him and his bike. This led to a second date and then a third, at which point a misfortune occurred: Horst met their mother. After that, instead of taking Tanja away on his bike, he wanted to see her at home, in their tiny shitty flat, with Annagret and the mother.

Inwardly, the mother was a hard and disappointed per-son, the widow of a truck mechanic who'd died wretch-edly of a brain tumor, but outwardly she was thirty-eight and pretty—not only prettier than Tanja but also closer in age to Horst. Ever since Tanja had failed her by not pursuing her education, the two of them had quarreled about everything imaginable, which now included Horst, who the mother thought was too old for Tanja. When it became evident that Horst preferred her to Tanja, she didn't see how it was her fault. Annagret was luckily not at home on the fateful afternoon when Tanja stood up and said she needed air and asked Horst to take her out on his bike. Horst said there was a painful matter that the three of them needed to discuss. There were better ways for him to have handled the situation, but probably no good way. Tanja slammed the door behind her and didn't return for three days. As soon as she could, she relocated to Leipzig.

After Horst and Annagret's mother were married, the three of them moved to a notably roomy flat where Annagret had a bedroom of her own. She felt bad for Tanja and disapproving of her mother, but her stepfather fascinated her. His job, as a labor-collective leader at the city's largest power plant, was good but not quite so good as to explain the way he had of making things happen: the powerful bike, the roomy flat, the oranges and Brazil nuts and Michael Jackson records he sometimes brought home. From her description of him, Andreas had the impression that he was one of those people whose self-love was untempered by shame and thus fully contagious. Certainly Annagret liked to be around him. He gave her rides on his motorcycle to and from the sports center. He taught her how to ride it by herself, in a parking lot. She tried to teach him some judo in return, but his upper body was so disproportionately developed that he was bad at falling. In the evening, after her mother had left for her night shift, she explained the extra-credit work she was doing in the hope of attending an *Erweiterte Oberschule*; she was impressed by his quick comprehension and told him he should have gone to an *EOS* himself. Before long, she considered him one of her best friends. As a bonus, this pleased her mother, who hated her nursing job and seemed increasingly worn out by it and was grateful that her husband and daughter got along well. Tanja may have been lost, but Annagret was the good girl, her mother's hope for the future of her family.

And then one night, in the notably roomy flat, Horst came tapping on her bedroom door before she'd turned her light out. "Are you decent?" he said playfully.

"I'm in my pajamas," she said.

He came in and pulled up a chair by her bed. He had a very large head—Annagret couldn't explain it to Andreas, but the largeness of Horst's head seemed to her the reason that everything always worked out to his advantage. *Oh, he has such a splendid head, let's just give him what he wants.* Something like that. On this particular night, his large head was flushed from drinking.

"I'm sorry if I smell like beer," he said.

"I wouldn't be able to smell it if I could have one myself."

"You sound like you know quite a bit about beer drinking."

"Oh, it's just what they say."

"You could have a beer if you stopped training, but you won't stop training, so you can't have a beer."

She liked the joking way they had together. "But *you* train, and *you* drink beer."

"I only drank so much tonight because I have something serious to say to you."

She looked at his large head and saw that something, indeed, was different in his face tonight. A kind of ill-controlled anguish in his eyes. Also, his hands were shaking.

"What is it?" she said, worried.

"Can you keep a secret?" he said.

"I don't know."

"Well, you have to, because you're the only person I can tell, and if you don't keep the secret we're all in trouble."

She thought about this. "Why do you have to tell me?"

"Because it concerns you. It's about your mother. Will you keep a secret?"

"I can try."

Horst took a large breath that came out again beer-smelling. "Your mother is a drug addict," he said. "I married a drug addict. She steals narcotics from the hospital and uses them when she's there and also when she's home. Did you know that?"

"No," Annagret said. But she was inclined to believe it. More and more often lately, there was something dulled about her mother.

"She's very expert at pilfering," Horst said. "No one at the hospital suspects."

"We need to talk to her about it and tell her to stop."

"Addicts don't stop without treatment. If she asks for treatment, the authorities will know she was stealing."

"But they'll be happy that she's honest and trying to get better."

"Well, unfortunately, there's another matter. An even bigger secret. Not even your mother knows this secret. Can I tell it to you?"

He was one of her best friends, and so, after a hesitation, she said yes.

"I took an oath that I would never tell anyone," Horst said. "I'm breaking that oath by telling you. For some years now, I've worked informally for the Ministry for State Security. I'm a well-trusted unofficial collaborator. There's an officer I meet with from time to time. I pass along information about my workers and especially about my superiors. This is necessary because the power plant is vital to our national security. I'm very fortunate to have a good relationship with the ministry. You and your mother are very fortunate that I do. But do you understand what this means?"

"No."

"We owe our privileges to the ministry. How do you think my officer will feel if he learns that my wife is a thief and a drug addict? He'll think I'm not trustworthy. We could lose this flat, and I could lose my position."

"But you could just tell the officer the truth about Mother. It's not your fault."

"If I tell him, your mother will lose her job. She'll probably go to prison. Is that what you want?"

"Of course not."

"So we have to keep everything secret."

"But now I wish I didn't know! Why did I have to know?"

"Because you need to help me keep the secret. Your mother betrayed us by breaking the law. You and I are the family now. She is the threat to it. We need to make sure she doesn't destroy it."

"We have to try to help her."

"You matter more to me than she does now. You are the woman in my life. See here." He put a hand on her belly and splayed his fingers. "You've become a woman."

The hand on her belly frightened her, but not as much as what he'd told her.

"A very beautiful woman," he added huskily.

"I'm feeling ticklish."

He closed his eyes and didn't take away his hand. "Everything has to be secret," he said. "I can protect you, but you have to trust me."

"Can't we just tell Mother?"

"No. One thing will lead to another, and she'll end up in jail. We're safer if she steals and takes drugs—she's very good at not getting caught."

"But if you tell her you work for the ministry, she'll understand why she has to stop."

"I don't trust her. She's betrayed us already. I have to trust you instead."

She felt she might cry soon; her breaths were coming faster.

"You shouldn't put your hand on me," she said. "It feels wrong."

"Maybe, yes, wrong, a little bit, considering our age difference." He nodded his big head. "But look how much I trust you. We can do something that's maybe a little bit wrong because I know you won't tell anyone."

"I might tell someone."

"No. You'd have to expose our secrets, and you can't do that."

"Oh, I wish you hadn't told me anything."

"But I did. I had to. And now we have secrets together. Just you and me. Can I trust you?"

Her eyes filled. "I don't know."

"Tell me a secret of your own. Then I'll know I can trust you."

"I don't have any secrets."

"Then show me something secret. What's the most secret thing you can show me?"

The hand on her belly inched southward, and her heart began to hammer.

"Is it this?" he said. "Is this your most secret thing?"

"I don't know," she whimpered, very frightened and confused.

"It's all right. You don't have to show me. It's enough that you let me feel it." Through his hand, she could feel his whole body relax. "I trust you now."

For Annagret, the terrible thing was that she'd liked what followed, at least for a while. For a while, it was merely like a closer form of friendship. They still joked

together, she still told him everything about her days at
school, they still went riding together and trained at the
sports club. It was ordinary life but with a secret, an extremely grown-up secret thing that happened after she'd
put on her pajamas and gone to bed. While he touched her,
he kept saying how beautiful she was, what perfect beauty.
And because, for a while, he didn't touch her with any part
of himself except his hand, she felt as if she herself were
to blame, as if the whole thing had actually been her idea,
as if she'd done this to them with her beauty and the only
way to make it stop was to submit to it and experience release. She hated her body for wanting release even more
than she hated it for its supposed beauty, but somehow the
hatred made it all the more urgent. She wanted him to kiss
her. She wanted him to need her. She was very bad. And
maybe it made sense that she was very bad, being the
daughter of a drug addict. She'd casually asked her mother
if she was ever tempted to take the drugs she gave her
patients. Every once in a while, yes, her mother had answered smoothly, if a little bit of something at the hospital
was left unused, she or one of the other nurses might take
it to calm their nerves, but it didn't mean the person was
an addict. Annagret hadn't said anything about anyone
being an addict.

For Andreas the terrible thing was how much the stepfather's pussycentrism reminded him of his own. He felt
only somewhat less implicated when Annagret went on
to tell him that her weeks of being touched had been
merely a prelude to Horst's unzipping of his pants. It was
bound to happen sometime, and yet it broke the spell that
she'd been under; it introduced a third party to their
secret. She didn't like this third party. She realized that it
must have been spying on the two of them all along, bid-
ing its time, manipulating them like a case officer. She
didn't want to see it, didn't want it near her, and when it

tried to assert its authority she became afraid of being at home at night. But what could she do? The pecker knew her secrets. It knew that, if only for a while, she'd *looked forward* to being tampered with. She'd half-wittingly become its unofficial collaborator; she'd tacitly sworn an oath. She wondered if her mother took narcotics so as not to know which body the pecker really wanted. The pecker knew all about her mother's pilferage, and the pecker was empowered by the ministry, and so she couldn't go to the authorities. They'd put her mother in jail and leave her alone with the pecker. The same thing would happen if she told her mother, because her mother would accuse her husband, and the pecker would have her jailed. And maybe her mother deserved to be jailed, but not if it meant that Annagret remained at home and kept harming her.

This was the latest chapter of her unfinished story, and it came out on the fourth evening of Andreas's counseling. When Annagret had finished her confession, in the chill of the sanctuary, she began to weep. Seeing someone so beautiful weeping, seeing her press her fists to her eyes like an infant, Andreas was gripped by an unfamiliar physical sensation. He was such a laugher, such an ironist, such an artist of unseriousness, that he didn't even recognize what was happening to him: he, too, was starting to cry. But he did recognize why. He was crying for himself—for what had happened to him as a child. He'd heard many stories of childhood sexual abuse before, but never from such a good girl, never from a girl with perfect hair and skin and bone structure. Annagret's beauty had broken something open in him. He felt that he was *just like her*. And so he was also crying because he loved her, and because he couldn't have her.

"Can you help me?" she whispered.

"I don't know."

"Why did I tell you so much if you can't help me? Why

did you keep asking me questions? You acted like you could help me."

He shook his head and said nothing. She put a hand on his shoulder, very lightly, but even a light touch from her was terrible. He bowed forward, shaking with sobs. "I'm so sad for you."

"But now you see what I mean. I cause harm."

"No."

"Maybe I should just be his girlfriend. Make him divorce my mother and be his girlfriend."

"No." He pulled himself together and wiped his face. "No, he's a sick fucker. I know it because I'm a little bit sick myself. I can extrapolate."

"You might have done the same thing he did . . ."

"Never. I swear to you. I'm like you, not him."

"But . . . if you're a little sick and you're like me, it means that I must be a little bit sick."

"That's not what I meant."

"You're right, though. I should go home and be his girlfriend. Since I'm so sick. Thank you for your help, Mr. Counselor."

He took her by the shoulders and made her look at him. There was nothing but distrust in her eyes now. "I want to be your friend," he said.

"We all know where being friends goes."

"You're wrong. Stay here, and let's think. Be my friend."

She pulled away from him and crossed her arms tightly.

"We can go directly to the Stasi," he said. "He broke his oath to them. The minute they think he might embarrass them, they'll drop him like a hot potato. As far as they're concerned, he's just some bottom-tier collaborator—he's nobody."

"No," she said. "They'll think I'm lying. I didn't tell you everything I did—it's too embarrassing. I did things to interest him."

"It doesn't matter. You're fifteen. In the eyes of the law, you have no responsibility. Unless he's very stupid, he's got to be scared out of his mind right now. You've got all the power."

"But even if they believe me, everybody's life is ruined, including mine. I won't have a home, I won't be able to go to university. Even my sister will hate me. I think it's better if I just give him what he wants until I'm old enough to move away."

"That's what you want."

She shook her head. "I wouldn't be here if that was what I wanted. But now I see that nobody can help me."

Andreas didn't know what to say. What he wanted was for her to come and live in the basement of the rectory with him. He could protect her, homeschool her, practice English with her, train her as a counselor for at-risk youth, and be her friend, the way King Lear imagined life with Cordelia, following the news of the court from a distance, laughing at who was in, who was out. Maybe in time they'd be a couple, the couple in the basement, leading their own private life.

"We can find room for you here," he said.

She shook her head again. "He's already upset that I don't come home until midnight. He thinks I'm out with boys. If I didn't come home at all, he'd turn my mother in."

"He said that to you?"

"He's an evil person. For a long time, I thought the opposite, but not anymore. Now everything he says to me is some kind of threat. He's not going to stop until he gets everything he wants."

A different sensation, not tears, a wave of hatred, came over Andreas. "I can kill him," he said.

"That's not what I meant by helping me."

"Somebody's life has to be ruined," he said, pursuing

the logic of his hatred. "Why not his and mine? I'm already in a kind of prison. The food can't be any worse in a real prison. I can read books at state expense. You can go to school and help your mother with her problem."

She made a derisive sound. "That's a good plan. Trying to kill a bodybuilder."

"Obviously I wouldn't warn him in advance."

She looked at him as if he couldn't possibly be serious. All his life, until now, she would have been right. Levity was his métier. But it was harder to see the ridiculous side of the casual destruction of lives in the Republic when the life in question was Annagret's. He was already falling in love with this girl, and there was nothing he could do with the feeling, no way to act on it, no way to make her believe that she should trust him. She must have seen some of this in his face, because her own expression changed.

"You can't kill him," she said quietly. "He's just very sick. Everyone in my family is sick, everyone I touch is sick, including me. I just need *help*."

"There is no help for you in this country."

"That can't be right."

"It's the truth."

She stared for a while at the pews in front of them or at the cross behind the altar, forlorn and murkily lit. After a time, her breaths became quicker and sharper. "I wouldn't cry if he died," she said. "But I should be the one to do it, and I could never do it. Never, never. I'd sooner be his girlfriend."

On more careful reflection, Andreas didn't really want to kill Horst, either. He could imagine surviving prison, but the label *murderer* didn't accord with his self-image. The label would follow him forever, he wouldn't be able to like himself as much as he did now, and neither would other people. It was all very well to be a *Assibräuteau-*

freißer, a troller for sex with the antisocial—the label was appropriately ridiculous. But *murderer* was not.

"So," Annagret said, standing up. "It's nice of you to offer. It was nice of you to listen to my story and not be too disgusted."

"Wait, though," he said, because another thought had occurred to him: if she were his accomplice, he might not automatically be caught, and even if he were caught her beauty and his love for her would forever adhere to what the two of them had done. He wouldn't simply be a *murderer*; he'd be the person who'd eliminated the molester of this singular girl.

"Can you trust me?" he said.

"I like that I can talk to you. I don't think you're going to tell anyone my secrets."

These weren't the words he wanted to hear. They made him ashamed of his fantasy of homeschooling her in the basement.

"I don't want to be your girlfriend," she added, "if that's what you're asking. I don't want to be anyone's girlfriend."

"You're fifteen, I'm twenty-seven. That's not what I'm talking about."

"I'm sure you have your own story, I'm sure it's very interesting."

"Do you want to hear it?"

"No. I just want to be normal again."

"That's not going to happen."

Her expression became desolate. The natural thing would have been to put his arms around her and console her, but nothing about their situation was natural. He felt completely powerless—another new sensation and one he didn't like one bit. He figured that she was about to walk away and never come back. But instead she drew a stabilizing breath and said, without looking at him, "How would you do it?"

In a low, dull voice, as if in a trance, he told her how. She had to stop coming to the church and go home and lie to Horst. She had to say that she'd been going to a church to sit by herself and pray and seek God's guidance, and that her mind was clearer now. She was ready to give herself fully to Horst, but she couldn't do it at home, out of respect for her mother. She knew a better place, a romantic place, a safe place where some of her friends went on weekends to drink beer and make out. If he cared about her feelings, he would take her there.

"You know a place like that?"

"I do," Andreas said.

"Why would you do this for me?"

"Who better to do it for? You deserve a good life. I'm willing to take a risk for that."

"It's not a risk. It's guaranteed—they'd definitely catch you."

"OK, thought experiment: if it were guaranteed they *wouldn't*, would you let me do it?"

"I'm the one who should be killed. I've been doing something terrible to my sister and my mother."

He sighed. "I like you a lot, Annagret. I'm not so fond of the self-dramatizing, though."

This was the right thing to have said—he saw it immediately. Not a full-bore burning look from her but unmistakably a spark of fire. He almost resented his loins for warming at the sight; he didn't want this to be just another seduction. He wanted her to be the way out of the wasteland of seduction he'd been living in.

"I could never do it," she said, turning away from him.

"Sure. We're just talking."

"You self-dramatize, too. You said you were the most important person in the country."

He could have pointed out that such a ridiculous claim could only be ironic, but he saw that this was only half true. Irony was slippery, the sincerity of Annagret was firm. "You're right," he said gratefully. "I self-dramatize, too. It's another way the two of us are alike."

She gave a petulant shrug.

"But since we're only talking, how well do you think you could ride a motorbike?"

"I just want to be normal again. I don't want to be like you."

"OK. We'll try to make you normal again. But it would help if you could ride his motorbike. I've never been on one myself."

"Riding it is sort of like judo," she said. "You try to go with it, not against it."

Sweet judo girl. She continued like this, closing the door on him and then opening it a little, rejecting possibilities that she then turned around and allowed, until it got so late that she had to go home. They agreed that there was no point in her returning to the church unless she was ready to act on their plan or move into the basement. These were the only two ideas either of them had.

Once she stopped coming to the church, Andreas had no way to communicate with her. For the following six afternoons, he went up to the sanctuary and waited until dinnertime. He was pretty sure he'd never see her again. She was just a schoolgirl, she didn't care about him, or at least not enough, and she didn't hate her stepfather as murderously as he did. She would lose her nerve—either go alone to the Stasi or submit to worse abuse. As the afternoons passed, Andreas felt some relief at the prospect. In terms of having an experience, seriously contemplating a murder was almost as good as going through with it, and it had the added benefit of not entailing risk. Between prison and no prison, no prison was clearly preferable. What tormented him was the thought that he wouldn't lay eyes on Annagret again. He pictured her studiously practicing her throws at the Judo Club, being the good girl, and felt very sorry for himself. He refused to picture what might be happening to her at home at night.

She showed up on the seventh afternoon, looking pale and starved and wearing the same ugly rain jacket that half the teenagers in the Republic were wearing. A nasty cold drizzle was falling on Siegfeldstraße. She took the rearmost pew and bowed her head and kneaded her pasty, bitten hands. Seeing her again, after a week of merely imagining her, Andreas was overwhelmed by the contrast between love and lust. Love turned out to be soul-crippling, stomach-turning, weirdly claustrophobic: a sense of endless-ness bottled up inside him, endless weight, endless poten-tial, with only the small outlet of a shivering pale girl in a bad rain jacket to escape through. Touching her was the farthest thing from his mind. The impulse was to throw himself at her feet.

He sat down not very close to her. For a long time, for several minutes, they didn't speak. Love altered the way he perceived her uneven mouth-breathing and her trembling hands—again the disparity between the largeness of her mattering and the ordinariness of the sounds she made, the everydayness of her schoolgirl fingers. He had the strange thought that it was wrong, wrong as in *evil*, to think of kill-ing a man who, in however sick a way, was also in love with her; that he instead ought to have compassion for that man.

"So I have to be at the Judo Club," she said finally. "I can't stay long."

"It's good to see you," he said. Love made this feel like the most remarkably true statement he'd ever made.

"So just tell me what to do."

"Maybe now is not a good time. Maybe you want to come back some other day."

She shook her head, and some of her hair fell over her face. She didn't push it back. "Just tell me what to do."

"Shit," he said honestly. "I'm as scared as you are."

"Not possible."

"Why not just run away? Come and live here. We'll find a room for you."

She began to shiver more violently. "If you won't help me, I'll do it myself. You think you're bad, but I'm the bad one."

"No, here, here." He took her shaking hands in his own. They were icy and so ordinary, so ordinary; he loved them. "You're a very good person. You're just in a bad dream."

She turned her face to him, and through her hair he saw the burning look, the full-bore burning look. "Will you help me out of it?"

"It's what you want?"

"You said you'd help me."

Could anyone be worth it? He did wonder, but he set down her hands and took a hand-drawn map from his jacket pocket.

"This is where the house is," he said. "You'll need to take the S-Bahn out there by yourself first, so you'll know exactly where you're going. Do it after dark and watch out for cops. When you go back there on the motorcycle, have him cut the lights at the last corner, and then go all the way back behind the house. The driveway curves around behind. And then make sure you take your helmets off. What night are we talking about?"

"Thursday."

"What time does your mother's shift start?"

"Ten o'clock."

"Don't go home for dinner. Tell him you'll meet him by his bike at nine thirty. You don't want anyone to see you leaving the building with him."

"OK. Where will you be?"

"Don't worry about that. Just head for the back door. Everything will be like we talked about."

She convulsed a little, as if she might retch, but she mastered herself and put the map in her jacket pocket. "Is that all?" she said.

"You suggested it to him. The date."

She nodded quickly.

"I'm so sorry," he said.

"Is that all?"

"Just one other thing. Will you look at me?"

She remained hunched over, like a dog that had been bad, but she turned her head.

"You have to be honest with me," he said. "Are you doing this because I want it, or because you want it?"

"What does it matter?"

"A lot. Everything."

She looked down at her lap again. "I just want it to be over. Either way."

"You know we won't be able to see each other for a very long time, whichever way it goes. No contact of any kind."

"That's almost better."

"Think about it, though. If you came here instead, we could see each other every day."

"I don't think that's better."

He looked up at the stained ceiling of the sanctuary and considered what a cosmic joke it was that the first person his heart had freely chosen was someone he not only couldn't have but wouldn't even be allowed to see. And yet he felt all right about it. His powerlessness itself was sweet. Who would have guessed that? Various clichés about love, stupid adages and song lyrics, flashed through his head.

"I'm late for judo," Annagret said. "I have to go."

He closed his eyes so that he didn't have to see her leave.

* * *

It was so easy to blame the mother. Life a miserable contradiction, endless desire but limited supplies, your birth
just a ticket to your death: why not blame the person who'd
stuck you with a life? OK, maybe it was unfair. But your
mother could always blame her own mother, who herself
could blame the mother, and so on back to the Garden.
People had been blaming the mother forever, and most of
them, Andreas was pretty sure, had mothers less blameworthy than his.

An accident of brain development stacked the deck
against children: the mother had three or four years to
fuck with your head before your hippocampus began
recording lasting memories. You'd been talking to your
mom since you were one year old and listening to her for
even longer, but you couldn't remember a single word of
what you or she had said before your hippocampus kicked
into gear. Your consciousness opened its little eyes for the
first time and discovered that you were headlong in love
with your mom. Being an exceptionally bright and recep-
tive little boy, you also already believed in the historical
inevitability of the socialist workers' state. Your mother
herself, in her secret heart, might not have believed in it,
but you did. You'd been a person long before you had a
conscious self. Your little body had once been deeper inside your mother than your father's dick had ever gone,
you'd squeezed your entire goddamned head through her
pussy, and then for the longest time you'd sucked on her
tits whenever you felt like it, and you couldn't for the life
of you remember it. You found yourself self-alienated
from the get-go.

Andreas's father was the second-youngest Party member ever elevated to the Central Committee, and he had
the most creative job in the Republic. As the chief state
economist, he was responsible for the wholesale massag-
ing of data, for demonstrating increases in productivity

where there weren't any, for balancing a budget that every year drifted farther from reality, for adjusting official exchange rates to maximize the budgetary impact of whatever hard currency the Republic could finagle or extort, for magnifying the economy's few successes and making optimistic excuses for its many failures. The top Party leaders could afford to be stupid or cynical about his numbers, but he himself had to believe in the story they told. This required political conviction, self-deception, and, perhaps especially, self-pity.

A refrain of Andreas's childhood was his father's litany of the unfairnesses with which the German workers' state contended. The Nazis had persecuted the Communists and nearly destroyed the Soviet Union, which had then been fully justified in exacting reparations, and America had diverted scarce resources from its own oppressed working class and sent them to West Germany to create an illusion of prosperity, luring weak and misguided East Germans across the border. "No state in world history has ever started at a greater disadvantage than ours," he liked to say. "Beginning with sheer rubble, and with every hand raised against us, we've succeeded in feeding and clothing and housing and educating our citizens and providing every one of them with a level of security that only the wealthiest in the West enjoy." The phrase *every hand raised against us* never failed to move Andreas. His father seemed to him the greatest of men, the wise and kindhearted champion of the conspired-against and spat-upon German worker. Was there anything more worthy of sympathy than a suffering underdog nation persevering and triumphing through sheer faith in itself? *With every hand raised against it?*

His father was overworked, however, and traveled a lot to Moscow and to other Eastern Bloc countries. Andreas's real love affair was with his mother, Katya, who was no less perfect and much more available. She was pretty and lively and quick; rigid only in her politics. She had boyishly short hair of unrivaled redness, blazing but natural-looking redness, the product of a Western bottle obtainable only by the very privileged. She was a jewel of the Republic, a person of great physical and intellectual charm who'd elected to stay behind while others like her were getting out. Nobody toed the Party line with greater ease. Andreas had gone to lectures of hers and seen the hold she had on her classes, the way she mesmerized them with the redness of her hair and the torrent of words she delivered without notes. She could quote whole chunks of Shakespeare from memory, whatever random lines her thought process happened to call for, and then freely translate them into German for the slower students, and everything she said was shot through with orthodoxy: the Danish tragedy a parable of false consciousness and its downfall, Polonius a travesty of the bourgeois intelligentsia, the blond prince a prophetic prefigurement of Marx, Horatio his Engels, and Fortinbras the Lenin-like fulfiller and guarantor of revolutionary consciousness, arriving at the Danish equivalent of the Finland Station. If anyone was put off by how obviously well Katya thought of herself, if anyone found her liveliness unsettling (safety lay in drabness), she had her position as chair of her division's political oversight committee to set their minds at rest.

She also came from heroic stock. In 1933, after the burning of the Reichstag and the banning of the Communist Party, the smart or lucky party leaders fled to the Soviet Union for advanced training by the NKVD while the others dispersed across Europe. Katya's mother held a British passport and managed to emigrate to Liverpool with her husband and their two girls. The father found work at the dockyards and did enough spying for the Soviets to stay in their good graces; Katya claimed to remember Kim Philby coming to dinner once. When the war broke out, the family was politely but firmly relocated to the Welsh countryside and waited out the war there. Minus Katya's older sister, who'd married a swing-band leader, the parents returned to East Berlin, marched in a celebratory parade, received public commendations for their resistance to fascism, and then were quietly exiled to Rostock by the NKVD-trained leaders whom the Soviets had installed in power. Only Katya was allowed to remain in Berlin, because she was a student. Her father hanged himself in Rostock in 1948; her mother had a nervous breakdown and was warehoused in a locked ward until she, too, died. Andreas later came to think it possible that the secret police had assisted his grandfather's suicide and his grandmother's breakdown, but such consolation was politically foreclosed to Katya. Her own star rose with the eclipse of her parents, who could now safely be remembered as martyrs. She became a full professor and eventually married a university colleague who'd weathered the war in the Soviet Union, along with his Wolf relatives, and learned his economics there.

Nothing about Andreas's childhood with her was ordinary. She permitted him everything, and in return she required only that he be with her constantly, asked only that he be delighted with her. The delight came naturally to him. Her tenure at the university was in *Anglistik*, and from the beginning she spoke both German and English at home with him, best of all in the same sentence. Mixing up the two languages was endless fun. *Du hast ein* bloody awful mess *gemacht!* The *Vereinigten Staaten* are rotten! Is that a fart *oder eine Ausfahrt* I smell? *Willst du ein* otheres *Stück* creamcake? What goeth in thy little head on? She refused to entrust him to day care, because she wanted him all to herself, and she had the privilege to get away with it. He started reading so young he didn't remember learning to do it. He did remember sleeping in her bed when his father was away; also remembered his father's snoring when he tried to join the two of them at night, remembered feeling scared of the snores, remembered her getting up and taking him back to his room and sleeping with him there. He was apparently incapable of doing anything she didn't like. When he had a tantrum, she sat down on the floor and cried with him, and if this upset him all the more, she became all the more upset herself, until finally the funniness of her make-believe distress distracted him from his own distress. Then he laughed, and she laughed with him.

One time he got so angry at her that he kicked her in the shin, and she stumbled around the living room in make-believe agony, crying, in English, "A hit, a palpable hit!" It was so funny and infuriating that he ran and kicked her again, harder. This time she collapsed on the floor and lay motionless. He giggled and thought about kicking her one more time, since they were having so much fun. But when she continued not to move he became worried and kneeled down by her face. She was breathing, not dead, but there was a strange empty look in her eyes. "Mama?"

"Do you like to be kicked?" she said in a low monotone.

"No."

She didn't say anything more, but he was highly precocious and immediately felt ashamed of kicking her. She never had to tell him what not to do, and she never did. He began to paw and prod her, trying to rouse her, saying, "Mama, Mama, I'm sorry I kicked you, please get up." But now she was weeping—real tears, not make-believe. He stopped pawing her and didn't know what to do. He ran to his bedroom and did some crying of his own, hoping she would hear him. He ended up howling, but she still didn't come to him. He stopped crying and went back to the living room. She was still on the floor, in the exact same position, her eyes open.

"Mama?"

"You didn't do anything wrong," she murmured.

"I didn't hurt you?"

"You're perfect. The world isn't."

She didn't move. The only thing he could think to do was to go back to his room and lie very still, like her. But this was boring, so he opened a book. He was still reading it when he heard his father come home. "Katya? *Katya!*" His father's footsteps sounded stern and angry. Then Andreas heard a slap. After a moment, a second slap. Then his father's footsteps again, and then his mother's, then a clatter of pots and pans. When he went out to the kitchen, his mother gave him a warm smile, her familiar warm smile, and asked what he'd been reading. At dinner the parental conversation was the same as ever, his father mentioning the name of some person, his mother saying something funny and slightly mean about this person, his father replying "From each according to his ability" or something similarly sententious and correct, his mother turning to Andreas and giving him the special wink she liked to give him. How he loved her! Loved both of them! The earlier scene had been a bad dream.

Many of his other early memories were of attending committee meetings at the university with her. She gave him a chair in the corner of the meeting room, away from the table, and he precociously read chapter-books—in German, Werner Schmoll, *Nackt unter Wölfen*, *Kleine Shakespeare-Fabeln für junge Leser*; in English, *Robin Hood* and Steinbeck—while the gathered professors outdid one another in proposing new ways to align the *Anglistik* curriculum with class struggle and better serve the German worker. Probably no meetings at the university were more suffocatingly doctrinaire, because no department was more inessential and embattled. Andreas developed an almost telepathic connection with his mother; he knew exactly when to look up from his book and receive her special wink, the wink that told him that she and he were suffering together and together were smarter than anyone else. Her colleagues probably didn't love having a child in the room, but Andreas had a preternaturally long attention span and was so in tune with his mother that he knew what might embarrass her and never did it. Only in extreme situations did he get up and tug on her sleeve so that she could take him to the ladies' room to pee.

At one of the longest of these meetings—so Katya's story went; Andreas didn't remember it—he became too drowsy to read and nestled his head on the armrest of his chair. One of Katya's colleagues, trying to be tactful in the presence of her son, and presumably unaware of his language skills, suggested in English that perhaps the boy should go lay down in her office. According to Katya, Andreas immediately sat up straight and shouted out, in English: "To say 'lay' when you mean 'lie' is a *lie!*" It was true that he'd learned the distinction between *lie* and *lay* at some point, and that his estimation of his own intelligence was very high, but he still couldn't believe that he'd been clever enough, at six, to say such a thing. Katya insisted that he had. It was one of many precocity stories that she liked to retell: how her six-year-old's English was better than her tenured colleague's. Her retellings didn't embarrass Andreas as much as he later came to feel they should have. He learned early to tune out her pride in him, to take it as a given and move on.

He saw less of her as he advanced through the regimentations and indoctrinations of lower school and afterschool programs, but by then he was already convinced that he had the world's best parents. He still loved coming home and matching wits with his mother bilingually, he was better able now to read her favorite plays and novels and be the person his father wasn't, a person who read literature, and although he could also see better that she wasn't entirely stable (there were further mental collapses, on the floor of her study, in the bathtub, and occasional unaccountable absences followed by unlikely explanations) he felt a kind of *noblesse oblige* toward his friends and classmates, taking it as a given that their mothers were less wonderful than his. This conviction persisted until puberty.

In theory, psychologists were unnecessary in the Republic of Bad Taste, because neurosis was a bourgeois malady, a morbid expression of contradictions that by definition could not exist in a perfect workers' state. Nevertheless, there were psychologists, a few of them, and when Andreas was fifteen his father arranged for him to see one of them. He stood accused of having tried to kill himself, but his presenting symptom was excessive masturbation. In his opinion, excess was in the eye of the beholder, and in his mother's opinion he was going through a natural adolescent phase, but he allowed that his father might be right in thinking otherwise. Ever since he'd discovered a secret passageway out of self-alienation, in the form of giving himself pleasure while also receiving it, he'd increasingly resented any activity that took him away from it.

The most time-consuming of these was football. No sport was less interesting to the East German intelligentsia, but by the age of ten Andreas had already absorbed his mother's disdain for the intelligentsia. He argued to his father that the Republic was a workers' state and football the sport of the working masses, but this was a cynical argument, worthy of his mother. Football's real attraction was that it separated him from classmates who fancied themselves interesting but weren't. He compelled his best friend, Joachim, for whom he was the glass of fashion and the mold of form, to sign on with him. They went to a sports center agreeably distant from Karl-Marx-Allee, and with their talk of Beckenbauer and Bayern München they made their classmates feel left out. Later on, after he saw the ghost, Andreas pursued the sport obsessively, practicing with his clubmates at the sports center and by himself at the Weberwiese, because he imagined himself as a star striker and it spared him from thinking about the ghost.

But he was never going to be a star striker, and the ease of masturbation only heightened his frustration with the defenders who kept thwarting his attempts to score. By himself, in his room, he could score at will. There, the only frustration was that he became bored and depressed when he'd scored too many times and couldn't do it again for a while.

To sustain his interest, he had the inspiration of making pencil drawings of naked girls. His first drawings were extremely crude, but he discovered that he had some talent, especially when he could work from a model in an illustrated magazine, undressing her as he copied, and that by drawing with one hand and touching himself with the other he could prolong the pleasurable suspense for hours. The less successful drawings he came on, balled up, and threw away. The better ones he saved and improved and delayed adding filthy captions to, because, although the idealized faces and bodies remained lovely to him, the words he imputed to them embarrassed him the next day.

He informed his parents that he was quitting football. His mother approved ipso facto of everything he did, but his father said that if he quit he would have to find other healthful and commensurately time-consuming activities, and so, one evening, on the way home from practice, he jumped off the Rhinstraße bridge and down into the trashy bushes

where, as it happened, he'd last seen the ghost. He broke
his ankle and told his parents that he'd jumped on a stupid dare.

The one thing everyone in the Republic had plenty of
was time. Whatever you didn't do today really could be
put off until tomorrow. Every other commodity may have
been scarce, but never time, especially if you had a broken ankle and were extremely intelligent. Homework was
a laugh for a boy who'd been reading since three and doing multiplication since five, there was a limit to the pleasure he could take in entertaining the boys at school with
his intelligence, the girls didn't interest him, and ever
since he'd seen the ghost he'd stopped enjoying conversations with his mother. She was as interesting as ever, she
dangled her interestingness at the dinner table like a piece
of luscious fruit, but he'd lost his appetite for it. He lived
in a vast proletarian desert of time and boringness, and
so he didn't see anything wrong or excessive in devoting
a good chunk of each day to producing beauty with his
hands, transforming blank paper into female faces that
owed their very existence to him, transforming his dinky
worm into something big and hard. He became so un-
ashamed of his drawings that he took to working on the
faces on the living-room sofa, sometimes touching his
pants to maintain a moderate level of stimulation, sometimes becoming so absorbed in his art that he forgot to
be stimulated.

"Whose face is that?" his mother asked him one day,
looking over his shoulder. Her tone was coy.

"No one's," he said. "It's just a face."

"It must be someone's face. Is it a girl you know at
school?"

"No."

"You seem very practiced. Is this what you've been
working on with your door closed?"

"Yes."

"Do you have other drawings that I can see?"

"No."

"I'm really impressed with your talent. Can't I see your other drawings?"

"I throw them away when I'm done with them."

"You have *no* others?"

"That's right."

His mother frowned. "Are you doing this to hurt me?"

"Honestly, the thought of you never crosses my mind. You should be worried if it did."

"I can protect you," she said, "but you have to talk to me."

"I don't want to talk to you."

"It's normal to be excited by pictures at your age. It's healthy to have urges at your age. I'm just interested in knowing whose face that is."

"Mother, it's an *invented face*."

"Your drawing looks so personal, though. Like you know very well who that's supposed to be."

Without another word, he put the drawing in a binder and went and shut himself in his bedroom. When he opened the binder again, the penciled face looked loathsome to him. Hideous, hideous. He tore up the paper. His mother knocked on the door and opened it.

"Why did you jump off the bridge?" she said.

"I told you. It was a dare."

"Were you trying to harm yourself? It's important that you tell me the truth. It would be the end of the world for me if you did what my father did to me."

"Joachim dared me, just like I said."

"You're too intelligent to do something so stupid on a dare."

"All right. I wanted to break my leg so I could spend more time masturbating."

"That's not funny."

"*Please* go away so I can masturbate." The words just popped out of his mouth, but the shock of hearing them jolted something loose in him. He jumped to his feet and came at his mother, trembling, grinning, and said, "*Please go away so I can masturbate. Please go away so I can—*"

"Stop!"

"I'm not like your father. I'm like *you*. But at least I keep to myself. I don't harm anyone but myself."

She blanched at the goal he'd scored. "I have no idea what you're talking about."

"No, of course not. I'm the crazy one. I can't even tell *a hawk from a handsaw*." He knew the line in English.

"Enough with the Hamletizing."

"*A little more than kin, a little less than kind.*"

"You have some thoroughly wrong idea," she said. "You got it from a book and it annoys me, all this hinting. I'm starting to think your father's right—I let you read things when you were too young for them. I can still protect you, but you have to confide in me. You have to tell me what you're really thinking."

"I'm thinking—nothing."

"Andreas."

"Please go away so I can masturbate!"

He was protecting her, not the other way around, and when his father came home from yet another round of factory tours and informed him that he had a date with a psychologist, he assumed that his mission in the counseling sessions would be to continue protecting her. His father wouldn't have entrusted him to anyone but the most politically rock-solid, Stasi-certified psychologist. However much Andreas was coming to hate his mother, there was no way that he was telling the psychologist about the ghost.

The Republic's capital wasn't just spiritually flat but

literally flat. Such few hills as it had were composed of rubble from the war, and it was on a minor one of these, a grassy berm behind the back fence of the football pitch, that Andreas had first seen the ghost. Beyond the berm were disused rail tracks and a narrow stretch of wasteland too irrationally shaped to have fit into any five-year development plan to date. The ghost must have come up from the tracks on the late afternoon when Andreas, winded from sprints, hung his hands on the fence and pressed his face into its links to catch his breath. At the top of the rise, maybe twenty meters away, a gaunt and bearded figure in a ratty sheepskin jacket was looking at him. Feeling his privacy and privilege invaded, Andreas turned around and put his back to the fence. When he returned to running sprints and glanced up at the hill, the ghost was gone.

But he appeared again at dusk the following day, again looking directly at Andreas, singling him out. This time some of the other players saw the ghost and shouted at him—"Stinking deviant!" "Go wipe yourself!" etc.—with the morally untroubled contempt that club members had for anyone not playing by society's rules. You couldn't get in trouble for reviling a bum; quite the opposite. One of the boys peeled off and went to the fence to shout abuse from a closer range. Seeing him approach, the ghost ducked behind the hill and out of sight.

After that, he appeared after dark, loitering at the point on the hill where the light from the pitch ended, his head and shoulders dimly visible. Running up and down the pitch, Andreas kept looking to see if the ghost was still there. Sometimes he was, sometimes he wasn't; twice he seemed to beckon to Andreas with a motion of his head. But he was always gone by the time the final whistle blew.

After a week of this peek-a-boo, Andreas took Joachim aside when practice ended and everyone else was leaving the pitch. "That guy on the hill," he said. "He keeps looking at me."

"Oh, so it's you he's after."

"Like he has something to say to me."

"Gentlemen prefer blonds, man. Somebody should report him."

"I'm going to jump the fence. Find out what his story is."

"Don't be stupid."

"There's something weird about the way he looks at me. It's like he knows me."

"Wants to *get* to know you. It's your curly golden locks, I'm telling you."

Joachim was probably right, but Andreas had a mother in whose eyes he could do no wrong, and by now, at the age of fourteen, he was accustomed to following his impulses and taking what he wanted, so long as he didn't directly disrespect authority. Things always turned out well for him: instead of falling on his face, he was praised for his initiative and creativity. He felt like talking to the ghost in the sheepskin jacket and getting his story, which was bound to be less boring than anything else he'd heard in the past week, and so, with a shrug, he went over to the fence and wedged a toe in its links.

"Hey, come on," Joachim said.

"Call the police if I'm not back in twenty minutes."

"You're unbelievable. I'm coming with you."

This was what Andreas had wanted, and, as usual, he was getting it.

From the top of the rise, they couldn't see much in the shadows along the rail tracks. A truck skeleton, urban weeds, small prospectless trees, some pale lines that might have been the remains of walls, and their own attenuated shadows from the pitch lights. Banks of medium-rise socialist housing were massed in the far distance.

"Hey!" Joachim shouted at the darkness. "Antisocial Element! You here?"

"Shut up."

Down by the tracks they saw a movement. They took the straightest line they could to it, picking their way slowly in the poor light, weeds grabbing at their bare legs. By the time they reached the tracks, the ghost was all the way down near the Rhinstraße bridge. It was hard to tell, but he seemed to be looking at them.

"Hey!" Joachim bellowed. "We want to talk to you!"

The ghost started moving again.

"Go back and shower," Andreas said. "You're scaring him."

"This is stupid."

"I'll only go as far as the bridge. You can meet me there."

Joachim hesitated, but in the end he almost always did what Andreas wanted. When he was gone, Andreas trotted down the tracks, enjoying his little adventure. He could no longer see the ghost, but it was interesting just to be in an unregulated space, in the dark. He was smart and knew the rules, and he wasn't breaking any by being here. He felt entitled to it, just as he felt entitled to be the player on the football pitch whom the figure stared at. He wasn't afraid; he felt unharmable. Still, he was glad of the safety of the streetlights on the bridge. He stopped in front of it and peered into its shadows. "Hello?" he said.

A foot scraped on something in the shadows.

"Hello?"

"Come under the bridge," a voice said.

"You come out."

"No, under here. I won't hurt you."

The voice sounded gentle and educated, which somehow didn't surprise him. It wouldn't have been appropriate for a person who wasn't intelligent to stare at him and beckon to him. He moved under the bridge and made out a human shape by one of the pillars. "Who are you?" he said.

"Nobody," the ghost said. "An absurdity."

"Then what do you want? Do I know you?"

"No."

"Then what do you want?"

"I can't stay here, but I wanted to see you before I go back."

"Back to where?"

"Erfurt."

"Well, here I am. You're seeing me. Do you mind if I ask why you're spying on me?"

The bridge above them shook and boomed with the weight of a passing truck.

"What would you say," the ghost said, "if I told you I'm your father?"

"I'd say you're a lunatic."

"Your mother is Katya Wolf, née Eberswald. I was her student and colleague at Humboldt University from 1957 until February 1963, at which time I was arrested, tried, and sentenced to ten years in prison for subversion of the state."

Andreas involuntarily took a step backward. His fear of political lepers was instinctive. No good could come of contact with them.

"Needless to say," the ghost added, "I did not subvert the state."

"Obviously the People thought otherwise."

"No, interestingly, no one ever thought otherwise. I went to prison for the crime of having relations with your mother before and after she was married. The *after* in particular was a problem."

A horrible feeling seized Andreas, part loathing, part pain, part righteous rage.

"Listen to me, dirtbag," he said. "I don't know who you are, but you can't talk about my mother that way. You understand? If I see you again at the football pitch, I'm calling the police. You understand?" He turned and stumbled back toward the light.

"Andreas," the dirtbag called after him. "I held you when you were a baby."

"Go fuck yourself, whoever you are."

"I'm your father."

"Go fuck yourself. You're filthy and disgusting."

"Do one thing for me," the dirtbag said. "Go home and ask your mother's husband where he was in October and November of 1959. That's all. Just ask him and see what he says."

Andreas's eyes fell on a scrap of lumber. He could bash the dirtbag's head in, nobody would miss an enemy of the state, nobody would care. Even if they caught Andreas, he could say it was self-defense and they'd believe him. The idea was giving him a stiffy. There was a murderer in him.

"You don't have to worry," the dirtbag said. "You won't see me again. I'm not allowed to enter Berlin. I'm almost certainly on my way back to prison, just for having disappeared from Erfurt."

"You think I care?"

"No. Why would you. I'm nobody."

"What's your name?"

"It's safer for you if you don't know."

"Then why are you doing this to me? Why did you even come here?"

"Because I sat in prison for ten years imagining it. I spent another year imagining it after I got out. Sometimes you imagine something for so long, you find that you have no choice but to do it. Maybe you'll have a son of your own someday. You might understand better then."

"People who tell filthy lies belong in prison."

"It's not a lie. I told you the question you need to ask."

"If you did something bad to my mother, you deserve all the more to be in prison."

"That's the way her husband saw it, too. You can understand why I might see things rather differently."

The dirtbag said this with a note of bitterness, and already Andreas could sense what later became transparent to him: the guy was guilty. Maybe not of the crime for which he'd been imprisoned, but certainly of having taken advantage of something unstable in his mother, and then of coming back to Berlin to make trouble; of caring more about getting even with his former lover than about the feelings of their fourteen-year-old son. He was a sleaze, a nobody, *a former graduate student of English studies.* At no point did Andreas dream of reestablishing contact with him.

All he said in the moment was "Thanks for ruining my day."

"I had to see you at least once."

"Fine. Now go back to Erfurt and fuck yourself."

Still muttering this phrase, Andreas hurried out from under the bridge and scrambled up the embankment to Rhinstraße. There was no sign of Joachim, so he made his way home, pausing twice in shadowed doorways to rearrange his underpants, because his homicidal stiffy was persisting in his football shorts. He had no intention of asking his father the question the ghost had suggested, but he was suddenly thinking of scenes from the past two or three years which had made so little sense to him that he'd dutifully put them out of his mind.

There was the time he'd gone out to the dacha on a Friday afternoon and found his mother sitting stark naked between two rosebushes, unable or unwilling to utter a word until his father finally arrived, after dark, and slapped her face. That was a weird one. And the time he'd been sent home from school with a fever and found his parents' bedroom door locked and later seen two workers in blue coveralls hastening out of the bedroom. And the time he'd gone to her office at the university to have a permission slip signed, and again the door was locked, and after some minutes a male student had come out, his hair plastered with sweat, and Andreas had tried to go through the door but his mother had pushed it shut from inside and locked it again.

And what she'd said afterward, the bewitching gaiety of her explanations:

"I was just smelling the roses, and it was such a lovely day I took my clothes off, to be closer to nature, and then when I saw you I was so embarrassed that I couldn't say a word to you."

"They were fixing the electricity and they needed me to stand by the light switch and flip it on and off and on and off, and they were so silly with their rules that they wouldn't even let me open the door. It was like I was their prisoner!"

"We'd had the most horribly excruciating disciplinary meeting, the poor boy is being expelled—you probably heard him crying—and I had to make some notes while it was still fresh in my mind."

He remembered the determined pressure of her office door, the irresistible force pushing him back. He remembered remembering, when he saw her pussy in the rose garden, that this wasn't the first time he'd seen it—that something he'd thought was a disturbing dream from his early childhood hadn't actually been a dream; that she'd shown it to him once before, to answer some precocious question of his. He remembered that although he'd been sprawled with his fever in the living room, in plain sight, the two workmen in coveralls hadn't said hello to him, hadn't even glanced at him, as they made their escape.

When he got home, Katya was sitting on their fake-leather faux-Danish sofa—so tacky and yet two cuts above most other sofas in the Republic—reading the *ND* and drinking her after-work glass of wine. She had an air of knowing that she looked like an advertisement for life in East Berlin. In the window behind her were the pretty lights of another superior modern building across the street. "You're still in your football clothes," she said.

Andreas moved behind a chair to conceal his stiffy. "Yeah, I decided to run home."

"You left your clothes at the pitch?"

"I'll get them tomorrow."

"Joachim just called. He wondered where you were."

"I'll call him back."

"Is everything all right?"

He wanted to believe in the image she was presenting, since it obviously meant so much to her: the ideal worker and mother and wife relaxing after a productive day within a system that provided better security than capitalism and was, to boot, in the best of ways, more serious. Her ability to read every last dull word in the *ND* with seeming interest was undeniably impressive. The true extent of his love was becoming evident only now, when the sight of her also revolted him.

"Everything couldn't be better," he said.

Retreating to the bathroom, he took out his stiffy and was saddened by how minor it seemed, compared to how prominent it had felt on the street. Nevertheless, it was what he had to work with, and he proceeded to work with it that night, and the next night, and the next, until he succeeded in banishing the thought of asking his parents where his father had been in the fall of 1959. The ghost from Erfurt may have been wronged, but Andreas himself hadn't been, not in any meaningful sense. Rather than stir up pointless trouble, rather than cause his parents anguish, he took what he knew and suspected about his mother and used it only to excuse his own solitary depravities. If she was entitled to entertain a random pair of workers in her bedroom on a Tuesday afternoon, he was certainly entitled to impute raunchy words to the women he drew and to shoot his seed all over them.

The psychologist, Dr. Gnel, had a spacious ground-floor office in the Charité complex and sat behind his desk in an impressively clinical white coat. Andreas, taking a seat opposite him, had the sense of being at a medical consultation or a job interview. Dr. Gnel asked him if he knew why his father had sent him here.

"He's being sensible and careful," Andreas said. "If I turn out to be a sex criminal, there'll be a record of his having intervened."

"So you personally don't feel there's any reason for you to be here?"

"I'd much rather be at home masturbating."

Dr. Gnel nodded and jotted on his notepad.

"That was a joke," Andreas said.

"What we choose to joke about can be revealing."

Andreas sighed. "Can we establish right away that I'm much smarter than you are? My joke was not revealing. The joke was that you'd take it to be revealing."

"But that in itself is revealing, don't you think?"

"Only because I want it to be."

Dr. Gnel set down his pen and notepad. "It seems not to occur to you that I might have had other very smart patients. The difference between them and me is that I'm a psychologist and they are not. I don't have to be as smart as you to help you. I only have to be smart about one thing."

Andreas felt unexpectedly sorry for the psychologist. How painful it must have been to know that your intelligence was limited. How shameful to have to confess your limitations to a patient. Andreas was well aware that he was brighter than the other kids at his school, but not one of them would have admitted it in the piteously limpid way that Dr. Gnel had. He decided that he would like the psychologist and try to take care of him.

Dr. Gnel returned the favor by pronouncing him not suicidal. After Andreas explained why he'd jumped from the bridge, the doctor simply complimented him on his resourcefulness: "There was something you wanted, you didn't see how you could get it, and yet you found a way."

"Thank you," Andreas said.

But the doctor had follow-up questions. Was he attracted to any of the girls at his school? Were there ones he felt like kissing, or touching, or having sex with? Andreas honestly answered that all his female classmates were stupid and repellent.

"Really? All of them?"

"It's like I see them through some distorting pane of glass. They're the opposite of the girls I draw."

"You wish you could have sex with the girls you draw."

"Absolutely. It's a great frustration that I can't."

"Are you sure you're not drawing self-portraits?"

"Of course not," Andreas said, offended. "They're totally female."

"I'm not objecting to your drawings. To me they're another example of your resourcefulness. I don't want to judge, I only want to understand. When you tell me you draw figments of your imagination, things that only exist inside your head, doesn't that sound a bit like a self-portrait?"

"Maybe in the most narrow and literal sense."

"What about the boys in your school? Are you attracted to any of them?"

"Nope."

"You say that so flatly, it's as if you didn't honestly consider my question."

"Just because I like my friends, it doesn't mean I think about having sex with them."

"All right. I believe you."

"You say that like you don't believe me."

Dr. Gnel smiled. "Tell me more about this distorting pane of glass. What do your female classmates look like through it?"

"Boring. Stupid. Socialist."

"Your mother is a committed socialist. Is she boring or stupid?"

"Not at all."

"I see."

"I don't want to have sex with my mother, if that's what you're suggesting."

"I didn't suggest that. I'm just thinking about sex. Most people think it's exciting to have it with a real flesh-and-blood person. Even if she bores you, even if she seems stupid to you. I'm trying to understand why you don't think that."

"I can't explain it."

"Do you think the things you want are so dirty that no real girl could possibly want them?"

The doctor may have been smart about only one thing, but Andreas had to admit that, within his narrow speciality, the doctor was apparently smarter than he was. He himself was feeling quite mixed up, because he had evidence that his mother herself wanted to do dirty things, and had in fact done them, which ought to have suggested that other females might also want to do them, and do them with *him*; but somehow he felt just the opposite. It was as if he loved his mother so much, even now, that he subtracted the things that were disturbing about her and mentally implanted them in other females to make them frightening to him, make him prefer masturbation, and let his mother remain perfect. This didn't make sense, but there it was.

"I don't even want to know what a real girl wants," he said.

"The same thing as you, maybe. Love, sex."

"I'm worried that there's something wrong with me. All I want to do is masturbate."

"You're only fifteen. That's very young to be having sex with another person. I'm not telling you it's what you should be doing. I just find it interesting that not one single classmate of yours, female or male, is attractive to you."

Years later, Andreas still couldn't say whether his sessions with Dr. Gnel had greatly helped him or grievously harmed him. Their immediate result, though, was that he started chasing girls. What he wanted above all was that *there not be something wrong with him*. Before the sessions had even ended, he applied his intelligence to the task of being more normal, and it turned out that Dr. Gnel was right: the real thing *was* more exciting—more challenging than drawing pictures, not as impossible as becoming a star striker. From dealing with his mother, he had a powerful arsenal of sensitivity, entitlement, and disdain to bring to bear on girls. Because there was so much time to talk and so little of interest to talk about, everyone at his school knew that his parents were important. This inclined girls to trust him and take their cues from him. They felt excited, not threatened, by his joking about the Free German Youth, or the senility of the Soviet politburo, or the Republic's solidarity with the rebels in Angola, or the eugenic physiques of the Olympic diving team, or the appalling petit bourgeois taste of his countrymen. It wasn't that he cared much, one way or another, about socialism. The point of his joking was to convey to his female listeners that he was capable of naughtiness, and to gauge their level of interest in being naughty with him. In his last years at the *Oberschule*, he got quite far with many of them. And yet, repeatedly, at the crucial moment, he ran aground on their narrow-minded working-class morality. The line they drew between finger fucking and real fucking was like the line between ridiculing German-Angolan brotherhood and calling the socialist workers' state a failure and a fraud. He found only two girls willing to cross the line, and both of them had dismayingly romantic visions of their future with him.

It was the quest for wilder girls that led him into Berlin's bohemian scene—to the Mosaik, the Fengler, the poetry readings. By then he was studying math and logic at the university, subjects "hard" enough to pass muster with his father and abstract enough to spare him from tedious political discussion. He got top marks in his classes, engaged intensively with Bertrand Russell (he'd turned against his mother but not against her Anglophilia), and still had copious free time. Unfortunately, he was by no means the only man to whom it had occurred to trawl the scene for sex, and although he did have the advantage of being young and good-looking he was also radiantly privileged. Not that anyone imagined the Stasi would be so dumb as to send a person like him undercover, but he sensed an aversion to his privilege everywhere he went, a feeling that he could get a person into trouble, whether he intended to or not. To succeed with the arty girls, he needed bona fides of disaffection. The first girl he set his sights on was a self-styled Beat poet, Ursula, whom he'd seen at two readings and whose ass was an amazement. Chatting her up after the second reading, he was inspired to claim that he wrote poetry himself. This was an outrageous lie, but it landed him a date to have coffee with her.

She was nervous when they met. Nervous somewhat on her own account but mostly, it seemed, on his.

"Are you suicidal?" she bluntly asked him.

"Ha. Only north-northwest."

"What does that mean?"

"Shakespeare reference. It means not really."

"I had a friend in school who killed himself. You remind me of him."

"I did jump off a bridge once. But it was only an eight-meter drop."

"You're more of a reckless self-harmer."

"It was rational and deliberate, not reckless. And that was years ago."

"No, but right now," she said. "It's almost like I can smell it on you. I used to smell the same thing on my friend. You're looking for trouble, and you don't seem to understand how serious trouble can be in this country."

Her face wasn't pretty, but it didn't matter.

"I'm looking for some other way to be," he said seriously. "I don't care what it is, just as long as it's different."

"Different how?"

"Honest. My father is a professional liar, my mother a gifted amateur. If they're the ones who are thriving, what does it say about this country? Do you know the Rolling Stones song 'Have You Seen Your Mother, Baby'?"

" 'Standing in the Shadow.' "

"The very first time I heard it, on RIAS, I could tell in my gut that everything they'd told me about the West was a lie. I could tell it just from the *sound*—there was no way a society that produced that kind of sound could be as oppressed as they said it was. Respectless and depraved, maybe. But happily respectless, happily depraved. And what does that say about a country that wants to forbid that kind of sound?"

He was saying these things just to be saying them, because he hoped they would bring him closer to Ursula, but he realized, as he said them, that he also meant them. He encountered a similar irony when he went home (he still lived with his parents) and tried to write something that Ursula might mistake for actual poetry: the initial impulse was pure fraudulence, but what he found himself expressing was authentic yearning and complaint.

And so he became, for a while, a poet. He never got anywhere with Ursula, but he discovered that he had a gift for poetic forms, perhaps akin to his gift for realistically drawing naked women, and within a few months he'd had his first poem accepted by a state-approved journal and made his debut at a group reading. The male bohemians still distrusted him, but not the females. There ensued a happy period when he woke up in the beds of a dozen different women in quick succession, all over the city, in neighborhoods he'd never dreamed existed—in flats without running water, in absurdly narrow bedrooms near the Wall, in a settlement twenty minutes by foot from the nearest bus stop. Was there anything more sweetly existential than the walking done for sex in the most desolate of streets at three in the morning? The casual slaughter of a reasonable sleep schedule? The strangeness of passing someone's hair-curlered mother in a bathrobe on your way to her heartrendingly hideous bathroom? He wrote poems about his experiences, intricately rhymed renderings of his singular subjectivity in a land whose squalor was relieved only by the thrill of sexual conquest, and none of it got him in trouble. The country's literary regime had lately relaxed to the extent of permitting this kind of subjectivity, at least in poetry.

What got him in trouble was a cycle of word puzzles that he worked on when his brain was too tired to do math. The soothing thing about the sort of poetry he wrote was that it limited his choice of words. It was as if, after the chaos of a childhood with his mother, he craved the discipline of rhyme schemes and other formal constraints. At another cattle-call literary event, where he was given only seven minutes at the podium, he read his puzzle poems because they were short and didn't betray their secrets to a listener, only to a reader. After the reading, an editor from *Weimarer Beiträge* complimented him on the poems and said she could fit a few of them into the issue she was closing. And why did he say yes? Maybe there really was something suicidal in him. Or maybe it was the looming of his military service, which it was already a small scandal that he'd deferred, given his father's lofty position. Even if, as was likely, he served in an elite intelligence or communications corps, he couldn't imagine himself surviving the military. (Poetic discipline was one thing, army discipline another.) Or maybe it was just that the magazine editor was about the same age as his mother and reminded him of her: somebody too blinded by self-regard and privilege to recognize what a total tool she was. She must have fancied herself a sensitive advocate of youthful subjectivity, a woman who really understood young people today, and it must have been inconceivable to her and her supervisors that a young man even more privileged than they were could wish to embarrass them, because none of them noticed what everyone else did within twenty-four hours of the magazine's distribution:

Muttersprache / Mother Tongue

I	Ich
connected	
her	danke
	es
with	deiner
inappropriate	immensen
desire,	Courage,
made	allabendlich.
every	Träume
	ermächtigen.
enthusiastically	
unnatural	Träume
response	hüten
entirely	eines
mine.	
	Muttersöhnchens
She	ohnmächtigen
observed	Schlaf.
zealously,	Träumend
if	
a	gelingt
little	Liebe
	ohne
irritably;	Reue:
she	In
made	Oedipus'
up	Unterwelt
such	singt
droll	ein
excuses;	jauchzender,
nobody	aberwitziger
	Chor

had	uns
ever	Lügen
really	aus
relished	Träumen
lying	ins
if	Ohr.
correct	Nur
hypocrisies	
sufficed	tags
	offenbaren
to	
evade	Yokastes
negativity.	Obsession
	und
She	Rasen
allowed	
me	sich,
everything;	ordnungshalber,
not	charakterlich.
every	Ich
radically	aber
grotesque	liege
upbringing	im
so	Schlaf,
succeeds.	Mutter.

The hullabaloo that followed was delicious. The magazine was yanked from every shelf and trucked away for pulping, the editor was fired, her boss demoted, and Andreas speedily expelled from the university. He left the office of his department chair wearing a grin so wide it made his neck hurt. From the way the heads of strangers swiveled toward him, from the way the students who knew him turned their backs at his approach, he could tell that the entire university had already heard the news of what he'd done. Of course it had—talking was pretty much the only thing that anyone in the Republic, except maybe his father, had to fill their days with.

When he went out onto Unter den Linden, he noticed a black Lada double-parked across from the main university entrance. Two men were in the car, watching him, and he gave them a wave that they didn't return. He didn't really see how he could be arrested, given who his parents were, but he also didn't mind the thought of it. If anything, he'd relish the opportunity to not recant his poems. After all, didn't he adore sex? Didn't he dearly love coming? And so, if you took him at his literal word, what more heartfelt tribute to socialism could he offer than to dedicate his *MoST gLoRIOUs* orgasm to it? Even his wayward dick rose to attention and saluted it!

The Lada tailed him all the way to Alexanderplatz, and when he emerged from the U-Bahn at Strausbergerplatz, a different car, also black, was waiting for him on the Allee. For the previous two nights he'd been hiding out at the Müggelsee, but now that his expulsion was official there was no point in avoiding his parents. It was February, and the day was unusually warm and sunny, the coal pollution mild and almost pleasant, not throat-burning, and Andreas was in such sunny spirits that he felt like approaching the black car and explaining to its occupants, in a lighthearted tone, that he was more important than they could ever hope to be. He felt like a helium balloon straining skyward on a slender string. He hoped he might never in his life be serious again.

The car tailed him to the Karl Marx Buchhandlung, where he went inside and asked a bad-smelling clerk if they had the latest issue of *Weimarer Beiträge*. The clerk, who knew his face but not his name, briskly replied that the issue wasn't in yet.

"Really?" Andreas said. "I thought it was supposed to be in last Friday."

"There was a problem with the content. It's being re-issued."

"What problem? What content?"

"You didn't hear?"

"Why, no, I didn't."

The clerk evidently considered this so unlikely as to be suspicious. He narrowed his eyes. "You'll have to ask someone else."

"I always seem to be the last person to find out . . ."

"A stupid adolescent vandal caused a lot of trouble and cost a lot of money."

What was it about bookstore clerks and their powerful body odor?

"They ought to hang the guy," Andreas said.

"Maybe," the clerk said. "What I don't like is that he got innocent people in trouble. To me, that's selfish. Socio-pathic."

The word landed in Andreas's gut like a punch. He left the store in a state of deflation and doubt. Was that what he was—a sociopath? Was that what his mother and mother-land had made him? If so, he couldn't help it. And yet he had a horror of diagnostic labels that suggested there was something wrong with him. As he headed up the Al-lee toward his parents' building, under a sun that now seemed wan, he mentally scurried to rationalize what he'd done to the magazine editor—tried to tell himself that she'd gotten only what every apparatchik deserved, that she was being punished for her own stupidity in failing to notice the obvious acrostics, and that, in any case, he was suffering consequences easily as dire as hers—but he couldn't get around the fact that he hadn't thought once, let alone twice, about what he might be doing to her by giving her his poems. It was as if he'd chosen to commit

vehicular suicide by swerving at high speed into a car
filled with children.

He racked his memory for an example of his having
treated another human being as anything but an instrumentality. He couldn't count his parents—his whole
childhood was a sense-defying brainfuck. But what about
Dr. Gnel? Hadn't he felt compassion for the psychologist
and tried to take care of him? Alas, the label *sociopath*
reduced the example of Gnel to shit. Seducing the shrink
who was investigating his sociopathy? His motives there
were suspect, to say the least. He thought of the women
he'd slept with on his poetry-sponsored spree and
how *grateful* he'd felt to each of them—surely his gratitude counted as evidence in his favor? Maybe. But he
couldn't even remember half their names now, and the
work he'd done to give them pleasure seemed in hindsight merely a device to heighten his own. He was dismayed to find no evidence at all of having cared about
them as people.

How strange that he went through life loving who he
was, savoring himself, enjoying his capabilities and levity, only to see something loathsome when a store clerk
uttered a chance word and he saw himself objectively. He
recalled his jump from the bridge—at first a delicious
sense of floating on air but then a merciless acceleration,
the ground lurching up at him viciously uncontrollable
momentum body impact pain. Gravity was objective. And
who had set him up to jump? It was so easy to blame the
mother. He was *her* instrumentality, the accouterment of
her sociopathy. There was a submerged but killing violence in what she'd done to him, but being a killer didn't
accord with her self-regard, and so, to help her out, he'd
jumped from the bridge, and so he'd published those
poems.

The black car shadowed him to their building and

stopped when he went inside. Upstairs, on the top floor, he found the flat filled unusually with cigarette smoke, an ashtray heaping on a faux-Danish end table. He looked for Katya in her bedroom, in her study, in his own room, and finally in the bathroom. She was on the floor by the toilet, in the half-uncurled position of a stillbirth, her eyes staring at the toilet's base.

For a moment, his guts twisted up. He was a four-year-old again, stricken at the sight of his beloved red-haired mother in distress. It all came back, especially the love. But the fact that it was coming back made him angry.

"Ah, so here we are," he said. "What happened—the cigarettes make you sick?"

She didn't move or answer.

"It's wise to go slowly when you take up a habit again after twenty years."

No response. He sat down on the edge of the bathtub.

"It's just like old times," he said jovially. "You on the floor in a fugue state, me not knowing what to do. It's remarkable how high-functioning you are, for an insane person. I'm the only one who gets to see you on the floor."

She breathed out and her lips grasped feebly at the exhalation, forming a few faint fricatives but nothing like a word.

"Sorry, didn't catch that," Andreas said.

Her next exhalation seemed to form the words *what's wrong with you*.

"What's wrong with *me*? I'm not the one on the floor in a fugue state."

No response.

"I bet you're rethinking your decision not to abort me, right around now. It turns out to be so much more painful to wait twenty years for me to do it myself."

Her eyes weren't even blinking.

"I'll be in my room if you want me," he said, standing

up. "Maybe you'd like to come and watch me masturbate—speaking of taking up old habits again."

In truth he had no inclination to jerk off and wasn't sure he ever would again. Nor was he sleepy or depressed—didn't feel like lying down. He was in a state unlike any he'd ever known, a state of having absolutely nothing to do. No point in studying math or logic, no point in writing poetry, no interest in reading, no energy for throwing things away, no responsibilities, nothing. He thought of packing a bag, but he couldn't think of a single thing he wanted to take to wherever he was going. He was afraid that if he went back into the bathroom he would kick his mother, and although it was true that his father could slap her out of her states, he somehow doubted that blows from him would do the trick. He perched on a windowsill and looked down at the black car on the street. The man in the passenger seat was reading a newspaper. This seemed to Andreas a poignant futility.

After a few hours, the telephone rang. He guessed that the caller was his father and that he wasn't supposed to answer the phone himself. This was convenient, because he was afraid of speaking to his father. And maybe he wasn't a total sociopath after all, because the thought of his father's anger and shame and disappointment brought tears to his eyes. His father was the earnest little German boy who believed in socialism. He worked hard, he had a disturbed wife, and he'd lovingly raised a child who wasn't his, not even spiritually. Beyond pity, Andreas had a sense of identification with him, for sharing the burden of Katya.

The phone rang and rang. It was a form of slapping but one so attenuated by distance that he counted more than fifty rings before he heard Katya stirring. The uncertain padding of her little feet. The ringing stopped, and he heard her murmur a few times and then hang up. Then sounds of her putting herself back together. By the time she approached his room, her steps were brisk, her false self reassembled.

"You have to leave here," she said from the doorway. She was holding a lighted cigarette and the ashtray, which she'd emptied.

"You don't say."

"For now, you're safe from arrest, thanks to your father. Of course, that could change at any time, depending on how you behave."

"Tell him I appreciate it. Seriously."

"He's not doing it for you."

"Even so. It's nice for me, too. He's been a good step-father."

Rather than take the bait, she dragged hard on the cigarette, not looking at him.

"How are those tasting, after all these years?"

"It's not out of the question that you can do your service now. It would be hard service, on the worst base, and you'd be watched. Your deferment was already a costly embarrassment to your father, and it would be an immense favor to me if you'd do the service now. You may recall that I interceded for you."

"When have you ever done anything but intercede for me? Everything I am I owe to you. Mother."

"You've put both him and me in a terrible position. Me especially, since I was the one who interceded for you. The best thing you can do now is accept this extremely merciful offer."

"*Hup*, two, three, four. Are you out of your mind?" He laughed and slapped his head. "Sorry, tactless question."

"Will you accept the offer?"

"How much do you want it? Enough to have an honest conversation with me?"

She snapped off a drag with the practice of a former smoker. "I'm always honest with you."

"See what I mean? It's not going to be so easy for you. But all you have to do is tell the truth for once, and I'll do the service for you."

She snapped off another drag. "That's no bargain at all if you refuse to believe the truth."

"Trust me. I'll know it when I hear it."

"The only other option is that you sever all contact with us permanently and take your chances on your own."

That she could say such a thing, and say it so coolly, was an unexpectedly painful blow to him. He saw that, in her own way, she really was being honest with him now: there was room for only one fuckup in the home of Undersecretary Wolf. His father had enough trouble covering for her, cleaning up her messes, talking her out of rose gardens. He'd had at least one lover of hers imprisoned, he'd performed untold further miracles of suppression, and Katya wasn't so bonkers that she didn't know a good thing when she had it. Andreas had been flattering to her when he was the world's most precocious boy, when he was in love with her, when he was her pretty prince. But as soon as she'd seen the pictures he was drawing, she'd ratted him out to his father and had him sent to a psychologist, and now there was nothing at all for her in him. The time had come to give him the boot.

And again tears came to his eyes, because, no matter how he'd come to hate her, he was also, even now, trying to impress her and win her praise, bringing her his Bertrand Russell papers as mother-flattering evidence of his outsize intellect, constructing his rhyme schemes. He'd even believed, at some level, that the cleverness of "Muttersprache" would please her. He was twenty years old and as duped as ever. And he didn't want to leave her. That was the saddest, sickest part of it. He was still a wanting four-year-old, still betrayed by shit that had happened to his brain before he had a self that remembered.

He watched her pretty fingers stub the cigarette out. The agony of withdrawal from her was a measure of the depth of his addiction.

"You were fucking a grad student for six years," he said. "You fucked him for so long that he grew up to be your colleague."

"No," she said calmly, almost as if she were bored. "I would never have done that."

"You were alone at home the entire fall when I was conceived."

"No. Your father never went on trips that long."

"And then, after I was born, you kept on fucking your colleague."

"That's entirely false," she said. "But I suppose it doesn't matter, since you have no intention of believing me. I do ask, though, that you not use the word *fuck* with your mother."

This reproach, mild though it was, was all but unprecedented. Her entire method as a mother was to abjure direct correction.

"Why would a well-educated man I've never seen," he said, "start following me around at the football pitch and tell me a story like that?"

Her face became masklike.

"Mother? Why would a person do that?"

She blinked and came to. "I have no idea," she said. "There are all kinds of strange people in the world. If this is what's been upsetting you all this time . . ." She frowned.

"Yes?"

"It occurs to me that we have a third option. We can have you admitted to a mental hospital."

He burst out laughing. "For real? That's the third option?"

"I'm afraid we may have ignored your cries for help for far too long. But now you've made one that we can't ignore, and it's not too late for help. Now that I think about it, getting you the help you need may be the most attractive of all our options."

"You think I'm mentally ill."

"No, never. Not a mental illness. But extreme emotional distress. You experienced some kind of trauma at the football pitch that you didn't tell us about. A thing like that can fester."

"Indeed."

Her gaze wandered away, out into the hallway. "Andreas, consider it," she said. "My family has a history of emotional distress. I'm afraid that some of that may have been passed on to you."

"Skipping a generation, of course."

"I think what you've done to your father and me qualifies as extreme disturbance. I think I have a right to lie down on the bathroom floor."

"When you go back there, take a pillow. It's a hard floor."

"I admit that I've had mood swings over the years. But that's all they are, mood swings. I'm sorry if that was hard to live with. I don't think it's enough to explain what you've done to us."

"I have my own unique mental illness."

"Well," she said, turning away from him. "Please consider it. I think it's good that we had this honest conversation."

It didn't speak well of his sanity that he actively had to squelch the impulse to run after her and kill her with whatever came to hand. Then again, he did squelch it, which spoke better of his sanity. And his next impulse—to run out to the street and find a girl he could bang—was not only reasonable but fully practicable. His bohemian credentials were golden now. He threw some clothes and books into a duffel bag. In the seven years that followed, he saw his mother only twice, accidentally, from a distance.

The drizzle persisted through the week, with intermittent harder showers, and for three nights he obsessed about the rain, wondering whether it was good or bad. When he managed to sleep for a few minutes, he had dreams which he ordinarily would have found laughably obvious—a body not in the place where he'd left it, feet protruding from under his bed when people entered his room—but which under the circumstances were true nightmares, of the sort from which he ordinarily would have been relieved to awaken. But being awake was even worse now. He considered the plus side of rain: no moon. And the minus side: deep footprints and tire tracks. The plus side: easy digging and slippery stairs. And the minus side: slippery stairs. The plus side: cleansing. And the minus side: mud . . . The anxiety had a life of its own, it churned and churned. The one thought that brought relief was that Annagret was unquestionably suffering even more. The relief was to feel connected to her. The relief was love, the astonishment of experiencing her distress more keenly than he experienced his own; of caring more about her than about himself. As long as he could hold that thought and exist within it, he could halfway breathe.

There is a divinity that shapes our ends . . .

At three thirty on Thursday afternoon he packed a knapsack with a hunk of bread, a pair of gloves, a roll of piano wire, and an extra pair of pants. He had the feeling that he'd slept not at all the previous night, but maybe he had, maybe a little bit. He left the rectory basement by the back stairs and emerged in the courtyard, where a light rain was falling. Earnest embarrassments were smoking cigarettes in the ground-floor meeting room, the lights already on.

On the train he took a window seat and pulled the hood of his rain parka over his face, pretending to sleep. When he got out at Rahnsdorf, he kept his eyes on the ground and moved more slowly than the early commuters, letting them disperse. The sky was nearly dark. As soon as he was alone he walked more briskly, as if he were out for exercise. Two cars, not police, hissed past him. In the drizzle he looked like nobody. When he rounded the last bend before the house and didn't see anyone on the street, he broke into a lope. The soil here was sandy and drained well. At least on the gravel of the driveway, he wasn't leaving footprints.

No matter how many times he'd gone over the logistics in his head, he couldn't quite see how they would work: how he could conceal himself completely and still be within striking distance. He was desperate to keep Annagret out of it, to keep her safe in her essential goodness, but he was afraid that he wouldn't be able to. His anxiety the previous night had swirled around the image of some awful three-person scrum that would leave her trust in him shattered.

He strung the piano wire between two railing posts, across the second of the wooden steps to the back porch. Tightening it at a level low enough that she could not too obviously step over it, he dug the wire into the wood of the posts and flaked some paint off them, but there was nothing to be done about that. In the middle of his first night of anxiety, he'd gotten out of bed and gone to the rectory's basement staircase to conduct a test of tripping on the second step. He'd been surprised by how hard he'd pitched forward, in spite of knowing he was going to trip—he'd nearly sprained his wrist. But he wasn't as athletic as the stepfather, he wasn't a bodybuilder . . .

He went around to the front of the dacha and took off his boots. He wondered if the two *VoPos* he'd met the previous winter were patrolling again tonight. He remembered the senior one's hope that they would meet again. "We'll see," he said aloud. Hearing himself, he noticed that his anxiety had abated. Much better to be doing than to be thinking about doing. He entered the house and took the key to the toolshed from the hook where it had hung since he was little.

He went outside again and put on his boots and stepped carefully around the edge of the back yard, mindful of footprints. Once he was safely in the toolshed, which had no windows, he groped for a flashlight and found one on the usual shelf. In its light, he checked inventory. Wheelbarrow—yes. Shovel—yes. He was shocked to see, by his watch, that it was already nearly six o'clock. He turned off the flashlight and took it out into the drizzle with the shovel.

The spot he had in mind was behind the shed, where his father had always piled yard waste. Beyond the pile the pines were sparse, their fallen needles lying thick on soil furrowed by the frost heaves of winters past. The darkness was near total here, the only light a few grayish panels between the surrounding trees, in the direction of the West's greater brightness. His mind was working so well that he thought to remove his watch and put it in his pocket, lest the shock of digging damage it. He turned on the flashlight and laid it on the ground while he cleared needles, setting aside the most freshly fallen in a separate pile. Then he turned out the light and dug.

Chopping through roots was the worst—hard work and loud work. But the neighboring houses were dark, and he stopped every few minutes to listen. All he heard was the rustle of rain and the faint generic sounds of civilization that collected in the basin of the lake. Again he was glad

of the soil's sandiness. He was soon into gravel, noisier to
dig through but harder to slip on. He worked implacably,
chopping roots, levering out larger stones, until he recalled, with some panic, that his sense of time was messed
up. He scrambled out of the hole for the flashlight. Eight
forty-five. The hole was more than half a meter deep.
Not deep enough, but a good start.

He made himself keep digging, but now his anxiety
was back, prompting him to wonder what time it was,
what time. He knew he had to hold out and keep *doing*,
not thinking, for as long as he could, but he soon became
too anxious to wield the shovel with any force. It still
wasn't even nine thirty, Annagret hadn't even met her
stepfather in the city yet, but he climbed out of the hole
and forced himself to eat some bread. Bite, chew, swallow, bite, chew, swallow. The problem was that he was
parched and hadn't brought water.

Fully out of his head, he dropped the bread on the
ground and wandered back to the shed with the shovel.
He could almost not remember where he was. He started
to clean his gloved hands on the wet grass but was too out
of his head to finish the job. He wandered around the edge
of the yard, stepped wrong and left a deep footprint in a
flower bed, dropped to his knees and madly filled it, and
managed to leave an even deeper footprint. By now he was
convinced that minutes were passing like seconds without
his knowing it. From a great distance he could still discern
his ridiculousness. He could picture himself spending
the rest of the night leaving footprints while cleaning
his hands after filling footprints he'd left while cleaning his
hands, but he also sensed the danger of picturing it. His
mind was drawn to silliness as if to some sweet infantile
distraction from anxiety. If he let the native hue of his
resolution be sicklied over with it, he was liable to put
down the shovel and go back to the city and laugh at the

idea of himself as a killer. Be the former Andreas, not the man he wanted to be now. He saw it clearly in those terms. He had to kill the man he'd always been, by killing someone else.

"Fuck it," he said, deciding to leave the deep footprint unfilled. He didn't know how long he'd knelt on the grass having extraneous and postponable thoughts, but he feared it was a lot more time than it had felt like. Again from a great distance, he observed that he was thinking crazily. And maybe this was what craziness was: an emergency valve to relieve the pressure of unbearable anxiety.

Interesting thought, bad time to be having it. There were a lot of small things he should have been remembering to do now, in the proper sequence, and wasn't. He found himself on the front porch again without knowing how he'd got there. This couldn't be a good sign. He took off his muddy boots and his slippery socks and went inside. What else, what else, what else? He'd left his gloves and the shovel on the front porch. He went back out for them and came inside again. What else? Shut the door and lock it. Unlock the back door. Practice opening it.

Extraneous bad thought: were the whorls of toeprints unique like those of fingerprints? Was he leaving traceable toeprints?

Worse thought: what if the fucker thought to bring a flashlight or routinely carried one on his bike?

Even worse thought: the fucker probably *did* routinely carry a flashlight on his bike, in case of a nighttime breakdown.

A still worse thought was available to Andreas—namely, that Annagret would be there and could use her body, could feign uncontrollable lust, to forestall any business with a flashlight—but he was determined not to entertain it, not even for the relief from his terrible new anxiety, because it would entail being conscious of an obvious fact, which was that she must *already* have used her body and feigned lust to get the fucker out here. The only way Andreas could stand to picture the killing was to leave her entirely out of it. If he let her into it—allowed himself to acknowledge that she was using her body to make it happen—the person he wanted to kill was no longer her stepfather but himself. For putting her through a thing like that; for dirtying her in the service of his plan. If he was willing to kill the stepfather for dirtying her, it logically followed that he should kill himself for it. And so, instead, he entertained the thought that, even with a flashlight, the stepfather might not see the trip wire.

He'd heard it said, possibly by Dr. Gnel, that every suicide was a proxy for a murder that the perpetrator could only symbolically commit; every suicide a murder gone awry. He was prepared to feel universally grateful to Annagret, but right now he was more narrowly grateful that she was bringing him a person worth killing. He imagined himself purified and humbled afterward, freed finally of the filth, freed of the sordid history of which this lakeside dacha was a part. Even if he ended up in prison, she would literally have saved his life.

But where was his own flashlight?

It wasn't in his pockets. It could be anywhere, although he surely hadn't dropped it randomly in the driveway. Without it, he couldn't see his watch, and without seeing his watch he couldn't ascertain whether he had time to put his boots back on and return to the back yard and find the flashlight and ascertain whether he did, in fact, have time to be looking for it. The universe, its logic, suddenly felt crushing to him.

There was, however, a small light above the kitchen stove. Turn it on for one second and check his watch? He had too complicated a mind to be a killer, too much imagination for it. He could see no rational risk in turning on the stove light, but part of having a complicated mind was understanding its limits, understanding that it couldn't think of everything. Stupidity mistook itself for intelligence, whereas intelligence knew its own stupidity. An interesting paradox. But it didn't answer the question of whether he should turn the light on.

And why was it so important to look at his watch? He couldn't actually think of why. This went to his point about intelligence and its limits. He leaned the shovel against the back door and sat down cross-legged on the mud rug. Then he worried that the shovel was going to fall over. He reached to steady it with such an unsteady hand that he knocked it over. The noise was catastrophic. He jumped to his feet and turned on the stove light long enough to check his watch. He still had at least thirty minutes, probably more like forty-five.

He sat down on the rug again and fell into a state like a fever dream in every respect except that he was fully aware of being asleep. It was like being dead without the relief from torment. And maybe the adage had it backward, maybe every murder was a suicide gone awry, because what he was feeling, besides an all-permeating compassion for his tormented self, was that he had to follow through with the killing to put himself out of his misery. He wouldn't be the one dying, but he might as well have been, because the relief that would follow the killing had a deathlike depth and finality in prospect.

For no apparent reason, he snapped out of his dream and into a state of chill clarity. Had he heard something? There was nothing but the trickle and patter of light rain. It seemed to him as if a lot of time had passed. He stood up and grasped the handle of the shovel. He was having a new bad thought—that, for all his care in planning, all his anxiety, he'd somehow neglected to consider what he

would do if Annagret and her stepfather simply didn't
show up; he'd been so obsessed with logistics that he
hadn't noticed this enormous blind spot, and now, because
the weekend was coming and his parents might be out
here, he was facing the task of refilling the hole he'd
dug for nothing—when he heard a low voice outside
the kitchen window.

A girl's voice. Annagret.

Where was the bike? How could he not have heard
the bike? Had they walked it down the driveway? The bike
was essential.

He heard a male voice, somewhat louder. They were
going around behind the house. It was all happening so
quickly. He was shaking so much that he could hardly
stand. He didn't dare touch the doorknob for fear of making a sound.

"The key's on a hook," he heard Annagret say.

He heard her feet on the steps. And then: a floor-
shaking thud, a loud grunt.

He grabbed the doorknob and turned it the wrong way
and then the right way. As he ran out, he thought he didn't
have the shovel, but he did. It was in his hands, and he
brought the convex side of its blade down hard on the dark
shape looming up in front of him. The body collapsed on
the steps. He was a murderer now.

Pausing to make sure of where the body's head was,
he raised the shovel over his shoulder and hit the head so
hard he heard the skull crack. Everything so far fully
within the bounds of planned logistics. Annagret was
somewhere to his left, making the worst sound he'd ever
heard, a moan-keen-retch-strangulation sound. Without
looking in her direction, he scrambled down past the body,
dropped the shovel, and pulled the body off the steps by
its feet. Its head was on its side now. He picked up the
shovel and hit the head on the temple as hard as he could,

to make sure. At the second crack of skull, Annagret gave a terrible cry.

"It's over," he said, breathing hard. "There won't be any more of it."

He dimly saw her moving on the porch, coming to the railing. Then he heard the strangely childish and almost dear sounds of her throwing up. He didn't feel sick himself. More like postorgasmic; immensely weary and even more immensely sad. He wasn't going to throw up, but he began to cry, making his own childish sounds. He dropped the shovel, sank to his knees, and sobbed. His mind was empty, but not of sadness.

The drizzle was so fine it was almost a mist. When he'd cried himself dry, he felt so tired that his first thought was that he and Annagret should go to the police and turn themselves in. He didn't see how he could do what still had to be done. Killing had brought no relief at all—what had he been thinking? The relief would be to turn himself in at the police station.

Annagret had been still while he cried, but now she came down from the porch and crouched by him. At the touch of her hand on his shoulder, he sobbed again.

"Shh, shh," she said.

She put her face to his wet cheek. The feel of her skin, the mercy of her warm proximity: his weariness evaporated.

"I must smell like vomit," she said.

"No."

"Is he dead?"

"He must be."

"This is the real bad dream. Right now. Before wasn't so bad. This is the real bad."

"I know."

She began to cry voicelessly, huffingly, and he took her in his arms. He could feel her tension escaping in the form of whole-body tremors. Her tension must have been unspeakably bad, and there was nothing he could do with his compassion except to hold her until the tremors subsided. When they finally did, she wiped her nose on her sleeve and pressed her face to his. She opened her mouth against his cheek, a kind of kiss. They were partners, and it would have been natural to go inside the house and seal their partnership, and this was how he knew for certain that his love for her was pure: he pulled away and stood up.

"Don't you like me?" she whispered.

"Actually, I love you."

"I want to come and see you. I don't care if they catch us."

"I want to see you, too. But it's not right. Not safe. Not for a long time."

In the darkness, at his feet, she seemed to slump. "Then I'm completely alone."

"You can think of me thinking of you, because that's what I'll be doing whenever you think of me."

She made a little snorting sound, possibly mirthful. "I barely even know you."

"Safe to say I don't make a habit of killing people."

"It's a terrible thing," she said, "but I guess I should thank you. Thank you for killing him." She made another possibly mirthful sound. "Just hearing myself say that makes me all the more sure that I'm the bad one. I made him want me, and then I made you do this."

Andreas was aware that time was passing. "What happened with the motorcycle?"

She didn't answer.

"Is the motorcycle here?"

"No." She took a deep breath. "He was doing maintenance after dinner. He didn't have it put back together when I went to meet him—he needed some new part. He said we should go out some other night."

Not very ardent of him, Andreas thought.

"I thought maybe he'd gotten suspicious," she said. "I didn't know what to do, but I said I really wanted it to be tonight."

Andreas again suppressed the thought of how she'd persuaded the stepfather.

"So we took the train," she said.

"Not good."

"I'm sorry!"

"No, it was the right thing to do, but it makes things harder for us."

"We didn't sit together. I said it was safer not to."

Soon other riders on the train would be seeing the missing man's picture in the newspaper, maybe even on television. The entire plan had hinged on the motorcycle. But Andreas needed to keep her morale up. "You're very smart," he said. "You did the right thing. I'm just worried that even the earliest train won't get you home in time."

"My mother goes straight to bed when she comes home. I left my bedroom door closed."

"You thought of that."

"Just to be safe."

"You're very, very smart."

"Not smart enough. They're going to catch us. I'm sure of it. We shouldn't have taken the train, I hate trains, people stare at me, they'll remember me. But I didn't know what else to do."

"Just keep being smart. The hardest part is behind you."

She clutched his arms and pulled herself to her feet. "Please kiss me," she said. "Just once, so I can remember it."

He kissed her forehead.

"No, on the mouth," she said. "We're going to be in jail forever. I want to have kissed you. It's all I've been thinking about. It's the only way I got through the week."

He was afraid of where a kiss might lead—time was continuing to pass—but he needn't have been. Annagret kept her lips solemnly closed. She must have been seeking the same thing he was. A cleaner way, an escape from the filth. For his part, the darkness of the night was a blessing: if he could have seen the look in her eyes more clearly, he might not have been able to let go of her.

While she waited in the driveway, away from the body, he went inside the house. The kitchen felt steeped in the evil of his lying in ambush there, the evil contrast between a world in which Horst had been alive and the world where he was dead, but he forced himself to put his head under the faucet and gulp down water. Then he went to the front porch and put his socks and boots back on. He found the flashlight in one of the boots.

When he came around the side of the house, Annagret ran to him and kissed him heedlessly, with open mouth, her hands in his hair. She was heartbreakingly teenaged, and he didn't know what to do. He wanted to give her what she wanted—he wanted it himself—but he was aware that what she ought to want, in the larger scheme, was to not get caught. It was painful to be older and more rational, painful to be the enforcer. He took her face in his gloved hands and said, "I love you, but we have to stop."

She shivered and burrowed into him. "Let's have one night and then be caught. I've done all I can."

"Let's not be caught and then have many nights."

"He wasn't such a bad person, he just needed help."

"You need to help me for one minute. One minute and then you can lie down and sleep."

"It's too awful."

"All you have to do is steady the wheelbarrow. You can keep your eyes shut. Can you do that for me?"

In the darkness, he thought he could see her nod. He left her and picked his way back to the toolshed. It would be a lot easier to get the body in the wheelbarrow if she helped him, but he found that he welcomed the prospect of wrangling the body by himself. He was protecting her from direct contact, keeping her as safe as he could, and he wanted her to know it.

The body was in coveralls, work clothes from the power plant, suitable for motorcycle maintenance but not for a hot date in the country. It was hard to escape the conclusion that the fucker really hadn't intended to come out here tonight, but Andreas did his best to escape it. He rolled the body onto its back. It was heavy with gym-trained muscle. He found its wallet and zipped it into his own jacket, and then he tried to lift the body by its coveralls, but the fabric ripped. He was obliged to apply a bear hug to wrestle the head and torso onto the wheelbarrow.

The wheelbarrow tipped over sideways. Neither he nor Annagret said anything. They just tried again.

There were further struggles behind the shed. She had to help him by pushing on the wheelbarrow's handles while he pulled from the front. The footprint situation was undoubtedly appalling. When they were finally beside the grave, they stood and caught their breath. Water was softly dripping from pine needles, the scent of the needles mixing with the sharp and vaguely cocoa smell of fresh-turned earth.

"That wasn't so bad," she said.

"I'm sorry you had to help."

"It's just . . . I don't know."

"What is it?"

"Are we sure there's not a God?"

"It's a pretty far-fetched idea, don't you think?"

"I have the strongest feeling that he's still alive somewhere."

"Where, though? How could that be?"

"It's just a feeling I have."

"He used to be your friend. This is so much harder for you than for me."

"Do you think he was in pain? Was he frightened?"

"Honestly, no. It happened very fast. And now that he's dead he can't remember pain. It's as if he'd never existed."

He wanted her to believe this, but he wasn't sure he believed it himself. If time was infinite, then three seconds and three years represented the same infinitely small fraction of it. And so, if inflicting three years of fear and suffering was wrong, as everyone would agree, then inflicting three seconds of it was no less wrong. He caught a fleeting glimpse of God in the math here, in the infinitesimal duration of a life. No death could be quick enough to excuse inflicting pain. If you were capable of doing the math, it meant that a morality was lurking in it.

"Well," Annagret said in a harder voice. "If there is a God, I guess my friend is on his way to hell for raping me. I'd personally be happier if he was in heaven. Putting him in a hole is enough for me. But they say God plays by tougher rules."

"Who told you that?"

"My father, before he died. He couldn't figure out what God was punishing him for."

She hadn't talked about her father before. If time hadn't been passing, Andreas would have wanted to hear everything, know everything about her. He loved that she wasn't consistent; was possibly even somewhat dishonest. This was the first time she'd used the word *rape*, and she was seeming less unfamiliar with religion than she'd made herself out to be, at the church. His wish to puzzle her out was as strong as his wish to lie down with her; the two desires almost amounted to the same thing. But time was passing. He didn't have a muscle that wasn't hurting, but he jumped into the grave and set about deepening it.

"I'm the one who should be doing that."

"Go in the shed and lie down. Try to sleep."

"I wish we knew each other better."

"Me, too. But you need to try to sleep."

She watched in silence for a long time, half an hour, while he dug. He had a confusing twinned sense of her closeness and complete otherness. Together, they'd killed a man, but she had her own thoughts, her own motives, so close to him and yet so separate. And again he felt grateful to her, because she wasn't just smart in his male way, she was smart in female ways he wasn't. She'd seen immediately how important it was to be together—what a ceaseless torture it would be to remain apart, after what they'd done—while he hadn't seen it until now. She was just fifteen, but she was quick and he was slow.

Only after she went to lie down did his mind shift back into logistics mode. He dug until three o'clock and then, without pausing, dragged and rolled the body into the hole and jumped down after it to wrestle it into a supine position. He didn't want to have to remember the face, so he sprinkled some dirt over it. Then he turned on the flashlight and inspected the body for jewelry. There was a heavy watch, not inexpensive, and a sleazy gold neck chain. The watch came off easily, but to break the chain he had to plant a hand on the dirt-covered forehead and yank. Fortunately nothing was real, at least not for long. Infinitesimally soon, the eternity of his own death would commence and render all of this unreal.

In two hours he had the hole refilled and was jumping on the dirt, compacting it. When he returned to the tool-shed, the beam of the flashlight found Annagret huddled in a corner of it, shivering, her arms around her knees. He didn't know which was more unbearable to see, her beauty or her suffering. He turned the light off.

"Did you sleep?"

"Yeah. I woke up freezing."

"I don't suppose you noticed when the first train comes."

"Five thirty-eight."

"You're remarkable."

"He was the one who checked the time. It wasn't me."

"Do you want to go over your story with me?"

"No, I've been thinking about it. I know what to say."

The mood between the two of them felt cold and chalky now. For the first time, it occurred to Andreas that they might have no future together—that they'd done a terrible thing and would henceforth dislike each other for it. Love crushed by crime. Already it seemed like a very long time since she'd run to him and kissed him. Maybe she'd been right; maybe they should have spent one night together and then turned themselves in.

"If nothing happens in a year," he said, "and if you think you're not being watched, it might be safe to see each other again."

"It might as well be a hundred years," she said bitterly.

"I'll be thinking of you the whole time. Every day. Every hour."

He heard her standing up.

"I'm going to the station now," she said.

"Wait twenty minutes. You don't want to be seen standing around there."

"I have to warm up. I'll run somewhere and then go to the station."

"I'm sorry about this."

"Not as sorry as I am."

"Are you angry at me? You can be. Whatever you need to be is fine with me."

"I'm just sick. They'll ask me one question, and everything will be obvious. I feel too sick to pretend."

"You came home at nine thirty and he wasn't there. You went to bed because you weren't feeling well . . ."

"I already said we don't have to go over it."

"I'm sorry."

She moved toward the door, bumped into him, and continued on outside. Somewhere in the darkness, she stopped. "So I guess I'll see you in a hundred years."

"Annagret."

He could hear the earth sucking at her footsteps, see her dark form receding across the back yard. He'd never in his life felt more tired. But finishing his tasks was more bearable than thinking about her. Using the flashlight sparingly, he covered the grave with older and then fresher pine needles, did his best to kick away footprints and wheelbarrow ruts, and artfully strewed leaf litter and lawn waste. His boots and jacket sleeves were hopelessly muddy, but he was too spent to muster anxiety about it. At least he could change his pants.

The mist had given way to a warmer fog that made the arrival of daylight curiously sudden. Fog was not a bad thing. He policed the back yard for footprints and wheelbarrow tracks. Only when the light was nearly full-strength did he return to the back steps to remove the trip wire. There was more blood than he'd expected on the steps, less vomit than he'd feared on the bushes by the railing. He was seeing everything now as if through a long tube. He filled and refilled a watering can at the outside spigot, to wash away blood.

The last thing he did was to check the kitchen for signs of disturbance. All he found was wetness in the sink from the drink he'd taken. It would be dry by evening. He locked the front door behind him and set out walking toward Rahnsdorf. By eight thirty he was back in the

basement of the rectory. Peeling off his jacket, he realized
that he still had the dead man's wallet and jewelry, but he
could sooner have flown to the moon than dispose of
them now; he could barely untie his muddy boots. He lay
down on his bed to wait for the police.

They didn't come. Not that day, that week, or that season—
they never came at all.

And why didn't they? Among the least plausible of
Andreas's hypotheses was that he and Annagret had committed the perfect crime. Certainly it was possible that his
parents hadn't seen what a wreck he'd made of the dacha's
back yard; the first heavy snow of the season had come
the following week. But nobody had noticed the unforget-
tably beautiful girl on either of her train trips? Nobody in
her neighborhood had seen her and Horst walking to the
station? Nobody had looked into where she'd been going
in the weeks before the killing? Nobody had questioned
her hard enough to break her? The last Andreas had seen
of her, a feather would have broken her.

Less implausible was that the Stasi had investigated the
mother, and that her addiction and pilferage had come to
light. The Stasi would naturally have interested itself in a
missing informal collaborator. If the mother was in Stasi
detention, the question wasn't whether she'd confess to the
murder (or, depending on how the Stasi chose to play it,
to the crime of assisting Horst's flight to the West). The
only question was how much psychological torture she'd
endure before she did.

Or maybe the Stasi's suspicions had centered on the
stepdaughter in Leipzig. Or on Horst's co-workers at the
power plant, the ones he'd reported on. Maybe one of them
was already in prison for the crime. For weeks after the
killing, Andreas had looked at the newspapers every day.

If the criminal police had been handling the case, they surely would have put a picture of the missing man in the papers. But no picture ever appeared. The only realistic explanation was that the Stasi was keeping the police out of it.

Assuming he was right about this, he had a further hypothesis: the Stasi had easily broken Annagret, she'd led them to the dacha, and they'd discovered who owned it. To avoid public embarrassment of the undersecretary, they'd accepted Horst's sexual predation as a mitigating circumstance and contented themselves with scaring the daylights out of Annagret. And to torture Andreas with uncertainty, to make his life a hell of anxiety and hyper-caution, they'd left him alone.

He hated this hypothesis, but unfortunately it made more sense than any of the others. He hated it because there was an easy way to test it: find Annagret and ask her. Already scarcely an hour of his waking days passed without his wanting to go to her, and yet, if he was wrong about his hypothesis, and if she was still under suspicion and still being closely watched, it would be disaster for them to meet. Only she could know when they were safe.

He went back to counseling at-risk youths, but there was a new hollowness at his core which never left him. He no longer taught the kids levity. He was at risk him-self now—at risk of weeping when he listened to their sad stories. It was as if sadness were a chemical element that everything he touched consisted of. His mourning was mostly for Annagret but also for his old lighthearted, libidinous self. He would have imagined that his primary feeling would be anxiety, the feverish fear of discovery and arrest, but the Republic appeared to be intent on spar-ing him, for whatever sick reason, and he could no longer remember why he'd laughed at the country and its taste-lessness. It now seemed to him more like a Republic of

Infinite Sadness. Girls still came to his office door, interested in him, maybe even all the more intrigued by his air of sorrow, but instead of thinking about their pussies he thought about their young souls. Every one of them was an avatar of Annagret; her soul was in all of them.

Meanwhile in Russia there was *glasnost,* there was Gorby. The true-believing little Republic, feeling betrayed by its Soviet father, cracked down harder on its own dissidents. The police had raided a sister church in Berlin, the Zion Church, and earnestness and self-importance levels were running high on Siegfeldstraße. There was a wartime mood in the meeting rooms. Secluding himself, as always, in the basement, Andreas found that his sorrow hadn't cured him of his megalomaniacal solipsism. If anything, it was all the stronger. He felt as if his misery had taken over the entire country. As if the state were choking on his crime; as if, unable or unwilling to arrest him, it were determined to rain misery down on everyone else. The embarrassments upstairs were surprised, and perhaps secretly disappointed, when the police failed to raid their own church. But he wasn't. The state avoided him like a toxin.

Late in the spring of 1989, his anxiety returned. At first he almost welcomed it, as if it were the companion of his AWOL libido, reawakened by warm nights and flowering trees. He found himself drawn to the television in the rectory's common room to watch the evening news, unexpurgated, on ZDF. The embarrassments watching with him were jubilant, predicting regime collapse within twelve months, and it was precisely the prospect of regime collapse that made him anxious. Part of the anxiety was straightforward criminal worry: he suspected that only the Stasi was keeping the criminal police at bay; that he was safe from prosecution only as long as the regime survived; that the Stasi was (irony of ironies) his only friend.

But there was also a larger and more diffuse anxiety, a choking hydrochloric cloud. As Solidarity was legalized in Poland, as the Baltic States broke away, as Gorbachev publicly washed his hands of his Eastern Bloc foster children, Andreas felt more and more as if his own death were imminent. Without the Republic to define him, he'd be nothing. His all-important parents would be nothing, be less than nothing, be dismal tainted holdovers from a discredited system, and the only world in which he mattered would come to an end.

It got worse through the summer. He could no longer bear to watch the news, but even when he locked himself in his room he could hear people in the hallway yammering about the latest developments, the mass emigration through Hungary, the demonstrations in Leipzig, the rumors of a coming coup, because they were all that anyone was talking about. People were still cowed by Honecker and still afraid of Mielke, but Andreas knew in his bones that the jig was almost up. Beyond his anxiety, and aside from his having had not one single thought about what he might do when the regime fell, he felt sadness and pity for the earnest little German socialist boy abandoned by the Soviets. He wasn't a socialist, but he might as well have been that little boy himself.

On a Tuesday morning in October, after the largest demonstration yet in Leipzig, the young vicar came tapping on his door. The guy ought to have been in giddy spirits, but something was troubling him. Instead of sitting down cross-legged, he paced the room. "I'm sure you heard the news," he said. "A hundred thousand people in the street and no violence."

"Hooray?" Andreas said.

The vicar hesitated. "I need to come clean with you about something," he said. "I should have told you a long time ago—I guess I was a coward. I hope you can for-give me."

Andreas wouldn't have figured the guy for an infor-mant, but his preamble had that flavor.

"It's not that," the vicar said, reading his thought. "But I did have a visit from the Stasi, about two years ago. Two guys who looked the part. They had some questions about you, and I answered them. They implied that I'd be ar-rested if you found out they'd been here."

"But now it turns out that their guns are loaded with daisy seeds."

"They said it was a criminal matter, but they didn't say what kind. They showed me a picture of that pretty girl who came here. They wanted to know if you'd spoken to her. I said you might have, because you're the youth coun-selor. I didn't say anything definite. But they also wanted to know if I'd seen you on some particular night. I said I wasn't sure—you spend so much time alone in your room. The whole time we were having this conversation, I'm pretty sure you were down here, but they didn't want to see you. And they never came back."

"That's all?"

"Nothing happened to you, nothing happened to any of us, and so I assumed that everything was OK. But I felt bad about talking to them and not telling you. I wanted you to know."

"Now that the ice is melting, the bodies are coming to the surface."

The vicar bristled. "I think we've been good to you. It's been a good arrangement. I know I probably should have said something earlier. But the fact is we've always been a little afraid of you."

"I'm grateful. Grateful and sorry for any trouble."

"Is there anything you want to tell me? Did something bad happen to the girl?"

Andreas shook his head, and the vicar left him alone with his anxiety. If the Stasi had come to the church, it meant that Annagret had been questioned and had talked. This meant that the Stasi had at least some of the facts, maybe all of them. But with a hundred thousand people assembling unhindered on the streets of Leipzig, the Stasi's days were obviously numbered. Before long, the *VoPos* would take over, the real police would do police work . . .

He jumped up from his bed and put on a coat. If nothing else, he now knew he had little to lose by seeing Annagret. Unfortunately, the only place he could think of to look for her was the *Erweiterte Oberschule* nearest to her old neighborhood in Friedrichshain. It seemed inconceivable that she'd proceeded to an *EOS*, and yet what else would she be doing? He left the church and hurried through the streets, taking some comfort in their enduring drabness, and stationed himself by the school's main entrance. Through the high windows he could see students continuing to receive instruction in Marxist biology and Marxist math. When the last hour ended, he scanned the faces of the students streaming out the doors. He scanned until the stream had dwindled to a trickle. He was disappointed but not really surprised.

He returned to the school the next morning, again with no luck. He went to the office of a family-services caseworker he particularly trusted, waited while she checked the central registry, and left empty-handed. For the next week, every afternoon and evening, he loitered outside judo clubs, at sports centers, at bus stops in Annagret's old neighborhood. By the end of October, he'd given up hope of finding her, but he continued to wander the streets. He trawled the margins of protests, both planned and spontaneous, and listened to ordinary citizens risking imprisonment by demanding fair elections, free travel, the neutering of the Stasi. Honecker was gone, the new government was in crisis, and every day that passed without violence made a Tiananmen-style crackdown seem less likely. Hungary had already liberated itself, the others would surely soon follow. Change was coming, and there was nothing he could do but wait to be engulfed by it. The Berlin air tasted hydrochloric to him.

And then, on November 4, a miracle. Half the city had bravely taken to the streets. He was moving through crowds methodically, scanning faces, smiling at a loud-speakered voice of reason rejecting reunification and calling for reform instead. On Alexanderplatz, toward the ragged rear of the crowd, among the claustrophobes and undecideds, his heart gave a lurch before his brain knew why. There was a girl. A girl with spikily chopped hair and a safety-pin earring, a girl who was nonetheless Annagret. Her arm was linked with the arm of a similarly coiffed girl. Both of them blank-faced, aggressively bored. She'd ceased to be the good girl.

WE MUST FIND OUR OWN WAY, WE MUST LEARN TO TAKE THE BEST FROM OUR IMPERFECT SYSTEM AND THE BEST FROM THE SYSTEM WE OPPOSED . . .

As if seeking relief from the boringness of the amplified voice, Annagret looked around the crowd and saw Andreas. Her eyes widened. He was smiling uncontrollably. She didn't smile back, but she did put her mouth to the ear of the other girl and break away from her. As she approached him, he could see more clearly how changed her demeanor was, how unlikely it was that she might still love him. She stopped short of embrace range.

"I can only talk for a minute," she said.

"We don't have to talk. Just tell me where I can find you."

She shook her head. Her radical haircut and the safety pin in her ear were helpless against her beauty, but her unhappiness wasn't. Her features were the same as two years ago, but the light in her eyes had gone out.

"Trust me," he said. "There's no danger."

"I'm in Leipzig now. We're only up for the day."

"Is that your sister?"

"No, a friend. She wanted to be here."

"I'll come and see you in Leipzig. We can talk."

She shook her head.

"You don't want to see me again," he said.

She looked carefully over one shoulder and then over the other. "I don't even know. I'm not thinking about that. All I know is we're not safe. That's all I can think about."

"We're safe as long as there's a ministry."

"I should go back to my friend."

"Annagret. I know you talked to the ministry. They came to the church and asked about me. But nothing happened, they didn't question me. We're safe. You did the right thing."

He moved closer. She flinched and edged away from him.

"We're not safe," she said. "They know a lot. They're just waiting."

"If they know so much anyway, it doesn't matter if we're seen together. They've already waited two years. They're not going to do anything to us now."

She looked over her shoulder again. "I should go back."

"I have to see you," he said for no reason except honesty. "It's killing me not to see you."

She hardly seemed to be listening; was lost in her unhappiness. "They took my mother away," she said. "I had to tell them some kind of story. They put her in a psychiatric hospital for addiction, and then she went to prison."

"I'm sorry."

"But she's been writing letters to the police. She wants to know why they didn't investigate the disappearance. She gets released in February."

"Did you talk to the police yourself?"

"I can't see you," she said, her eyes on the ground. "You did a big thing for me, but I don't think I can ever see you again."

"Annagret. Did you talk to the police?"

She shook her head.

"Then maybe we can fix it. Let me try to fix it."

"I had the most horrible feeling when I saw you. Desire and death and *that thing*. It's all mixed up and horrible. I don't want to want things like that anymore."

"Let me make it go away."

"It will never go away."

"Let me try."

She murmured something he couldn't hear above the noise. Possibly *I don't want to want it*. Then she ran back to her friend, and the two of them walked away briskly, without looking back.

But there was hope, he decided. Buoyed by it, he started running and kept running all the way to Marx-Engels Platz. Every single person in the street was a hindrance to him. All he cared about was seeing Annagret again. The reason he had to make the murder case go away was that he couldn't have Annagret unless he did.

But her mother, to whom he now saw that he'd given insufficient thought, was a serious problem. The mother would have no reason to stop pushing for an investigation, and she would soon be out of prison. Pushing, pushing. When the Stasi collapsed, the police could take the case file and initiate their own investigation. Even if he stayed ahead of them, even if he could somehow move the body, the file was bound to surface when the government went down. And what was in the file? He realized that he should have asked Annagret what exactly she'd told the Stasi. Did they know about the dacha? Or had they shut down their investigation as soon as they'd traced her to him?

He went back to Alexanderplatz, hoping to find her again. He searched the crowds until nightfall, to no avail. He considered going to Leipzig—it wouldn't be hard to locate her sister's flat, where she presumably was living—but he was afraid he would lose her altogether, lose her permanently, if he tracked her down and pestered her with questions.

And so began two months of impotence and dread. On the night the Wall was breached, he felt like the one sober man in a city of falling-down drunks. Once upon a time, he would have laughed at how ridiculously twenty-eight years of national internment had ended, an improvised remark by an exhausted Schabowski demolishing the entire apparatus, but in the event, when he heard the shouting in the rectory, and when the vicar came running downstairs to break the blessed news to him, he might have been a cosmonaut hearing a space rock puncture the metal skin of his capsule. Air whooshing out, the void invading. While the rectory emptied, everybody hastening to the nearest checkpoint to see for themselves, he stayed huddled in a corner of his bed, his knees drawn up to his chin.

He had not one particle of desire to cross the border. He could have gone to Leipzig and found Annagret, the two of them could have crossed over to the West and never come back, could have found a way to go and live in Mexico, Morocco, Thailand. But even if she wanted a life on the lam, what would be the point? Only in his motherland did his life make sense. It didn't matter that he hated her, he still couldn't leave her. In his mind, the only way to save himself was to come to Annagret as the man who'd guaranteed her safety, so that the two of them could walk in public with their heads held high. More than ever, in the chaotic days following the breach, he saw in Annagret his only hope.

He started taking the U-Bahn out to Normannenstraße and mingling with the protesters at the Stasi compound, collecting rumors. The Stasi was said to be shredding and burning documents around the clock. It was said to be hauling them by the truckload to Moscow and Romania. He tried to imagine the scenario in which his own file was destroyed or deported, but the Stasi was undoubtedly being methodically German and working from the top down, attending first to the documents that compromised its own officers and spies, and there were surely enough of those to fill the shredders and furnaces and trucks for months.

When the weather was decent, larger crowds of concerned citizens gathered outside the compound. On ugly afternoons only the hard core showed up, always the same faces, men and women who'd been interrogated and imprisoned for bad reasons and bore adamantine grudges against the ministry. The one Andreas liked best was a guy his own age who'd been spirited off the street in his late teens, after he'd defended a female classmate from the sexual advances of a Stasi commander's son. He'd been warned once, and he'd ignored the warning. For this, he'd spent six years in two prisons. He retold his story incessantly, to anyone who would listen, and it never failed to move Andreas. He wondered what had become of the girl.

And then one evening in early December, returning to the church, he opened his door and saw, sitting on his bed, calmly reading the *Berliner Zeitung*, his mother.

His breathing stopped. He just stood in the doorway and looked at her. She was perilously thin but smartly dressed and generally well put together. She folded the newspaper and stood up. "I was curious about where you've been living."

She was still diabolically lovely. Her hair the same unbelievable red. Her features sharper but her skin unwrinkled.

"You have books I'd like to borrow," she said, moving to his shelves. "It does my heart good to see how many of them are English." She pulled a title off a shelf. "Do you admire Iris Murdoch as much as I do?"

He found his breath and said, "What brings you here?"

"Oh, I don't know. Desire to see my only child, after nine years? Is that so strange?"

"I wish you would leave."

"Don't say that."

"I wish you would leave."

"No, don't say that," she said, reshelving the book. "Let's sit and talk a little bit. Nothing bad can happen to us now. You of all people should be aware of that."

She was violating the room, violating him, and yet some traitorous part of him was overjoyed to see her. Had spent nine years pining for her. Had looked for her in fifty-three girls without finding her. It was terrible how much he loved her.

"Sit with me," she said, "and tell me how you are. You look wonderful." She smiled warmly as her gaze moved up and down him. "My beautiful strong son."

"I'm not your son."

"Don't be silly. We've had some hard years, but that's all behind us now." The warmth left her smile. "Forty years of living with the swine who drove my father to suicide—that's all behind us. Forty years of appeasing the stupidest, boringest, meanest, ugliest, most stink-cowardly self-satisfied philistines the world has ever seen. All behind us. Poof!"

Her stream of pejoratives ought to have counted as refreshing honesty, but the self-regard that impelled them was unchanged, and so to him they only deepened her offense. In the old days, she'd been similarly gaily vicious about the U.S. government. He thought he might have to strangle her, to stop her from emitting her toxic self-regard, to save his life. The second murder was always easier than the first.

"So let's sit and talk," she said.

"No."

"Andreas," she said lullingly. "It's over. It's been terribly hard for your father, obviously. The one man in this country with real intelligence and integrity. The one person truly trying to serve his country and not himself. He's inconsolable. I wish you'd come and see him."

"Not going to happen."

"Can you not understand and forgive him? You put him in a terrible position. It seems so silly now, but it wasn't silly then. He could either serve his country or be the father of a state-subverting poet."

"Not a difficult choice, given that I'm not even his son."

She sighed. "I wish you'd stop with that."

He saw that she was right: it didn't matter. He no longer cared who his father was, couldn't begin to connect with the younger self to whom it had mattered. Maybe it had to do with his having crushed a man's skull with a shovel, but his old anger was gone. All that was left were the more basic emotions of love and loathing.

"We'll be fine," Katya said. "Even your father. These are just difficult days for him. He's known for at least five years that the end was coming, but it's killing him to watch it happen. The new cabinet wants to keep him, but he's planning to resign at the end of the year. We'll be fine—he has a brilliant mind, he's not too old to teach."

"*All's well that ends well.*"

"He didn't do anything wrong. There were murderers and thieves in the government, but he wasn't one of them."

"Although he did abet them for forty years."

She pulled herself up straight. "I still believe in socialism—it's working in France and Sweden. If you want to blame someone, blame the Soviet swine. Your father and I did our best with what we had. I'll never apologize for that."

Politics, collective guilt, collaboration—the whole subject bored him more than ever.

"Anyway," Katya said, "I thought you might want to come home. You can have your old room back, it's certainly more comfortable than this . . . room. I imagine you'll be going back to school, and you can stay with us rent-free. We can start over as a family."

"That sounds good to you?"

"Honestly, yes. You could stay in the dacha instead if you'd prefer, but that's a long train ride. There's also a chance that we'll be selling it."

"What?"

"I know, it's hard to believe, but Wessi speculators are already sniffing all over the city. One of them was out at the Müggelsee, talking to our neighbors, promising hard currency."

"You'd sell the dacha," he said dully.

"Well, it's ugly. Your father doesn't think so, but that's just sentimentality. The speculator was talking about bulldozing all the lakefront houses for a golf course. The Wessis aren't so sentimental."

Beyond his dread at the thought of bulldozers, he felt betrayed by the Republic. Everything it touched turned to shit. It couldn't even defend itself against Wessi speculators. He'd known all along how ridiculously inept it was, but its ineptitude wasn't funny now.

"What are you thinking?" Katya said with a note of coyness.

There was only one thing to be done. He stepped all

the way into the room and closed the door behind him. "You want me to come home," he said.

"It would mean the world to me. It's time for you to thrive again. With the mind you have, you could have a doctorate in three years."

"Thriving would be nice, I agree. But you have to do something for me first."

She pouted. "I'm not sure I like it when you bargain with me."

"It's not what you think. I don't care what you've done. Truly I don't. What I have in mind is something else entirely."

He watched as a strange thing happened in her face, a subtle but crazy-looking modulation of expressions, some interior struggle made visible—her fantasy of being a loving mother, her resentment at the bother of it. He almost felt sorry for her. She wanted things to be easy for her and had no strength or patience when they weren't.

"I'll come home," he said, "but first I need something from State Security. I need everything they have on me. Every file. I need it in my hands."

She frowned. "What do they have?"

"Some bad things, possibly. Things that would make it hard for me to thrive. Things that would embarrass you."

"What did you do? Did you do something?"

He was greatly relieved to hear her ask. Evidently, the Stasi had suspended its investigation on its own initiative, without informing his parents.

"You don't need to know," he said. "You just need to get me the files. I'll take care of it from there."

"Everybody wants their file now. All over the country, collaborators are quaking in their hideous shoes, and the Stasi knows it. Those files are its insurance policy."

"Yeah, but I'm guessing that members of the Central

Committee are not so afraid. At this point, a request for my files would almost be routine."

She searched his face with frightened eyes. "What did you do?"

"Nothing you wouldn't be proud of, if you knew the facts. But the rest of the world might see it differently."

"I can ask your father," she said. "But he's barely recovered from your last transgression. This might not be the best time to mention a new one."

"Don't you love me, Mother?"

Cornered by the question, she agreed to try to help him. Before she left the church, it seemed necessary to both of them that they embrace, and what an odd embrace it was, what a sick transaction. She, who wasn't capable of real love, pretended to love him while he, who really did love her, exploited her pretended love. He took refuge in the chamber of his mind where his purer love of Annagret was locked away.

A week went by, and then another week. Christmas came and went, and still he heard nothing from his mother. Was it possible she'd already gotten the files and read them? Was she rethinking whether she wanted him in her life again? She'd already decided once before that she could live without him.

He finally called her on the day before New Year's.

"It's your father's last day of work," she said.

"Yeah, I'm a little worried about that," he said. "His lack of leverage as a private citizen."

She didn't reply.

"Mother? Should I be worried?"

"I'm feeling somewhat bullied, Andreas. I feel as if you're taking advantage of my wish for reconciliation."

"Did you ask him or didn't you?"

"I've been waiting for the right moment. He's terribly

discouraged. It might be better if you came and asked him yourself."

"You mean, now that it's too late?"

"Why don't you just tell me what you think is in the files. I'm sure it's not so bad."

"I can't believe you let three weeks go by!"

"Please don't shout at me. You're forgetting who your relatives are."

"Markus has nothing to do with domestic operations."

"His name carries weight. Your family is still royalty in this pigsty. And your father is still on the Central Committee."

"Well, then, please ask him."

"First I'd like to know what it is you're hiding."

If he'd thought it would help him, he would happily have told her the story, but his instincts told him not to do it—specifically, not to refer in any way to Annagret's existence. And so he said, instead, "I'm going to be famous, Mother." This hadn't occurred to him until this moment, but he recognized the truth of it immediately: he had it in him to be famous. "I'm going to thrive and be famous, and you're going to be very glad to be my parent. But if you don't get me the files, I'm going to be famous in a different way. A way you won't like."

Two further weeks of waiting followed. Now even on dark days the crowd on Normannenstraße was large, and then suddenly, one miserable raw afternoon, it was enormous. Near the main gate of the compound, Andreas stepped up onto the bumper of a truck to gauge it. People were massed as far as he could see. Thousands of them. Banners, pickets, chanting, TV crews.

Stasi RAUS. Stasi RAUS. Stasi RAUS . . .

People were pushing on the plate-metal gate, scaling it by the handle and hinges, shouting at the guards within.

And then, inexplicably, and to his horror, the gate swung inward.

He was still standing on the bumper of the truck, many layers of body away from the gate. He jumped down and joined the crowd pressing forward, keeping his hand on a leather jacket ahead of him, preserving some space in case of a crush from behind.

A young woman to his left spoke to him affectionately. "Hey, you."

Her face was sweet but only vaguely familiar, maybe not familiar at all. "Hello," he said.

"My God," she said. "You don't even remember me."

"Sure I do."

"Yeah." She smiled, not nicely. "Sure you do."

He hung back long enough for another forward-pushing body to replace her at his side. The voices around him were subdued, maybe with reverence, maybe out of old habit of submission, but after he'd squeezed through the gate and entered the courtyard he could hear rowdy shouting in the building ahead of him. By the time he made it inside, there was already broken glass on the floor and spray paint on the walls. The trend of the crowd was up the central stairs, up to the floors where the offices of Mielke and other senior officers were said to be. Papers were falling from above, the single sheets floating lazily, the bunched ones plummeting. When he reached the stairs, he turned back and looked at the faces coming at him, faces so vivid they seemed to be moving in slow motion, faces red or gray with cold, faces of wonder, triumph, curiosity. Near the front door, uniformed guards were observing with stony indifference. He bucked the flow and approached one. "Where are the archives?" he said.

The guard raised his hands and spread them, palms up.

"Oh come on," Andreas said. "Do you think you're going to undo what's happening here?"

The guard shrugged again with his hands.

Outside again, in the courtyard, through which citizens were continuing to pour like pilgrims, he considered what was happening. To appease the crowd, someone had made the decision to open the main administration building, which had presumably been cleansed of anything compromising. The entire action was symbolic, ritual, maybe even scripted. There were at least a dozen other buildings in the compound, and nobody was trying to get into them.

"The archives!" he shouted. "Let's find the archives!"

Some heads in the crowd turned to him, but everyone kept moving forward, intent on the symbolic penetration of the inner sanctum. In the light of TV cameras and photo flashes, papers were drifting down from broken windows. Andreas went to the fence at the south end of the courtyard and looked at the largest and darkest of the other buildings. Even if he could somehow lead a charge into the archives, his chances of locating his files on his own were close to nil. They were in there somewhere, but the opening of the gate hadn't helped him in the slightest. It had only weakened his friend, the Stasi.

Twenty minutes later, he was pressing a button in the vestibule of his parents' building. The voice that crackled over the intercom was his father's.

"It's me," Andreas said. "Your son."

When he got to the top floor, an old man in a cardigan was standing at the open door of his parents' flat. Andreas was shocked by the change in him. He was shorter, frailer, stooped, with hollows on his cheeks and throat. He extended a hand to shake, but Andreas put his arms around him. After a moment, his father returned the embrace.

"Your mother is at a lecture tonight," he said, ushering Andreas inside. "I was just eating a blood sausage. I can boil you one if you're hungry."

"I'm fine. Just a glass of water."

The new decor in the flat was leather and chrome, with overly bright older-person lighting. A purplish pool of sausage matter was congealing on a lonely plate. His father's hands trembled as he poured from a bottle of mineral water and handed him a glass.

"You should eat your sausage while it's warm," Andreas said, sitting down at the table.

His father pushed his plate aside. "I can boil another later if I'm hungry."

"How are you doing?"

"I'm physically well. Older, as you see."

"You look great."

His father sat down at the table and said nothing. He'd never been an eye-contact kind of man.

"I take it you're not watching the news," Andreas said.

"I lost my appetite for news some months ago."

"They're storming Stasi headquarters as we speak. Thousands of people. They're in the main building."

His father merely nodded, as if in assent.

"You're a good man," Andreas said. "I'm sorry I've made life harder for you. My problem was never with you."

"Every society has rules," his father said. "A person either follows them or he doesn't."

"I respect that you followed them. I'm not here to accuse you. I'm here to ask a favor."

His father nodded again. Down on Karl-Marx-Allee, cars were honking in what sounded like celebration.

"Did Mother tell you that I need a favor?"

His father's face became sad. "Your mother had a lengthy file of her own," he said.

Andreas was so startled by the non sequitur that he didn't know what to say.

"Over the years," his father continued, "she has had repeated episodes during which she behaved irresponsibly. She's a committed socialist and a loyal citizen, but there have been embarrassments. Quite a number of them. I suspect that you're aware of this."

"It does me good to hear it from you."

His father made a demurring gesture with his fingers. "We have had, for some years, issues of command and control with the Ministry for State Security. I've been fortunate in my dealings with it, thanks to my cousin and to my oversight of its budget. But the ministry has considerable autonomy, and a relationship is a two-way street. I've asked many favors of it, over the years, and I now have very little to offer it in return. I'm afraid that such goodwill as I still had was exhausted when I obtained your mother's file for her. She still has many years of professional life ahead of her, and it was important to her, going forward, that no record of her past behavior come to light."

However much Andreas had hated Katya in the past, he'd never hated her more than he did right now. "So, wait," he said. "You're saying you know what I'm here for."

"She mentioned it," his father said, withholding eye contact.

"But she didn't care about me. She just cared about protecting herself."

"She did intercede on your behalf as well, once we had her records."

"First things first!"

"She is my wife. You need to understand that."

"And I'm not really your son."

His father shifted uncomfortably. "I suppose that may be correct, in a technical sense."

"So I'm fucked. She fucked me over."

"You chose not to play by society's rules, and you don't seem to have repented of it. When your mother is her true self, she repents of what she's done when she was not herself."

"You're saying there's nothing you can do for me."

"I'm reluctant to go back to a well I fear is dry now."

"Do you know why it matters to me?"

His father shrugged. "I have guesses, based on your past behavior. But, no, I don't."

"Then let me tell you why," Andreas said. He was furious with himself for having waited five weeks for his mother to rescue him—would he ever stop being the dumbfuck four-year-old? But he was down to only two choices, either get out of the country or trust the man who wasn't really his father, and so he told him the story. Told it with major embellishments and omissions, carefully framing it as a parable of a good socialist judo girl *who had followed all the rules* and been raped by a Stasi-abetted incarnation of pure evil. He made a case for his own reformation, spoke of his good work with at-risk youth, spoke of his successes, his genuine service to society, his refusal to mix with the dissidents: his attempt to become, in the church basement, a son worthy of his father. He cast his state-subverting poetry as a regrettable response to having had a mentally ill mother. He said he did repent of it now.

When he was finished, his father said nothing for a long time. Cars were still honking in the street now and then, the pool of cold blood sausage darkening toward black.

"Where did this . . . event occur?" his father said.

"It doesn't matter. A safe place in the countryside. Better if you don't know where."

"You should have gone straight to the Stasi. They would have punished the individual severely."

"She wouldn't do it. She'd followed the rules all her life. She just wanted to have a good life in society as it existed. I was trying to give her that."

His father went to a sideboard and returned with two glasses and a bottle of Ballantine's. "Your mother is my wife," he said, pouring. "She will always come first."

"Of course."

"But your story is affecting. It puts a different light on things. It makes me question, to some extent, the idea I've had of you. Should I believe it?"

"The only things I left out were to protect you."

"Did you tell it to your mother?"

"No."

"Good. It would only upset her, to no purpose."

"I'm more like you than I am like her," Andreas said. "Can you see that? We're both dealing with the same difficult person."

His father emptied his glass with one gulp. "These are difficult times."

"Can you help me?"

His father poured more scotch. "I can ask. I fear the answer will be no."

"That you would even ask—"

"Don't thank me. I would be doing it for your mother, not for you. The law is the law—we can't take it into our own hands. Even if I'm successful, you should go to the police and make a full confession. The act would be all the more commendable if you performed it when you no longer had to fear discovery. If the facts really are the way you've represented them, you can count on considerable leniency, especially in the current climate. It would be hard on your mother, but it would be the right thing to do."

Andreas thought, but didn't say, that in fact he was more like his mother, not his father, because he had no interest at all in doing the right thing if the wrong thing would save him from public shame and prison time. His life seemed to him a long war between two sides of him, the sick side that he had from his mother, the scrupled side that he had from a nongenetic father. But he feared that at base he was all Katya.

He'd taken leave of his father and was walking to the elevator when the door of the flat opened behind him. "Andreas," his father called after him.

He went back to the door.

"Tell me the name of the individual," his father said. "It occurs to me that you'll also want the file on his disappearance."

Andreas searched his father's face. Did the old man intend to turn him in? Unable to find an answer, Andreas spoke the full name of the man he'd killed.

Late the following afternoon, the vicar came down to his room to tell him that he had a phone call.

"I think I've done it," his father said, on the phone. "You won't be sure until you actually go to the archive. They wouldn't remove the files from there, and it's quite possible that you won't be allowed to take them with you. But they will show them to you. So, at least, they say."

"I don't know how to thank you."

"Thank me by never speaking of it again."

At eight o'clock in the morning, following his father's instructions, Andreas went back to Normannenstraße and presented himself at the front gate. A television crew was eating hard rolls by a van. He gave the name he'd been told to give, Captain Eugen Wachtler, and submitted to a pat down, relinquishing the knapsack in which he'd hoped to carry the files away.

Captain Wachtler came to the gate twenty minutes later. He was bald and precancerously gray and had the faraway expression of someone enduring chronic pain. There was a small stain on the lapel of his suit jacket. "Andreas Wolf?"

"Yes."

The captain gave him a security pass on a lanyard. "Put this on and follow me."

Without further words, they crossed the courtyard and went through an unlocked gate and then a gate that Wachtler unlocked and relocked behind them. There were further locks at the entrance of the main archive building, one that Wachtler had a key for, another operated by a guard behind a thick glass window. Andreas followed the captain up two flights of stairs and down a corridor of closed doors. "Exciting times here," Andreas ventured to say.

Wachtler didn't respond. At the end of the hall, he unlocked yet another door and beckoned Andreas into a small room with a table and two chairs. On the table were four file folders, neatly stacked.

"I will be back in exactly one hour," Wachtler said. "You are not to leave this room or remove any materials from it. The pages are numbered. Before we leave, I will examine them to make sure that nothing is missing."

"Got it."

The captain left and Andreas opened the topmost folder. There were only ten pages in it, pertaining to the disappearance of Unofficial Collaborator Horst Werner Kleinholz. The second folder also contained ten pages, a carbon copy of the first file. As soon as Andreas saw the carbon copy, he knew that there was hope. He'd been instructed not to remove anything, but there was no reason to give him the duplicate if they expected him to follow the instruction. The carbon copy was a clear signal that this was all they had and they were giving it to him. He was flooded with love and pride and gratitude. His father had worked for forty years within the system, playing by the rules, to bring about this moment. His father still had influence, and the Stasi had come through for him.

He took out the plastic shopping bag that he'd stuffed in his boot and put both copies of the investigation file in it. The other two folders on the table were thicker. They contained the two halves of his own file, continuously numbered. These, too, he put in the plastic bag.

His heart was pounding and he was getting a major stiffy, because the rest was a game. The rules of the game were that he was breaking the rules, stealing materials without the Stasi's knowledge or consent, materials that he was only supposed to look at, not take with him. It wouldn't be the Stasi's fault if they went missing.

He had a flicker of worry that the captain had locked him in the room, but the door wasn't locked, the game was on. He stepped out into the corridor. The building was weirdly silent, not a voice to be heard, just a low institutional humming. He retraced his steps to the stairs and down the two flights. From the main hallway he heard footsteps and voices, employees arriving for work. He stepped boldly into it and headed for the front door. Incoming workers gave him cold, incurious looks.

He tapped on the window at the door where the guard sat. "Can you let me out?"

The guard half stood to read the pass hanging from Andreas's neck. "You'll have to wait for your escort."

"I'm not feeling well. I might throw up."

"There's a bathroom down the hall to your left."

He went to the bathroom and locked himself in a stall.

If the game was on, there had to be some way for him to escape. He still had his stiffy, and he felt a curiously strong impulse to take it out and ejaculate, most gloriously, into a Stasi toilet. It had been three years since he'd felt so wildly aroused, but he told himself—spoke it out loud— "Wait. Soon. Not yet. Soon."

Returning to the hallway, he saw an open door with daylight spilling through it, suggesting a window he might climb out of. Again boldly, he walked to the door. It was a conference room, with windows on the courtyard. The windows had heavy grates, but two of them had been opened, as if to let in more light. When he stepped into the room, a female voice spoke sharply, "Can I help you?"

A thick middle-aged woman was placing biscuits on a glass plate.

"No, sorry, wrong room," he said, retreating.

More workers were entering the building, dispersing into stairwells and side hallways. He stationed himself at the end of the main hallway, keeping an eye on the conference room, waiting for the woman to step out. He was still waiting when a commotion developed at the far end of the hall, at the entrance. He hurried toward it, plastic bag in hand.

Eight or ten men and women, manifestly not Stasi, were making their way through the portal. A smaller group of Stasi officers, in decent suits, was standing inside to greet them. Andreas recognized several of the visitors' faces—this had to be the ad hoc Citizens' Committee of Normannenstraße, making its first inspection of the archives, under strict supervision. The committee members were holding themselves erect, with self-importance but also with awe and trepidation. Two of them were shaking Stasi hands when Andreas pushed past them and through the inner door.

"Stop," came the voice of the guard behind glass.

An officer was locking the outer door but hadn't got the job done yet. Andreas shoved him aside, turned the handle, and pushed through. He sprinted across the courtyard with his plastic bag. There was shouting behind him.

The gate in the fence was locked, but there was no barbed wire, no concertina. He scrambled up and vaulted down and sprinted for the main gate. The guards merely watched as he ran out to the street.

And there were the TV cameras. Three of them, pointing at him.

A phone was ringing at the guard station.

"Yes, he's right here," a guard said.

Andreas glanced over his shoulder and saw two guards coming for him. He dropped his bag, raised his hands, and addressed the cameras. "Are you rolling?" he shouted.

One television crew was scrambling. A woman in another gave him a thumbs-up. He turned to her camera and began to speak.

"My name is Andreas Wolf," he said. "I am a citizen of the German Democratic Republic, and I am here to monitor the work of the Citizens' Committee of Normannenstraße. I'm coming directly from the Stasi archives, where I have reason to fear that a whitewash is occurring. I'm not here in an official capacity. I'm not here to work *with*, I'm here to work *against*. This is a country of festering secrets and toxic lies. Only the strongest of sunlight can disinfect it!"

"Hey, stop," called a member of the crew that had been scrambling. "Say that all again."

He said it all again. He was utterly improvising, but the longer he spoke and the more his image was recorded, the safer he was from being seized by the guards behind him. It was his first moment of media fame, the first of many. He spent the rest of the morning on Normannenstraße, giving interviews and rallying onlookers,

demanding that sunlight be shined on the abscess of the
Stasi. By the time the members of the Citizens' Committee emerged from the compound, they had no choice but
to welcome him to their cause, because he'd already stolen
their media moment.

His plastic shopping bag was visible in thousands of
frames of video that day. It was firmly under his arm
when, late in the afternoon, he ran home to the basement
of the church. He was almost free. His only worry now
was the unsecurely buried body, he was very close to having Annagret, his libido was back. He didn't even glance
at the files in the bag, just shoved them under his mattress
and ran outside again. In a state of sex-mad lightness,
he crossed the old border at Friedrichstraße and made his
way west to the Kurfürstendamm, where he met the good
American Tom Aberant.

Too Much
Information

Ordinarily, Leila looked forward to traveling on assignment. She was never more of a professional, never more defensibly excused from her caretaking duties in Denver, than when she was locked in a hotel room with her green-tea bags, her anonymized Wi-Fi connection, her two colors of ballpoint, her Ambien stash. But from the moment she arrived in Amarillo, on a commuter jet from Denver, something felt different. It was as if she didn't even want to be in Amarillo. The normally pleasurable economies of her competence, the preferred-customer getaway from the rental-car lot, the optimal route she took to the small house of Janelle Flayner, the swiftness with which she secured Flayner's trust and got her talking, weren't pleasurable. Late in the afternoon, she stopped at a Toot'n Totum convenience mart and bought a chef salad in a polyethylene box. In her hotel room, which a recent occupant had smoked in, she uncapped the cup of salad dressing and felt nailed by the product's targeting of her demographic: the solitary 50+ female looking for something sensible to eat. It occurred to her that what she was feeling wasn't generic loneliness. She had a new research assistant, Pip Tyler, and she was wishing she could have brought the girl along.

With a little ache in her throat, for which only work was a remedy, she set out after dinner to meet the former girlfriend of Cody Flayner. She left her room lights burning and the privacy card on her doorknob. Outside, the sky was cloudless and nicked with random dull stars, their contextualizing constellations obscured by light and dust pollution. The Texas Panhandle was in year five of a drought that might soon be upgraded to permanent climate change. Instead of April snowmelt, dust.

While she drove, she Bluetoothed her phone into the car stereo and listened uncomfortably to her interview of Cody Flayner's ex-wife. She considered herself a good-hearted person, an empathetic listener, but in playback she could hear herself manipulating.

Helou—what kind of last name is that?

It's Lebanese . . . Christian. I grew up in San Antonio.

You know, I was just sitting here thinking you sound Texan.

But Leila no longer sounded Texan, except when she was interviewing Texans.

Layla, if you don't mind my saying, you don't strike me as the kind of gal who picks wrong.

Ha. Take a closer look.

So you know what cheated-on feels like.

Anything that's unhappy and has to do with marriage—yes.

It's a sisterhood, all right. That phone of yours close enough?

We don't have to use it if—

I told you, I want it on. It's about time somebody listened to me—I'd started thinking nobody cared. If you want to put me on the Internet saying Cody Flayner is a DEADBEAT CHEATER MORON, you be my guest.

I hear he's become very active in a Baptist church.

Cody? Gimme a break. The Ten Commandments is like his personal to-do list. I know for a fact he's having relations with a nineteen-year-old girl in that congregation. He only joined that church because his daddy made him.

Tell me about that.

Well, you know. We wouldn't be talking if you didn't know. They caught him with his pants down. He could of started World War Three, taking that thing home on his precious Ram truck. And the plant didn't even fire him! Fired his boss, but all Cody got was "reassignment." It sure helps when your dad's a muckety-muck at the plant. And I'll say this for the old man, he drove a good bargain. First time I been getting my payments since the day Cody walked out on us.

He's started paying child support.

For now. We'll see how long his newfound faith'll last. I reckon about as long as his little buddy in Christ don't completely blimp out.

Does this girl have a name?

Porky Bonehead.

But on her driver's license?

Marli Copeland. Just an "i" at the end. You're probably thinking it's bad of me to even have that information.

No, I totally get it. He's the father of your children.

But that girl won't talk to you, no way. Not if Cody don't.

To drive east on Amarillo Boulevard was to pass, in quick succession, the high-security Clements Unit prison complex, the McCaskill meat-processing facility, and the Pantex nuclear-weapons plant, three massive installations more alike than different in their brute utility and sodium-vapor lighting. In the rearview mirror were the evangelical churches, the Tea Party precincts, the Whataburgers. Ahead, the gas and oil wells, the fracking rigs, the over-grazed ranges, the feedlots, the depleted aquifer. Every facet of Amarillo a testament to a nation of bad-ass firsts: first in prison population, first in meat consumption, first in operational strategic warheads, first in per-capita carbon emissions, first in line for the Rapture. Whether

American liberals liked it or not, Amarillo was how the rest of the world saw their country.

Leila liked it. She came from the blue part of Texas, and from a time when the blue part was larger, but she still loved the whole state, not just San Antonio and the Gulf-softened winters and the burning green of the mesquite in spring but the in-your-face ugliness of the red parts. The embrace of ugliness; the eager manufacture of it; the capacity of Texan pride to see beauty in it. And the exceptional courtesy of the drivers, the enduring apartness of the old republic, the assurance of being a shining example to the nation. Texans looked down on the other forty-nine states with a gracious kind of pity.

Phyllisha's one of them girls that all she has to do is shake her goldy locks and the men all lose their mind. You know the expression "one-trick pony"? That's her with her hair. Shakey-shakey-shakey. And Cody's dumber than a post. A post knows it's dumb and Cody don't. And I suppose I'm the dumbest of all, because I married him.

So after Cody was "reassigned," Phyllisha Babcock left him?

It was Mr. Flayner Senior made Cody break it off. That was part of their bargain if he wanted to keep working at the plant. That girl is some bad news. Not enough to wreck his home, she had to try and wreck his career.

No sources were more reliably forthcoming than ex-wives. The former Mrs. Flayner, a dyed redhead whose facial features were somehow concave, giving her a look of bashful apology, had baked a coffee cake for Leila and held her captive at her kitchen table until her kids came home from school.

Arranging to see Phyllisha Babcock had been harder. Since her break with Flayner, she'd shacked up with a controlling guy who screened her calls at the only number findable for her. All the boyfriend would say to Leila, the three times she called, was "I don't know you, so good-bye." (Even he was not without Texan courtesy; he could have said worse.) Phyllisha had also—another red flag of the controlling boyfriend—vanished from social media. But Pip Tyler was a very good researcher. By tedious trial and error, she'd located Phyllisha's new place of work, a drive-in Sonic in the town of Pampa.

Two weeks before going to Amarillo, at the dead hour of eight on a Tuesday night, Leila had reached Phyllisha by phone at the drive-in. She'd asked if they might talk a little bit about Cody Flayner and the July Fourth incident.

"Maybe not," Phyllisha had said, which was encouraging. The only words that truly meant no were *fuck you*. "Maybe, if you were from the Fox channel, but you're not, so."

Leila explained that her employer, Denver Independent, was a foundation-supported investigative news service. She mentioned that DI had partnered with many national news outlets, including *Sixty Minutes*, in breaking stories.

"I don't look at *Sixty Minutes*," Phyllisha said.

"Why don't I just stop by the Sonic some weeknight. Nobody has to know we even spoke. I'm just trying to get the story right. It can be as off the record as you like."

"I don't like that you even know where I work. And my boyfriend doesn't like me talking personal to people he doesn't know."

"Sure. I respect that. I wouldn't want to get you in trouble with him."

"No, I know, it's kind of dumb. Like, what am I going to do, run off with you?"

"Rules are rules."

"That's for damned sure. For all I know, he's sitting across the street right now, wondering who I'm on the phone with. Wouldn't be the first time."

"I won't keep you, then. But if I come by some Tuesday, maybe this time of night?"

"What did you say the name of your magazine was?"

"Denver Independent. We're online only, no print version."

"I don't know. Somebody ought to tell about the crazy shit that happens at that plant. But I got to worry about myself first. So I guess that's a no."

"I'll stop by. You can decide when you see me. How's that sound?"

"It's nothing personal. I'm just kind of in a situation."

The first Leila had seen of Phyllisha Babcock was in the Fourth of July pictures that Cody Flayner had posted on his Facebook page the previous summer. She was wearing a patriotically colored bikini and drinking beer. Her body looked to be only a healthy diet and some regular exercise away from greatness, but her face and hair were on the verge of confirming a wicked little dictum of Leila's: Blondes don't age well. (Leila saw middle age as the Revenge of the Brunettes.) Phyllisha was mostly in the foreground of the pictures and mostly in focus, but the autofocus had erred in one shot, clearly revealing that the large object on the bed of Flayner's Dodge pickup, in the background, parked in the driveway, was a B61 thermonuclear warhead. In the blurred background of another shot, Phyllisha was straddling the warhead and appeared to be making a show of licking its tip.

Leila had been on assignment in Washington when Pip Tyler came to Denver to interview for a research internship, but word of the interview had quickly spread. Pip had brought screen shots of Flayner's photos with her, as an example of a story she might like to pitch, and DI's head of research had asked her how she'd come by them. Pip explained that she had friends in the Oakland nuclear-disarmament community who had hacker friends with access to object-recognition software and (illegally) to the inner workings of Facebook's content delivery network. She said she'd already friended Cody Flayner through an antinuke friend who'd friended him under false pretenses. In response to her private query about the warhead pictures, which had long since been scrubbed from Flayner's Facebook page, Pip had received a one-line answer: "It aint a real one, sugar." Pip's clips and her other credentials were excellent, and the head of research had hired her on the spot.

The following week, returning from Washington, Leila had gone straight to the corner office of Tom Aberant, the founder and executive editor of Denver Independent. It was no secret at DI that she and Tom had been a couple for more than a decade, but the two of them kept things professional at work. She really just wanted to say, "Hi, I'm back." But as she approached the open door of Tom's office she caught a strange vibe.

A girl with long and lustrous hair was sitting with her back to the doorway. Leila had the distinct impression that Tom was ill at ease with her; and the thing about Tom was that nothing scared him. Leila herself was afraid of death, but Tom wasn't. The threat of lawsuits and injunctions didn't scare him, corporate money didn't scare him, firing employees didn't scare him. He was Leila's mighty fortress. But in his haste to stand up, before she was even through the doorway, she sensed a perturbation. Uncharacteristic also his fumbling for words: "Pip—Leila—Leila—Pip—"

The girl had a strikingly deep suntan. Tom hurried around his desk and did a herding thing with his arms, bringing the two women together while also moving them toward the doorway, as if eager to get Pip away from him. Or as if to underline that he wasn't trying to hide her from Leila. The girl's face was honest and friendly and less than threateningly beautiful, but she seemed discomfited herself.

"Pip's already turned up more good stuff in Amarillo," Tom said. "I know you're slammed, but I thought maybe the two of you should work together."

Leila queried him with a frown and caught something in his averted eyes.

"I'm very busy this week," she said pleasantly, "but I'm happy to try to help."

Tom herded them through his doorway. "Leila's the best," he said to Pip. "She'll take good care of you." He looked at Leila. "If you don't mind?"

"I don't mind."

"Great."

And he closed his door behind them. The door he almost never closed. A few minutes later, he came out to Leila's work space for the exchange of greetings they ought to have had in his office. She knew she shouldn't ask if he was OK, since she hated being asked this herself and had trained Tom never to do it: *How about I just tell you if I'm ever not OK.* But she couldn't help doing it.

"Everything's fine," he said. His eyes were masked by the reflection of the overhead lighting on his wire-frame glasses. The glasses were of an awful seventies design and of a piece with the military buzz he gave to his remaining hair; another thing he wasn't afraid of was anyone's opinion of how he looked. "I think she's going to be terrific."

She. As if Leila's question had referred to her.

"And . . . which of my other stories would you prefer that I neglect?"

"Your choice," he said. "She says she owns the story, but we have no way of knowing who else knows about it. I don't want us to be chasing it after it goes viral."

"*Broken Arrow II.* That's quite the first pitch from a research intern."

Tom laughed. "Right? Not Strangelove—*Broken Arrow.* That's our association now." He laughed again, sounding more like his usual self.

"I'm just saying it seems a little too good to be true."

"She's Californian."

"Hence the impressive suntan?"

"Bay Area," Tom said. "It's like the flu viruses coming out of China—pigs, people, and birds all living under one roof. The Bay Area is where you'd expect a story like this to come from. All that hacker capability mingling with the Occupy mentality."

"I guess that makes sense. It's just interesting that she came to us. She could have taken the story anywhere. ProPublica. California Watch. CIR."

"Apparently she has a boyfriend she followed here."

"Fifty years of feminism, and women are still following their boyfriends."

"Who better than you to straighten her head out? If you really don't mind."

"I really don't mind."

"What's one more person on the long list of people Leila's nice to?"

"You're absolutely right. It's just one more person."

And so the handoff to Leila had occurred. Had Tom been vaccinating himself against the girl by teaming her with his girlfriend? Pip was by no means the most attractive intern to have worked at DI, and Tom had often stated, in the hard-fact-stating voice he had, that his type was Leila's type (slight, flat, Lebanese). What could it be about Pip that had required vaccination? Eventually it dawned on Leila that the girl might be a *former* type of Tom's, a type like his ex-wife. And it wasn't quite true that nothing scared him. Anything to do with his ex-wife made him nervous. He squirmed whenever someone on TV reminded him of her; he talked back at the screen. As soon as Leila understood that she was doing him a favor by assuming responsibility for Pip, she went ahead and took the girl under her care.

Did Cody talk about perimeter security when you were married? Were you surprised when you heard he'd taken a weapon home with him?

There's nothing so dumb that Cody could do it and surprise me. One time he was stripping paint off our garage and tried to light a cigarette with the blowtorch—took him a while to notice he'd set his shirt collar on fire.

But the perimeter?

They had a lot of parameters that him and his dad used to talk about. Parameter is a word I definitely overheard. Exposure parameters, and . . . what else? Something with protocols?

But the gates, the fences.

Oh, my. Perimeter. *You meant* perimeter *and here I'm talking about* parameters. *I don't even know what a parameter is.*

So did Cody ever talk about people sneaking things in or out?

Mostly in. They have enough bombs in there to turn the whole Panhandle into a smoking crater. You'd think they'd be a little nervous and alert, but it's the opposite, because the whole point of the bomb is to make sure we never have to use it. The whole show is kind of a big huge nothing, and the people who work there know it. That's why they have their safety competitions, their softball league, their canned-food drives—to keep it interesting. The work's better than meat packer or prison guard, but it's still boring and dead-end. So they've had some problems with contraband coming in.

Alcohol? Drugs?

No booze, they'd catch you. But certain illegal stimulants. Also clean pee for the drug tests.

And what about things coming out?

Well, Cody had a whole chest of nice tools with a little bit of radioactive in 'em, enough so OSHA said they couldn't use 'em anymore. Perfectly good tools.

But no bombs going missing.

Lord, no. They have bar codes, they have GPS, they have all these sheets you have to sign. They know where every bomb is every minute. I know about that because that's where Cody worked.

Inventory Control.

That's right.

Leila turned off the recording as she approached the town of Pampa. This part of the Panhandle was so flat that it was paradoxically vertiginous, a two-dimensional planetary surface off which, having no trace of topography to hold on to, you felt you could fall or be swept. No relief in any sense of the word. The land so commercially and agriculturally marginal that Pampans thought nothing of wasting it by the half acre, so that each low and ugly building sat by itself. Dusty dead or dying halfheartedly planted trees floated by in Leila's headlights. To her they were Texan and therefore lovely in their way.

The Sonic parking lot was empty. She'd decided not to risk spooking Phyllisha by calling her a second time; if she happened to be off work, Leila could come back tomorrow. But Phyllisha was not only there but was hanging halfway out the drive-in window, trying to touch the ground without falling all the way out.

As Leila approached the window, she saw the dollar bill below it. She picked it up and put it in Phyllisha's hand.

"Thank you, ma'am." Phyllisha levered herself back inside. "Can I help you?"

"I'm Leila Helou. Denver Independent."

"Whoa. I would of sworn you'd be Texan."

"I am Texan. Can we talk?"

"I don't know." Phyllisha leaned out the window again and scanned the parking lot and the street. "I told you about my situation. He's picking me up at ten, and sometimes he's early."

"It's only eight thirty."

"You're not supposed to stand here anyway. This is for cars only."

"Why don't I come inside, then."

Phyllisha shook her head pensively. "It's one of those things that only makes sense when you're inside it. I can't explain it."

"It's like being a willing prisoner."

"Prisoner? I don't know. Maybe. The Prisoner of Pampa." She giggled. "Somebody oughta write a novel about me and call it that."

"How into him are you?"

"I'm kind of nuts about him, actually. Part of me doesn't even mind the prisoner part."

"I get that."

Phyllisha looked into Leila's eyes. "Do you?"

"I've been in situations myself."

"Well, shit. I don't care. You can sit on the floor, down out of sight. The manager won't see you if you come in through the back. Everybody else back here is Mexican."

The leading occupational hazard of Leila's job was sources who wanted to be friends with her. The world was overpopulated with talkers and underpopulated by listeners, and many of her sources gave her the impression that she was the first person who'd ever truly listened to them. These were always the single-story sources, the "amateurs" whom she seduced by appearing to be whomever

they needed her to be. (She also dissembled with the professionals, the agency staffers, the congressional aides, but
they used her as much as she used them.) Many of her
colleagues, even some she liked, were brutal in betraying
their sources afterward and severing all contact with
them, adhering to the principle that it was actually kinder
not to return a call from a person you'd slept with if you
didn't intend to sleep with him again. In reporting, as in
sex, Leila had always been a caller-back. The only way
she could morally tolerate her seductions was honestly to
be, at some level, the person she was pretending to be.
And then she felt obliged to return her sources' calls and
emails, even their Christmas cards, after she was done
with them. She was still getting mail from the Unabomber,
Ted Kaczynski, well over a decade after she'd written a
sympathetic story about his legal plight. Kaczynski had
been barred from serving as his own counsel at his trial,
effectively muzzled from airing his radical opinions about
the U.S. government, by reason of insanity. And the proof
of his insanity? His belief that the U.S. government was a
repressive conspiracy that muzzled radical opinion. Only
an insane person would believe that! The Unabomber had
really, really liked Leila.

What Phyllisha told her, while she sat on the floor amid
ketchup smears and Mexican music, was that Cody
Flayner was an all-hat loser she'd counted the days till she
could get away from. Between his fine ass and his soft
eyes and his droopy little puppy eyelashes, she hadn't been
able to resist getting in the sack with him. But she swore
to Leila that she'd never meant for him to leave his wife
and kids. He'd surprised her with that, and then, for a
while, she was stuck with him. All she'd wanted was a
good time, and here she'd wrecked people's lives. She felt
bad about it, and so she lived with Cody for six whole
months.

"You stayed with him because you felt guilty?" Leila said.

"Kind of! That and free rent and lack of immediate other options."

"You know, I did the same thing when I was your age. Wrecked a marriage."

"Maybe if it *can* be wrecked, it *oughta* be wrecked."

"There are different schools of thought on that."

"So how long'd you stick around? Or did you not even feel guilty?"

"That's the thing." Leila smiled. "I'm still married to him."

"Well, that's a happy ending."

"Safe to say there's been some guilt along the way."

"You know, you seem OK to me. I never met a reporter before. You're not what I expected."

That's because I'm freaking good at getting people to open up, Leila thought.

Phyllisha interrupted herself to serve a carload of teenagers and then to scold her co-workers. "Hey fellas, no quiero la musica. Menos loud-o, por favor?"

That Cody was the best thing that ever happened to Phyllisha was a conviction of his that she did not reciprocate. The more he tried to impress her, the less impressed she got. He picked a bar fight in her presence to show her how well he could take getting the crap beaten out of him. His wife, the baboon face, hadn't managed to get his wages garnished for child support—count on Big Government to screw things up—and he bought Phyllisha piles of bling and other stuff, including a brand-new iPad, to impress her. The whole idea behind his July Fourth surprise was to impress her. She knew that he worked at the bomb plant and had the most boring of all the jobs there. He could jaw for hours about *variable yields* and *bunker busters* and *kilotonnage*, making himself out to be per-

sonally responsible for keeping the nation safe. She finally
got fed up and told him the truth, namely, that he was a
nobody and she wasn't impressed with these bombs that
he didn't actually have anything to do with. She hurt his
feelings, but she didn't care. She'd already exchanged
meaningful eye contact with his friend Kyle, who lived
over in Pampa.

On the night of July 3, coming home late from drinking
with her girlfriends, she found Cody waiting for her on
the front steps. He said he had another present for her.
He took her around to the back yard, where something big
and cylindrical was lying on a blanket. Cody said it was
a fully armed B61 thermonuclear warhead, and what did
she think of *that*?

Well, she was afraid, was what.

Cody said, "I want you to touch it. I want you to get
buck-naked and lay on it, and then I'm gonna do you like
you never been done in your whole life."

She hedged by saying she didn't want to get radiation
poisoning or whatnot.

Cody said the warhead was totally safe to handle and
be around. He made her touch it with her hand and explained to her about one-point safety and permission action links. It was the usual all-hat routine, talking about
stuff he didn't really understand and had nothing to do
with, except that this time there was an actual thermonuclear warhead on a blanket in his yard.

"And I know how to set it off," he said.

You do not, Phyllisha said.

"There's a way if you got the codes, and I got the codes.
I can wipe old Amarillo right off the map. Right now."

Why would you do that, Phyllisha wanted to know. She
half believed him and two-thirds didn't.

"To make you see how much I love you," Cody said.

Phyllisha said she didn't see the connection between

loving her and blowing up Amarillo. She thought that, conceivably, by saying this, by buying time, she was saving tens of thousands of innocent Amarillo lives, her own not least among them. She was listening out of one ear for police sirens.

Cody then assured her that he wasn't going to do it. He just wanted her to know that he *could* do it. He, Cody Flayner. He wanted her to feel the kind of power he had at his disposal. He wanted her to take off all her clothes and put her arms around the bomb and stick her little tail up in the air for him. Didn't the bomb's terrible, dangerous power make her want that?

It did, actually, when he put it like that. She went ahead and did what he'd said, and they hadn't had such a good time since before he'd surprised her by moving out on his wife. To be that close to so much potential death and devastation, to have her sweaty skin against the cool skin of a death-bomb, to imagine the whole city going up in a mushroom cloud when she orgasmed. It was pretty great, she had to say.

At the same time, it was obviously a one-night-only thing. Either Cody would be hauled off to jail or he'd have to take the B61 back to where it belonged, and that would be the end of them having orgasmic sex with her face mashed up against the casing of a 300-kiloton death-bomb. To enjoy it while it lasted, they went at it a second time. Cody got her all wound up but afterward she felt sad for him. He wasn't very bright, and she'd already made up her mind to go with Kyle.

Baby, she said, they're going to put you in jail.

"No they ain't," Cody said. "Not for borrowing a fake."

A fake?

"Yeah, for training purposes. It's a perfect replica, except for the fissile core."

She got upset then. Was he trying to make her feel

stupid now, or what? He'd told her it was a fully armed death-bomb!

"Nobody takes out a real bomb on their pickup, sweetheart."

So the bomb was just a fake? Well, that was just like him.

"Yeah, and what difference did it make?" he said. "You sure didn't seem like you were fakin' it. Talk about Fourth of July fireworks—whoo hee!"

Leila was writing furiously in her notebook. "And how long did he keep the replica? We have pictures of it from the Fourth of July."

"He took it back the next night," Phyllisha said. "The plant's real quiet on the Fourth, and he knew the people at the gate. But first he had to show the thing off to his friends, at the barbecue. Kyle says Cody's always been like a little dog that follows you around, doing stuff on dares to try to make people respect him."

"And were his friends impressed?"

"Kyle wasn't. He had a notion of what Cody and me had done the night before, because Cody was all but bragging about it. Calling it the afrodizziac bomb."

"Lovely. But, just so we're clear, in one of the pictures, you seem to be . . ."

Phyllisha blushed. "I know the picture. I was doing that on Kyle's account. Looking him right in the eye."

"Cody couldn't have been happy about that."

"I can't say I'm proud of my behavior. But I was scared Kyle might think Cody and I were A-OK again. I did what I had to do."

"And that's why Cody broke up with you?"

"Who the heck told you that? Kyle helped me pack up while Cody was taking the bomb back. That very same night. I've been in Pampa ever since. I still feel bad about it, but at least Cody's last memories of me are good ones. Neither of us will ever forget the night with the death-bomb. It's like a memory we can always treasure."

"Do you have any idea how the plant found out about it?"

"Well, you can't pull a stunt like that without word getting around. Plus it was on Facebook. Can you imagine?"

Taking leave of Phyllisha, her short-term memory aching like an unmilked cow, Leila moved her car out of the Sonic lot and parked it farther down the street. Using a red ballpoint, she filled out and clarified the scribbles in her notebook. The work couldn't wait until she returned to Amarillo; her precise recall of interviews lasted less than an hour. Before she was finished, a vintage pickup rumbled into the Sonic lot and then out again. As it passed by Leila, she saw Phyllisha, not on the passenger side of the bench but scooched toward the middle, with her arm around the driver's neck.

Leila was just old enough to have lived through the Watergate hearings at an age where she could understand them. Of her mother she could remember little more than a jumble of fear and sadness, hospital rooms, her father's sobbing, a funeral that seemed to last for days. Only in the summer of Sam Ervin and John Dean and Bob Haldeman did she become a fully remembering person. She'd begun watching the hearings as a way to escape interaction with her father's crone cousin Marie. Her father, who had a busy practice and was also on the research faculty at the dental school, had brought Marie over from the old country to keep house for him and care for Leila. Marie frightened Leila's friends, licked her knife at the dinner table, wore clicking dentures that she refused to exchange for better ones, complained incessantly about the air-conditioning, and was unacquainted with the concept of letting a child win at games. Summers with her were long, and Leila never forgot the thrill of realizing that everything the adults in Washington were saying on TV made sense to her; that she could follow the conspiracy. A few years later, when her father took her to see *All the President's Men*, she made him leave her at the theater so she could sneak back in to watch the next screening.

Her father had approved of her sneaking. He operated by Old World rules, the blurring of right and wrong into whatever you could get away with; he stole hotel towels and bought a radar detector for his Cadillac and was merely annoyed, not embarrassed, when the IRS caught him cheating on his taxes. But he could also seem New World. When Leila, under the spell of *All the President's Men*, declared her ambition to be an investigative reporter, her father replied that journalism was a male business and that she should *therefore* go into it, to show what a Helou woman was capable of. He said that America was a butter the hot knife of her mind was made to cut through, America the place where a woman didn't have to live like Marie, on a cousin's charity.

His message was feminist, and yet he wasn't a feminist. As Leila proceeded through college and into newspaper work, she couldn't shake the sense that she was proving something for *him*, not for herself. When she landed a real reporting job, at the *Miami Herald*, and her father was disabled by a stroke, she knew it was his wish and expectation that she quit the job and return to San Antonio. Marie was dead by then, but her father had two sons from his first marriage, in Houston and Memphis. They could have taken him in, if they hadn't been men.

To fill her evenings in San Antonio, while her father languished, she began to write short stories. She later felt so mortified to have imagined herself as a fiction writer that she recalled these stories with revulsion, as scabs that she couldn't stop picking but was too ashamed to make bleed. She couldn't reconstruct her reasons for writing them, apart from a wish to rebel against her father's ambitions for her and to punish him for getting in their way. But after he died, of a second stroke, she decided to spend a good chunk of her inheritance—from an estate heftily diminished by delinquent taxes and shared with her half brothers and two women she'd scarcely known, one of them a dental hygienist her father had long employed—to pursue a degree in creative writing at a program in Denver.

She was already older than most of the other students in Denver and not only had more real-world experience but was sitting on more family unhappiness and immigrant lore. She also considered herself more attractive than the quality of her past boyfriends would suggest. When one of her first-semester teachers, Charles Blenheim, singled out and praised the work of a younger "experimental" female writer in the workshop, it activated a hereditary competitive streak in Leila. Among the Helous, the main form of family interaction was playing cards and board games, at which it was assumed that everyone was trying to cheat. Leila worked hard on her fiction and even harder on her comments on her younger rival's work. She learned exactly where to stick the needle, and soon she had Charles's attention.

Charles was at the apex of his career, coming off a Lannan Fellowship year and a front-page *Times* review that had anointed him as the heir of John Barth and Stanley Elkin, but he didn't know it was the apex. In the bright light of his prospects, his marriage of fifteen years was seeming lackluster and unbecoming to him, a contract entered into when Blenheim stock was undervalued. Leila had come along at just the right time to put an end to it. While she was at it, she permanently turned his two daughters against him. She understood how she must have looked to them, and to his wife, and she was sorry about it—she hated being hated—but she didn't feel especially guilty. It simply wasn't her fault that Charles was happier with her. Not to choose his happiness and her own happiness over his family's would have required very strict principles. At the crucial moment, when she'd looked into herself for a clear understanding of right and wrong, she'd instead found the mess her father had bequeathed her.

She was wild about Charles, for a while. Among all his female students, he'd chosen *her*. His older man's bulk made her own slightness agreeable to her; made her feel amazingly sexy. He rode a Harley-Davidson to class, he wore his corn-silk hair down to the shoulders of his leather jacket, he referred to literary giants by their first names. To spare him from institutional embarrassment, she quit the writing program. A week after his divorce went through, she rode on the back of his Harley to New Mexico and married him in Taos. She went to conferences with him and performed what she was slow to realize was her function at them: to be younger and fresh and somewhat exotic, to excite the envy of male writers who hadn't traded in their wives yet or hadn't done so recently. She'd published enough of her scratchings, in small journals where a word from Charles carried weight, to introduce herself as a fiction writer.

When Charles's several honeymoons had ended, he settled down to write the *big book*, the novel that would secure him his place in the modern American canon. Once upon a time, it had sufficed to write *The Sound and the Fury* or *The Sun Also Rises*. But now bigness was essential. Thickness, length. Leila would have been well advised, before marrying a novelist or imagining herself as one, to wait and sample life in a house where a *big book* was being contemplated. A day of frustration was mourned with three large bourbons. A day of conceptual breakthrough and euphoria was celebrated with four large bourbons. To dilate his mind to the requisite bigness, Charles needed to spend weeks on end doing nothing. Although the university asked very little of him, it asked for more than nothing, and the tiniest unperformed tasks became torments to him. Leila took over every task she could and many that she shouldn't have, but she couldn't, for example, teach his workshops. For hours, their three-story Craftsman echoed with his groans at the prospect of teaching. The groans came from every floor of it and were at once heartfelt and intended as humor.

It was Charles's saving grace, and the heart of Leila's weakness for him, to be funny. On a rare good day, he might produce a long paragraph—disconnected, like all its fellows, from any other paragraph—that made her hoot with laughter. Much more often, there was no paragraph. Instead, during the small scrap of time when she was free to toil on her scratchings, at the child-size desk of his older daughter, in what had been the daughter's bedroom, and to self-hatingly contrast her flat reportorial style with the "twinned muscularity and febrility" (*New York Times Book Review*, front page) of her husband's paragraphs, even though he'd failed to string together two of them since before she'd married him, she heard the door of his book-lined third-floor study open, followed by the Trudge. He retarded this Trudge, knowing she could hear it, to make the very sound of it funny. Finally he stopped outside her closed door and—as if it could be imagined that she hadn't heard the Trudge approaching—hesitated for some minute or minutes before knocking. Even after he'd opened the door, he didn't enter the room immediately but stood and slowly turned his gaze on every corner of it, as if wondering whether he might write bigger in a child's bedroom, or as if to refamiliarize himself with the strange little world of being Leila. Then suddenly—

his timing always comic—he looked at her and said, "You busy?" She never said she was. He entered the room and fell onto the dust-ruffled single bed and groaned cartoonishly. He was good about apologizing for disturbing her, but she detected, in his apologies, an undercurrent of resentment at her ability to perform household tasks while managing, in her flat reportorial way, to string a few paragraphs together. Sometimes they discussed the etiology of his blockage, his obstacle *du jour,* but only as a prelude to what he'd come downstairs for, which was to fuck her on the dust-ruffled bed, or on the Douglas-fir flooring, or on the child-size desk. She liked doing it with him. Liked it a lot.

After a year of *big book* ignition failure, she'd had enough of fiction writing. As a feminist, she couldn't imagine merely being Charles's wife, so she went to work at the *Denver Post* and quickly thrived there, doing journalism for herself now, not for her father. Without her in the house, pages of the *big book* began to coalesce, albeit slowly and at the cost of stepped-up bourbon intake. After she won a prize for her reporting (Colorado State Fair mismanagement), she dared to excuse herself from the dinners that Charles was obliged to host for visiting writers. Oh, the drinking at those ghastly dinners, the inevitable slighting of Charles, the addition of yet another name to his hate list. Practically the only living American writers Charles didn't hate now were his students and former students, and if any of the latter had some success it was only a matter of time before they slighted him, betrayed him, and he added them to his list.

Given his sinking confidence and rising self-pity levels, she might have worried that he'd do to her, with some fresh female student, what he'd done to his first wife. But he remained almost maniacally arousable by her. It was as if he were a big cat and she, with her slightness, her littleness, the mouse on which he compulsively pounced. Maybe it was a novelist thing or maybe just Charles, but he couldn't leave her alone. Even when they weren't having sex, he was forever poking and probing her, getting his fingers in her spirit, leaving nothing unsaid.

As if in self-defense, she reached the point of wanting him to make her pregnant. She had friends at the *Post* with babies, toddlers, six-year-olds. She'd held them in her arms and inwardly melted at the trust and innocence with which they put their hands on her face, their faces on her breast, their feet between her legs. Nothing, she came to think, was sweeter than a child, nothing more precious and worth having. But when—on a night carefully selected for having followed a day of thousand-word progress on his book—she took a deep breath and raised the subject of children with Charles, he became especially dramatic. He turned his head with comical slowness and gave her his glowering Look. The Look was supposed to be funny but it also scared her. The Look meant *Think about what you just said.* Or *You must be joking.* Or, more sinisterly, *Do you realize you're speaking to a major American novelist?* The frequency with which she'd received the Look of late was making her wonder what she was to him. She'd thought he was attracted to her talent and toughness and maturity, but she worried that it was principally her slightness.

"What?" she said.

He squeezed his eyes shut so tightly that his whole face wrinkled. Then he blinked them open. "Sorry," he said. "What was the question?"

"Whether we might talk about having a kid."

"Not now."

"OK. But do you mean 'now' as in 'tonight,' or 'now' as in 'this decade'?"

He sighed dramatically. "What exactly is it about my

profoundly non relationship with my existing children that makes you think I'm dad material? Did I not notice something?"

"But this is me. This isn't her."

"I'm aware of the distinction. Are you aware of the pressure I'm under?"

"It's kind of hard to miss."

"No, but can you *conceive* . . . can you *imagine* me, for one second, finishing the book with a baby in the house?"

"Obviously, it wouldn't happen for at least nine months. Maybe a medium-term deadline would help you."

"I'm already three years past one of those."

"A real deadline. One you believed in. I'm saying this is something I want with you. I want you to finish the book and us to maybe have a kid. The two things don't have to be opposed. Maybe they could be connected, in a good way."

"*Leila.*" He barked the name sternly but also ironically: to be funny.

"What."

"I love you more than anything in this world. Please tell me you know that."

"I know that," she said in a slight voice.

"So hear me, please. Please hear this: every further minute this particular conversation lasts is going to be a day of lost work in the coming week. One minute, one day; I can feel it. When you suffer, I suffer—you know that. So can we please just put an end to it right here?"

She nodded, and then cried, and then had sex with him, and then cried some more. A few months later, when the *Post* offered her a five-year stint as its Washington correspondent, she accepted. She hadn't entirely stopped loving Charles, but there was only so long that she could stand to be around him with an ache in her chest. She felt loyal to a baby in her that hadn't even been conceived yet. To a possibility.

It came along to Washington with her, the possibility, and it flew home with her to Denver once a month, for staff meetings and conjugal obligations. She didn't want to think about being divorced in her early forties, working sixty and seventy hours a week and wanting a kid, and yet her trajectory was like a thing she had no control over, a hurtling into deeper space, a feeling of nearly achieved escape velocity. She knew but didn't want to know where it was taking her. When she spoke on the phone with Charles, late at night, she could tell that he was lonely, because he'd never been so attentive to her reporting work, so eager to be of help. But when he came east in the summer, and again the next summer, her little apartment on Capitol Hill became the sour-smelling cage of a big cat too depressed to groom itself. Charles spent his days in his boxer shorts and bitched about the weather. For the first time, she felt physically averse to him. She invented reasons to stay out late, but he was always waiting for her, anxious, obsessive, when she came home. He'd finally delivered the *big book*, but his editor wanted revisions and he couldn't make up his mind about the smallest change. He asked her the same editorial questions over and over, and it did no good for her to answer them, because he had the very same questions again the next night. Both of them were relieved when he returned to Denver, where a fresh crop of students was waiting to hang on his words.

She met Tom Aberant in February 2004. Tom was a well-regarded journalist and editor who'd come to Washington to poach talent for a nonprofit investigative news service he was starting, and Leila, who by now had won a shared Pulitzer (anthrax, 2002), was on his wish list. He took her to lunch and told her he had $20 million in seed money. He currently lived in New York, but he was divorced and childless and thinking of situating his non-profit in Denver, his hometown, where the overhead would be lower. Having done his homework, he knew that Leila had a husband in Denver. Might she be interested in going home and working at a nonprofit, insulated from the impending collapse of print-ad revenues, freed from space constraints and daily deadlines, and paid a competitive salary?

The offer ought to have appealed to her. But Charles's *big book* had been published just the week before and was getting slaughtered by reviewers ("bloated and immensely disagreeable," Michiko Kakutani, *New York Times*), and Leila was in a state of medium-grade dread. She'd been calling Charles three and four times a day for pep talks, telling him how sorry she was that she couldn't be with him. But it was clear, from the repugnance she felt toward Tom's offer, that she wasn't really sorry at all. She didn't want to be the woman who abandoned her husband after his magnum opus tanked. But there was no hiding, from herself or from Tom, how unready she was to give up Washington.

"You're pretty sure it has to be Denver," she said.

Tom's face was fleshy, his mouth somehow turtlish, his eyes narrow in a way that conveyed kindly amusement. The hair he still had farther back on his head was closely buzzed and mostly dark. The thing about men in their prime was that, within rather wide limits, it didn't matter if they weren't conventionally handsome. They could also get away with bellies and even with high-pitched voices, if they were scratchy high-pitched, as Tom's was.

"Pretty sure, yeah," he said. "I've got a sister and a niece there. I miss the West."

"It sounds like an amazing project," Leila said.

"Do you want to think it over? Or are you just going to say no right now."

"I'm not saying no. I'm . . ."

She felt utterly exposed.

"Oh, this is *terrible*," she said. "I know what you must be thinking."

"What am I thinking?"

"Why wouldn't I want to go home to Denver."

"I'm not going to lie to you, Leila. You'd be a keystone hire for me. I thought Denver would be a selling point."

"No, it's great, and I think you're absolutely right about the industry. We had a monopoly on classifieds for a hundred years. Roll the presses, print the money. And now we don't. But . . ."

"But."

"Well, this is coming at a bad moment for me."

"Trouble at home."

"Yeah."

Tom put his hands behind his head and leaned back, straining the buttons of his dress shirt. "So tell me if this sounds familiar," he said. "You love the person but you can't live with him, the person is struggling, you think a separation will make it better, let the two of you recover. And then it finally comes time to get back together, because the separation was only supposed to be temporary, and you discover that, no, in fact, you were lying to yourself the whole time."

"Actually," Leila said, "I've suspected for quite a while that I've been lying to myself."

"So women are smarter than men. Or you're just smarter than I was. But to spin out the hypothetical scenario a little further—"

"I think we both know who we're talking about."

"I'm a fan of his," Tom said. "*Mad Sad Dad*—great book. Hilarious. Gorgeous."

"Super funny, definitely."

"And yet now here you are in Washington. And his new book's getting kicked in the head."

"Yes."

"Fuck the reviewers. I'm still going to buy it. But, speaking hypothetically, is there someone else in town here I should know about? If he's good and does investigative, I'd be happy to look at his CV. I have nothing in principle against couple hires."

She shook her head.

"No, there isn't anybody?" Tom said. "Or no, he's not a journalist?"

"Are you trying to ask if I'm available in some other way?"

He crumpled forward and covered his face with his hands. "I deserved that," he said. "I was actually *not* asking that, but the question wasn't straight, either. It's just a thing with me—I'm kind of a connoisseur of guilt. I shouldn't have asked you that."

"If you could see my guilt levels, I think you'd find them quite appealingly high."

The flirtation with which she made this statement made it true. It was appalling, an almost autonomic thing, the way she was warming to the first sweet, funny, successful, unmarried man she'd met since the wave of caustic adjectives ("stale," "obese," "exhausting") had crashed over the *big book*. But no matter how guilty it made her, she couldn't help it: she resented Charles for having failed. She resented that she now had to feel like a shallow, success-chasing woman just because she was liking Tom Aberant. If Charles's book had been glowingly reviewed and short-listed for prizes, she could have continued on her outbound trajectory without feeling guilty. No one would have blamed her. To the contrary, it would have been blameworthy to go *back* to him—to have fled to Washington while he was suffering and then to swoop back in to enjoy his success. And so she couldn't help wishing that Charles didn't exist. In a world where he didn't exist, she could have said yes to Tom's extremely attractive job offer.

What she did instead was suggest that she and Tom get together again over drinks. She wore a short black dress to the bar. Later, from her apartment, she sent Tom a long and disclosive email. She delayed calling Charles that night. In her growing sense of guilt about delaying, *in the guilt itself*, she found the will and motive not to call him at all. (Even though the sufferer of guilt could stop the suffering whenever she chose, simply by doing the right thing, the suffering was still real while it lasted, and self-pity wasn't picky about the kind of suffering it fed on.) The next day, she didn't open Tom's return email but went to work, called Charles three times, and ate a late dinner with a source. At home, she called Charles a fourth time and finally opened Tom's email. It wasn't disclosive, but it was invitational. She took a Friday-night train to Manhattan (somehow the guilt that should have *followed* infidelity not only existed *before* the infidelity but was hounding her *into* it) and spent the night at Tom's apartment. She spent the whole weekend with him, leaving his side only to go to the bathroom to pee or call Charles. Her guilt was so large that it was gravitational, warping space and time, connecting through non-Euclidian geometry to the guilt she hadn't felt while wrecking Charles's marriage. This guilt turned out not to have been nonexistent but pre-forwarded, by way of time-and-space warp, to Manhattan in 2004.

She couldn't have borne it without Tom. She felt safe with Tom. He was both the cause of her guilt and the balm for it, because he understood it and was living it himself. He was only six years older than Leila, younger than his hair loss made him look, but he'd started so early on his marriage that its ending, after twelve years, was in the fairly distant past. His wife, Anabel, had been an artist, a promising young painter and filmmaker, who came from one of the families that owned McCaskill, the biggest food-products company in the world. On paper, she was absurdly rich, but she was estranged from her family and refused on principle to take money from them. By the time Tom escaped from the marriage, her art career was going nowhere, she was in her late thirties, and she still wanted children.

"I was a coward," he said to Leila. "I should have left her five years earlier."

"Is it cowardly to stay with a person you love and who needs you?"

"You tell me."

"Hmm. I'll get back to you on that."

"If she'd been thirty-one, she could have put her life together and met somebody else and had her baby. I waited just long enough to make that very difficult."

"It wouldn't have helped that she was rich?"

"She was insane about the money. She'd sooner have died than take it from her father."

"But then that's her choice. Why should you feel guilty for a choice *she's* making?"

"Because I knew she'd make that choice."

"And did you cheat on her?"

"Not until we'd separated."

"Then, I'm sorry, but I think I've got you beat in the guilt race."

But there was something else, Tom said. Anabel's father had always liked him and tried to help him out financially. Tom couldn't accept any help as long as he stayed with Anabel, but when the father had died, more than a decade after the divorce, he'd left Tom a bequest to the tune of $20 million, and Tom had taken it. It was the seed money for his nonprofit venture.

"And you feel *guilty* about that?"

"I could have said no."

"But you're doing an amazing thing with the money."

"I'm enjoying money my wife could never take. Not just enjoying it, doing well with it professionally. Increasing my male professional advantage."

Although Leila appreciated Tom's company, his guilt seemed a little overwrought to her. She wondered if he might be exaggerating it (and downplaying the sexual hold that Anabel had had on him) for her sake. On her second weekend in New York, she asked him if she could flip through his box of old snapshots. There were pictures of a young man so skinny and boyish and thick-haired she barely recognized him. "You look like a completely different person."

"I was a completely different person."

"But, like, not the same DNA, even."

"That's how it feels."

As soon as Leila saw Anabel, she understood Tom's guilt better. The woman was *intense*—fiery-eyed, full-chestedly anorexic, Medusa-maned, mostly unsmiling. In the background of the pictures was student housing, slum housing, wintry pre-9/11 New York skyline.

"She does look a little scary," Leila said.

"Terrifying. I'm having a PTSD thing just looking at these."

"But you! You were so young and sweet."

"That's kind of my marriage in a nutshell."

"And where is she now?"

"No idea. We didn't have any friends in common, and we broke off all contact."

"So maybe she took her money after all. Maybe she owns an island somewhere."

"Anything's possible. But I don't think so."

Leila wanted to ask if she could keep one snapshot of Tom, an especially sweet one taken by Anabel on the Staten Island Ferry, but it was too soon to ask for a picture. She closed the box and kissed his turtle mouth. Sex with him was not the drama it had always been with Charles, the pouncing, the bouncing, the screaming of the prey, but she already thought she might prefer this other way. It was quieter, slower, more like a meeting of minds via bodies.

She had a deep sense of rightness with Tom—it was the thing, among many things, that she felt guiltiest about, because it meant that Charles was not right, had never been right. Tom's reserve, his willingness to leave her be, was soothing to her maritally poked and probed spirit. And he seemed to have the same sense of rightness with her. They were journalists and spoke a common language. But she couldn't help wondering why a catch like him had never remarried. Before she burned any bridges with Charles, she asked Tom why.

He replied that he hadn't stayed with any woman for longer than a year since his divorce. According to his ethics, one year was the limit, at least in New York, for any uncommitted relationship; and his bad marriage had made him commitment-shy.

"So what are you saying?" she said. "I've got ten months before you show me the door?"

"You're already in a committed relationship," he said.

"Right. Funny. Is this rule of yours something you led with on first dates?"

"It's a tacit rule in New York dating. I'm not the author of it. It's a way to avoid chewing up five years of a woman's life and *then* showing her the door."

"As opposed to, say, getting over your commitment phobia."

"I tried. More than once. But apparently I'm textbook PTSD. I had actual panic attacks."

"Textbook toxic bachelor is what it sounds more like."

"Leila, they were younger. I knew things they didn't know, I knew what can happen. Even if you weren't married, it wouldn't be the same with you."

"No, that's right. Because I'm forty-one. I'm already past the sell-by date. You won't have to feel so guilty when you dump me."

"The difference is that you've been through a marriage."

A light went on in Leila. "No, here's what it is," she said. "What's different is that I'm older than your wife when you divorced her. You didn't trade up to some twenty-eight-year-old. With me you're trading *down*. You don't have to feel so guilty."

Tom said nothing.

"And you know how I know that? Because I make the same kind of calculations myself. Whatever it takes to get away from my guilt, even for five minutes, my mind will do it. There was a review of Charles's book in *The Adirondack Review*, online. Glowing. He sent the link in an email blast to everyone in his address book, and I didn't see it until I was on my way up here to sleep with you. He needed somebody to tell him not to send that email blast. He needed *me, his wife,* to tell him, 'Better not to do that.' But I was otherwise engaged, on the phone, talking to you. And where's *my* little rule to help me out of that one? I don't have a little rule."

She was putting on clothes, repacking her overnight bag.

"I'm done with the rule," Tom said. "I only mentioned it because I trusted you to understand it. But you're right, it does help that you're forty-one. I'm not going to deny it."

His honesty seemed directed at the ghost of his ex-wife, not at Leila.

"I think I'm just going to leave before you make me cry," she said.

What drove her away from his apartment that night was an instinct about Tom. If his reserve had simply been his fundamental nature, she could have relaxed and appreciated it. But he hadn't always been reserved. He'd been open to intensity in his marriage, so open that he now felt traumatized by it, and Anabel clearly still had a grip on his conscience. He'd had something with Anabel that he didn't intend to have with anyone else, and an instinct told Leila that she would always feel secondary—that here was a competition she could never win.

But Tom kept calling her that winter, updating her on the progress of his nonprofit, and she couldn't pretend that she would rather have been talking to anyone else. In early May, three and a half months after they'd first met, he came down to Washington again. When she went to Union Station and saw him ambling up the platform, in wrinkled khakis and an old fifties sport shirt specifically chosen for its ugliness, as a private joke at the expense of good taste, a little chime sounded in her head, a single pure note, and she knew she was in love with him.

He'd booked a room at the George, so as not to presume that he could stay with her, but he never checked in. He spent a week in her apartment, using her Internet connection and reading on her sofa, his glasses perched upon his bald dome, his fingers curled over the spine of his book, holding it close to his bad eyes. She felt as if he'd always been there on the sofa; as if, when she came home and saw him sprawled on it, she was finally truly coming home, for the first time in her life. She agreed to leave the *Post* and go to work for his nonprofit. If there had been other things to agree to, she would have agreed to them.

She wanted (but didn't yet say she wanted) to try to have
a baby with him. She loved him and wanted him to never
leave. Now there was only the matter, much discussed
but still not acted on, of having the conversation with
Charles. And maybe, if she'd managed to have that conversation in time, she could have married Tom. But she
was cowardly—as cowardly as Tom said he'd been in not
ending his own marriage. She delayed having the conversation, delayed giving notice at the *Post*, and on a warm
Colorado night in late June, on a foothill road behind
Golden, Charles went over the front of the XLCR 1000
he'd bought with the last third of his U.K. advance and
was paralyzed below the hips. He'd been drinking.

The fault was his but also undeniably hers. While falling in love with someone else, she'd allowed her husband's
life to spin out of control. She immediately had herself
reassigned to Denver, and as long as Charles was in the
hospital, and then in rehab, she couldn't tell him about
Tom; she needed to keep his spirits up. But suppressing
the fact of Tom made the prospect of divulging it ever
scarier. She performed the role of loving wife perfectly—
she saw Charles briefly every morning and for hours
every evening, she sold their three-story house and bought
a more suitable one, she infused morale and sneaked him
whiskey, she befriended his doctors and caregivers, she
ran herself ragged—and meanwhile, at the pretty house
that Tom had bought in Hilltop, in part with money
from his former father-in-law, she had sex with someone
else.

Charles's accident ended up costing her a year of fertility. It was unthinkable, as long as he was recovering, to
bring him the news that she was carrying someone else's
child. Unthinkable to add a baby to an already overstressed
life. And then unthinkable not to live with Charles after she
brought him home to his new house. But she still wanted

a baby, and when, by and by, Tom asked her how long she intended to keep living with Charles, she found herself replying with a question of her own.

"No," Tom said.

"That's it?" she said. "No?"

He gave her many sensible reasons—their dedication to their work, their already overfull lives, the danger of birth defects for older couples, the global cataclysms that climate change and overpopulation would likely unleash in a child's lifetime—but the reason that actually made him angry was that she was still living with Charles and hadn't told him about their affair. How could he think of having a kid with a woman who couldn't even leave her husband?

"The minute I got pregnant, I'd tell him everything," she said.

"Why not tell him now?"

"He's suffering. Would you have abandoned Anabel if she'd landed in a wheelchair? Charles needs me."

"But can you not see how this looks to me? I'm ready to go, right now. I'm ready to marry you tomorrow. And you don't even have a *timeline* for getting out of your marriage."

"Well, and I'm telling you how you could help me with that."

"And I'm telling you there's something wrong if that's what you need to help you."

She was in a weak position, wanting a baby and running out of time. If it didn't happen with Tom, it wouldn't happen at all. She felt grief at the death of the possibility, pain at Tom's refusal, and anger at him for not wanting what she wanted. He didn't seem to understand the bind she was in. She was convinced that his avowed reasons for not wanting a kid were bogus—that his actual reason was to avoid the guilt of having the child he'd denied his ex-wife—but he refused to credit her own guilt about Charles.

And so they started fighting. Hotly on her side, coldly on his. Again and again the same impasse: she wouldn't leave Charles, he wouldn't try to have a baby. Tom never lost control, never even raised his voice, and his explanation for this—that he'd already done five lifetimes' worth of fighting with Anabel and refused to do it anymore—made Leila lose control for both of them. Charles had never driven her to shriek with rage; nobody had; but competing with Anabel did. She detested the sound of her shrieking so much that she broke up with Tom. A week later, they reconciled. A week after that, they broke up again. She was right for him, he was right for her, but they couldn't find a way to be together.

For nearly two months, they didn't communicate in any way. Then one night, after she'd put Charles to bed and cleaned his errant shit off the toilet and found herself weeping, she yielded to an impulse to call Tom. She picked up the phone, but there was something wrong with it—no dial tone.

"Hello?" she said.

"Hello?"

"*Tom?*"

"Leila?"

Two months of no contact, and they'd picked up the phone at the same moment. She didn't believe in signs, but this had to be a sign. She blurted out that she couldn't divorce Charles but couldn't live without Tom. He in turn said he didn't care if she ever divorced Charles, he couldn't live without her, either. It felt like coming home again.

The next morning, she told Charles that she was getting a place of her own and leaving the *Post* to work for a new nonprofit service. She didn't say why, but Charles poked and probed and made her confession for her. She continued to spend every second weekend with him, but from then on she lived mainly at Tom's, not as the co-keeper of his house, not as a person who made decorating decisions, but as a kind of permanent special guest. The two of them buried the fundamental conflict that their fighting had exposed; buried it deep. She never quite forgave him for not wanting a child with her, but in time it stopped mattering. They were both busy building DI into a nationally respected news service, and she was additionally busy taking care of Charles; sometimes she even found herself feeling grateful to be unburdened with children.

Her life with Tom was strange and ill-defined and permanently temporary but therefore all the more a life of true love, because it was freely chosen every day, every hour. It reminded her of a distinction she'd learned as a child in Sunday school. Their marriages had been Old Testament, hers a matter of honoring her covenant with Charles, Tom's a matter of fearing Anabel's wrath and judgment. In the New Testament, the only things that mattered were love and free will.

Early in the morning after her visit with Phyllisha, she drove to the house that Earl Walker had bought, for a price publicly recorded at $372,000, after losing his job at the weapons plant. The house had a triple garage and a sprinkler system whose early-morning overshoot had left the street wet where she parked. Apparently, in Amarillo, when lawns dried out in a drought, the obvious thing to do was water them. On Walker's driveway was a newspaper with a rubber band around it. After Leila had sat for a few minutes, a very heavy woman in her fifties came out and picked it up, gave Leila a hard look, and went back inside.

Walker had been Cody Flayner's boss in Inventory Control. This information Leila had from Pip, who had also learned that Walker had sold his previous home for $230,000. People who'd lost their job didn't typically turn around and buy a larger house, nor were they good candidates for a larger mortgage, and no probated will from the previous three years could account for the additional $142,000 Walker had paid. This amounted to a fact nearly as interesting as the Facebook pictures. Another fact, unearthed by Pip in an inspector general's report from January, was that "a minor irregularity in Inventory Control" had occurred at the plant the previous summer; according to the report, the irregularity had been "satisfactorily addressed" and was "no longer an issue." At Leila's suggestion, Pip had shown the Facebook pictures to an auto mechanic and learned that, unless Flayner's pickup had a custom suspension, the load on its bed had probably been less than the nine hundred pounds of a real B61. "It aint a real one, sugar" was still the only statement that Leila or Pip had gotten from Flayner directly. Leila's one phone call to him had quickly ended with threats and curses.

Walker, too, had said no to her, but merely "no," and merely "no" meant "maybe." She sat in her car, drinking green tea and replying to emails about other stories, until Walker himself came out of his house and strode straight toward her, across his sodden lawn. He was Jack Sprat lean and wearing a sweat suit with the purple and white of Texas Christian University. The Horned Frogs. She powered down her window.

"Who are you?" Walker said. He had a whiskey drinker's complexion not unlike her husband's.

"Leila Helou. Denver Independent."

"That's what I thought, and I already told you I got nothing to say to you."

With whiskey, the capillary bloom was more diffusely rosy than with gin and less purple than with wine. Every university dinner party was a study in blooms.

"I have just a couple of very quick and straightforward questions," Leila said. "Nothing that's going to cause you any trouble."

"You're already trouble. I don't want you on my street."

"But if we could meet for a cup of coffee somewhere? Any time today is good for me."

"You think I'm going to sit in public with you? I'm asking you politely to please go away. I couldn't talk to you even if I wanted to."

Not on my street. Not in public. Not allowed to talk.

"You've got a beautiful house," she said. "I've been admiring it."

She gave him a pleasant smile and touched the hair at her temple for no other reason than to let him see her fingers in her hair.

"Listen," he said. "You seem like a nice lady, so I'm going to spare you a deal of trouble here. There's no story. You think there's something but there's not. You're barking up the wrong tree."

"Easy, then," she said. "Let's clear it up. I'll tell you why I think there's something, you can explain to me why there's not, and I can be home tonight in Denver, sleeping in my own bed."

"I'd prefer you just start up your car and move it off this street."

"Or not explain, if you don't want to. You can just nod or shake your head. There's no law against shaking your head, is there?"

She smiled again and demonstrated how to shake a head. Walker sighed as if unsure what to do.

"Here, I'm starting my car," she said, starting it. "See? I'm going to leave your street."

"Thank you."

"But maybe there's someplace you need to be? I can give you a lift."

"I don't need a lift."

She turned off the engine, and Walker sighed more heavily.

"I'm sorry," she said. "But I wouldn't be a responsible journalist if I didn't hear your side of the story."

"There is no story."

"Well, see, but that's a side itself. Because other sides are saying there *is* a story. And some of those sides are telling me that you were paid off not to talk about it. And I'm wondering why the money, if there's no story. You see what I'm saying?"

Walker bent down closer to her. His face was like a stained map of somewhere densely populated. "Who you been talking to?"

"I don't betray sources. That's the first thing you need to know about me. When you talk to me, you're safe."

"You think you're smart."

"No, in fact, I'm fairly female-brained about this stuff. I could really use your help to understand it."

"Smart lady from the big city."

"Just tell me a time and a landmark. Somewhere I can meet you. Somewhere anonymous."

Anonymous was a preferred word of hers with male sources. It had all the right connotations. Anonymous was the opposite of the wife in Walker's house. Who, at that very moment, opened the front door and called out, "Earl, who is that?"

Leila bit her lip.

"Reporter lady," Walker shouted back. "She needs directions out of town."

"You tell her you got nothing to say to her?"

"What I just *said* to you."

After the door had closed again, Walker spoke without looking at Leila. "Behind the Centergas depot on Cliffside. Be there at three. You don't see me by four, you may as well head on home to that bed of yours in Denver."

As Leila drove away from his house, on the rush of his yes, the kind of rush she lived for as a journalist, she had to tell herself not to speed. Who could have guessed that, of the ten tricks she'd tried, dropping the word *bed* would be the one that got to him?

Back in her hotel room, she speed-dialed with the letter P.

"This is Pip Tyler," Pip said in Denver.

"Hello, hello. I just landed a date with Earl Walker."

"Hey!"

"I also got Phyllisha Babcock's story."

"*Nice*."

"The most hilarious thing you ever heard. Flayner borrowed the weapon as a sex aid."

"She told you that?"

"It would have been TMI if there were such a thing in this business. But she did also confirm the weapon was a dummy."

"Oh."

"It's still a good story, Pip. If a worker can take a dummy out, he could take a real one, too. It's still a story."

"I guess it's good to know the world is safer than I thought."

As Leila filled her in on the details, she was glad, as a person, if not as a boss, that Pip seemed in no hurry to get back to the research she was doing for another reporter on the credentialing of coroners.

"I should let you read your autopsy reports," Leila said finally. "How's that going?"

"Borink."

"Well. You have to pay your dues."

"I'm describing, not complaining."

Leila resisted a surge of emotion. Then she surrendered to it. "I miss you."

"Oh—thank you."

She waited, hoping for more.

"I miss you, too," Pip said.

"I wish I'd brought you with me."

"It's OK. I'm not going anywhere."

Leila felt keenly, after the call, that she liked the girl too much. "I miss you" was already more than she had a right to elicit from a subordinate and still not as much as she wanted to hear. She felt dissatisfied and exposed and somewhat nuts. The tenderness she felt with children had always had a physical component, situated close in her body to the part that wanted intimacy and sex. But the reason she felt such tenderness was that, no matter how she warmed to a child in her arms, she knew she would never betray and exploit its innocence. This was why nothing could replace having kids—this structural insatiability, both painful and delicious, of parental love.

Uncannily enough, Pip's actual name was Purity. (She called herself Pip Tyler on her résumé, but Leila had looked at her college transcript.) The name seemed apt to Leila without her being able to say exactly why. Certainly Pip was no innocent sexually. She was shacked up in Denver with a boyfriend about whom she'd been resolutely tight-lipped, saying only that he was a musician named Stephen. She'd also been living in serious squalor in Oakland, surrounded by dirty anarchists, and her pictures of Cody Flayner's barbecue had been obtained by lawless hacking. Leila wondered if the innocence she sensed in Pip was actually her own innocence at the age of twenty-four. Back then, she'd had no concept of how little she knew, but she could see it clearly now in Pip.

She wanted to be a good feminist role model and give Pip the direction she herself had lacked at that age. "The irony of the Internet," she'd said to her at lunch one day, "is that it's made the journalist's job so much easier. You can research in five minutes what used to take five days. But the Internet is also killing journalism. There's no substitute for the reporter who's worked a beat for twenty years, who's cultivated sources, who can see the difference between a story and a non-story. Google and Accurint can make you feel very smart, but the best stories come when you're out in the field. Your source makes some offhand remark, and suddenly you see the *real* story. That's when I feel most alive. When I'm sitting at the computer, I'm only half alive."

Pip listened to Leila attentively but noncommittally. She had the modern college grad's reluctance to express a strong opinion, for fear of being uncool or disrespectful. It did occur to Leila that Pip wasn't actually innocent at all—that, to the contrary, she was wiser than Leila, that she and her peers were well aware of what a terminally fucked-up world they were inheriting, and that Leila herself was the innocent one. But she persisted in thinking that Pip's coolness was merely a generational style, and looking for ways to break through it.

Pip seemed to drink either not at all or way too much. Leila had been treating her to dinners out, to make sure she got some good meals, and had drunk alone at them. But the previous week, on Thursday night, Pip had ordered a glass of wine and dispatched it in two minutes. After she'd done the same to a second glass, she asked if she could order a bottle; she offered, ridiculously, to pay for it. An hour later, the bottle empty, her dinner barely touched, she was crying. Leila reached across the table and put her hand on her flushed face. She said, "Oh, honey."

Pip pushed away from the table and ran to the bathroom. When she returned, she asked if she might, this once, come home with Leila and sleep on her sofa or something.

"Oh, honey," Leila said again. "Won't you tell me what's wrong?"

"Nothing's wrong," Pip said. "I just feel so alone here. I miss my mom."

Leila preferred not to think about the girl's mother. "It's fine if you want to come home with me," she said. "There are just some things you need to know about my situation."

Pip quickly nodded.

"Or maybe you've already heard about it."

"Some of it."

"Well, ordinarily I'd be at Tom's tonight—I'm presuming that's part of what you know. But I don't think that's such a good idea."

"It's OK. I shouldn't have asked."

"No! It's lovely that you asked. But I'm sort of a guest at the other house. If you could live with a little bit of sneaking . . ."

"I wasn't thinking."

"I wouldn't offer if it weren't all right with me."

Charles's house was three blocks from the creative-writing offices. He could have wheeled himself to and from work—could also have retired—but he preferred to conduct his workshops and office hours from home. The house was a lair that he did his best never to leave; he said he'd rather be the absolute ruler of a 2,000-square-foot kingdom than be that wheelchair dude in the outside world. He had fair control of his bowels, remarkable abdominal and shoulder strength, and great dexterity with his chair. He still drank too much, but he'd cut back because he intended to live a long time. His paraplegia had objectified his grievance with the literary world, which, he believed, wanted more than ever for him to simply go away, and he wasn't going to give it that satisfaction.

Leila still spent half her weekends at Charles's, but she didn't sleep with him. She had her own—slight—room at the front of the hallway leading to the big cat's bedroom. She would have liked to slip Pip into the house unobserved, but it was only ten o'clock and the living-room lights were on when they pulled into the driveway.

"Well," she said. "It looks like you'll meet my husband. Are you sure you're up for that?"

"I'm curious, actually."

"That's the journalistic spirit."

Leila knocked on the front door, unlocked it, and stuck her head in to warn Charles that he had two visitors. They found him lying on the sofa with a pile of student writing on his chest and a red pencil in his hand. He still had his looks and his long hair, which he wore in a nearly white ponytail. Near at hand was a whiskey bottle, stoppered. Books were shelved floor to ceiling and standing in stacks on the floor.

"This is one of our research interns, Pip Tyler," Leila said.

"Pip," Charles boomed, looking the girl up and down in open sexual appraisal. "I like your name. I have *great expectations* of you. Aieee—you must get that a lot."

"Seldom so neatly put," Pip said.

"Pip needs a place to sleep tonight," Leila said. "I hope you don't mind."

"Are you not my wife? Is this not our house?" Charles laughed less than nicely.

"Anyway, so," Leila said, edging toward the front hall.

"Are you a *reader*, Pip? Do you read *books*? Is the sight of so many books in one room at all *frightening* to you?"

"I like books," Pip said.

"Good. Good. And are you a big fan of *Jonathan Savoir Faire*? So many of my students are."

"You mean the book about animal welfare?"

"The very one. He's a novelist, too, I'm told."

"I read the animal book."

"So many *Jonathans*. A plague of literary *Jonathans*. If you read only the *New York Times Book Review*, you'd think it was the most common male name in America. Synonymous with talent, greatness. Ambition, vitality." He arched an eyebrow at Pip. "And what about *Zadie Smith*? Great stuff, right?"

"Charles," Leila said.

"Sit with me. Have a drink."

"A drink is more or less exactly what we don't need. And you've got stories to read."

"Before my *long and restful* night's sleep." He picked up a student story. " 'We were doing lines as long and fat as milk-shake straws.' The flaw in this simile: can we spot it? Pip? Can you tell me what's less than airtight about this simile?"

Pip seemed to be enjoying the show that Charles was putting on for her. "Is there a difference between milk-shake straws and other straws?"

"Good point, good point. The hobgoblin of spurious specificity. And the *tubularity* of a drinking straw, the dull sheen of its plastic—the suspicion creeps in that the author is personally unacquainted with the physical properties of powder cocaine. Or that he's confused the substance with the tool for nasally delivering the substance."

"Or he's just trying too hard," Pip said.

"Or trying too hard. Yes. I'm going to write those very words in the margin. Would you believe that I have colleagues who won't make marginal notations? I actually *care* about this student. I think he could do better, if he could only see what he's doing wrong. Tell me, do you believe in the *soul*?"

"I don't like to think about it," Pip said.

"Charles."

He gave Leila a look of comically sorrowful reproach. Must she deny him, the wheelchair dude, his iota of pleasure? "The soul," he said to Pip, "is a chemical sensation. What you see lying on this sofa is a glorified *enzyme*. Every enzyme has its special job to do. It spends its life looking for the specific molecule it's designed to interact with. And can an enzyme be *happy*? Does it have a *soul*? I say yes to both questions! What the enzyme you see lying here was made to do is find bad prose, interact with it, and make it better. That's what I've become, a *bad-prose-correcting enzyme*, floating in my cell here." He nodded at Leila. "And she worries that I'm not happy."

Pip's eyes widened with swallowed comment.

"She's still looking for her molecule," Charles continued. "I already know mine. Do you know yours?"

"I'm going to set Pip up in the basement room," Leila said.

"Safe, but not completely safe," he said. "I've conquered those stairs more than once."

In the basement, Leila put Pip to bed and then sat near her, under an afghan, drinking from a bottle of wine that she'd opened out of nervous agitation and shared with Pip against her better judgment. The wine and the bed and the girl's proximity brought out something predatory in her, something ardent and greedy, the same inherited Helou thing that had once landed her Charles and, later, Tom. She told Pip how she'd ended up with two men, the husband whose care she managed and the boyfriend she loved. She didn't mention having wanted children, because the story of her disappointment felt too personal and too relevant to what she was doing at this moment:

sitting at the bedside of a daughter-aged girl. But she kept drinking and told Pip a lot. She told her that if she ever had to choose between men she'd probably choose Charles, because she'd made a vow to him and had arguably ruined his life, and that Charles was OK with this. That he still needed her and was still sometimes capable of sex. That he'd sussed out a lot about Tom and enjoyed baiting her about him, and that, although she did acknowledge that Tom existed, she never referred to him by name. That in more than a decade the two men had never met. That the molecule for which she was evidently the matching enzyme was the care of disabled older men. That, contrary to Charles's theory, interacting with this molecule didn't make her happy. That happy would have been a life entirely with Tom.

"The job is mine, though," she said. "His children never forgave him for leaving their mother, and they're pretty screwed up anyway. I'm all he's got."

Hearing this, Pip began to cry again. Leila took her wineglass away from her, obviously too late, and held her hand. "Won't you tell me what's upsetting you tonight?"

"I've just been feeling really alone."

"It's hard when the only person you know in a town is your boyfriend."

Pip didn't respond to this.

"Are things OK with you two?"

"I'm thinking I might have to go back to California soon."

"Because things aren't working out with your boyfriend?"

Pip shook her head and reluctantly divulged. Her student debt, she said, was so large that most of her small intern salary was going to payments on it; she couldn't afford to be in Denver unless she lived rent-free. Her debt was from both college and the private high school she'd attended in Santa Cruz—her mother had kept telling her not to worry about the money. And her mother, though not technically disabled, was emotionally handicapped and had no support network. There was no one but Pip to look after her, and all Pip could see in her own future was nursing her. "It makes me feel like I'm already an old person myself," she said.

"You're the opposite of old."

"But I feel so guilty being this far away from her. Like, what am I even doing here? It's some kind of unsustainable fantasy."

How Leila wished that she could offer to let Pip live with her. But even though she seemed to have two homes, she had none that was actually hers. Not the finest of feminist role-modeling. "It's only been two months," she said. "Surely you can be away from California for longer than two months."

"You don't understand," Pip said. "What makes me feel so guilty is that I don't *want* to go back there. I love working with you and learning from you. But when I think about not going back, it just breaks my heart to think of her alone in our cabin, missing me."

"I do understand," Leila said. "You're describing my daily life."

"But at least you're in the same *town*. You had bad luck, but you found the right way to deal with it. Sometimes I wish . . ."

"What do you wish?"

Pip shook her head. "I've already kept you up way too late."

"Not the other way around?"

"Sometimes I wish I'd gotten to have a parent more like you."

The little basement room seemed to spin, and not just from the wine in Leila's head.

"Well," she said briskly, patting Pip's hand and standing up, "I wouldn't have minded having a daughter like you, either, so."

"Thank you for the dinner and the wine."

"You're very welcome."

"We'll both be sorry tomorrow."

"Just hungover. Not sorry, I hope."

Leila gave a false little laugh for which she punished herself, as she climbed the basement stairs, by striking her forehead with the heel of her hand. Upstairs, Charles was snoring on the sofa, the student stories on the floor, the whiskey bottle damaged. She woke him with a kiss on his forehead. "Ready to go to bed?"

"Ready to *piss*."

He didn't require her help in getting into his chair, but he appreciated it. There was a narrow but deep way in which she was closer to him than she would ever be to anyone else. The two of them had no secrets. Over the years, being a novelist, Charles had guessed and gleefully trumpeted pretty much every feeling she'd ever had about Tom. If she still declined to speak Tom's name, it was to protect his privacy, not hers. It was a little game that Charles was fine with playing.

The master-bedroom end of the house had a faint but inexpungible scent of skin lotions and fart. In the bathroom, she stood by the railinged toilet and watched Charles's urine issue from his penis in a healthy stream. It did both of them good for her to witness his bodily functions. It was a way of doing something for each other. Even when she handled the penis to ejaculation, it wasn't just for him. He was the baby she'd got.

"When I heard your car," he said, "I thought, 'Thursday! What a nice surprise.'"

"I appreciate your letting her stay here."

"Then I thought, 'Trouble on the Other Home Front?'"

"You weren't kidding about needing to pee."

"My continence speaks to the existence of a Deity for which evidence is otherwise scant."

"I'm a little nuts about that girl."

He raised an eyebrow. "You thinking of jumping the fence?"

"God, no. She's more like a lost puppy that found its way to me."

"You can keep her in the basement, but you'd have to do the house-training."

"Where did Rosie put the clean pajamas?"

"They're right in front of you."

"Ah, yes. They're right in front of me."

The next morning, somewhat hungover, she went to Tom and told him he had to hire Pip as a full-fledged researcher, with a salary she could live on. Tom pointed out that Pip hadn't finished her internship. Leila said, "She's good, she's worth it, and she needs the money right now." And Tom, with a shrug, assented. Before he could change his mind, she went and found Pip and told her the good news.

"That's great," Pip said in a small voice.

For a moment, Leila wondered whether she was doing something selfish, something disturbed even, by trying to keep Pip in Denver. But the girl herself had said she didn't want to leave.

"Now let's find you a place to live," Leila said cheerfully. "We can start by asking around the office."

Pip nodded, seeming underjoyed.

The meeting with Earl Walker, behind the propane depot on Amarillo's outskirts, lasted less than fifteen minutes. Walker stayed in his truck, speaking through the open window, and left the engine running. He admitted to having accepted a $250,000 severance payment after he'd remarked to plant management that everyone would be happier if he was happy. He further admitted to having been fired for cause, the cause being that he'd done some drinking, *once*, while on the job. *One time*, Cody Flayner had had to cover for him, and Flayner, having a taste for blackmail and being a generally nasty little shit, had made him pay for it by doing the egress paperwork on the mock B61, so that Flayner could play a prank on his girlfriend. Walker wasn't proud of himself, but he insisted that he'd done nothing dangerous. The mock B61 had been shipped in error from Kirtland Air Force Base in Albuquerque, and a carload of Air Force investigators had come by to examine it, but Kirtland hadn't yet dispatched a truck to repossess it. If Flayner hadn't been so stupid as to show the thing off to his buddies, and post pictures of it, there would have been no harm, no foul.

"You did not hear any of this from me," Walker said, shifting his truck into drive.

"Absolutely not," Leila said. "Your wife can attest to the fact that you refused to talk to me."

Her mind was already moving on to a story she was developing on mining-industry ties to the Colorado Department of Natural Resources. She still needed to interview plant management about the mock B61, but the smallness of the Flayner story was becoming apparent. It would disappoint Pip, the smallness, and Leila decided to let the girl write it and share the byline.

Back in her hotel room, she tried calling Pip and Tom and then texted them. That both texts went unanswered for some hours, while she plowed through the tax filings and COI disclosure statements that Pip had dug up for her, became noteworthy only when Tom returned her call, around ten thirty Denver time.

"Where you been?" she asked.

"Out to dinner," he said. "I took your girl to dinner."

Leila immediately had a bad feeling, as if she'd felt a tooth crack.

"I always take new hires to dinner," Tom said.

"Right. Of course. And where'd you go?"

"Place That Used to Be the Corner Bistro."

The Place That Used to Be the Corner Bistro was her and Tom's place. They liked to reward it for its name.

"I have no imagination for restaurants," he said. "My mind becomes a perfect blank."

"It's kind of funny to think of you there without me." There was a tremor in Leila's voice.

"I had the same thought. I don't think I've ever been there without you."

But he'd taken other new hires to dinner, and in each case he'd had enough imagination to think of restaurants other than the one where he and Leila went. Although the two of them never fought—hadn't fought in so many years that she'd thought they never would again—she was remembering the foretaste now, the constriction of her chest.

"Maybe I was wrong," she said, "but I had the sense you weren't even comfortable around Pip."

"Not wrong. You're never wrong."

"She reminds you of Anabel."

"Of Anabel? No."

"She's the same type. If *I* can see it, you can definitely see it."

"Completely different personality. And you were right—I'm glad we hired her."

"Always Listen to Leila."

"The words I live by. But I ran something by her. Tell me what you think of this. I said I'd run it by you, too."

"Move her out of research and into reporting?"

"Ah, no. That's worth discussing, but no. I asked her if

she might want to live with you and me for a while. I gather she's beyond broke."

Fighting was like vomiting. The prospect grew more dreadful with each year that passed without her doing it. Even when she finally fell ill and needed to throw up, and even though she rationally knew that it would bring relief, she struggled to hold the vomit in as long as possible. And fighting was even worse, because fighting didn't bring relief. Fighting was more like death in that regard: just keep postponing.

"*Your* house," she said, trying to steady her voice. "Pip living in *your* house."

"Our house. Didn't you tell me you wished you could take her in?"

"Actually, what I said was that I wished I had a place that I could offer her. I don't think of your house as a place I can offer."

"I think of it as *our* house."

"I know you do. And you know I don't. Which is a long discussion I don't feel like having right now."

"I didn't promise her anything."

"Well, I'm not loving the position that puts me in. Of being the one who nixed it, and her knowing it was me."

"I can tell her I had second thoughts myself, so you're not in that position. But help me understand why you're nixing it? I thought you wanted her to live with you."

"You didn't even like being in the same *room* with the girl until tonight. It seems like a pretty fast one-eighty on your part."

"Leila. Come on. You're the one who's smitten with her. I'm not going to take her from you. And she couldn't take me from you if she made it her entire life's mission. She's a *child*."

Leila didn't know who to be more jealous of, Tom or

Pip. But together the two jealousies made her feel like simply bowing out.

"It's fine with me," she said. "Do whatever you want."

"When you say it like that?"

"What do you want me to say? That there's something wrong with my head? That I'm *smitten* with a girl I've only known two months? That I'm *jealous*? I'm not going to fight about this. You just caught me by surprise."

"She and I talked about you."

"How nice."

"She wants to be like you."

"She must be out of her mind."

"Well, there is one thing. Or rather, isn't. She should probably tell you this herself, but she's so in awe of you that she's afraid to. There isn't any boyfriend."

"What?"

"She's in a Lakewood share with two other girls. She made up the whole thing about a boyfriend. Or, to be precise, there is a guy, who is named Stephen. But he lives in California and has a wife."

"She told you this?"

"I have some skill at eliciting things myself."

Leila ought to have felt betrayed, but mostly she felt sorry for Pip. Happy people didn't tell lies. "Why did she do that?"

"Didn't want to seem overeager to be in Denver. Didn't want you to know how alone she is. Didn't want to seem pathetic to you. I gather the reason she wanted to get out of California was her situation with the married guy there. But this is part of why it occurred to me that she could live with us. She's very talented but kind of a mess."

"You're not attracted to her."

"I can't even describe how far off the radar that is."

The risk of a fight was waning. To talk about something else, Leila mentioned her meeting with Earl Walker and her idea of letting Pip write the story, since it was small.

"Why did Walker meet with you?" Tom said.

As soon as he said it, she saw it.

"Ah," she said. "You're good."

"All I said was 'Why did he meet with you?' "

"No, but that's it. I was so fixated on Pip, on her being disappointed. It's a good question."

"Happy to help."

"Because there was one thing Walker said. He said Albuquerque had sent over a car full of investigators. It just sailed right past me."

"You were fixated on Pip."

"OK, OK."

"We're the team, right? I'm not the enemy."

"I said OK."

"Reinterview."

When she got off the phone, she saw that a text from Pip had come in: I have a confession to make. Good girl, Leila thought. Good for her.

She herself was off her game. She'd totally botched her meeting with Walker. He'd been rushed and flighty, but this didn't excuse her not having asked the obvious question: *Why did Kirtland AFB ship a dummy weapon to Amarillo in the first place?* This was the question that Walker had met with her to be asked. The plant wouldn't have paid a quarter-million dollars to shut him up about some harmless prank. But a weapon that had gone missing in Albuquerque? Swapped out for a training dummy?

Even more embarrassing was why she hadn't thought to ask the question. She'd assumed that the reason that Walker was meeting with her was her self-presentation, her feminine wiles. She'd taken his allusion to her bed in Denver straight, when in fact it had been sarcastic. She was fifty-two. The hair she'd made a show of toying with was graying.

Ugh. Ugh.

Ambien normally knocked her right out, but on the nights when it didn't she had no recourse; she'd heard too many somnambulism stories to take another dose. She lay and tossed on the drought-dry bed, which somehow smelled more strongly of cigarettes than it had the previous night, and considered the fact that Pip had lied to her. That Pip had fallen for somebody's husband; had done or tried to do to a marriage what Leila herself had once done. That she herself was now the older, drier, pouchier-faced woman who once had been, as Pip was now, a mobile destabilizing menace, a kind of rogue warhead . . .

How terribly easy it had turned out to be to transform naturally occurring uranium into hollow spheres of plutonium, pack the spheres with tritium and surround them with explosives and deuterium, and do it all in such miniature that the capacity to incinerate a million people could fit on the bed of Cody Flayner's pickup. So easy. Incomparably easier than winning the war on drugs or eliminating poverty or curing cancer or solving Palestine. Tom's theory of why human beings had yet to receive any message from extraterrestrial intelligences was that all civilizations, without exception, blew themselves up almost as soon as they were able to get a message out, never lasting more than a few decades in a galaxy whose age was billions; blinking in and out of existence so fast that, even if the galaxy abounded with earthlike planets, the chances of one civilization sticking around to get a message from another were vanishingly low, because it was too damned easy to split the atom. Leila neither liked this theory nor had a better one; her feeling about all doomsday scenarios was *Please make me the first person killed*; but she'd forced herself to read accounts of

Hiroshima and Nagasaki and what it was like to have had your skin burned off entirely and still be staggering down a street, alive. Not just for Pip's sake did she want the Amarillo story to be large. The world's fear of nuclear weapons was unaccountably unlike her fear of fighting and vomiting: the longer the world lasted without ending in mushroom clouds, the *less* afraid people seemed to be. The Second World War was remembered more for the extermination of Jews, more even for the firebombing of Dresden or the siege of Leningrad, than for what had happened on two August mornings in Japan. Climate change got more ink in a day than nuclear arsenals did in a year. To say nothing of the NFL passing records that Peyton Manning had broken as a Denver Bronco. Leila was afraid and felt like the only one who was.

Or almost the only one. Pip was afraid, too. The mother who'd named her Purity appeared to have taught her very little about how the world worked, and this meant that Pip looked at things with eyes unclouded by preconception. She saw a planet on which there were still seventeen thousand nukes, probably enough to wipe vertebrate life off the face of it, and thought *This can't be good*.

There had been a time when taking in a houseguest would have inhibited Leila and Tom; when they'd drawn the blinds and curtains and walked around his house naked for the pleasure of entrusting each other with the sight of their no longer so young bodies; when the refrigerator door and the living-room floor had been viable surfaces against which to brace herself for him. Although that time was long gone, they'd never formally acknowledged its passing—so much remained unspoken behind the glare on Tom's glasses—and Leila couldn't help feeling hurt that he'd unilaterally acknowledged it by inviting the girl to live with him.

Fusion chain reactions were natural, the source of a

sun's energy, but fission chain reactions weren't. Fissile plutonium atoms were nature's unicorns, and nowhere in the universe could a critical mass of them naturally assemble itself. People had to force it to occur, and to force the mass further, with explosives, into a superdense state in which the chain reaction could proceed through enough generations to ignite fusion. And how quickly it all happened. Jiggling atomic droplets of plutonium ingesting neutron newcomers, cleaving into smaller atomic droplets, spewing further neutrons. Skinless people staggering down the street with their entrails and eyeballs hanging out . . .

They should have had a baby. In a way, it was an immense relief not to have had one, not to have brought another life to a planet that would be incinerated quickly or baked to death slowly; not to have to worry about that. And yet they should have done it. Leila loved Tom and admired him beyond measure, she felt blessed by the ease of her life with him, but without a child it was a life of leaving things unspoken. Of cuddling in the evening, watching cable dramas together, inhabiting broad areas of agreement, avoiding the few hots spots of past disagreements, and drifting toward old age. Her sudden ardor for Pip was irrational but not senseless, not sexual but intense; compensatory. She didn't know what exactly would come of permitting a newcomer into the nucleus of her and Tom, but she pictured a mushroom cloud.

Three and a half weeks after Pip moved in, Leila went to Washington. Along with the warhead story, she was reporting a statistics-driven piece about the lax enforcement of tax law in the tech industry. All the Washington hotels in her permitted price class were dispiriting, and she was staying in one of them. She would have liked to go home to Denver sooner, but her favorite senator, the most liberal member of the Armed Services Committee, had promised her fifteen Friday-afternoon minutes before he followed the rest of Congress out of town. She'd arranged the meeting in person, with his chief of staff, so as not to leave a phone or email trail. Since the advent of NSA dragnets, she'd operated more and more by Moscow Rules. Members of Congress were especially attractive sources, because they weren't polygraphed.

Working her Pentagon contacts, some of whom she'd known since her *Post* days, she'd pieced together a sanitized version of what had happened in Albuquerque. Yes, ten B61 weapons had been trucked to Amarillo for scheduled refurbishment and circuitry upgrades. Yes, one of them had turned out to be an unarmed facsimile normally stored on the base near the real weapons, for use in training the accident-response team. Yes, bar coding and microchip self-identifiers had been tampered with. Yes, there had ensued eleven days when a real weapon was off the grid and presumably stored in a poorly secured shed. Yes, heads had rolled. Yes, the weapon was now "fully accounted for" and had never been less than fully safed. No, the Air Force would not provide any details of the theft or disclose the identity of the perpetrator(s).

"There's no such thing as 'fully safed,'" Ed Castro, a nukes expert at Georgetown, had told her. "Safe from detonating if you whack it with a hammer, sure. Safe from circumventing the code mechanisms, probably. We also suspect that later-generation bombs 'poison' their own cores if you tamper with them. But the thing about mid-period weapons like the B61 is that they're sickeningly simple at heart. All the really high technology comes in prior to the assembly of the weapon. Creating and refining the plutonium and hydrogen isotopes: unbelievably difficult and costly. Designing the lens geometry of the high explosives: difficult. But putting the pieces together and making them go boom? Sadly, not so difficult. If you've got time and a couple of PhDs, reverse engineering the ignition circuitry is eminently doable. The result won't be so elegant and miniature, and the yield might be reduced, but you'll have a working thermonuclear weapon."

"Who would want one?" Leila said, half rhetorically.

Castro was the kind of quote hound reporters loved. "The usual suspects," he said. "Islamic terrorists. Rogue states. James Bond movie villains. Would-be extortionists. Conceivably antinuke activists hoping to prove a point. These are the end users, and thankfully they're a fairly feckless lot. The more interesting thing to think about is who their potential suppliers would be. Who's really good at getting and moving stuff they're not supposed to have? Who goes around *collecting* that kind of stuff in case it comes in handy?"

"The Russian Mob, for example."

"In the years before Putin took over, I used to wake up in the morning and marvel that I was still alive."

"But then the Russian Mob became indistinguishable from the Russian government."

"The kleptocracy has definitely improved nuclear security."

Reporting was imitation life, imitation expertise, imitation worldliness, imitation intimacy; mastering a subject only to forget it, befriending people only to drop them. And yet, like so many imitative pleasures, it was highly addictive. Outside the Dirksen Building, on Friday afternoon, Leila saw other Hill reporters milling in little clouds of self-importance that she could discern because she was inhabiting one herself and was affronted by the sight of others. Had they, like her, removed the batteries from their smartphones, to hide their location from the dragnet? She doubted it.

The senator was only twenty-five minutes behind schedule. His staff chief, apparently preferring deniability, didn't join him and Leila in his office.

"You're annoying the Air Force," the senator said when they were alone. "Nice work."

"Thank you."

"Obviously we're strictly on background. I'm going to give you the names of other people who've been briefed, and you need to leave an electronic trail of contacting every one of them. I want this story told, but it's not worth losing a committee seat over."

"Is it that big a deal?"

"It's not that big a deal. Medium-size, maybe. But the mania for secrecy is out of control. Are you aware that the agencies don't just number and watermark the classified reports we get now? They do something with the spacing between the letters of each copy—the kerning?"

"Kerning, yes."

"Apparently it creates a unique signature for each copy. In Technology We Trust. Need to put that on the new hundred-dollar bill."

Over the years, Leila had come to believe that politicians were literally made of special stuff, chemically different stuff. The senator was flabby and bad-haired and acne-scarred and yet completely magnetic. His pores exuded some pheromone that made her want to look at him, keep hearing his voice, be liked by him. And she did feel liked. Everyone he wanted to be liked by did.

"So you could have heard this from any number of people," he said when she'd written down the names. "The problem is we trust technology. We put our trust in the safing of the warheads, and we neglect the human side, because tech problems are easy and human problems are hard. That's where the whole country is right now."

"Easier to put journalists out of work than to find something to replace us with."

"Drives me crazy. I don't have to tell you what morale is like in the bomber and silo crews. We don't trust technology quite enough to replace them with machines. We may yet reach that point, but in the meantime those postings are career suicide. You get the worst and the least bright, safeguarding our most terrible weapons and bored out of their minds. Cheating on their exams, breaking rules, flunking urine tests. Or not flunking them."

"In Albuquerque?"

"If you're thinking crystal meth, think again. These are career officers. Don't even write down the name Richard Keneally, but remember it. The Man Who Can—apparently there's at least one on every base. I hope you don't mind that I'm summarizing many pages of a report that has a unique typographical signature, rather than letting you read it?"

"You have a plane to catch."

"The drugs are almost all prescription stuff. Adderall, OxyContin. Drugs to help you pass the time while your classmates from the academy are flying actual missions or eating Lockheed's shrimp. You know my feelings about the nation's drug laws. Suffice it to say, we're talking about officer drugs, not grunt drugs. But still, whatever the legal inequities, they're a no-no in the armed services. They'll still light up a tox screen. Which, if you're the Man Who Can, is the real ceiling on the growth of your business. What to do about that?"

Leila shook her head.

"Have the friendly friends who supply you with the drugs quietly take over the lab that tests the urine."

"Really," Leila said.

"I wish I could show you the report," the senator said. "Because it gets better, which is to say worse. Who are the friendly friends? I hate the word *cartel*, it's completely wrong. We should call them *DHLes Especiales* or *FedExes Extralegales*, because that's what they are. If you're manufacturing fake cancer drugs in Wuhan and you need to get a container of your product to the American consumer, who are you going to call? DHL Especial. Same thing for weapons, designer knockoffs, underage prostitutes, and, obviously, drugs of all kinds. One call serves all. The American middle-class appetite for illegal drugs provided the capital to build some of the most sophisticated and effective companies on earth. Their business is delivering the goods, and their offices aren't far south of the border. And our Man Who Can, Richard Keneally, whose name you're remembering but not writing down, was doing business with them for several years, right under the noses of sundry inspectors general, and it only came to light because a training-replica B61 turned up where it shouldn't have."

"Did the real weapon leave the base?"

"Fortunately no. The story is extremely sad and disturbing but also funny in a way. DHL Especial may or may not have had a buyer for the weapon—we'll never know. But before Richard Keneally could even try to get the 'replica,' which is to say the real weapon—before he could get it off the base, he tripped on a parking stop and fell on a bottle of tequila he was carrying. The broken glass severed an artery, he nearly bled out, and he was stuck in a hospital for a week. That's the part that's a little bit funny. The part that isn't is that Keneally apparently couldn't deliver the warhead as scheduled, and he had no way of letting the Especiales know why he hadn't. His two sisters had both disappeared, one in Knoxville, one in Mississippi, around the time the warhead swap occurred. Apparently they were kidnapped as security for the deal.

They both ended up dead behind a car dealership in Knox-ville, with single gunshots to the back of the head. One of the sisters had three children. The only bright spot is that the children weren't harmed."

Leila was writing as fast as she could. "Good God," she said.

"It's terrible. But to me it's as much a story about the utter failure of the war on drugs, about trusting in tech-nology instead of taking care of people, as it is about our nuclear arsenal."

"I see that," Leila said, still writing.

"It was all going to come out even if you hadn't come here with your questions. The *WaPo*'s already on the de-motion and reassignment of the officers Keneally sold to. They know about the drug dealing. Only a matter of time before someone leaks the rest."

"You've talked to the *Post*?"

The senator shook his head. "Still being punished by this office for something unrelated."

"Why did Keneally do it?"

"The speculation is partly money, partly fear for his life."

"Are you saying he's not in custody?"

"You'll have to ask someone else."

"That sounds like a no."

"Draw your own conclusions. And let me reiterate that none of this goes on your site until you have independent confirmation."

"We don't like single-source stories. We're old-fashioned that way."

"This is known to us. It's one reason you and I are sitting here. Or have been." The senator stood up. "I actually do have a plane to catch."

"How was Keneally going to get the weapon off the base?"

"That's it, Leila. You already have more than you need to get the rest of it."

He was right about that. One of the best stories of her career was in the bag. The rest would be routine triangulate-and-bluff—"I'm just confirming that I have my facts right"—while she endured the sick-making anxiety that the *Post* or someone else, someone less scrupulous about multiple-sourcing, would scoop her.

Leaving the Dirksen, she thought about canceling her trip home to Denver, but the work she had to do now, to confirm the senator's story, could only be done with in-person meetings, and on a mild and sunny spring weekend nobody she needed to see would be staying in D.C. Better to spend the weekend in Denver, writing and lining up interviews, and fly back on Sunday night.

Or so she rationalized it. The unfortunate, unflattering fact was that she didn't want to leave Tom and Pip alone together for a weekend. She'd already been feeling resentfully beleaguered by how much she had to do—too many stories, a caregiver crisis at Charles's house, the usual email and social-media onslaught (the former Mrs. Cody Flayner was writing to her daily, sending recipes and pictures of her kids)—and the new urgency of the Albuquerque story only added to her workload. The story was demanding and she its single parent. Even going home, she wouldn't have much time for Tom or Pip. Their unscheduled freedom on the weekend seemed sybaritic in comparison. She knew it was important to resist jealousy and resentment and self-pity, but she was having a hard time of it.

On the Metro, her hand shook so much that it was hard to fill out the scribbles in her notebook, hard to tap out texts to Tom and Pip. By the time she boarded her Denver flight, her anxiety about being scooped was nearly disabling. There wasn't enough room between seats for her to work without being observed by the businessman next to her, and her mind was too jumpy to concentrate on tech-industry taxes, and so she bought a split of wine and stared uselessly at the crawl of the jet icon across the route map on the seat-back screen. She bought a second split and applied it to her anxiety.

She had no rational case against Pip as a houseguest. The girl had yet to leave an unwashed dish or spoon in the sink, a light burning in an empty room. She'd even offered to do Tom and Leila's laundry for them. They'd recoiled at the thought of her handling their underwear, but she explained that she'd never lived in a house with a functioning washer and dryer ("Total luxury") and so they let her do the sheets and towels. She had little of the unearned entitlement for which kids of her generation were laughed at, but she didn't apologize for being in the house or thank them too profusely for letting her be there. During the week, at least on the nights when Leila was home, she prepared her own separate dinner, retreated to her room, and didn't show herself again. Come Friday night, though, she plunked herself down on a stool in the kitchen, let Tom shake her one of his perfect Manhattans, chopped garlic for Leila, and opened up with funny tales of squatter life in Oakland.

Leila ought to have been pleased with the arrangement. But she had reason to believe that, on the nights she worked late or had to be at Charles's, Pip wasn't staying in her room all evening. Twice already in a month, Leila had learned of important news—the unofficial approval of a $7.5 million grant to DI from the Pew Foundation, the selection of an unfriendly judge for a First Amendment case that DI was co-defending—not directly from Tom but from Tom by way of Pip. Having herself once been the beneficiary of an older man's experience, Leila knew how nice it felt to be specially apprised of things, and how unaware the girl was of what a privilege it was, how unaware that people might resent her for it. Leila wondered if the guilt she'd come to feel about what she'd done to Charles's first wife wasn't guilt at all but anger; anger at the younger Leila who'd been granted entrée to the literary world because she was attractive to Charles; an older woman's feminist anger at her younger self. She felt some of this anger as she watched Pip absorbing Tom's wisdom and basking in the pleasure he took in her young company.

This wasn't just theoretical. Twice already in a month, Tom had pounced on Leila in Charles-like ways. Once while she was standing at the bathroom mirror, removing her makeup, and he'd come up behind her with his cock already escaping from his pajamas, and again just a few nights later, when she'd turned out her reading light and felt his hand on her collarbone, which he liked, and on her neck, which he liked even more. This had been Tom's way only in the beginning. Other understandings had long since superseded that one, and very minimal paranoia was required to connect the sudden change in Tom to the radiating presence, two doors down the hallway, of a full-chested, creamy-skinned, regularly menstruating twenty-four-year-old. If Leila had lived alone with Pip, she might have been happy to see the girl making herself at home, going braless under her sweatshirt after showering, digging her bare feet between sofa cushions while she lay and worked with the tablet device DI had issued her, the shampoo fragrance of her damp hair filling the room. But with Tom in the mix, the spillage of Pip around the house made Leila feel merely old.

The girl was doing nothing wrong, just being herself, but Leila could feel herself turning against her, envying her time alone with Tom, envying that she, not Leila, was getting to enjoy him. She believed that both he and Pip liked her too much to betray her, but it didn't matter. Scarcely more than minimal paranoia was needed to imagine that Pip's physical resemblance to Tom's ex-wife had reawakened something in him, was curing him of his post-traumatic aversion to Anabel's type, making it possible for him to again be attracted to it, and that this type was more truly his type, and that his preference for Leila's type had been, all along, a reaction against the awfulness of his marriage: that Pip was the perfect avatar of young Anabel, his fundamental type without any Anabel baggage. When he'd asked Leila if she would mind his taking Pip to *One Night in Miami*, since Leila was going to be in Washington, she'd felt pinioned by her circumstances. How could she object to Tom going out with Pip when she herself spent so much time at Charles's? Still gave the man hand jobs from time to time! She was stuck with an embittered wheelchair dude and could buy herself free time only at the cost of sleeping fewer hours, while Pip, who had no other friends, and Tom, who left the office promptly at seven every night, had plenty of free time and could hardly be faulted for spending it with each other.

Her resentment would have been more demonstrably irrational if she hadn't persisted in feeling secondary in Tom's inner life. Guilt wasn't the only reason she'd stayed married to Charles. She'd never quite got over her suspicion that, however much Tom loved her for her own sake, it mattered to him that she hadn't been young when he met her; that Anabel couldn't fault him for being with her. Just as Anabel couldn't fault him for operating an impeccably worthy news service with the money her father had left him. These moral considerations were still operative in him, and so her commitment to Charles continued to be strategic, a way of ensuring that she, too, like Tom, had someone else. But she was ruing it now.

The girl seemed largely unaware of her jealousy. Midway through her second Manhattan, the night before Leila had left for Washington, Pip had gone so far as to declare that Tom and Leila gave her hope for humanity.

"Say more," Tom had said. "I think I can speak for Leila in saying we'd both like to offer hope to humanity."

"Well, the work you do, obviously," Pip said, "and the way you go about it. But all I've ever seen of couples is bad things. Either it's lies and misunderstanding and abusiveness, or it's this stifling, I don't know, *niceness*."

"Leila can be stiflingly nice."

"I know. You're making fun of me. But it's like, with the really close couples I know, there's no room for anybody else. It's all about their wonderfulness as a couple. There's kind of an old-sock smell to them, a this-morning's-pancakes smell. I'm trying to say it's nice for me to see it doesn't have to be that way."

"You're making us very proud of ourselves."

"Don't tease her for giving us a compliment," Leila said crossly.

"Anyway," Pip said.

They were in Tom's kitchen, and Leila, sensitive to Pip's vegetarian inclinations, was making a zucchini frittata for dinner. Both she and Tom had noticed that whenever food was about to be sautéed, Pip went upstairs and shut the door of her bedroom. "You seem to be very sensitive to smells," Tom said now. "Pancake smells, sock smells . . ."

"Smell is hell," Pip said. She raised her Manhattan glass as if toasting the sentiment.

"I used to be married to someone who felt that way," Tom said.

"But smell is also heaven," Pip said. "I found that—" She stopped herself.

"What?" Leila said.

Pip shook her head. "I was just thinking about my mother."

"Is she a super-smeller, too?" Tom said.

"She's super anything to do with sensitivity. And she tends to be depressed, so smell is always hell for her."

"You're missing her," Leila said.

Pip nodded.

"Maybe she'd like to come out here and visit you."

"She doesn't travel. She doesn't drive, and she's never set foot on an airplane."

"She's afraid of flying?"

"It's more like she's one of those mountain people who never leaves the mountains. She said she'd come to my college graduation, but I could tell how nervous the idea made her, riding the bus or asking somebody to take her, and I finally told her she didn't have to. She was incredibly apologetic, but I could tell she was also incredibly relieved. And Berkeley's not even two hours away."

"Ha," Tom said. "I would have loved not having my mother at my college graduation. She herself described it as the worst day of her life."

"What happened?" Pip said.

"She had to meet the person I ended up marrying. It was a very bad scene."

He said more about the scene, and Leila could hardly listen to it, not because she'd heard the story before but because she *hadn't*. He'd had a decade-plus to tell her the story of his college graduation, and she was hearing it only as he recounted it to Pip. She wondered what other interesting things he'd told the girl while she was not around.

"You know, the wine's not working for me," she said from the stove. "Will you make me a Manhattan?"

"I'll do it," Pip said eagerly.

Leila had been drinking more since she'd met Pip. At the dinner table that night, she found herself ranting about the false promise of the Internet and social media as substitutes for journalism—the idea that you didn't need Washington journalists when you could read the tweets of congressmen, didn't need news photographers when everyone carried a phone with a camera, didn't need to pay professionals when you could crowdsource, didn't need investigative reporting when giants like Assange and Wolf and Snowden walked the earth . . .

She could feel herself targeting Pip with her rant, losing her cool by way of attacking Pip's noncommittal coolness, but there was an undercurrent of grievance with Tom as well. He'd told her, a long time ago, that he'd met Andreas Wolf in Berlin, back when he was still married. All he would say was that Wolf was a magnetic but troubled person, with secrets of his own. But the way he said it gave Leila the impression that Wolf had meant a great deal to Tom. Like Anabel, Wolf belonged to the dark core of Tom's inner life, the pre-Leila history against which she contended. Because she appreciated that he didn't poke and probe her, she didn't poke or probe him. But she couldn't help noticing how closely Tom guarded his memories of Wolf, and she felt some of the same competitive jealousy she did toward Anabel.

This had already come to the surface a year ago, when she'd been honored with an interview by the *Columbia Journalism Review*. In response to a question about leakers, she'd laid into the Sunlight Project rather viciously. Tom was unhappy with her when he read the interview. Why antagonize the true believers who had nothing better to do with their days than to mischaracterize the "Luddites" who disagreed with them? Wasn't Denver Independent just as wedded to the Internet as the Sunlight Project was? Why expose herself to cheap criticism? Leila had thought but hadn't said: *Because you don't tell me anything.*

As she continued her Manhattan-fueled rant at the dinner table, extending it to male-dominated Silicon Valley and the way it exploited not only female freelancers but women more generally, seducing them with new technologies for chitchat, giving them the illusion of power and advancement while maintaining control of the means of production—phony liberation, phony feminism, phony Andreas Wolf—Pip stopped eating and stared unhappily at her plate. Finally Tom, himself quite drunk, interrupted.

"Leila," he said. "You seem to think we don't agree with you."

"*Do* you agree with me? Does Pip agree with me?" She turned to Pip. "Do you have an actual opinion to offer on this?"

Pip's eyes widened and stayed fixed on her plate. "I understand where you're coming from," she said. "But I guess I don't see why there can't be room for both journalists and leakers."

"Exactly," Tom said.

"You don't think Wolf is competing with you?" Leila said to him. "Competing and *winning*?" She turned to Pip again. "Tom and Wolf have a history."

"You do?" Pip asked.

"We met in Berlin," Tom said. "After the Wall came down. But that has nothing to do with this."

"Really?" Leila said. "You hate Assange, but somehow Wolf gets a free pass. Everyone gives him a free pass. He gets carried around on people's shoulders and hailed as a hero and a savior and a mighty feminist. And I don't buy it for one second. I especially don't buy his feminism."

"No other leaker in the last decade has broken a bigger and better variety of stories. You're just annoyed because he has as good a record as we do."

"Uploading some dentist's selfies of his thingy in the face of a female patient on Propofol? I guess you could call that a feminist act. But maybe *feminist* isn't the *best* word to describe an upload like that?"

"He does better things than that. The Blackwater and Halliburton leaks were game changers."

"But always with the same flimflam. Shining his pure light on a world of corruption. Lecturing other men on their sexism. It's like he wants there to be a world full of women and only one man who understands them. I know that kind of guy. They give me the creeps."

"What happened in Berlin?" Pip said.

"Tom doesn't talk about it."

"That's true," Tom said. "I don't talk about it. Do you want me to talk about it now?"

Leila could see that the only reason he was offering was that the girl was there.

"With you here," she said to Pip with a wretched little laugh, "I'm learning all sorts of things I didn't know about Tom."

Pip, no dummy, sensed the danger. "I don't need to hear about Berlin," she said. She reached for her wineglass and managed to knock it over. "Shit! I'm so sorry!"

Tom was the one to jump up and get paper towels. Charles, even before his accident, would have let Leila mop up the wine—Charles who almost never taught books by women, while Tom hired more female journalists than male ones. Tom was a strange hybrid feminist, behaviorally beyond reproach but conceptually hostile. "I get feminism as an equal-rights issue," he'd said to her once. "What I don't get is the theory. Whether women are supposed to be exactly the same as men, or different and better than men." And he'd laughed the way he did at things he found silly, and Leila had remained angrily silent, because she was a hybrid the other way around: conceptually a feminist but *one of those women* whose primary relationships had always been with men and who had benefited professionally, all her life, from her intimacy with them. She'd felt attacked by Tom's laughter, and the two of them had been careful never to discuss feminism again.

Another thing not spoken of, in a life of things unspoken, a life that Leila had enjoyed until the girl became a part of it. Pip seemed very happy to be with them and had stopped making noises about returning to California; it wouldn't be so easy to get rid of her. But Leila, to her sorrow, had started wishing that they could.

When the plane touched down in Denver, she checked her work email and then her texts. There was one from Charles: Does Cesar exist?

As soon as she was off the plane, she called him. "Is César there yet?"

"Still not," Charles said. "It's a matter of indifference to me, but I know how you like to bite them people's heads off. And nibble on they tiny feet."

"Fuck these people. What is so hard about getting someone to show up?"

"Rowrr!"

César, the new aide, was supposed to have been at Charles's at six to give him a bath, PT, and a hot dinner. It was now eight thirty. The trouble with Charles was that he didn't like having aides but didn't dislike it so much that he forbade Leila to employ them and oversee them. As a result, she did a lot of work for little thanks.

Striding down the concourse, she called Tom's home number and was shunted straight to voice mail. Next she called the agency.

"People Who Need People, this is Emma," said a girl who sounded about twelve.

"This is Leila Helou and I want to know why César isn't at Charles Blenheim's."

"Oh hi, Mrs. Blenheim," Emma said cheerfully. "César should have been there at six."

"I'm aware of that. But he was not there at six. He's still not there."

"OK, no problem. I'll see if we can find out where he is."

" 'No problem'? It is a problem! And this is not the first time."

"I'll find out where he is. It's really no problem."

"Please stop saying 'no problem' when we have a problem."

"We're a little shorthanded tonight. One sec . . . Oh, I see what happened. César had to fill in for another aide who got sick. He should be getting to Mr. Blenheim's pretty soon."

The agency couldn't foresee a staff shortage? Thought it was OK to send someone three hours late and not notify them? Made a practice of pulling aides off scheduled visits and sending them to other clients? Didn't even train its desk personnel to apologize?

Leila knew better than to ask these questions. She was halfway into the city when Emma called back. "OK, so, unfortunately it looks like César won't be able to get away. But we do have someone else we can send out. She can't do lifting, but she can help Mr. Blenheim with other things and keep him company."

"Mr. Blenheim doesn't need company. Mr. Blenheim only needs lifting."

"OK, no problem. Let me reach out to César again."

"Just forget the whole thing. Send a male aide out at nine tomorrow morning, and never mention the name César to me again. Can you do that for me? Is it no problem?"

Charles was perfectly capable of feeding himself and getting himself into bed, and Leila could feel that she was spiting herself by letting Tom and Pip enjoy an extra hour or two at home without her. But she did it anyway. She found Charles sitting in his chair in the hallway off his kitchen, where he'd randomly stopped. A smell of canned beef stew was in the air.

"God, you look depressing," she said. "Why are you sitting in the hallway?"

"I've become kind of obsessed with this nonexistent César. There's that great passage in Proust where Marcel talks about imagining the face of the girl you've only glimpsed from behind. How beautiful the unseen face always is. I have yet to experience the disappointing reality of César."

"You must have been on your way somewhere when you stopped here. Maybe you want to go there?"

"It's been nice getting better acquainted with the hallway."

"What do you need?"

"A real bath, but that's not going to happen. I suppose I could have a drink. Haven't played the drink card yet."

He wheeled himself into the living room, and she brought him his bottle and a glass.

"You should run along to your guy and your gamine," he said.

"First tell me what else I can do for you."

"You didn't have to come here at all. In fact, it's interesting that you did. Is everything OK on the other home front?"

"Things are fine."

"You've got that parenthetical frown between your eyebrows."

"I'm just really tired."

"I don't know your guy—haven't had the pleasure. But the gamine has a daddy thing. Even the wheelchair dude was getting somewhere, in the few short minutes you gave me with her. I've always had a knack for bringing out daddy issues."

"Huh. Thanks for that."

"I didn't mean you." He frowned. "Was that what I was for you? Daddy?"

"No. But I probably did have issues."

"None that I could smell the way I could with this girl. I'd advise keeping close watch."

"Have you ever been tempted to leave a thought unspoken?"

"I'm a writer, baby. Voicing thought is what I'm poorly paid and uncharitably reviewed for."

"It just seems like it must get very tiring."

When she finally arrived at Tom's, the only light she could see was from the kitchen. She loved his house and had made herself at home in it, but its very niceness was eternally a reminder that Anabel's father's money had paid for part of it. This may have been why she felt reluctant to so much as hang a picture of her own choosing in it, and why, for years, she'd tried to get Tom to accept rent checks from her. Since he refused them, she instead paid for Charles's caregivers and sent large sums to EMILY's List, to NARAL and NOW and Barbara Boxer, to ease her feminist conscience.

At the back door, before she went inside, she massaged the skin between her eyebrows, feeling grateful, not sore, that Charles had told her she was frowning. It occurred to her that she'd stayed married to him less for reasons of guilt or strategic balance than because she simply couldn't bear to part with a person who still loved her.

The kitchen was empty. Water simmering in the pasta pot, an untossed salad on the island countertop. "Hell-o-oh," she called with the silly lilt with which she and Tom announced arrivals.

"Hello," Tom called from the living room, without the lilt.

She wheeled her suitcase out to the front hall. It took her a moment, in the semidarkness, to see Tom stretched out on the sofa.

"Where's Pip?" she said.

"Pip is out with the interns tonight. I drank too much, waiting for you, and had to lie down."

"I'm sorry I'm so late. We can eat right away."

"No rush. There's a drink for you in the freezer."

"I won't pretend I don't want it."

She took her suitcase upstairs and changed into jeans and a sweater. Maybe it was only because she'd expected to find Pip here, but the house seemed ominously sound-swallowing, the banalities of homecoming unreverberating. When she went back downstairs and claimed her drink, Tom was still on the sofa.

"You got my text," she said.

"I did."

"Two women are dead. The guy in the middle of it is probably dead, too. It's a drug story as well as a nukes story. Really scary stuff."

"That's great, Leila."

He sounded far away, but she drank her drink and gave him the details. He said the right things in response, but not in the right voice, and then a silence fell. The house was so quiet that she could hear the faint rattle of the pasta-pot lid.

"So what's happening," she said.

It was a while before Tom answered. "You must be very tired."

"Not so bad. The drink is waking me up."

A longer silence fell, a bad one. She felt as if she'd walked into someone else's life, someone else's house. She didn't recognize it. Pip had done something to it. Suddenly the distant rattle of the pot lid was unbearable.

"I'm going to go turn the stove off," she said.

When she came back, Tom was upright on the sofa, rubbing his eyes with one hand and holding his glasses in the other.

"You want to tell me what's going on?" she said.

"Always Listen to Leila."

"What's that mean?"

"It means you were right. Having her here was a bad idea."

"How so?"

"It's making you unhappy."

"A lot of things do. If that's all it is, let's move on."

Silence.

"So, she's uncannily like Anabel," Tom said. "Not the personality but the voice, the gestures. When she yawns, it could be Anabel yawning. Same thing when she sneezes."

"Not knowing Anabel, I'll have to take your word for that. Do you want to have sex with her?"

He shook his head.

"You sure?"

To her dismay, he seemed to need to think about it.

"Oh, fuck," Leila said. "*Fuck.*"

"It's not what you think."

It was as if, all of a sudden, with no warning, she were vomiting. The wave of rage, the old fighting feeling.

"Leila, there's—"

"Do you have any idea how sick of this life I am? Do you have the foggiest fucking clue? What it's like to live with a man still haunted by a woman he hasn't seen in twenty-five years? To feel like the sum of what I mean to you is that I'm not her?"

He didn't have to rise to this. He knew how to stay cool

and to defuse. But he must have drunk quite a lot before she came home.

"Yeah, I do, a little bit," he said unsteadily. "A little bit, yeah. I know what it's like to sit around here waiting all evening while you stop and see your husband for no reason."

"His caregiver didn't show up."

"That's funny. Who could have foreseen such a thing? When has a thing like that ever happened before?"

"It's unfortunate that it happened tonight."

"Nothing I'm not used to."

"Well, good, because it's never going to change. Why would I change it now? Why did I even come home? Why didn't I stay over with a person who's never going to hurt me? Who never hurts me. A person I'm number one with."

"Why not indeed?"

"Because I'm not in love with him! And you know it. This has nothing to do with Charles."

"No, it does, a little bit, I think."

"Nothing, nothing, nothing. I take care of Charles because he needs me. You hold on to Anabel because you never stopped loving her."

"That is preposterous."

"It's preposterous to deny it. I could see it the first second I saw you and Pip in the same room. *No one stays haunted by a person they're not still in love with.*"

"I'm not the one still giving my husband hand jobs."

"God!"

"If indeed that's all you give him."

"God damn it! I knew I never should have told you!"

"Never mind the telling. I'm talking about the doing. You don't think there's a bit of a double standard here?"

"I told you because it didn't matter. You yourself said it didn't matter. You said it was no different than feeding him mashed peas with a spoon. Those were your exact words."

"I'm just saying, Leila. Don't talk to me about being haunted. You practically have to invent reasons to be over there with him."

"He needs care."

"He doesn't even *want* half the things you do for him."

"Well, I'm sorry, but you had your chance. You had your chance to give me someone more appropriate to take care of. And the only reason you didn't—"

"Ah. Here we go."

"The only reason you didn't—"

"There were a lot of good reasons, and you know it."

"The only reason you didn't is Anabel. Anabel, Anabel, Anabel. What is so wonderful and amazing about Anabel? Please answer me. I'd like to know."

He sighed heavily. "After the first couple of years, I was almost never happy with her. I'm almost always happy with you. You make me happy every time you walk into the room."

"Like when I walked in just now? That made you happy?"

"Right now we seem to be having a fight."

"Because Anabel's in the house—you said it yourself. Same voice, same gestures. You can be happy with me as long as we're alone, but put her in the same house with us—"

"I already said it was a mistake to bring Pip here."

"So in other words: Yes. Yes, I'm only good enough as long as you're not reminded of her."

"Not true. Wholly wrong."

"You know what I feel like doing? I feel like letting the two of you live here alone and work it out. I can live with my husband, she can have the daddy she never had, and you can have a nice fresh incarnation of the woman you never got over. You can listen to her yawns and imagine you're with Anabel."

"Leila."

"I'm actually not kidding. I'm thinking that's what I might do. It's kind of refreshing to think of not having to be the boss's mistress for a change. To not have that be *the very first thing* that every new intern learns about me. Maybe I can make some new female friends while I'm at it, so I don't have to walk around feeling like such an embarrassing betrayal of the sisterhood. There are a whole lot of things I could do with five more nights and one less man in my week."

"Leila."

"In fact, I've already got my bag packed. You can wait up for Pip. I'll go home—*home*." She drained her drink and stood up. "In case you hadn't noticed, I'm not so into her anymore."

"I've noticed. She's noticed, too."

"Oh, that's great."

"She went out tonight so you and I could be alone. Hence the irony and irritation of your important business at your husband's. But she's not stupid. She's not insensitive."

"No, she's lovely in every way. Why not go ahead and fuck her brains out?"

"The last thing she wants is to come between us. She looks up to you—"

"Have a baby with *her*, now that you've expended all your guilt on me—"

"She looks up to you, and she can sense that you don't want her here. It's making her miserable."

"You know, that's very nice. But I don't like hearing that you talk about me, and I like even less that you're doing it. Maybe you can do me a favor and talk about Anabel instead."

"You're upset," he said. "I'm upset. I got pissed off and jealous waiting for you. I'm sorry about that. You come home with huge news, you're understandably exhausted, and what do we do? We fight."

"Oh, I'll be back. You know I will. It's just, every once in a while, I come up against how much I hate this life, even though it's a good life. Do you feel that, too?"

He shook his head.

"I'm worn out," she said. "And I have to work all weekend. Right now, the only thing I can think is that there's a little room that's all mine, one hundred percent mine, and it's not here. I'm sorry."

He sighed again. "Before you go?"

"Yeah?"

"Try not to get angry when I say this."

"Just hearing that, I start to get angry."

He set his glasses on a cushion and covered his face with his hands, rubbing his eyes.

"You're going to think I buried the lede," he said. "You're going to think I'm insane. But I think she might be my daughter."

"Who might be your daughter?"

He put his glasses back on and stared straight ahead. A ghost was in the room with them. "It's not possible," he said. "I don't have a daughter, and even if I somehow did, what are the chances of her living under my roof?"

"Zero."

"Exactly."

"And so?"

"She's Anabel's daughter," he said. "Her mother is definitely Anabel. And I'm the father. I'm pretty sure of that, too."

Leila had to sit down to steady the room. "That can't be."

"Now you see why I was so impatient for you to get home."

Even sitting down, she could feel the floor tilting beneath her, as if it were trying to tumble her out of the house. Was it possible that everything was over? That she would go home to Charles and never come back? It seemed possible.

"It started with 'Smell is hell,'" Tom said. "And the fact that her mother is nutty and living underground. And so, on Wednesday, after the theater, I asked her why her mother changed her identity. She said her mother's afraid that her father will 'take her away from her.' Sound like Anabel? More than a little, right? And so I asked her if she had a picture of her mother—"

"I don't want to hear it," Leila said.

"And she did, on her phone."

"I really don't need to hear this." She was already thinking that if Tom had known that Anabel had a kid, he wouldn't have been so averse to having one himself. Already thinking that this was the end of her and him.

"So who's the father?" Tom said. "I'll spare you the details, but there's no way it could be me. And yet I'm pretty sure it's me."

"Why is that."

"Because Pip is the right age, and because I know Anabel. The way she vanished makes more sense now, knowing she was pregnant—"

"I'll say this one more time. It is a torture for me to hear about Anabel."

Tom sighed. "I can't tell you how strange it was to see her picture on Pip's phone. I only looked for one second, but one second was enough. I don't know what I said, but Pip was completely casual about it. She wasn't trying to hide anything. I asked to see the picture, she showed it to me. Which makes me think—"

"She has no idea."

"Exactly. Either that, or she's a really good liar. Because

I started to think about the boyfriend thing, the fact that she lied to us. It made me wonder if she *does* know who I am."

"You didn't ask her?"

"I wanted to talk to you first."

Leila thought of the emergency cigarettes that she kept in the freezer. The drink had stunned her. Tom's news had stunned her.

"This has nothing to do with me," she said dully. "This is your life, your real life, the life that matters to you. I was always just a sideshow. Even if you didn't want your real life back, it's coming to get you. And you don't have to worry about me—I know how to exit quietly."

"I would like nothing better than to never see Anabel again."

She gave a brittle laugh. "It sounds like you'll be seeing quite a lot of her now."

"Pip's a good researcher. It's possible she managed to figure out who Anabel is, which led her to me. But if she's good enough to figure that out, she's good enough to figure out that there's a billion-dollar trust set up in Anabel's name."

"A billion dollars."

"If Pip knew about it, she wouldn't be here in Denver. She'd be trying to get her mother to pay off her miserable little student loan. Which tells me that she doesn't know anything."

"A billion dollars. Your ex-wife is worth a billion dollars."

"I've told you that."

"You told me it was a *lot*. You didn't say a billion dollars."

"That's just a guess, based on McCaskill's revenues. It was already pushing a billion when her father died."

Leila was accustomed to feeling slight, but she didn't think she'd ever felt slighter than she did at this moment.

"I'm sorry," Tom said. "I know it's a lot to hear."

"A lot to hear? You have a *child*. You have a daughter you didn't know about for twenty-five years. A daughter who's living under your own roof now. I'd say, yes, that's quite a lot for me to hear."

"This doesn't have to change anything."

"It's already changed everything," Leila said. "And it'll be good. You can normalize things with Anabel, have a nice relationship with Pip, stop being haunted. Spend your holidays together. It'll be great."

"Please. Leila. I need you to help me think about this. *Why did she come to Denver?*"

"I have no idea. Bizarre coincidence."

"No way."

"OK, so she knows, and she's a good liar."

"You really believe she's that good?"

She shook her head.

"So she doesn't know," Tom said. "And if she doesn't know . . . then how the fuck did she end up in our house?"

Leila shook her head again. Whenever the time came to vomit, it wasn't just the thought of food that sickened her; it was the thought of wanting *anything*. Nausea the negation of all desire. And so, too, fighting. She was remembering the old desolation and feeling it again now, the conviction that love was impossible, that however deeply they buried their conflict it would never go away. The problem with a life freely chosen every day, a New Testament life, was that it could end at any moment.

Moonglow
Dairy

But smell had also been heaven. Not outside the airport of Santa Cruz de la Sierra, where the waftings of cow shit from adjacent pastures mingled with the smellable inefficiencies of engines banned from California long before Pip was born; not in the Land Cruiser sure-handedly piloted by a taciturn Bolivian, Pedro, through diesel particulates on the city's ring boulevards; not along the Cochabamba highway, where every half kilometer another brutally effective speed bump gave Pip a chance to smell fruit rotting and things frying and be approached by the sellers of oranges and fried things who'd installed the speed bumps in the first place; not in the swelter of the dusty road that Pedro veered onto after Pip had counted forty-six bumps (*rompemuelles* Pedro called them, her first new word in Spanish); not when they reached a ridge and headed down a narrow road as steep as anything in San Francisco, the noontime sun boiling plastic volatiles out of the Land Cruiser's upholstery and vaporizing gasoline from the spare can in the cargo area; but when the road, after plunging through dry forest and through cooler woods half cleared for coffee plantings, finally bottomed out along a stream leading into a little valley more beautiful than any place Pip could have imagined: then the heaven had commenced. Two scents at once, distinct like layers of cooler and warmer water in a lake—some intensely flowering tropical tree's perfume, a complex lawn-smell from a pasture that goats were grazing—flooded through her open window. From a cluster of low buildings on the far side of the valley, by a small river, came a trace of sweet fruitwood smoke. The very air had a pleasing fundamental climate smell, something wholly not North American.

The place was called Los Volcanes. There were no volcanoes, but the valley was enclosed by red sandstone pinnacles five hundred meters high or more. The sandstone absorbed water during the rainy season and released it year-round into a river that meandered through a pocket of wet forest, an oasis of jungle in otherwise dry country. Well-maintained trails branched through the forest, and during Pip's first two weeks at Los Volcanes, while the other Sunlight Project interns and employees did their shadowy work and she had only small menial jobs to do (because Andreas Wolf was away, in Buenos Aires, and she hadn't yet had the entry interview at which he told new interns what to do), she hiked the trails every morning and again late in the afternoon. To keep herself from dwelling on what she'd left behind in California, the piteous maternal cries of "Purity! Be safe! Pussycat!" that had followed her down the lane when she left for the airport, she immersed herself in smells.

The tropics were an olfactory revelation. She realized that, coming from a temperate place like the other Santa Cruz, her own Santa Cruz, she'd been like a person developing her vision in poor light. There was such a relative paucity of smells in California that the interconnectedness of all possible smells was not apparent. She remembered a college professor explaining why all the colors the human eye could see could be represented by a two-dimensional color wheel: it was because the retina had receptors for three colors. If the retina had evolved with four receptors, it would have taken a three-dimensional color *sphere* to represent all the ways in which one color could bleed into another. She hadn't wanted to believe this, but the smells at Los Volcanes were convincing her. How many smells the earth alone had! One kind of soil was distinctly like cloves, another like catfish; one sandy loam was like citrus and chalk, others had elements of patchouli or fresh horseradish. And was there anything a fungus couldn't smell like in the tropics? She searched in the woods, off the trail, until she found the mushroom with a roasted-coffee smell so powerful it reminded her of skunk, which reminded her of chocolate, which reminded her of tuna; smells in the woods rang each of these notes and made her aware, for the first time, of the distinguishing receptors for them in her nose. The receptor that had fired at Californian cannabis also fired at Bolivian wild onions. Within half a mile of the compound were five different flower smells in the neighborhood of daisy, which itself was close to sun-dried goat urine. Walking the trails, Pip could imagine how it felt to be a dog, to find no smell repellent, to experience the world as a seamless many-dimensional landscape of interesting and interrelated scents. Wasn't this a kind of heaven? Like being on Ecstasy without taking Ecstasy? She had the feeling that if she stayed at Los Volcanes long enough she would end up smelling every smell there was, the way her eyes had already seen every color on the color wheel.

For a week, because nobody was paying much attention to her, she let herself go a little nuts. In the evening, after the sudden fall of tropical night, she tried to interest the other young women at dinner (which was breakfast for the hacker boys) in her olfactory discoveries, her pursuit by nose of previously unsmelled smells, and her theory that there was actually no such thing as a bad smell: that even the supposedly worst smells, like human shit or bacterial decay or death, were bad only out of context; that in a place like Los Volcanes, where the smellscape was so richly complete, it might be possible to find the good in them. But the other girls—every one of whom was, perhaps not incidentally, beautiful—seemed not to have noses like hers. They agreed that the flowers and the rain smelled nice here, but she could see them exchanging glances with one another, forming judgments. It was like her first week in college dining hall all over again.

She was only slightly below the median age of the Project staff. She was surprised by how many of the others mentioned *making the world a better place* when she asked why they were working for Andreas. She thought that, however laudable the sentiment was, this particular phrase ought to have been ridiculed off the face of the earth by now; apparently a sense of irony was low on the list of employment qualifications here. If Pip had been Andreas, she might have started to make the world a better place by hiring some females to do tech work. With the exception of a beautiful gay male Swede, Anders, who had some journalism chops and wrote the digests of the Project's leaks, the division of labor by gender was perfect. The boys went to a windowless and heavily secured building beyond the goat pasture and wrote code there, while the girls hung out in the refurbished barn and did community development and PR and search-engine optimization, source verification and liaising, website and bookkeeping chores, research and social media and copywriting. To a person, they had backgrounds more fascinating than Pip's. They were Danish and British and Ethiopian, Italian and Chilean and Manhattanite, and they appeared to have spent their college years not going to class (they'd already read and reread *Ulysses* at twelve while attending private academies for the supergifted) but taking semesters off from Brown or Stanford to fabulously work for Sean Combs or Elizabeth Warren, combat AIDS in sub-Saharan Africa, or sleep with college-dropout founders of billion-dollar Silicon Valley start-ups. Pip saw that TSP couldn't possibly be creepy or cultish, because the other young women weren't the kind who made mistakes.

Her own history and expectations were achingly unfabulous. She asked people if Annagret had recruited them, but nobody had heard of Annagret. They'd all come to Bolivia by personal referral or direct application. Pip attempted to amuse them by telling the story of Annagret's questionnaire and ended up feeling like a complainer. The others weren't complainers. If you were incredibly attractive and privileged and wanted only to make the world a better place, complaint was unbecoming.

At least the animals were poor like her. She befriended Pedro's dogs and tried to get the goats to like her. There were blue iridescent butterflies the size of saucers, smaller ones in every color, and tiny stingless bees whose hive on the back veranda of the main building, Pedro said, produced a kilo of honey every year. Prowling the riverbank and pursuing agoutis was an adorable dark-furred mini-wolverine sort of mammal that Pedro's dogs, though twice its size, were very afraid of. The forest was populated with Dr. Seuss birds, huge guans that clambered in fruit trees, tinamous that tiptoed in the shadows. Screeching acid-green parakeets executed group dives from cliff faces, their wings hissing loudly as they swooped past. Circling at the zenith were condors, wild condors, not captive-bred like the ones in California. Taken together, the animals reminded Pip that she was an animal herself; the multitude of shames she'd left behind in Oakland seemed of smaller consequence at Los Volcanes.

And the place was amazingly clean. What looked from a distance like litter would turn out to be a fallen paper-white blossom, or fluorescent orange fungi shaped like industrial earplugs, or a dew-covered spiderweb imitating a scrap of cellophane. The river, which flowed out of a vast uninhabited park to the north, was clear and swimmably warm. Pip bathed in it before dinner and then got even cleaner in the well-water shower in the four-person room she'd been assigned. The room had white walls, red tile floors, and exposed beams cut from timber that had fallen on the property. Her roommates were a little messy but not dirty.

The word around the compound was that Andreas was in Buenos Aires for the shooting of the East Berlin scenes for a movie that was being made about him. The word was that he was having an affair with the American actress Toni Field, who was playing his mother in the movie, and that the affair, which had been rumored in the press, was good PR for the Project. "It's his first movie star," Pip's roommate Flor explained to her one night. "All the women he has affairs with stay loyal to him, even after he ends them, so this should open doors for us in Hollywood."

"Which presumably is a good thing?" Pip said.

Flor was a tiny American-educated Peruvian; if Disney ever made an animated feature for the South American market, its heroine would look like her. " 'Every hand is raised against the leaker,' " she said. "That's the first thing you learn from him. We take our friends wherever we can find them."

"Nice for him that he does the dumping and women do the staying loyal."

"His own loyalty is to the Project."

"You know, my mother was convinced he only brought me down here to have sex with him."

"That won't happen," Flor said. "You'll see when you meet him. He's all about the work we do. He would never do anything to compromise it."

"So it's about avoiding bad press?"

"I'm sorry if you're disappointed."

"I'm not disappointed. But he did come on pretty strong in his emails."

Flor frowned. "He sent you emails?"

"Yeah, a whole bunch of them."

"That would be unusual for him."

"Well, I emailed him first. Annagret gave me his address."

"Do you have a lot of experience in work like this?"

"No, none. I'm more like somebody who wandered in off the street."

"Who is this Annagret?"

"Somebody he apparently used to sleep with. I just assumed everyone here had taken her questionnaire."

"She must be somebody from before he set up in Bolivia."

Pip was seeing Annagret in a new and sadder light, as a middle-aged person inflating her importance to the Project, playing up her past importance to Andreas, remaining loyal after being discarded.

"Before Toni Field," Flor said, "it was Arlaina Riveira. And Flavia Corritore, who writes for *La Repubblica*. Philippa Gregg, who wanted to be his biographer—I don't know what the status of that book is. And before that it was Sheila Taber—she's got the most followers on Twitter of any professor in America. All these people are helping us now."

It seemed to Pip that Flor was enumerating Andreas's successful women to punish her for getting emails from him.

The first person after Pedro to be nice to her was an older girl, Colleen, who smoked cigarettes and had her own private bedroom in the main building. Colleen had grown up on an organic farm in Vermont and was, it went without saying, very pretty. She was TSP's business manager, overseeing the kitchen and Pedro and the other local staff. Because she reported directly to Andreas, and because social status at TSP appeared to be a function of proximity to him, whatever table she sat down at for dinner was the first to fill up. She was different from the rest, and Pip wondered what the secret was of being different in a way that attracted people, as opposed to her own way.

Colleen always had two cigarettes after dinner, on the back veranda, where Pip had taken to sitting and listening to the frogs and owls and stridulators, the nocturnal orchestra. Colleen neither said much to her nor seemed to mind her being there. After her second cigarette, she went back inside and spoke to the staff in a Spanish whose fluency made Pip feel envious and discouraged. She didn't wish she were any of the other women, because it would have meant forsaking irony, but she could see wanting to be Colleen.

One night, between cigarettes, Colleen broke her silence and said, "It's a crap world, isn't it?"

"I don't know," Pip said. "I was just sitting here thinking it's amazingly beautiful."

"Give it time. You're still in sensory overload."

"I don't think I'll ever get tired of it."

"It's all crap."

"What's crap about it?"

In the dark, Pip heard the scrape of a lighter, the smoker's gasp. "Everything," Colleen said. "We're a clearinghouse for crap. Nobody leaks good news. All we get is crap news, day after day, crap pouring in. It wears you down."

"I thought the idea was that sunlight disinfected it."

"I'm not saying it shouldn't be done. I'm saying it wears you down. The infinite variety of human badness."

"Is it possible you've been here too long? How long have you been here?"

"Three years. Almost since the beginning. I've become the resident depressed person, it's practically my whole function. Everyone else can look at me and think, *Thank God I'm not like her*, and feel good about themselves."

"You could leave."

"Yeah. I could leave."

"What's he like?" Pip said. "Andreas?"

"He's an asshole."

"Really."

"I'm saying that purely descriptively. How could he not be? To do a thing like TSP, you have to be an asshole."

"But you still can't leave."

"I'm being strung along. I'm aware of it every minute of the day, that he's stringing me along. It's approaching *Guinness Book of World Records* proportions, my willingness to be strung along. I get to be first among nobodies to him. I have my own room. I even know where the money comes from."

"Where does the money come from?"

"I get to be the most special of the never-to-be-special. He really knows how to play a person."

A silence fell. Frogs in the night were calling, calling, calling.

"So what brings you here?" Colleen said. "You seem a little challenged in the entitlement department. I mean, compared to the others."

Pip, grateful to be asked, poured out her story, omitting nothing, not even her recent hideous actions in Stephen's bedroom in the squatter house.

"So basically," Colleen summarized, "you don't know what the fuck you're doing here."

"I'm looking for my other parent."

"That should stand you in good stead. Having something besides a hunger for Dear Leader's love and approval. My advice? Keep your eyes on what you came for."

Pip laughed.

"What?"

"I was just thinking about Toni Field," Pip said. "It's like if they were making a movie about me and I was sleeping with the actor who played my father. Isn't that a little weird? Sleeping with the person who's playing his mother?"

"He's a weird dude. Ours is not to wonder why."

"I think it would be very weird. But Flor seems to think it's some outstanding coup."

"Flor's like some single-minded carnivore whose meat is fame. She doesn't need money—her family owns half of Peru. They're big in minerals. She's like, 'Fame? Do I smell fame? Is there fame here? Will you share it with me?' To her, Andreas hooking up with Toni Field is almost as good as hooking up with Toni Field herself."

Pip was thrilled to be dishing, even though the mechanism was dismal, her feeling specially confided in by Colleen, who herself was treated specially by Andreas, who was off in Buenos Aires having sex with his virtual mother. To impress Colleen, she said she was going down to the river and swim.

"Now?" Colleen said.

"You want to come with me?"

"Not sure I'm up for being attacked by the *hurón*."

"He always runs away when I see him."

"He's just trying to lull you into the water at night."

"I'm going to do it." Pip stood up. "You sure you don't want to?"

"I hate dares."

"I'm not daring you. Just asking."

Pip waited in suspense for Colleen's answer. For all her disadvantages in life, she did have the advantage of having swum in the dark a lot, at the swimming hole in the San Lorenzo, in Henry Cowell Redwoods State Park, on summer nights when the temperature lingered in the eighties and the river hadn't yet dried out and scummed over. Oddly enough, her mother had often swum with her, perhaps because her body was less *visible* at night. Pip remembered the surprise of realizing, while her mother floated on her back in her black one-piece bathing suit, that her mother had once been a girl like her.

"OK, fuck it," Colleen said, standing up. "I'm not going to let you win this."

The moon had risen above the eastern pinnacle, whitening the lawn and making the darkness under the trees by the river even inkier. To get to the bathing spot, Pip and Colleen crossed the water on a chainsaw-hewn plank that was tethered by a rope to a tree in case of flooding. While she undressed, Pip sneaked glances at Colleen. Her hunched shoulders, her almost cowering posture, suggested a body image more like Pip's own and less like those of her roommates, who stepped out of the shower with their shoulders thrown back and their heads held high.

Colleen put a toe in the river. "Where did I get the idea this water is warm?"

Pip did what had to be done, which was to run and dive and fully submerge herself. She remembered the feeling of expecting to be bitten by any number of things, at any moment, and the pleasure, then, of not being bitten; the emergence of trust in the dark water. Colleen, still cowering, her moonlit arms folded across her chest, stepped forward and sank slowly to her knees, like an Aztec virgin submitting not very happily to sacrificial death.

"Isn't it great?" Pip said, paddling about.

"Horrible. Horrible."

"Put your head all the way under."

"No fucking way."

"This has got to be the most beautiful place on earth. I can't believe I get to be here."

"That's because you haven't met the snake yet."

"Just dive. Get your head under."

"I'm not like you, nature girl."

Pip reared up, feeling all fleshy appendage, and grabbed Colleen by the arm.

"Don't," Colleen said. "I mean it."

"OK," Pip said, letting go.

"This is what I do, this is who I am. I go in up to my knees and no farther. I get the worst of both worlds."

Pip clothed herself in water again. "I know the feeling," she said. "But I'm not having it right now."

"I don't see how you're not afraid of being mauled by the *hurón.*"

"It's the upside of having poor impulse control."

"I'm going to go have another cigarette," Colleen said, leaving the water. "Just scream with blood-curdling terror if you need me."

Pip thought Colleen would change her mind, but she didn't. Left by herself, enveloped by the chirping of frogs and the murmur of flowing water and the smells, the smells, Pip experienced a moment of happiness purer than any she'd ever felt. It had to do with being naked in clean water and far away from everything, in a remote valley in the poorest country in South America, but also with her courage to be alone in the river, as contrasted with Colleen's neurotic fear. It made her feel grateful to her mother, made her miss her and wish that she could be here, floating near her. The love that was a granite impediment at the center of her life was also an unshakable foundation; she felt blessed.

She continued to feel blessed on subsequent evenings, on the back veranda, as she learned more about Colleen's crap childhood. The farm in Vermont was something between collective and cult, the land owned by her father, who fashioned himself as a cross between Henry David Thoreau, a many-wived biblical patriarch, and the psychologist Wilhelm Reich. His ongoing self-actualization took the form of leaving the farm in Colleen's mother's hands for months at a time, returning with younger women who helped him channel his orgone energy into the farm's rocky soil, to make it more fecund, and randomly knocking up Colleen's mother. Colleen was homeschooled until she turned sixteen and ran away, first to Boston and then to Hamburg, in Germany, where she worked as an au pair. Then she attended Wellesley on a full scholarship and graduated when she was still just twenty-two. The irony of her position now, performing a role similar to her mother's at a patriarchal place, wasn't lost on her. She seemed almost to revel in the crappiness of it.

Pip, for her part, felt she was finally finding a friend who could understand her own strange childhood. She was attracted to Colleen's cigarette-smelling darkness, and now she didn't have to worry about where she sat at dinner, because Colleen saved the place next to hers. She could tell that Colleen liked her sarcasm, and she played it up for her. Colleen invited her to her room, which was sweet and low-ceilinged, to dish and drink beer and watch TV shows streamed over the private fiber-optic line that Andreas had obtained in a deal to upgrade Bolivian army comms. If Colleen had been a boy, Pip would have slept with him. As it was, she was going to bed long after midnight, waking up late and somewhat hungover, and blowing off her morning hikes.

Then one night, after returning from a hike so long that she'd done the last part of it by feel in the dark, she went to the dining room and saw that her usual place beside Colleen had been taken by Andreas Wolf. Her heart jumped at the sight of him. He was listening seriously to another woman at the table, listening and nodding, and Pip immediately got what Annagret's boyfriend had meant about his charisma. It was partly a matter of his still-boyish German good looks, but there was an ineffable something else, a glow of charged fame particles, or a self-confidence so calm and mighty it altered the geometry of the dining room, drawing every sight line to itself. No wonder Colleen didn't care whether he was an asshole. Pip wanted to keep looking at him herself.

Colleen was slouched low in her chair, her face averted from Andreas, and was tapping a finger on the table, her food untouched. Pip was hurt that she hadn't saved the place to her other side for her. She took the only available seat, beside her roommate Flor. A bowl of beef stew was being handed around the table, along with the usual yuca and potatoes and onion and tomatoes. Pip had basically thrown in the towel on vegetarianism. At least the beef in Bolivia was grass-fed.

"So Dear Leader is back," she said.

"Why do you call him that?" Flor said sharply. "This isn't North Korea."

"She does it because Colleen does it," a person named Willow said.

Pip felt slapped in the face. "It's good to see we're evolved past eighth grade."

"You can bet Colleen would never say 'Dear Leader' to his face," Willow said.

"I bet you'd be wrong," Pip said. "I bet he'd just laugh. I was insulting in my emails, and it wasn't like my invitation was retracted."

Flor did some private, not-nice eye-widening, and Pip saw that she wasn't doing herself any favors by continuing to mention her email correspondence with Andreas.

"Why even stay here if you're just going to be negative?" Willow said.

"What does it say about this place that a little bit of humor is so threatening?"

"It's not threatening. It's boring. *30 Rock* already did North Korea. The laughs have been had."

Never having seen *30 Rock*, Pip was rejoinderless and squished. All through dinner, fame and charisma rays from the direction of Andreas warmed the back of her neck. She knew she ought to hurry and go back to her room, to return Colleen's snub and not appear needy, but she also wanted to meet Andreas, and so she lingered at the table, eating two lime-flavored custards, after the others had left. Behind her, Andreas and Colleen were speaking German. This finally made her feel so excluded and irrelevant that she pushed away from her table and headed for the door.

"Pip Tyler," Andreas said.

She turned back. Colleen was looking aside again, tapping her finger, but Andreas's blue eyes were on her. "Come sit down with us," he said. "We haven't met."

"I'll be on the veranda," Colleen said, standing up.

"No, stay with us," Andreas said.

"Need to smoke."

Colleen left the room without a glance at Pip. Andreas beckoned to her. "Will you have an espresso with me?"

"I didn't even know there *was* espresso here."

"All you have to do is ask. Teresa!"

Pedro's wife, Teresa, stuck her head out of the kitchen, and Andreas raised two fingers. Pip sat down in the chair farthest from him at his table. The nerve she'd had in writing emails to him was so far gone that she didn't even want to shake his hand. She just hunched her shoulders and waited to be spoken to.

"Colleen tells me you've been enjoying yourself here."

She nodded.

"Did I not tell you it's the most beautiful place?"

"No, you definitely told me."

"I'm sorry I wasn't here when you arrived. Making the Argentinean capital look like nineteen-seventies East Berlin—they needed a lot of advice."

"It's cool that they're making a movie about you."

"Very strange but, yes, very cool. Also very dull. You stand around for ten hours waiting for twenty minutes of action, and even then you don't see it directly. You're at the back of a crowd in a trailer, trying to see a monitor."

"Still and all," Pip said.

"Still and all, intensely gratifying to the ego."

"I'm guessing it's in pretty good shape, your ego."

"No complaints."

Pedro's wife came out with two espressos, and Andreas told her in Spanish that she was looking very well. Teresa, normally the picture of long-suffering, appeared inordinately grateful for the compliment, and Pip caught a glimpse of how the world must seem to Andreas: like one of those stadium crowds where every person had a colored board that they could flip in concert with everyone else and form messages. The message he was forever getting was that he was special and great. He walked into the stadium, and suddenly the sea of random bodies became the words WE LOVE YOU, MAN. Pip felt a prickle of resentment.

"So what's Toni Field like?" she said.

"Lovely. Talented."

"She's playing your mom, right?"

"Yes."

"Was your mom as hot as Toni Field?"

Andreas smiled. "I knew I was going to like you."

Pip was trying to stay mindful of *asshole*, of *stringing along*. "What's that mean?"

"You ask good questions. You're more angry than careful."

She didn't know what to say to this.

"I'm tired," he said. "We'll do your entry interview in the morning." He drained his espresso cup. "Unless you feel you've had your vacation and just want to go home."

"Not yet."

"Good. Come to the barn in the morning."

When he was gone, Pip went out to the veranda and sat down by Colleen, who was staring at the dark river. The night was warm, and so many frogs were chirping that the wall of their sound was seamless.

"So the cat's back," Pip said. "Does this mean the mice don't get to play anymore?"

Colleen lit her second cigarette and didn't answer.

"Is it just me," Pip said, "or are you giving me a weird vibe?"

"I'm sorry," Colleen said. "Have you ever seen a man ballroom-dancing with a woman who's passed out? I feel like that woman. He moves my arms, he leads me around the floor. My head's flopping like a rag doll's, but I'm doing the usual dance moves. Like everything's OK. Good old Colleen, still running the show."

"I thought you might be mad at me for something."

"No. Pure self-absorption."

This was some consolation to Pip, but not much. She'd alienated all the undark girls by getting closer to Colleen, but Colleen was too dark to get very close to. In little more than two weeks, she'd managed to replicate her social situation in Oakland.

"I thought we could be friends," she said.

"I'm not worth it."

"You're the only person here I like."

"That feeling is fairly mutual," Colleen said. "But you know what I'm going to do, one of these days, when they least expect it? I'm going to go back to the States and work for a big law firm and marry some dull guy and have kids with him. That's the future I'm postponing."

"Don't you have to go to law school first?"

"I have a law degree from Yale."

"Criminy."

"I keep hanging on here, hoping there's some more interesting existence for me. But there isn't. It's only a matter of time before I go and do the gutless thing. The boring thing."

"A great job and a family doesn't sound so bad to me."

"You should do something better with the guts you've got."

"I don't usually think of myself as having guts."

"People with guts seldom do."

They listened to the frogs for a while.

"Can I keep sitting here with you?" Pip said.

"*Criminy.* You're the first person I've ever heard say *criminy*." Colleen lifted a hand, hesitated, and then patted Pip's hand. "You can keep sitting here."

In the morning, after an early hike, Pip went looking for Andreas. The tech building, where the boys worked, was powered by a special generator situated in a sound-proofing bunker and fueled by a natural gas line, courtesy of the Bolivian government, that branched off a ten-inch pipeline that ran along the ridge. The barn and the other buildings were powered by micro hydroelectric and a field of solar panels halfway up the access road. Andreas was much admired for declining to have a private office. He underscored that the Project was a collective, not a top-down organization, by working on a laptop in the barn's loft, where there were sofas and a kitchenette that anyone could use. Pip picked her way through the panoply of female beauty on the main floor, all the girls mousing and clicking, many of them in pajama bottoms that they would wear all day, and climbed the stairs to the loft.

Andreas was in conference with further girls in pajama bottoms. "Ten minutes," he said to Pip. "Feel free to join us."

"No, I'll wait outside."

Scraps of morning cloud and mist were shredding themselves on the sandstone pinnacles, the sun gaining the upper hand; the world here seemed created afresh every day. Pip sat on the grass and watched a bird with a long forked tail follow the goats, eating flies. It would do this all day; its job and its place in the world were secure. Pedro, crossing the lawn with a chainsaw and one of his sons, gave Pip a friendly wave. He seemed similarly secure.

Andreas came outside and sat down by her. He was wearing good narrow jeans and a close-fitting polo shirt that emphasized the flatness of his belly. "Nice morning," he said.

"Yah," Pip said. "The sunlight feels especially disinfectant today."

"Ha."

"You know, I've always hated the word *paradise*. I thought it was just stupid born-again-speak for *dead*. But now I'm having to rethink that, a little bit. Like that bird there—"

"Our fork-tailed flycatcher."

"It seems perfectly contented. I'm starting to think paradise isn't eternal contentment. It's more like there's something eternal about feeling contented. There's no such thing as eternal life, because you're never going to outrun time, but you can still escape time if you're contented, because then time doesn't matter. Does that make any sense?"

"A lot of sense."

"So I envy animals. Dogs especially, because nothing smells bad to them."

"I'm glad you like it here," Andreas said. "Did Colleen get your automatic wire transfers sorted out?"

"Yes, thank you for that. Bankruptcy is being staved off as we speak."

"So let's talk about what you might do for us."

"Besides being the resident dogperson? I already told you what I really want. I want to find out who my father is, or at least what my mother's real name is."

Andreas smiled. "I see how that helps you. But how does it help the Project?"

"No, I know," Pip said. "I know I have to work."

"Do you want to be a researcher? There's a lot you could learn from Willow. She's fantastic at finding things."

"Willow doesn't like me. Actually, nobody here much likes me, except Colleen."

"I don't believe that."

"Apparently I'm too sarcastic. I wrinkle my nose at the Kool-Aid. I also talk about smell too much."

"Nobody here has ill intentions. Every person here is extraordinary in some way."

"You know, that's the first actually creepy thing you've said to me."

"How so?"

"If I were in charge of your image management? I'd hire some fat people, some ugly people. I wouldn't set up camp in the most beautiful valley on earth. It gives me the creeps, all this beauty. It makes me not like you."

Andreas stiffened. "Well, we can't have that, can we."

"Well, or maybe we can. Maybe not liking you is the way I can be helpful. I'm pretty sure I'm not the only person who'd be creeped out by the scene here. Didn't you tell me you wanted me to help you understand how the world sees you? I can be your personal disliker. I have some real skills in that line."

"It's funny," he said. "The more you dislike me, the more I like you."

"I got that from my last boss, too."

"There are no bosses here."

"Oh, please."

He laughed. "You're right—I'm the boss."

"Well, and as long as we're being honest, I never paid much attention to your Project. What the world thinks of it is your problem, not mine. I mean, it's nice you wanted me here. But the main reason I came is because Annagret said you could help me answer my questions."

"You don't admire the Project even a little bit?"

"Maybe I don't understand it yet. I'm sure it's very admirable. But some of your leaks are so small, it's almost like those revenge-on-the-cheating-boyfriend websites."

"That's a bit harsh, don't you think? We were just discussing a new upload—Australian government emails on the subject of endangered species. Wallabies, parrots. How to pretend to care about protecting them while they sell them out to the ranchers and hunters and mining interests. This is not a trivial leak. But the only way we get it, the only way we remain relevant, is by delivering the goods every day. We have to do the small things to get the big things."

"I agree that it's too bad about the endangered animals of Australia," Pip said. "But I'm still smelling something else."

"Ah, this nose of yours. What exactly is it telling you?"

She thought before she answered. She didn't really want to be his personal disliker—she could see what a tiring and alienating job it would be. She'd come to Bolivia willing to admire the Project; it was mainly the chokingly high admiration levels of the other interns that made her hostile. And yet her hostility did help her stand out from the crowd. It could be a way to gratify her own miserable little ego and be liked by him.

"There was this place," she said. "This dairy called Moonglow Dairy, near where I lived when I was growing up. I guess it was a real dairy, because they had a lot of cows, but their real money didn't come from selling milk. It came from selling high-quality manure to organic farmers. It was a shit factory pretending to be a milk factory."

Andreas smiled. "I don't like where you're going with this."

"Well, you say you're about citizen journalism. You're supposedly in the business of leaks. But isn't your real business—"

"Cow manure?"

"I was going to say fame and adulation. The product is you."

In the tropics, there was a specific minute in the morning when the sun's warmth stopped being pleasant and turned fierce. But this minute hadn't arrived yet. The perspiration popping out on Andreas's face had come from something else.

"Annagret was right," he said. "You really are the person I wanted here. You have courage and integrity."

"I bet you say that to all the girls."

"Not true."

"Not to Colleen?"

"Yes, all right." He nodded slowly, his eyes on the ground. "Maybe to Colleen. Does that make it easier for you to believe me?"

"No. It makes me want to go pack my suitcase. Colleen is totally unhappy."

"She's been here too long. It's time for her to move on."

"And now you need a new Colleen? To exploit and string along? Is that the idea?"

"I feel bad for her. But I didn't do anything to her. She

wants something I've always been very clear about not being able to give her."

"That's not how she tells it."

He raised his eyes and looked at her. "Pip," he said. "Why don't you like me?"

"It's a fair question."

"Is it because of Colleen?"

"No." She could feel her self-control slipping away. "I think I'm just generally hostile these days, especially with men. It's a problem I'm having. Couldn't you tell from my emails?"

"Tone is hard to judge in emails."

"I was fairly happy here until last night. And now suddenly it's like I'm back in all the shit I tried to run away from. I'm still an angry person with poor impulse control. I'm sure it's great what you're doing for the wallabies and parrots—right on, Sunlight Project. But I'm thinking I should go and pack my suitcase."

She stood up to leave before she had a full-on outburst.

"I can't stop you," Andreas said. "All I can do is offer you the truth. Will you sit down again and let me tell you the truth?"

"Unless the truth is very long, I might stay standing up."

"Sit down," he said in a much different voice.

She sat down. She was unused to being commanded. She had to admit that it was kind of a relief.

"Here are two true things about fame," he said. "One is that it's very lonely. The other is that the people around you constantly project themselves onto you. This is part of why it's so lonely. It's as if you're not even there as a person. You're merely an object that people project their idealism onto, or their anger, or what have you. And of course you can't complain, can't even talk about it, because you're the one who wanted to be famous. If you try to talk about it anyway, some angry young woman in Oakland, California, will accuse you of self-pity."

"I was just calling it like I saw it."

"Everything conspires to make the famous person ever more alone."

She was disappointed that his truth had to do with him, not her. "What about Toni Field?" she said. "Do you feel lonely with her? Isn't that why famous people marry each other? To have someone to talk to about the terrible pain of being famous?"

"Toni's an actress. Sleeping with her is a mutually flattering transaction."

"Wow. Does she know that's how you think about it?"

"We both know the terms of the transaction. Those have been the terms for me with everyone since Annagret. Things were different with Annagret because I was nobody when I met her. It's the reason I trust her. It's the reason I trusted her when she told me we should invite you here."

"I didn't trust her at all."

"I know. But she saw something special in you. Not just talent but something else."

"What does that even *mean*? The more you try to tell me the truth, the weirder this gets."

"I'm simply asking you to give me a chance. I want you to keep being yourself. Don't project. Try to see me as a person trying to run a business, not some famous older man you're angry with. Take advantage of the opportunity. Give Willow a chance to teach you some research skills."

"I'm really questioning this Willow idea."

Andreas took her hands in his and looked into her eyes. She didn't dare do anything with her hands except leave them completely limp. His eyes were beautifully blue.

Even subtracting the vision-distorting effects of his charisma, he was a good-looking man.

"Do you want some more truth?" he said.

She looked aside. "I don't know."

"The truth is that Willow will be extremely nice to you
if I tell her to be. Not fake nice. Genuinely nice. All I have
to do is press a button."

"Whoa, whoa," Pip said, pulling her hands away.

"What am I supposed to do? Pretend it's not true? Deny
my own power? She projects like crazy onto me. There's
nothing I can do about it."

"Whoa."

"You came here for truth, didn't you? I think you're
strong enough to hear it undiluted."

"Whoa."

"Anyway," he said, standing up. "I'll see you at lunch."

The sun had turned fierce. Pip fell over onto her side
as if pushed by the force of its heat, her head swimming.
She felt as if, for a moment, she'd had her skull opened
up and her brains given a vigorous stir with a wooden
spoon. She was still a long way from submitting to him,
a long way from being his for the taking, but for a moment he'd been deep enough inside her head that she could
feel how it could happen—how Willow might change her
feelings like an octopus changing color, just because he
told her to, and how Colleen could be trapped in a scene
she hated by a wish for a thing she knew she'd never get
from a person she thought was an asshole. For a moment,
an appalling divide had opened up in Pip. On one side
was her good sense and skepticism. On the other was a
whole-body susceptibility different in category from any
she'd experienced. Even at the height of her preoccupation with Stephen, she hadn't wanted to be his *object*;
hadn't fantasized about *submitting* and *obeying*. But these

were the terms of the susceptibility that Andreas, his fame and confidence, had revealed in her. She understood better why Annagret had been so contemptuous of Stephen's weakness.

She forced herself to sit up and open her eyes. Every color around her was both itself and blazing white. In the forest beyond the river, the chainsaw was moaning. How could she have imagined that she had any idea where she was? She had no idea. The place was a cult the more diabolical for pretending not to be one.

She stood up and returned to the barn, appropriated the nearest free tablet, and took it down into the riverside shade. Every second day since her arrival, she'd sent a cheerful email to her mother at her neighbor Linda's address. Linda had written back a few times, reporting that her mother was "kinda low" but "hangin' in there." Pip had concocted the fiction that it was impossible to make phone calls from Los Volcanes—what was the point of being here if she had to call her mother every day?—and she hesitated now before activating TSP's equivalent of Skype. To break down and call her mother was almost to admit that she couldn't survive here, that she was already on her way out. But the situation seemed to qualify as urgent. She didn't like having her brains stirred with a wooden spoon.

"Pussycat? Is everything all right?"

"Everything's fine," Pip said. "Pedro had to go into town for supplies. I'm calling from a pay phone there. Here, I mean. Here in town."

"Oh, I can't believe I'm hearing your dear voice. I thought it could be months and months before I did."

"No, well, here it is."

"Dearheart, how are you? Are you really all right?"

"I'm great. You can't imagine how beautiful everything

is, I made a friend, Colleen, I told you about her, she's really smart and funny—she has a law degree from Yale. Everyone here is well educated. Everyone has parents they're in touch with."

"Do you know when you're coming home yet?"

"Mom, I just got here."

There ensued a silence in which she imagined her mother remembering her purpose in coming to Bolivia, the angry things she'd said before leaving with her suitcase.

"So anyway," Pip said, "Andreas came back last night. Andreas Wolf. I finally got to meet him. He's actually really nice."

Her mother said nothing, and so Pip chattered on about the movie in Buenos Aires, about Toni Field and other Wolf women, hoping to imply that he wasn't preying on the interns. That she wanted to imply this, when the whole reason she'd called her mother was that she was afraid of being preyed on, was a good illustration of their relationship.

"So anyway," she said.

"Purity," her mother said. "He's a lawbreaker. Linda printed out an article for me to read. He's in very serious trouble with the law. His fans don't seem to care about that—they think he's a hero. But if you break the law, just by helping him, you might never be able to come home. You need to think about this."

"I haven't seen any reports of interns returning in handcuffs."

"Violating federal law is not a joke."

"Mom, everyone here is seriously rich and well educated. I really don't think—"

"Maybe their families can afford expensive lawyers. I'm not going to have a good night's sleep until you're safely back home."

"Well, at least now you've got some *reason* for not sleeping."

This was a moderately cruel thing to say, but Pip could now see, as she should have seen before she made the mistake of calling, that her mother had nothing helpful to offer.

"Whoops," she said. "Pedro's waving to me—gotta go."

She was heading up to the barn when Willow came out of it. She was wearing a polka-dot jumper in which she looked oppressively fantastic.

"Hey Willow how's it going."

"Pip, I need to talk to you."

"Oh, Christ, let me guess. You want to apologize."

Willow frowned. "For what?"

"I don't know—for being mean to me last night?"

"I wasn't being mean. I was being honest."

"Jesus. Fuck me."

"Seriously," Willow said. "What did I say to you that wasn't honest?"

Pip sighed. "I don't even remember. I'm sure you're right."

"Andreas just told me that he wants us to work together. I think it's a great idea."

"Yeah, I bet you do."

"What do you mean?"

"He told you to like me, and now you like me. How am I not supposed to find that creepy?"

"I already wanted to like you," Willow said. "We all did. It's just that your hostility is kind of hard to take."

"It's who I am. It's what I live and breathe."

"Well, then, explain it to me. If I understand better where it's coming from, it won't bother me anymore. Do you want to go for a walk now and tell me about it?"

"Willow." Pip waved a hand in front of her eyes. "Hello? You're totally creeping me out. You're fucking with my head. You were mean to me last night—my senses did not deceive me. And now you want to be my friend? Because Andreas told you to?"

Willow laughed. "He told me to remember that you're funny—that that's the way your mind works. And he's right. You're really funny."

Pip broke away and marched up toward the barn. Willow ran after her and grabbed her by the arm.

"Let go of me," Pip said. "You're worse than Annagret."

"No," Willow said. "We're going to be spending a lot of time together. We have to find a way to like each other."

"I'm never going to like you."

"Why not?"

"You don't want to know."

"I do want to know. I want you to be honest. That's the only way this works. Come sit with me and tell me everything you hate about me. I already told you I don't like your hostility."

To Pip there seemed to be only two choices, either pack her bag or do what Willow asked. If she hadn't called her mother, she might have imagined there was something to go home to. But she'd come here hoping to get information, she hadn't got it yet, and according to both Colleen and Andreas she had courage. So she sat down with Willow in the shade of a flowering tree.

"I hate that you're way prettier than I am," she said. "I hate that there were always these alpha girls and you're one of them and I'm not. I hate that you went to Stanford. I hate that you don't have to worry about money. I hate that you'll never really get how privileged you are. I hate that you love the Project and aren't bothered by how weird this place is. I hate that you don't have to be snarky. I hate that you can't imagine what it's like to be poor and owe money, and have a depressive single parent, and be so angry and weird that you can't even have a boyfriend—oh, never mind." Pip shook her head with disgust. "This is obviously all just my own self-pity."

But Willow's face had become a purplish-red prune of hurt. "No," she said. "No. You're only saying what I've always known people think about me."

She squeezed her eyes shut and began to cry. Pip was horrified.

"I didn't *ask* to be pretty," Willow snuffled. "I didn't *ask* to be privileged."

"No, I know," Pip said consolingly. "Of course not."

"What can I do to make up for it? What can I possibly ever do?"

"Well. Actually. Do you happen to have a hundred and thirty thousand dollars you can spare?"

Willow smiled while continuing to cry. "That's funny. You really are funny."

"I take it that's a no."

"I suffer, too, you know. Believe me, I suffer." Willow took Pip's hands and rubbed her palms with her thumbs. It seemed to be a Sunlight Project thing, this invasive grabbing of hands. "But can I be really honest with you?"

"Seems only fair."

"There's another reason I sort of hate you. It's because he likes you."

"He seems to like you, too."

Willow shook her head. "The way he talked to me about you—I could tell. Even before that, I could tell. You obviously didn't care about the Project. And then, when we heard he writes you emails . . . It's going to be a little hard to work with you, knowing how much he likes you."

A complex fear was stealing over Pip, the fear that Andreas really did specially like her, along with the fear of being disliked for it; of having to apologize for it, especially to Colleen. "OK," she said. "Now *I'm* starting to feel guilty."

"It's no fun, is it?"

Willow smiled and leaned forward and gave her a sisterly hug. Pip had the corrupt sensation of being bought off with the prospect of the friendship of an alpha girl, the promise of social acceptance. But she was no longer *distrusting* Willow. This seemed like a step forward.

In the evening, on the veranda, Pip told Colleen almost everything the day had brought.

"Willow's by no means the worst," Colleen said. "Did she tell you one of her brothers was killed three years ago?"

"God, no."

"Snowboarding accident. She's still on major meds. And of course this is known to the Wolf. The Wolf can always spot the weak lamb in the flock."

Pip was impressed, almost confounded, that Willow hadn't played the dead-brother card with her. Had simply sat there under the tree and taken her punishment. It spoke to the intensity of whatever Andreas had said to her.

"I'm understanding a little better how you're stuck here," she said.

"Yeah, well. From what you're telling me, I suspect my days have been numbered since you got here."

"Colleen. You know I'd rather be your friend than his."

"You say that now. But he's only been back for one day."

"I don't want to be here if you're not here."

"Really? If what you need is time away from your mother, you should try to hold out longer than two weeks."

"I don't have to go back to California. Maybe we could both go somewhere else."

"I thought you had a missing parent to find."

"Maybe Flor can give me a hundred and thirty thousand dollars, and then I won't have to."

"You've got a lot to learn about rich people," Colleen said. "Flor won't even share her dental floss."

When Pip went to the barn the next morning, after her early hike, Willow was outwardly unchanged and yet seemed like a different person, a fragile person on anti-depressants, a guilty survivor of her little brother's death. This time it was Pip who initiated the hug. She couldn't tell whether it was good that she'd overcome some of her hostility or sordid that she was now on hugging terms with a member of the in crowd; whether she was evolving or being corrupted. But Willow's research chops were awesome. She typed and moused and clicked so rapidly, bouncing among so many windows at once—Australian property transfers, rosters of Australian corporate direc-torships, Australian business-news archives, dark-Web Australian government databases—that Pip could see it would be weeks before she could follow what Willow was doing in real time.

Andreas didn't speak to her privately that day, nor the next day, nor for ten days after that. He was constantly conducting hushed powwows with the other girls, com-ing and going between the barn and the tech building, and having long informational conversations with Willow while Pip sat beginnerishly in a chair beside her. That he ignored only her, as if to emphasize that she was the only intern not contributing materially to the Project, was ob-viously deliberate. He was obviously trying to sharpen her appetite for further personal contact, further moments of intoxicating honesty. But she couldn't bring herself either to confront him or to resent him. He'd got inside her head with a wooden spoon. She wanted more of what he was withholding. Not a whole lot more, she told herself. Just another taste, to be reminded of how it felt—to see if he could have that effect on her a second time.

And then one night he was gone again.

"Toni Field came to town," Colleen explained after dinner.

"Really? To Santa Cruz? Why didn't she just come here?"

"It's part of his firewall between business and recreation. And apparently Toni needs special handling. She's a little too into him. Doesn't seem to understand who gets to set the rules. She way overstepped them by following him to Bolivia. He's probably terminating their relationship as we speak. In the nicest way imaginable, of course."

"He told you that?"

"He tells me a lot, sister. I'm still first among nobodies. Don't you be forgetting that."

"I hate you."

"You're kind of breaking my heart here, Pip. I gave you fair warning about him. And now you say a thing like that."

Two mornings later, returning from her hike, Pip found Pedro waiting for her with the Land Cruiser on the grass in front of the main building. She still couldn't understand every word Pedro said, but she gathered that El Ingeniero (as he called Andreas) wanted her to join him in Santa Cruz right away.

"*¿Yo? ¿Está seguro?*"

"*Sí, claro. Pip Tyler. Va a necesitar su pasaporte.*"

Pedro was impatient to leave, but she begged permission to take a shower and put on fresh clothes. She was so out of her head that she found herself shampooing her hair a second time without intending to. She couldn't even frame the question of why she'd been summoned. Her thoughts were jostling fragments. Too late to ask Colleen if interns ever traveled with Andreas. Too late to ask Pedro if she was supposed to bring anything but her passport, or what she should wear. She looked down at her left palm and saw that she'd filled it with shampoo a third time.

The inbound drive felt less epically long than the outbound had. Civilization reassembled itself in the form of dusty roadwork, cheap loudspeakers blasting *música valluna*, billboard ads for mobile devices, posses of kids in school uniforms, a deepening particulate pall. Not until they were into Santa Cruz's ringed boulevards, passing stores that were simply small warehouses with the front wall removed, did Pip hazard to ask Pedro why he supposed El Ingeniero wanted her in town.

Pedro shrugged. "*Negocios. Él siempre tiene algún 'negocito' que atender.*"

In a less raw and more shaded neighborhood was a low-rise hotel called the Cortez. Pedro helped her register and instructed her to wait in her room for a call from El Ingeniero. She searched Pedro's face for evidence of custodial worry, but he just smiled and told her to enjoy the city.

She'd never stayed in a hotel. Wandering through the lobby and bar, her knapsack on her shoulder, she heard conversations in English and possibly Russian. Out in the courtyard were jacaranda trees and a large fiberglass stork whose belly was a pay phone. She thought she saw Andreas at a table by the swimming pool, but it wasn't him.

Having her own hotel room, cleaned expressly for her, was possibly the happiest-making gift she'd ever been given. There was a *desinfectado*-certifying strip of paper across the toilet seat, crisp paper wrappings on the drinking glasses, a TV, a built-in air conditioner, a minibar, total luxury. She remembered her high-school friends' descriptions of Hawaiian resorts, her college friends' raptures about room service, and how deprived she'd felt listening to them. Even poor people sometimes stayed at Motel 6. But her mother wouldn't travel, and while her friends were taking spring-break road trips she'd always dutifully gone home to Felton.

She kicked off her shoes and rolled around on the bed, luxuriating in the cleanness of the pillowcases. She closed her eyes and saw a tropical highway with *rompemuelles*. She expected the phone to ring soon, but it didn't, and so she lay for a while and listened to Aretha. She tried to watch soap operas that her Spanish wasn't quite up to. She drank a beer from the minibar and finally cracked the Barbara Kingsolver novel that Willow had pressed on her. The sunlight in her window was mellowing to apricot by the time Andreas called.

"Good, you're there."

"Yah," Pip said. Her voice sounded sultry from hours in a hotel-room bed. There was a bit of the wooden spoon simply in his having made her stay in bed all day.

"I had a very long meeting with an assistant defense minister."

"That's impressive. What about?"

"I'll be in the bar. Come down when you can."

When she hung up the phone, her hands were shaking, her whole arms, really, from the shoulders down. Again the sensation of having no idea where she was. She could *almost* see the thing her mother had claimed to see, the not-right thing about Andreas's interest in her. The swiftness with which she'd arrived at this moment, the straightness of the line from Annagret's questionnaire to a room at the Hotel Cortez, definitely gave her a feeling of no-control. And yet she'd emailed Andreas of her own free will. She'd come to Bolivia for good reasons of her own, and there was honestly nothing so outstanding or attractive about her. Was it simply that she was proving to be the weakest lamb?

Andreas was at a table in a corner of the bar, typing on a tablet. As Pip crossed the room, she heard the words

Toni Field from a table of three American businessmen.
They were looking at Andreas, and it compounded her
disorientation to be the person plunking her unfamous self
down by him. He typed a little more before he turned off
the tablet and smiled at her. "So," he said.

"Yeah, so," she said. "This is fully weird."

"Do you want a drink?"

"Can we stay here if I don't?"

"Certainly."

She crossed her arms to suppress their shaking, but this
only transferred the shaking to her jaw. She felt quite
miserable.

"You look terrified," Andreas said. "Please don't be. I
know this seems strange to you, but I brought you here
for business only. I needed to talk to you, and I can't do it
at home. I've created a beehive of surveillance there."

"There's always the woods," Pip said. "I seem to be the
only one who walks in them."

"Trust me. This is better."

"Trust is kind of the opposite of what I'm feeling now."

"I'm telling you: this is business. How are you liking
working with Willow?"

"Willow?" She glanced over her shoulder at the American men. One of them was still looking at Andreas. "It's
just like you promised. She likes me. Although I do wonder
if she'll still like me after I've been in a hotel with you. I
know Colleen won't. I'm already pretty well compromised
just by being here."

Andreas looked at the Americans and gave them a little
wave. "There's a nice *churrasquería* around the corner.
It will be empty at this hour. Are you hungry?"

"Yes and no."

Walking with the Bringer of Sunlight on the city
streets, carrying her dumb knapsack, she felt like a true
San Lorenzo Valley yokel. A flock of green-and-orange

parrots wheeled overhead, screeching louder than the buses and scooters. She wished that she could join their flock. At the *churrasquería*, in a secluded corner booth, Andreas ordered a bottle of wine. She knew she shouldn't drink, but she couldn't resist.

"Honestly?" she said when the wine was poured. "I don't know why I'm here, but I wish I wasn't."

"It was your choice," he said. "You didn't have to get in the Land Cruiser."

"How was that my choice? You're the boss, you're making my loan payments. You have all the power. You've got everything, I've got nothing. But it still doesn't mean I want to be your special girl."

He watched her drink without drinking from his own glass. "Is it so bad to be special?"

"Have you seen any kids' movies lately?"

"I sat through *Frozen* with a woman I was seeing."

"They're all about being the special one, the chosen one. 'Only you can save the world from Evil.' That kind of thing. And never mind that specialness stops meaning anything when every kid is special. I remember watching those movies and thinking about all the unspecial characters in the chorus or whatever. The people just doing the hard work of belonging to society. They're the ones my heart really goes out to. The movie should be about *them*."

He smiled. "You should have grown up in East Germany."

"Maybe!"

"But what if ordinariness is an unrealistic ambition for you?"

"I'm telling you what you can do to help me, if you really want to help me. Just leave me alone. Don't make me sit around in a hotel room all afternoon, waiting for you. I'd rather be part of the hive."

"That's unfortunate," he said. "I do understand what you're saying. But I need your help, too."

Pip refilled her glass. "OK. I guess we're on to plan B."

"I'm going to tell you something that I've only told one other person, ever. After you hear it, I want you to think about which one of us has the real power over the other. I'm going to give you the power you say you don't have. Do you want it?"

"Oh boy. More truth?"

"Yes, more truth." He looked around the empty restaurant. The waiter was polishing glasses, and dusk had fallen on the street. "Can I trust you?"

"I haven't told anyone about you and your mom's vagina."

"That was nothing. This is something."

He picked up his wineglass, held it in front of his eyes, and drained it.

"I killed a person," he said. "When I was twenty-seven. I killed a man with a shovel. I planned it carefully and did it in cold blood."

The wooden spoon was in her head again, and this time it was worse, because this time it felt as if the disturbance were emanating from his own head. There was torment in his face.

"I've lived with it half a lifetime," he said. "It never goes away."

He looked so anguished, so much like a person, so little like a famous figure, that she reached across the table and squeezed his hand.

"The victim was Annagret's stepfather," he said. "She was fifteen, he was sexually abusing her. He worked for the Stasi, and she had no recourse. She came to the church where I worked. I murdered him to protect her."

What he was saying couldn't possibly be true, but Pip suddenly didn't want to be touching him. She withdrew her hand from his and put it on her lap. One day when she was in high school, an ex-convict had come to talk to her civics class about conditions in California's prison system. He was a well-spoken middle-class white guy who happened to have served fifteen years for shooting his stepfather in the heat of an argument. When he described the trouble he now had with women, the question of whether to cop to being an ex-con and a murderer before a first date, Pip's skin had crawled at the thought of dating him. Once a killer, always a killer.

"What are you thinking?" he said.

"This is very disturbing," she said.

"I know."

"Am I really the only person you've ever told about this?"

"With one terrible exception, yes."

"It's not, like, some initiation thing you do with everyone who works for you?"

"No, Pip. It's not."

She was remembering that after the ex-con had made her skin crawl she'd felt guilty and compassionate for him. How hard it must have been to carry around forever a thing he'd done once on an impulse. She did things on impulse all the time.

"So," she said. "This must be the real reason you trust Annagret."

"That's right. I didn't tell you everything about us."

"Annagret knows what you did."

"Indeed. She helped me do it."

"Criminy."

He refilled their wineglasses. "We got away with it," he said. "The Stasi had suspicions, but my parents protected me. I eventually got the case files, and the case went away. But there was a problem. I made a horrible mistake, after the Wall came down. I met a guy in a bar and told him what I'd done. An American . . ." He covered his face with his hands. "Horrible mistake."

"Why'd you tell him?"

"Because I liked him. I trusted him. I also needed his help."

"And why was it a mistake?"

Andreas lowered his hands. His expression had hardened. "Because now, all these years later, I have reason to think he intends to destroy the Project with his information. He's already made one rather pointed threat. Are you starting to see why I need an intern I can trust?"

"I sure don't see why it's me."

"I can take you to the airport right now. We'll send your bag after you. I'll understand if you want to leave now and never have anything to do with me again. Would you like that?"

Something was very wrong, but Pip didn't know what. It didn't seem possible that Andreas had killed a man with a shovel, but it also didn't seem possible that he would just make up the story. Whether the story was true or not, she sensed that he was trying to do something to her by telling it. Something not right.

"The questionnaire," she said. "You didn't really ever use it with anybody else. It was just for me."

He smiled. "You were a special case."

"Nobody else had to take it."

"I can't tell you how happy I am that you came here."

"But why *me*? Wouldn't you rather have a true believer?"

"Precisely not. We've had some anomalies in our internal network. Little things missing, transmission log discrepancies. This is going to sound extremely paranoid, but it's really only moderately paranoid. I have some reason to worry that we have a journalist embedded with us."

"No, that's fairly high-grade paranoia."

"Think about it. Somebody who wants to come and spy on us would pretend to be the truest of believers. That's how they'd get in. And all I have is true believers."

"What about Colleen?"

"She came as a true believer. I almost completely trust her. But not quite."

"Jesus. You really are paranoid."

"Sure." Andreas smiled again, more broadly. "I'm out of my fucking mind. But this guy who I confessed to in Berlin—who *got* me to confess—he was a journalist. And do you know what he does now? He runs an investigative-journalism nonprofit."

"Which one?"

"It's better if you don't know, at least for a while."

"Why not?"

"Because I just want to you to listen. Keep your ears open, without preconceptions. Tell me your sense of what's going on. I already know you have very good sense."

"So basically be a horrid spy."

"Maybe. If you want to use that word. But *my* spy. The person I can talk to and trust. Would you do that for me? You can keep learning from Willow. We'll still help you try to find your father."

She thought of good old mentally ill Dreyfuss—*There was something not right about those Germans.* She said, "You didn't actually kill anyone, did you."

"No, I did, Pip. I did."

"No, you didn't."

"It's really not a matter of opinion."

"Hmm. And you say Annagret helped you?"

"It was terrible. But yes. She did. Her mother had married a very evil person. I have to live with what I did, but part of me doesn't regret it."

"And if the story comes out, that's the end of Mr. Clean."

"It destroys the Project, yes."

"And the Project is you. You're the product."

"So you say."

Something in Pip's chest spasmed, almost retched. "I don't like you," she said involuntarily. She was having an outburst with no advance warning. She scrambled out of the booth, reached back into it for her knapsack, and ran to the door of the restaurant and out onto the sidewalk. Was she sick to her stomach? Yes, she was. She dropped to her knees beneath a streetlight and spat up a dark rope of liquid.

She was still on her hands and knees when Andreas crouched beside her and put his hands on her shoulders. For a while he didn't say anything, just gently massaged her shoulders.

"We should get some food in you," he said finally. "I think it would help."

She nodded. She was at his mercy—it wasn't like there was anywhere else she could go. And the way he was rubbing her shoulders was undeniably tender. No man old enough to be her father had ever touched her like that. She allowed herself to be led back to the booth, where he ordered her an omelet and french fries.

After she'd eaten part of the omelet, she started drinking again, really putting it away. In the haziness that ensued, there were the actual words he spoke, many more words about his crime, about Annagret, about East Germany, about the Internet, about his mother and his father, about honesty and dishonesty, about his breakup with Toni Field, and then there was the deeper nonverbal language of intention and symbol which constituted the wooden spoon. The working over her brain was getting now was far more prolonged and thorough than the first one. Each of the two languages, the verbal and the non-verbal, kept distracting her from the other, and she was in any case increasingly drunk, and so it was hard to follow what was being said in either language. But when a second bottle of wine had been emptied, and Andreas had paid the waiter, and they'd walked back to the Hotel Cortez, where Pedro was waiting with the Land Cruiser, she found that it didn't matter whether or not she liked Andreas.

"You'll be home by midnight," he was saying. "You can make up whatever story you like. A broken tooth, emergency dental work—whatever you like. Colleen will still be your friend."

Pedro was holding open the door of the Land Cruiser.

"Wait," Pip said. "Can I go to my room and lie down first? Just for an hour. My head's a little spinny."

Andreas looked at his watch. It was clear that he wished she would leave now.

"Just for an hour," she said. "I don't want to be sick on the highway."

He nodded reluctantly. "One hour."

As soon as she was in her room, she felt sick again and threw up. Then she drank a Coke from the minibar and felt much better. But instead of going downstairs, she sat on the bed and waited for some time to pass. Making Andreas impatient seemed to her the only form of resistance available, the only way to assert herself against the spoon. But was resisting what she even wanted? The longer she waited, the more erotic the suspense felt. The mere fact of waiting in a hotel room implied sex—what else was a hotel room for?

When the phone rang, she ignored it. It rang fifteen times before it stopped. A minute later, there was a knock on the door. Pip stood up and opened it, afraid it would be Pedro, but it was Andreas. He was pale, tight-lipped, furious.

"You've been here an hour and a half," he said. "You didn't hear the phone ring?"

"Come in for a second."

He looked up and down the hallway and came in. "I need to be able to trust you," he said, locking the door. "This is not a good start."

"Maybe you just won't be able to trust me."

"That's not acceptable."

"I have poor impulse control. This is a known fact about me. You knew what you were getting into."

Still pale, still angry, he moved toward her, backing her into the corner behind the TV. He grasped her arms. Her skin felt alive to his, but she didn't dare be the one to make the move.

"What are you going to do?" she said. "Strangle me?"

He could have found this funny, but he didn't. "What do you want?" he said.

"What does every girl want from you?"

This did seem to amuse him. He let go of her arms and smiled wistfully. "They want to tell me their secrets."

"Really. I find that hard to relate to, not having any myself."

"You're an open book."

"Pretty much."

He walked away and sat down on the bed. "You know," he said, "it's difficult to trust a person with no secrets."

"I find it hard to trust people, period."

"I'm not happy that Pedro knows I'm up here with you. But now that I'm here, we're not leaving until I know I can trust you."

"Then we could be here quite a while."

"Do you want to hear my theory of secrets?"

"Do I have a choice?"

"My theory is that identity consists of two contradictory imperatives."

"OK."

"There's the imperative to keep secrets, and the imperative to have them known. How do you know that you're a person, distinct from other people? By keeping certain things to yourself. You guard them inside you, because, if you don't, there's no distinction between inside and outside. Secrets are the way you know you even have an inside. A radical exhibitionist is a person who has forfeited his identity. But identity in a vacuum is also meaningless. Sooner or later, the inside of you needs a witness. Otherwise you're just a cow, a cat, a stone, a thing in the world, trapped in your thingness. To have an identity, you have to believe that other identities equally exist. You need closeness with other people. And how is closeness built? By sharing secrets. Colleen knows what you secretly think of Willow. You know what Colleen secretly thinks of Flor. Your identity exists at the intersection of these lines of trust. Am I making any sense?"

"Sort of," Pip said. "But it's a pretty weird theory for a person who exposes people's secrets for a living."

"Were you not listening in the restaurant? I got trapped into this job. I hate the Internet as much as I hated my motherland."

"I guess you did say that."

"Were you not even listening to yourself? I'm not doing this job because I still believe in it. It's all about me now. It's *my* identity."

He made a gesture of self-disgust.

"I don't know what to say to you," Pip said. "I already told you my secret. I told you my real name."

"Your name is nothing to be ashamed of."

"I also went through a shoplifting phase in middle

school. I had quite a masturbation thing going when I was ten."

"Didn't everyone?"

"OK, so there's nothing. I'm boring and ordinary. Like I said, you knew what you were getting into."

Suddenly, without her quite knowing how he'd traversed the distance between them, he was pressing her into the corner again. He had his mouth to her ear and his hand wedged between her legs. There was a weird suspenseful moment of adjustment. She couldn't breathe, but she could hear him breathing heavily. Then his hand moved up to her belly and down again into her jeans and underpants.

"What about this," he murmured in her ear. "Is this not a private thing of yours?"

"Fairly private, yes," she said, heart pounding.

"This is the reason I trust you?"

She couldn't believe what was happening. He was putting a fingertip inside her, and her body wasn't exactly saying no to it.

"I don't know," she whispered. "Maybe."

"Do I have your permission for this?"

"Um . . ."

"Just tell me what you want."

She didn't know what to say, but she probably should have said something, because, in the absence of a response, he was unzipping her jeans with his free hand.

"I know I was asking for it," she whispered. "But . . ."

He drew his head back. There was an avid gleam in his eyes. "But what?"

"Well," she said, squirming a little, "isn't it kind of customary to kiss a person before you stick your finger in her?"

"That's what you want? A kiss?"

"Well, I guess, between the two things, right at this moment, yes."

He brought his hands up to her face and cupped her cheeks. She could smell her own private scent as well as his male body smell, a European smell, not unpleasant. She closed her eyes to receive his kiss. But when it came, she didn't respond to it. Somehow it wasn't what she wanted. Her eyes opened and found his looking into them.

"You have to believe this wasn't why I brought you here," he said.

"Are you sure it's what you want even now?"

"In strict honesty? Not as much as I want to kiss a different part of you."

"Whoa."

"I think you'd like it. And then you could leave, and I could trust you."

"Is this the way you always are with women? Was this how things went with Toni Field?"

He shook his head. "I told you. I'm not myself in transactions like that. I'm showing my true self to you because I want us to trust each other."

"OK, but, I'm sorry—how does this make you trust *me*?"

"You said it yourself. If Colleen finds out about this, she won't forgive you. None of the interns will. I want you to have a secret that only I know."

She frowned, trying to understand the logic.

"Will you give me that secret?" He put his hands on her cheeks again. "Come lie down with me."

"Maybe it's better if I just go back."

"You're the one who wanted to go to your room. You're the one who made me come up here."

"You're right. I did."

"So come lie down. The person I honestly am is a person

who wants his tongue in you. Will you let me do that?
Please let me do that."

Why did she follow him to the bed? To be brave. To
submit to the fact of the hotel room. To have her revenge
on the indifferent men she'd left behind in Oakland. To
do the very thing her mother had been afraid would happen. To punish Colleen for caring more about Andreas
than about her. To be the person who'd come to South
America and landed the famous, powerful man. She had
any number of dubious reasons, and for a while, on the
bed, as he slowed down the action, kissing her eyes and
stroking her hair, kissing her neck, unbuttoning her shirt,
helping her out of her bra, touching her breasts with his
gaze and his hands and his mouth, tenderly easing down
her jeans, even more tenderly peeling off her underpants, her reasons were all in harmony. She could feel
his hands trembling on her hips, feel his own excitement,
and this was something—it was a lot. He seemed honestly
to want her private thing. It was really this knowledge,
more than the *negocitos* he was expertly transacting
with his mouth, that caused her to come with such violent
alacrity.

But after it was over, the sensation of not liking him
returned. She felt embarrassed and dirty. He was kissing
her cheeks and her neck, thanking her. She knew what the
polite thing to do was, and she could tell, from his unabated urgency, that he wanted it. Not to deliver would
be selfish and perverse of her. But she couldn't help it: she
didn't feel like fucking what she didn't like.

"I'm sorry," she said, gently pushing him away.

"Don't be sorry." He pursued her and climbed onto
her, moving his clothed legs between her bare ones.
"You're remarkable. You're everything I could have
hoped for."

"No, that was definitely great. That felt really nice. I

don't think I've ever come so fast or so hard. It was like, wowee-zowee."

"Oh God," he said, shutting his eyes. He took her head in his hands and humped her a little with the hardness in his pants. "God, Pip. God."

"But, um." Again she tried to push him away. "Maybe I should go back now. You said I could go back after you did that."

"Pedro and I worked out a story about a broken truck axle. We have hours if you want them."

"I'm trying to be honest. Isn't that the point here?"

He must have tried to hide the look that appeared on his face then, because it was gone again immediately, replaced by that smile of his. For a moment, though, she'd seen that he was crazy. As if in a bad dream, a dream in which some guilty fact is forgotten and then suddenly remembered, it occurred to her that he had actually once murdered someone; that this was real.

"It's fine," he said with that smile.

"It's not that I didn't like the way you made me feel."

"Truly, it's fine." Without kissing her, without even looking at her, he got up and went to the door. He straightened his shirt and hitched up his pants.

"Please don't be angry with me."

"I'm the opposite of angry," he said, not looking at her. "I'm mad for you. Quite unexpectedly mad for you."

"I'm sorry."

In the Land Cruiser, to salvage some shred of dignity, she told Pedro that El Ingeniero had needed help with his *negocios*. Pedro, in reply, seemed to say that El Ingeniero's work was very complicated and beyond his understanding, but that he didn't have to understand it to be a good overseer at Los Volcanes.

When they got home, long after midnight, a light was still burning in Colleen's room. Deciding that lies were better told fresh than stale, Pip went straight up the stairs to the room. Colleen was in bed with a workbook and a pencil.

"You're up late," Pip said.

"Studying for the Vermont bar. I've had this book for a year. Tonight seemed like a good night to finally open it. How was Santa Cruz?"

"I wasn't in Santa Cruz."

"Right."

"I lost a big filling at breakfast. Pedro had to take me to the dentist. And then he hit a speed bump too hard and broke an axle. I spent like six hours sitting outside a garage."

Colleen carefully made a mark in the workbook with her pencil. "You're a terrible liar."

"I'm not lying."

"There isn't a *rompemuelles* within two hundred miles that Pedro doesn't know."

"He was talking to me. He didn't see it."

"Just get the fuck out of my room, all right?"

"Colleen."

"It's not personal. You're not the person I'm hating. I knew this would happen sometime. I'm just sorry it was you. There was a lot to like about you."

"I like you so much, too."

"I said get out of here."

"You're being crazy!"

Finally Colleen looked up from the workbook. "Really? You want to lie to me? You want to prolong this?"

Pip's eyes filled. "I'm sorry."

Colleen turned a page in her book and made a show of reading. Pip stood for a while longer in the doorway, but Colleen was right. There was nothing else to say.

In the morning, instead of taking a hike, Pip went to breakfast with the others. Colleen wasn't there, but Pedro was. He'd already told the story of his and Pip's ill-fated trip to the dentist. If Willow and the others were suspicious, they didn't show it. Pip was sick with general dread and specific guilt about Colleen, but to everyone else it was just another day of Sunlight.

Colleen left two days later. She'd been discreet about her reasons, saying only that it was time to move on, and once she was safely gone the other girls were frankly patronizing about her depression and her lovesickness for Andreas; their consensus was that her departure was a much-needed step toward restoring her self-esteem. Which, in a way, it was. But Pip inwardly burned with loyalty to her, and with guilt.

When Andreas returned, he gave Colleen's job as business manager to the Swede, Anders. But since no one imagined that Anders was specially dear to Andreas, Colleen's position at the top of the pecking order went to the person whom everybody knew Andreas particularly liked, the person whose presence at Los Volcanes was known to be more extraordinary than their own. Now it was Pip beside whom Andreas sat down for dinner, Pip whose table filled up first. To her vast amusement, tiny Flor was suddenly eager to be her friend. Flor even asked to join her on a hike, to experience for herself the smells that Pip had raved about, and once Flor had hiked with her the other girls vied for the same privilege.

The less than healthy satisfaction Pip took in being socially central for once in her life was linked in her mind to the memory of Andreas's tongue and how explosively her body had responded to it. Even the dirtiness she'd felt afterward was agreeable in hindsight, in a wicked sort of way. She imagined an arrangement whereby she continued to receive the favor from time to time, and he could trust her, and she could have her dirty pleasure. He'd implied it himself: he was one of those cunnilingus guys.

Surely some mutually satisfactory arrangement could be worked out.

But the weeks went by, August becoming September, and though Pip was now a full-fledged researcher, handling simpler assignments on her own and devoting her free time to laborious searches of databases for the name Penelope Tyler, Andreas still avoided talking to her one-on-one the way he did with Willow and many of the others. She understood that she was supposed to be spying for him, and that they should never be seen having hushed conspiratorial talks. But the spying thing seemed ridiculous to her—the only vibe she ever got off anyone was overpowering sincerity—and she began to feel that she was being punished by him; that she'd hurt him and shamed him by refusing to have sex with him. His unfailingly warm and affectionate manner with her meant nothing; she knew very well that he was a master dissembler; he'd all but said it himself, and his incessant talk of trust and honesty only proved it. Underneath, she became convinced, he was angry with her and regretted having trusted her.

And so, day by day, seduced by tongue and popularity, she formed the resolve to give him everything he wanted the next time they were alone. *Quite unexpectedly mad for you*: that still had to be operable, didn't it? She wasn't mad for him, but she was curious, sexually botherated, and increasingly resolute. She began looking for opportunities to accost him in private. Someone always seemed to follow him out of the barn to the tech building; Pedro or Teresa always seemed to be within earshot when he was alone in the main building. But one afternoon, toward the end of September, she looked out a window and saw him sitting by himself in a far corner of the goat pasture, facing the forest.

She hurried outside and crossed the pasture so briskly

that the goats scattered. Andreas must have heard her coming, but he didn't turn around until she reached him and saw that he'd been crying. It reminded her of something; of Stephen crying on their front porch in Oakland.

He patted the grass. "Sit down."

"What is it?"

"Just sit down. I got bad news."

Mindful of their visibility, she sat down at some distance from him.

"My mother is sick," he said. "Kidney cancer. I just found out."

"I'm so sorry," Pip said. "I didn't know you were even in touch with her."

"She doesn't hear from me. But I still hear from her."

"Should I leave you alone?"

"Was there something you wanted?"

"It's not important."

"I'd much rather hear about you than think about her."

"Is it bad, her cancer? What stage is it?"

He shrugged. "She wants to come and see me. Does that sound good? It's not as if I can travel to her. That's some small blessing. I'm spared that decision."

"I feel like hugging you. But I don't want to be seen doing it."

"That's good. You've been very good, by the way."

"Thank you. Although . . . Are you mad at me?"

"Certainly not."

She nodded, wondering whether to believe him.

"I've spent most of my life hating her," he said. "I told you some of the reasons I hate her. But now I get this email and I remember that they weren't the real reasons, or not the whole reason. They're half the reason. The other half is that I can never stop loving her, in spite of all those other reasons. I forget about this, for years at a time. But then I get this email . . ."

He expelled air, either a laugh or a sob. Pip didn't dare look to see which it was. "Maybe the love is more important than the hate," she said.

"I'm sure for you it would be."

"Well, anyway. I'm sorry."

"Did you need to talk to me privately? Should we make some arrangement?"

"No. Either I'm a terrible spy or you were just being paranoid."

"Then what did you want?"

She turned to him and showed him, with the look on her face, what she wanted.

His eyes, which were bloodshot, widened. "Oh," he said. "I see."

She looked down at the ground and spoke in a low voice. "I feel really bad about what happened the other time. I think it could be better. I mean, if that's at all interesting to you."

"It is. Absolutely. I'd hardly dared hope."

"I'm sorry. You asked what I wanted, but I shouldn't have answered. Not now."

"No, it's fine." He sprang to his feet, his grief apparently forgotten. "I have to go to town next week, to see her. I was dreading that, but now I'm not. Let me think about how to get you there with me. How does that sound?"

Pip struggled to find breath to answer. "Sounds good," she said.

One of the insaner things about the Project was that private electronic communication was impossible. The internal network was designed so that all chats and emails were viewable by anyone on the network, because everything was viewable to the tech boys and it wasn't fair to give them an advantage. If a girl wanted to hook up with a boy (and it happened quite a bit, though the boys were physically a less prepossessing lot), she arranged it either openly on the network or in person. And so it was that Andreas pressed a handwritten note into Pip's hand when she was leaving the main building the following night.

> *Be happy: your spying days may be over. No plausible story is available. You're coming with me because I'm meeting potential investors and you're the intern whose judgement I most trust. But think carefully about whether you're ready for the others to see you differently. I'll accept whatever you decide. Please burn this.—A.*

On the veranda, above the dark river, Pip burned the note with a lighter that Colleen had left behind. She missed Colleen and wondered if she herself was in for three years of being strung along, but she also felt victorious and capable. She'd gone deeper into the dark river than Colleen had, deeper than just her knees, and she was pretty sure she'd already gone farther with Andreas. It was all very strange and would have felt even stranger if her life hadn't been so strange to begin with. To her the strangest thought of all was that she might be extraordinarily appealing. It went against everything she believed in—or at least against everything she *wanted* to believe in; because, deep down, in her most honest heart, maybe every person considered herself extraordinarily appealing. Maybe this was just a human thing.

"Do I get to meet your mother?" she asked Andreas a week later, when Pedro was driving them up the steep road out of the valley.

"Do you want to? Annagret was the only woman of mine who ever did. My mother was very kind to her, until she wasn't."

Pip was too disturbed by the phrase *woman of mine* to

answer. Did the phrase now apply to her? It sounded like it did.

"She's very seductive," Andreas said. "You'd probably like her. Annagret liked her a lot—until she didn't."

Pip rolled down her window, put her face to the cool early-morning air, and whispered, "Am I your woman." She didn't think Andreas could hear her, but it was possible he had.

"You're my confidante," he said. "I'd be interested in what your good sense has to say about her."

He put his hand on her upper thigh and left it there. Pretty much every thought she'd had in the last week had led back to one thing. She was experiencing stronger symptoms of being in love, a queasiness more persistent, a heart more racing, than she remembered having had with Stephen. But the symptoms were ambiguous. A condemned person walking to the gallows had many of the same ones. When Andreas's hand crept, thrillingly, to the inside of her thigh, she had neither the courage nor even the inclination to place a corresponding hand on his leg. The rightness of the phrase *preyed upon* was becoming evident. The feelings of prey in the grip of a wolf's teeth were hard to distinguish from being in love.

Her Spanish was enough improved that she followed everything Andreas said to Pedro. Pedro was to be at the Cortez at six o'clock the next morning. Andreas would probably be waiting for him, but if he wasn't, Pedro was to proceed to the airport with a sign that said KATYA WOLF and bring her to the hotel.

Evidently Andreas intended to spend all day and all night and possibly the next morning with Pip alone. How absurd that they first had to sit together in the back seat for three hours while Pedro braked for speed bumps. What a torture, these *rompemuelles*.

I am in love, she decided. *I'm the least beautiful girl*

at Los Volcanes, but I'm funny and brave and honest and
he chose me. He can break my heart later—I don't care.

At the Cortez, he instructed her to wait in the lobby
for fifteen minutes before joining him in his room. She
watched damp-haired, morning-faced travelers surrender-
ing room keys. It seemed to be no time of day in no place
on earth. A Latin businessman idling by the reception
desk was looking intently at her chest. She rolled her eyes;
he smiled. He was an insect compared to the man who
was waiting for her.

She found him sitting with his tablet at the desk in his
room. A tray of sandwiches and cut-up fruit was on the
bed. "Have some food," he said.

"Do I seem hungry?"

"Your stomach seems sensitive. It's important that
you eat."

She hazarded some papaya, which according to her
mother was soothing to the stomach.

"What would you like to do today?" he said.

"I don't know. Is there a particular church or museum
I'm supposed to see?"

"I don't love being seen in public. But, yes, the old town
center is worth seeing."

"You could wear sunglasses and a funny hat."

"Is that what you want?"

The papaya made her burp. She felt that she had to stop
being prey, to somehow take the initiative. She was still
disinclined to touch him, but she walked over behind him
and forced herself to put her hands on his shoulders. She
ran them down onto his chest. It had to be done.

He took hold of her wrists so she couldn't get away.

"I thought you never laid a hand on interns," she said.
"I thought it was bad press."

"Serially bedding them would be bad press," he said.
"Falling in love with one of them is a very different story."

Her knees quaked. "Did you actually just say that?"

"I did."

The wooden spoon, the wooden spoon.

"OK, then," she said, sinking to the floor.

He let go of her wrists, extricated himself from the desk, and kneeled in front of her.

"Pip," he said. "I know I'm old. Probably as old as your father. But I have a young heart—I don't have much experience with real love. Probably not much more than you do. This is new and frightening for me, too."

The wooden spoon. Her brain was churning. It was more a father than a lover to whom she now pressed herself in her fear; more a father whom she clutched for safety. And yet, the night before, she'd trimmed her personal hair for him with a razor. She was massively confused. He held her tightly, stroking her head.

"Do you like me at all?" he said.

She nodded because she knew he wanted her to.

"A lot?" he said. "Or just a little?"

"Quite a lot," she said for the same reason.

"I like you, too."

She nodded again. But even though he'd made her do it, she felt bad about lying to him. If he truly was falling in love with her, it was a mean thing to do. To make up for it, she tried to say something both honest and nice. "I really liked the way you made me feel the other time. I can't stop thinking about it. I'm fairly obsessed with it. I want you to do it again."

His body tensed at this. She worried that she'd said the wrong thing—that he'd seen through her attempt to turn their talk away from love, and was hurt. And so she kissed him. Urgently, forwardly, offering him her tongue, opening herself to him, and he responded in kind. But the sensible side of her was still semi-functioning. A laugh came out of her before she could stifle it.

"What?" he said, smiling.

"I'm so sorry," she said. "I'm just wondering if we're both trying to do what neither of us actually wants."

He seemed alarmed. "What do you mean?"

"No, just the kissing part," she hastened to say. "You didn't seem so into the smooching last time. You were honest about that. And, honestly, it's fine with me too if we skip it."

It happened again. Again, for a second, for less than a second, before he could turn his face away, she saw a wholly different person, a crazy person.

"You're a remarkable woman," he said, face averted.

"Thank you."

He stood up and walked away from her. "I mean it," he said. "I've never felt so off balance in my life. You make me feel smaller, in a good way. I'm supposed to be the great teller of truth, and you keep cutting me down. I hate it, but I love it. I love you." He turned back to her and said it again. "I love you."

She blushed. "Thank you."

"That's it?" he said wildly. "*Thank you?* Who made you this way? Where did you come from?"

"The San Lorenzo Valley. It's quite the humble, democratic place."

He strode back over to her and yanked her to her feet. "You're driving me crazy!"

"All is not so well inside my own head, either."

"So what are we? How do we do this? What is the way we're going to be together?"

"I don't know."

"*Take off your fucking clothes*—does that work?"

"It has some promise."

"So do it. Slowly. I want to watch you. Take your panties off last."

"OK. I can do that."

She liked taking orders from him. Liked it more than anything else about him. But as she did as she'd been told, unbuttoning one button of her shirt, and then a second button, she wasn't sure that she liked that she liked it. She wished she could unhear what Stephen had said to her, in his bedroom, about needing a father. A dread began to build in her as she undid a fourth button, and then the last. She beheld an emotional vista in which she was angry at her missing father, at all older men, and provoked and punished this father-aged man, drove him wild, induced him to offer himself as the person missing from her life; and her body responded to the offer; but it was icky to respond to him that way. She let her bra fall to the floor.

"My God you're beautiful," he said, staring.

"I think you mean I'm young."

"No. The inside of you is even more beautiful than the outside."

"Keep talking," she said. "It's helping."

When she was finally fully naked, he dropped to his knees and pressed his face to her crotch. "You shaved for me," he murmured gratefully.

"Who said it was for you?" she said with a faltering laugh. Being so liked by him, she was liking herself quite a lot, but it deepened her sense of dread to hear herself continuing to provoke him, and to feel the effect her provocation had. His hands were trembling on her butt. He was kissing her, inhaling her, and she could feel how it would all happen again, the same as last time, except that this time she would have to submit to the whole deal; there would be no going back on her word.

All at once, at the prospect of being fucked by him, she experienced a different kind of climax. The lack of friction with which she'd arrived at this moment, the speed and directness with which he'd arranged an assignation with her, the ease with which he'd got her standing naked in a hotel room, combined with a complex of misgivings—*father, killer, spoon-wielder, fugitive, crazy person*—to produce a simple thought: she didn't want to be his woman.

In the sober light of this thought, what they were doing seemed ridiculous.

"Um," she said, stepping away from him. "I think I need a small time-out."

He slumped. "Now what."

"No, seriously, I've been looking forward to this for a month and a half. I've been touching myself every night, thinking about it. Imagining I'm you. But now—I don't know. I'm wondering if touching myself might be enough."

He slumped further. She picked up her bra and put it on. She put on her jeans, not bothering with the underpants, which were still right in front of him.

"I'm really sorry," she said. "I don't know what's wrong with me."

"So what would you like to do instead?" His voice was strained with self-control. "Visit the picturesque town center?"

"Honestly I hadn't thought past going to bed with you."

"It's still an option."

"Maybe if you order me to. I like it when you give orders. I think I may have a slave personality."

"That's not an order I can give. I don't want it if you don't want it. You said you wanted it."

"I know."

He sighed heavily. "What changed your mind?"

"It just suddenly didn't feel right to me."

"Am I too old for you?"

"God, no. I like your age. If anything, maybe a little too much. Plus you've got that ageless German male thing going. You've got those blue eyes."

He bowed his head. "So you just don't like who I am."

She felt terribly sorry. She kneeled by him and petted his shoulders and kissed his cheek. "Everybody likes you," she said. "Millions of people like you."

"They like a lie. You're the person I showed my true self to."

"I'm so sorry. I'm so sorry." She hugged his head to her chest and rocked him a little. Her heart was reengaging with him, and she wondered if a mercy fuck was in the offing. She'd never done one, but she now saw how it happened. An ulterior part of her was further considering that, at some later date, she might take retrospective satisfaction in having fucked the famous outlaw hero, and that this was her chance to do it, and that, conversely, this future self of hers would writhe with remorse if all she'd done was lead him on and chicken out. Chicken out *twice*.

He had his face between her breasts, his hands down the back of her jeans. The fact that she'd chickened out *twice* seemed significant. She thought of what her mother had said before she left Felton with her suitcase. "I know you're very angry with me, pussycat, and you have a right to be. I worry about you in the jungle, on a different continent. I worry about you with Andreas Wolf. But the one thing I never worry about is your good moral sense. You've always been a loving person, with a clear sense of right and wrong. I know you better than you know yourself. And that's what I know about you." Pip, who could see nothing but the mess her bad behavior made of every relationship in her life, had felt quite sure, in the moment, that her mother knew nothing at all about her. But to have recoiled from Andreas *twice*, when everything argued for submitting—didn't this mean something? Maybe her mother was right. Maybe she did have a clear moral sense. She could remember having loved Ramón and even Dreyfuss pureheartedly. What had ruined things in Oakland was her lust for Stephen, her anger at an older man.

She kissed the curly top of Andreas's head and untangled herself from him. "It's just not going to happen," she said. "I'm sorry."

She put on her shirt and went down to the lobby. Her decision seemed irrevocable, not even in her power, and she was prepared to sit in the lobby all day and all night if she had to. But Pedro was back with the Land Cruiser in less than an hour. She couldn't face sitting in the front with him; her body felt prickly and contaminating. She lay down in the back and waited to be overwhelmed with shame and guilt and second-guessing.

When the feelings came, they were even worse than she'd foreseen. For two days she did little but lie in bed, unresponsive to her roommates' comings and goings. She'd been flying high, liking herself, as long as she'd been liked by Andreas, but now, having incurred his displeasure, she fell into a pit of displeasure with herself. Even though she'd been the rejecter, not the rejected, the scene in the hotel room had been as bad as the one in Stephen's bedroom. It played over and over in her head, particularly the moment when she'd been naked and he'd been on his knees.

On the third day, when she managed to drag herself to dinner, she found herself unpopular again. She ate with her head down and went back to bed. Nobody was honest with her now. She couldn't tell if she was being ostracized because she was believed to have seduced Andreas or because he was known to be unhappy with her. Either way, she felt she deserved it. She composed an email epistle to Colleen, a full confession, before she realized that Colleen would only hate her more for it. She cut all but a few sentences:

You did the right thing, leaving. He really is a weird dude.
All I did with him was talk, and that's all it's ever going
to be. I'm not long for this place myself.

When Andreas returned, three days later, he was the
same as before with her, cordial but distant, which made
her feel all the guiltier. She believed that he really had told her
a secret he'd told no one else at Los Volcanes—that he
really had specially wanted her—and that, behind his
smile, he had to be feeling hurt and ashamed. Unable to
relive the moment of her decision, she fell to thinking that
she'd made a ghastly mistake. What if she'd gone ahead
and been his lover? What if she'd learned to be deliriously
happy with him? Now his desire was bottled up inside him
and she couldn't enjoy it. She thought of begging him for
a third chance, but she was afraid she'd chicken out a third
time. She walked around for a week with a lump of near-
clinical depression in her throat. She pretended to go for
hikes but sat down after the first bend in the trail and wept.

He discovered her on one of these crying jags. It was
late afternoon and getting dark; rain was falling from the
outskirts of a thunderhead. He came around the bend in
a yellow slicker and rubber boots and saw her with her
back against a tree, her arms around her knees, getting
soaked.

"I came looking for you." He crouched down by her.
"I didn't realize you were so close."

"I don't hike anymore," she said. "I just come here
and cry."

"I'm sorry."

"No, I'm the one who's sorry. I ruined everything."

"Don't blame yourself. I'm a grown man. I can take
care of myself."

"I'm never going to betray you," she blubbered. "You
can trust me."

"I won't pretend that I don't love you. I do love you."

"I'm sorry," she blubbered.

"But here, enough of that." He took off his slicker, draped it over her, and sat down. "Let's think about what you want to do now."

She wiped her nose with her hand. "Just send me home," she said. "I had one big opportunity here, and I blew it."

"Willow tells me the search for your missing parent isn't going well."

"Sorry, two opportunities. Two things I failed at."

"I'm afraid that Annagret and I did you a disservice, telling you we could help. What you're looking for is pre–digital era, which makes it very hard. I spoke with Chen about you." Chen was the chief hacker. "I asked if we could do a facial-recognition search with an older picture of your mother. It would take a lot of pirated computing power, and I'm willing to do it for you. But Chen thinks it would be a waste of time."

In the clear gray light of her depression, Pip saw that she'd done again what she'd done with Igor at Renewable Solutions—had fallen for an employer's empty sales pitch.

"It's OK," she said. "Thank you for asking him."

"I'll keep making your student loan payments as long as you're here. But we should think about your next step. You're a good writer, and Willow says you're a very fast learner. You were miserable at your sales job. Have you ever thought about being a journalist?"

She managed a wan smile. "Isn't the Project destroying the field of journalism?"

"Journalism will survive. There's a lot of nonprofit money going into it now. Somebody as capable as you can find a job if she wants one. I'm thinking that old media might be more suited to you anyway, given how little you like what I'm doing."

"I wanted to like it. I'm so sorry I can't."

"Enough of that." He took her hand and kissed it. "You are what you are. I love what you are. I'm going to miss it."

She started crying all over again. From somewhere in the mist came the thundercrack sound of sandstone splitting off the face of a pinnacle, followed by a muffled crash. She'd been on trails where shards of rock had fallen so close to her that she could hear the whistle of their plummeting.

"Can you order me?" she said.

"What?"

"Give me an order. Say I have to do journalism. Can you do that? I still want you to give me orders . . ." She squeezed her eyes shut. "I'm such a mess."

"I don't understand you," he said. "But, yes, if you insist. I can order you to do it."

"Thank you," she whispered.

"So let's work on that. I have a little present for you, to get you started. Talk to Willow. She'll show it to you."

"You're being really nice to me."

"Don't worry. There's something in it for me, too. Do you see what it is?"

She shook her head.

"You'll figure it out," he said.

He must have given Willow another talking-to that afternoon. After ten days of coolness to Pip, she'd saved her a place at dinner and was eerily friendly to her again. In the evening, in the barn, she showed Pip a set of photographs deleted by a Facebook user but still retrievable, by the likes of Chen, from Facebook's bowels. On the back of a pickup truck, at somebody's party in Texas, was what appeared to be an operational nuclear warhead. It couldn't possibly be a real one, but it looked exactly like the real ones Pip had seen in presentations at her study group in Oakland.

In the weeks that followed, she tried to teach herself journalism. With the help of a hacker boy, she friended the Facebook user who'd put up the pictures, but this went nowhere. She had no idea how to approach the Air Force or the weapons plant with questions, and, even if she had, she would have been calling without credentials on a Skype-like connection from Bolivia. This gave her new respect for real journalists but was personally discouraging. She might have given up if Andreas hadn't then connected her with a Bay Area whistle-blower who had information about groundwater contamination at a Richmond landfill. Using the information, and making phone calls to less intimidating local authorities—she wasn't afraid of cold-calling; she'd developed at least one usable skill at Renewable Solutions—she produced a story that then magically appeared online at the *East Bay Express*, whose editor was a fan of Andreas. The *Express* also ran her next piece, "Confessions of an Outreach Associate," which Willow had helped her with by failing to laugh at it until she'd made it genuinely funny.

Early in January, after she'd written two further, shorter pieces for the *Express*, on subjects supplied by the editor and reportable by telephone, Andreas went for a walk with her and suggested that she apply to work as a research intern at an online magazine called Denver Independent. "It specializes in investigative journalism," he said. "It wins prizes."

"Why Denver?" she said.

"There's a very good reason why."

"*East Bay Express* seems to like me. I'd rather be closer to my mom."

"Are you asking me to order you?"

It was three months since their morning at the Cortez, and she was still wishing he'd ordered her to go to bed with him.

"Denver's just a name to me," she said. "I don't know anything about the place. But sure. Tell me what you want, and I'll do it."

"What I want?" He looked up at the sky. "I want you to like me. I want you never to leave me. I want to get old with you."

"Oh!"

"I'm sorry. I had to say that once before you left."

She wished she could believe him. He seemed to believe himself. But her inability to trust him was in her marrow; in her nerves.

"Anyway," she said.

"Anyway, I'm not asking for much. If you get the job in Denver, which I think you will, I want you to open an attachment I'll send you when you have an office email account. The editor and publisher is a man named Tom Aberant. All you really have to do is open the attachment. But if you want to keep your ears open, and get a sense of whether Denver Independent is coming after me, I'd be grateful for that, too."

"He's the other person who knows what you did. He's the journalist."

"Yes."

"You want me to be your spy."

"Whatever you feel comfortable with. If it's nothing, so be it. The only thing I ask, besides opening the attachment, is that you not tell anyone that you were down here. You never left California. Telling Aberant you were here is the one thing that could actually harm me. Harm you, too, needless to say."

A dark thought occurred to her.

"Don't get me wrong," she said. "I'm liking being a

journalist. But is this person in Denver the real reason you suggested it?"

"The real reason? No. But part of the reason? Of course. It's good for you *and* good for me. Do you have a problem with that?"

In the moment, it didn't seem like much for him to ask. She'd withheld her heart and her body from him, and she remembered, from her experience with Stephen, the ache and desolation of being denied the heart and body you desired. She may not have trusted Andreas, but she had compassion for him, including his paranoia, and if a click of a mouse would suffice to make her less indebted to him, less guilty for hurting him, she was willing to click. She thought it might help close the books on her and him. And so she went to Denver.

When she returned to Tom and Leila's house, very late, after a night of drinking with the Denver Independent interns, she was surprised to find Leila on the steps outside the kitchen, bundled in a thick fleece jacket, with cigarette smoke in the vicinity.

"Aha, you caught me," Leila said.

"You *smoke*?"

"About five a year." In a white cereal bowl next to Leila were four stubbed butts. She covered the bowl with her hand.

"What is it like to be so moderate?" Pip said.

"Oh, it's just another thing to feel insecure about." Leila gave a self-disliking laugh. "The interesting people are always immoderate."

"Can I sit here with you?"

"It's freezing. I was about to go inside."

Following Leila into the house, Pip worried that she herself was the cause of Leila's smoking. She'd sort of fallen in love with Leila, in the same way she had with Colleen in Bolivia, but ever since she'd moved in with her and Tom she'd had the sense that she was causing trouble between them. She was a little bit in love with Tom, too, because she could afford to be, because she wasn't physically attracted to him—he was both older and *safe*—and Leila, of late, had been all too visibly jealous of one or both of them. Pip knew she should just move somewhere else. But it was hard to let go of the family she'd fallen into.

In the kitchen, Leila poured the butts and ashes onto a sheet of foil and balled it up. Aided by the four margaritas in her, Pip asked her if she could ask her something.

"Of course," Leila said, taking coffee from the refrigerator.

"Would you rather I find my own place to live? Would that help?"

For a moment, Leila froze. She seemed pretty in a very particular way to Pip. Not irritating-pretty like the Sunlight Project interns; older-pretty; lovely in a way to be aspired to. She looked at the coffee can in her hand as if she didn't know how it had got there. "Of course not," she said. "Does it seem like I want you to?"

"Um. Well. Yeah. A little bit."

"I'm sorry." Leila moved briskly to the coffee maker. "You're probably just picking up on insecurities that have nothing to do with you."

"Why are you insecure? I admire you so much."

The coffee can fell to the floor.

"This is what I get for smoking," Leila said, bending down.

"Why are you smoking? Why are you making coffee at one thirty in the morning?"

"Because I know I'm not going to sleep anyway. I might as well work."

"Leila," Pip said plaintively.

Leila gave her a look worse than annoyed; a fierce look. "*What?*"

"Is something wrong?"

"No. Nothing." Leila composed herself. "Did you get my text from Washington?"

"Yeah! It sounds like this is bigger than we thought."

"Well, that's all it is. I'm half out of my mind with fear that somebody's ahead of us on the story."

"Is there something I can do to help?"

"*No!* Go to bed. It's late."

In the upstairs hallway, Pip could hear Tom snoring off whatever he'd drunk. She sat on the edge of her bed and typed out an email to Colleen, the latest of many, all of them unanswered.

> Yes, me again. I thought of you because I just caught
> Leila smoking behind the house and it made me miss you.
> I keep missing you. I know all I do is betray people. But
> I can't stop wishing you'd give me another chance. Much
> love, PT

Emailing drunk was never a good idea, but she went ahead and hit Send.

Her problem was that it was true: all she did was betray people. Almost as soon as her email account at Denver Independent had been activated and she'd clicked on the attachment from Andreas, she'd regretted it. The symphony she'd failed to hear in Bolivia had commenced immediately in Denver. Her fellow interns were ordinary young people, not goddesses or prodigies. The reporters and editors were lumpy and sarcastic, the division of labor gender-neutral, the office atmosphere serious and professional but not remotely cool. Though Andreas liked to tell his interns that *every hand was raised against the leaker*, to stake his claim to the sympathy accorded underdogs, the Project was too cool and famous to be an underdog. The real underdogs were the journalists. Though much was made of Andreas's personal penury, the purity of his service, it was the ordinary financial stresses of the journalists, their child-support and mortgage payments, the four-dollar sandwiches they ate for lunch, that reminded Pip of her mother and her struggling neighbors in Felton. After six hours she felt more at home at DI than she had in six months at TSP.

And Leila: lovely in body and soul, motherly in a way that felt sisterly, not suffocating, a Pulitzer-winning journalist whose personal life was even stranger than Pip's. And Tom: earnest about his work but silly in private, indifferent to anyone's opinion of what he said or how he looked, his manner as reserved and ironic as Andreas's was invasive and self-important, his commitment to Leila the more obvious for being unspoken. Pip loved them both, and when they asked her to move in with them she felt as if, after a life of constraints and poor decisions and general ineffectiveness, she'd finally caught a major break.

Which made it all the more disastrously unfortunate that she'd planted spyware on DI's computer system, pretended to be responsible for finding the warhead pictures that Andreas had given her, and told Tom and Leila a dozen other lies. She'd succeeded in walking back the smaller lies without undue damage or embarrassment, but the biggest lies—and presumably the spyware—remained in place. And now Leila was turning against her, and now Tom, too, was suddenly uncomfortable around her; the two things, taken together, made her afraid that, although she respected Tom too much to have flirted with him or laid her authority-questioning shtick on him, he might have developed a romantic interest in her. Two nights ago, he'd taken her to the theater, and as if it weren't unsettling enough to be there *as his date*, he'd lowered his guard on the drive home and asked her personal questions, had seemed distinctly pale when she said good night to him, and had been avoiding her ever since.

There was also the matter of the email Willow had sent her recently. It was newsy and surprisingly sentimental and came with a picture attached, a selfie that Willow had taken with Pip outside the barn. The caption could have been "Alpha Girl with Beta Girl." But Willow had been party to the fabrication of Pip's journalistic credentials; surely she knew that encrypted texting was the only safe way for anyone at the Project to communicate with her. So why an email? And why the clunky business of sending an attachment? Pip had been doing her best to forget that she'd opened it at home, using Tom's private Wi-Fi.

All things considered, she was proud of having drunk only four margaritas with the interns tonight. Between her lies and the tensions in the house, it seemed only a matter of time before she found herself jobless and on the street again, her major break squandered. And she knew what she had to do. She had to betray Andreas and tell Tom and Leila everything. But she couldn't bear to disappoint them.

By saying nothing, she was protecting a killer, a crazy person, a man she didn't trust. And yet she was reluctant to lose her connection with him. He'd messed with her head, and it brought her an unwholesome pleasure to mess with *his* head—to be the person in Denver who knew his secrets and had to be worried about. Without his daily presence to remind her of her distrust, his power and his fame and his special interest in her were all the more conducive to sexual fantasy. He scored zeroes in certain important love metrics but was off the charts in others.

She texted him every night at bedtime and didn't turn off her phone until he'd texted back. She'd come to think it would have been less bad to sleep with him, less of a moral surrender, than to open the email attachment he'd sent her. Why, why, why hadn't she slept with him when she had her chance? Running away from Bolivia seemed all the more regrettable now that she knew that his fear of Tom was unfounded. Planting spyware was a pointless and truly vile sin that she could have obviated by staying with Andreas and committing a pleasurable sin.

> There is no embedded journalist. There is no investigation.

You sure?

> T seems to like you! He hasn't even told L what happened in Berlin.

Are you quite sure of that?

> Yes. Trust me.

What did he say about Berlin?

> That he knew you.

That's all?

> Yes! You can stop being paranoid.

If only it were that easy.

She had to fight the temptation to sext him a picture of her private thing. She was the latest of those women who stayed loyal to him. The alteration of her brain by wooden spoon was apparently ongoing.

It wasn't hard to conceal the state of her brain from Tom and Leila, but its alteration was the reason she'd flown directly from Bolivia to Denver without stopping to see her mother. Her mother could be scarily perceptive about her state of mind. No sooner had Pip arrived in Denver than she'd been forced to conceal it from her.

"Purity," her mother had said on the telephone. "When you told me you couldn't find anything out about your father in Bolivia, were you lying to me?"

"No. I don't tell lies to you."

"You didn't find anything out?"

"No!"

"Then tell me why you had to go to Denver."

"I want to learn to be a journalist."

"But why did it have to be Denver? Why *that* online magazine? Why not someplace closer to home?"

"Mom, this is the time when I need to be on my own for a while. You're getting older, I'm going to be there for you. Can't I have a couple of years where I get to be away?"

"Did Andreas Wolf want you to go to that place?"

Pip hesitated. "No," she said. "They just happened to have an intern position I applied for."

"It was the only news service in the country accepting applications?"

"You just don't like it because it's in a different time zone."

"Purity. I'm going to ask again: are you telling me the truth?"

"Yes! Why are you asking me?"

"Linda helped me use her computer, and I looked at the website. I wanted to see for myself."

"And? It's a great site, right? It's serious long-form investigative journalism."

"I have the feeling you're not telling me things you should be telling me."

"I'm not! I mean, I'm *not* not."

However sensitive to smells her mother was, she had an even keener nose for moral failings. She could smell that Pip was doing something wrong in Denver, and Pip resented her for it. She'd already denied herself Andreas because of something her mother had said. To live up to her mother's ideal, she'd behaved more worthily than she'd had to, and she felt she deserved credit for it, even though her mother knew nothing about it. She was in no mood to be lectured.

But her mother had been sulking ever since. Not returning phone messages and then, when Pip did reach her, not joyfully ejaculating but making her displeasure known with sighs and silences and monosyllabic answers to Pip's dutiful questions. Pip had finally gotten angry and stopped calling altogether. She hadn't even told her mother she'd moved in with Tom and Leila. For a while, living with them, she'd felt vindicated in her belief that she could have been a well-adjusted and effective person if she'd had a pair of parents like these. They'd already done so much to help her that finding her real father had ceased to be a burning priority. But preferring them as parents made her pity her mother, who was alone in Felton and had done her best with the poor resources she had. Pip's life seemed like a conspiracy to betray every single person in it. And now Tom seemed to have a thing for her, which amounted to yet another betrayal, a betrayal of Leila that Pip hadn't intended and couldn't control. It was all making her even more dependent on her nightly textings with Andreas and the self-touching she often did afterward.

Tom was still snoring when she ventured out to the bathroom. From downstairs came a smell of coffee and the faint patter of a keyboard. Pip felt pity for Leila, too. And for Tom, if he was attracted to her. And of course for Andreas, and for Colleen. Apparently pity and betrayal were related.

Back in her bed, she texted Andreas. It was too late at night to expect a reply, and she should have just gone to sleep, but instead she appended further texts.

> Is there a way to make your spyware self-destruct?

> I mean, since T's not hiding anything.

> It puts me in a hard position. These are good people.

> I'm worried that T has a thing for me.

> I want to feel you hard inside me. I want to

She was erasing the last message, which she'd typed only as a masturbation aid, when a reply came in from Los Volcanes.

> Do you have a thing for him too?

She was surprised. It was four in the morning in Bolivia.

> No! He's Leila's.

> I would have no objection.

> I'm not into him anyway.

> You don't have to pretend on my account.

> Not pretending. You know which older man I'm into.

She waited ten minutes, second-guessing herself, for his reply to her temerity. She knew she was behaving badly, trying to keep him interested after having twice rejected him. But right now their texting was the closest thing she had to a sex life. She typed more:

> Sorry about that. TMI. Are you still there? Were you ignoring my other texts? Is there a way for the spyware to uninstall itself?

> I don't want you anymore.

His text was like a sock in the jaw. Her hands jumped away from her device, letting it fall between her legs. Was he jealous of Tom? It seemed important to set the record straight, and so she picked up the device again. She cursed the errors her trembling finger made.

> I'm sexually obsessed with you. I'm dying of regret.

> Get over it. I don't want you.

> Are you mad at me?

> Not mad. Just honest. Don't text me anymore. I won't answer.

She fell on her side with a whimper and pulled the comforter over her head. She couldn't figure out what she'd done wrong—she'd *said* she wasn't interested in Tom. Why was Andreas punishing her now? She writhed under the comforter, trying and failing to make sense of what he'd written, until the comforter became a tormentor. Sweating all over, she threw it off and went downstairs to the dining room, where Leila was working.

"You're still awake?" Leila said.

Her smile was troubled but not phony. Pip sat down across the table from her. "Can't sleep."

"Do you want an Ambien? I have a veritable cornucopia."

"Will you tell me what you found out in Washington?"

"Let me get you an Ambien."

"No. Just let me sit here while you work."

Leila smiled at her again. "I like that you can be honest about what you want. It's something I still struggle with."

Her smiles were taking some of the sting off Andreas's brutal words.

"But let me try it," Leila said. "I want you to not sit here while I work."

"Oh," Pip said, very hurt.

"It makes me self-conscious. If you really don't mind?"

"No, I'll leave. It's just—" Outburst Alert. Outburst Alert. "I don't know why you're being so weird to me. I didn't do anything to you. I would never do anything to hurt you."

Leila was still smiling, but something was glittering in her eyes, something awfully similar to hatred. "I'd appreciate it if you'd just let me work."

"Do you think I'm a home-wrecker? Do you think I'd ever in a million years do that to you?"

"Not intentionally."

"Then why are you being this way, if it's not my fault?"

"Do you know who your father is?"

"My *father*?" Pip made an insultingly baffled face and gesture.

"Are you ever curious?"

"What does any of this have to do with my father?"

"I'm just asking."

"Well, I wish you wouldn't. I already feel like I walk around in life with this sign hanging from my neck, BEWARE OF DOG, DIDN'T HAVE FATHER. It doesn't mean I want to have sex with every older man who comes my way."

"I'm sorry."

"I can pack my things and move out tomorrow. I'll quit my job, too, if that would help."

"I don't want you to do either of those things."

"Then what? Wear a burka?"

"I'm going to be spending more time with Charles. You and Tom can have the house to yourselves to work out whatever you have to work out."

"*There is nothing to work out.*"

"The point is simply—"

"I thought you guys were sane and normal. That's part of what I love about you. And now it's like I'm a lab rat you're leaving alone in a cage with another rat to see what happens."

"That's not what I'm doing."

"Sure feels like it."

"Tom and I are having some trouble. That's all it is. Can I get you an Ambien?"

Pip took the Ambien and woke up alone in the house. In the windows was a pale gray Colorado morning sky of the sort from which she'd learned not to predict the afternoon weather—it could snow or turn shockingly warm—but she was grateful for the bright overcast; it matched her spirits. She'd been terminated by Andreas but also released; she felt both bruised and cleaner. After reheating and eating some frozen waffles, she went out walking toward downtown Denver.

The air smelled like spring, and the Rockies, behind her, all snowy, were there to remind her that she still had many things to do in life, such as going up to Estes Park and experiencing the mountains from close range. She could do this after she made her confession to Tom and before she returned to California. In the crisp air, she saw clearly that the time to confess had come. As long as she'd had her late-night textings and touchings, she'd had some *reason* to have planted the spyware and to avoid the awfulness of telling Tom about it: she was bewitched and enslaved by Andreas. Now there was no reason, nor any sense in trying to preserve the life she had going in Denver, however eagerly she'd taken to it. The whole thing was built on lies, and she wanted to come clean.

Her resolve was firm until she arrived at DI and was reminded that she loved the place. The overhead lights were off in the main space, but two journalists were in the conference room and Pip could hear Leila's pretty telephone voice in her task-lighted work space. Pip hesitated in the corridor, wondering if she could still avoid confessing. Maybe if the spyware disappeared? But whatever was upsetting Leila wasn't going away. If she was upset about Tom liking Pip too much, a full confession would certainly put an end to that. Pip took the long way around to his office, avoiding Leila.

His door was standing open. As soon as he saw Pip, he reached quickly for his computer mouse.

"Sorry," she said. "Are you in the middle of something?"

For a moment, he seemed totally guilty. He opened his mouth without saying anything. Then, collecting himself, he told her to come in and shut the door. "We're in battle mode," he said. "Or Leila's in battle mode. I'm in Leila-care mode. Her engine runs hot when she's afraid of being scooped."

Pip shut the door and sat down. "I gather she got something big yesterday."

"Ghastly thing. Major story. Bad for everyone except us. It's very good for us, assuming we're the ones to break it. She'll fill you in—she's going to need your help."

"An actual weapon went missing?"

"Yes and no. It never left Kirtland. Armageddon was averted." Tom leaned back in his chair, catching the fluorescent light on his terrible glasses. "This was probably before your time, but there used to be a countdown-to-Armageddon clock. Union of Concerned Scientists, I believe. It would be four minutes to midnight, and then there'd be a new round of arms-control talks, and the clock would go back to five minutes before midnight. It all seems vaguely cheesy and ridiculous now, like everything else from those years. What kind of clock runs backward?"

He seemed to be free-associating to conceal something.

"They still have that clock," Pip said.

"Really."

"But you're right, it feels dated. People are more advertising-literate these days."

He laughed. "Plus it turns out that it wasn't actually five minutes to midnight in 1975, otherwise we'd all be dead now. It was nine fifteen or something."

Pip's own countdown-to-confession clock was stuck at one second before midnight.

"Anyway, Leila's on the ragged edge," Tom said. "She comes across as so unthreatening that people don't realize how competitive she is."

"I'm realizing it, a little bit."

"A couple of years ago, she was way out in front on the Toyota recall story, or she thought she was. She thought she had time to nail it down tight and break it complete. And then suddenly she starts hearing from her contacts in the agencies. *They're* calling *her* to tell her they just

heard an amazing story from the *Journal*'s guy. These
were people who hadn't known anything, hadn't told
her anything, and now they had the whole story! She's
hearing that the *Journal*'s guy was up all night drafting.
She's hearing that the *Journal* is already lawyering it.
And there's no worse feeling. No worse thing to write
than a story where you have to credit the guy you were
way ahead of until two days ago. Apparently the *WaPo*'s
on the Kirtland story—Leila found that out yesterday.
We're still ahead, but probably not by much."

"Is she drafting?"

"That's what sleepless nights are for. I'd almost rather
get scooped than see her in the state she's in. You need to
help me try to keep her halfway sane."

Pip was starting to feel bad about having lashed out at
Leila; to wonder if she was simply overstressed by work.

"But listen," Tom said, leaning forward. "Before you
go, I want to ask you a personal question."

"I actually had something to—"

"We were talking about your dad the other night. And
I've been thinking—you're a great researcher. Have you
ever tried to find him?"

She frowned. Why did people keep asking her about
her father? In her guilty frame of mind, she had the curious thought that *Andreas* was secretly her father. That this
was why her mother was so hostile to him. That Tom and
Leila had discovered the spyware and knew more about
her than she herself did. Andreas as her dad: the thought
was crazy but had a certain logic, the logic of ick, the logic
of guilt.

"Yeah, I've tried," she said. "But my mom covered her
tracks really well. The only thing I've got is her made-up
name and my approximate date of birth. I always seemed
to be the right size for the grade I was in. But I know my
birth certificate is fake."

The look Tom was giving her was worrisomely loving. She lowered her eyes.

"You know," she said, "I'm not a very good person."

"What are you talking about? What's not good about you?"

She took a deep breath. "I don't always tell the truth."

"About what? About your father?"

"No, that part is true."

"Then what?"

Just say it, she thought. *Say: I was in Bolivia, not California . . .*

There was a tap on the door.

Tom jumped to his feet. "Come in, come in."

It was Leila. She looked at Pip and spoke to Tom. "I was on the phone with Janelle Flayner. I was thinking last night about something she'd said to me. Something like 'It's about time someone listened.'"

"Leila," Tom said gently.

"Hear me out. This is not paranoia. She said that, and I called her, and it turns out that, yes, she did communicate with someone else. Before me. While Cody's pictures were still up on Facebook, she sent a message to the *famous leaker*. 'The Sunshine Boys?' That's what she said. The Sunshine Boys. The place that everybody sends their tips to."

Pip had one of those double blushes, a mild one followed by a burning whole-body wave.

"So what?" Tom said, less gently.

"Well, Mrs. Flayner didn't hear back. Nothing ever happened."

"Good. Happy ending. He couldn't do shit from Bolivia. To cover a story like this, you need boots on the ground."

"Well, but Wolf never put the pictures up. He puts up

twenty things a day—there's no filter. But for some reason he didn't put this one up."

"I'm serenely unworried."

"I'm radically worried."

"Leila. He's had the information for almost a year. Why would he suddenly decide to float it in the next five days?"

"Because these stories have a boiling point. Suddenly everyone starts talking overnight. If he gets one more leak, he can spit in the soup. It's bad enough if the *Post* does it to me. But if *that guy* gets there first—"

"The world looks very scary when you haven't slept. You're the one who's sitting on the elephant. You're the only one who can connect the dots from Amarillo to Albuquerque."

"People steal elephants. It happens all the time."

"If you want to worry about something, worry about the *Post*."

Leila laughed raggedly. "I'm all over that, too. They've got to be days ahead of me on the Kirtland drug scandal. Probably weeks. There's no way I can cover it when I'm also confirming the nuke story."

"You'll pick up enough of it collaterally. It's fine if the *Post* has more detail on it, so long as we're first. Let them add the salt to our soup. Worst case, they're out in front with a drug story, and we follow with an Armageddon story."

"You're sure you don't want to do a co-op with them?"

"With a Jeff Bezos joint? I can't believe you're even asking."

"Then prepare for me to be a wreck."

Leila left, and Tom gazed after her. "I hate to see her like this," he said. "It feels like the end of the world to her when she gets beaten."

Pip wondered if she'd been mistaken. He wasn't seeming like a man in love with anyone but Leila.

"Do you have your phone?" he said.

"My phone?"

"I want to make some calls to the *Post*. Dial some numbers and see who's there on a Saturday. If the people I have in mind aren't there, she can worry a little less."

Even though Pip had come here to confess, she was tempted to say she didn't have her device with her; it was radioactive with incriminating texts. But to claim not to have it was dumb and implausible. When she handed it over to Tom, it felt like a small bomb, and when she left his office she stationed herself outside the door, hoping her proximity would inhibit him from reading her texts.

She saw that she'd lost her nerve and wouldn't be confessing anything today. If, as she now suspected, she'd been mistaken about Tom's interest in her, there might be nothing so terrible about her situation that uninstalling Andreas's spyware couldn't fix it. When Tom emerged from his office, smiling, she took her phone to the ladies' room and locked herself in a stall.

> You'll think I'm being a bitch because you don't want me. Maybe I am. But you have to tell me if you can uninstall your spyware. If you can, you have to do it. You've put me in a horrible position. I want it to be like I never met you. I want to delete all that and have a life here. If you care about me at all, you'll write back to me. If I don't hear from you, I'll have to tell T everything. Yes, that's a threat.

She sent the text and went to Leila's work space, where Leila was on the phone again. Pip stood in the corridor with her head bowed, trying to look penitent.

"I'm sorry if I make you self-conscious," she said when

Leila was off the phone. "Are you too upset with me to let me help you?"

Leila seemed about to say something angry that she reconsidered. "We're not going to talk about that," she said. "You need to be a journalist this week. Not a researcher, not a houseguest. Do you think you can work with me?"

"I love working with you."

The first task Pip was given was to gather basic facts about the execution-style killing of two women in Tennessee. The facts turned out to be consistent with the appalling story Leila told her. The women, sisters with the maiden name Keneally, had been abducted within minutes of each other in different cities; neither body showed signs of sexual trauma, and officially the police had no leads. As Pip proceeded to learn what she could about the hospitalization and disappearance of the sisters' brother, Richard, she began to think she'd been petulant and childish in threatening to quit her job. Although living with Tom and Leila was clearly a mistake, the job wasn't.

She kept retreating to the ladies' room to check messages, but it wasn't until she and Tom had gone home for a late dinner and she was in bed, at the usual texting hour, that Andreas's reply came in.

I'll ask Chen what he can do.

She turned off the device without replying. She'd forced him to break his vow not to text her again, and she felt good about it. Less like a child, more like an adult who had some power. Not like a rigorously moral person, certainly; but moral absolutism was childish. Downtown, at her desk, Leila was gutting out some private misery, sitting alone at the office after midnight, drafting her story, because Leila was an adult. Her toughness made Pip see

Andreas in a new light, as a kind of child-man, obsessed with spilling secrets. She squirmed with displeasure at the recollection of his hand in her pants. She could see—she thought she could see—that what adults did was suck it up and keep their secrets to themselves. Her mother, a gray-haired child in so many ways, was an adult in this one regard at least. She kept her secrets and paid the price. Pip imagined herself continuing to work at DI, knowing what she knew, having done what she'd done, and not confessing it, just as Leila had said: *We're not going to talk about that.*

Her new feeling of adultness persisted through the days that followed, as Leila went back to Washington to confirm her story, returned home triumphant but even more anxious (one of her sources had uttered the words "You might not be alone"), and pulled yet another all-nighter to finish her draft. By Thursday morning the lawyer was on it. Pip had slept very little herself and was going to be rewarded with an additional-reporting byline. She hadn't had an unexhausted moment to think about Andreas or whether the spyware was still installed; she was fact-checking like a madwoman. The suspense in the office seemed both silly and exciting. Silly because the whole thing was just a game that had nothing to do with social utility (what did it matter if they beat the *WaPo* by an hour or a day?) but exciting in the way the Manhattan Project must have been exciting: they'd been building their information bomb for months, and now they were waiting to explode it.

She was still checking less essential facts when the story went up on Friday morning.

**THEFT OF THERMONUCLEAR WEAPON IN
NEW MEXICO THWARTED BY ACCIDENT**
MISSING PERPETRATOR TIED TO MEXICAN CARTEL
AND DRUG ABUSE AT KIRTLAND AFB; ALARM FIRST
RAISED AT WEAPONS PLANT IN TEXAS

Leila had gone home with a fever that she hoped to sleep off in time for interviews with NPR and cable news. The social-media team was manning its battle station, and more phones than usual seemed to be ringing, but the office was otherwise unshaken by the detonation of the information bomb. Other reporters still had their own stories, and Tom had been closeted in his office for more than an hour. The blast wave and radiation pulse were occurring in cyberspace.

Pip was on the phone with a Sonic Drive-In manager, trying to reach Phyllisha Babcock, whose tale of death-bomb sex had squeaked into the article in one-graf form, when the office IT manager, Ken Warmbold, came by her desk. He waited while she wrote down the hours of Phyllisha's shift, and then he told her that Tom wanted to see her. She left her desk reluctantly. Fact-checking had tapped into her compulsion for cleanliness. It was making her crazy to have the article up with even tiny facts unchecked.

Tom was sitting at his desk with his fingers knit together and pressed to his mouth. His interlocked knuckles were white with the force he was applying to them. "Shut the door," he said.

She obeyed him and sat down.

"Who sent you here?" he said.

"Just now?"

"No. To Denver. I know the answer, so you might as well tell me."

She opened her mouth and closed it. She'd been so deep in fact-checking, it hadn't occurred to her to wonder why Tom was closeted with the IT manager.

"Obviously I'm upset," he said, not looking at her. "But I'm willing to consider the possibility that you're not entirely to blame. So just say what you have to say."

She tried to speak. Swallowed. Tried again. "I wanted to say it. On Saturday. I'm sorry I didn't."

"So say it now."

"I don't want to."

"Why is that?"

"You'll hate me. Leila will hate me."

He tossed some stapled pages across his desk. "This is Ken's report on the office network. We have extremely good security here. We're protected against every form of spyware known to man. But apparently there's one not known to man. It has a completely alien signature. It took some finding, but Ken found it."

Pip's eyes weren't working right. The words of the report were just a blur.

"Did you know about this?" Tom said.

"Not for positive. But I did worry. I opened an attachment I shouldn't have."

He tossed another document at her. "What about this? This is the report on my home computer. Did you open any suspicious attachments at home?"

"There was one . . ."

He slammed his hand down on his desk. "Say the name!"

"I don't want to," she whimpered.

"My home hard drive's been scraped for two weeks. My business network's been an open book since three days after we hired you. And who brought me the story I just broke? Who was the intern who brought me the Facebook pictures? What is the name of the leaker who we now know had those pictures last summer?"

"I don't know."

"Say it!"

She burst into tears. "I'm sorry! I'm so ashamed!"

Tom pushed a box of tissues toward her and waited, with crossed arms, for her tears to abate.

"I lied," she said, sniffling. "I was in Bolivia for six months. The Sunlight Project. That's where I got the Facebook pictures. From *him*. I lied to you about that. I lied about everything, and I'm so sorry. I know it's a disaster."

"Do you really?"

"Yes! All our confidential sources, all our databases, everything. I know. *I get it*. I'm so sorry."

Tom's eyes were fixed on some unseen presence, not her.

"I met this German woman in Oakland," she said. "She wanted me to go to Bolivia. She said the Project could help me find my father. And so I went there, and he was—"

"Say the name."

"I can't. But he took this special interest in me, and he told me something. I think you may know it."

"Say it."

"That he killed someone. That there was one other person he'd told, and it was you. And then I gave up on finding my father and I wanted to leave, and he told me to come here. He was afraid you wanted to expose him. He sent me an email attachment. I knew what it was, and I opened it anyway. But I swear to you that's all I did."

Tom pressed his fingertips to his forehead. "And why would you do this for him?"

"I don't know! I felt bad for him—he came on really strong with me. I thought I had to respond. I did respond, I was bad. I mean, he's really famous, I couldn't help it. But then I didn't like him, and he was hurt, and, I don't know, I guess I felt I owed him something. And then I was so happy here—the whole thing started seeming like this horrible dirty dream."

"Dirty."

"I didn't sleep with him. I didn't."

"Why would I care who you sleep with?"

The phone rang. Tom looked at it, unplugged it, and continued to look at it.

"Well, anyway," she said. "I was a willing accomplice. You can call the police if you want."

"What would that serve?"

"To punish me."

"I admit that I have no patience with liars. I think it's best if you hand in your resignation and go home to your mother. But I'm not interested in punishing you."

Pip had never been arrested, never sent to a principal's office, never yelled at by a father. She'd done some bad things in her life but nothing so bad that she hadn't been able to get away with it by being cute, or pitiable, or obviously well-meaning. She'd always managed to avoid scenes of harsh discipline; and now she was getting what she deserved. But still it seemed cruel and unusual that Tom was the man she was in trouble with. She couldn't think of anyone whose standards she would have wanted less to run afoul of. His maturity and manliness, his fleshy shaved cheeks, his bald head, his crookedly knotted tie, his fashion-defying glasses all seemed to brook no nonsense. She felt wretchedly sad that this had to be the man, of all men, whom she'd betrayed and disappointed.

He was flipping through one of the IT reports. "The office breach doesn't worry me too much," he said. "The guy's whole business depends on protecting his sources. I think he'll protect mine. At worst, he'll try to poach them. What concerns me is the home computer."

"I'm sorry," Pip said. "That was so dumb of me. One of the Project girls sent me an email attachment. I never should have opened it."

"Have you had access to my home computer since then?"

"Me? No! I mean, how could I? Don't you have passwords?"

"The software records keystrokes."

"I don't know anything about it. I didn't even know there *was* spyware. I mean, I was worried, but I wasn't sure."

"He didn't send you any passwords?"

"No."

"So you haven't seen anything on my hard drive. He hasn't sent you any documents from it."

"No! We broke off contact!"

"Why should I believe you? You've done nothing but lie to us."

"You and Leila are my heroes. I would never spy on you. I would never read anything I wasn't supposed to. I adore you guys."

"And what if he sent you a document now? What would you do?"

"If I knew it was yours," she said, "I wouldn't read it."

Tom released a long sigh, his shoulders caving inward around the loss of the air that he'd been holding in. Again he was staring at some invisible presence. Pip wondered what document of his could be so explosive that he had to worry about her reading it. She couldn't imagine that he, of all men, had anything to hide.

[le1o9n8a0rd]

My affair with Anabel had begun as soon as our divorce decree came through. In exchange for stipulating that I'd abandoned her—"abandonment" being one of the few grounds for divorce that New York state law recognized, and the one that Anabel felt best captured the wrong she'd suffered—I'd been permitted to reclaim our valuable rent-controlled tenement in East Harlem while Anabel went off to live by herself in the woods of New Jersey. Since there could be no talk of inflicting Manhattan on her, I had to take the bus across 125th Street and the subway up to 175th, followed by a much longer and invariably nauseating bus ride over the Hudson and out through increasingly raw developments to the hills northwest of Netcong.

I'd made this trip twice in February, twice in March, and once in April. On the last Saturday in May, my phone rang around seven in the morning, not long after I'd gone to bed drunk. I answered it only to stop the ringing.

"Oh," Anabel said. "I thought I was going to get your machine."

"I'll hang up and you can leave a message," I said.

"No, this is only going to be thirty seconds. I swear I will not get drawn in again."

"Anabel."

"I just wanted to say that I reject your version of us. I utterly reject it. That's my message."

"Couldn't you have rejected my version by just never calling me again?"

"I'm not getting drawn in," she said, "but I know the way you operate. You interpret silence as capitulation."

"You don't remember me promising I'd never interpret your silence that way. The very last time we spoke."

"I'm hanging up now," she said, "but at least be honest, Tom, and admit that your promise was a low trick. A way of having the last word."

I laid the phone on my mattress, next to my ear and mouth. "Are we at the point yet where I get blamed for this conversation lasting more than thirty seconds? Or do I still have that to look forward to?"

"No, I'm hanging up," she said. "I wanted to say for the record that you're completely wrong about us. But that's all. So. I'm going to hang up."

"OK, then. Good-bye."

But she could never hang up, and I could never bear to do it for her.

"I'm not blaming you," she said. "You did consume my youth and then abandon me, but I know you're not responsible for my happiness out here, although in fact I'm having a good time and things are going pretty well, unbelievable as it may sound to a person who considers me, quote, 'unequipped' to deal with the, quote, 'real world.'"

"'Consumed my youth and then abandoned me,'" I quoted back. "But this is not a provocation. You just wanted to leave a thirty-second message."

"Which I would have done! But you *reacted*—"

"I reacted, Anabel—do I need to point this out? I reacted to your picking up a telephone and dialing my number."

"Right, I know, because I'm so needy. Right? I'm so pathetically needy."

I couldn't have named one instant of happiness or ease from our previous togetherness binge, four weeks earlier. I emerged from these binges feeling bruised and harrowed, with worrisome bomb craters in my memory but also a vague, sick craving for a do-over.

"Look," I said. "Do you want to get together? Do you want me to come out? Is that why you called?"

"No! I do not want to get together! I want to hang up the phone if you would please just let me!"

"Usually, in the past, though, when you've called," I said, "you've started out saying you didn't want to get together, and then, after a couple of hours on the phone, it's come out that you did actually, all along, underneath, want to get together."

"If *you* want to come out and see *me*," she said, "you should have the decency to say so in so many words—"

"And by then, of course—"

"Like any polite man who wants to spend time with a woman he respects, instead of making your invitation some sort of icky *accusation*—"

"By then, of course," I said, "it's gotten to be pretty late in the day, which means that by the time we actually do get together, which is what you've secretly wanted all along, it's *very* late, and when we then, inevitably, go ahead and sleep together—"

"Instead of insidiously twisting things around," she said. "So that it looks like *my* neediness rather than yours, *my* lousy life rather than your own lousy life—"

"Inevitably go ahead and sleep together—"

"I don't want to sleep with you! I don't want to see you! That's not why I called! I called to say a simple thing which—"

"It's three or four in the morning before we actually get around to the sleeping part of sleeping together, which, with three hours of travel and a workday ahead of me, has tended, in the past, to become kind of a bad scene. Is all I'm trying to remind you."

"If you want to come out and go for a hike with me," she said, "that would be very nice. I would like that. But you have to say it's what *you* want."

"But I didn't call you," I said.

"But you were the one who brought up getting together. So just be honest with me now."

"Is this something you want?"

"Not unless you want it and you say so like a human being."

"But that perfectly mirrors my own sentiments. So."

"Look, I *called*," she said. "You could at least—"

"What could I do?"

"Do you think I'm going to *harm* you if you let your defenses down for one tiny half second? I mean, what do you think I'm going to do? Make you my slave? Force you to be married to me again? It's a hike, for God's sake, it's just a hike!"

Simply to avoid the two-hour version of this conversation—wherein Party A tried to prove that Party B had made the fatal statement that prolonged the conversation in the first place, and Party B challenged Party A's version of events, and this, in turn, there being no actual transcript, compelled Party A to reconstruct from memory the conversation's overture and Party B to offer a reconstruction that differed from Party A's in certain crucial respects, which then necessitated a time-devouring joint effort to collate and reconcile the two reconstructions—I agreed to go out to New Jersey and take a hike.

Anabel was cleansing her spirit on land that belonged to the parents of her younger friend and only fan, Suzanne. One of my first actions after requesting a divorce was to sleep with Suzanne. She'd asked me out to dinner as a kind of ambassador for Anabel, intending to talk me into reconsidering the divorce, but she was so worn out from listening to Anabel's complaints about me and about the New York art world, in nightly two-hour phone calls, that I ended up talking her into betraying Anabel. I must have been trying to make Anabel want a divorce as much as I did, but things hadn't worked out that way. She'd terminated her friendship with Suzanne and accused me of refusing to rest until I'd stolen or polluted every last thing she had. But the upshot, according to her curious moral calculus, was that both Suzanne and I owed her. I continued to take Anabel's calls and get together with her, and Suzanne allowed her to keep living on the New Jersey property, which Suzanne's parents, who'd relocated to New Mexico, were trying to sell at an unrealistic price.

The frosty bus ejected me at a nowhere little intersection in the woods. For a split second my eyeballs fogged up in the humidity. A kind of atmospheric curfew had been imposed by the heat—everything felt close and lush. Greenhouse. I saw Anabel step out of some trees where she'd been hiding. She was smiling broadly and, all things considered, inappropriately. My face did something grotesque and inappropriate in reply.

" 'Hello, Tom.' "

" 'Hello, Anabel.' "

Her extraordinary mane of dark hair, whose intricate care and increasingly frequent colorings probably occupied her more than any activity except sleeping and meditating, was all the thicker and more splendid in the steam of summer. Between the top of her beltless corduroys and the bottom of a tight plaid short-sleeved shirt was a strip of naked belly that could have been a thirteen-year-old's. She was thirty-six. I was two months short of thirty-four.

"You're allowed to come closer to me," she said at the moment I was about to come closer.

"Or not," she added, at the moment I was deciding not to.

Bus fumes lingered in the buggy road cut.

"We're sort of perfectly out of sync here," I said.

"Are we?" she said. "Or is it just you? I don't feel out of sync."

I wanted to point out that, by definition, a person couldn't be in sync with a person who was out of sync with her; but there was a logic tree to consider. Every utterance of hers gave me multiple options for response, each of which would prompt a different utterance, to which, again, I would have multiple options in responding, and I knew how quickly I could be led eight or ten steps out onto some dangerous tree branch and what a despair-inducingly slow job it was to retrace my steps back up the branch to a neutral starting point, since the job of retracing the steps would itself result in utterances to which I would inevitably produce a certain percentage of complicating responses; and so I'd learned to be exceedingly careful about what I said in our first moments together.

"I should tell you right now," I said, "that I absolutely have to catch the last bus back into the city tonight. It's a really early bus, like eight o'clock."

Anabel's face became sad. "I won't stop you."

In the minute I'd been off the bus, the sky had steadily grown less gray. Sweat was popping out all over me, as if somebody had turned on a broiler.

"You always think I'm trying to detain you," Anabel said. "First I bring you out here when you don't want to come here. Then I make you stay here when you want to be gone. You're the one who's always coming and going, but somehow you have the idea that I'm the one pulling the strings. Which, if *you* feel powerless, just imagine how I feel."

"I wanted to get it said," I said carefully. "I had to say

it sometime, and if I'd said it later, it might have seemed like I'd been trying to hide it from you."

She tossed her mane with displeasure. "Because of course it would disappoint me. Of course it would break my heart if you had to catch the eight eleven bus. You're standing there wondering: What is the best moment to convey this heartbreaking news to your clinging, suffocating, former whatever-I-am?"

"Well, as you're kind of demonstrating right now," I pointed out, "both approaches carry their own risk."

"I don't know why you think I'm your enemy."

Cars were approaching on the main road. I moved up the smaller road toward Anabel, and she asked me if I'd thought she would be *disappointed* that I wasn't spending the night.

"Possibly, a little bit," I said. "But only because you'd mentioned that you didn't have anything planned all day tomorrow."

"When do I ever have anything planned?"

"Well, exactly. And that's why the fact that you went so far as to mention it—"

"Instantly became translated in your mind into the threat of recrimination if you decided not to spend tomorrow with me, too."

I inhaled. "There's an element of truth to that."

"Well, good," she said. "And I'm suddenly not sure I want to see you at all, so."

"That's fine," I said, "although I wish you'd told me that before you'd invited me out here and I'd spent half a day on buses."

"I didn't invite you. I accepted your offer to come out. There's a big difference there. Especially when you show up so full of animosity, and the first thing out of your mouth is how soon you have to leave. The first thing out of your mouth."

"Anabel."

"*You* rode the bus all day. *I* sat here waiting for you. Who has it worse? Who's more pathetic?"

It was humiliating to do the logic tree with her. Humiliating how ready I was to contest the pettiest point, humiliating to still be doing it after having done it so infernally much in the previous twelve years. It was like beholding my addiction to a substance that had long since ceased to give me the slightest kick of pleasure. Which was why our meetings now had to take place in the strictest secrecy. Anywhere else but deep in the woods, we would have been too ashamed of ourselves.

"Can we just hike?" I said, shouldering my knapsack.

"Yes! Do you think I want to stand here talking like this?"

The little road ran near the boundary of Stokes State Forest. We'd had a wet spring, and the plant kingdom of the ditches and the successional meadows and the stonier-sloped woods was fantastically green. Obscene amounts of pollen were in the air, the trees burdened with the bright dust of their own fertility, the swollenness of their leaves. We squeezed through the jaws of a rusty gate and went down an old dirt road so badly washed out that it was more like a creek bed. Weeds liable to repent of their exuberance very soon—weeds already bigger than they ever ought to have been, weeds on steroids, weeds about to lean and buckle and be ugly—shouldered in so high on both sides that we had to walk single file.

"I don't suppose I'm allowed to ask you why you 'have to' go back tonight," Anabel said.

"Not really, no."

"It would be just too painful for me to hear you have a brunch date with Winona Ryder."

My presumptive interest in dating much younger pretty girls, now that I was divorced, had become a leitmotif of

Anabel's. But my actual date the next day was for dinner, not brunch, and was not with a girl but with Anabel's father, whom she loathed and hadn't seen in more than a decade. Despite our well-demonstrated pattern of recidivism, I'd allowed myself to believe that I really wouldn't ever hear from her again, and that I could see her father without fear of being castigated for it.

"Isn't that what the girlies like to do now?" Anabel said. "Meet for 'brunch'? I do believe there's no more sickening word in the English language. The mingled smells of quiche lorraine and sausage grease."

"I have to go back because I need to get some sleep, not having had any last night."

"Oh, right. I woke you up. I still need to be punished for that."

I managed not to respond. I was starting to remember chunks of binge that I'd blacked out from my previous visit, but it felt less like remembering than reliving. Past and future mingled in the land of Tom and Anabel. The New Jersey sky was a low-hanging steambath of churning flocculence, darkening and then yellowly brightening in random places that gave no clue about the sun's actual location or, thus, about what time it was or where east and west might be. My disorientation deepened when Anabel led me up into woods once haunted by the Lenape tribe. It was simultaneously five and one and seven and last month and tomorrow afternoon.

Anabel stayed ahead of me, her corduroy butt directly in my line of sight. She led me along deer trails, long-legged like a deer herself, skirting anything that looked like poison ivy. She was no longer life-threateningly malnourished the way she'd been in the years leading up to our separation, but she was still thin. Around her ribs and waist were curves of the kind that wind carves in snowdrifts.

We were coming down a spongy rust-brown hillside of pine needle when I saw that she'd unbuttoned her shirt. Its little tails fluttered at her sides. She didn't turn back but started running down the hill. How oppressively hot the woods were, compared to the road! I followed my ex-wife into a small clearing by a lake that appeared to have dried up, though not before drowning all the trees that had once stood in the basin. It was a forest of big gray sticks, the same metallic color as the sky. A silvery heron lifted itself into the air.

"Here," Anabel said. There was moss and rock and bare dirt underfoot. She shrugged off her shirt and turned around and showed herself to me. Her areolae were too big and outrageously red-red to bear looking at. It was as if her skin were a cream-colored silk into which the blood from matching punctures had seeped extensively. I averted my eyes.

"I'm trying to become less shy with you," she said.

"Seems to be going pretty well today."

"So look at me."

"All right."

Her blush was highlighting the long, thin line of scar tissue on her forehead—a vestige of the same childhood horse-riding accident that had cost her most of her two front teeth, which had been capped expensively, if not altogether imperceptibly. Between these two teeth was a gap that to me had always been a sexy thing. Her little come-hither gap. The continual suggestion of a tongue.

She shook her breasts at me and shuddered with shyness and turned away, embracing the trunk of a beech tree. "Look, I'm a tree hugger," she said.

This was the point at which we were supposed to reverse course and scamper back down to the unitary trunk of the logic tree, all the yes-no branchings converging in assent: yes yes yes. I took off my clothes and discovered that although we were divorced I'd packed six condoms in my little knapsack.

Anabel, lying prone on moss and dirt, offering herself like an original Lenape woman, told me these weren't necessary.

"How so not necessary?"

"Just not," she said.

"To be discussed later," I said, tearing open a package.

I was still so thin in 1991 that I didn't really have a body at all. What I had was more like an armature of coat-hanger wire with a few key sensory parts attached to it—a lot of head, a fair amount of hands, an erection either tyrannical or absent, and nothing else. I was like a thing drawn by Joan Miró. I was all idea. Six times now, this weird contraption had hauled itself out to the scenic Delaware Water Gap region to be part of some bad idea that Anabel and I now jointly had about ourselves. It wasn't snuggly, it wasn't nice. It was her lying down on something hard or squalid and the coat-hanger-wire contraption jumping on furiously.

I asked if I was hurting her.

"Not . . . *damaging* me. . . . . . . as far as I can tell . . ."

She said this with an ironic twinkle. There was a football-size rock near her head. I wondered if she'd deliberately lain down by this rock to suggest a thing that she was still too shy with me to ask for. I wondered if the idea was for me to pick up the rock and smash her skull with it.

"How about now?" I said, thrusting hard.

"Now damage possible."

All we ever argued about was nothing. As if by multiplying zero content by infinite talk we could make it stop being zero. In order to have sex again we'd had to separate, and in order to have frenzied and compulsive sex we'd had to get divorced. It was a way of raging against the giant nothing that arguing had ever done to save us. It was the one argument that each of us could lose with honor. But then it was over and there was nothing again.

Anabel was lying facedown on the rocks and dirt, quietly sobbing, while I sorted out the topology of pants legs and underwear. I knew better than to ask why she was crying. We'd be here until nightfall if I did that. Much better to start hiking again and actually cover some ground while we had the conversation about why I hadn't asked her why she was crying.

She stood up to put her shirt on. "So," she said. "Now you've had your treat, and you can go back to the city."

"Please don't try to tell me you didn't want that yourself."

"But it was the *only* thing you wanted," she said. "And so now you can go back. Unless you want to do it again right now and then go back."

Slapping a mosquito on my forearm, I looked at my watch and couldn't read what it plainly said.

"Tell me why we never had children," Anabel said. "I don't remember what your explanation was."

I felt suddenly light-headed. Even by Anabel standards, her broaching of the subject of children seemed an exorbitantly high price for me to pay for a few minutes of sex. She was also presenting the bill brutally soon.

"Do you remember?" she said. "Because I don't remember any real discussion."

"So let's have a five-hour discussion about it right now," I said. "This would be a great time and a great place."

"You said, 'To be discussed later.' And now it's later."

I killed another mosquito. "I'm suddenly getting bit."

"I've been getting bitten the whole time."

"I didn't realize you meant that kind of discussion."

"What did you think I meant?"

I touched the plump knotted rubber in my pants

pocket. "I don't know. Some possible-other-partners, epidemiological type of thing."

"Safe to say I don't want to hear about that."

"Lot of mosquitoes here," I said. "We should move."

"Do you even know where we are? Can you find your way back?"

"No."

"So I guess you need me after all. If you want to catch your bus."

Strict vigilance was needed to avoid getting lost in the logic tree, but Anabel's heat, the heat of her back and of our liquid interfacing, and the scent of the Mane 'n Tail shampoo in her hair, which was always faint but never entirely absent, had dulled my thinking. I'd eaten the opium of Anabel, with predictable consequences. I said, somewhat desperately, "Look, I already know there's no way you're letting me catch that bus."

"Letting you. Ha."

"Not you," I said, "I meant *us*. There's no way we're letting me catch the bus."

But the mistake had been made. She kicked her feet into her sneakers. "We'll go right back and wait," she said. "Just to spare me a tiny bit of your hatred for once in my life. So for once I don't have to be blamed for making you miss your bus."

Anabel refused to see that there was simply something broken about us, broken beyond repair and beyond assignment of blame. During our previous binge, we'd talked for nine hours nonstop, pausing only for bathroom breaks. I'd thought I'd finally succeeded in showing her that the only way out of our misery was to renounce each other and never communicate again; that nine-hour conversations were themselves the sickness that they were purportedly trying to cure. This was the version of us that she'd called me this morning to reject. But what was her version? Impossible to say. She was so morally sure of herself, moment by moment, that I perpetually had the feeling that we were getting somewhere; only afterward could I see that we'd been moving in a large, empty circle. For all her intelligence and sensitivity, she not only wasn't making sense but was unable to recognize that she wasn't, and it was terrible to see this in a person to whom I'd been so profoundly devoted and had made a vow of lifelong care. And so I had to keep working with her to help her understand why I couldn't keep working with her.

"Here's what's fucked up," I said as we climbed out of the ruined basin and up to a less buggy height. "Just speaking for myself. A month goes by, and I'm feeling so freakish and depressed and ashamed, because of the last time we got together, that I can barely show my face to another human being. And so I have to come out here, and once I'm here it's practically *biological* that I'm going to end up staying thirty-six hours, and raising all sort of false hopes and expectations—"

Anabel spun around. "Shut up! Shut up! Shut up!"

"Do you want me to kill you?"

She shook her head emphatically, no, no, she didn't want to be killed.

"Then don't call me."

"I wasn't strong enough."

"Don't get me out here again. Don't do this to me."

"I wasn't strong enough! For God's sake! Do you have to rub my face in how weak I am?" And she walked in a small circle with her hands bent into claws near her face, which looked as if a swarm of hornets had somehow got inside her head and were stinging her brain.

"Have pity on me," she said.

I seized her and kissed her, my Anabel. She was snotty and teary and hot-breathed and dear. Also quite seriously disturbed and all but unemployable. I kissed her to try to make the pain stop, but in no time I also had my hands down the back of her corduroys. Her hips were so narrow that I could take her pants down without unbuttoning them. We'd been little more than children when we fell in love. Now everything was ashes, ashes of ashes burned at temperatures where ash burns, but our full-fledged sex life had only just begun, and I would never stop loving her. It was the prospect of another two or three or five years of sex in the ashes that made me think of death. When she pulled away from me and dropped to her knees and unzipped my knapsack and took out my Swiss Army knife, I thought she might be thinking of it, too. But instead she was stabbing the five remaining condoms dead.

The apartment on Adalbertstraße was hostage to a stomach. When Clelia closed her eyes at night, she could picture it hovering in the darkness above her cot. Outwardly taut and glossy, a pale pink digestive aubergine with darkish veins stemming off it, the stomach was red and shredded on the inside, awash in caustic liquids and liable to convulse like a raging baby at any hour, especially a wee one. This unhappy organ had its residence in the body of Clelia's mother, Annelie. Clelia slept in the corner of the living room nearest to her mother's bedroom, so that when Annelie called out for milk and zwieback in the night she wouldn't wake the younger children or her brother, Rudi, in their bedrooms, only Clelia.

The stomach was keenly attuned to Clelia's self-pity. It could hear her when she cried herself to sleep, it didn't like her doing this, it threw up blood and bile onto her mother's bedsheets, which Clelia then had to strip and soak. There was no arguing with blood. No matter how cruel her mother was to her, she held the bloody trump card of actually being ill.

Nor was there any arguing that Clelia needed to have a job. Even if she hadn't been denied entry to the university—the university that her father had attended, the four-hundred-year-old university that she passed every morning on her way to the bakery—the family couldn't have afforded to let her go full-time. Uncle Rudi worked for the city in a street-paving capacity, proud in his bright blue coveralls, the German worker's uniform, the true uniform of tyranny in the socialist workers' state, and he took care of his ailing sister to the extent of paying the rent. But he drank and had girlfriends, and so it fell to Clelia to put food on the table. Her brother was fifteen and her sister was still a little girl.

By day Clelia waited on customers at the bakery, by night she waited on the stomach. Only on Saturday afternoons and Sundays did she have a few hours to herself. She liked to walk along the river and, if the day was sunny, find a patch of clean grass to lie down on and close her eyes. She didn't need to see more people, she took money from hundreds of people at the bakery, men who stared at her indecently, old women who tweezed coins from cloth pouches as if picking a nose with thumb and finger. Most of Clelia's *Oberschule* friends were now at the university and strangers to her, the rest kept their distance because her father's family was bourgeois, and she preferred to be by herself anyway, so she could dream of the man who would take her away from Adalbertstraße to Berlin, to France, to England, to America. A man like her father, whom she could still remember following up their building's stairs and hearing gently say, through the grudging one centimeter that their upstairs neighbor had opened his door, "My wife is very sick tonight. Her stomach. If you could not be quite so loud?" A man like that.

On a very warm June Saturday, not long after Clelia had turned twenty, she took off her apron at the bakery and told the manager she was leaving early. Already, in 1954, workers in Jena were learning that no harm would come of leaving early; all it meant was that customers had to wait in longer lines, at worst at the cost of work time at their own jobs, where it likewise didn't matter if they were absent. Clelia hurried home and changed into her favorite old faded lavender summer dress. Her uncle had taken her brother and sister fishing and left her mother, whom the stomach had kept awake all night, asleep in bed. Clelia made a pot of the blackberry tea that her mother claimed was calming to the stomach, although it contained tannic acid and caffeine, and took it to her bedroom with a plate of dry biscuits. She sat on the edge of her mother's bed and stroked her hair the way she remembered her father doing. Her mother awoke and pushed her hand away.

"I brought you some tea before I go out," Clelia said, standing up.

"Where are you going?"

"Out."

Her mother's face was still pretty when the stomach was off duty. She'd suffered for enough years to be ancient now, but she was only forty-three. For a moment, it seemed that she might be about to smile at Clelia, but then her eyes fell to Clelia's body, and her face immediately assumed its customary contours. "Not in that dress you're not."

"What's wrong with this dress? It's a hot day."

"If you had any sense, the last thing you'd do is call attention to your body."

"What's wrong with my body?"

"Its chief defect is that there's rather a lot of it. A girl with any intelligence would seek to minimize its effect."

"I'm very intelligent!"

"No, in fact," her mother said, "you're a stupid goose. And I predict with some confidence that you'll make a present of yourself to the first stranger who says two kind words to you."

Clelia blushed and, blushing, felt herself to be unquestionably a stupid goose: breasty and tall and absurd, with long feet and too much mouth. Goose that she was, she persisted in honking: "Two kind words is more than I ever heard in my whole life with you!"

"That's unjust, but never mind."

"I *wish* some stranger would say kind words to me. I would *love* to hear kind words."

"Oh, yes, it's very nice," her mother said. "Every once in a long while, the stranger might even be sincere."

"I don't care if he's sincere! I just want to hear kind words!"

"Listen to yourself." Her mother felt the pot of tea and filled her cup. "You haven't cleaned the bathroom yet. Your uncle makes a mess of the toilet. I can smell it from in here."

"I'll do it when I get back."

"You'll do it now. I don't understand this 'pleasure first and duty second.' You'll clean the bathroom and wash the kitchen floor, and then, if there's time, you can change your clothes and go out. I don't see how you can enjoy a pleasure when you know there's work to do."

"I won't be gone long," Clelia said.

"Why the hurry?"

"It's such a beautiful warm day."

"Are you going to buy something? Are you worried that the store will close?"

Annelie was good at intuiting the one question Clelia didn't want to answer truthfully, and asking it.

"No," Clelia said.

"Bring me your pocketbook."

Clelia went to the parlor and came back with the pocketbook, which contained some small bills and change. She watched while her mother counted pfennigs. Although her mother hadn't hit her since she became the family's breadwinner, Clelia's expression was all animal edginess, the distraction of cornered prey.

"Where is the rest of it?" her mother said.

"This is all there is. I gave you the rest of it."

"You're lying."

All of a sudden, in the left cup of Clelia's bra, six twenties and eight tens began to stir like crisp-winged insects preparing for flight. She could hear the rustle of their paper wings, which meant that her sharp-eared mother could hear them too. Their scratchy legs and hard heads dug into Clelia's skin. She willed herself not to look down.

"It's the dress," her mother said. "You want to buy the dress."

"You know I can't afford that dress."

"They'll take twenty marks and let you pay installments."

"Not for this, they won't."

"And how do you know that?"

"Because I went and asked! Because I want a nice dress!" Clelia looked down in dismay as her right hand, entirely of its own volition, rose from her side and came to rest on the guilty bra cup. She was such an open book, such a guileless and everywhere-spilling mess, that her mother simply said:

"Show me what you have there."

Clelia took the bills from her bra and gave them to her mother. In the rear of the clothing shop on their street was a particular sundress cut Western or what passed for Western in godforsaken Jena, certainly too Western to be placed on display. Clelia brought the shop lady fresh pastries that she said were old and had to be disposed of, and the shop lady was kind to her. But Clelia was such a stupid goose that she'd described the sundress to her little sister, as an example of what could be found in the rear of stores in the socialist republic, and her mother, though no fan of the socialist republic, had taken note. She was better at surveillance than the socialist republic was. Calm in victory, she put the money in the pocket of her robe, took a sip of tea, and said, "Did you want the dress for some particular assignation? Or just for walking the streets?"

The money didn't rightfully belong to Clelia and was, to this extent, unreal to her, and she felt that she deserved the punishment of having it taken away from her—indeed, she'd reached into her bra with a sense of penitent relief. But seeing the money disappear into her mother's pocket made it real to her again. Six months it had taken her to save it up without being caught. Her eyes filled.

"*You're* the streetwalker," she said.

"I beg your pardon?"

Horrified with herself, she tried to take it back. "I meant, you like to walk in the street. I like to walk in the park."

"But the word you just used. It was?"

"Streetwalker!"

Warm dark tea slapped Clelia full across the bodice of her lavender dress. She looked down, wide-eyed, at the destruction.

"I should have let you starve," her mother said. "But you ate and ate and ate, and now look at how much there is of you. Was I supposed to let my children starve? I couldn't work, and so I did the only thing I could. Because you ate and ate and ate. You have no one but yourself to blame for what I did. It was your appetite, not mine."

It was true enough that her mother had no appetite. But she spoke with such fairy-tale cruelty, in a voice so exacting and controlled, that it was as if there were no mother there at all: as if the person in bed were merely a flesh-and-blood dummy through which the vengeful stomach spoke. Clelia waited to see if some human remnant of her mother might reconsider what she'd said and apologize for it, or at least mitigate it; but her mother's face distorted with a sudden writhing of the stomach. She gestured feebly toward the teapot. "I need hot tea," she said. "This isn't hot enough."

Clelia fled the bedroom and hurled herself onto her cot.

"You're a dirty—*whore!*" she whispered. "*A dirty whore!*"

Hearing herself, she immediately sat up and clamped her mouth shut with her fingers. Tears in her eyes gave trembling, diaphanous wings to the bars of sunlight leaking in around the heavy curtains that the stomach insisted be kept closed. My God, she thought. How can I say that? I'm a terrible person! And then, throwing herself back down on the narrow mattress, she expelled more words into her pillow: "*A whore! A whore! A filthy whore!*" At the same time, she beat on her head with her knuckles. She felt herself to be the world's most terrible person, also one of the most unlucky and ridiculous. Her legs were so long that to sleep on the cot she had to bend them or leave her feet hanging off the end. She was more than one and three-quarters meters tall, a ridiculous goose in the too-small cage of her cot, with the ugliest name any girl was ever given. People at the bakery had the impression that she was stupid because she giggled for no reason and tended to blurt out whatever came into her head.

She wasn't stupid. She got excellent marks in school and could have been taking classes at the university if the committee had let her. The official word was that her father was bourgeois, but her father was dead and her mother and uncle came from the correct social class. The real stigma was that her mother had granted favors to one and then another black-uniformed officer in the worst years. Clelia's little sister was the daughter of the second one. And, yes, Clelia had eaten the meat and butter and candy, but she'd been a child, unversed in evil. It was to the evil stomach that one of the officers had brought an entire case of authentic *Pepto-Bismol*. Annelie had sold herself for the stomach, not for her children.

In my mother's many tellings of this story to me, she always stressed that when she'd changed out of her ruined dress and dropped one hard roll and two books into her purse, she hadn't been intending to abandon her siblings, hadn't been acting on any long-contemplated plan. She just wanted an evening away from the stomach, at most a night and day of relief from an apartment that made her both wholly conscious of the misery of being German and wholly unable to imagine not being German. Until that Saturday in June, the worst thing she'd ever plotted was to buy a Western sundress. Now she'd never have the dress, but she could still go walking in the West, the American sector was only a train ride away.

With thirty marks in her shoulder bag, she hurried downhill to the center of town, which was still being re-built, with socialist unhurry, from the pummeling it had received for harboring the manufacturer of bomb sights and rifle scopes for the war. The round-trip ticket to Berlin cost her nearly all her money. With the little that remained she bought a small bag of candy that left her all the hun-grier by the time the train reached Leipzig. So little had she planned to run away, one dry roll was the only other food she had. But what she mainly yearned for now was fresh air. The air in her train compartment stank of so-cialist underarm, the air from the open window was hot

and rank with heavy industry, the air at the Friedrichstraße station was befouled with cheap tobacco smoke
and bureaucratic ink. She had no sense of being one drop
in the bucket of brains and talent that was draining out of
the republic in those years. She was just a blindly running
goose.

The West was even more ruined than the East, but the
air really was a little fresher, if only because night had
fallen. The impression Clelia had on Kurfürstendamm
was of a place that had experienced a hard winter, not permanent socialist ruination. Already, like the first green
shoots of spring, like snowdrops and crocuses, the vital
signs of commerce were emerging on the Ku'damm. She
walked up the length of it and back down again, never
stopping, because to stop would mean to think about how
hungry she was. She walked and walked, through darker
streets and neighborhoods more demolished. Eventually
she became aware that, in some unthinking animal
way, she was looking for a bakery, because bakeries
dumped their stale *Schrippen* after closing hour on Saturdays. But why, when a person was desperately seeking
one particular kind of store in an unfamiliar city, did she
invariably choose the best route to not find it? Every intersection was another opportunity for error.

Error by error, Clelia blundered into the extremely dark
and deserted neighborhood of Moabit. A light rain had
started falling, and when she finally stopped walking,
under a mutilated linden tree, she had no idea where she
was. But the city seemed to know—seemed only to have
been waiting for her to stop walking. A black sedan, windows open, roof poxed with raindrops, pulled up alongside
her, and a man leaned out from the passenger side.

"Hey there, Legsy!"

Clelia looked around to see if the man might be ad-
dressing someone else.

"Yes—you!" the man said. "How much?"

"Excuse me?"

"How much for the two of us?"

Smiling politely, because the two men were smiling in such a friendly way themselves, Clelia glanced over her shoulder and started walking again in that direction. She stumbled and began to hurry.

"Oh, hey, wait, you're fantastic—"

"Come back—"

"Legsy—Legsy—Legsy—"

She felt she was being impolite, even though the two men appeared to have mistaken her for a prostitute. It was an honest mistake and understandable given the circumstances. I should go back, she thought. I should go back and make sure it really was a mistake, and try to think of the right thing to say, because otherwise they're going to feel embarrassed and ashamed, even though it's my own stupid fault for walking on this street . . . But her legs kept carrying her forward. She could hear the sedan turning around and coming after her.

"Apologies for the misunderstanding," the driver said, slowing the car to match her pace. "You're a decent girl, aren't you?"

"Pretty girl," the other man averred.

"This is no kind of neighborhood for a decent girl to walk in. We'll give you a ride."

"It's raining, sweetheart. Don't you want to get out of the rain?"

She kept moving, too embarrassed to look in their direction, but also unsure of herself, because it really was raining and she was very hungry; and maybe this was how it had started for her mother, too, maybe her mother had once been a girl like she was now, lost in the world and needing something from a man . . .

On the dark sidewalk in front of her another man

loomed up. She stopped and the car stopped. "You see
what I mean?" the driver said to her. "It isn't safe to walk
alone here."

"Come, come," the other one urged. "Come with us."

The man on the sidewalk wasn't physically imposing,
but he had a broad, honest face. And this would have been
my father: even on a dark and rainy night in sinister
Moabit, he was unmistakably trustworthy. I'm helpless to
picture him on that street in anything but cheerfully terrible clothes, his L.L.Bean walking shoes, his khaki high-
water pants, and one of those fifties sport shirts whose
collar tabs opened wide and flat. After sizing up the situation with a frown, he spoke to Clelia in self-taught German: *Entshooldig, fraulein. Con ick dick helfen? Ist allus
okay here? Spreckinzee english?*

"A little," she said in English.

"D'you know these guys? D'you want 'em here?"

After a hesitation, she shook her head. Whereupon my
father, who was in any case physically fearless, and who
believed, moreover, that if you treated people in a rational and friendly manner they would treat you the same
way, and that the world would be a better place if everyone would do this, went over to the sedan and shook the
men's hands, introduced himself in German as Chuck
Aberant of Denver, Colorado, and asked them if they lived
in Berlin or were just visiting like he was, listened with
genuine interest to their answers, and then told them not
to worry about the girl; he would personally vouch for her
safety. It was exceedingly improbable that he would ever
see the men again, but, as my father said, you never knew.
Always worth approaching every man you met as if he
might become your best friend in the world.

My mother, who at twenty had already witnessed the
bombing of Jena, the Red Army's arrival, her mother being doused with the contents of a neighbor's chamber pot,

a dog eating a child's corpse, pianos hacked apart for fire-
wood, and the rise of the socialist workers' state, liked to
say to me that she had never in her life seen anything more
amazing than the American man's warmth toward the two
creeps in their sedan. His kind of trust and openness was,
for a Prussian, inconceivable.

"What's your name?" my father asked her when they
had the street to themselves.

"Clelia."

"Oh my, what a beautiful name," my father said. "That's
a *great* name."

My mother happily smiled and then, certain that she
looked like a mouthsome Tyrannosaur, tried to stretch
her lips down over her hundred teeth; but concealment
was a lost cause. "Do you really think?" she said, smiling
all the more widely.

My father hadn't said two kind words, it was more like
ten. It still wasn't very many. In the back pocket of his
khakis was a map of Berlin, the kind with the patented
folding system (my father loved innovations, loved to see
inventors rewarded for improving the human condition),
and he was able to lead my mother to Zoo Station and buy
her some wurst at the all-night food kiosk there. In a mix
of English and German, followable only spottily by my
mother, he explained that this was his first day in Berlin
and he was so excited to be here that he could have walked
all night. He was a delegate to the Fourth World Congress
of the Association for International Understanding (which
wouldn't survive to hold a fifth congress, owing to its exposure, the following autumn, as basically a Communist
front). He'd left his two little girls, from his first marriage,
in the care of his sister, and had flown to Berlin on his
own nickel. He'd had some disappointments in life, he'd
hoped to contribute more to the world than teaching high-
school biology, but the wonderful thing about teaching

was that it gave him whole summers to get *out*, out into the world, out into nature. He delighted in meeting foreigners and uncovering common ground; at one point, he'd studied Esperanto. His girls, only four and six, were already great little campers, and when they were older he intended to take them to Thailand, to Tanzania, to Peru. Life was too short for sleeping. He didn't want to waste one minute of his week in Berlin.

When my mother told him she'd run away from Jena, my father's first impulse was to think of his own daughters and insist that she go home again in the morning. But when he learned that her mother had beaten her and that she'd never go to college, he reconsidered. "Golly, that's rough," he said. "Something wrong with a system that makes a bright, vital girl like you work behind the counter in a bakery. I'm an old-fashioned camper—a blanket and a piece of level ground's enough for me. My hotel's not much, but it does have beds. Why don't you sleep in mine, and we'll see how things look to you tomorrow. I can get a little shut-eye on the floor."

His motives were almost certainly benign. My father was a good man: a tireless teacher and loyal husband, a seeder of independence in my sisters, a sucker for stories of injustice, a reflexive giver of the benefit of the doubt, a vigorous raiser of his hand when there was unpleasant work to be volunteered for. And yet I'm haunted by the fact that, all his life, he did exactly what he pleased. If he wanted to take his students to Honduras to dig sewage lines, or to a Navajo reservation to paint houses and brand cattle, even if it meant leaving my mother alone for weeks with the kids, he did it. If he wanted to stop the family car and chase a butterfly, he did it. And if he felt like marrying a pretty woman young enough to be his daughter, he did it—twice.

He was originally from Indiana. Hoping to make a

contribution to agriculture, he'd pursued entomology, but the road to a PhD in entomology is long. Certain stages in the life cycle of the caddis flies he was studying could be collected only for a week or two each year, and to support himself while the years went by he took a job with the Colorado Department of Agriculture. He was living in Denver when he finished his dissertation and sent his collection to his committee in Indiana, which couldn't grant a degree without seeing specimens. The package, which represented eight years of work, disappeared in the U.S. mail without a trace. His dream had been to teach at a university and do pure research, but instead he ended up as an ABD in the Denver public school district.

Sometime in the late thirties, he took under his protection a bright but vulnerable girl whose stepfather was an alcoholic brute. He had conferences with her mother, he arranged for the girl to live with a different family, and he encouraged her to apply for college. But the girl turned out to be amenable to rescue only temporarily, because her boyfriend was in prison. As soon as he got out, they ran away to California. My father served four years in the Army Signal Corps, the last of them in Bavaria, and when he returned to his job in Denver he learned that the young woman was living at home again; her boyfriend was now in military prison for nearly killing someone in a bar fight. My father, who I suspect had been in love with her from the beginning, invited her on long hikes in the mountains and by and by proposed to her. Trying to turn her life around, and under pressure from her mother, the young woman may have felt that she had no choice but to accept. (She looked like an angel in the one picture I ever saw of her, but there was something empty in her eyes, a deadness, the despair of the disparity between what she looked like and what she felt herself to be.) The daughters she'd had with my father were one and three when her boyfriend finished his sentence and resurfaced in Denver. My father never told even my mother, let alone me, what happened then. All I know is that he ended up with sole custody of my half sisters.

He was more than twice my mother's age, but she was a couple of inches taller, and maybe this helped equalize and normalize things. In Berlin, he blew off the plenary sessions of the Fourth Congress, which even by the standards of international do-goodery must have set new records for tediousness and pointlessness, and together he and my mother walked the city. They took the boat rides that must be taken in Berlin, they ate at restaurants that seemed first-class to her. On their fifth evening, he sat her down and made a little speech.

"Here's what I want to do," he said. "I want to marry you, and, no, don't worry, I'm not trying to pull anything dishonorable. I just have a feeling that if you stay here you're going to get in trouble and find yourself back in Jena in no time, and there goes your whole life. So, and then we'll see about getting you a passport and so forth. I'll fly back here next week with my little girls, and you can see if you want to come back to the States with me. If you don't want to, no hard feelings, we'll annul the marriage. I just think you're a swell girl, with a good head on your shoulders, and I have a feeling I'd be happy to stay married to you. I think you're pretty darned wonderful, Clelia."

"My mother was right," my mother said to me much later, when my father was long dead. "I was a stupid-innocent goose. I was so thirsty for kindness, but I'd still never imagined a man could be as kind as your father. I thought I'd run into the kindest man in the world. On a dark street in Moabit! Some kind of miracle! And you know how thick his wallet always was—all those things he never took out of it, business cards from important people, clippings from important publications, all those tips for self-improvement, all those recipes for a better world. And money. Well, it was more than I'd ever seen—more than we had at the bakery at the end of the day. A price-subsidized Communist bakery with one cash register: that was my idea of a lot of money! I didn't even know the hotel we were in was terrible, he had to tell me it was terrible, and even then I blamed it on the congress, not him. What did I know about strong dollars, weak currencies? And I couldn't follow everything he said, so I thought the entire city of Denver had elected him to be its representative at an important world congress. I thought he was rich! I'd never seen a thicker wallet. I didn't know the Association for International Understanding had exactly four dues-paying members in the state of Colorado. I didn't know anything. He had my heart in his hand in five minutes. I would have crawled on my knees to America to be with him."

It took some years for my mother's passion to wane and the marriage to fully polarize. In the early years, she was engulfed by child care and by night school, where she eventually earned a degree in pharmacology. But by the time of the first presidential election I remember, she was voting for Barry Goldwater. She'd seen enough of social-ism to foresee its ultimate failure, she knew the Soviets to be thieves, rapists, and murderers, and she never got over the shock of discovering that my father was rich only in comparison to Jena, only the way most Americans were rich. In her disappointment with him, she idealized the truly wealthy, attributing improbable virtues to them. She'd cashed in her youth and her looks for life in a cramped three-bedroom house with a tin-pot progressive too good and kind to be divorced, and in her rage against her stupid-innocence she found better men to admire: Goldwater, Senator Charles Percy, later Ronald Reagan.

Their conservatism appealed to her German belief that nature was perfect and that all the troubles in the world were caused by man. During my school hours, she worked at the Atkinson's Drugs on Federal Boulevard, and what she saw there was diseased human beings parading to the counter where she took their scripts and gave them drugs. Human beings busily poisoning themselves with cigarettes and alcohol and junk food. They weren't to be trusted, the Soviets weren't to be trusted, and she arranged her politics accordingly.

My father knew that nature wasn't perfect. During his years with the Ag Department, he'd stood in parched fields amid plants that were dying of thirst because they lost too much water through their stomata, because their use of carbon dioxide was grossly inefficient, because the chlorophyll molecule's left hand didn't know what the right hand was doing—its left hand took in oxygen and emitted CO_2 while its right hand did the opposite. He foresaw the day when deserts would bloom because of smarter plants, plants perfected by human beings, plants implanted with better, more modern chlorophyll. And he knew that Clelia knew her chemistry, he defied her to refute his proof of nature's imperfection, and so they would argue about chemistry, with rising voices, at the dinner table.

Sadly, she wasn't a very good stepmom to my sisters. She herself was like a plant in a parched field, craving the rain of my father's attention, which my sisters soaked up so much of. But it was worse than that: she criticized my sisters the way her own mother had criticized her; she found particular fault with their clothes. This had to do partly with the rebellious sixties, hard years for a conservative, and partly with the rebellion of one of her own organs, her colon. I'm told I was a colicky baby, and no sooner was she past the stress of this than she suffered an ectopic pregnancy. Physical stress, life disappointment, money worries, genetic predisposition, bad luck: her bowel became inflamed and gave her trouble for the rest of her life. It pulled the strings in her face that her mother's stomach had pulled in hers, and she became, with everyone but me, the voice of its unhappiness.

When I think about Anabel and the warning signs I ignored on the road to marrying her, I keep coming back to my polarized family: my sisters out doing world-bettering things with my dad, me at home with my mom. She spared me the shameful details of her suffering (she would have preferred, I'm sure, to have had her mother's stomach, which ejected nothing worse than blood, not foul-smelling filth, not the very foundation of German expletive, humor, and taboo), but of course I could sense that she wasn't happy, and my father always seemed to be out at some meeting or away on an adventure. I spent a thousand evenings alone with her. She was mostly very strict with me, but we had a strange little game that we played with the tony magazines she subscribed to. After we'd paged through an entire *Town & Country* or *Harper's Bazaar*, she had me pick out the one house and one woman I most wanted. I soon learned to choose the most expensive house, the greatest beauty, and I grew up feeling as if I could redeem her unhappiness by getting them. What was striking about our game, though, was what a gushing, hopeful, big-sisterly girl she seemed like, leafing through the pages. When I was older and she told and retold me the story of her flight from Jena, the person I imagined was that girl.

I betrayed Anabel before I even met her. At the end of my third year at Penn, I'd run for the top job at *The Daily Pennsylvanian* on a platform of paying more attention to the "real" world, and once I was installed as executive editor, after a summer in Denver with my mother (my father had died two years earlier), I created the position of city editor and assigned articles about ticket scalping at the Spectrum, mercury and cadmium in the Delaware, a triple murder in West Philly. I thought my reporters were breaking the hermetic campus bubble of seventies self-indulgence, but I suspect that, to the people they pestered for interviews, they seemed more like kids whose over-priced candy bars you had to buy so they could go to summer camp.

In October, my friend Lucy Hill alerted me to an interesting story. Across the river, in Elkins Park, the dean of the Tyler School of Art had come to his office one morning and found a body wrapped in brown butcher paper. Scrawled on the paper in red crayon were the words YOUR MEAT. The body was warm and breathing but nonresponsive. The dean summoned security, which tore away enough paper to reveal the face of a second-year grad student, Anabel Laird. Her eyes were open, her mouth taped shut. Laird was already known to the dean for a series of letters denouncing the underrepresentation of women on the faculty and the disproportionate number of fellowships awarded to male MFA students. Further judicious tearing seemed to indicate that Laird was wearing nothing but the butcher paper. After some collective hand-wringing, security carried away the package and put it in a room with a female secretary who unwrapped the student, untaped her mouth, and covered her with a blanket. Laird refused to speak or move until late afternoon, when a second female student arrived with some clothes in a plastic bag.

Since Laird was an old friend of Lucy's, I should have edited the story myself, but I'd fallen behind with my class work and left the *DP* in the hands of the managing editor, Oswald Hackett, who was also my roommate and best

friend. The Laird story, written by a notably amoral sophomore, was by turns salacious and snarky, with an as-
sortment of tasty blind quotes from Laird's fellow students
("nobody likes her," "poor little trust-fund girl," "a sad cry
for the attention she's not getting with her films"), but the
reporter had checked the requisite boxes, getting lengthy
quotes from Laird and a bland statement from the dean,
and Oswald ran it in full on our front page. When I read
it the following afternoon, I had only a fleeting sense of
guilt. Not until I stopped by at the *DP* and found phone
messages from both Laird and Lucy did I realize—all at
once, with a lurch in my heart—that the piece had been
really cruel.

A fact of my life was that I had a morbid fear of reproach, especially from women. Somehow I persuaded
myself that I could get away with not returning either of
the women's messages. Nor did I bring the matter up with
Oswald; being so afraid of reproach myself, I hated to inflict it on a friend. It seemed possible that Lucy, who lived
off campus, might have cooled down by the next time I saw
her, and it didn't occur to me that a woman militant
enough to wrap herself in butcher paper might show up
at the *DP* in person.

As the executive editor, I had an actual office I could
use as a study room. If Anabel had come to it in bib overalls, the Penn uniform of feminist militancy, I might have
guessed who she was, but the woman who knocked on my
door, late on a Friday afternoon, was dressed expensively,
in a white silk blouse and a snug below-the-knee skirt that
struck me as Parisian. Her mouth was a slash of crimson
lipstick, her hair a dark cascade.

"I'm looking for Tom Ab*err*ant."

"*Ab*erant," I corrected.

The woman registered her surprise with the bulging
eyes of a hanged person. "Are you a *freshman*?"

"Senior, actually."

"Good Lord. Did you come here when you were thirteen? I'd pictured somebody bearded."

My baby face was a sore subject. My freshman roommate had suggested that I age myself by manufacturing a dueling scar in the nineteenth-century manner, by cutting myself with a saber and laying a hair in the cut to keep it from healing cleanly. I believed my face to be the main reason why, although I was good at befriending women, I wasn't having sex with any of them. I got physical attention exclusively from very short girls and queer guys. One of the latter had walked up to me at a party and, without a word, put his tongue in my ear.

"I'm Anabel," the woman said. "The person whose message you didn't return."

My chest constricted. Anabel shut the door behind her with a chicly booted foot and sat down with her arms crossed tightly, as if to conceal what her blouse wanted to reveal. Her eyes were large and brown, like a deer's, and her face rather long and narrow, also like a deer's; she shouldn't have quite been pretty but somehow was. She was at least two years older than me.

"I'm sorry," I said wretchedly. "I'm sorry I didn't return your message."

"Lucy told me that you were a good person. She said I could trust you."

"I'm sorry about the article, too. The fact is, I didn't even read it until after it was out."

"Are you not the editor?"

"Authority is delegated in various ways."

I was avoiding her eyes, but I could feel them blazing at me. "Was it necessary for your reporter to mention that my father is the president and chairman of McCaskill? And that I'm not a well-liked person?"

"I'm *sorry*," I said. "As soon as I saw the story, I realized it was cruel. Sometimes, when you're in the thick of putting a story together, you forget that someone's going to read it."

She tossed her dark mane. "So, if I hadn't read it, you wouldn't be sorry? What does that mean? You're sorry you were caught? That's not sorry. That's cowardly."

"We shouldn't have used those quotes if we couldn't attribute them."

"Oh, well, it makes for a fun guessing game," she said. "Which person thinks I'm a spoiled rich girl, which person thinks I'm a nut job, which person is so sure my art is bad. Of course, it's maybe not so fun to sit in the same room with the people who said those things, and know they're still thinking them, and feel them *looking* at me. To have to sit there with those eyes on me. To be visible like that."

She still hadn't lowered her arms from the front of her blouse.

"You're the one who showed up naked in the dean's office," I couldn't help pointing out.

"Only after they ripped the paper off me."

"I'm saying you wanted publicity and you got it."

"Oh, it's not like I'm surprised. What's more interesting than a nude female body? What better to sell papers? You proved my point better than I could have proved it myself."

This was the first of the ten thousand times I had the experience of not quite following Anabel's logic. Because it was the first time and not the ten thousandth, and because she seemed so ferociously sure of herself—it hurts me to remember the ferocity and assurance she still had then—I assumed the fault was mine.

"We're a free paper," I said lamely. "We don't worry about selling."

"*Actions have consequences*," she said. "There's a high

road and a low road, and you took the low road. You're the editor, you put those things in print, and I read them. You hurt me and you're going to have to live with it. I want you never to forget it, the same way I'm never going to forget what you printed. You didn't even have the decency to return my phone call! You think because you're male and I'm female, you can get away with it." She paused, and I saw a pair of tiny tears dissolving her mascara. "You may not think so," she said more softly, "but I'm here to tell you you're a *jerk*."

Her looks and her superior age gave the accusation a particular sting. In truth, though, I was already primed to doubt my goodness. One Easter, when I was in seventh grade, the younger of my older sisters, Cynthia, had come home from college transformed into a hippie, with octagonal wireframes and a biblically bearded boyfriend. The two of them took a friendly clinical interest in me as one of the first new men of tomorrow. Cynthia asked me about my air rifle: Did I like to shoot and kill my enemies with it? Did I like to blow their heads off? How did I think it felt to have your head blown off? Like a game?

The boyfriend asked me about the butterfly collection I halfheartedly kept in an attempt to please my father: Did I like butterflies? Really? Then why did I murder them?

Cynthia asked me what my ambitions for life were: I wanted to be a reporter or a photojournalist? That was cool. But what about being a nurse? What about being a first-grade teacher? Those jobs were for girls? Why only for girls?

The boyfriend asked me if I ever thought about trying out to be a cheerleader: It wasn't allowed? Why not? Why couldn't a boy be a cheerleader? Couldn't boys jump, too? Couldn't boys cheer?

Together, the two of them made me feel like a stodgy old man. This seemed mean of them, but I also had the guilty sense that there was something wrong with me. One afternoon, a few years later, I came home late from school to a rodent emergency in the attic, my belongings spread across the floor of my bedroom, my closet door open, my father's legs visible on a stepladder. I allowed myself to hope that he'd somehow overlooked the worn copy of *Oui* magazine that I'd shoplifted from the back of a used-book store and hidden in the closet, but after dinner he came to my room and asked me what I thought it was like to be the women in a pornographic magazine.

"I hadn't thought about it," I said truthfully.

"Well, you're at the age where you'd better start thinking about it."

Everything about my dad was repelling and embarrassing me that year. His Mission Control eyewear, his petrochemically slicked hair, his wide gunslinger's stance. He reminded me of a beaver, all uncorrected overbite and senseless industry. Building another dam *why*? Gnawing tree trunks *why*? Paddling around with a big grin *why*, exactly?

"Sex is a great blessing," he said in his teaching voice. "But what you see in a porno magazine is human misery and degradation. I don't know where you got the magazine, but simply by owning it you've materially participated in the degradation of a fellow human being. Imagine how you'd feel if this were Cynthia, or Ellen—"

"OK, I get it."

"Do you really? Do you understand that these women are somebody's sisters? Somebody's daughters?"

I had a sense of moral injury, of being mistaken for a worse person than I was, because I had not, in fact, materially participated in anyone's degradation. To the contrary, by stealing the magazine, I'd financially *punished* the bookstore for its bulk purchase of secondhand porn; I was, if anything, a virtuous recycler, and any private uses to which I then put the stolen *Oui* were my own business and amounted, arguably, to further punishment of the exploiters, since my reliance on stolen goods obviated any cash purchase of freshly exploitational matter, not to mention saving virgin forests from being clear-cut and pulped.

A few days later, I stole more magazines. I liked *Oui* because the girls in it seemed realer—also more European, hence more cultured, intelligent, and soulful—than the ones in *Playboy*. I imagined deep conversations with them, I imagined them attracted to how compassionately I listened to them, but there was no denying that my interest in them died at the instant of orgasm. I felt as if I was up against a structural unfairness; as if simply being male, excitable by pictures through no choice of my own, placed me ineluctably in the wrong. I meant no harm and yet I harmed.

It got worse. With college looming, I made a bloodless but nonetheless exciting pact to exchange virginities with my senior-prom date, Mary Ellen Stahlstrom, whose romantic sights were set on someone unattainable, and so it happened that, on the last possible weekend of the summer, in an Estes Park cabin belonging to the parents of a mutual friend, at the crucial moment of entry, I accidentally delivered a sharp masculine poke to the very most sensitive and off-limits part of Mary Ellen. She gave a full-throated shriek, recoiling and kicking me away. My attempts to comfort her and apologize only fed her hysteria. She wailed, she thrashed, she hyperventilated, she kept babbling a phrase that I finally deciphered, to my immense relief, as a wish to be taken home to Denver right away.

Mary Ellen's anally violated shriek was ringing in my ears when I matriculated at Penn. My father had suggested that I choose a smaller college, but Penn had offered me a scholarship and my mother had seduced me with talk of the wealthy, powerful people I would meet at an Ivy

League school. In my first three years at Penn, I made not one wealthy friend, but my intimations of male guilt were given a firm theoretical foundation. From lectures both in and out of classrooms, beginning with an orientation-week sex talk delivered by a female senior in bib overalls, I learned that I was even more inescapably implicated in the patriarchy than I'd realized. The upshot was that, in any intimate relationship with a woman, my motives were a priori suspect.

Not that intimate relationships turned out to be a problem. Apparently, only to girls less than five feet tall did I not look heinously young. One of them, a fellow staffer on the *DP* during my second year, started giving me significant looks, tilting her head to one side, and finally passed me a note in which she alluded to the "danger" of getting "badly hurt" by me. I obliged her by making out with her in the middle of the Green one night, partly out of guilt for not being more interested in having sex with her—for being such an objectifying male that I couldn't see past her shortness—and partly with the vile male motive of finally having sex with someone, but I was unable to oblige her with the avowals that she then, with tilted head, solicited, and so I ended up guiltily hurting her with nothing to show for it. She went so far as to quit the paper.

I took refuge in beer, the pool tables in Houston Hall, and the *DP*. As working journalists in a student body doing frivolous student things, my friends and I achieved levels of self-importance that I wouldn't encounter again until I met people from the *New York Times*. We had nougat cores of innocence, of course, but we'd all bragged about our high-school sexual exploits and it never occurred to me that, since I had lied, my friends might also have lied. The one person who saw through me was Lucy Hill. She'd been a scholarship student at Choate Rosemary Hall and had waitressed for two years before starting at Penn. She had a boyfriend who was nearly thirty, a self-taught hippie carpenter who looked a lot like D. H. Lawrence, her favorite writer. Lucy's friendly clinical interest in me was more explicit and forgiving than my sister Cynthia's. When I confessed to her what I'd done to Mary Ellen Stahlstrom, she laughed and said that Mary Ellen had shrieked because I was giving her the kind of intercourse she couldn't admit she wanted. Lucy was now intent on finding me somebody with whom to *fuck like bunnies*. I didn't love the sound of *fuck like bunnies*, and I vaguely resented the condescension implicit in Lucy's project, but I had no one else to talk to about sex, and so I kept going to her off-campus house for weak coffee and mushy *Moosewood Cookbook* desserts.

Neither Anabel nor I knew it when she left my office, after pronouncing her judgment on my character, but I was exactly the guy she wanted. Outside my window, the sun had gone down in its sudden October way, and I sat in the twilight and suffered shame. I was prepared to believe I was a jerk, and yet it rankled to have been called one by an older and very attractive (and rich, can't forget rich, it was there from the beginning) woman who'd made a special trip across the Schuylkill to denounce me. I didn't know what to do. Calling Lucy would simply invite further reproach. I couldn't get *you're a jerk* out of my head. The mental picture of Anabel's nude body in butcher paper also gave me no rest.

Stopping only briefly at the dining hall to eat two chicken cutlets and a slice of cake, I returned to my dorm room and dialed Anabel's number, which I'd copied onto the palm of my hand. I counted ten rings on her phone before I hung up. When Oswald came back after dinner, he found me sitting in the dark.

"Mr. Tom, he brooding," he said. "Something has 'got his goat.' Something is 'stuck in his craw.'" He referenced, not for the first time, a *Get Smart* episode about an East Asian evildoer named the Claw: "*Not 'the Craw'! The CRAW!*"

I wanted to tell Oswald that he'd fucked up and exposed me to humiliation, but he was in such high spirits, so completely unaware of having fucked up, that I couldn't bring myself to ruin his evening. Instead, I vented my hatred of the author of the article.

"He's very like a little sharp-toothed mink," Oswald concurred. "If there were any justice in the universe, he wouldn't write such clean copy."

"The blind quotes about Laird were really mean. I'm wondering if we should print some sort of apology."

"Oh, don't do that," Oswald said. "You've got to stand by your reporter, even if he is a little beady-eyed mink."

Oswald and I had come up together on the *DP*, tearing apart each other's prose. Neither of us ever fell into a mood so bleak that the other couldn't talk him out of it, and Oswald soon had me laughing with his impression of the Broncos' backup quarterback Norris Weese (Oswald was a Nebraskan and a fellow Broncos fan) and his savage quotation of classmates dumber and more popular than us. Oswald's gift for ressentiment was redeemed by his Eeyore-like self-esteem levels. His long sexual drought had recently ended with his bedding of a sophomore poet who was obviously going to shred his heart but hadn't got around to it yet. Out of respect for my own drought, still ongoing, he rarely mentioned her to me, but when he left me alone again I knew that he was going to her, and I fell back into a pit of remorse.

Around ten o'clock I managed to reach Anabel on the phone.

"Listen," I said, "I'm feeling really bad about not protecting you better. I want to try to make it up to you."

"The damage is done, Tom. You already made your choice."

"But I'm not the person you think I am."

"Who do you think I think you are?"

"A bad person."

"I'm only going by the evidence," she said with a hint of playfulness, a possible softening of her judgment.

"Do you want me to resign? Would you believe me then?"

"You don't have to do that for me. You can just try to be a better editor in the future."

"I will. I will."

"All right, then," she said. "I don't forgive you, but I do appreciate your returning my call."

This was where the conversation ought to have ended, but Anabel, even back then, had a specific lack of resolve when it came to hanging up a telephone, and I didn't want to hang up without having been forgiven. For some seconds, neither of us spoke. As the silence lengthened it began, for me at least, to pulse with possibility. I strained to hear the sound of Anabel's breath.

"Do you ever show your art?" I said when the silence had become unbearable. "I'd be interested in seeing your films."

" 'Come up to my room and see my etchings.' Is that why you called me back?" Again the playful lilt. "Maybe you want to come over and see my art right now."

"Seriously?"

"Give it some thought and decide if you think I'm serious."

"Right."

"My art doesn't hang on a wall."

"Right."

"And no one goes in my bedroom but me."

She said this as if it were a prohibition, not a circumstance.

"You seem like an interesting person," I said. "I'm sorry we hurt you."

"I should be used to it by now," she said. "It seems to be what people do."

Again the conversation might have ended. But there was a factor in play which never would have occurred to me: Anabel was lonely. She still had one friend at Tyler, a lesbian named Nola who'd been her confederate in the butcher-paper incident, but the pressure of Nola's prospectless crush on her made her difficult to take in high doses. All the other students, according to Anabel, had turned against her. They had reason to resent the special status she'd wangled as a filmmaker at a school that didn't have a film program, but the real problem was her personality. People were attracted to her looks and wicked tongue and to the real-seeming possibility that she was an artistic genius; she had a way of drawing all eyes to her. But she was fundamentally far shyer than her self-presentation led anyone to imagine, and she kept alienating people with her moral absolutism and her sense of superiority, which is so often the secret heart of shyness. The instructor who'd encouraged her to make films had also later propositioned her, which (a) was piggish, (b) was apparently not unusual, and (c) destroyed her faith in his assessment of her talent. She'd been on the institutional warpath ever since. This had clinched her pariah status, since, according to her, the other students cared only about professorial validation, the professorial nod, the professorial referral to a gallery.

I learned some of this and many other things in the thrilling two hours we spoke that night. Though I didn't feel myself to be an interesting person, I did have listening skills. The more I listened, the more her voice softened toward me. And then we uncovered an odd co-incidence.

She'd grown up in Wichita, in a stately house on College Hill. She belonged to the fourth generation of one of the two families that wholly owned the agribusiness conglomerate McCaskill, the country's second-largest privately held corporation. Her father had inherited a five percent share of it, married a fourth-generation McCaskill, and gone to work for the company. As a girl, Anabel said, she'd been very close to her father. When the time came to send her away to Rosemary Hall, which her mother had attended before its merger with Choate, she said she didn't want to go. But her mother was insistent, her father uncharacteristically unwilling to indulge her, and so she arrived in Connecticut at the age of thirteen.

"For the longest time, I had everything turned around exactly wrong in my mind," she told me. "I thought my mother was terrible and my father was wonderful. He's extremely smart and seductive. He knows how to have his way with people. And when he started betraying my mother, after I went away to school, and when my mother started drinking after breakfast, I realized that she'd been trying to protect me by sending me away. She never admitted it to me, but I know that's what it was. He was killing her, and she didn't want him to kill me, too. I was so unjust to her. And then he killed her. My poor mother."

"Your father killed your mother?"

"You have to understand the way McCaskill works. They're obsessed with keeping the business in the family, so nobody on the outside can know what they're doing. It's all about secrets and family control. When a Laird marries a McCaskill, it has to be forever, because they're obsessed with family solidarity. So after I went away to school and my father started cheating on my mother, there really wasn't anything for her to do but drink. That's the

McCaskill way. That and drugs and dangerous hobbies like piloting helicopters. You'd be surprised how much of my extended family is strung out on something. At least one of my brothers is strung out as we speak. You either go to work for the company and increase the family riches—which is what *they* call the McCaskill way—or else you kill yourself with hedonism, because there's no reality principle to hold you back. It's not like anybody in the family needs to make a living."

I asked what had happened to her mother.

"She drowned," Anabel said. "In our pool. My father was out of town—no fingerprints."

"How long ago was this?"

"A little over two years ago. In June. It was a nice warm night. Her blood alcohol would have knocked a horse down. She passed out in the shallow end."

I said I was very sorry, and then I told her that my dad had died in the same month as her mother. He'd retired only two weeks earlier, after counting the years to his sixty-fifth birthday, never speaking of "retirement," only of "retirement from teaching," because he still had so much energy. He was looking forward to reconstructing his caddis-fly collection and finally getting his PhD, to learning Russian and Chinese, to hosting foreign-exchange students, to buying an RV that met my mother's requirements for outdoor comfort. But the first thing he did was volunteer for a two-month zoological mission to the Philippines. He wanted to scratch his old itch for exotic travel while I was still young enough to be spending summers at home, so that my mother wouldn't be alone. When I drove him to the Denver airport, he told me that he knew my mother could be difficult but, if I ever felt impatient with her, I had to remember that she'd had a rough childhood and wasn't in the best of health. His speech was loving and the last I ever heard from him. A day later, he was in a small plane that hit the side of a mountain. A four-paragraph story in the *Times*.

"What day did this happen?"

"It was June nineteenth in the Philippines. June eighteenth in Denver."

Anabel's voice became hushed. "This is extremely weird," she said. "My mother died on the same day. We were both half orphaned on the exact same day."

It now seems to me somehow crucial that the day was arguably *not* the same—her mother had died on the nineteenth. And until that Friday night I'd never been a superstitious person. My father had waged a personal war against the overvaluation of coincidence; he had a classroom riff, sometimes repeated at home, in which he "proved" that chewing Juicy Fruit gum causes hair to be blond, by way of illustrating proper scientific inference. But when Anabel spoke those words, after an hour and a half in which my world had been shrinking to the size of her voice in my ear—and here again it seems crucial that we had our first real conversation on the phone, which distills a person into words passing directly into the brain—I shivered as if my fate were overtaking me. How could the coincidence not be significant? The interesting person who'd pronounced me a jerk not six hours earlier had now been confiding in me, in her lovely voice, for an hour and a half. It felt incredible, magical. After the shiver had passed, I had an erection.

"What do you think it means?" Anabel said.

"I don't know. Maybe nothing. That's what my dad would say. Although—"

"It's very weird," she said. "I wasn't even planning on going to your office today. I was coming back from the Barnes Collection, which is a different story, why anybody still thinks Renoir *père* needs to be looked at, but there is such a person at Tyler and I have the misfortune of being in his lecture class, not having taken it last year when everyone else did. I'd imagined that an exception might be made, but, safe to say, nobody's in a mood to make exceptions for me now. But I was on the platform at Thirtieth Street, and I got so upset thinking about what you'd done to me that I let my train go by. And that seemed like a sign that I should go and find you. Because I missed the train. I've never gotten so involved in a thought I've missed a train."

"That does seem like a sign," I said, at the urging of my erection.

"*Who are you?*" she said. "Why did this happen?"

In the state her voice had put me in, I didn't consider these questions nutty, but I was spooked by their seriousness. "I am an American, Denver-born," I said. And added, pompously, "Saul Bellow."

"Saul Bellow is from Denver?"

"No, Chicago. You asked me who I am."

"I didn't ask who *Saul Bellow* is."

"He won the Pulitzer Prize," I said, "and that's what I want to do." I was trying to seem a tiny bit interesting to her, but instead I sounded idiotic to myself.

"You want to be a novelist?" Anabel said.

"Journalist."

"So I don't have to worry about you taking my story and putting it in a novel."

"Not going to happen."

"It's my story. My material. It's what my art comes out of."

"Of course it is."

"But journalists betray people for a living. Your little reporter betrayed me. I thought he was interested in what I was trying to express."

"That's not the only kind of journalist."

"I'm trying to figure out whether I should be hanging

up now. Whether these are *bad* signs. Betrayal and death, those are bad signs, aren't they? I think I should be hanging up on you. I'm remembering that you hurt me."

But of course she couldn't hang up.

"Anabel, please," I said. It was the first time I'd spoken her name. "I want to see you again."

I saw her again, but not before going to Lucy's house for weak coffee and some sort of brown Betty with oatmeal in it. Lucy's house was overwarm and reeked, to me, of fucking like bunnies. "You shouldn't feel bad about the article," she told me. "I only called you to warn you a righteous tornado was heading your way. Anabel needs to read Nietzsche and get over her thing about good and evil. The only philosopher she ever talks about is Kierkegaard. Can you imagine going to bed with Kierkegaard? He'd never stop asking, 'Can I do this to you? Is this OK?'"

"I still feel bad," I said.

"She called me yesterday to talk about you. Apparently you had some sort of marathon conversation?" Lucy helped herself to more brown Betty. She wasn't fat, but she was getting a little Moosewoody in the face and thighs. "She asked me if you're Good, capital G, which I took to mean she might want you in her pants. You certainly need to be in someone's pants, but I'm not sure that hers are the right ones. I know what I'm talking about. I was head over heels for her myself, our senior year at Choate. All the teachers were in awe of her, and she always had funds and got these crazy-strong buds they've started growing hydroponically. She had trouble relating to people, but not when she was stoned. She'd get massively stoned at parties, sort of dangerously stoned, and then have sex with somebody, and then get up at six in the morning and write college-level papers. I wanted to sleep with her myself, but she'd sworn off sex by the time we roomed together. Now she's given up pot, too. She's become Saint Anabel. I still love her, and I felt bad about the article, but it was really her fault for talking to your reporter. She sets herself up for these things."

"Does she have a boyfriend?"

"Not for the longest time," Lucy said. "I asked her how often she masturbates, and she acted all appalled with me for asking. As if she hadn't been one of the wildest girls in the history of Choate. But I think she's sort of messed up sexually from that. She was too young and she also got VD. It's unfortunate, but the upshot is I don't think she's a great candidate for you."

I was still processing this information when Lucy took my hand and led me out of the kitchen, away from its towers of crusty cookware, and up to the room she shared with her boyfriend, Bob. The bed was unmade, the floor strewn with clothes. "I have a new plan," she said. She pressed her forehead into mine and propelled me backward onto the bed. "We can start slowly and see how this goes. What do you think?"

"What about Bob?"

"That's my problem, not yours."

Just a week earlier, I might have been down with the plan. But now that Anabel was in the picture, I felt disappointed by the idea that sex, which had assumed such fearsome proportions in my mind, was supposed to be as natural and homey as eating brown Betty. There was also no escaping the conclusion that Lucy was trying to keep me away from Anabel. She was all but saying so. We necked on her paisley sheets for no more than ten minutes before I excused myself.

"This is fun, though, don't you think?" Lucy said. "We should have thought of this months ago."

"Definitely fun," I said. To be polite, I added that I looked forward to the next time.

How different my Sunday afternoon with Anabel was.

We met at the art museum under a cold gray sky. Anabel came clad in a black-trimmed crimson cashmere coat and strong opinions. I'd asked for instruction in art, and she swept through the galleries impatiently, issuing blanket dismissals—"snore," "wrong idea," "religion blah blah blah," "meat and more meat"—until we came to Thomas Eakins. Here she stopped and visibly relaxed.

"This is the guy," she said. "This is the only male painter I trust. I guess I also don't mind Corot and his cows. He gets the sadness of being a cow. And Modigliani, too, but that's only because I used to have a crush on his work and wished he could have painted me. All the rest of them, I swear to you, are telling lies about women. Even when they're not painting women, even when they're painting a landscape: it's lies about women. Even Modigliani, I don't know why I forgive him, I shouldn't. I guess because he's Modigliani. It's probably good I never met him. Later on, I can show you all the women painters in this collection—oh, wait." She snorted. "There are no women painters. This entire collection is an illustration of what happens without women on the scene to keep men honest. Except for this guy here. God, he's honest."

I took it as a heartening sign that she liked at least one male painter; that she could make an exception. She was a terrible art-history instructor, but if you were going to look at only one artist in that museum, Eakins wasn't a bad choice. She pointed out the geometry of rower and oar and scull and wake, and how honest Eakins was about the atmospherics of the lower Delaware valley. But the main thing for her was Eakins's bodies. "People have been depicting the human body for thousands of years," she said. "You'd think we would have gotten really good at it by now. But it turns out to be the hardest thing in the world to do right. To see it the way it really is. This guy not only saw it, he got it down in paint. Somehow, with everybody else, even photographers, or actually especially with photographers, some *idea* gets in the way. But not with Eakins." She turned to me. "You're a Thomas also, or just plain Tom?"

"Thomas."

"Am I allowed to say I'm glad I don't have your last name?"

"Anabel Aberant."

She thought about this. "Actually, Anabel Ab*err*ant might not be so bad. Kind of my entire story in two words."

"You're allowed to pronounce it any way you want."

As if to dispel any coded allusion to future marriage, she said, "You really are bizarrely young-looking. You know that, don't you?"

"Sadly, yes."

"I think it was a character thing with Eakins. I think to paint this honestly, you have to have a good character. He may have had sexual issues, but his heart was pure. People are always saying Vincent had a pure heart, but I don't believe it. His brain was full of spiders."

I was beginning to feel like the flavorless kid brother of someone Anabel was doing a favor by seeing me. That she'd called Lucy to ask about me, or that she might be trying to impress me, was hard to credit. As we made our way back outside, I remarked that she and Lucy were very different.

"She has a really fine mind," Anabel said. "She was the only person at Choate whose ambition I could recognize. She was going to make documentaries and change the face of American cinema. And now her ambition is to make babies with Handyman Bob. I'd be surprised if he has a single good chromosome left after all the psychedelics he's done."

"I think she and Bob may be having trouble."

"Well, I hope they hurry up with that."

Snowflakes, the first of the season, were slanting across the museum steps. In Denver a day like this would have delivered six to twelve inches, but in Philadelphia I'd learned to expect a turn to rain. As we proceeded down the Benjamin Franklin Parkway, the most desolate of Philly's many soul-oppressing avenues, I asked Anabel why she didn't have a car.

"You mean, where's my Porsche?" she said. "That's what you mean, isn't it. Nobody ever taught me how to drive. And I might as well tell you, in case you have the wrong idea about me, that I'm in the process of weaning myself from the family teat. My father's paying for my last semester, but that'll be the end of it."

"Daughters don't inherit?"

She ignored this small temerity. "The money is already ruining my brothers. I'm not going to let it ruin me. But that's not even the reason. The reason is the money has blood on it. I can smell it in my checking account, the blood from a river of meat. That's what McCaskill is, a river of meat. They trade in grain, too, but even there a lot of it goes to feed the river. You probably had McCaskill meat for breakfast today."

"They have a thing called scrapple here. It's said to be made out of organs and eyeballs."

"That's the McCaskill way, use everything."

"I think scrapple is more Pennsylvania Dutch."

"Have you ever been to a pig factory? Chicken farm? Stockyard? Slaughterhouse?"

"I've smelled them from afar."

"It's a river of meat. I'm making my thesis film about it."

"I'd like to see this film."

"It's unwatchable. Everybody hates it, except Nola, who's vegan. Nola thinks I'm a genius."

"Remind me what vegan is?"

"No animal products of any kind. I know I need to go that way myself, but I basically live on toast and butter, so it's not easy."

Everything she said fascinated me. We seemed to be heading toward the train station, and I was afraid that we'd part ways without my having fascinated her at all.

"I can assign a story on scrapple," I said. "Investigate where it comes from, what it's made of, how the animals are treated. I could write it myself. Everybody complains about scrapple, nobody knows what it is. That's the definition of a good story."

Anabel frowned. "It's sort of my idea, though. Not yours."

"I'm trying to make amends here."

"First I'd need to find out whether McCaskill makes scrapple."

"I'm telling you, it's Pennsylvania Dutch. I was the one who brought it up, anyway."

She stopped on the sidewalk and faced me full-on. "Is this what we're going to do? Are we going to compete? Because I'm not sure I need that."

I was happy that she spoke of us as something potentially ongoing; distressed that we might be something she didn't need. Somehow, already, the decision was hers to make. My interest in her had quietly been assumed.

"You're the artist," I said. "I'm just the journalist."

Her eyes searched my face. "You're very *pretty*," she said, not kindly. "I'm not sure I trust you."

"Fine," I said, smarting. "Thank you for showing me Thomas Eakins."

"I'm sorry." She pressed a gloved hand to her eyes. "Don't be hurt. I just suddenly have a bad headache and need to go home."

When I got back to campus, I thought of calling her to

see how she was feeling, but the word *pretty* was still rankling, and our date had been so unlike what I'd hoped for, so much not the dreamlike continuation of our phone call, that the needle of my sexual compass was swinging back toward Lucy and her plan. My mother had lately taken to warning me not to make the mistake she'd made and fall too hard for a person at too tender an age—to think of my career first, by which she meant that I should first make money and *then* choose the most expensive house, etc.—and I certainly felt safe from falling too hard for Lucy.

In my Sunday-night call to Denver, I mentioned that I'd been to the art museum with one of the heirs of the McCaskill fortune. This was weak of me, but I felt I'd disappointed my mother by failing to make the right sort of Ivy League friends. I seldom had news that cheered her.

"Did you like her?" my mother asked.

"I did, actually."

"Your father's friend Jerry Knox spent his entire career with McCaskill. They're well known for having the highest ethical principles. Only in America can you find a company like that . . ."

I settled in for another lecture. Since my father died, my mother had become a droner, as if to fill the hole in her life with verbiage. She'd also frosted her hair a yellowish gray to make herself look older, more like a widow, but she was still only forty-four and I hoped she would remarry, this time choosing somebody rich and politically right of center, after the expiration of whatever she deemed a proper interval of bereavement. Not that she'd done much actual grieving. She'd used the interval instead to be angry at my father and the *pointless* way he'd died. It had fallen to me and my sisters to be devastated by the plane crash. I'd already begun to take a kinder view of my father when it happened, and when I arrived at the high-school auditorium for his memorial service and saw the overflow crowd of colleagues and former students, I felt proud to be the son of a man who never met a person he didn't want to like. My sisters both gave eulogies whose effusion seemed pointed at his widow, who sat next to me and chewed her lip and stared straight ahead. She was still dry-eyed when the service ended. "He was a *very good man*," she said.

I'd since spent three increasingly unbearable summers with her. The highest-paying job I could find was at the Atkinson's Drugs branch where she herself worked. I stayed out late every evening with my friends and returned home after midnight to foul smells in our bathroom. My mother's colon was unhappy not only with me but with my sisters. Cynthia had dropped out of grad school to become a labor organizer in California's Central Valley; Ellen was living in Kentucky with a gray-bearded banjo player and teaching remedial English. Both of them seemed happy, but all my mother could see, and drone about, was the waste of their abilities.

I owed my drugstore job to Dick Atkinson, the owner of the chain. During my second summer with my mother, her bowel's irritation was aggravated by Dick's courtship of her. Dick was a nice guy and a staunch Republican, and I felt that my mother, who'd always admired his entrepreneurship, could do a lot worse. But Dick was twice divorced, and she, who had stuck it out with my father, disapproved of discarding spouses and wanted no part in it. Dick considered this ridiculous and believed that he could wear her down. By the end of the summer, she'd worked herself into such a state that her gastroenterologist had to put her on prednisone. A few months later, she'd quit her job at the pharmacy. She was now working, at what I suspected were slave wages, for the congressional campaign of Arne Holcombe, a developer of downtown

Denver office space. When I'd gone home for a third summer with her, I'd found her health improved but her idealization of Arne Holcombe so over the top, so incessantly and droningly expressed, that I worried for her sanity.

"What are the polls showing?" I asked her when she'd exhausted the subject of McCaskill's contributions to the moral fiber of the nation. "Does Arne have a chance?"

"Arne has run the most exemplary campaign the state of Colorado has ever seen," she said. "We're still suffering from the aftereffects of a lowlife president who put his lowlife cronies' interests before the public good. What a *gift* that was to the special-interest-pandering Democrats and their sickening, grinning peanut farmer. Why any rational person would think that Arne has anything to do with Watergate, it mystifies me, Tom, it really does. But the other side slanders and slanders and panders and panders. Arne refuses to pander. Why would he pander? Is it really so hard to understand that a person with twenty million dollars and a thriving business only descends into the gutter of Colorado politics if he's animated by civic responsibility?"

"So, that's a no?" I said. "The polls aren't looking good?"

I could never get a straight answer from her anymore. She droned on about Arne's honesty and integrity, Arne's fiercely independent mind, Arne's sensible business-based solution to the problem of stagflation, and I hung up the phone still not knowing what the polls showed.

The following Saturday night, Lucy and Bob threw a Halloween party at their house. Oswald and I put on suits and dark glasses and earphones and went as Secret Service agents. Bob's many friends, people who'd been living within a mile of their alma mater for nearly a decade, people for whom it was a political statement to invest their energies in absurdities and trivialities, had come in

ungainly conceptual costumes ("I am the Excluded
Middle," a guy sandwiched between slabs of Styrofoam
informed us gravely at the door) and were filling the
place with reefer smoke. Bob himself was wearing moose
antlers, signifying Bullwinkle, with Lucy as his sidekick,
Rocky. She'd blackened her nose, covered the rest of her
face with brown greasepaint, and dressed in brown stretch
pajamas with a tail of real animal fur attached above her
butt. She scampered over to Oswald and me and offered
to let us touch her tail.

"Must we?" Oswald said.

"I'm Rocky the Flying Squirrel!"

She seemed possibly stoned. I was already embarrassed to be there with Oswald, who had no patience with
counterculture zaniness. I scanned the living room for
younger, edgier faces and was surprised to see Anabel,
standing alone in a corner, her arms crossed firmly. Her
costume was no costume—jeans and a jean jacket.

Lucy could see where I was looking. "You know what
her costume is? 'Ordinary person.' Get it? She can only
pretend to be ordinary."

"That's Anabel Laird," I explained to Oswald.

"Hard to recognize without the butcher paper."

Anabel caught sight of me and widened her eyes in her
hanged-person way. It was interesting to see her in
denim—it really did look like a costume on her.

"I should go talk to her," I said.

"No, she needs to try to mingle," Lucy said. "This happened at our Bastille Day party, too. People can tell she's
worth talking to, they're coming up to me and asking who
she is, but they're afraid to go near her. I don't know why
she bothers coming to parties where she doesn't think
anyone's good enough for her."

"She's shy," I said.

"That's one word for it."

Anabel, seeing that we were talking about her, turned her back on us.

"Take us to your beer," Oswald said.

I was following him to the kitchen when Lucy grabbed my hand and said she had something to show me. We went upstairs to her bedroom. In the harsh light of its ceiling fixture, she looked like Lucy but also like a small animal. I asked what she wanted me to see.

"My tail." She turned around and wagged the fur at me. "Don't you want to touch my tail?"

Who doesn't enjoy touching fur? I stroked her tail, and she backed into me, grinding her butt against my thighs, dislodging the tail. This was sort of hot and sort of not. She brought my hands up to her breasts, which were lolling free under the pajamas, and declared, "I'm the little squirrel that loves to fuck!"

"Wow, OK," I said. "But aren't you also, like, hosting a party?"

She turned herself around in my arms, took off my shades, and pressed her face to mine. Her greasepaint had a strong crayon smell. "Has anybody ever lost their virginity to a squirrel?"

"Hard to know," I said.

"Would it even count?"

She put her tongue in my mouth and then led me to the bed. Sex with a squirrel who had exciting breasts beneath her little-kid pajamas was not without its appeal, and I was feeling strangely unconcerned about Anabel; I intuited that being pounced on by someone else might even advance my cause with her. But when Lucy got around to drawing my hand under the waistband of her pajamas, saying, "Feel what a furry little animal I am," I couldn't help seeing her silliness through the appalled eyes of Oswald, whose personality made me think of Anabel's, her judgments, her hanged-person eyes, which made me pull my hand away. I stood up and put my shades back on. "I'm sorry," I said.

Lucy was too programmatic about sex to betray, or possibly even to feel, any hurt. "That's OK," she said. "We don't have to do anything you're not ready for."

I could smell the greasepaint on my face; I must have looked like I'd been eating shit. When I went to the bathroom to clean myself up, I discovered a large brown smudge on the collar of my dress shirt, the only good one I owned.

Downstairs the music was King Crimson, a favorite of Bob's. Anabel was nowhere to be seen. Oswald was near the front door with the Excluded Middle, who was holding a rubber-banded bundle of pamphlets.

"Our friend here has published a chapbook of poetry," Oswald explained to me.

"Poetry should be free," the Excluded Middle said, handing me a chapbook. "This is my gift to you."

"Read the first one for Tom," Oswald urged him. "I love the joie de vivre."

"*My bare soles squoosh the black spring muck,*" the Excluded Middle recited. "*The earth is my WHOOPEE CUSHION!*"

"There you have it," Oswald said. "A miracle of poetic compression."

"Did you see Anabel?" I said. "Anabel Laird?"

"She just walked out."

"Wearing a jean jacket?"

"The very one."

I hurried out to the street. When I got to the corner of Market Street, I saw Anabel at the next corner, waiting for the light. I could feel that she'd become, in the space of half an hour, the person in the world it mattered most to me to catch sight of. She must have heard my running footsteps, but she didn't look at me, even when I reached her side.

"How could you leave?" I said, breathing hard. "We hadn't talked yet."

She angled her face away from mine. "What makes you so sure I wanted to talk to you?"

"I was attacked by a rabid squirrel. I'm sorry."

"You can still go back," Anabel said. "She seems very determined to take you. I'm guessing you're the problem she and the Handyman are having? I saw him in those ridiculous antlers and I thought: that is more perfect than he even knows."

"Can we go somewhere?" I said.

"I'm going home."

"Right. OK."

"I can't stop you from taking the same train, though. If you follow me to my door and ask politely, I might let you sit in my kitchen."

"Why did you come to the party?" I said. "You knew you'd hate it."

"Do you want me to say it was because I thought you'd be there?"

"Was that the reason?"

She smiled, still not looking at me. "I'm not going to draw your conclusions for you."

Her apartment was on the top floor of a well-maintained old house, not a student place, and her kitchen was a vision of cleanliness. She took her shoes off at the door and asked me to do the same. In a rustic white pottery bowl on the table were three perfect apples, on the windowsill two volumes of *The Vegetarian Epicure*, on the stove a gleaming copper-clad skillet. There was also, on the largest wall, a poster from a butcher shop, a diagram of a cow segmented and labeled as cuts of beef. I studied it, learning where the brisket and the chuck were, while Anabel left the kitchen and came back with an expensive-looking bottle.

"Here we have Château Montrose," she said. "The same vintage as my birth year. My father sent me a whole case for my birthday, which I'd be doing him a favor if I said was no worse than insensitive and symbolically grotesque, given how my mother died. I suspect his actual motives were more sinister. But I won't drink alone, for obvious reasons, and Nola is the only person who ever comes here, and she can't drink red wine with the medication she's on, so I still have ten bottles. It's your lucky night."

"What happened to the other two?"

"I took them to Lucy on Bastille Day. She's one of my oldest friends, I wanted to bring her something nice. But she was too grateful, if you know what I mean. One or two references to my *amazing generosity* would have been enough. After that it became a hostile comment on my privilege. Not just my privilege—me personally. I have to say, I know you're still friends with her, but I'm at the point where she's literally turning my stomach."

"Me too, a little bit," I said.

"Are you aware that you have squirrel on your collar?"

"She took some fending off."

"You'll notice I didn't ask why *you* were at the party."

"Look where I am now," I said. "I'm here, not there."

"Undeniably."

We clinked glasses, and I wished her a belated happy birthday. This led to our comparing birth dates. Hers turned out to be April eighth. Mine is August fourth.

The symmetry of 4/8 and 8/4 had a powerful effect on Anabel. "Good Lord," she said, staring at me as if I were an apparition. "Did you just make that up? Is your birthday really August fourth?"

The signs meant more to her than they did to me. For her they were a way for us to be about more than just chemistry, to be something in the stars, while for me they served mainly to confirm the chemistry of my feelings for her. When the wine had warmed her up and she took off her jean jacket, I saw my fate not in calendrical coincidence but in the thinness of her upper arms, in what they did to my heart.

Under the influence of wine and mystical sign, she set about improving me that night. To be with her, I'd need better ambitions. When she learned that I was applying to journalism school, she said, "And then what? You go to city council meetings in Topeka for five years?"

"It's an honorable tradition."

"But is that what you want? What do you *want*?"

"I want to be famous and powerful. But you have to pay your dues first."

"What if you could start your own magazine? What would you do with it?"

I said I would try to serve the truth in its full complexity. I told her about the politically polarized house I'd grown up in, my father's blind progressivism, my mother's faith in corporations, and how effectively the two of them could poke holes in each other's politics.

"I could tell your mother a thing or two about corporations," Anabel said darkly.

"But the alternative doesn't work, either. You get the Soviet Union, you get the housing projects, you get the Teamsters union. The truth is somewhere in the tension between the two sides, and that's where the journalist is supposed to live, in that tension. It's like I *had* to be a journalist, growing up in that house."

"I know what you mean. I had to be an artist for the same reason. But that's why I can't see you wasting five years in Topeka or wherever. If you already know you want to serve the truth, you should serve it. Start a magazine like nobody else's. Not liberal, not conservative. A magazine that pokes holes in both sides at the same time."

"*The Complicater.*"

"That's good! You should remember that. I'm serious."

In the glow of her approval, it seemed almost possible that I could start a magazine called *The Complicater.* And would she be talking about my future if she didn't think she might be a part of it? The thought of this future, the love it would imply, led me to the thought of reaching across the table and touching her hand. I was just about to do it when she stood up.

"I have a project, too." She went over to the diagram of the beef cuts. "This is my project."

"I was wondering why a vegetarian had a cow poster in her kitchen."

"I don't have it all figured out yet. And it's going to take me fifteen years to complete. But if I can do it, it's going to be like your magazine: like nothing the world has ever known."

"Can you tell me what it is?"

"Let's see if I ever see you again first."

I stood up and joined her by the diagram. "Do I have to stop eating beef?"

She turned to me in surprise. "Yes, now that you mention it. That would be a requirement."

"And what sort of thing would you give up?"

"A *lot*," she said, retreating to the table. "I've gotten good at being alone. This kitchen smells the way I want it to smell. I have a problem with smells, I smell things that nobody else can. I'm smelling greasepaint on you right now. It's nice to be able to control my smell environment, and I can hear myself think better when it's quiet. It wasn't easy to become a person who's OK being alone on a Saturday night, but I did the work, *I got there*, and now some part of me is wishing I hadn't gone out tonight. Some part of me wants you not to be here. But it's like you were fated to be here." She took a breath and looked me directly in the eye. "I waited at that corner for you, Tom. I looked at my watch, and I said I'm waiting five minutes. And you came in four. Four eight, eight four."

My heart began to pound. I was becoming a sign, I was losing my self, and although I was obviously excited to learn that Anabel had waited for me, the surge of blood in my groin might have been the erection they say men get at the moment of being executed. That was how it felt.

I went to her and dropped to my knees. No less powerful than my desire for her was my wish, now on the verge of being granted, to be the person she allowed into her private world—to mean something in the story she was telling herself. When she put her hands on my shoulders and knelt down in front of me I experienced the gravity of what it meant to her to do this, and was excited even more for her sake than for mine. I looked into her eyes.

She said, "This is our fourth encounter, you know."

"If you count the phone call."

"Are you going to kiss me?"

"I'm afraid to," I said.

"I'm afraid, too. I'm afraid of you. I'm afraid of us."

I brought my face closer to hers.

"You break it, you pay for it," she whispered.

I could have kissed her all night. I did kiss her all night. How the hours can pass with mere kissing is lost to me now, along with the rest of my youth. And there were pauses, certainly. There was gazing into each other's eyes, there was pleasurable discussion of when exactly we'd become inevitable. There was the bounty of her hair, the pure Anabel smell of her skin, the little gap in her front teeth, the physical outskirts with which I needed to acquaint myself before proceeding deeper. There were new apologies and small confessions. There was her sudden, mad, amusing licking of the linoleum to prove to me how clean Anabel Laird kept a kitchen floor. Later there was a move to the sofa in her living room. There was the closed door of the bedroom that nobody but Anabel entered. But mostly we just kissed until dawn exposed us to our raw-eyed selves.

Anabel sat up and reassembled her composure like a cat after an awkward leap. "You need to go now," she said.

"Of course."

"I can't let you in all at once. You can apparently go straight from Lucy to me without skipping a beat, but I'm out of practice."

"I wouldn't call myself practiced."

She nodded seriously.

"I have something to confess and something to ask you," she said. "I need you to know that Lucy told me things about you. I wanted to scream at her, Shut up! shut up! But she told me you're a virgin."

How I hated that word. It sounded outmoded and ob-scene and accurate.

"Well, so here's my confession: it matters to me. It's why I waited for you at the corner. I mean, I waited be-cause I wanted to see you. But also because I thought you might be a person I could start over with. Do you even understand how clean you are?"

My underpants were sticky from hours of steady seep-age, but Anabel was right: my dick and I were barely on speaking terms. The stickiness, like the dick itself, was a male embarrassment and seemed to have little to do with the tenderness I felt toward her.

"But that's not my question," she said. "My question is what did Lucy tell you about me."

"She told me"—I chose my words carefully—"that

you'd had some bad experiences in high school and hadn't had a boyfriend in a long time."

Anabel gave a little shriek. "*God* I hate her! Why did I stay friends with this person?"

"I don't care what you did at Choate. I won't talk about you again with her."

"I hate her! She's a gutter with no grate. She has to drag everything down to her level. I *know* her. I know exactly what she told you." Anabel squeezed her eyes shut, pushing out mascara tears. "You have to go now, OK? I need to be in my room."

"I'll go, but I don't understand."

"I want us to be different. I want us to be like nothing else." She opened her eyes and smiled at me timidly. "It's really OK if you don't want to. You're just a very nice person, Denver-born. I'd understand if you didn't want any of this."

My communication lines with my dick were maybe not so very bad, because my response was to pull her face into mine, force her swollen lips into my sore ones. I can't help thinking that if we'd done the sensible thing and gone ahead and fucked there, on the floor, we might have had a happy life together. But everything in the moment argued against it—my inexperience, my suspicion of my motives, Anabel's strange notions of purity, her wish to be left alone, my wish not to harm her. We separated, breathing hard, and glared at each other.

"I want it," I said.

"Don't hurt me," she said.

"I won't hurt you."

Back on campus, I slept away the morning and went to the dining hall just in time to get food. I found Oswald at the table we preferred, and he greeted me with headlines.

"*Aberant to Friend: Enjoy the Party.*"

"Really sorry about that."

"Apologetic Aberant Cites Secret Laird Summit."

I laughed and said, *"Hackett Found Guilty in Laird Hatchet Job."*

"You're blaming *me* for that?" Oswald batted his eyelashes.

"Not anymore."

"Please tell me some butcher paper came into play."

The Monday issue of the *DP* was light work, because we had all weekend for it. By late afternoon we'd put it to bed and I was able to call Anabel. She'd slept until three and should have had nothing to report, but lovesickness makes the most minor thoughts and doings worthy of narration. We talked for an hour and then discussed whether to get together that night, since I wouldn't have another free night until Friday.

"So it begins," she said.

"What does?"

"Your important responsibilities, my waiting. I don't want to be the person who waits."

"I'm the one who'll be waiting until Friday night."

"You'll be busy, I'll be waiting."

"You don't have work to do?"

"Yes, but tonight is my one chance to make *you* wait. I want you to have one little taste of what it's going to be like for me."

If the logic had been anyone else's, I might have become impatient, but I, too, wanted us to be like nothing else. To prolong an essentially semantic disagreement for half an hour, as we proceeded to do, didn't frustrate me. It led me deeper into her singularity, our soon-to-be joint singularity. It meant keeping her voice in my ear.

When we'd finally compromised by agreeing to meet for drinks in Center City—whence I imagined myself following her home again and this time gaining entry to her bedroom, gaining permission to put my hands on more highly charged parts of her body, maybe even gaining everything I wanted, provided she wanted it as much as I did—I ate a quick dinner and went to my room to read Hegel for an hour. I'd barely sat down when the call came from my sister Cynthia.

"Clelia's in the hospital," she said. "They admitted her last night around midnight."

I was in such an Anabel state that my thought was: we had our first kiss around midnight. It was as if my mother had somehow known. Cynthia explained that my mother had been in the bathroom for four hours with a rising fever, unable to get away from the toilet. She'd finally managed to phone her gastroenterologist, Dr. Van Schyllingerhout, who was old-school enough to make house calls and fond enough of my mother to do it at eleven on a Saturday night. His diagnosis was not just an acute bowel inflammation but a complete nervous breakdown—my mother couldn't stop deliriously defending Arne Holcombe from some unnamed accusation.

"So I just got off the phone with the campaign manager," Cynthia said. "Apparently Arne exposed himself to a female staffer."

"My God," I said.

"They tried to keep it from Clelia, but somebody told her. She kind of went out of her mind. Twenty-four hours later, she can't leave the toilet long enough to call for help."

Cynthia was hoping I could fly to Denver. She had a big vote on unionization coming up on Friday, and Ellen was still furious with my mother for some remark she'd made about banjo players. (Ellen's position then and ever after was: She's a bitch to me, and she's not actually my mother.) Cynthia had never entirely stopped being dubious of me morally, albeit in a friendly way, and she probably already feared (with good reason) that she'd end up

stuck with the primary emotional care of her stepmother.
I agreed to call the hospital.

First, though, I called Anabel and luckily caught her
before she'd left to meet me. I explained the situation and
asked if she might come and see me in my dorm instead.
Her response was dead silence.

"I'm sorry," I said.

"Now you see what I mean about it beginning," Anabel
said.

"But this is an actual emergency."

"Try to imagine me in your dorm. The eyes on me. The
smell of those showers. This is something you can imagine me doing?"

"My mom is in the hospital!"

"I'm sorry about that," she said more kindly. "I'm
just sick about the timing. It's like everything is some
sort of sign with us. I know it's not your fault, but I'm
disappointed."

I consoled her for nearly an hour. I believe this was the
first time I ever really spoke ill of my mother; she'd previously been nothing worse than an embarrassment I'd
kept to myself. I must have wanted to show Anabel that
my loyalties were hers for the taking. And Anabel, though
she identified with her own suffering mother, not only said
nothing in defense of mine but helped me to sharpen my
complaints with her. She groaned when I told her that my
mother subscribed to *Town & Country*, and that she considered paper napkins déclassé and put out cloth ones,
with napkin rings, at every meal, and that her idea of a
chic department store was Neiman Marcus. "You need to
tell her," Anabel said, "that the people she admires all fly
to New York and shop at Bendel's." Anabel may have
renounced her privilege, but she was still defending it
from parvenus. When I recall her snobbery, the innocent
cruelty of it, she seems very young to me, and I even

younger for feeling intoxicated by it and using it against my mother.

The voice in Denver was hoarse and slurred with sedatives. "Your dumb old mother is in the hospital," it said. "Doctor Schan . . . *Vyllingerhout* took one look at me . . . 'I'm taking you to the hospital.' He's the most wo'r'ful man, Tom. Lef' his bridge game for me, plays bridge on Saturday night . . . They don't make physissans like that anymore. He doesn't have to work—sisty-sis years old. A real arissocrat, I think I told you his family . . . very old family, Belgium. He comes on Saturday night straigh' from his bridge game to dumb old me. Saturday night he makes a house call. Says I'm going to get better, not giving up until I'm better. Honestly, I'm so discouraged with this dumb old thing . . . He really is my savior."

I was encouraged that she seemed already to be moving on from Arne Holcombe to Dr. Van Schyllingerhout. I asked if she wanted me to come and see her.

"No, sweetie. You're sweet to offer but you have your magazine. To edit . . . your newspaper I mean. I'm so proud you're editor in chief. It will really impress . . . the law schools."

"Journalism schools all the more."

"I'm just happy to think of you with your fine, interesting, ambitious friends . . . all your bright prospects. You don't have to come and see dumb old me. Rather you not see me this way. Not my best . . . you can come when I'm better."

I'm not proud to have seized on permission granted under sedation not to go and see her. I think she did genuinely want me to have my own life, but this doesn't lessen the offense of my fear of being around her, my fear of implication in her sickness and recovery, and I ought to have known—did know, but pretended I didn't—that Cynthia, who was a very good person like our dad, would take up my slack and drive to Denver in her VW minibus after her union vote.

Not that I gave it much thought. My head was a radio playing Anabel on every station. There was no magazine in the world in whose pages I wouldn't have pointed to her picture and said: That one. No words in the language that stopped my heart like ANABEL CALLED on my office message board. (Never ANNABELLE. She was vain about her name and spelled it for whoever took the message.) We spoke every night and I began to resent the *DP* for interfering. I stopped eating beef and much of anything else; I was constantly half nauseated. Oswald clucked over me, but I was half nauseated with everything, including my best friend. I only wanted Anabel Anabel Anabel Anabel Anabel. She was beautiful and smart and serious and funny and stylish and creative and unpredictable and liked me. Oswald delicately called my attention to signs that she might be somewhat crazy, but he also showed me an article in the business section of the *Times*: McCaskill, still swimming in profits from Soviet grain sales, had an estimated value of $24 billion, and its dynamic president, David M. Laird, was aggressively expanding its operations overseas. I did the math on David—five percent, four heirs—and arrived at a figure of *three hundred million dollars* for Anabel, and felt even sicker.

I had to see her three more times before she let me in her bedroom. She was no doubt mindful of the number four, but there was also a peculiar circumstance that I learned of some hours into our third meeting as a couple, after I'd emerged victorious from protracted struggle with fear and feminist self-scrutiny and dared to ease my hand up under the maroon velvet dress she was wearing. When my fingers finally reached her underpants and touched the source of the heat between her legs, she drew breath sharply and said, "Don't start."

My hand retreated immediately. I didn't want to harm her.

"No, it's OK," she said, kissing me. "I want you to feel me. But only for you, not for me. You don't want to start with me."

I took my hand out of her dress altogether and stroked her hair, to impress on her that I wasn't in a hurry, wasn't selfish. "Why not?" I said.

"Because it won't work. Not tonight."

She sat up on her sofa and pressed her knees together with her hands flat between them. She made me promise that, no matter what happened, I would never tell any-one what she had to tell me. Ever since she was thirteen, she said, her periods had been in perfect sync with the phases of the moon. It was a very weird thing: her bleed-ing invariably began nine days after the moon was full. She said she could be trapped in a cave for years and still know what day of the lunar month it was. But there was something even weirder: ever since she'd had her unhappy disease in high school (this was her phrase, "my un-happy disease"), she could only achieve satisfaction in the three days when the moon was fullest, no matter how hard she tried on other days of the month. "And believe me, I've tried," she said. "There's nothing but frustration at the end of what you were starting."

"It's a half-moon tonight."

She nodded and turned to me with worry in her eyes, what I took to be the endearing worry that she was strange or damaged, or the even more endearing worry that I might be repulsed by her. But I wasn't repulsed. I was thrilled that she'd confided in me and wanted me enough to worry about repulsing me. I thought I'd never heard of anything more amazing and singular: in perfect sync with the moon!

She must have felt relieved by how ardently I kissed her

and reassured her, because her actual worry had to do with the rather obvious corollary to her confession: if I was committed to complete mutuality, to doing nothing with her that she couldn't equally join in, I was going to be getting laid three days a month at best. She assumed that I could see this corollary. I didn't see it. But even if I had, three days a month would have looked pretty great from where I was sitting that night. (Later, indeed, when we were married, it did come to look pretty great, in the rearview mirror.)

A week later, arriving early at Thirtieth Street for the SEPTA train, I had an impulse to buy something for Anabel in honor of our fourth date. I wandered down to the book-and-magazine store, hoping it might have a copy of *Augie March*, which Oswald had taught me to consider the finest novel by a living American, but it didn't. My eye was caught instead by a stuffed animal, a miniature black plush-toy bull with stubby felt horns and sleepy eyes. I bought it and put it in my knapsack. On the train, crossing the Schuylkill, I saw the full moon gilding fair-weather clouds over Germantown. I was already so far gone that the moon seemed to me the personal property of Anabel. Like something I could touch and was about to.

Anabel, in her kitchen, wearing a stunning black dress, opened another bottle of Château Montrose. "This is the last bottle," she said. "I gave the other eight to the winos behind the liquor store."

Eights and fours, everywhere eights and fours.

"They must have thought you were their angel," I said.

"No, in fact, they hassled me because I didn't have a corkscrew."

I'd expected the night to be magical through and through, but instead we had our first fight. I made a joking offhand allusion to her father's wealth, and she became upset, because everywhere she went she was hated as the rich girl, *and I was not to joke about it*, she couldn't be with me if that was how I thought of her, she hated the money enough without my reminding her of it, she was already knee-deep in the blood of it. After my tenth unavailing apology, I found some backbone and got angry. If she didn't want to be the rich girl, maybe she should stop wearing a different dress from Bendel's every time I saw her! She was shocked by my anger. Her deer's eyes bulged at me. She poured her wine into the sink and then upended the bottle over it. *For my information*, she hadn't bought a new dress since her senior year at Brown, but this clearly didn't matter to me, I clearly had my own idea about her, and I'd dragged my wrong idea into what was supposed to have been a perfect night. Everything was ruined. *Everything.* And so on. She finally stormed out of the kitchen and locked herself in the bathroom.

Sitting by myself, listening to the sound of her showering, I had the opportunity to replay our fight in my head, and it seemed to me that everything out of my mouth had been the words of a *jerk*. I was gripped by my old sense of ineluctable male wrongness. My only hope of cleansing was to dissolve my self in Anabel's. It seemed that black and white to me. Only she could save me from male error. By the time she came out of the bathroom, wearing lovely white flannel pajamas with pale-blue piping, I was shivering and crying.

"Oh dear," she said, kneeling at my feet.

"I love you. I love you. I'm sorry. I just love you."

I was in wretched earnest, but my dick was eavesdropping in my corduroys and sprang to life. She rested her cheek and damp hair on my knee. "Did I hurt you?"

"It was my fault."

"No, you were right," she said. "I'm weak. I love my clothes. I'm going to give up everything, but I can't give up my clothes yet. Please don't think badly of me. I didn't mean to hurt you. We just needed to have a fight tonight, that's all. It was a test we had to go through."

"I love your clothes," I said. "I love how you look in them. I'm so in love with you I'm sick to my stomach."

"I can stop wearing them in public," she said. "I'll only wear them when I'm with you, and it won't have to mean anything, because you'll know it's only me not being strong enough yet."

"I don't want to be the person who tells you what you can't do."

She kissed my knee gratefully. Then she saw the lump in my pants.

"I'm sorry," I said. "It's embarrassing."

"Don't be embarrassed. Boys can't help it. I only wish I could unlearn everything I know about it for you."

She then suggested I take a shower, which seemed perfectly reasonable, since she'd taken one herself. After I'd dried myself with one of her luxurious towels, I put all my clothes back on, not wanting to appear presumptuous. When I stepped out of the bathroom, I found the apartment lit only by the moon. Her bedroom door, which had always been shut, was now open the width of one finger.

I went to it and stopped at the threshold, my ears full of the sound of my heart, which seemed to be pounding with the impossibility of what had happened to me. Nobody went in Anabel's bedroom, but she'd left the door open for me. For me. My head was so full of significance I thought it might explode, the way the world would have to when it encountered an impossibility. It was as if no one existed, had ever existed, except Anabel and me. I pushed open the door.

The bedroom was a dream of purity in strong monochrome moonlight. The bed was a high four-poster with a calico quilt under which Anabel was lying on her side.

There were sheer curtains on the dormer windows, one Amish rug on the floor, a spindly chair and desk (the latter bare except for the watch and earrings she'd been wearing), and a high antique dresser topped with a lace cloth. Sitting on the dresser were a threadbare teddy bear and an eyeless and equally threadbare toy donkey. On the wall were a pair of unframed paintings, one of a horse from an unsettling close-up perspective, the other of a cow from a similar perspective, both of them unfinished-looking, with bare patches of canvas, which was Anabel's way as an artist. The spareness of the room felt rural-Kansan, nineteenth-century, especially in the moonlight. The animals reminded me that I hadn't given Anabel her present.

"Where are you going?" she called out plaintively when I went to retrieve my knapsack.

I came back with the little plush bull and sat on the edge of the bed like a father with his girl. "Forgot I had a present for you."

She sat up in her pajamas and took the bull. For a moment I thought she was going to hate it; was going to be scary Anabel. But she wasn't that Anabel in her bedroom. She smiled at the bull and said, "Hello, little one."

"It's OK?"

"He's perfect. I haven't had a new animal since I was ten." She glanced at her dresser. "The others are too worn out to talk to me anymore." She stroked the bull. "What's his name?"

"Not Ferdinand."

"No, not Ferdinand. Only Ferdinand is Ferdinand."

I don't know why the name Leonard popped into my head, but I said it.

"Leonard?" She peered into the bull's sleepy eyes. "Are you Leonard?" She turned its plushy face toward mine. "Is he Leonard?"

"Yes, I am Leonard," I said in the Belgian accent of my mother's gastroenterologist.

"You're not an American bull," Anabel said coyly.

Leonard explained, through me, that he came from a very old aristocratic cow family in Belgium, and that a series of misfortunes had brought him to Thirtieth Street Station in severely straitened circumstances. Leonard turned out to be a terrible snob, appalled by the ugliness of Philadelphia and the tackiness of America, and he was delighted with the prospect of entering Anabel's employ— he could tell she was a kindred spirit.

Anabel was entranced, and I was entranced to be entrancing her. I was also afraid to set Leonard aside, afraid of what came next, and I now see that I couldn't have found a better way to make Anabel feel safe than to play with a stuffed animal in her little girl's room. I'd blundered into being perfect for her. When we finally dismissed Leonard and she pulled me down on top of her, there was a new look in her eyes, the unconcealable and unfakable look of a woman seriously in love. It's not something a man sees every day.

I wish I could remember the sensation of being taken by her, or maybe it's more accurate to say that I wish I could go back to that moment as the person I am now, could be in that state of trembling wonder but also have enough experience to appreciate how it felt to be inside a woman for the first time; to enjoy it, basically. But it wasn't as if I'd enjoyed my first beer or my first cigar, either. The beauty of Anabel naked literally made my eyes hurt, and I was nothing but a thousand worries. If I remember anything from the moment at all, it's the dreamlike sensation of walking into a room where two figures had been for my entire life, two figures who knew each other well and were talking about realistic adult things I knew nothing about, two figures indifferent to my very late arrival.

These figures were the things so graphically *down there*, my dick and Anabel's cunt. I was the young and excluded third party, Anabel a distant fourth. But this may have been some actual dream from some other time.

What I do remember clearly is what a full moon did for Anabel, how she came and came. I was too clumsy to manage it in the purely thrusting way I would have liked to, but she showed me different ways. It seemed inconceivable that such a total pleasure machine couldn't come at other times of the month, but later experience seemed to bear this out. She was a nearly silent comer, not a screamer. In the warmer light of dawn, she confessed to me that during her now-ended years of celibacy she'd sometimes waited for her best day and spent the entirety of it in her bedroom, masturbating. The vision of her beautiful, endless, solitary self-pleasuring made me wish I could be her. Since I couldn't, I fucked her for a fourth and last sore time. Then we slept until the afternoon, and I stayed in her apartment for another two days, sustaining myself with buttered toast, not wanting to waste the moon's fullness. When I finally got back to campus, I resigned from the *DP* and let Oswald take over.

My mother had warned me that her face had swollen up from the high doses of prednisone that Dr. Van Schyllingerhout had her on, but I was still shocked when I met her at the airport. Her face was a ghastly fat cartoon of itself, a miserable moon of flesh, her cheeks so bloated they pushed her eyes half shut. Her apologies to me were piteous. She said she was *sick* about the state she was in for an *Ivy League graduation* she'd so looked forward to.

I told her not to worry, but I was sick about it, too. No matter how often you remind yourself that a face is just a face, that it has nothing to do with the character of the person within, you're so used to reading people through their faces that it's difficult to be fair to a deformed one. My mother's new face repelled the very sympathy it ought to have elicited from me. She was like a shameful secret of mine, a pumpkin-headed scarecrow in a checkered pants suit, when I walked her across the Green to my Phi Beta Kappa induction. I avoided meeting anyone's eyes, and when I'd deposited her in a seat in College Hall, I had to force myself to walk, not run, away from her.

After the ceremony, in what felt like a straightforward purchase of my freedom from her, I gave her my Phi Beta Kappa key. (She wore it on a fine gold chain for the rest of her life.) I left her in her assigned room in the Superblock to freshen up—the weather was bludgeoningly hot and humid—while Oswald and I set up our dorm rooms for a wine-and-cheese party. I'd conceived of the party as a way to introduce my mother and Anabel in a casual setting. Anabel was dreading it, but my mother had no reason to. She disapproved of Anabel without even having met her, and I'd been too cowardly to tell her that Anabel was coming to the party.

Back in November, I'd imagined that my mother would be pleased that I was officially dating a McCaskill heir. But she'd heard from my sister how Anabel and I had met. Cynthia had been amused by the butcher-paper story, but all my mother could see in it was kookiness, radical feminism, and public nudity. In her weekly dronings to me, she promulgated a new, invidious distinction between *entrepreneurial* wealth and *inherited* wealth. She also rightly suspected that I'd quit the job of executive editor because of Anabel. I explained that I wanted to focus on my reportorial skills—I was writing, with Anabel's blessing, a major piece on scrapple—but my mother could smell our sex acts all the way from Denver. When I went home for Christmas and informed her that I'd not only be-

come a vegetarian but was returning to Philly after only
a week, her colon flared up badly again.

Let it not be thought that I didn't know what I was getting into with Anabel, or that I made no effort to escape
it. Three days a lunar month we were a pair of junkies
who'd scored the cleanest shit ever, but on the other
twenty-five I had to contend with her moods, her scenes,
her sensitivities, her judgments, her so easily hurt feelings.
We seldom actually fought or argued; it was more often a
matter of processing, endlessly, what I or someone else
had done to make her feel bad. My entire personality reor-
ganized itself in defense of her tranquillity and defense
of myself from her reproach. It's possible to describe this
as an emasculation of me, but it was really more like a dissolution of the boundaries of our selves. I learned to feel
what she was feeling, she learned to anticipate what I was
thinking, and what could be more intense than a love
with no secrets?

"A word about the toilet," she'd said one day, early on.

"I always raise the seat," I said.

"That's the problem."

"I thought the problem was guys who think they can
aim through the seat."

"I appreciate that you're not one of them. But there's
a spatter."

"I wipe the rim, too."

"Not always."

"OK, room for improvement."

"But it's not just on the rim. It's on the underside of the
rim and on the tile. Little drops."

"I'll wipe there, too."

"You can't wipe the whole bathroom every time. And
I don't like the smell of old urine."

"I'm a guy! What am I supposed to do?"

"Sit down?" she suggested shyly.

I knew this wasn't right, couldn't be right. But she was hurt by my silence and became silent herself, in a more grievous way, with a stony look in her eyes, and her hurt mattered more to me than my rightness. I told her I would either be more careful or start sitting down, but she could sense that I was resentful, that my submission was grudging, and there could be no peace in our union unless we *truly agreed about everything.* She began to weep, and I began the long search for the deeper cause of her distress.

"*I* have to sit down," she said finally. "Why shouldn't *you* sit down? I can't not see where you spatter, and every time I see it I think how unfair it is to be a woman. You can't even see how unfair it is, you have no idea, no idea."

She proceeded to cry torrentially. The only way I could get her to stop was to become, right then and there, a person who experienced as keenly as she did the unfairness of my being able to pee standing up. I made this adjustment to my personality—and a hundred others like it in our early months together—and henceforth I peed sitting down whenever she could hear me. (When she couldn't, though, I peed in her sink. The part of me that did this was the part that ultimately ruined us and saved me.)

She was more lenient of difference in the bedroom. It was certainly an unhappy day when she connected the dots for me and explained that we couldn't have intercourse when only one of us could take satisfaction in it. At my suggestion, after hours of pained discussion and silences, we tried it anyway, and I had to suffer the guilt of her sobbing when I came inside her. I asked if she'd had *no* pleasure, to which she sobbed that the frustration outweighed the pleasure. We had the whole unfairness conversation again, but this time I was able to point out that, by her own admission, she wasn't normal, i.e., that we weren't dealing with a structural gender imbalance. In the end, since she loved me, and was probably afraid of losing me to someone more normal, she agreed to make other arrangements for me. These were a little strange but very creative and, for a while, satisfactory. First I had to take a shower, then we had to converse with Leonard and get his amusing Belgian bull's-eye take on the news of the day, then we undressed, and then she—there's no other way to put it—played with the dick. Sometimes it was a camera slowly panning over her body and then shooting its favorite parts. Sometimes she wrapped it in her cool, silky hair and milked it. Sometimes she nuzzled it until it wet her face, as if it were a shower head. Sometimes she took it in her mouth, her gaze not moving from it to my eyes until the moment she swallowed. She was affectionate to the dick in much the same way she was affectionate to Leonard. She told me it was pretty like I was pretty. She claimed that my semen smelled cleaner than other semen she'd had the misfortune of smelling. But the strangest thing, in hindsight, was that she always made the dick not part of me. She didn't like me to kiss her while she was touching it; she preferred that I not even touch her with my hands until she was finished with it. And always, as I discovered, she was counting. When a full moon came around again, restoring normalcy, she informed me when an orgasm of hers had equalized our tallies for the month. And then everything was OK with us. Then we were one again.

Two other crises bear noting. The first was my acceptance by the journalism school at the University of Missouri, an excellent school that my mother had encouraged me to apply to because it was affordable and not so far from Denver. I may have been besotted with Anabel, and I may have turned against my maleness as an impediment to our union of souls, but the male part of me was still there and well aware that she was strange, that I was young, and that a vegetarian diet wasn't agreeing with my stomach. I imagined regrouping in Missouri, becoming a lean and mean reporter, sampling some other girls before deciding whether to commit to a life with Anabel. I made the mistake of breaking the Missouri news to her on the night before a full moon. I tried to jolly her into her bedroom, but she went silent. Only after hours of sulking and prodding, hours we could have spent in bed, did she lay out my thinking for me in its full male vileness. She didn't miss a thing. "You'll be there having your excellent journalist's life, you'll be *happy* not to be with me, and I'll be here waiting," she said.

"You could come with me."

"You can see me living in Columbia, Missouri? As your tagalong girl?"

"You could stay here and work on your project. It's only two years."

"And your magazine?"

"How am I going to start a magazine with no money and no experience?"

She opened a drawer and took out a checkbook.

"This is what I have," she said, pointing to a figure of some $46,000 in the savings ledger. I watched her write me a check for $23,000 in her elegant artist's hand. "Do you want to be with me and be ambitious?" She tore out the check and handed it to me. "Or do you want to go to Missouri with all the other hacks?"

I didn't point out that checkbook gestures aren't so meaningful coming from a billionaire's daughter. Doubting her vow not to accept more money from her father was as grievous a wrong as doubting her seriousness as an artist. She'd already trained me never to do it. She was rabid on the subject.

"I can't take your money," I said.

"It's *our* money," she said, "and this is the last of it. Everything I have is yours. Use it well, Tom. You can go

to school with it if you want to. If you're going to break
my heart, this is the time to do it. Not from Missouri a
year from now. Take the money, go home, go to journalism school. Just don't pretend you're in this with me."

She went and locked herself in her bedroom. I don't
know how many times I had to promise I wasn't leaving
her before she let me in. When she finally did, I tore up
the check—"Don't be a fool, that's good money!" Leonard cried from the headboard—and seized her body with
a new sense of possession, as if becoming more hers had
made her more mine.

My mother was furious about my decision. She saw me
starting down the path of indigence my sisters were tread-
ing, the path of my father's stupid idealism, and it did me
no good to cite the many famous journalists who hadn't
gone to grad school. She was even more upset, a month
later, when I told her I was coming to Denver only for a
week that summer. I'd spent all of eight days with her
since her hospitalization, and I felt I owed her (and Cynthia) a month at home, but Anabel had been counting on
our starting a life together the minute I graduated. She
took my proposal of a month apart as a catastrophic betrayal of everything we'd planned together. When I suggested that she join me in Denver, she stared at me as if
I, not she, were the insane one. Why I didn't resolve the
crisis by breaking up with her is hard to fathom. My brain
was apparently already so wired into hers that even though
I knew she was being unreasonable and heartless, I didn't
care. All drugs are an escape from the self, and throwing
myself away for Anabel, doing something *obviously
wrong* to make her feel better, and then reaping the ecstasy of her renewed enthusiasm for me, was my drug. My
mother cried when I told her my travel plans, but only
Anabel's tears could change my mind.

Anger with the two of us was broadcast in my mother's

swollen face at the graduation party. There was no safe way to explain to my friends and their normal-looking parents that she didn't always look like this. Everyone was sweating mightily by the time Anabel arrived, wearing a drop-dead sky-blue cocktail dress and accompanied by Nola. They went straight to the wine, and it was a while before I could pry my mother away from Oswald's parents and lead her to the corner where Anabel was sitting in Nola's little cloud of disaffection. I made the introduction, and Anabel, stiff with shyness, rose and took my mother's hand.

"Mrs. Aberant," she bravely said. "I'm so glad to finally meet you."

My poor disfigured pants-suited mother, confronting the vision of that sky-blue cocktail dress: Anabel could never forgive her for what she did, but eventually I could. Something resembling a condescending smile appeared on her bloated face. She released Anabel's hand and looked down at Nola, who was dressed in punky black. "And you are . . . ?"

"The depressive friend," Nola said. "Pay me no mind."

Anabel had wanted to make a good impression on my mother; she just needed a modicum of coaxing out of her shyness. None was forthcoming. My mother turned away and told me she wanted to change her clothes before dinner.

"You need to talk to Anabel," I said.

"Maybe another time."

"*Mom*. Please."

Anabel had sat down again, her eyes wide with injured disbelief.

"I'm sorry I'm not at my best," my mother said.

"She came all the way over here to meet you. You can't just walk away."

I was appealing to her sense of propriety, but she was

too sweaty and miserable to heed it. I gestured to Anabel to join us, but she ignored me. I followed my mother out into the hallway.

"Just tell me how to get back to my room," she said. "You stay at your nice party. I'm so happy to have met Mr. and Mrs. Hackett. They're fine, interesting, responsible people."

"Anabel is extremely important to me," I said, trembling.

"Yes, I can see she's quite pretty. But so much older than you."

"She's *two years* older."

"She looks so much older, sweetie."

Half blind with hatred and shame, I led my mother outside and over to her room. By the time I got back to the party, Anabel and Nola were gone—a relief, since I was hardly in a mood to defend my mother. At dinner with the Hacketts, my mother's face was an unreferred-to elephantine presence, and I refused to say a word to her directly. Afterward, in the humid shade of the Locust Walk, I informed her that I couldn't spend the evening with her, because Anabel's thesis project was being screened at Tyler at nine thirty. I'd dreaded telling her this, but now I was glad to.

"I'm sorry your mother is such an embarrassment," she said. "This dumb condition of mine is ruining everything."

"Mom, you're not embarrassing me. I just wish you could have talked to Anabel."

"I can't stand having you angry at me. It's the worst thing in the world for me. Do you want me to come and see her movie with you?"

"No."

"If she means so much to you that you won't even speak to me at dinner, maybe I should go."

"No."

"Why not? Is her movie immoral? You know I can't stand nudity or gutter language."

"No," I said, "it's just not going to make sense to you. It's about the visual properties of film as a purely expressive medium."

"I love a good movie."

Both of us must have known she'd loathe Anabel's work, but I managed to persuade myself to give her a second chance. "Just promise you'll be nice to her," I said. "She's worked all year on this, and artists are sensitive. You have to be really, really nice."

Anabel's project was titled, at my suggestion, "A River of Meat." She'd wanted to call it "Unfinished #8," because in her view the film wasn't quite finished, because she never quite finished anything, because she got bored and moved on to the next artistic challenge. I told her that only she would know that her film wasn't finished. She'd obtained two short 16 mm film clips, one of a cow being bolt-gunned in the head in a slaughterhouse, the other of Miss Kansas being crowned Miss America 1966, and she'd labored for the better part of a year to reprint and hand-doctor and intercut the two clips. Her favorite filmmakers were Agnès Varda and Robert Bresson, but her project owed more to the hypnotic musical tapestries of Steve Reich. She alternated a single frame with its negative one to one, one to two, two to one, two to two, and so on, and she introduced other rhythmic variations by reversing the frames, rotating them by ninety degrees, running them backward, and hand-coloring the frames with red ink. The resulting twenty-four-minute film was radically repellent, a full-scale assault on the visual cortex, but you could also see genius in it if you looked at it right.

My mother's all-time favorite movie was *Doctor*

Zhivago. During the last minutes of the screening, I could
hear her muttering angrily. When the lights came up, she
hurried to the door.

"I'll just wait outside," she said when I caught up with
her.

"You need to say something nice to Anabel first."

"What can I say? That is the most horrible, disgusting
thing I've seen in my entire life."

"A little nicer than that would be good."

"If that's art, then there is something wrong with art."
A wave of anger came over me.

"You know what?" I said. "Just tell her that. Tell her
you hated it."

"I'm not the only person who would hate it."

"Mom, it's fine. She's not going to be surprised."

"Do *you* think it's art?"

"Definitely. I think it's amazing."

Down at the front of the screening room, Anabel was
standing with Nola, not looking at us, some terrible scene
with me no doubt brewing inside her. The few students
and professors in the audience had fled for their lives. My
mother spoke to me in a low voice.

"I don't even recognize you, Tom, you've changed so
much in the last six months. I'm very disturbed by what's
happened to you. I'm disturbed by a person who would
make a movie like that. I'm disturbed that she's the reason you suddenly quit the fine job you worked so hard to
get, and you're not pursuing your graduate studies."

I, for my part, was disturbed by my mother's steroidal
ugliness. My life was lovely Anabel, and I could only hate
the bloat-faced, slit-eyed person who questioned it. My
love and my hatred felt indistinguishable; each seemed to
follow logically from the other. But I was still a dutiful
son, and I would have taken my mother back to Penn if
Anabel hadn't come stalking up the aisle.

"That was great," I said to her. "It's amazing to see it on the big screen."

She was glaring at my mother. "What did *you* think?"

"I don't know what to say," my mother said, frightened.

Anabel, her shyness now dispelled by moral outrage, laughed at her and turned to me. "Are you coming with us?"

"I should probably take my mom home."

Anabel flared her long nostrils.

"I can meet you later," I said. "I don't want her taking the train by herself."

"And she couldn't possibly take a cab."

"I've got like eight dollars on me."

"She has no money?"

"She didn't bring her purse. She has this idea about Philly."

"Right. All those scary black people."

It was wrong to be talking about my mother as if she weren't there, but she'd wronged Anabel first. Anabel stalked back down the aisle, opened her knapsack, and returned with a pair of twenty-dollar bills. What do they say at NA meetings? The thing you promise yourself you'll never go so low as to do for drugs is the very thing you end up doing? I would have said that it was bad in eight different ways to take money from Anabel and hand it to my mother, but that's what I did. Then I called a cab and waited with her in silence in front of President's Hall.

"I've had some rough days," she said after a while. "But I think this has been the worst day of my life."

The moon above us, in the Philly haze, was a dissolving beige lozenge. My response to its fullness was Pavlovian, a quickening of the pulse that was hard to distinguish, in the moment, from my fear of my mother's pain and from the thrilling cruelty of what I was doing to her. My chest felt too tight for me to say anything, even that I was sorry.

I met Anabel's father later that summer. For two months, she and I had played house with some of her remaining forty thousand dollars, sleeping until noon, breakfasting on toast, trolling thrift stores to improve my wardrobe, escaping the heat at double features at the Ritz, and perfecting our wok skills. On my birthday, we made a plan to become more serious about our work. I began to write a manifesto for *The Complicater* while she embarked on the year of reading she needed to do for her grand film project. She went to the Free Library every weekday afternoon, because we'd decided it was healthy to be apart for some hours and she didn't want to wait for me at home like a housewife.

David Laird called on one of those afternoons. I had to explain to him that Anabel had a boyfriend and that I was that person.

"*Interesting*," David said. "I'm going to tell you a little secret: I'm glad to hear a male voice. I was afraid the wind was blowing in the direction of that mentally-ill dyke friend of hers, just to spite me."

"I don't think that was ever in the cards," I said.

"Are you black?" he said. "Handicapped? Criminal? Drug addict?"

"Ah, no."

"*Interesting*. I'll tell you another secret: I like you already. I take it you're in love with my daughter?"

I hesitated.

"Of course you are. She's quite something, isn't she? To call her a handful is the understatement of a lifetime. They really broke the mold with that one."

I could already hear why Anabel hated him.

"But listen," he went on, "if *she* likes you, *I* like you. Hell, I was even prepared to like the mentally-ill girl, although, praise the Lord, it didn't come to that. Anabel'd do almost anything to spite me, but she won't go so far as to cut off her nose, if you know what I mean. I know her, I know that pretty nose of hers. And I want to know the guy she's living with. What do you say to dinner at Le Bec-Fin next Thursday? The three of us. The reason I called is I've got some business over in Wilmington."

I said I'd have to ask Anabel.

"Aw, hell, Tom—it's Tom, right? You're going to need to grow some serious gonads if you're going to live with my girl. She'll eat you alive if you're not careful. You just tell her you said you'd have dinner with me. Can you say those words to me? 'Yes, David, I will have dinner with you'?"

"I mean, yeah, sure," I said. "If it's OK with her."

"No, no, no. Those aren't the words. You and I are having dinner, period, and she can come along if she wants to. Believe me, there's no way in hell she's letting the two of us go out alone. That's why it's important that you say the words to me. If you're this afraid of her now, it'll only get worse later."

"I'm not afraid of her," I said. "But if she doesn't want to see you . . ."

"OK. All right. Here's a different argument. Here's another secret for you: she does want to see me. It's been more than a year since she got to spray me in the face with cat piss. That's what she does. And she doesn't like to admit it, but she enjoys it. She's got a lot of cat piss, and there's only one face she wants to spray. So when she says she doesn't want to see me, you tell her you're going to see me anyway. It'll be our little secret that we're really doing it for her."

"Wow," I said. "I'm not sure that's a good argument."

David laughed loudly. "Oh, come on, I'm just fooling around. Let's go and have a great meal at the best place in Philadelphia. I miss my Anabel."

Of course she threw a scene when she learned I'd spoken to him. He was a *seducer*, she said, and when he couldn't seduce he *bullied*, and when he couldn't bully he *bought*, and although she was on to him and had built up her defenses, she didn't trust me not to be seduced or bullied or bought. And so on. I'd been offended by much of what he'd said, but I also couldn't get it out of my head; who else, after all, could I talk to about Anabel? I experimentally grew some gonads and said it was hurtful and insulting not to trust that I loved her, not him. I experimented further and told her I'd given my word to have dinner with him. And, exactly as he'd predicted, she agreed to come along.

I tasted my first $3,000 wine at Le Bec-Fin. David had handed Anabel the wine list, and she was reading it when the sommelier came by. "Give her a minute while she finds your cheapest bottle," David said to the sommelier. "In the meantime, Tom and I will have the '45 Margaux."

When I sought Anabel's approval for this, she widened her eyes at me unpleasantly. "Go ahead," she said. "I don't care."

"It's a little game she and I play," David explained. He was a tall, trim, vigorous man with nearly white hair, a distinguished male version of his daughter, much better-looking than your average billionaire. "But here's an interesting fact for your future reference. At a place like this, the very cheapest bottle on the list is often sensational. Not sure why that is. It's the mark of a great restaurant, though."

"I'm not looking for something sensational," Anabel said. "I'm looking for something I won't gag on the price of."

"Nice for you that you'll probably get both," David said. He turned to me. "Ordinarily, I'd order that bottle myself. But then she and I couldn't play our little game. You see what she makes me do?"

"Funny how women are always to blame for what men do to them," Anabel remarked.

"Has she told you how she broke her teeth?"

"She has."

"But did she tell you the best part? She got back on the horse. Blood all over her face, her mouth full of broken tooth, and she gets right back on the horse. And she gives that bridle a yank like she's going to rip its head off. She almost broke its neck. That's my Anabel."

"Dad, shut up, please."

"Honey, I'm speaking well of you to your boyfriend."

"Then don't omit the part about my never getting on a horse again. I still feel bad about what I did to that poor beast."

Given Anabel's hatred of David, I was surprised by their intimate way together. It was like watching a pair of Hollywood execs abuse each other—you had to be powerful to take the abuse with a laugh. When David mentioned, offhandedly, that he'd remarried, Anabel's response was "To one person, or several?"

David laughed. "One is all I can afford."

"You'll need at least three in case you have to kill a couple more."

"I married a dipsomaniac," David explained to me.

"You *created* an alcoholic," Anabel said.

"Somehow men are always to blame for what women do to them."

"Somehow it's always true. Who's the lucky lady?"

"Her name's Fiona. You'll want to meet her."

"I won't want to meet her. I'll just want to sign over my birthright to her. Just show me the dotted line."

"Not going to happen," David said. "Fiona signed what they call a prenuptial agreement. You're not going to be rid of your birthright that easily."

"Watch me," Anabel said.

"You must talk her out of this madness, Tom."

I was having trouble fitting into their banter. I didn't want David to think I was too earnest or subservient to Anabel, but I couldn't be too at ease with him without appearing disloyal to her. "That's not in my job description," I said carefully.

"But you do agree it's madness?"

My eyes met Anabel's. "No, I don't," I said.

"Give it time. You will."

"No, he won't," Anabel said, looking into my eyes. "Tom's not you. Tom is clean."

"Ah, yes, the blood on my hands." David held his hands up for inspection. "Funny, I'm not seeing it tonight."

"Look more closely," Anabel said. "I can smell it."

David seemed disappointed in me when he learned that I didn't eat meat, and outright annoyed when Anabel ordered nothing but a plate of vegetables, but his foie gras and his veal chop restored his spirits. It may only have been a form of billionaire narcissism, but he demonstrated cover-to-cover familiarity with *The New Yorker*, spoke knowledgeably of Altman and Truffaut, offered to get us tickets to *The Elephant Man* in New York, and seemed genuinely interested in my opinions about Bellow. It occurred to me that something tragic had happened in the Laird family—that Anabel and her father ought to have been the best of friends. Was she his bitter enemy, and her brothers three disasters, not because he was a monster but because he was too fabulous? Anabel had never claimed that he wasn't likable, only that he seduced people with his likability. He told me stories of bad business moves he'd made—the selling of a Brazilian sugar mill a year before it became wildly profitable, his torpedoing of a partnership with Monsanto because he thought he knew more about plant genetics than Monsanto's head of R&D did—and made fun of his own arrogance. When the conversation turned to my career plans and he offered, first, to get me a job at the *Washington Post* ("Ben Bradlee's an old friend of mine") and then, after I'd declined that offer, to fund the start-up of my contrarian magazine, I had the feeling that he was daring me to be fabulous like him.

Anabel thought otherwise. "He just wants to buy you," she said on our train ride home. "It's always the same. I let my guard down a tiny bit, and I loathe myself afterward. He wants to get his fingers into everything I have, the same way McCaskill's got its fingers into everything the world eats. He won't rest till he has everything. It's not enough to be the world's leading supplier of turkey meat, he has to have Truffaut and Bellow. You flatter his intellectual vanity. He thinks if he can have you, he'll get *me*, and then he'll have everything."

"Did you hear me saying yes to him?"

"No, but you liked him. If you think he's going to leave you alone now, think again."

She was right. Not long after our dinner, I received, by express mail, a package containing four hardcover first editions (*Augie March*, H. L. Mencken, John Hersey, Joseph Mitchell), two tickets to *The Elephant Man*, and a letter from David in which he'd recorded his thoughts on rereading *Augie March*. He also mentioned that he'd spoken on the phone to Ben Bradlee about me, and he invited me and Anabel to New York for a weekend of theater the following month. When Anabel had finished tearing up the tickets, she pointed out the initials in the lower corner of the letter's second page. "Don't flatter yourself too much," she said. "He dictated it."

"So what? I can't believe he went and reread *Augie March* for me."

"Oh I can."

"You're not tearing up the books, though."

"No, those you can keep if you can get the blood off them. But if you ever take anything more than token gifts from him, you will destroy me. And I mean destroy me."

He continued to call me now and then, and I considered not telling Anabel about it, but I was already peeing in the sink and didn't want to keep more secrets from her. Instead, I reported on his fabulous doings and then concurred in her condemnation of them. But I secretly liked him, secretly loved the loving way he spoke of Anabel, and she—he'd been right about this—secretly enjoyed having fresh doings to condemn.

My manifesto for *The Complicater* wasn't going well. It was long on contrarian rhetoric and short on facts. If I really intended to found a new magazine, I ought to have been maintaining my friendships from the *DP* and cultivating relationships with local freelancers. *The Complicater* was an obvious nonstarter unless Anabel relented and let David fund it, and so I passed my days in the vague hope that she would relent. Oswald, who'd gone home to Lincoln to pay down his college debt, sent me droll letters to which I couldn't summon the energy to respond. I would make it my *one task* for the afternoon to write him a letter, and I wouldn't manage to write one sentence until five minutes before Anabel came home from the library. I didn't have anything to report to anybody except that I was besotted with her.

Having spent the previous ten months shaping my personality to fit with hers, sanding away the most prominent points of friction, I was mostly blissful in her presence that fall. We were developing our routines, our shared opinions, our private vocabulary, our store of phrases that

had been funny on first utterance and seemed scarcely less
funny on the hundredth, and every word and every belonging of hers was colored by the sex I'd had with her
and no one else. When I was alone in the apartment,
though, I felt depressed. Anabel had limitless money but
intended never to take any of it, I was mad for her body
but could have it only three days a month, I liked her dad
but had to pretend I didn't, her dad had fabulous connections but I wasn't allowed to use them, I had a supposedly
ambitious project but no chance of making it happen,
and whenever my mother dared to question what I was
doing—I continued to call her every Sunday night—I
took it as a criticism of Anabel and angrily changed the
subject.

Our joint plan was to be poor and obscure and pure and
take the world by surprise at a later date. Anabel was so
convincing that I believed in our plan. My only fear was
that she'd realize I wasn't as interesting as she was and
leave me. She was the amazing thing that had happened
to me, and I intended to support her and defend her from
a world that didn't understand her, and so, on the anniversary of Lucy's Halloween party, I withdrew the last
$350 from my old savings account and bought a ring with
a pitiful little phonograph-stylus diamond. By the time
Anabel came home from the library, I'd tied the ring to
Leonard's neck with a white ribbon and left him standing
in the center of our bed.

"Leonard and I have something for you," I said.

"Aha, you've been out," she said. "I thought I smelled
city on you."

I led her into the bedroom.

"Leonard, what do you have for me?" She picked him
up and saw the ring. "Oh, Tom."

"I am not, of course, a beast of burden," Leonard said.
"I am an ornament of society, not a common toiler. But

when he requested that I be your ring bearer, I could hardly refuse."

"Oh, Tom." She set Leonard on the nightstand and put her arms around my neck and looked into my eyes. Her own were lustrous with tears and ardor.

"It's our first anniversary," I said.

"Oh, my darling. I knew you'd remember, but I also wasn't sure you would."

"Will you marry me?"

"A thousand times!"

We tumbled onto the bed. It wasn't the right time of month, but she said it didn't matter. I thought that maybe now that we were going to be married she might get past her problem, and I think she thought so too, but it wasn't to be. She said she was happy anyway. She lay on her back with our little bull between her breasts and untied the ribbon.

"I'm sorry the diamond is so small," I said.

"It's perfect," she said, putting the ring on. "You picked it out for me, and so it's perfect."

"I can't believe I get to be married to you."

"No, I'm the lucky one. I know I'm not an easy person."

"I love your difficulty."

"Oh, you're perfect, you're perfect, you're perfect!" She kissed me all over my face, and we made love again. The ring on her finger had magical powers. I was fucking my *betrothed*, there was a new dimension to the joy of it, an immeasurably deeper chasm into which to throw my self, and no end to the falling. Even when I finished, I kept falling. Anabel cried softly—with pure happiness, she said. What I now see is a pair of kids who'd been snorting the powder for a year, losing their connections to reality one by one and becoming (at least in my case) depressed about it. How, by the logic of addiction, could we not have proceeded to the needle and the vein? But in the moment all I was aware of was the rush the ring brought. While it lasted, I gathered my courage and asked Anabel to come with me to Denver for Christmas, announce our engagement, and give my mother another chance. To my delight, Anabel not only didn't resist but smothered me with kisses, saying she'd do anything for me now, anything, anything.

In her own way, she tried. She was prepared to like my mother if my mother would appreciate her. She even bought her own separate Christmas presents for her—a volume of Simone de Beauvoir, some fruit-scented soaps, a lovely old brass pepper mill—and when we got to Denver she was good about offering to help my mother in the kitchen. But my mother, still traumatized by "A River of Meat," declined the offers. She seemed determined to play the role of martyred working mom—she'd gone back to her job at the pharmacy, Dick Atkinson having married someone else—to Anabel's indolent rich girl. She also, though I'd been explaining it to her for months, refused to grasp that Anabel had become a vegan and I a vegetarian. For our first dinner, I caught her making baked whitefish for me and macaroni and cheese for Anabel.

"No flesh for me, no animal products for Anabel," I reminded her.

She was still somewhat moonfaced, but we were getting used to it. "It's nice fish," she said, "not meat."

"It's dead animal. And cheese is an animal product."

"Then what is 'vegan'? Does she eat *bread*?"

"The macaroni is fine, the problem is the cheese part."

"So, she can just eat the macaroni. I'll cut away the crust."

Fortunately my sister Cynthia was there, too. After I'd introduced her to Anabel, she'd pulled me aside and whispered, "Tom, she's *beautiful*, she's *wonderful*." Cynthia took up the defense of our dietary restrictions, and when

I announced our engagement, at the dinner table, she ran to the kitchen for a bottle of pink champagne that my mother had bought in expectation of an Arne Holcombe victory. My mother herself simply stared at her plate and said, "You're very young to be doing this."

Anabel evenly asked her how old she'd been when she got married.

"I was very young, and so I know," my mother said. "I know what can happen."

"We're not you," Anabel said.

"That's what everyone thinks," my mother said. "They think they're not like other people. But then life teaches you some lessons."

"Mom, be happy," Cynthia called from the kitchen. "Anabel's fantastic, this is great news."

"You don't need my blessing," my mother said. "All I can give you is my opinion."

"Noted," Anabel said.

Somehow we got through the holiday on civil terms. I slept in the basement so that Anabel could have her own bedroom. We assented to this maintenance of propriety to keep the peace, but every night, in the basement, as if to show my mother who was boss, Anabel gave me a blow job. This was probably the all-time peak of her carnality with me, the only time I remember her getting down on her knees. My mother was less than fifteen feet away from us, as the gamma ray flies; we could hear her footsteps, the toilet flushing, even the sounds of her bowel. After Cynthia left, Oswald came over from Nebraska for two nights, and my mother was so pointedly affectionate to him that Anabel remarked to me, "She'd rather you were marrying Oswald."

On our last day, alone with my mother, we made our favorite stir-fry for dinner, and she began to drone on about money. She could understand our living on Anabel's assets and doing something socially beneficial, she said, and she could understand our finding responsible jobs and supporting ourselves, but she could *not* understand our living in voluntary poverty and pursuing unrealistic dreams.

"We still have some savings," I said. "If we run out, we'll get jobs."

"Have you ever had a job?" my mother asked Anabel.

"No, I grew up obscenely rich," Anabel said. "It would have been a joke to have a job."

"Honest work is never a joke."

"She works incredibly hard on her art," I said.

"Art isn't work," my mother said. "Art is something you do for yourself. I'm not saying you have to work, if you're lucky enough not to have to. But if there's money coming to you, you should accept the responsibilities that come with it. You need to do *something*."

"Art *is* something," I said.

"Part of my artistic performance," Anabel said, "is not to touch money that has blood on it. To be the person who rejects it."

"I don't understand that," my mother said.

"There's such a thing as collective guilt," Anabel said. "I didn't personally keep farm animals in hellish conditions, but as soon as I found out about the conditions I accepted my guilt and decided to have nothing to do with it."

"I can't believe McCaskill is any worse than other companies," my mother said. "It's helping feed a hungry world. And what about wheat? And soybeans. Even if you don't like the meat business, your money isn't all bad. You could take some of it for yourself and do something charitable with the rest. I don't see what you gain by rejecting it."

"The Nazis improved the German economy and built

a great highway system," Anabel said. "Maybe they were only half bad, too?"

My mother bristled. "The Nazis were a terrible evil. You don't have to tell me about the Nazis. I lost my father in Hitler's war."

"But you don't have any guilt yourself."

"I was a child."

"Oh, I see. So there *isn't* such a thing as collective guilt."

"Don't talk to me about guilt," my mother said angrily. "I left behind a sister and a brother and a sick mother who needed me. I don't know how many letters I wrote to apologize, and they never wrote back."

"Neither did six million Jews, I guess."

"I was a *child*."

"So was I. And now I'm doing something about it."

My own brand of collective guilt had to do with being male, but I could see that my mother had a point about work. When Anabel and I returned to Philadelphia and I again faced the impossibility of *The Complicater*, I was seized with a new plan: *write a novella*. Begin it in secret and surprise Anabel with it on our wedding day. It would give me new work to do, solve the problem of a wedding present for Anabel, prove to her that I was interesting and ambitious enough for her to marry, and maybe even reconcile her with my mother—because the novella I envisioned was a Bellovian treatment of the only good story I knew: my mother's guilty flight from Germany. I already had the first sentence of it: "The fate of the family on Adalbertstraße was in the hands of a raging stomach."

We'd chosen the Washington's Birthday weekend for our wedding party, so that our friends from out of town could comfortably attend. Besides Nola, Anabel still had three reasonably good friends, one from Wichita, two from Brown. (She would terminate two of these friendships within months of our marrying; the third would remain on probation until a baby put an end to it.) Since she was inviting no one from her family to the party, and since my mother didn't even like her, Anabel thought it was unfair to invite my own family, but I made the case that Cynthia did like her and that I was my mother's only child.

Then one evening Anabel brought me a letter from our mailbox.

"It's interesting," she said, "that your mother still writes just to you, not to both of us."

I opened the letter and scanned it: *Dearest Tom . . . house seems so empty with you gone from it . . . Dr. Van Schyllingerhout . . . higher dose of . . . I tried to say nothing but every nerve in my body . . . to compare her childhood of inherited privilege and luxury to my childhood in Jena . . . unspeakable carnage of the War with modern farming methods . . . deeply offended . . . no choice but to speak my heart freely to you . . . You are making a TERRIBLE MISTAKE . . . quite attractive and very alluring to an inexperienced young man . . . you ARE very inexperienced . . . see nothing but unhappiness in your future with a pampered, demanding, EXTREME person raised in extreme wealth and privilege . . . already so skinny and pale from the kooky diet she has you . . . when a person is not experienced sometimes the sex instinct clouds their judgment . . . I beg you to think hard and realistically about your future . . . want nothing more than for you to find a loving, sensible, mature, REALISTIC person to make a happy life with . . .*

With suddenly cold hands, I folded the letter and put it back in its envelope.

"What does she say?" Anabel asked.

"Nothing. Her colon's flared up again, it's really bad."

"Can I read the letter?"

"It's just her being her."

"So we're getting married in six weeks, and I can't read a letter from your mother."

"I think the steroids make her a little crazy. You don't want to read it."

Anabel gave me one of her frightening looks. "This isn't going to work," she said. "We're either full partners or we're nothing. There is no letter that anyone could send me that I wouldn't want you to read. None. Ever."

She was preparing to rage or to cry, and I couldn't stand either, and so I handed her the letter and retreated to the bedroom. My life had become a nightmare of exactly the female reproach I'd dedicated it to avoiding. To avoid it from my mother was to invite it from Anabel, and vice versa; there was no way out. I was sitting on the bed, kneading my hands, when Anabel appeared in the doorway. She didn't look hurt, just coldly angry.

"I'm going to use this word once in my life," she said. "Exactly once."

"What word?"

"*Cunt.*" She clapped her hands to her mouth. "No, that's a terrible word, even for her. I'm sorry I said it."

"I'm so sorry about the letter," I said. "She's really not well."

"But you understand I'm not going to see her again. I'm not going to buy her little Christmas presents. She's not coming to our wedding party. If we ever have a family, she's not going to see my children. You understand that, don't you?"

"Yes, yes," I said eagerly, in my relief that Anabel hadn't turned against *me*.

She knelt at my feet and took my hands. "People have strong reactions to me," she said, more gently. "It hurts me, but I'm used to it. What I can't stand is what her letter says about *you*. She has no respect for your taste or your judgment or your feelings. She thinks she still owns you and can tell you what to do. And that makes me very angry. She refuses to see who you are."

"I really do think she's miserable because she's sick."

"Her feelings *make* her sick. You've said it yourself."

"She was polite to you in Denver. This has to be the steroids talking . . ."

"I'm not saying you can never see her again. You're a loving person. But I can't see her anymore. Ever. You understand that, don't you?"

I nodded.

"We were both half orphaned on the same day," she said. "And now we'll be full orphans together. Will you do that with me?"

The next day, I wrote a very formal letter to my mother, retracting her invitation to the wedding party.

We were married on Valentine's Day, with two ladies from the clerk's office as witnesses. We had dinner at home, spaghetti with spinach and garlic and olive oil, to symbolize the thrift that we intended to embrace, but Anabel had once mentioned that she liked Mumm champagne, and I'd bought her a bottle to mark the occasion with some small luxury. After dinner, she gave me my present, a new Olivetti portable typewriter. I was immediately aware of a more troubling symbolism: both of our gifts had to do with *my* work, not hers. But my novella had taken an unexpected turn—the young woman in Jena came from the town's richest family, and her father was a brute—and I believed that Anabel would be able to recognize it as a loving tribute to her. So I bravely handed over a manila envelope to which I'd glued a white bow.

She opened it with a puzzled frown. "What is this?"

"The first half of a novella. I wanted to surprise you."

She took out the manuscript, read some of the first page, and then simply stared at it without reading; and I saw that I'd made a terrible mistake.

"You're writing fiction," she said dully.

"I want to be with you in everything," I said. "I don't want to be a journalist, I want to be *with* you. Partners—"

I reached for her hand, but she pulled it away.

"I think I need to be alone now," she said.

"The novella is a tribute to you. To the two of us."

She stood up and headed toward the bedroom. "I really just need to be alone right now."

I heard her close the bedroom door behind her. Our marriage, four hours old, couldn't have been going worse, and I felt entirely to blame. I hated my novella for having done this to her. And yet I'd been happy working on it, had been markedly less depressed in the six weeks since I'd abandoned *her* plan for me, *The Complicater*. I sat for an hour at the kitchen table, in a deepening cold fog of depression, and waited to see if Anabel might come out of the bedroom. She didn't. Instead I began to hear the sharp gasps of her unsuccessfully resisting tears. Full of pity for her, I went into the bedroom and found it dark. She was crumpled up on the bare floor by the windows.

"What have I done?" I cried.

Her answer came out slowly, in fragments punctuated by my apologies and her tears: I'd lied to her. I'd kept secrets from her. Both of our wedding presents were about *me*. I'd broken my promises to her. I'd promised that she was the artist and I was the critic. I'd promised that I wouldn't steal her story, but she could tell from one paragraph that I'd stolen it. I'd promised that we wouldn't compete, and I was competing with her. I'd deceived her and ruined our wedding day . . .

Each reproach landed like acid on my brain. I'd heard it said that there is no pain worse than mental torture, and now I believed it. Even the worst of our premarital scenes had been nothing like this; it had always been fundamentally OK me dealing with temperamental Anabel. Now I was experiencing her psychic pain directly as my own. The heaven of soul-merging was a hell. Clutching my head, I ran away from her and threw myself on the living-room sofa and lay there for some hours, experiencing mental torture, while Anabel did the same in the bedroom. I kept thinking, this is our wedding night, this is our wedding night.

It must have been two in the morning before I worked up enough hatred of my novella to stand up and start burning it, page by page, on the kitchen stove. Anabel eventually smelled the smoke and came staggering in, very pale, and watched me in silence until the last page was burned and I burst into tears.

She was immediately all over me, full of comfort, desperate with love. How I craved that love! How we both craved it! Better than the best drug after the agony of withdrawal from it: the smell of her teary face, the soft avidity of her mouth, the warm solidity of her body, the naked fact of her. It was almost as if we'd deliberately manufactured unspeakable pain to achieve this level of wedding-night bliss.

Without being aware of it, however, I'd made a second terrible mistake, which came to light at our party, two nights later. The party was already uncomfortably weighted against the distaff, because Nola had failed to show up (she'd moved to New York, in part to get over her feelings for Anabel) and one of Anabel's Brown friends had bailed at the last minute, while Cynthia and five of my Penn friends and three of my Denver friends had come from near and far. But Oswald had brought good mix tapes and seemed to be developing a brother's-best-friend thing for Cynthia, which was fun to watch happening, and Anabel had drunk enough to be enjoying my other friends' stories about me, rather than feeling threatened by them, and I was proud of how beautiful she looked in her strapless party dress.

I was clearing the floor for dancing when our buzzer rang. Anabel, hoping it was Nola, ran to the intercom in the kitchen. I couldn't hear her over the party noise, but she came back pale with fury. She beckoned me into the bedroom with a jerk of her head and shut the door behind us.

"How could you?" she said.

"What?"

"It's my *father*."

"Oh no."

"The only way he could have known is if you told him. You!" Her face twisted up. "I can't believe this is happening to me!"

It was true: David, in a recent phone call, had coaxed out of me the date of our party, so that he could send us, he said, a very small wedding present. I'd emphasized that the party was for friends, not family.

"I specifically told him he wasn't invited," I said.

"My God, Tom, how could you be so stupid? Haven't you learned *anything* about him?"

"I'm sorry. I'm sorry. But can we just try to make the best of it?"

"No! The party is over. I'm pulling the plug. This is my worst nightmare."

"Did you let him in?"

"I had to! But I'm not leaving this room until he's gone."

"Let me deal with it."

"Oh right, good luck with that."

Out in the living room, David had set down a load of small presents and a jeroboam of Mumm and was jovially introducing himself to our guests. His face lit up further at the sight of me. "There he is! The groom! Congratulations! You're looking very dashing, Tom, as well you should." He gave me a crushing handshake. "I meant to be here two hours ago, we had a problem with the plane. Where's my little girl?"

I tried to answer coldly, but my tone was simply factual. "She doesn't want you here."

"Doesn't want her only parent at her wedding party?" David looked around the room, appealing to our silent guests. The stereo was playing "Remote Control." "She's my favorite person in the world. How could I miss her wedding party?"

"I really think it's better if you go."

David stepped around me and rapped on the bedroom door. "Anabel, honey? Come out and join us before the wine gets warm."

To my surprise, the door opened immediately. Anabel drew her head back and spat in David's face. The door slammed shut again.

Everybody saw it, nobody said a word. "Remote Control" continued to play while David wiped spit from his eyes. When he lowered his hand, he looked a decade older. He smiled at me weakly. "Enjoy the years," he said, "until she does the same to you."

Her long months of preliminary reading done, Anabel went to work on her ambitious project. It was a film about the body. She couldn't get over how strange it is that a person can live for fifty or seventy or ninety years and die without having made the most basic acquaintance with the body that is the sum of her existence: that there are so many places on the body—certainly places on the head and back that she can't directly see, but even places on her arms and legs and torso—to which, in all those years, she won't have paid as much attention as a butcher pays to cuts of beef.

The surface area of her own body was about sixteen thousand square centimeters, and her plan was to inscribe a grid of 32-square-centimeter "cuts" on it with a fine-tipped black marker. Except on her feet and face and fingers, these "cuts" would be simple 57×57 millimeter squares. All five hundred of them would appear in her film. She intended to take a full week to acquaint herself with each one—to neither slight nor privilege any one 32-cm^2 part of her body; to be able to say, when she died, that she'd truly known all that could be seen of it—and she'd assigned herself the daunting task of doing something fresh and compelling with every cut. The differences might be purely filmic, but more often they'd involve images relating to the thoughts and memories that a particular cut inspired. In this respect, the project was closer to performance art than to film. If she could stick to her schedule, the performance would last ten years, the creative challenge steadily increasing. She didn't know how long the final film would be, but she was aiming for twenty-nine and a half hours, an hour for each day of the lunar month. Her larger ambition was to reclaim possession of her body, cut by cut, from the world of men and meat. After ten years, she'd own herself entirely.

I loved the idea, and she loved me for loving it. One hot July afternoon, she let me be the one to make the first black mark on her body, a grid encompassing two of her left toes, whose surface area it had taken her half a day to determine accurately; she'd left ink dots that I connected. "Now you have to leave me alone with it," she said.

"I want to know every inch of you myself."

"I'll always come back to you," she said gravely. "In ten years I'll be all yours."

I kissed the toes and left her alone with them. What was ten years?

If she could have worked faster, and if artists like Cindy Sherman and Nan Goldin hadn't risen to prominence, and if video art hadn't suddenly all but extirpated experimental film, and if she hadn't been paralyzed by jealousy of my smaller but completable journalism projects, it's conceivable that her film would have come to something. But a year went by and she was still on her left ankle. I now see that she must have quickly become bored with the surface of her body—there's a reason we go through life without paying much attention to it—but to her it felt as if the world were out to thwart her.

Naturally, I bore the brunt of this. A wrong word at the breakfast table or a distracting smell from something I was cooking ("Smell is hell," she liked to say) could ruin a workday. Even a capsule newspaper review of a "competitor" could shut her down for a week. With her tacit permission, I took to vetting *The New Yorker* and the arts section of the *Times* and tearing out potentially upsetting items before she could read them. I also answered our phone, paid our bills, and did our taxes. When we moved into a larger space, I soundproofed the windows of her project room, and when, six months later, she decided that Philadelphia was depressing her and retarding my career, I went to New York and found us our apartment in East Harlem. There, too, I soundproofed her room. And none of this resentfully, all of it true-believingly, because she was the hedgehog and I was the fox. But it was more than that: as with the toilet seat, I was making amends for a structural unfairness. It *hurt* her that I had practical skills, and because it hurt her it hurt me, too.

My greatest capacity was for earning money. I was so hungry for advancement and had so much time on my hands (seven days a week, Anabel closeted herself with her 16 mm Beaulieu) that I broke in rather easily at *Philadelphia* magazine. I could have become a news editor there, or later at the *Voice*, but I didn't want an office job, because some mornings, before closeting herself, Anabel needed to spend several hours discussing an incorrect look I'd given her or a disturbing news item that had slipped past my censoring, and I had to be available for that. So I worked from home and became a skilled reporter. Since I wasn't competing with Anabel creatively, she encouraged me to be ambitious and gave me good notes on everything I wrote. In return, I covered our rent and utilities and food. For film stock and processing, she burned through her remaining savings and then started selling off the jewelry she'd been given by her father and inherited from her mother. I was shocked to learn how much the jewelry was worth, and a tiny bit resentful, but it wasn't as if I'd entered our marriage with any jewelry of my own.

Need I mention that our sex life went straight downhill? Our problem wasn't typical marital boredom. It was partly that she spent all day deeply contemplating her body and just wanted to read a book or watch TV in her free time, but mostly that our souls were merged. It's hard to feel as if you *are* someone and at the same time *want* her. By the mid-eighties, our only halfway decent sex was of the homecoming variety, after one of my reporting trips or my annual summer visit to Denver; for a few hours, we were unlike enough to reconnect. In the years after that, when she was starving herself and exercising three hours a day, she simply stopped having her periods. Then there was never a good time of month for her, then we put Leonard in a shoe box and didn't take him out again, then all we did was talk and talk, like a two-person emotional bureaucracy. The smallest of questions ("Why did you wait ten minutes to tell me your good news instead of telling me immediately?") triggered a full formal investigation, with every response filed in triplicate and the review period extended and re-extended while the archives were searched.

And we were isolated. To get dressed up and mingle with other sexual beings might have helpfully separated us. But Anabel became ever shyer and less sure of herself, ever more ashamed to speak of a project that she and I believed was genius but no one else could see; and inevitably, since our only friends were *my* friends, she felt slighted by their greater interest in me. I started meeting them alone for lunch or early drinks. I told absolutely no one about my home life. It would have been a betrayal of Anabel, and I was ashamed of the strangeness of my marriage and, worse, of how I sounded when I answered a friend's polite question about her and her work. I sounded like a person making excuses for her, a person who couldn't see that his spouse wasn't actually the genius he was convinced she was. I was still convinced, but, oddly, I didn't sound convincing.

Even David, who hadn't stopped calling me, seemed to have lost interest in Anabel. His three sons were continuing to enact every known cliché of rich-kid misbehavior, and his daughter had spat in his face. I was his most plausible remaining object of paternal pride. He never failed to offer me funding, connections, a good job at McCaskill, sometimes all three. Under his leadership, McCaskill was expanding its Asian operations, trading in Peruvian fish meal and German flaxseed oil, diversifying into financial services and fertilizer, widening the river of meat, pouring beef and eggs into the gullet of McDonald's and turkey into the maw of Denny's. By my calculation, David's stake in the company was approaching three billion dollars.

And then suddenly I was in my thirties. I had dozens of professional friends but nobody to talk to about Anabel except our building's super, Ruben, who doubled as the manager of an underground lottery that was operated by our building's owner and pegged to the Dominican Lotería Nacional. The building was kept safe by the constant presence of Ruben and his runners—a toothless alcoholic nicknamed Low Boy, a couple of retired hookers. Ruben was courtly with Anabel and respectful of the man who'd married her; he called me Lucky. Anabel's other fan was her new friend, Suzanne, whom she'd met at an improv class that I'd implored her to take after she'd been stymied with her project for an entire fall. She'd finally filmed her way to the top of her left leg and couldn't bring herself to inscribe a "cut" near her genitals. Her food intake had dwindled to coffee with soy milk in the morning and a small dinner in the evening. During the day she was often disabled by "bloatation" and stomach cramps, but she became frantic if anything (i.e., too many hours of discussion with me) impeded her 5 p.m. to 8 p.m. exercise regime, which involved workout tapes by Jane Fonda, runs in Central Park, and a secondhand rowing machine that now dominated her work space.

She had as much body fat as a Shaker chair, her periods were a thing of the past, and whole seasons came and went in which the closest I came to fucking her was Ruben's imagination, but this didn't stop us from discussing a potential baby. She wanted to have a family with me, but first she had to finish her project, reclaim her body, and achieve a success to match or exceed my own; otherwise she'd be stuck at home with diapers while I had my splendid male career. I didn't see how we could wait for her to finish—she hadn't even looked at much of her hundred hours of raw footage, let alone begun to edit it, and at the rate she was proceeding she'd still be filming at seventy—but I couldn't point this out without stoking her panic. All I could do was try to calm her, so that she could get on with the contemplation and filming of her genitals.

For our eighth anniversary, after my first sale of an article to *Esquire*, I prevailed on Anabel to come to Italy with me. We'd never had a honeymoon, and I thought that

Europe might revive us. The trip was touristically successful—we had the Gothic sculpture of Tuscany and the ancient ruins of Sicily to ourselves—but Anabel got hunger headaches every afternoon, and every evening I had to accompany her on three-hour power walks in the dark, our abdomens cramping while we scouted for a restaurant filled with locals, because this was our honeymoon and she needed her one meal of the day to be a great one.

We returned to New York determined to make our own Sicilian-style spaghetti with fried eggplant and tomatoes, a dish so delicious that we wanted to eat it twice a week. Which we did, for several months. And here was the thing: I didn't get sick of it slowly. I got sick of it suddenly, radically, and permanently while eating a plateful whose first bites I'd enjoyed as much as ever. I set down my fork and said we needed a break from fried eggplant and tomatoes. The dish was perfect and delicious and not to blame. I'd made it poison to me by eating too much of it. And so we took a monthlong break from it, but Anabel still loved it, and one very warm evening in June I came home and smelled her cooking it.

My stomach heaved.

"We overdid it," I said from the kitchen doorway. "I can't stand it anymore."

Symbolism was never lost on Anabel. "I'm not spaghetti with eggplant, Tom."

"I'm literally going to throw up if I stay here."

She looked frightened. "All right," she said. "But will you come back later?"

"I will, but something has to change."

"I agree. I've been having thoughts."

"Good, I'll come back later."

I ran down five flights of stairs and over to the 125th Street station with no plan, no friend good enough to go and confide in, just a need to get away. There was, in those years, a ragged band of funk musicians who busked irregularly on the station's downtown platform. Always a bass player and guitarist, often a drummer with a trap set that looked rescued from a dumpster, sometimes a singer with gold teeth and a soiled sequined dress. Only the singer ever interacted with their audience, the others seemed wrapped up in painful private histories from which the music was a momentary respite. The guitarist knew how to pitch a groove above the rumble of the trains and not let up on it, no matter how he sweated.

That evening they were a trio. Dollar bills had collected in an open guitar case, and I threw in a bill and retreated up the platform with the respect incumbent on the white in Harlem. I've since searched, to no avail, for the song they were playing. Maybe it was their own song, never recorded. It had a simple minor-seventh riff that spoke of beauty amid incurable sadness, and in my recollection they played it for twenty minutes, half an hour, long enough for many local and express trains to come and go. Finally there came a perfect storm of drafts from uptown and downtown, a big humid uric wind that swept the platform and then reversed itself, and reversed itself again, so that the dollar bills came levitating out of the guitar case and drifted up and down the platform like leaves in autumn, tumbling and skidding, while the band played on. It was perfectly beautiful and perfectly sad, and everybody on the platform knew it, nobody bent down to touch the money.

I thought of my suffering Anabel, alone in the apartment. I saw my life and walked back up the stairs.

She was standing right inside our front door as if she'd been expecting me. "Will you help me?" she said immediately. "I know that something has to change, and I can't do it without you. Will you look at what I'm doing and tell me what I'm not seeing?"

"Just don't make me eat any more fried eggplant," I
said.

"I'm serious, Tom. I need your help."

I agreed to help her. We went into her workroom, which
had long been off limits to me, and she shyly showed me
some impressive film clips. An underexposed black-and-
white close-up of a "cut" on her left thigh which she'd
hand-doctored to create the impression of dark ocean
swells. An imperfectly synched but very funny monologue
on kneecaps. A disturbing montage of subway-platform
footage intercut with her corpse-white big toe tagged with
her name, as if to suggest that she'd thought about jumping in front of a train. I was so warmly encouraging that
she opened her notebooks for me.

These had always been strictly private, and it was a
measure of her desperation that she let me see them, because they weren't the elegantly lettered and story-boarded
pages I'd imagined. They were a diary of torment. Entry
after entry began with a daily to-do list and devolved into
increasingly illegible self-diagnoses. Then she'd start a
fresh page with a neat chart of film cuts, fill in only the
first few squares, and then scribble revisions to them, and
then cross out the revisions and scribble new ones in the
margins, with lines connecting various thoughts and key
points triple-underlined; and then she'd draw a big angry
X through the entire thing.

"I know it doesn't look like it," she said, "but there are
good ideas in here. This looks like it's crossed out, but
it's not really crossed out, I'm still thinking about it. I have
to leave it crossed out because otherwise it puts too much
pressure on me. What I really need to do is go through
all the notebooks"—there were at least forty of them—
"and then try to keep everything in my head and make
a clear plan. It's just that there's so *much*. I'm not crazy.

I just need some way to organize it that doesn't put too much pressure on me."

I believed her. She was smart and had good ideas. But, leafing through those notebooks, I could see that she had no chance of finishing her project. She, who for so long had seemed all-powerful to me, wasn't strong enough. I felt responsible for having failed to intervene sooner, and now, even though I was sick of the marriage to the point of heaving, I couldn't leave until I'd helped her out of the stuck place I'd allowed her to fall into. The marriage I'd hoped would lead me out of guilt had led me only deeper in.

And yet: guilt must be the most monstrous of human quantities, because what I did to relieve my guilt then—stay in the marriage—was precisely the thing I felt guiltiest about later, when the marriage was over. After the night of spaghetti and eggplant, as if she'd seen for the first time that I might leave her, she began to speak of a date, eighteen months in the future, when she and I could set about having a little baby girl (she never imagined a boy). The idea was partly to give herself a goal and deadline for advancing her project above her abdomen, but she was also trying, for my sake, to be more realistic; we couldn't wait forever to get pregnant. I could see that a baby might be just what we needed, a baby might save us, but I could also see that I was likely to be doing the bulk of the child care as long as her project was unfinished. And so, whenever she brought up the baby question, I changed the subject to her project. Whether I wanted her to hurry up and finish it so that we could share the care of a baby, or whether I just wanted her to be OK enough that I could safely divorce her, I honestly can't remember. But I do know that I could summon up the sickening smell of fried eggplant simply by thinking of it. If I'd heeded my stomach and cut her loose, she might have had time to find some-one else to have her baby with.

"Bold proposal," I'd said in her workroom, the morning after the spaghetti night. "You increase the size of your 'cuts' by a factor of ten. I can help you plan the whole thing, I can draw it out for you so it's not all in your head. And then you do it in two years and you're done."

She shook her head dismissively. "I can't change the size of the cuts halfway in."

"But if you make them ten times bigger, you can redo the whole leg in two months. You can cherry-pick the best nonbody shots you already have."

"I'm not throwing away eight years of work!"

"But it's not even finished work." I gestured toward her towers of processed but unopened film boxes. "You need to do whatever it takes to be finished."

"You know I've never finished anything in my life."

"Good time to start, don't you think?"

"*I know what I'm doing*," she said. "What I need your help with isn't throwing away eight years of work. It's helping me organize the ideas I *already have*. And it was obviously a mistake to ask you. Oh! Oh! I'm so stupid."

She beat her fists on her offending head. It took me two hours to talk her down and then a further hour to emerge from the sulk she'd put me in by suggesting that my aes-thetic was vulgar. Then, for three hours, I helped her block out a rough schedule for completing her project, and then, for another hour, I began the transfer of important thoughts from the first of her forty-odd notebooks into a new note-book, written by me. Then it was time for her three hours of exercise.

We had many days like this in the year that followed. For ten hours I worked out sequences for her, sequences that seemed to me totally doable, only to hear her say, when it was time for her to exercise, that we seemed to be making my journalistically organized film, not her film, which led to another day of discussion in which she tried to describe the sequences *she* wanted, and I couldn't follow her overall logic, and she explained it all again, and I still couldn't follow it, and it was time for her to exercise. I cut back on my own work, passing up an opportunity to follow the Dukakis campaign for *Rolling Stone*, and I was losing friends the way addicts do, by canceling dates at the last minute. We'd entered the squalid maintenance phase of our addiction, not a particle of pleasure in the morning, just a sick sense of unresolved issues from the day before. It went on and on and on and would have gone on even longer if my mother hadn't gotten a death sentence.

She called, unusually, on a weekday afternoon. "Oh, this terrible body of mine," she said. "It's given me nothing but trouble, and now it's going to kill me. Tom, I'm so sorry. I'm letting you down, I'm letting Cynthia down, I'm letting everyone down. Dr. Van Schyllingerhout has been so patient with me, he's tried so hard, he says I'm one of the reasons he won't retire. He's almost eighty, Tom, and still seeing patients. I'm such a disappointment to you all. But your dumb old mother has *cancer*."

More pitiable even than her cancer was her impulse to apologize for it. I probed her news for a silver lining, but apparently there wasn't one. She'd simply had rotten luck. Because the steroids had put her at high risk for cancer, Dr. Van Schyllingerhout had been giving her biennial colonoscopies, but the cancer must have appeared immediately after her previous one. In two years it had spread beyond her colon and was likely inoperable. They were going to open her up to relieve her blockage, blast her with radiation, and then do further surgery to see what could be salvaged, but the prognosis was poor.

"I'll be there tomorrow," I said.

"Tom, I'm so sorry. I hate to burden you with this. I want to live to see you happy and successful. But this dumb old body of mine, always the same dumb thing . . ."

I walked into Anabel's workroom and sat down and cried. Anabel later told me that my tears had terrified her—she was afraid I'd come in to say I couldn't live with her anymore—but once I gave her the news she put her arms around me and cried with me. She even offered to come to Denver.

"No," I said, drying my face. "You stay here. This will be good for both of us."

"That's what I'm worried about," she said. "That I'm going to work better without you, and you're going to be happier without me. And that'll be the end of us. You'll think, Why am I with this crazy woman who can't do her work? And I'll remember how much better I worked when I got to be alone all the time." She began to cry again. "I don't want to lose you."

"You won't lose me," I said. "It's just some time apart."

The argument I made to her, and to myself, was that we needed to reconstruct our separate identities in order to go on together. I genuinely believed this, but my reasons for believing it were bad. I was postponing for as long as possible the guilt of abandoning her. I was also hoping, unrealistically, that she might spare me from this guilt by being the one to leave.

In a hospital corridor in Denver, while my mother was in post-op, I conferred with Dr. Van Schyllingerhout. He was a compassionate-eyed bald man with an aquiline nose. He'd been good to my mother, but he was unmistakably *pissed off* about her cancer. "The surgeon is unhappy," he said in an accent less like Leonard's than I'd remembered. "He wanted to take more, but your mother is adamant about not wanting a stoma. It's a quality-of-life choice we have to respect. She doesn't want the bag.

But you hate to tie a surgeon's hands. Her chances are worse now."

"How bad?"

He shook his head, pissed off. "Bad."

"I appreciate your respecting her wishes."

"Your mother is a fighter. I've had many patients not as sick as her give up and take the colostomy. And of course you know the story of her leaving Germany. She was in a situation of indignity that she refused to accept. With the will she has, she should have lived another thirty years."

So began my admiration of my mother. It's odd to say this, given how sick she was, but she gave me hope about my own life. My situation with Anabel was surely no more of a torment to me than her bowel was to her, and abandoning her mother and siblings couldn't have been easier than what I had to do to Anabel. If my mother could fight through it, so might I.

Her surgery seemed to have excised the phrase *dumb old mother* from her vocabulary, along with others like it. She came home from the hospital without her self-deprecation. Under the influence of Cynthia, who was now a single mom and living in Denver with her daughter, her political views had also softened. "I'm starting to think that money really is the root of all evil," she said to me one night. "As soon as you have money, you have envy. That's the problem with the Communists, they envy the rich, they're obsessed with redistributing money. And, I'm sorry, but I look at Anabel's family and all I see is the harm the money did to it."

"That's why she rejected it," I said.

"But rejecting money is just another way to be obsessed with it. It's just like the Communists. The productive workers get exploited by the lazy ones. I'm sorry to say this, but it's not right that Anabel doesn't work—that *you're* the one who has to make up for her obsession. She would have been better off not having money in the first place."

"Her family is messed up, for sure. But she's not lazy."

"When I'm gone, you're going to have a little money from this house. And I do not want that money going to support Anabel. That money is for *you*. It's not much, but your father worked hard, I worked hard. Please promise me you won't give it to the daughter of a billionaire."

I considered my hardworking parents. "All right," I said.

"Do you promise?"

I made the promise, but I wasn't sure I would keep it.

That summer, I started eating meat again. I went to Nevada and wrote a story for *Esquire* about the proposed Yucca Mountain nuclear-waste repository. I also nursed my mother through her radiation sickness and saw a lot of Cynthia and her little girl. Now it was Anabel to whom I made Sunday-night phone calls. She claimed to be having productive thoughts, and only when she said things like "Don't forget me, Tom" was it less than nice to hear her voice. She wouldn't have guessed that I was eating meat again, and I didn't mention it.

My mother continued to surprise me. After she'd recovered from her second, conclusively discouraging surgery, in October, she asked me to take her to Germany before she died. She'd been following the political developments there, the swelling exodus of East Germans through Czechoslovakia, and for the first time in many years she'd tried sending another letter to her family at its old address. Three weeks later, she got a long letter back from her brother. He and his wife were still living in the old place, his mother had died in 1961, his little sister was twice divorced, his older son had been admitted to the university. At least as my mother translated it to me, his letter was devoid of resentment, as if her disappearance were just another fact from a difficult childhood he'd long since put behind him. There was no mention of the many earlier letters he hadn't answered. I wondered if he might never have been resentful, only fearful that the Stasi would frown on his corresponding with an escapee. And now people had stopped being afraid of the Stasi.

On the strength of my three semesters of college German and my mother's story, I contracted with *Harper's* to write a firsthand account of communism's collapse. My mother had lost a lot of weight and was looking truly scarecrowish, but her bowel was still functioning somehow, and she didn't have a stoma. One evening, when I was helping her put her simple affairs in order, she set down her pen and said to me, "I think I'm going to die in Germany."

"You don't know that," I said.

"I'm done here," she said. "Cynthia is a good mother, a fine person, and you're on your way to a fine career. I think Denver and I have had enough of each other. A life is a funny thing, Tom. People talk about putting down roots, but people aren't trees. If I have any roots, they aren't here."

She worried that she'd forgotten her German, but she was so good at language, had learned English so well, that I considered this unlikely. On our last night in Denver, Cynthia came over to our house without her daughter. When it was time for her to say good-bye, forever, I tried to leave her alone with my mother.

"No, stay with us," my mother said. "I want you to hear what I have to say." She turned to Cynthia. "I want to apologize for not being a better mother to you when you were young. I made excuses for it, but that's all they were, excuses, and I don't deserve any of what you've done for me since then. You've been the best daughter a mother could ever ask for. You were the great gift your father gave me. If I've been lucky in nothing else, I've been lucky in you and Tom. I want you to know how deeply I appreciate everything you've done, and how sorry I am that I was ever unkind to you. You're a wonderful person, more wonderful than I deserve."

Cynthia's face had crumpled, but my mother remained dry-eyed, dignified. German. In the shadow of death, she was no longer the person I'd known. She'd become the person I hadn't known, the German person. The decades of her unhappiness, the years of her dronings, now seemed like a long failure to find a good way to be American.

By the time we left for Berlin, the Wall had been breached. (I mentally rearranged my unwritten story, as journalists do, to make it more about young Clelia.) After resting for a day in Berlin, we proceeded by train to Jena. Looking out the window at a town shrouded in coal smoke, my mother commented, "Thirty-five years they've had to make it even uglier. Thirty-five years, my God, of manu-facturing ugliness. People will forget, but I don't want you to forget: this part of Germany paid for its guilt."

I wrote this down in a notebook. East Germany may have been a giant penitentiary administered by the Rus-sians, the Stasi may have embodied the worst excesses of German authority and bureaucratic thoroughness, and anyone with brains or spirit may have fled the country be-fore the Wall went up, but the inmates who'd remained behind to expiate the country's collective guilt had para-doxically been liberated from their Germanness. The ones I met in Jena were humble, unpunctual, spontaneous, and generous with what little they had. The country's economy had been a sham from the start, and although the inmates had played along with the rules, attending the political-education meetings, licking their attendance stamps and

pasting them into little books that reminded me of the
Green Stamps of my youth, their real loyalties were to
one another, not to the state. My uncle Klaus and his wife
cleared out of the bedroom that had once been Annelie's
and gave it to my mother. They had a telephone but rarely
used it. Friends simply appeared at the door and were
ushered in to the weeklong house party with which my
mother's return was celebrated. There was endless beer
and bad white wine and cream cakes. My presence was
awkward, since I couldn't understand much of the conversation, and I was relieved when, at the end of the week,
my mother proposed that I leave her alone with her brother
and come back to visit only on Saturday nights and Sundays. "You need to write your article," she said. "They've
offered to take care of me, but I want them to have a break
every week."

"You're sure this is what you want to do."

"That's how they do things here," she said. "They take
care of each other."

"You're sounding like an old Communist."

"It's been forty years of terrible waste," she said, "a
whole country of wasted lives. It's a country of big children, people being naughty behind the teacher's back,
people tattling on each other, people getting their dumb
certificates for being good little socialists. People submitting to the system because they're German and because
it's a system. The whole thing was stupid and a lie. But
they're not arrogant, not know-it-alls. They give what they
have and they take me the way I am."

The closer she came to dying, the more sure of herself
she became. She'd concluded that the meaning of a life
was in the form of it. There was no answering the question of why she'd been born, she could only take what
she'd been given and try to make it end well. She intended

to die in her mother's bedroom, in the company of her brother and her only offspring, without the indignity of a colostomy bag.

I went back to Berlin, teamed up with a couple of young French journalists I'd met, and ended up squatting with them in a Friedrichshain apartment whose tenants had simply walked away from it and showed no sign of returning. For a month I made the weekly trip down to Jena, with an extra trip at Christmas, while my mother grew ever thinner and grayer. Thankfully, her pain was mostly tolerable. When she had a sharper attack of it, she rubbed her gums with the morphine that Dr. Van Schyllingerhout had given her to smuggle along with us.

My last meal with her was breakfast on the second Sunday of January. She'd been up a few times in the night, doing things that her dignity precluded my witnessing, and her eyes were hollow, the contours of her skull crisply visible beneath her thin skin, but she was still bright Clelia, her heart still beating, her brain still oxygenated and filled with her life. I was happy to see her eat an entire hard roll with butter.

"I need to know what you and Anabel are going to do," she said.

"I'm not thinking about that now."

"Yes, but you'll have to think about it soon."

"She needs to finish her project, and then we're still hoping to have a family."

"Is that what you want?"

I thought about this and said, "I want to see her happy again. She used to be amazing, and now she's all beaten down. I think if she were happy and successful I'd be happy with her."

"Your happiness shouldn't depend on hers," my mother said. "You were a happy little boy, and I know your father and I weren't the easiest parents, but I don't think you were harmed. You have a right to be happy for yourself. If you're with someone who can't be happy, you need to think about what you're going to do."

I promised to think about it, and my mother went to lie down in her mother's bedroom while I struggled to read a German newspaper. Half an hour later, I heard her go into the bathroom. A while after that, I heard her scream. The scream has stayed with me, I can still play it in my head exactly as I heard it.

She was on the toilet, doubled over and rocking with agony. She'd been on a toilet in distress countless times in her life, but this was, remarkably, the first time I'd ever seen her on one. She would have wished that I hadn't, and I was and remain sorry, for her sake, that I did. She looked up at me, wild-eyed, and said, with a gasp, "Tom, my God, I'm dying."

I helped her up by the armpits and half carried her into the bedroom, leaving behind a bowl of blood and worse. Her breathing was rapid and shallow. Some part of her jerry-rigged colon had ruptured, and she was dying of sepsis. I rubbed morphine into her gums and stroked her fragile head. Her head was still so warm, I wondered what was happening inside it, but she didn't speak to me again. I said it was OK, I said I loved her, I said not to worry about me. Her breathing became slower and more labored, and then, just past noon, it stopped altogether. I laid my cheek on her chest and held her for a long time, not thinking anything, just being an animal that had lost its mother. Then I got up and called the number my uncle had given me to get a message to him at his little weekend cottage.

Klaus and I thought it was better to have no funeral than a tiny funeral. After the cremation, he and I walked along the river, among the lawns where my mother had sunned herself as a girl, and scattered half of the ashes

along the riverbank. The other half I put aside for scattering in Denver with Cynthia. On the morning I left Jena, I
thanked Klaus, in halting German, for everything he'd
done. He shrugged and said my mother would have done
the same for him. It occurred to me to ask what she'd been
like as a girl.

"*Herrisch!*" He laughed. "Now you see why I had to
help her."

I looked up the unfamiliar word later. *Bossy.*

On the train back to Berlin I stood at the rear of the
last car the whole way, watching the receding track sig-
nals change from red to green. It didn't feel so bad to be
an orphan. It felt like the first day of a long vacation, a
day as empty as the January sky was clear and sunny. The
only cloud, Anabel, was in a different hemisphere. My
sense of liberation was partly financial—Cynthia and
Ellen and I would divide an estate worth more than
$400,000—but it was larger than that. My parents had
both bowed out now, leaving the entire field to me, and
I could see that I'd been hobbling myself for Anabel's
sake, for fear of getting too far ahead of her.

I'd promised to call her that afternoon, but scattering
my mother's ashes had made me aware of something
childish and fundamentally irrelevant in the body-filming
project, and I was afraid of betraying this if we spoke.
My own body felt so vital, so far from its own death,
that I went out walking instead, retracing my mother's
long-ago steps, mingling with foreign gawkers along
the Wall in Moabit and then finding my way to the
Kurfürstendamm.

Near the western end of it, I stopped in a pub to eat a
sausage and record my journalistic impressions in a notebook. At some point I noticed a man alone at the next
table, a young German with a high forehead and loosely
curly hair. He was watching the pub's television with his

arms draped across the chairs on either side of him. The wide-openness of his posture, the sense of ownership it broadcast, kept drawing my eyes to him. Finally he saw me looking and gave me a smile. As if letting me in on a joke, he pointed up at the TV screen.

His face was on the screen as well. He was being interviewed on a city street, above a tag of ANDREAS WOLF, DDR SYSTEMKRITIKER. I couldn't make out much of what he was saying, but I caught the word *sunlight*. When the news program cut away to a wide shot of what I recognized as the national headquarters of the Stasi, I looked over and saw that he'd spread his arms even wider. I stood up with my notebook and went over to his table. "*Darf ich?*"

"Certainly," he said in English. "You're an American."

"That's right."

"Americans are entitled to sit wherever they want."

"I don't know about that. But I'm curious what you were saying there. My German isn't great."

"Your notebook," he said. "Are you a journalist?"

"I am."

"Excellent." He extended a hand. "Andreas Wolf."

I shook his hand and sat down across from him. "Tom Aberant."

"Can I buy you a beer?"

"Let me buy you one."

"I'm the person celebrating. Never been on television, never been in the West, never spoken to an American. It's my lucky night."

I bought us some beers and got him talking. He told me he'd been part of the storming of Stasi headquarters, where he'd found himself the de facto spokesman of the Citizens' Committee demanding oversight of the archives, and had rewarded himself by making his first trip out of the East. He'd barely slept in sixty hours, but he didn't seem tired. I was feeling similarly buoyant. The luck of meeting an East German dissident in his first hours in the West, before any other Western journalist had had a crack at him, was making my mood on the train from Jena seem prophetic.

We finished the beers and went out to the street. Andreas didn't walk so much as *strut*, in his tight jeans and army jacket, with his shoulders thrown back. The city's atmosphere was still lingeringly festive, and he kept tossing his head at the foreigners and East Berliners on the Ku'damm, as if daring them not to recognize him. When we passed good-looking women, he pivoted sharply to stare after them. I had a feeling that Anabel wouldn't like him, not one bit, and that I was furthering my liberation simply by walking with him.

On a quieter block, he stopped in front of a BMW showroom. "What do you think, Tom? Should I try to want one of these cars? Now that there's no East, only West?"

"It's your duty as a consumer to want them."

He gazed at the ultimate driving machines. "I've never seen anything more terrifying in my life. Everyone else couldn't wait to come here. Everyone else was too stupid to be terrified."

"How would you feel about my writing down what you're saying?"

"That's what you want?"

"You seem like a person with stories to tell."

He laughed. "*And let me speak to the yet unknowing world how these things came about: so shall you hear of carnal, bloody, and unnatural acts . . .* Who am I quoting?"

"I believe that is Horatio's final speech."

"Very good!" He hit me, flat-handed, on the shoulder. "Is it just you, or am I going to like every American?"

"Probably somewhere in between."

"You'd laugh if you could see my image of America. Skyscrapers and a wretched underclass. Brechtian exploitation. Gorkian lower depths, Mick Jagger as the devil. *Puerto Rican girls just dyin' to meetchoo.*"

"I recommend lowering your expectations."

"Should I go there?"

"To New York? Definitely. I can show you all around."

I was aware of benefiting, in his estimation, from being an American; aware also of the shame I would feel if he came to New York and witnessed the kind of life I had with Anabel. He gave the finger to the shiny BMWs and kept the finger raised above his shoulder as we proceeded down the sidewalk.

What he'd told me already—that he'd spent his twenties as a designated antisocial citizen, living outside the socialist grid, in the basement of a church—was going straight into my *Harper's* piece. And yet journalism was the least of the reasons why, when we parted ways at Friedrichstraße, I asked him to meet me there again the following afternoon. Andreas looked nothing like Anabel, except that he was skinny, but his self-assurance was so reckless that it gave the impression of something damaged or anguished underneath, something that reminded me of the charismatic damaged girl I'd fallen for. Or maybe he just reminded me of what a crush felt like.

Like it or not, I absolutely had to call Anabel the next day. This could only be done from a booth at a post office, and while Andreas showed me around the center of East Berlin, pointing out the church where he'd counseled at-risk teens, the privileged *Oberschule* he'd attended, the youth club where frowned-upon bands had played, the bars where the *Asoziale* had congregated, I became nervous about finding a post office before closing time. Finally I said as much to him.

"What will happen if you don't call her?"

"More trouble than not calling her is worth."

"OK, serious question: is this what being married is like?"

"Why? Are you considering it yourself?"

His expression became earnest. We were on a street in Prenzlauer Berg littered with the crap furniture that people had been throwing out their windows since the Wall came down. "Not marriage," he said. "But there is a girl. She's very young, I hope you'll get to meet her. If you meet her, you'll see why I'm asking."

It was a measure of how much I was liking him that his mention of a girl made me jealous. I had no doubt that she was unbelievably beautiful and as keen for sex as Anabel wasn't. I envied him for that. Weirder, and indicative of the raw place where losing my mother had landed me, was that I also envied the girl for the entrée that being female gave her to his private life.

"Call your wife," he said. "I'll wait for you."

"No, fuck it," I said. "I'll do it tomorrow."

"Do you have a picture of her?"

I did, in my wallet, a snapshot from Italy, a flattering picture. Andreas studied it and nodded with approval, but I saw or imagined that I saw something relax in him, as if he now knew for sure he had the better woman; had won that particular competition. I felt sorry for Anabel but sorry for myself as well, for having to be her defender.

He handed back the snapshot. "You're loyal to her."

"So far."

"Eleven years—fantastic."

"A vow is a vow."

"It won't be easy for me to live up to your standard."

Already he, too, seemed to be thinking we might be friends. As we continued to walk, in the underlit streets, he alluded to his country's pollution, its literal and spiritual pollution, and to his own personal pollution. "You don't even know how clean you are."

"I haven't had a bath in three days."

"You worry about calling your wife. You nurse your mother when she's dying. These things seem obvious to you, but they're not obvious to everyone."

"It's more like a morbidly overdeveloped sense of duty."

"Your mother—how old was she?"

"Fifty-five."

"Shit luck. Good mother?"

"I don't know. I always thought she was a problem, and now I can't think of one bad thing she ever did to me."

"How was she a problem?"

"She didn't like my wife."

"And you were loyal to your wife."

"You've got me wrong," I said. "I'm sick of clean. I'm sick of my marriage. I've been wasting my life."

"I know the feeling."

"I'm so fucking sick of who I am."

"I know that feeling, too."

"Do you want to get a beer?"

He stopped walking and looked at his watch. It hurt my pride to be so much the asker, but I was determined to be his friend. He had an irresistible magnetism and an air of secret sorrow, secret knowledge. Years later, when he became internationally famous, I wasn't surprised. The whole world seemed to feel what I'd felt for him, and I was never able to begrudge him his success, because I knew that underneath, inside him, something was broken.

"Yeah, OK, a beer," he said.

We went into a bar, aptly named the Hole, and there I proceeded to lacerate myself. I told Andreas how I'd ignored my mother's warnings about Anabel and then all but abandoned her for eleven years. How I'd ignored Anabel's father's warnings, ignored my own instinctual liking for him, and pledged my allegiance to a nutty woman. I was betraying Anabel with every word I said, and the terrible thing was how good betrayal felt. It was as if all I'd needed was some plausible alternative to her, some potential male friend for whom I had a crushlike feeling, to admit to myself how angry I was at her; how angry I perhaps had always been.

My confession was no less sincere for having a tactical dimension. I'd never spoken to a source about my marriage, but openness was my modus, my way of encouraging sources to open up in turn. It didn't mean I was manipulative; it meant I had a personality made for journalism. And I could tell, from the raptness of Andreas's attention, that my American style was effective with a German. It had been my father's style, too, and my mother, at twenty, had been defenseless against it.

"So what are you going to do?" Andreas said when I was finished.

"Anything that's not going back to Harlem sounds good to me."

"You should call her tomorrow. If you're really not going back."

"Yeah, all right. Maybe."

He was looking at me intensely. "I like you," he said. "I'd like to help you write the truth about my country. But I'm afraid that if you knew my own story, you wouldn't like me."

"Why don't you tell it and let me be the judge."

"If you could meet Annagret, you might understand. But I'm not allowed to see her yet."

"Really."

"Yes, really."

The bar had filled up with cigarette smoke, cancerous-looking men, and girls with haircuts that only a day ago

I would have considered ghastly. Now, when I permitted myself to imagine sleeping with one of those haircuts, it seemed like something I would soon be doing, if I didn't leave Berlin.

"It's good to talk about things," I said.

He shook his head. "I can't tell you."

We were in territory familiar to a journalist. Sources who bothered to allude to stories they couldn't tell me almost always ended up telling them. The important thing was to talk about anything that wasn't the untold story. I bought us another round of beers and got him laughing with an attack on twentieth-century British literature, which he seemed to know inside out and was shocked by my dismissal of. Then I defended the Beatles while he extolled the Stones, and we found common ground in ridiculing the Dylan worshippers, both American and German. We talked for three hours, while the Hole emptied out and the untold story hovered in the vicinity. Finally Andreas covered his face and pressed hard on his closed eyes. "All right," he said. "Let's get out of here."

It was curious, in retrospect, how little I'd identified with my father; how wholly I'd sided with my mother. But now she was dead, and as I walked into the dark Tiergarten with Andreas I could have been my dad on the night he'd met her. A chance meeting, a tall young woman from the East, a city alive with possibility. He must have been amazed to have her at his side.

We sat down on a bench.

"This is not for publication," Andreas said. "This is simply to help you understand."

"I'm here as a friend."

"A friend. Interesting. I've never had a friend."

"Never?"

"When I was in school, people liked me. But I found them contemptible. Cowardly, boring. And then I became an outcast, a *dissident*. No one trusted me, and I trusted them even less. They were cowardly and boring, too. A person like you couldn't have existed in that country."

"But now the dissidents have won."

"Can I trust you?"

"You have no way of knowing it, but, yes, you absolutely can."

"See if you still want to be my friend when you hear what I have to tell you."

In the darkness, in the center of a city too diffuse and underpopulated to fill the sky with its noise, he told me how well connected his parents had been. How privileged he himself had been until he'd thrown away his life with an act of political defiance. And how, after his expulsion from the university, he'd drifted into a Milan Kundera world of pussy; how he'd then met a girl who'd changed his life, a girl whose soul he loved, and how he'd tried to save her from the stepfather who'd abused her. How the stepfather had pursued them to his parents' dacha. How he'd killed the stepfather in self-defense, with a shovel that happened to be at hand, and buried the body behind the dacha. He told me about his subsequent paranoia and his good fortune in retrieving his police and surveillance files from the Stasi archives.

"I did it to protect her," he said. "My life is not worth protecting, but hers is."

"But it was self-defense. Why didn't you just report it?"

"For the same reason she hadn't gone to the authorities. The Stasi protect their own. The truth is whatever they want it to be. We both would have gone to prison."

I'd interviewed convicted murderers in the past. I'd been a little scared of each of them, in a purely instinctive way, as if their history might repeat itself on me. But in the state I was in, after so much beer and conversation,

I found myself strangely envious of Andreas, for the largeness and extremity of the life he'd led.

He'd begun to cry, voicelessly.

"It was bad, Tom," he said. "It never goes away. I didn't mean to kill him. But I did it. I did it . . ."

I put my arm around his shoulders, and he turned to me and clung to me.

"It's all right," I said.

"Not all right. Not all right."

"No, no. It's all right."

He cried for a long time. I stroked his head and held him close. If he'd been a woman, I would have kissed his hair. But strict limits to intimacy are the straight man's burden. He pulled away and composed himself.

"So that's my story," he said.

"You got away with it."

"Not quite. She won't see me until I know we're safe. We're almost safe, but there's still a body in my parents' yard."

"Jesus."

"Worse than that. They may be selling the house to speculators. There's talk of digging up the ground. If I want to see her again, I have to move the body."

"I'm sorry I can't help you with that."

"No, you're clean. I would never involve you."

There was a note of tenderness in his voice. I asked what he planned to do about the body.

"I don't know," he said. "I could learn to drive a car, but that would take time. I'm worried that I'm going to lose her. I guess I could do it with two suitcases, a trip on a train."

"That would be some high-stress train trip."

"I have to see her again. Whatever is needed, I'll do it. That's my only plan—to see her again."

I felt another twinge of jealousy. Of exclusion; of competition with the girl. How else to explain what I said then?

"I can help you."

"No."

"I just cremated my mother. I'm up for it."

"No."

"I'm an American. I have a driver's license."

"No. It's a dirty business."

"If you've been telling me the truth, it's a thing worth doing."

"I have to do it alone. I have no way to repay you."

"No repayment necessary. I'm offering as a friend."

Somewhere in the distance, in the dark trees and bushes behind us, a cat cried out faintly. Then there came a second cry, somewhat louder, not a cat. It was a woman receiving pleasure.

"What about the archives," Andreas said.

"What about them?"

"The committee is going to Normannenstraße again on Friday. I could get you in."

"I don't see them letting an American do that."

"Your mother was German. You represent the people who escaped. They have files, too."

"This doesn't have to be a quid pro quo."

"Not quid pro quo. Friendship."

"It would certainly be a journalistic coup."

Andreas jumped up from the bench. "Let's do it! Both things." He leaned over me and clapped me on the arms. "Shall we do it?"

The woman in the distance was crying out again. I had the thought that I could have this very woman, or one just like her, if I stayed with Andreas in Berlin.

"Yes," I said.

Early the next morning, in Friedrichshain, I woke up

in a state of remorse. The linens on my bed hadn't been clean to begin with, and I'd never washed them; had simply accustomed myself to squalor. If the person I'd fallen for had been female, and had been lying next to me in bed, naked, I might have been able to block out thoughts of Anabel. As it was, the only way I could get back to sleep was to resolve to call Anabel later in the day and try to make amends for what I'd said to Andreas about her.

But when I did get up, around noon, the prospect of hearing her voice, its tremolo of injury, was repellent to me. The voice I wanted to hear and the face I wanted to see were Andreas's. I went over to West Berlin and rented a car, making sure I was permitted to take it outside the city limits. Returning home, I found a telegram addressed to me on the floor of the vestibule.

CALL ME.

I lay down in my unclean bed, the telegram beside me, to wait for the city's coal smoke to thicken into darkness and the post offices to drop their shutters.

Driving out to the suburbs, under the cover of night, I swerved around a stopped streetcar and nearly mowed down the riders who came bursting out of its doors. They shouted angrily, and I waved my hands in American apology. With the help of my father's old patented-fold Berlin map, I navigated through endless neighborhoods of German penitence. The streets near the Müggelsee were more built up and heavily trafficked than I'd imagined; I was relieved to find the Wolfs' summer house secluded by overgrown conifers.

I cut the lights and drove the car onto the frozen lawn and around behind the house, as Andreas had instructed me. From there I could see the iced-over lake, mottled white beneath a dome of urban cloud, and a toolshed in the rear corner of the lot. Andreas was standing by the shed with a shovel and a tarp.

"Any trouble?" he said cheerfully.

"A near-fatal accident, but no."

"You're good to do this for me."

"Thank me later."

He led me into the woods behind the shed. There was a pile of dirt and a corresponding hole. "My hands are terrible," he said. "The dirt on top was frozen hard. But now I think we can just lift the thing out by the clothes. I already lifted up both ends."

I looked down into the hole. There was enough ambient light to see that the body's coveralls, now impregnated with sandy mud, had once been blue. They gave the bones the shape and some of the bulk of a body. There looked to be some shreds of skin still on the hand bones. The smell wasn't bad, a faint rot on rot, like moldy cheese. Only one thing was missing.

"Where's the head?"

Andreas nodded over his shoulder. "In a plastic bag. No need for you to see that."

I appreciated his consideration. Having sat so recently with my mother's body, I was still in a penumbra of inurement to death. But a skull, perhaps with bits of hair on it, would have been a bad sight. The bones were more safely abstract without it. I felt that in making myself look at them, I was ensuring that I could never go back to Anabel.

Nevertheless, my jaw was shuddering, and not simply from the cold. Andreas spread the tarp, and we straddled the hole and tugged on the coveralls. They must have been rotten underneath. They came apart in the middle, dumping bones and various lumps of unidentifiable substance.

"Fuck this," I said.

"Yeah, OK. Leave it to me."

I stood at the edge of the lake while Andreas heaved and shoveled things out of the hole. I didn't go back until he'd rolled up the tarp and was filling the hole with dirt again. I helped him with that, to speed things along.

"I got us some sandwiches," he said when we'd stowed the tarp and its contents in the trunk of the car.

"I can't say I have much appetite."

"Force yourself. We have a long drive."

We washed our hands with a bottle of mineral water and ate the sandwiches. I was cold again, and in the cold it occurred to me, as it somehow hadn't before, that I was about to commit a serious crime. I felt a pang, not a large one, but a definite pang of homesickness for Anabel. Bad as our life had become, it was domestic, predictable, monogamous, uncriminal. In a corner of my mind, a rat of a thought scurried: that I'd met Andreas forty-eight hours ago, that I didn't really know him, and that he might have not told me the whole truth; that, indeed, he might have been working me all along, as his ticket back to Annagret.

"Reassure me about the police," I said. "I'm picturing a routine traffic stop. *Please open the trunk.*"

"The police have bigger things to worry about these days."

"I did almost kill about six people on the way over here."

"Would you be happier if I said I'm scared out of my mind?"

"Are you?"

"A little bit, yeah." He punched me in the arm. "You?"

"I've had funner evenings."

"I won't forget what you're doing for me, Tom. Never."

In the car, with the heat blasting, I felt better. Andreas told me more about his life, the bizarrely literary terms in which he understood it, and his yearning for a better, cleaner life with Annagret. "We're going to find a place to live," he said. "You can stay with us for as long as you want. It's the least we can do for you."

"And you'll do what for a living?"

"I haven't thought so far ahead."

"Journalism?"

"Maybe. What's it like?"

I told him what it was like, and he seemed interested, but I sensed a faint, unspoken distaste, as if he had grander ambitions that he was tactfully refraining from mentioning. It was the same sense I'd had when he looked at Anabel's picture: he was happy to admire what I had as long as what he had was even better. This might not have boded well for a future friendship of equals, but there at the beginning, in the very warm car, it was consonant with my experience of crushes—the feeling of inferiority, the hope of being found worthy nonetheless.

"The Citizens' Committee is meeting tomorrow morning," he said. "You should come along with me, so they know who you are on Friday. How's your German?"

"Eh."

"*Sprich. Sprich.*"

"*Ich bin Amerikaner. Ich bin in Denver geboren—*"

"The *r* is wrong. Say it more in the throat. *Amerikaner. Geboren.*"

"My *r*'s are the least of my problems."

"*Noch mal, bitte: Amerikaner.*"

"*Amerikaner.*"

"*Geboren.*"

"*Geboren.*"

For a good hour, we worked on my pronunciation. It makes me sad to think of that hour. Judging from his arrogant street presentation, I would never have guessed what a patient teacher he was. We were already assuming that I would stay on in Berlin, but I could also feel that he liked both me and his language and wanted us to get along.

"Let's work on your English accent," I said.

"My accent is flawless! I'm the son of an English professor."

"You sound like the BBC. You've got to flatten your *a*'s. You haven't really lived until you've said *a* like an American. They're one of the glories of our nation. Say *can't* for me."

"Can't."

"Aaaaa. Caaaan't. Like a bleating goat."

"Caaaaan't."

"There you go. The British have no concept of what they're missing."

On the outskirts of a no-account town, we stopped at a shuttered gas station so that Andreas could dig into a trash bin and bury the skull in it. Waiting in the car, I felt convinced that I was performing a good deed. If my mother hadn't emigrated, if I'd been born in a Stasi-shadowed country, I might have killed a Stasi rat in self-defense myself. Helping Andreas seemed to me a way of atoning for my American advantages.

"You didn't leave the engine running," he remarked when he was back in the car.

"Didn't want to be conspicuous."

"It's a question of efficiency. Now you have to warm it up again."

I put the car in gear and smiled at knowing better. "In the first place," I said, "what heats a car is excess engine heat. The added fuel use is zero. You might know this if you'd ever driven one. More to the point, it's never efficient to maintain heat in a cold environment."

"That's completely false."

"No, in fact it's true."

"Completely false." He seemed eager to spar. "If you're heating a house, it's much more efficient to maintain a temperature of sixteen degrees overnight than to raise the temperature from five degrees in the morning. My father always did it at the dacha."

"Your father was wrong."

"He was the chief economist of a major industrialized nation!"

"I'm understanding better why the nation failed."

"Trust me, Tom. You're wrong about this."

It happened that my own father had explained to me the thermodynamics of home heating. Without mentioning him, I pointed out to Andreas that the rate of caloric transfer is proportional to temperature differential—the warmer the house, the more profusely it bleeds calories on a cold night. Andreas tried to fight me with integral calculus, but I remembered the basics of that, too. We tussled while I drove. He advanced ever-more esoteric arguments, refusing to accept that his father had been wrong. When I finally defeated him, I could feel that something had changed between us, some hook of friendship set. He seemed both confounded and admiring. Until then, I don't think he'd believed I was a worthy intellectual adversary.

It was after midnight when we reached the Oder valley. We crossed a decrepit wooden bridge to an island used only in the summer, by farmers growing hay. The crusted snow on the dikes between frozen marshes was virgin. I didn't like the tracks we were leaving, but Andreas said that the forecast was for rain and warmer weather. On the far side of the island was a tangle of woods that he remembered from a nature walk he'd taken while attending an elite summer camp. "It was the height of privilege," he said. "We had border guards with us."

Whatever the East German army was doing now, it was doing it somewhere else. We hustled the rolled-up tarp and two shovels up into a ravine where our footprints wouldn't be visible. From there, we struggled through leafless brambles and into the woods.

"Here," he said.

The digging was hard but also warming. I was ready to stop when we were one foot down, but Andreas insisted on digging deeper. An owl was calling from somewhere near, but the only other sound was the crunch of our shovels and the crack of the tree roots we encountered.

"Now leave me alone," he said.

"I don't mind helping. It's not like not helping will lessen my criminal offense."

"I'm burying what I was before I knew Annagret. This is personal."

I walked away from the grave and stayed away until he was throwing dirt on the remains. Then I helped him finish the burial and cover the spot with leaves and dirty snow. By the time we returned to the road, a fog had gathered, brighter in the east where the night was ending. We stowed the shovels in the trunk. After Andreas had slammed down the lid, he let out a falsetto whoop. He jumped up and down and whooped again.

"Jesus, shut up," I said.

He grasped me by the arms and looked me in the eye. "Thank you, Tom. Thank you, thank you, thank you."

"Let's get out of here."

"You need to understand what this means to me. To have a friend I can trust."

"If I tell you I understand, can we hit the road?"

His eyes were shining strangely. He leaned into me, and for a moment I thought he might kiss me. But it was merely a hug. I returned it, and we stood for a while in awkward embrace. I could feel him breathing, feel the humidity of his sweat escaping from beneath his army jacket. He put a hand on the back of my head, his fingers closing around my hair the way Anabel's might have. Then, abruptly, he broke away from me. "Wait here."

"Where are you going?"

"One minute," he said.

I watched him run back up the ravine and kick through the brambles. I hadn't liked his whooping, and I liked this additional delay even less. I lost sight of him in the trees, but I could hear sticks snapping, the rustle of his jacket on branches. Then a deep rural silence. And then, faintly but distinctly, the clink of a belt buckle. The sound of a zipper.

To avoid hearing more, I walked up the road in the direction of our tire tracks. I tried to put myself in Andreas's position, tried to imagine the relief and exhilaration he was feeling, but there was simply no squaring his avowed remorse with defiling his victim's final grave.

His business was done in a few minutes. He came running up the road, running and jumping. When he reached my side, he turned in a complete circle with his arms in the air and the middle finger of each hand extended. He whooped again.

"Can we leave?" I said coolly.

"Absolutely! You can drive twice as fast now."

He seemed not to notice that my mood had changed. In the car, he was manically voluble, bouncing from subject to subject—how it could work for me to live with him and Annagret, how exactly he was going to get me into the archives, and how the two of us could collaborate, him unlocking the forbidden doors, me writing the stories. He urged me to drive faster, to pass trucks on blind curves. He recited old poems of his and explicated them. He recited long passages of Shakespeare in English, banging out the blank-verse rhythm on the dashboard. Every now and then, he paused to whoop again, or to pummel me in the arm with two fists.

When we finally reached his church in Berlin, on Siegfeldstraße, my mouth tasted metallic with exhaustion. He wanted to grab a quick breakfast and go straight to the

Citizens' Committee meeting, but I said, truthfully, that I had to lie down.

"Leave it to me, then," he said.

"OK."

"I'm never forgetting this, Tom. Never, never, never."

"Don't mention it."

I popped the trunk lid and got out of the car. Seeing Andreas take out the shovels in full daylight, I wondered, belatedly, which one of them had been the murder weapon. In my sleep-deprived state, it seemed very bad that I might have used that particular shovel.

He clapped me on the shoulder. "You all right?"

"I'm fine."

"Get some sleep. Meet me here at seven. We'll have dinner."

"Sounds good."

I never saw him again. When I awoke, in my filthy sheets, it was an hour before the rental-car office closed. I returned the car and walked back to my squat in the dark. I still had a hankering to see Andreas's face and hear his voice—I have it even as I write this—but the sadness from which I'd been running was hitting me so hard that I could barely stand upright. I lay down on the bed and wept for myself, and for Anabel, and for Andreas, but above all for my mother.

The approach of thunderstorms was making the New Jersey sky three-dimensional, a many-tiered vault of variously shaded cloud, gray and white and hepatic green, when Anabel led me out of the woods and up through a pasture to Suzanne's parents' house. She claimed that she wanted to show me something quickly before taking me back to catch my bus, but I knew that my actually catching the 8:11 bus was as arrant a fantasy as our ever finding a way to live together again, if only because the business of escaping from her, of enforcing my right to leave, was so painful that I shied from it like a brutalized animal. Anything at all was preferable, and there was also the prospect of further sex, which promised minutes of relief from consciousness.

And still I balked at the door of the house. It was a sixties-modern summer place with a mountain view and some apple trees behind it. Anabel went right in, but I hung in the doorway, my stomach suddenly upset like the sky, my heart racing with what I now think was straightforward PTSD.

"Won't you come inside with me?" she said in a tone whose very sweetness was insane.

"I think after all maybe not."

"Do you realize you left your toothbrush here last time?"

"My dentist keeps me well supplied."

"The man who 'forgets' his toothbrush in a woman's house is a man who wants to come back."

My panic intensified. I looked over my shoulder and saw a fractal of lightning on the next ridge over; I waited for the thunder. When I looked into the house again, Anabel was not in sight. I considered, quite seriously, strangling her to death while I fucked her and then throwing myself in front of the 8:11 bus. The idea was not without its logic and appeal. But there were the bus driver's feelings to consider . . .

I stepped into the house and closed the screen door behind me. With my help, she'd cleared the furniture from the living room, leaving only a mat for her yoga and meditation. She hadn't officially abandoned her film project, it was merely on hold while she sought to regain her calm and centeredness. She was living on the half of my inheritance I'd given her as part of our divorce settlement. After returning from Berlin, I'd needed no more than a day with her to recognize that my homesickness had been grounded in a fantasy. She'd said she wasn't spaghetti with eggplant, but to me she really was. And so I'd built us a new fantasy of divorce as our only hope of reuniting.

Anabel was convinced that I'd been unfaithful to her in Berlin—that this was why I hadn't called her. To defend myself against this baseless charge, I'd told her more about Andreas than I should have. Not about the murder, not about my having been an accessory after the fact, but enough about his personality and history to explain both why I'd been attracted to him and why I'd run away from him. She'd concluded that he was a jerk who'd brought out the jerk in me, the jerk who'd returned from Berlin and asked for a divorce. But the person I'd actually been a jerk to was Andreas. I'd stood him up for our dinner date, and then I'd waited two months before sending him a stilted letter of apology, reassurance, and "warm wishes."

I could hear Anabel showering in the bathroom. There being nowhere to sit in the living room, I went and sat down on her bed. Outside, the sky seemed to have taken on the black solidity of a hillside you could walk right up. All the books on the nightstand were self-help and spirituality, titles Anabel would have sneered at just a few years earlier. I felt very sorry for her.

She came out of the bathroom naked, her hair in a towel. "The shower's nice," she said. "You should take one, too."

"I'll wait until I get back tonight."

"You don't have to be afraid of me. I'm not going to lock you in the bathroom." She moved close to me, her pubic hair commanding my field of vision. "If you like me," she said, "you'll take a shower."

I didn't like her, not anymore, but I still hadn't found a way to say so. "Do you have any form of contraception that you haven't destroyed with a pocket knife?"

"First take a shower, and then I'll tell you if I do."

There was a blast of thunder directly over the house.

"You said you had something to show me," I said. "That's the only reason I came inside."

"But now it's raining and there's lightning."

"Being struck by lightning doesn't sound too bad to me right now."

"It's your choice," she said. "Take a shower or be struck by lightning."

A middle was being excluded, and the middle was reality. I took a shower, listening to the thunder, and put my clothes back on. When I returned to the bedroom, Anabel was sitting cross-legged on the bed in her old Japanese silk robe, which she'd disarranged with poignantly transparent seductive intent, a breast hanging halfway out. Beside her was a shoe box.

"Look who I found," she said.

She opened the box and took out Leonard. It was five or six years since I'd last seen him. Sheets of rain were ripping themselves on the apple trees outside the window.

"Come say hi to him," Anabel said, smiling at me with love.

"Hello."

She picked up the bull and looked into his face. "Do you want to say hello to Tom?"

I couldn't breathe, let alone speak.

Anabel frowned at Leonard with coy reproach. "Why aren't you saying hello?" She looked up at me. "Why isn't he talking?"

"I don't know."

"Leonard, say something."

"He doesn't talk anymore."

"He must be angry that you're not with us anymore. I think he wants you to come home." She cuddled the bull. "I wish you'd say something to me."

Don't talk to me about hatred if you haven't been married. Only love, only long empathy and identification and compassion, can root another person in your heart so deeply that there's no escaping your hatred of her, not ever; especially not when the thing you hate most about her is her capacity to be hurt by you. The love persists and the hatred with it. Even hating your own heart is no relief. I don't think I'd ever hated her more than I did for exposing herself to the shame of my refusing to speak in Leonard's voice.

"I'm seeing your father tomorrow," I said.

"That's not Leonard's voice," she said, frightened.

"No. It's my voice. Put that thing away."

She set the toy aside. Then she picked it up again. Then she set it down again. Her fear and indecision were terrible to see. Or maybe it was my own power that was terrible.

"I don't want to know about it," she said. "Can you please just spare me?"

I'd intended to spare her, but I hated her too much now. "He's bringing me a check," I said.

She moaned and fell over as if I'd hit her. "Why are you doing this to me?"

"A large check," I said.

"Shut up! For God's sake! I try to be nice to you and you spit in my face!"

"He's giving me money to start a magazine."

She sat up again, her eyes blazing now. "You're a *jerk*," she said. "That's what you are. A jerk! You always were and you always will be!"

I'd thought that nothing could be worse than the sight of her being hurt and shamed by me. But in fact I hated her even more for hating me.

"Maybe twelve years is enough years of being made to feel that way," I said.

"It's not what you feel, it's what you *are*. You're a jerk, Tom. You're a fucking asshole journalistic jerk. You ruined my life and now you're spitting on me, you're *spitting* on me."

"You're the one who did the spitting, as you may recall."

To her credit, her honesty and morality were still functioning. She said, more quietly, "You're right. I was young and he ruined our wedding party, but you're right, I did literally spit on someone." She shook her head. "And now you're making me pay for it. Both of you. Now the men are doing the spitting, because I was weak. I was always weak. I'm weak now. I failed. But the person I spat on had *everything*, while you're spitting on somebody when she's down. There's a difference there."

"One obvious difference being that I'm not actually spitting," I said coldly.

"I'm so far down, Tom. How can you do this to me?"

"I keep looking for a way to make you never call me again. I keep thinking I've found it, but then, no, the fucking phone rings."

"Well, you finally may have found it. Taking his money may do it for you. I'm thinking you'll never hear from me again. There was still one thing in my life that you hadn't perverted or stolen or destroyed. Now there's nothing. I'm totally alone with nothing. Job well done."

"I hate you," I said. "I hate you even more than I love you. And that's saying something."

After a moment, her face turned red and she began to cry piteously, like a little girl, and it didn't matter that I hated her, I couldn't stand to see her in such pain. I sat down on the bed and held her. The rain had gone away, leaving behind a blue-gray curtain of cloud that looked almost wintry. I thought of winter as I held her, grew bored with holding her. The winter of no Anabel in my life.

As if sensing it, she began to kiss me. We'd always relied on pain to heighten the pleasure that followed it, and it seemed to me we'd reached the limit of the psychic pain we could inflict. When she lay back and opened her robe, I looked at her breasts and hated their beauty so intensely that I squeezed a nipple and twisted it hard.

She screamed and hit me in the face. I was murderously aroused and hardly felt it. She hit me again, on the ear, and glared at me. "Are you going to hit me back?"

"No," I said. "I'm going to fuck you in the ass."

"No, I don't want that."

I'd never spoken so violently to her. We'd reached the end of the road of our feminist marriage. "You wrecked the condoms," I said. "What am I supposed to do?"

"Give me a baby. Leave me with something."

"No way."

"I think it could happen tonight. I have a sense about these things."

"I think I'd sooner kill myself than sign on for that."

"You hate me."

"I hate you."

She was still in love with me. I could see it in her eyes, the love and the pure inconsolable disappointment of a child. I had all the power, and so she did the only thing still available to her to stab me in the heart, which was to roll over submissively and raise the skirt of her robe and say, "All right, then. Do it."

I did it, and not once but three times before I escaped from the house the next morning. After each assault, she went straight to the bathroom. My state of mind was that of the crack addict crawling on the floor, looking for crumbs. I wasn't raping Anabel, but I might as well have been. Pleasure was low on the list of what either of us was after. I was after what she'd been after with her film, a final and complete exhaustion of the subject of the body. What she was after, it seemed to me, was the sealing of her moral victimhood.

At dawn, to a chorus of birds, I got up and dressed without washing. Anabel was facedown on the sweaty bed, corpse-still, but I knew she wasn't sleeping. I loved her terribly, loved her all the more for what I'd done to her. My love was like the engine of a hundred-dollar car that had no business starting up and yet kept starting up. The murder and suicide I imagined weren't figurative. I would keep going back, and it would be worse each time, until finally we were driven to the violence that released our love to the eternity it belonged to. Standing by the bed, looking down at my ex-wife's body, I thought it might happen as soon as the next time I saw her. I thought it might even happen now if I said anything to her. So I picked up my knapsack and left the house.

The full moon was setting in the west, a mere white disk, its light-casting power defeated by the morning. Halfway down the driveway, I entered golden sunlight and saw a bright red bird mating with a yellow female on a dead tree branch. The birds were too busy to mind my approach. The head feathers of the male, sticking straight out, a scarlet Mohawk, seemed to be sweating pure testosterone. Finished with the female, he flew straight at me, kamikaze style, barely missing my head. He landed on a different branch and glared in a blaze of aggression.

The day was even hotter than the day before, and the air-conditioning on the bus was broken. When I finally got back to 125th Street, the sidewalk was crowded with sweat-gleaming women and children emerging from storefront churches. A stench of rotten cantaloupe was in the air, gastric and cloying, cut with exhaust from a Kennedy Fried Chicken. The pavement was shiny with a blackish vulcanized glaze of chicken grease, sputum, spilled Coke, and trashbag leakage.

"My man Lucky," Ruben said to me in my building's lobby, which was littered with Sunday-morning betting slips. "You look like shit warmed over."

My answering machine was showing one new message. I was afraid it was from Anabel, but it was from a woman who sounded Jamaican, asking me to tell Anthony that her husband had died last night and that the funeral would be on Tuesday afternoon at such-and-such church in West Harlem. She repeated that I should tell Anthony that her husband had died. This was it, the only message, a Jamaican woman informing me, in a calm and very tired voice, that her spouse had died.

I turned on the AC and left a message at the Carlyle for David Laird. Then I fell asleep and dreamed that I was in a many-roomed house where a party was happening. I'd fallen into a deep flirtatious conversation with a young dark-haired woman who seemed to like me, seemed ready to leave the party with me. The only impediment to effortless happiness with her was something I may or may not have said, something that made her think I might be a *jerk*. To my joy, I was able to tell her that a different man had said it. Andreas Wolf had said it. I knew this for a fact, and she believed me. She was falling in love with me. And just as I was beginning to understand that she must be Annagret, Andreas's young girl, I realized instead that she was Anabel—a younger, softer Anabel, at once pliant and sportive, instilled with the best kind of knowledge about me, knowledge that felt loving and forgiving—except that she couldn't possibly be Anabel, because the real Anabel was standing in a doorway, witnessing my flirtation. The dread I felt of her judgment, and of the punishment of interacting with her nuttiness, came directly from life. She looked stricken with betrayal and hurt. Worse yet, the girl had seen her and vanished.

David returned my call late in the afternoon.

"I can't do it," I said.

"An eight o'clock table at Gotham? Are you kidding me? Of course you can do it."

"I can't take the money."

"What? That is beyond ridiculous. It's criminally foolish. You can dedicate every one of your issues to sullying the good name of McCaskill, I still want you to have the money. If you're worried about Anabel, just don't tell her."

"I already told her."

"Tom, Tom. You can't listen to what she says."

"I'm not. She's going to think I took the money, and I'm OK with that. I just don't want to take it."

"Stupidest thing I ever heard. You need to come to the Gotham and be plied with martinis. The check's burning a hole in my briefcase."

"Not gonna do it."

"And this change of heart?"

"I can't have anything to do with her," I said. "I appreciate how good you've been to—"

"I'll be frank with you," David said. "I'm more than a little disappointed in you. I thought you'd finally quit trying to out-Anabel Anabel, now that you're divorced. But everything you're saying to me is bullshit."

"Look, I—"

"Bullshit," he repeated, and hung up on me.

The next time I heard from David, four months later, it was through an intermediary, a retired New York City cop who worked as a private detective. His name was DeMars and he showed up at my door one afternoon without warning, having bullied his way past Ruben. He was walrus-mustached and intimidating. He said the simplest thing would be for me to show him my datebook and receipts for the previous four months. "It's entirely routine," he said.

"I don't see anything routine about it," I said.

"You been in Texas recently?"

"I'm sorry—who are you?"

"I work for David Laird. I'm especially interested in the last two weeks of August. Best thing for you is if you can show me you weren't in Texas at any point then."

"I'm going to call David right now, if you don't mind."

"Your ex disappeared," DeMars said. "She sent her dad a letter that appears to be authentic. But we don't know the circumstances of the letter, and, nothing personal, but you're the ex. You're the man we go to."

"I haven't seen her since the end of May."

"Easiest for both of us if you can document that."

"It's hard to prove a negative."

"Do your best."

Having nothing to hide, I handed over my receipts and credit-card statements. When DeMars saw that my August was richly documented—I'd been in Milwaukee with half the journalists in America, reporting on Jeffrey Dahmer for *Esquire*—he became less obnoxious and showed me copies of a postmarked envelope and the handwritten note it contained.

> *To David Laird: I'm not your daughter. You won't hear from me again. I'm dead to you. Don't look for me. I won't be found. Anabel.*

"Postmark is Houston," DeMars said. "I need you to tell me who she knows in Houston."

"No one."

"You sure about that?"

"Yes."

"Well, see, here's why I'm involved. David says he hasn't seen her in more than a decade. He's dead to her anyway, so why the letter? Why now? And why is she in Houston? I thought maybe you could shed some light."

"We just went through a bad divorce."

"Violent bad? Restraining-order bad?"

"No, no. Just emotionally painful."

DeMars nodded. "OK, so an ordinary divorce. She wants to make a clean break, start a new life, and so on. But the way I read this letter is she's afraid people are gonna think that someone did away with her. That's the only reason to write it: 'Don't worry, I'm not actually dead.' But why would anyone think that in the first place? You see what I mean?"

Anabel was so impractical and such a recluse that it was hard to imagine her in Houston. But something had clearly changed in her, because she hadn't called me in four months.

"We have her in New York on July 22," DeMars continued, "taking five thousand in cash out of her bank. Same day, she leaves keys, no note, just the keys, at the building of her friend Suzanne. You didn't see her in New York that day, did you?"

"We've had no contact of any kind since May."

"But, see, if she doesn't send that letter, nobody looks for her. My impression is she's not exactly Miss Congeniality. It could have been years before anybody noticed she was missing."

"At the risk of sounding self-important, I think she wrote the letter as a message to me."

"How's that work? Why not just write *you* a letter? Did she write you a letter?"

"No. She's trying to prove that she's capable of not having any contact with me."

"Kind of an extreme way of going about that."

"Well, she's extreme. It's also possible she was trying to protect me, in case someone like you came looking for her."

"Bingo." DeMars snapped his fingers. "I was hoping you'd be the one to say that. Because that's my problem with the letter. Painful divorce, irreconcilable differences, and yet here she is, going out of her way to protect you? I don't see it. Your typical angry ex, she'd like nothing better than to have people wondering if you'd offed her."

"That's not Anabel. Her whole thing is being morally irreproachable."

"What about you? Any friends in Texas?"

"Not to speak of."

"You'll show me your address book and phone bills."

"I will. But you'd do her a kindness if you stopped looking for her."

"She's not the person paying me."

DeMars wanted more from me—wanted contact information for every person Anabel had ever known—and I worried that I made myself suspicious by refusing to provide it. But there was an air of due diligence, of nose-holding, in his questioning of me. He seemed already to have concluded that Anabel was nutty and a pain in the ass, and that the entire case was nothing more than family nonsense. He called me a couple of times to follow up, and then I never heard from him again; never learned if he'd succeeded in locating her. I hoped for her sake that he hadn't, because I really did think that her letter to David was a message to me. I may have left the marriage before she did, but she was determined to one-up me and be the really radical leaver. I hated her for the hatred implicit in this, but I still felt guilty about leaving her, and it eased my guilt, a tiny bit, to imagine her succeeding in something, if only in disappearing. I'd escaped the marriage but the moral victory was hers.

I didn't hear from David again until 2002, a year

before he died. This time the intermediary was a lawyer, writing to inform me that I'd been named the sole trustee of an inter vivos trust that David had created in Anabel's name. I dialed the number on the letter and learned that she was still missing, eleven years after her disappearance, and that David intended her to have one-quarter of his estate anyway, in the hope that she'd eventually show up and claim it.

"I don't want to be the trustee," I said.

"Well, now," the lawyer said with a lovely Kansan twang. "You might want to hear the terms first."

"Nope."

"You're gonna make my life harder if you don't, so please just hear me out. The trust consists entirely of McCaskill stock. Seventy percent of that is illiquid, the other thirty percent can be offered by way of the company's ESOP program but doesn't have to be. Just going by book value, you're looking at nearly a billion dollars. Five-year average dividend comes in at four point two percent, which the company is nominally committed to increasing. Based on that simple average alone, you've got about forty-two million annually in cash dividends. Trustee's fee shall be one point five percent of that. So we're talking, what, three-quarters of a million a year for the trustee, probably a million soon enough. Since the stock either can't be sold or doesn't have to be, the trustee's responsibilities are nugatory. Nothing more than ordinary shareholder responsibilities. To put it plainly, Mr. Aberant, you get a million a year for doing nothing."

My salary then, as the managing editor at *Newsday*, was less than a quarter of that. I was still making mortgage payments on the Gramercy Park one-bedroom that I'd bought after landing my first editing job at *Esquire* and had held on to through my years at the *Times* magazine and at the *Times*. If I'd still believed that a journal of opin-

ion called *The Complicater* could change the world—if I
hadn't instead come to feel that covering daily news re-
sponsibly was a worthier and more embattled cause—I
could have funded a fine quarterly with a million a year.
But David had been right: I was trying to out-Anabel
Anabel. Trying to stay clean in case she ever happened to
find out what I'd been doing since I left her. Trying to
prove her wrong about me. I repeated to the lawyer in
Wichita that I wanted nothing to do with the trust.

I never quite figured David out. He was fabulously
good at making money, and he really did love Anabel, for
many of the same reasons I did, but the cruelty and the
vengeance in giving her a billion unwanted dollars, and
in naming the person she most hated as trustee, were unmistakable. I couldn't decide whether he intended to keep
punishing her from beyond the grave, or whether he nur-
tured the sentimental hope that she might one day return
and claim her birthright. Maybe it was both. I do know
that money was the language he spoke and thought in. A
year after I'd heard from his lawyer, he died and left me
twenty million dollars, free and clear, "for the establish-
ment of a quality national newsmagazine." The bequest
seemed to have more to do with rewarding me than with
punishing Anabel—so, at least, I chose to construe it—
and this time I didn't say no.

About Anabel the obituaries of David reported only
that her address and occupation were unknown, but press
coverage of the Laird family continued to be findable if
you were curious and did a little looking. Anabel's three
brothers had blossomed into larger-scale failures. The oldest, Bucky, was briefly in the news for trying and failing
to buy the Minnesota Timberwolves and move them to
Wichita. The middle one, Dennis, dropped $15 million on
a Republican primary Senate campaign that he still managed to lose by double digits. The youngest, Danny, the

former drug addict, had gone to work on Wall Street and shown a knack for joining firms on the brink of going down in flames. Three years after David's death, presumably using the money he'd inherited, he partnered into a hedge fund that soon went down in flames. Around the same time, I happened to meet Bucky Laird at a leadership-conference boondoggle in California. We chatted a little, and he told me, quite matter-of-factly, that he and his brothers had always assumed I'd murdered Anabel and got away with it. When I denied it, he seemed neither to believe me nor particularly to care.

I've never stopped wondering where Anabel is and whether she's alive. I know that if she is alive she takes satisfaction in my being unaware of it—a satisfaction great enough, I suspect, to keep her living even if she has no other reason to. I remain convinced that I'll see her again someday, even if I never see her again. She's eternal in me. Only once, and only because I was very young, could I have merged my identity with another person's, and singularities like this are where you find eternity. I couldn't go on and have children with anyone else, because I'd prevented her from having them. I couldn't settle down with anyone significantly younger than me without proving that my wish to do this was the reason that I'd dumped her. She'd also left me with a lifelong allergy to unrealistic women, an allergy that tended to compound itself, since the minute I detected a hint of fantasy in a woman and had my reaction to it, I rendered any hopes she had for me unrealistic. I wanted nothing to do with anyone like Anabel, and even when I found someone truly unlike her, a woman with whom it's an inexpressible blessing to share a life, Anabel's sadness and her moral absolutism continued to color my nighttime dreams. Her act of disappearance and negation becomes more significant and wounding, not less, with every year that passes without a sign of her existence. She may have been weaker than me, but she managed to outplay me. She moved on while I stayed stuck. I have to hand it to her: I feel checkmated.

The Killer

When the two-way radio chirped and erupted in the burry voice of Pedro, it seemed to awaken Andreas from a dream that was aware of having lasted too long and was trying to end itself. "*Hay un señor en la puerta que dice que es su amigo. Se llama Tom Aberant.*"

On the table by his bed was a sandwich with one bite taken out of it. He couldn't have said what day of the week it was. The system that had placed him under house arrest was in his head. Hearing the name Tom Aberant barely moved him. He seemed to remember investing enormous obsessional energy in Tom Aberant, for months, maybe for years, but the recollection was faint and flavorless. He no more hated Tom or feared him than he did anything else now. He had only an intolerable, chest-crushing anxiety. That, and a wan perception of the cruelty of being visited, for whatever reason, by a journalist. He no longer met the fundamental requirement of an interviewee, which was to like yourself.

"*Hacelo pasar,*" he told Pedro.

Before he'd quit doing interviews, the previous fall, he'd taken to dropping the word *totalitarian*. Younger interviewers, to whom the word meant total surveillance, total mind control, gray armies in parade with medium-range missiles, had understood him to be saying something unfair about the Internet. In fact, he simply meant a system that was impossible to opt out of. The old Republic had certainly excelled at surveillance and parades, but the essence of its totalitarianism had been more everyday and subtle. You could cooperate with the system or you could oppose it, but the one thing you could never do, whether you were enjoying a secure and pleasant life or sitting in a prison, was not be in relation to it. The answer to every question large or small was socialism. If you substituted *networks* for *socialism*, you got the Internet. Its competing platforms were united in their ambition to define every term of your existence. In his own case, when he'd started to be properly famous, he'd recognized that fame, as a phenomenon, had migrated to the Internet, and that the Internet's architecture made it easy for his enemies to shape the Wolf narrative. As in the old Republic, he could either ignore the haters and suffer the consequences, or he could accept the premises of the system, however sophomoric he found them, and increase its power and pervasiveness by participating in it. He'd chosen the latter, but the particular choice didn't matter. He was in relation to the Revolution either way.

In his experience, few things were more alike than one revolution to another. Then again, he'd experienced only the kind that loudly called itself a revolution. The mark of a legitimate revolution—the scientific, for example— was that it didn't brag about its revolutionariness but simply occurred. Only the weak and fearful, the illegitimate, had to brag. The refrain of his childhood, under a regime so weak and fearful it built a prison wall around the people it allegedly had liberated, was that the Republic was blessed to be in history's vanguard. If your boss was a shithead and your own husband was spying on you, it wasn't the regime's fault, because the regime served the Revolution and the Revolution was at once historically inevitable and terribly fragile, beset with enemies. This ridiculous contradiction was a fixture of bragging revolutions. No crime or unforeseen side effect was so grievous that it couldn't be excused by a system that *had to be* but *easily could fail*.

The apparatchiks, too, were an eternal type. The tone of the new ones, in their TED Talks, in PowerPointed product launches, in testimony to parliaments and congresses, in utopianly titled books, was a smarmy syrup of convenient conviction and personal surrender that he remembered well from the Republic. He couldn't listen to them without thinking of the Steely Dan lyric *So you grab a piece of something that you think is gonna last*. (Radio in the American Sector had played the song over and over to young ears in the Soviet sector.) The privileges available in the Republic had been paltry, a telephone, a flat with some air and light, the all-important permission to travel, but perhaps no paltrier than having *x* number of followers on Twitter, a much-liked Facebook profile, and the occasional four-minute spot on CNBC. The real appeal of apparatchikism was the safety of belonging. Outside, the air smelled like brimstone, the food was bad, the economy moribund, the cynicism rampant, but inside, *victory over the class enemy was assured*. Inside, *the professor and the engineer were learning at the German worker's feet*. Outside, the middle class was disappearing faster than the icecaps, xenophobes were winning elections or stocking up on assault rifles, warring tribes were butchering each other religiously, but inside, *disruptive new technologies were rendering traditional politics obsolete*. Inside, decentralized ad hoc communities were *rewriting the rules of creativity*, the revolution *rewarding the risk-taker who understood the power of networks*. The New Regime even recycled the old Republic's buzzwords, *collective*, *collaborative*. Axiomatic to both was that a

new species of humanity was emerging. On this, apparatchiks of every stripe agreed. It never seemed to bother
them that their ruling elites consisted of the grasping, brutal old species of humanity.

Lenin had been a risk-taker. Trotsky had been one, too,
until Stalin had made him the Bill Gates of the Soviet
Union, the excoriated crypto-reactionary. But Stalin himself hadn't needed to take so many risks, because terror
worked better. Although, to a man, the new revolutionar-
ies all claimed to worship risk-taking—a relative term in
any case, since the risk in question was of losing some
venture capitalist's money, at worst of wasting a few pa-
rentally funded years, rather than, say, the risk of being
shot or hanged—the most successful of them had instead
followed Stalin's example. Like the old politburos, the
new politburo styled itself as the enemy of the elite and
the friend of the masses, dedicated to *giving consumers
what they wanted*, but to Andreas (who, admittedly, had
never learned how to want stuff) it seemed as if the Internet was governed more by fear: the fear of unpopular-
ity and uncoolness, the fear of missing out, the fear of
being flamed or forgotten. In the Republic, people had
been terrified of the state; under the New Regime, what
terrified them was the state of nature: kill or be killed, eat
or be eaten. In both cases, the fear was entirely reasonable; indeed, it was the *product* of reason. The full name
of the Republic's ideology had been Scientific Socialism,
a name pointing backward to *la Terreur* (the Jacobins,
with their marvelously efficient guillotine, may have been
executioners, but they fashioned themselves as executors
of Enlightenment rationality) and forward to the terrors
of technocracy, which sought to liberate humanity from
its humanness through the efficiency of markets and the
rationality of machines. This was the truly eternal fixture

of illegitimate revolution, this impatience with irrationality, this wish to be clean of it once and for all.

It was Andreas's gift, maybe his greatest, to find singular niches in totalitarian regimes. The Stasi was the best friend he'd ever had—until he met the Internet. He'd found a way to use both of them while standing apart from them. Because it reminded him of his similarity to his mother, Pip Tyler's remark about the Moonglow Dairy had wounded him, but she was right: for all the good work the Sunlight Project did, it now functioned mainly as an extension of his ego. A fame factory masquerading as a secrets factory. He allowed the New Regime to hold him up as an inspiring example of its *openness*, and in return, when it couldn't be avoided, he protected the regime from bad press.

There were a lot of could-be Snowdens inside the New Regime, employees with access to the algorithms that Facebook used to monetize its users' privacy and Twitter to manipulate memes that were supposedly self-generating. But smart people were actually far more terrified of the New Regime than of what the regime had persuaded less-smart people to be afraid of, the NSA, the CIA—it was straight from the totalitarian playbook, disavowing your own methods of terror by imputing them to your enemy and presenting yourself as the only defense against them—and most of the could-be Snowdens kept their mouths shut. Twice, though, insiders had reached out to Andreas (interestingly, both worked for Google), offering him dumps of internal email and algorithmic software that plainly revealed how the company stockpiled personal user data and actively filtered the information it claimed passively to reflect. In both cases, fearing what Google could do to him, Andreas had declined to upload the documents. To salvage his self-regard, he'd been honest with the leakers: "Can't do it. I need Google on my side."

Only in this one respect, though, did he consider himself an apparatchik. Otherwise, in interviews, he disdained the rhetoric of revolution, and he inwardly winced when his workers spoke of making the world a better place. From the example of Assange, he'd learned the folly of making messianic claims about his mission, and although he took ironic satisfaction in being famed for his purity, he was under no illusions about his actual capacity for it. Life with Annagret had cured him of that.

Three days after Tom Aberant had helped him bury the bones and rotted clothes of her stepfather in the lower Oder valley, he'd gone to Leipzig to look for her. He'd intended to go even sooner, but he was already much in demand for interviews with the Western press. Already, on the strength of his once having published a few naughty poems in *Weimarer Beiträge*, lived in a church basement, and blundered out of Stasi headquarters at the right moment, he was labeled PROMINENT EAST GERMAN DISSIDENT. Already, too, there were grumblings among the old embarrassments on Siegfeldstraße, mutterings that he'd done little but sleep with teenagers while the others were risking persecution. But none of them had a father on the Central Committee, none of them a résumé as sexy as the story of his acrostic poems, and by giving a dozen interviews back to back, always under the label of PROMINENT DISSIDENT (and always taking care to acknowledge the bravery of his Siegfeldstraße comrades), he made himself so much realer than the embarrassments that they had little choice but to accept the media's version. His fame soon changed even their memories of him.

Annagret didn't live with her sister in Leipzig, but the sister directed him to a teahouse frequented by feminists, a group until recently even more demoralized than environmentalists; polluted though it was, the Leipzig sky was less gray than the Republic's leadership was grayly male. It was two in the afternoon when he pushed open the tea-house's squeaky door. Annagret came out from the kitchen in back, wiping her hands on a dish towel.

Smile, Andreas thought.

She didn't smile. She looked around the room, which was empty. On the walls were a picture of Rosa Luxemburg, a poster celebrating Women of Heavy Industry, and slightly more daring images of Western female musicians and activists. Everything faded and filmed over with the sadness he'd once mistaken for ridiculousness. A Joan Baez tape played quietly.

"We don't have to talk now," he said. "I just want you to know I'm here."

"Now is fine," she said, not looking at him. "We may not have much to say."

"I have things to say."

She faintly smirked. " 'Good news.' "

"Yes, good news. Should I come back later?"

"No." She sat down at a table. "Just tell me your good news. I think I already know some of it. I saw you on TV."

"I know," he said, sitting down, "I'm an overnight sensation. And you didn't believe me when I said I was the most important person in the country. Do you remember that?"

"I remember that." She wouldn't look at him. "I remember everything. Do you?"

"Yes."

"Then why are you here?"

"Because we're safe now. We're safe and I love you."

She stared for a while at the tabletop. Then she nodded.

"Do you want to know why we're safe?"

"No," she said.

"I have the case files, and I've moved what needed to be moved."

She nodded again.

"You're not happy to hear that?"

"No."

"Why not?"

"Because of what we did."

"Annagret. Please look at me."

She shook her head, and he understood that the problem had never been that they weren't safe. The problem was that he reminded her of what he'd put her through.

"It's better if you just go," she said.

"I can't go," he said. "I can't imagine life without you."

Before she could reply, the front door squeaked open and two women came in, talking about the New Forum. Annagret jumped up and disappeared into the kitchen. Soon other regulars arrived, all women. Though they didn't seem actively hostile, Andreas felt like a foreign body in an organism quietly trying to rid itself of him. A midge in a watering eye.

A girl he recognized, the friend he'd seen with Annagret in Berlin two months ago, arrived and joined her in waiting tables. The friend asked him if he wanted anything.

"Nothing, thank you."

"I don't want to be rude," the friend said. "But maybe you should leave now."

"Yeah, OK."

"It's not personal. It's just the kind of place we are."

The midge was as relieved to be expelled as the watering eye was to expel it. Outside, in a cold drizzle, he considered taking the train back to Berlin and resuming his role as a PROMINENT EAST GERMAN DISSIDENT, giving Annagret more time to think. If Tom Aberant hadn't vanished on him, he might have done it. Having even one real friend, a friend who knew his secret and had volunteered to help him bury it forever, might have lessened the urgency of his need for Annagret. But Tom hadn't kept his date for dinner. Andreas had waited for hours for him to show up. The next day, returning from a round of interviews, he'd asked every person at the church whether an American had come around to look for him. He hadn't had the sense, not at all, that Tom was merely seducing him for journalistic purposes. Even if he was, it made no sense for him to disappear before Andreas had got him into the Stasi archives. The explanation had to be that Tom had gone home to his wife: he hadn't liked Andreas as much as he liked the woman he supposedly was sick to death of. The sting of this rejection was a measure of the swiftness and depth of the liking Andreas had taken to him. To be rejected by Annagret as well was simply not an option.

He went to the Leipzig train station and fished newspapers from trash cans and read them, feeling fortified when he saw his own name. Who could resist the temptation of believing one's own press? In the evening, he returned to the teahouse and waited outside until it went dark and Annagret and her friend were lowering its shutters.

"Go away," the friend said to him. "She doesn't want to see you."

"That sounds personal," he said.

"Yes, now it's personal."

"I have to go back to Berlin. There's a lot going on, and I need to be part of it. My name is Andreas, by the way."

"I know who you are. We saw you on TV."

"Annagret," he said. "I have to go back. Won't you at least take a walk with me?"

"She doesn't want to," the friend said.

"A short walk," he said. "We have some private family

things to talk about. The three of us can get together later on."

"All right," Annagret said suddenly, pulling away from the friend.

"Annagret—"

"He's not like the others. And he's right—there is a family thing."

Andreas noted, not for the first time, that she had some skill at lying. When he and she were alone, walking under umbrellas, she apologized for the friend. "Birgit is just very protective."

"She seems particularly good at keeping men away."

"I can do that myself. But it gets tiring, the constant attention. It's nice to have some help."

"The attention is that constant?"

"It's disgusting. It's actually been worse in Leipzig. Yesterday a guy pulled up next to me on his bike and asked me if I'd marry him."

Although Andreas would have liked to break the guy's nose, he couldn't help feeling proud of the testament to Annagret's beauty. "That's very hard," he said. "It's hard to be you."

"He didn't even know me."

They walked in silence for a while.

"The thing we did," she said. "I did it for you."

He was sorry to hear it, but also the opposite of sorry.

"I was out of my mind," she said. "I was crazy for you. And I did a thing that ruined my life, and now it's all I can think of when I see you. The thing I did for you."

"But I did what I did for you, too. I'd do it again right now. I'd do anything to protect you."

"Hmm."

"Come to Berlin with me. Leipzig is a shithole."

"You're not going to leave me alone, are you."

"There's no other way. We were meant to be together."

She stopped walking. No one else was on the sidewalk, and he'd already lost track of where they were. "The most terrible thing of all?" she said. "I like that you're a killer."

"I think I'm more than that."

"But that's the reason I'll go with you, if I go. Isn't that terrible?"

It did seem a little terrible, because only now, when she called him a killer, was he overcome with lust for her. He steeled himself against the urge to take her in his arms.

"We have to try to make amends," she said. "We have to do good things."

"Yes."

"Lots and lots of good things. Both of us."

"That's what I want. To be good with you."

"Oh God." A sob escaped her. "Please go back to Berlin. Please, An—"

She'd been about to say his name. He realized that he'd never heard her say it.

"Can you say my name?" he said, pursuing an instinct.

She shook her head.

"Just look at me and say my name. Then I'll go back to Berlin. I'll wait however long I have to."

She ran away from him. Suddenly, full speed, holding her umbrella to one side. He lost a few seconds in deciding to chase after her, and she was so young and so fleet, his judo girl, that he would never have caught up with her if she hadn't come to a red light and taken too sharp a turn at the corner. The drizzle must have frozen there. Her feet went out from under her, and it sickened him to see her fall.

She was still on the ground, clutching her hip, when he reached her.

"Are you all right?"

"No. Or actually, yes. I'm all right." And there it

was—the smile he'd longed to see. "You told me not to self-dramatize. Do you remember?"

"Yes."

"I remember everything. Every word."

He crouched down and took her cold hands in his and let her look into his eyes. He saw that he could have her. But instead of a symphony of joy and gratitude, he heard a horrid little voice of doubt: *Are you sure you really love her? No sooner does she chide herself for being self-dramatizing than she claims to remember every single word you ever said to her! She has no sense of humor— don't you think this might become oppressive?* He tried to deafen himself to the voice. She was, after all, uniquely beautiful. Two years ago, when he'd presented her with a menu of options that included murder, she'd picked murder. She was a good girl who was also dirty and a liar. Other men's interest disgusted her, but somehow his didn't. She knew he'd been bad and she wanted him anyway; was offering him a better life.

"Let's go to your place and pack your bags," he said.

"Birgit will hate me."

"Not as much as she hates me."

For two or three years, he was happy with her. She was very young and didn't know anything about anything, certainly not how to share a life with a man, and although he himself had never shared a life with a woman, he was older and she presumed that he knew everything. She had a way of gazing solemnly into his eyes while he was on top of her, inside her, completely having her, and the mere recollection of this gaze turned him on for reasons he was slow to understand. As long as her idealistic ardor lasted, he let her buy little things, bedspreads, earthenware mugs, lampshades, that he knew were ugly. He praised the dismal Indian meals she'd taught herself to cook. He took pleasure in watching her find her way in Berlin, making new friends and reuniting with old ones, joining collectives, going to work at a women's support services center. When they were out together, he felt proud, not oppressed, that she held him by the arm and never looked at any man but him. When they were at home, she was heartbreakingly eager to please. She seemed to have the idea that the more they made love, the more it confirmed that they were meant to be a couple and that she hadn't done a bad thing in succumbing to the killer of her stepfather. For two or three years, he was the happy beneficiary of this idea more nights than not.

But the problem with sex as an idea was that ideas could change. By and by, Annagret developed a different and much drearier idea, of total honesty in bed, with heavy emphasis on discussion. He indulged it at first, trying to be a good man, trying to live up to an ideal image that he, too, still had of himself, but there was finally no way around it: endless discussion with a humorless twenty-three-year-old bored him. During the day, when they were apart, he kept picturing her solemn gaze, but when he came home he found a person with no resemblance to the object he'd desired. She was tired, had cramps, had evening plans, some needy woman's hand to hold somewhere, some no-chance cause to organize another protest for. Or, even worse, wanted to discuss her feelings. Or, worst of all, wanted to discuss *his* feelings.

To escape domestic boredom, he attended overseas conferences, in Sydney and São Paulo and Sunnyvale. Besides his work on the Gauck Commission, administering the Stasi archives, he did transitional-justice consulting all over the former Eastern Bloc, sitting in overlit conference rooms identical in every respect but the languages on the mineral-water bottles from which unreconciled antagonists were pouring. Because reporters and cameras were so fond of him, he was starting to hear directly from

corporate and governmental whistle-blowers in reunified
Germany, and because committee work didn't suit his personality (he was singular, not collegial) he was thinking
about setting up on his own, becoming a clearinghouse
for secrets, omitting the committees and dealing directly
with the media. But his domestic problem, the disparity
between the nighttime object he desired and the daylight
actuality of Annagret, followed him everywhere. Even
when he was alone in a hotel room in Sydney, turned on
by the recollection of her solemn gaze, he had only to call
home and hear her voice for two minutes to be bored with
her. The boredom was immediate and overwhelming.
Whatever they were talking about was *wildly* irrelevant,
intolerably irrelevant, to what he wanted.

He saw that he'd trapped himself. He'd set up house
less with a woman than with a wishful concept of himself as a man who could live happily ever after with a
woman. And now he was bored with the concept. Although he never raised his voice with Annagret, he began to sulk and take offense at inoffensive things. He
made subtly mocking comments about her work and was
unfair to her female friends, whom he considered losers
and resented for exploiting the weak link of Annagret to
latch on to his fame. He gave lame excuses for avoiding
them, and when a social outing couldn't be avoided he was
alternately cold, silent, or insulting. He behaved like a jerk
and paid a price for it in self-regard, but he persisted in it,
hoping that she would recognize it as a well-known sign
of trouble in a relationship, and that maybe, eventually, he
would be able to escape the trap.

But she was relentlessly good to him. When she got
angry, it was rarely for long. She, who was otherwise a stal-
wart feminist, surrounded by man-distrusters, continued
to carve out an exception for him. She took his work seriously and gave him helpful advice. She washed the dirty

clothes and dishes he'd taken to leaving scattered around the flat. And the nicer she was, the more deeply he was trapped. Trapped by his gratitude for her high esteem and his fear of forfeiting it, trapped also by the early promises and avowals he'd made, the fuel with which he'd fired her idealism (and, for a while, his own). And because there were very few women who could top her combination of beauty and youth, and none at all from whom he wouldn't have had to conceal that he was a murderer, and because he was in any case already famous enough that word of an affair was liable to get back to Annagret and shatter her idealization of him, other women seemed foreclosed to him.

Completing his entrapment was Annagret's friendship with his mother. Back in 1990, after they'd set up house in Berlin and accustomed themselves to appearing in public together, unlearning the fear of incriminating themselves by doing so, he'd taken her to meet his parents. For the sake of his father, to whom he felt grateful and whose good opinion he prized, he ran the risk that his mother would be jealous of Annagret and cruel to her. But Katya was charming. She seemed to welcome Annagret's beauty, which made her a suitable Wolf ornament, and Annagret's youthful pliancy, which made Andreas's own hostility seem perverse. She wanted Annagret to go back to school, and when Annagret demurred, saying she preferred to roll up her sleeves and help other people, Katya gave her a wink and said, "We'll allow that. But you have to promise to attend my university instead. You can study with me in your free time, we'll work on your English, and everything you learn will be interesting. Believe me, I know where the boring things are." She winked again.

Instinctively alarmed by the proposal, Andreas took Annagret home and told her his worst Katya stories, the

ones he'd been holding back for fear that they'd reveal the
family sickness in him. Annagret listened earnestly and
said she liked Katya anyway. She liked her for having
given birth to him. She liked her—no matter what he
said—for obviously loving him as much as she did. And
he was still so new to the miracle of possessing Annagret's body, the miracle of feeling capable of love, that he
assented to the proposal. He managed to imagine that he
might solve the problem of Katya by farming it out to
Annagret.

Annagret's own mother was a disaster. As threatened,
she'd pushed the police to investigate her husband's
disappearance, but she was a known thief and drug addict,
fresh out of prison, and made a poor impression. The
police said honestly that the case file was lost and there
was little they could do except circulate her husband's
photograph. The mother tried to enlist the help of her
husband's widowed mother and learned that the Stasi,
two years earlier, had told his mother that he'd escaped to
the West; she was still waiting to hear from him. Soon
enough, Annagret's mother was using again. She came to
Annagret and Andreas and badgered them for money.
Annagret coldly suggested that her mother get sober and
look for work in a foreign country where nurses were in
short supply. Annagret's hatred of her was both genuine
and convenient, since it protected her from the guilt of
having had her husband murdered. The mother continued to harass them, turning up at their door to descant
on Annagret's ingratitude, until she succeeded in trading
her looks for drugs and lodging with a Polish carpenter
who also used.

Katya, by comparison, was an angel to Annagret. After
Andreas's father died, in 1993, she kept the old flat on
Karl-Marx-Allee. She'd resigned from the university and
endured a decent two-year interval of rehabilitation be-

fore resuming work as a *Privatdozent* and publishing a
book-length study of Iris Murdoch to admiring reviews.
She power walked eight kilometers every morning and
traveled often to London with her Lhasa apso, Lessing.
Annagret saw her at least once a week when she was in
Berlin. The arrangement that Andreas had envisioned,
whereby Annagret took over the distasteful job of keeping up family appearances, was working out much the
way he'd hoped—except that he became insanely jealous
of how close the two women were.

He hadn't seen this coming. Annagret's earnestness
was never more unbearable to him, their wrongness as a
couple never more evident, than on the evenings when she
was at his mother's. He blamed her both for liking his
mother and for being liked by her. And he had no acceptable outlet for his jealous rage. Even when they fought,
his voice merely became chalkily rational. She detested
this chalky voice, but it was effective in contrast to her
red-faced blurting: he was a good man, in firm control of
his temper and everything else. But if she happened to
stay at Katya's even half an hour later than expected, he
descended into a state of such eye-widened, heart-thudding
rage that all he could do was sit with his arms pressed to
his sides and try not to explode. It was so extreme that he
began to suspect there was something inside him, some
other self that had always been in him, that wasn't in other
people. Was very unusual and sick and particular to him.

This thing, which he came to think of as the Killer, was
like a neutrino or an esoteric boson, detectable only by
inference. Observing his subatomic self with rigorous
honesty, investigating the deep structure of his unhappiness, taking note of certain strange and evanescent fantasies, he slowly pieced together a theory of the Killer and
the paradoxical equivalencies and time-bendings that
characterized it. Boredom and jealous rage, for example,

were equivalent. Both had to do with the Killer's frustration at not getting its object of desire. The Killer was enraged with Katya for depriving him of the object and no less enraged with Annagret herself. And what was this object? According to his theory, it was the fifteen-year-old girl he'd killed for. He'd believed he was attracted to her goodness, for its potential to redeem him, but to the Killer she was a fellow killer and liar and seducer. Her solemn gaze turned him on because it took him back to the night behind his parents' dacha, to the body of the man whom she'd seduced and lied to and helped him kill. The more she became her own person, became his mother's friend and many other women's friend, the harder it was to see her as that fifteen-year-old.

Denied this particular satisfaction, he was prone to Killer-sponsored fantasies, some of them so offensive to his self-image (for example, the fantasy of coming on Annagret while she was sleeping) that it took a huge exertion of honesty to clock them before he suppressed them. All of the fantasies, without exception, involved darkness at night, the darkness at his parents' dacha, the darkness of a hallway down which he was eternally walking to a bedroom. In his subatomic self, no chronology was stable. The object he wanted predated the piercings, the hair choppings, the gauzy Indian smocks she'd taken to wearing, and not because he "secretly" preferred fifteen-year-olds (if he ever had, he'd outgrown it) but because it was Annagret the socialist judo girl who'd helped him kill. Had *made* him kill; was *equivalent* to killing. The older Annagret, who was going to absurdly altruistic lengths to atone for the murder, didn't suit the Killer's purposes one bit, and so the Killer, in its fantasies, reversed the arrow of time and made her fifteen again. And more than that: when he examined certain fantasies closely, it was sometimes not he but her stepfather who walked down the dark hallway to the bedroom where she was sleeping. He was at once the man he'd killed and the man who'd killed him, and since another dark hallway existed in his memory, the dark hallway between his childhood bedroom and his mother's, there was a further twisting of chronology whereby his mother had given birth to the monster who was Annagret's stepfather, he was that monster, and he'd killed him in order to become him. In the shadowy world of the Killer, nobody was ever dead.

He would have loved not to believe in his theory, would have loved to lump it with the mumbo-jumbo of contemporary physics and dismiss it, but the thing he loved most about himself was his refusal to lie to himself, and no matter how busy he got and how much he traveled, there always seemed to come another night when he found himself alone at home, in the grip of a homicidal rage that he had no other way of explaining.

On one such night, Annagret returned from his mother's with an especially earnest look on her face. He was sitting on the sofa, not even pretending to be reading something. It was all he could do not to punch a wall; it was that bad.

"I thought you were coming home at nine," he managed to say.

"We got to talking about things," Annagret said. "I asked her about the fifties, what the country was like then. She told me all sorts of interesting things. But then—this is very strange. It's important. Do you mind talking to me now?"

He could feel her looking at him, and he willed his lips to curl upward, to smile. "Of course not."

"Have you eaten?"

"Not hungry."

"I'll make us some noodles later." She sat down on the sofa by him. "Your mother was talking about your father's career, how brilliant he was, how busy he was. And then suddenly she stopped and said, 'I had a lover.'"

The rage inside him was titanic. How to keep from exploding? What a relief exploding was. How excellent it must have been for him to crush a man's skull with a shovel. If only he could recall—reexperience—the relief of doing that! He couldn't recall it. But the thought of it slightly calmed him; gave him something to hold on to.

"That's interesting," he murmured.

"I know. I couldn't believe she was telling me. You said she's always claimed it never happened. I was too afraid to ask her to say more about it, and she didn't. Just 'I had a lover.' And then she changed the subject. But then she kept looking at me, I don't know, like she wanted to make sure I'd noticed what she'd said."

"Mm."

"But listen. Andreas. I know we can't tell anyone our secret. I know that. But I see her so often, she's in her seventies, she is your mother. I had an impulse to tell her, and the impulse felt right. She would never tell anyone else, I'm sure of it. Do you think it's all right if I tell her?"

He didn't think so, not one bit. That Annagret could even imagine telling Katya! Previously unguessed vistas of female closeness opened up to his mind's eye. Katya having her way with him by way of pliant Annagret. Annagret so credulous, so earnest, so ready to betray him. Coming home at ten thirty when she'd promised to be home by nine—so many hours with Katya. Talking, talking, talking. Cunts, cunts, cunts. He was out of his mind.

"Are you out of your mind?" he said.

"No, I'm not," she said, immediately on guard. "And she isn't, either. I actually think she's better. I know she was difficult when you were little, but that was a long time ago."

She knew? *Difficult?* She didn't know. Nobody could

know what having Katya as a mother had been like. What it was like to be psychically fucked with, day after day, and to be not only too young and weak to fight it but unable even to be angry, because she'd seduced him into wanting it. Annagret had wanted it from her stepfather for a week or two, a month at most. Andreas had wanted it throughout his childhood. And yet again he was trapped, because, unlike Annagret, he hadn't been physically raped. He had to live with the possibility that there had never been anything so monstrous about Katya. Her version of reality was seamless, especially in old age, her youthful peccadilloes now forgotten or rendered harmless by a nice French word like *lover*. She'd always insisted that the disturbance was in him, not her; that it was sick of him not to believe she was a good and loving mother. And indeed it was he who'd been sitting for hours in a jealous rage, waiting for the ladies to finish with their cozy chat.

"It can be a relief to confess things," Annagret said. "Sometimes I think you forget that you got to confess to your father. I don't get to confess to *anyone*."

COULD KILL HER WITH BARE HANDS RIGHT NOW

"Once you start confessing," he said chalkily.

"What?"

"Where does it stop?"

"I'm saying we tell *one* person. Your own mother. Don't you want to? Your father was very understanding, and you felt better. I bet your mother would be all the more understanding, because she knows what it's like to make mistakes."

Suddenly his mind changed temperature, as minds will do. In a cooler state, he imagined his mother knowing what they'd done. Katya was truly the last person in the world he had reason to be ashamed in front of, Katya who to him was vileness personified, and yet he imagined himself ashamed of being a killer. Ashamed of everything, every particle of himself, right up to this moment. Strangle his sweet judo girl to silence her? What was wrong with him?

Without looking at her face, he rotated toward her and buried his own face in her chest. He swung his legs up onto her lap and hung his arms around her neck. He looked like that stupid picture of John Lennon in Yoko's arms but who cared. He needed to be held. She was better than good, because she hadn't always been good. Had known badness and chosen goodness.

"I'm sorry," she whispered, stroking his hair, babying him. "I didn't mean to upset you."

"Shh."

"Are you all right?"

"Shh, shh."

"What is it?"

"We can't tell her," he said.

"We can, though. We should."

"Please, no. We can't."

He began to cry. The Killer stirred in him again, sensing opportunity in his tears, his regression. The Killer liked regression. The Killer liked it when he was four and Annagret fifteen. Blindly, with his eyes squeezed shut, he sought her lips with his. For a moment, hers were open and available, but then, as if she were prey, instinctively sensing a Killer she couldn't see, she averted her face. "We have to finish discussing this," she said.

Discuss, discuss, discuss. Talk, talk, talk. He hated her. Needed her, hated her, needed her, hated her. Eyes still shut, he tried to kiss her again.

"I'm serious," she said, trying to stand up. "Get off my lap."

He got off her lap and opened his eyes. "Go to a priest," he said.

"What?"

"If you want to confess. Find a Catholic church, go to the confessional, say what you have to say. You'll feel better."

"I'm not Catholic."

"I can't stop you from seeing her, but I don't like it."

"She worships you! You're practically her Jesus."

"She worships what she sees in a mirror. We're just useful objects to her. The more you tell her, the more she can use us."

"I'm sorry, but I think you're very wrong."

"Fine. I'm wrong. But I can't keep living with you if you tell her what we did."

Her face went red. "Then maybe we shouldn't live together!"

"Maybe not. Maybe you should live with her instead."

"I'm trying to have a close relationship with your mother, because you can't do it. I'm doing you a big favor, and now you're jealous!"

"I'm not jealous."

"I think you are."

"Not true. Not true."

Everything she said was accurate, every word of his a lie. And yet he was a well-paid transitional-justice consultant, and everywhere he went people were happy to see him. They fawned over his honesty and openness, they laughed at his irreverent humor, they took flattering pictures of him. He was trapped from all sides.

Meanwhile the leaks kept coming, in plain brown envelopes and cartons without return addresses. Being German, and East German at that, he was technologically conservative and still thought in terms of paper documents and physical computer disks. As late as the summer of 2000, he shared a home computer and email address with Annagret. She, with her community-organizing, her fringe causes, was the tech-savvy one. More and more often, he came home to find her typing and clicking away, in her absurdly limber posture on a chair, knees drawn up to her chin, arms reaching around them, a tea mug by her computer mouse, and thought: *My God, is this the rest of my life?* To the Killer in him, it seemed as if she'd armed herself with the Internet to defend herself against the person he really was. There was no prying her away from it.

But then she did him a seemingly lifesaving favor. She made him buy his own powerful computer and take full advantage of it. Which he proceeded to do. By night, he developed a network of malcontents and hackers and created the Sunlight Project; by day, while Annagret was off holding hands at her community center, he viewed pornography. It was really the latter more than the former that sold him on the Internet and its world-altering potential. The sudden wide availability of porn, the anonymity of access, the meaninglessness of copyright, the instantaneity of gratification, the scale of the virtual world within the real world, the global dispersion of file-sharing communities, the sensation of mastery that mousing and clicking brought: the Internet was going to be huge, especially for bringers of sunlight.

It was only much later, when the Internet had come to signify *death* to him, that he realized he'd also been glimpsing *death* in online porn. Every compulsion, certainly his own viewing of digital images of sex, which quickly became day-devouringly compulsive, smacked of death in its short-circuiting of the brain, its reduction of personhood to a closed loop of stimulus and response. But there was also already, in the days of file-transfer protocols and "alt" newsgroups, a sense of the unfathomable vastness that would characterize the mature Internet and the social media that followed it; in the uploaded images of somebody's wife sitting naked on a toilet, the charac-

teristic annihilation of the distinction between private and
public; in the mind-boggling *number* of wives sitting naked on toilets, in Mannheim, in Lübeck, in Rotterdam, in
Tampa, a premonition of the dissolution of the individual
in the mass. The brain reduced by machine to feedback
loops, the private personality to a public generality: a
person might as well have been already dead.

And death, of course, was catnip to the Killer. The images on the screen of his computer distracted him from
thoughts of dark hallways and secret defilements, and for
a while he believed that he'd found a way to make life with
Annagret livable in the long run. He could preserve his
ideal self in his own eyes by remaining mindful of the
male exploitation of women he was witnessing on his
screen, deploring it even as it stimulated him, and then,
after discharging his urges, he could preserve the ideal in
Annagret's eyes as well. To paraphrase Frank Zappa, she'd
thought it was a man she wanted, but instead it was a muf-
fin. Maybe she was punishing him for forbidding her to
confess their crime to Katya, or maybe it was gender politics or maybe just the normal course of things, but she
seemed not to care if they ever had sex again. What she
wanted—explicitly asked for, in her concept-heavy way—
was *closeness* and *togetherness*. These could be achieved
by cuddling, and Andreas, with his needs met elsewhere,
was fine with cuddling. The Internet had made it easier
for both of them to be like children.

It took him half a year to realize that, far from escaping, he'd trapped himself more deeply. He believed that if
he couldn't make a life work with beautiful Annagret,
wedded to her by their secret and by his old hope of re-
demption, he'd never again muster enough hope to make
a life work with anyone. To leave her would be to admit
that something had always been wrong with him. But
something *was* wrong with him. He was even more of a

compulsive masturbator now than he'd been as a teenager. Repetition was objectively boring but he couldn't stop it. The right-thinking incantations that had worked for a while, his scrupulous efforts to imagine the circumstances under which a teenage girl would permit three thuggish Russian men to ejaculate on her face in front of a camera, and to feel compassion for such a girl, no longer worked. What happened in the virtual world, where beauty existed for the purpose of being hated and besmirched, was more compelling than what happened in the real world, where beauty seemed to have no purpose at all. He became afraid of being touched by Annagret. He took a deep breath whenever he saw it coming, so that he wouldn't flinch. Closeness and togetherness were precisely what he couldn't bear now, and it was all the more desperately important that she not find this out and leave him in disgust. Without her idealization, there was no hope for him. He began to wonder if suicide, his own death, was what the Killer really wanted.

Although he knew the Killer was his enemy, he could never quite bring himself to hate it. Whenever he tried to tell himself that he hated it, his mind took a step back and saw that he was lying: he didn't honestly want to be anything but exactly who he was. This was especially evident in the lack of guilt he felt about killing Horst Kleinholz. He was never able to wish he hadn't done it. Indeed, when he was being fully honest with himself, he was immensely glad he had. And the same was true of the afternoons he spent jerking off at his powerful computer. He condemned what he was doing by the principles he wanted to believe in, but he could never hate it in the moment. Instead he resented Annagret, resented his own moral considerations, resented his other responsibilities, for standing in the way of his compulsion. And yet it was complicated, because when his watchful self stepped back from the computer over which he was hunched with his pants around his ankles, he hated what he saw. He wasn't constituted to hate himself subjectively, but he did hate the object he was in the world. The shameful, loathsome object with which something was very wrong. And it was beginning to occur to him that Annagret and his mother might be better off without that object; that he should have chosen a higher bridge to jump from as a teenager.

In something near desperation, he wrote a letter to Tom Aberant. Over the years, he and Tom had kept up a postcard correspondence. Tom's cards had the wry American tone that Andreas had liked in him, but they lacked the confessional warmth that had incited him to make his own confession. In his letter, he tried to revive the warmth. He said he now understood what had happened in Tom's marriage; he mentioned, with what he hoped was self-deprecating humor, that he was somewhat overly preoccupied with Internet porn; he pretended he had business that might soon take him to New York. It shouldn't have been hard for Tom to read between the lines and discern a plea for help. But the postcard Tom sent in reply was wry and distant and contained no invitation to New York.

It fell to Andreas's mother, of all people, to rescue him. At her invitation, he went to her flat for lunch on a rainy September Friday, four days before Al Qaeda's masterstroke. He was late because he'd found it necessary to experience orgasm one more time before he left, to bring himself as low as he could. Depression could be a sort of narcotic, dulling the impulse to argue with Katya and contradict her. The less he said to her, the better. Best of all would have been not to have lunch with her, but she'd told him that they needed to discuss Annagret's future privately. She'd hinted that it had to do with drawing up a new will.

Naturally, this turned out to have been a lie. At her flat, while she was setting out the prepared foods she'd bought at the Galeria, Andreas asked her, dully, about her will.

"I didn't invite you here to talk about my will," she said. "That's my own business."

He sighed. "I only asked because you mentioned it when you called me."

"The two things were not related. I'm sorry if you thought they were."

The narcotic was working. He didn't argue.

"You look so tired," she said.

"Life in the computer age."

When they sat down to eat, her little dog came over to her. She smiled at Andreas. "We go through the same charade at every meal."

"Which charade is that?"

"The charade of withholding and discipline."

"I remember it well."

"Lessing," she said to the dog. "Begging does not become you."

The dog barked and put its paws on her linen-clad thigh.

"It's terrible," she said. "It's as if I'm her pet, not the other way around." She gave the dog a morsel of roast potato. "Be happy with that potato," she told it. "That's all you're getting."

"So," Andreas said, "I'm not very hungry, and I have a lot of work to do."

"Yes, all right. Silly me for thinking you might spend a few hours with your only parent."

"You know you'd rather read about me than experience me in person. Why pretend?"

The dog had its paws on her thigh again. She gave it more potato.

"I'll come to the point," she said. "I'm concerned about Annagret."

Dulled though he was, spent though he was, it occurred to him that if the lunch were a short one he might still have some free hours with his computer before Annagret came home. There was certainly nothing to like about the real world he was inhabiting.

"Andreas," Katya said. "I think she might have to leave you."

"Excuse me?"

"You know how fond I've always been of her—almost as if she were my own daughter. In a sense, she's *been* my daughter. She really doesn't have another mother."

"So—what? I've been sleeping with my sister?"

"Leave it to you to have a thought like that and say it out loud. You know that's not what I meant. I meant that we've become very close."

"I've noticed."

"And I also know *you* better than anyone else in the world does."

"So you like to say."

"I never worry about what will happen to you. You're a dominant person, born to dominate, and everyone can sense it. You can do whatever you want, and somehow the world will find a way to love you for it. You've been extraordinary since the day you were born."

He pictured this extraordinary, dominant person forty-five minutes earlier, pants down, whacking away. "So you like to say," he said.

"Well, Annagret isn't like you. She's bright but not brilliant. She admires you but isn't like you. And I'm afraid—I can only assume—that she's decided she doesn't belong with a person so brilliant and dominant. There's no other explanation. And—" Katya's face hardened. "I hate to say this. But I think she's right."

"Do go on," Andreas said.

"We're speaking in confidence."

"Of course."

"Lessing—" She gave an entire pork cutlet to the dog, which scampered away with it. "Are you happy now?" she called after it mockingly.

"It's becoming less of a mystery how you stay so trim," Andreas said.

"Annagret confessed something to me."

He felt light-headed.

"I promised her I wouldn't tell you. I'm breaking that promise now, but I won't apologize for it. *Those that betray them do no treachery.*" Katya was quoting something in English. "Besides which, I think she knew I would tell you. She said it was weighing on her conscience—but why tell *me*? She knows very well that I'm your mother."

He frowned.

"She isn't right for you, Andreas. I thought I would be the last person ever to say that. But she's not right, and I'm very angry with her now. In a sense, she betrayed me, too."

"What exactly are we talking about?"

"I'm sure there are strains in your life with her. No couple can live for ten years without any strains at all. But look at you!" She sized him up with a fanatical blaze in her eyes. "She shouldn't love anyone but you!"

There seemed to be no end to the ways his mother could disturb him. He kept thinking that he must have seen it all, that she'd finally exhausted her supply. But there was always more.

"Annagret thinks better of me than I deserve," he said quietly. "I'm not an entirely well person."

"I can only imagine what she was thinking, but she appears to be in some sort of relationship with a woman at her community center. I don't know how far it's gone, but

obviously it's far enough that she needed to confess it—
to me. Well, I didn't know what to say. I asked her if she
thought she might be a lesbian. She said she didn't think
she was. It didn't really make sense, what she was saying,
but I gather that the woman is older and they have some
sort of friendship-that's-more-than-just-friendship. She
kept using the phrase *a special kind of closeness*, whatever that means. And she wanted me—me!—to tell her
what it meant."

He knew the person in question. "The woman's name
is Gisela?"

"Andreas, I've been studying literature my entire life.
I know a thing or two about human psychology. What I'm
seeing is that Annagret isn't right for you and she knows
it. But I'm not the one to tell her that. In fact, I'm not sure
I ever need to see her again."

If Katya was to be believed (admittedly a big if), Annagret had given him an amazing gift, a deus ex machina,
a way out of the trap. But he was wary of it. It seemed as
if Annagret knew more about him than he'd realized, and
was disgusted by him, and had consciously gone to someone else for what he wasn't giving her. Would she feel
guilty enough to keep her mouth shut after she was free
of him?

"People have affairs all the time," he said. "You had
affairs and stayed married. It doesn't have to mean anything."

"If you were the one doing it," Katya said, "it wouldn't
necessarily mean anything. You have the soul of an artist, beyond good and evil. But she's too small for you. She
knows it. She's said it to me herself, how hard it is to live
in your shadow."

"I haven't seen any sign of that."

"She wouldn't tell you. She did tell me. And she turned
for comfort to this special friend of hers, and she told me

about that, too. You're gifted at math—you tell *me* what two plus two is."

"This is so sick. That we're having this conversation."

"I'm sorry. I know how much you care about her. But I really don't think I need to see her anymore. My loyalty is to you, not to the person who finds it necessary to betray you."

He stood up and walked away from the table. If Katya was to be believed, Annagret blamed herself and still idealized him. The exit door was open wide. But all at once he felt terribly sorry for her. That she still revered him and considered herself small by comparison and had been so lonely that she crawled to Gisela: he felt restored to the sweet compassion he'd experienced in the church sanctuary on Siegfeldstraße, and with it to all the hope he'd invested in Annagret, to the innocence of his yearning to be a better person, before he'd descended into filth and doubt. His darling lost judo girl.

"Andreas," his mother said softly.

He turned to her, struggling not to cry. "It was *wrong* of you to tell me."

"Nothing a person does out of love can be wrong."

"Wrong! Wrong!"

He fled through the front door, past the elevator, and into the stairwell, where he could sob without fear of being discovered by his mother. It was years since there had been a shred of evidence that he was happy with Annagret. Everything about his miserable existence, down to the rawly chafed dick in his underpants at this very moment, argued against them. He couldn't be any more miserable without her than he already was, and she'd be happier without him, too. But none of this lessened his grief. He'd never experienced grief like this. It seemed as if he really loved her after all.

Grief passed, however. Before he was even home again,

he could see his future. He would never again make the mistake of trying to live with a woman. For whatever reason (probably his childhood), he wasn't suited for it, and the strong thing to do was to accept this. His computer had made a weakling of him. He also had a vague, shameful memory of climbing onto Annagret's lap and trying to be her baby. Weak! Weak! But now his mother, with her meddling, had given him the pretext he needed to be free of both her and Annagret. A double deus ex machina—the good luck of a man fated to dominate. It was ironic, of course, that the person who'd recalled him to his stronger self and made his weakness visible to him was Katya. Ironic that, although she was a liar, he'd recognized the truth of her description of him. Ironic that he would owe his new freedom to her. But this didn't make her meddling any less despicable. She'd played herself out of any future with him.

At home, he cleansed his hard drive of downloaded obscenity. His new sense of purpose and sobriety felt well worth the compulsive binge it had cost him to attain it. He washed the dishes in the sink and dried them. He saw that he would soon be bringing other women to wherever he lived, one after another—the repetition of a strong man—and that his new place would have to be clean and orderly, to signify self-mastery.

He was sitting straight-backed at the computer, bringing self-mastery to bear on his email queue, when Annagret came home with some dismal "bio" vegetables in a string bag.

"I'm only here to change clothes," she said. "We have a protest for the rent strikers."

"That's fine," he said. "But sit down for a minute first."

She sidled into the living room and perched on the edge of a chair and fixed her eyes on the floor. It seemed to him that she was radiating guilt. Interesting that he hadn't perceived it sooner. He'd carefully thought through the wording of what he had to say to her, but now that it was time to say it, he hesitated. He still had grief in him, and he wondered if he shouldn't be saying something very different with his newly regained sense of command: *Enough bullshit, enough cuddling. Strip naked for me. We're going to do things differently now.* Conceivably she might welcome it; conceivably it could save them. But more likely she'd refuse, which would hurt him and shame him, and there were, in any case, many other women to whom he could speak like that. Their appeal, too, was perceptible in a way it hadn't been before.

"We're not happy together," he said.

She bowed her head and shifted uncomfortably. "It's been difficult lately, I know. We haven't been so close. I know that. But . . ."

"I know about you and Gisela."

She blushed intensely, and he felt another surge of compassion for her, but also, for the first time, anger. She'd betrayed him, just as Katya had said. Until this moment, he hadn't been angry at all.

"Go to her," he said coldly. "Stay with her. I'll find another place to live."

She bowed her head further. "It's not what you think . . ."

"I don't care what it is. It's just a pretext anyway. We shouldn't be together."

"But who told you?"

"People come to me with dirt. It's my job to know things."

"Did Katya tell you?"

"Katya? No. It doesn't matter anyway. Do you honestly like being with me?"

It was a while before she answered. "It used to be

better," she said, "when we felt closer . . . I think you're a good person . . . A great person. It's just . . ."

"What?"

"Sometimes I wonder why you wanted to be with me in the first place."

Hearing this, the Killer in him became alert.

"You were the one who said we had to be together," she said. "I knew in my heart that it was wrong. I thought there was a way for us to not be so guilty, if we stayed apart, but as soon as we got together it meant we'd been guilty from the beginning."

"I was in love with you. I made a mistake."

"I was in love with you, too. But it was never right, was it."

"No."

She began to cry. "And now we'll never get over what we did."

"Not as long as we stay together."

"I'm so tired of living with it. I'm sorry I did this new bad thing, it's not even what you think. I guess I thought, 'I'm guilty anyway—what does it matter what I do?'"

"It's good you did it. I wouldn't have had the guts."

He wondered if he should go ahead and mention the computer now, make a clean breast of his own transgressions and give her some consoling company in her guilt. But the Killer said no. The Killer had only one objective now: to make sure she never had moral cause to betray him by telling someone else about the killing. Although it pained him to see her crying and apologizing, it was also reassuring. She still suffered from a sense of worthlessness for having wanted Horst, for having been abused, and even as Andreas was pitying her for this he was savoring his coming freedom. The sweet freedom of getting away with everything, of never having to see her

dowdy and earnest friends again, of never having to have
another discussion.

"We could have spent ten years in prison," he said. "Instead we spent ten years together. Maybe that was our
prison. Maybe we've served our sentence. You're only
twenty-eight—you can do whatever you want now."

"You're right. It did start to feel like prison. It . . . Oh!
I'm sorry!"

"Things will be better when you're out of it."

"I'm sorry!"

"Don't be sorry. Just go. Go to your protest."

The grief returned when she was gone. He welcomed
it, almost luxuriated in it, because it was a real emotion,
untainted by doubt about his secret motives. Like the
compassion it grew out of, it suggested that there might
not, after all, be anything so wrong with him. Maybe, if
he took care never to live with another woman, he could
succeed in living up to the image other people had of
him. Maybe the Killer had been merely a figment, a pro-
jection of his embattled but still fundamentally sound
moral sense, an artifact of the misfortune that the love of
his life was also the person with whom he'd committed a
murder. A misfortune, certainly. But maybe it was enough
to explain his vile feelings, his rage, his jealousy, his
radical doubt, his sick urges. Maybe, with self-mastery,
he could put all that behind him now.

After the planes hit New York and Washington, Annagret ran home to make sure he was OK. This was irrational but not unusual that day; there was a sense that
with crazy things happening in America they could be
happening anywhere, to anyone. But he and Annagret had
been growing apart for so long that when the thread of
togetherness was snapped they elastically sprang even
farther apart, finding themselves with no friends or even
any interests in common. All he had left, really, was the

sentimental and periodically grief-inducing conviction that she had been the love of his life.

Cutting the cord with Katya wasn't as easy. He deleted her phone messages without listening to them, and when she came to him in person he closed his door in her face and threw the bolt loudly; a week later, he moved to a new and more secure flat in Kreuzberg. But it wasn't hard to find his phone number, and later in the fall, after he'd been in the headlines for breaking the news of German computer sales to Saddam Hussein, one of his first big Internet leaks, he got a call from a man who said he had a document of interest to him.

"If it's paper, put it in the mail," Andreas said. "If it's digital, email it to me."

The caller had a Berlin accent and vocal cords that sounded slack with age. "I'd prefer to bring it to you in person."

"No. As you might imagine, I have some fear for my personal safety these days."

"I'm not bringing you a bomb. Just a document. It concerns you personally."

"Mail it."

"I'm not sure you understand. The revelations in this document refer to you personally."

Andreas didn't know who besides Tom Aberant could still expose his old crime. Captain Wachtler, who'd brought him his files at Stasi headquarters, was long dead—Andreas had used his position on the Gauck Commission to track the downward progress of Wachtler's health—but there were an indeterminate number of nameless functionaries above and below him on the old chain of command. They would all be older men with Berlin accents. It was possible that he was speaking to one of them now.

"What exactly do you want?" he said as levelly as he could.

"I want you to help me publish the document."

"Even though it concerns me."

"Yes."

Andreas agreed to meet the caller at the Amerika Haus library, where security was heavy. The man he found waiting there, the following afternoon, had a handsome, ruined, clean-shaven drinker's face. He looked to be in his late sixties and was dressed in tired Beatnik garb, a red turtleneck, a leather-elbowed corduroy blazer. Emphatically not former Stasi. There was a briefcase in front of him on the library table.

"So we meet again," he said, with a smile, when Andreas was seated across from him.

"We've met?"

"I was younger. I had a beard. I'd spent a week sleeping under a bridge."

Andreas never would have recognized him.

"How are you, my son?" his father said.

"Not so bad, until this moment."

"I've been following your exploits. I hope you won't mind that I've permitted myself some pride in you. Pride and a certain gloating satisfaction, given that the last time we met, you were so uninterested in learning secrets. How the world turns, eh? Now secrets are your business."

"I'm aware of the irony. What do you want?"

"Some occasional contact with you wouldn't be unwelcome."

How to explain the distaste he felt at the prospect? It wasn't just the red turtleneck, the elbow patches. It was that he sided with the memory of his other father. "Not interested," he said.

His father's smile became more pained. "Of course you're an arrogant son of a bitch. You grew up privileged, everything's always gone your way. How could you be anything else?"

"That pretty well sums it up."

"You're still on good terms with your mother, I suppose?"

"Hardly."

"It's shocking how little she's changed."

"You've seen her?"

"Through her doorway, briefly."

"What do you want?"

His father opened his briefcase and took out a manuscript three fingers thick. "You're not curious," he said. "But I can tell you that not everything has gone my way. I was sent back to prison. Got out again and drove a taxicab until the Stasi was no more. Married a girl who was kind but a drinker. Became quite a drinker myself. I'm sober now—thank you for asking. I have a son—another son—with serious congenital disabilities. My wife took care of him until she died, two years ago. Our boy is in a facility now, not a very nice one, but the best I could manage. After the Turn, I was able to get work teaching English to eighth and ninth graders. I have a bit of a pension now from that, but mostly I live on federal charity."

"That's a tough story," Andreas said with feeling. "I'm sorry."

"Not your responsibility. I didn't come here to accuse you. I'm sure it wasn't easy having Katya as a mother. I was destroyed after only six years of her. Or, no, that's not fair. I was crazy about her the whole time. The side of her she'd never show a child was really something."

"I think I saw some of that side."

"She's sublime in her way. But, of course, she also destroyed me."

"So . . ."

With a trembling hand, his father pushed the manuscript across the table. "In my retirement, I've taken to writing. This is my memoir. Have a look."

The Crime of Love. By Peter Kronburg. Andreas was sorry to see his father's name. Without a name, his existence had been conveniently spectral.

"I want you to read it," Peter Kronburg said. "It won't be a chore—I'm a good, clear writer. Your mother always said so."

"No doubt. And presumably there are detailed scenes of sex with her? The very title seems to promise it."

Peter Kronburg reddened slightly. "Only as pertinent to a larger story about the private life of the Central Committee."

"My mother wasn't on it."

"Her husband was. The descriptions of sex stay within bounds of good taste, and that's only half the book anyway. The rest is about prison and socialist 'justice.'"

"And me. You said it pertained to me."

Peter Kronburg reddened further. "At the end, I tell the story of our first meeting, and I admit that I've mentioned this aspect in my inquiries to publishers. I'm told it's important to describe a potential marketing plan in the query letter."

"*The untold story of Wolf's sordid origins.* And you want my help?"

"With your name attached to the marketing plan, I believe the book could be a bestseller. I have a disabled son to provide for when I'm gone. The book simultaneously partakes of *Ostalgie* and represents a searing critique of it. We're at a perfect historical moment for publishing it."

"It's astonishing that you haven't created a bidding war."

Peter Kronburg shook his head. "I get the same answer again and again. It seems that every publisher already has too many East memoirs coming out. Only one publisher even asked to see the manuscript, and some very young-sounding woman sent it back with the comment that it wasn't enough about *you*."

Andreas was feeling sad for his father. For his smallness in relation to the largeness of his son. For his grasping after the main chance from a position of marginality, his talk of a *marketing plan*. It was heartbreaking to see old Ossis trying to ape the thinking of Wessis, trying to master the lingo of capitalist self-promotion.

"*I met my son a second time, at the Amerika Haus library*," Andreas said. "This meeting itself could be the coda to your book."

Peter Kronburg shook his head again. "The purpose of the book isn't to shame you. I'm not angry at you. At your mother, at your father, at the Stasi, yes. But not at you. Unless you care about protecting Katya, the book won't hurt you in the slightest. Quite the contrary, I think."

"How does that work?"

"As I understand it, your own marketing plan is sunlight. If you endorse the book, if you help me present it to publishers again—to high-level editors, not frightened twenty-three-year-olds—you'll demonstrate that no secret is so sacred that you won't expose it. You'll be even more famous. Your legend will only grow."

And yours along with it, Andreas thought. Maybe his father wasn't quite as clueless as he'd imagined. Not quite so different from him. Maybe not different at all, just less lucky.

"And if I don't help you?" he said. "You'll go to *Stern* and tell them I'm a hypocrite?"

"I'm doing this for my son—my other son—and for justice. And I'm not sure that justice is so important at this point. It isn't news to anyone that the Stasi and people like your parents were evil. But in the world that's come after them, money is very important."

"I have no money for you."

"I suspect in time you will."

Andreas riffled the dot-matrixed pages of the manuscript. His eye fell on the sentence *She was a wildcat on her hands and knees*. No need to read any more of that. But he was curious, a little bit, about the red-turtlenecked man across the table from him. Had he always been on the make? Had he imagined that he could ride Katya's coattails, as her lover, to power and prestige within the socialist system? To be sent to prison as a state-subverter wasn't an *injustice* if you really were a state-subverter. Injustice was to have been an apparatchik and not received your promised reward.

"I won't give you money," he said. "I don't want to see you again, either. I buried my father, and I don't need another one. But I'll read the book and do what I can."

With evident emotion, Peter Kronburg extended a trembling hand across the table. Andreas grasped the hand, as a parting gift to him. Then he took the manuscript and left without another word.

A decade earlier, he'd carefully read his own Stasi file. It was mostly tedious, because he'd never been the target of a full operation, but there were some surprises. At least two of the fifty-three "at-risk" girls he'd slept with had been unofficial collaborators, confounding his theory that the Stasi rarely employed females and never such young ones. One of the informants had reported that he told inappropriate jokes at the expense of the state, sowed disrespect for Scientific Socialism among his counselees, and exploited his church authority to prey on them sexually; that after *endeavoring to gain his more complete trust by submitting to relations with him* and discovering that he had *aberrant sexual tendencies* (by which she'd presumably meant that he preferred eating her state-subverting pussy to kissing her state-sanctioned mouth), she'd feigned a strong interest in environmental activism; and that he'd laughed and said *the only green thing that interested him was pickles*. It turned out that this informant had been twenty-two; he remembered only her name, not her face. The other one, whom he remembered better, had been legitimately seventeen. She'd reported that he didn't *fraternize with other antisocial elements at the church*, didn't *encourage questioning of the guiding principles of Marxist-Leninist thought*, and *presented himself as a monitory example of the consequences of frivolously counterrevolutionary behavior*. Not coincidentally, she'd had no complaints about the sex, either.

The other small surprise in his file was that, until September 1989, his mother had received a visit from the Stasi on the first Friday of every month, simply to attest that she'd had no contact with her son. The reports on those visits, of which there were more than a hundred, were brief and basically identical, except that for the first three years they'd included annotations, typed on a different typewriter, confirming that the wiretap on her office telephone was negative for communication with AW. On the first report without an annotation, someone had scrawled *telephonic monitoring of KW suspended at request of Undersecy W.*

Andreas had been moved, in spite of himself, to learn of the extent to which Katya herself had been oppressed by the Stasi. He could never quite blind himself to the many ways in which she was a victim—of her own mental instability, of parents who'd dragged her back to the Republic instead of leaving her in England, of a secret police that had exiled and possibly killed those parents, of a husband she didn't love but was compelled to obey, of a system that stifled her native brilliance, of a lover who'd come back to Berlin to turn her son against her, and, finally, of that son himself. Mostly he hated her, but the potential for compassion continued to lurk in him.

Compassion for the broken, lost, victimized girl she'd been. Sometimes he even wondered if he'd seen a young Katya in the fifteen-year-old Annagret; if this was the real idea behind his idea of her.

As he carried Peter Kronburg's manuscript home to his flat, his compassion was afoot. Although he could see that Kronburg was right, that getting *The Crime of Love* published might help his own career, he could also see that he wasn't going to read it himself. Partly he felt squeamish, but mostly he felt protective. The few friends Katya had nowadays were Brits and old Wessis—she wanted nothing to do with *Ostalgie*—and she would probably lose them if they read the book. Even in an era of forgive and forget, collaborating to put an innocent man in prison for ten years, as she must have done, could not, once remembered, be so easily forgiven. The proud mother of the Bringer of Sunlight would become the reviled mother.

And so, although he'd vowed to himself not to, he went to see her one more time. When she came to the door, she was pouty about his having avoided her for three months, but her pouting turned to anger after he'd sat her down and explained the situation.

"It's because I refused to see him again," she said. "He must have gone home and taken the only revenge he could."

"My understanding is that money is his motive."

"He preyed on me before, and now he's doing it again."

"*It takes two to tango*," Andreas said in English.

"I'm not going to discuss this with you. I just shudder to think of you reading his version."

"Truth is a tricky thing, isn't it?"

"He had subversive levels of contact with the West. He was infatuated with America, the music especially. He's lying if he says there was any other reason for his heavy sentence."

"Oh, Mother."

"What?"

"That's the best you've got? He deserved ten years in prison for being an Elvis fan?"

Katya tossed her head. "It was a very frightening time, and he was disloyal. He wanted to leave the country with me, and then, when the Wall went up, he became desperate. He tried to destroy me. Destroy *us*, your father and me. I don't imagine you read any of this in his version."

Again and again, her dishonesty was the acid dissolving his compassion. He'd come to her with a wish to protect her from embarrassment. If she'd been authentic for just one moment, if she'd admitted that she'd made a mistake and regretted what she'd done to Peter Kronburg, he would have protected her.

"You loved him enough to keep his baby," he suggested.

"Don't say 'his.' You were my baby, not his."

"Ha. If I could have resigned from that position, I'd have done it in a heartbeat."

"You're thriving. You're magnificent. How bad a childhood could you have had?"

"Good point. I'm a famous credit to your mothering skills. But if I don't help him publish his memoir, he can make me look like a hypocrite. Would you like that?"

She shook her head. "It's an empty threat. He wouldn't do that. Just burn the manuscript and ignore him. People have stopped caring about our dirty laundry. This will blow over."

"Possibly. But here's a thought experiment for you: would you rather that I look bad, or that you look bad? Think about it carefully before you answer."

She stared straight ahead, her jaw set.

"Knotty little problem, right?"

She slumped against the rear cushions of her sofa,

continuing to stare blankly. It was as if he were witnessing his question's short-circuiting of her troubled brain.
He imagined the fugue: *A loving mother always puts her
son's welfare first, and to be a loving mother looks good,
but in this case putting my son's welfare first would entail my looking bad, and the whole point is not to look
bad, and yet to worry about looking bad is not to put my
son's welfare first, and a loving mother always puts
her son's welfare first* . . . Around and around like that.

"No-answer is an answer," he said, standing up. "I'm
going to leave now."

She didn't stop him; didn't say anything at all. The last
look he'd seen on her face had been so desolate that he
wouldn't have been surprised if she'd jumped out a window to her death. But the difference between him and her
was her capacity for self-deception. She didn't kill herself.
Instead, after he'd worked his magazine connections and
found a book publisher for *The Crime of Love*, and after
it had spent twelve weeks on the *Spiegel* bestseller list and
he'd reaped universal praise for promoting it, she moved to
London and rented a flat near the house of her widowed
sister. She published—in the *London Review of Books*, no
less—a long and self-justifying and chokingly dishonest
essay on the unreliability of East German memory. She
kept living, living.

He did, too. There were plenty of women who really
liked sex and wanted it with him, and there was global
fame to be pursued. Both were compulsions but not pathological ones. For a long time, while talented young
people flocked to the Sunlight Project, and while he applied his math and logic skills to becoming a crack tech-
nologist and a pretty good writer of code, and while the
excitement of leaking increased with the pervasiveness of
the Internet, until he had a bodyguard to protect him from
crazies and a team of pro bono lawyers to defend him

against the governments and corporations he lived to taunt, his ten years in prison with Annagret and the Killer seemed to him like a long bad dream that he'd awakened from. He never saw his mother, but in the great decade that followed the nineties, as he savored the ease of serial monogamy and the joy of consistently winning at the fame game, he sometimes thought back on her rhetorical question: how bad could his childhood have been? Even when he fled arrest in Germany, fled extradition from Denmark, found precarious refuge in Belize, luck was with him.

And then one day, in Belize, the Killer was back. Probably it had never been away, but he didn't become aware of it until he was leaving the beachside compound of Tad Milliken, after a delicious lunch. Tad Milliken was the Silicon Valley venture capitalist who'd retired to Belize to avoid the inconvenience of a statutory-rape charge pending against him in California. He was certifiably insane, an Ayn Rander who fancied himself an *Übermensch* and "the Singularity's chosen avatar," but he was surprisingly good company if you kept him on topics like tennis and fishing. He considered Andreas the second-most world-historical person residing in Belize, a fellow *Übermensch*, and wanted to be his friend, but this was awkward. Andreas badly needed money and hoped that Tad might give him some, and Tad still had Internet apologists who remembered him fondly as a father of the Revolution and insisted that he had an airtight insanity defense on the rape charge, but Tad had recently been in the news again for shooting a neighbor's pet macaw with the silver-plated Colt .45 he carried with him everywhere, and Andreas couldn't afford to be seen in public with him. Creepy sex stuff had already tarred Assange's reputation. Andreas imagined people googling "tad milliken," seeing "Andreas Wolf" and "statutory rape" on the first page of results, conflating his blondness and his line of work with the unfortunate orthographic proximity of "Andreas" to "Assange," and receiving the subliminal impression that he had a thing for fifteen-year-olds. Which he no longer did. And so he went to socially contortionate lengths to conceal from Tad his wish to see him only at his compound or on his fishing boat. It helped that, whenever they had a date, Tad sent a driver in a dark-windowed Escalade.

Tad was a self-documentarian. He had a self-activating camera in the Yankees cap he always wore and a tiny video device on a lanyard around his neck. At lunch, which was served poolside by a barefoot beauty named Carolina, conceivably as old as sixteen, Andreas had asked whether Tad might, for once, turn the cameras off. Tad, who was wearing a Hawaiian shirt unbuttoned to show off his sea-turtle belly, his tanned and heavily crunched abdominals, laughed and said, "You have something to hide today?"

"I'm just wondering where all this data goes."

"Let the sun shine in, man. You're on *Candid Camera*." Tad laughed again.

"It's not that I don't trust you. But if something were to happen to you . . ."

"You mean, if I die? I'm never going to die. That's the whole point of life-logging."

"Right."

"The data's in the cloud, and the cloud is eternally self-renewing. The error rate compared to DNA self-replication? Five orders of magnitude lower. Everything will be there, pristinely preserved, when they reboot me. I want to remember this lunch. I want to remember Carolina's little toes."

"I see what's in it for you. But from my point of view—"

"You don't care for the cloud."

"Not so much."

"It's still in its infancy. You'll love it when they reboot you."

"I already spend every day fishing unsavory things out of it."

"Ah, speaking of fish—"

Carolina had appeared with a platter of grilled fish on banana leaves. She moved Tad's silver gun to one side and set down the platter, and he pulled her onto his lap and kissed the side of her neck. Her smile seemed somewhat pained. Pulling the low-cut bodice of her dress away from her chest, Tad pointed his video device down inside the dress. "I'm going to want to remember these, too," he said. "These especially."

Carolina slapped away the camera and wordlessly extricated herself.

"She's still mad at me about the bird," Tad said, watching her go.

"I can't say it's playing well in the press, either."

"Oh, it wasn't that she liked the bird. It was worse than living next door to a sheet-metal plant, the shrieking of that thing. She just didn't think I could bag it without a shotgun. It was almost religious-superstitious. Thou shalt not use a revolver on a bird. She was deaf to my argument that a revolver is more sporting."

Andreas took some fish. "Let's talk about Bolivia."

"The country has no coast," Tad said. Possibly the most repellent thing about him was the dainty way he stabbed at food and poked it into his mouth, as if contact with it were a necessary evil. "It had a coast, but Chile stole it. Anyway, I can't live there. I need the sea. But there's a place in the mountains, Los Volcanes. Used to be owned by a German guy who does ecological survey work. I'd hired him when I was thinking I could corner the world market in lithium. He told me he'd been flying in a small plane and seen this little Shangri-la valley and said to himself, What the *fuck*? Bought it for thirty-five thousand American, unbelievable. I took an extra day to go and see it, and he was right. The place is unearthly. I offered him a million, he settled for one and a half. Some things you see and you just gotta have 'em."

"Does it have electricity? Cable?"

"Nothing. But the country has a president you can do business with. He was president of the coca growers' association when he got elected. Did he stop being president of the association? No way! That's what I call style. President of Bolivia *and* the coca growers' association. He screwed me on the lithium thing, but it was the right thing to do if you were him. And now he owes me. I can make the introduction. I can lease you Los Volcanes for a dollar a year. Throw in ten million for infrastructure improvements and operating expenses—you'll want to lay a fiber-optic line."

"Why would you do this for me?"

"You need a secure base. I need black-swan insurance. Belize is working for me now, gotta love the police here, but we're still pre-Singularity. If people like you and me are going to re-create the world, we may need a place where we can ride out transitional disruptions. Also, I don't see Greenland melting down before the Singularity, but if it does, nuclear weaponry could be utilized. We've backed away from nuclear-winter capability, but there could still be a nuclear autumn, a nuclear November, in which case the equator's where you want to be. Isolated valley in the center of an untargeted continent. Make sure you've got some comely young females, some spare parts, some goats and chickens. You can make the place cozy. I'd hate to have to join you there, but it could happen."

Tad stopped talking to stab at his fish and consume it with distrustful, snapping lunges with his mouth. Then he pushed his plate away as if disavowing something shameful.

"I'm not sure how to say this except bluntly," Andreas said, "or why I'm bothering to say it with your cameras sending this conversation to the cloud. But it would be important to me that no one know where the money is coming from."

Tad frowned. "Do I embarrass you?"

"No, of course not. I think we understand each other. But I have my own identity in the world, and . . . how to say this? Your legal troubles don't mesh well with it."

"My legal troubles are nothing compared to yours, my friend."

"I violated German official-secrets law and American anti-hacking law. That plays well even in the mainstream media. Certainly better than a sex charge."

"The old media live to smear me. I am the Primary Disruptor, and they know it."

"I get some of that, too. Which is why—"

"Of all the antenimbusian systems, the legal system is the most intellectually offensive to me. 'One size fits all'—my God. It's even worse than brick-and-mortar commerce. Why on earth, when we have the computing power to individually tailor everything else, do people still think the law should apply equally to everyone? Not every fifteen-year-old is alike, believe me. And am I exactly the same as every other sixty-four-year-old male?"

"It's an interesting point."

"And the rules of evidence—it's not a search for truth, it's an affront to truth. I *have* the truth, I have it recorded. And the lawyers cover their ears with their hands, literally cover their ears, and tell me they don't want to hear about it. Can a system *be* any more fubar than that? I am counting the days until a 'trial' consists of nothing more than sitting down and viewing the digital truth."

"But in the meantime . . ."

"It's fine," Tad said, somewhat crossly. "You can keep my name out of it. The Volcanes place is registered to a Bolivian corporation I set up to get around their foreign-ownership nonsense. There's three layers of shell there. The Bolivian entity can disburse the money."

"You really don't mind?"

"We're both truth-tellers, but I'm the more radical one. I have the guts to look you in the eye and tell you that your form of truth-telling is lesser than mine. But you're more likable. You can be truth-telling's friendlier public face."

"Sounds good to me," Andreas said.

The bad incident occurred after he and Tad had walked out to the compound's main gate. Not seeing the Escalade there, Tad phoned the driver, who said he was returning from a gas station. A few minutes later, as the gate was opening inward and the Escalade coming through it, a bald man with a camera, a gringo in a many-pocketed khaki vest, popped out from behind a palm tree across the road. He auto-fired at least ten shots of Andreas and Tad, with Tad's house behind them, before Andreas took cover behind the Escalade.

How could he have been so stupid as to stand in plain sight? It was bad, and it got worse. Tad had assumed a firing stance, aiming his revolver at the photographer, whose shutter Andreas continued to hear clucking. "Drop the camera, asshole," Tad shouted. "You think I wouldn't do it? You think I'm afraid?"

The gun was surprisingly unsteady. Tad's driver jumped out of the Escalade, looking bewildered. There was a scuffle of footsteps from the road. Tad lowered the gun and ran to the cages along the wall by the gate and released two of his Rottweilers.

Thus endeth my run of good luck, Andreas thought.

He and the driver followed Tad through the gate and watched the dogs tearing up the road after the photographer. This was the point at which the Killer made its presence known. The photographer stumbled against a parked minivan, and the dogs caught up with him and lunged without hesitation, one of them biting his arm, the other his leg. Andreas found himself hoping the dogs would kill him.

Tad was hustling up the road with his gun.

Andreas got in the Escalade and told the driver to do the same. By the time they were through the gate, the dogs were mewling and staggering—the photographer must have pepper-sprayed them—and the minivan was heading straight at Tad, who seemed to have lost interest in confrontation. He wandered off the road, his gun hanging loosely in his hand. The driver had to jerk the wheel of the Escalade to avoid collision with the minivan.

"Turn around and follow him," Andreas said.

The driver nodded, not very happily, and didn't hurry. By the time he'd turned the vehicle around, the road was empty. "He's gone," he said, as if this settled the matter.

Apparently nothing had changed. The Killer hadn't gone anywhere. Andreas felt like a dreamer awakening to an existence that had grown all the more desperate in the decade he'd been happily asleep. Instead of love, he had fame. Instead of a wife or children or real friends, like the friend Tom Aberant could have been, he had Tad Milliken. He was alone with the Killer.

He instructed the driver to take him to the nearest clinic. The photographer's minivan was parked outside it. Drops of fresh blood on the asphalt led to a red smear on the linoleum inside the door. Two Belizean women and four sick children were in the waiting room.

"I need to see my friend," Andreas told the receptionist. "The one who was bitten."

This being Belize, he was ushered right in to an examination room where a young doctor was cleaning a gnarly wound, one of several, on the photographer's arm. "Please wait outside," the doctor said without looking up.

The photographer, on his back, rolled his head toward Andreas. His eyes widened.

"I'm a friend," Andreas said. "I want to make this right."

"Your *friend* tried to kill me."

"I'm sorry. He's insane."

"You think?"

"Please wait outside," the doctor said.

The camera was sitting on a chair. Easy enough to walk away with it, but the pictures were only part of the problem. Money would have helped with the rest of the problem, but he was famed for having none. Famed for the Gandhian simplicity of his existence, the suitcase and briefcase in which his earthly possessions fit. Mostly this worked in his favor, but it wasn't working now.

Out in the parking lot, under a roasting sun, he called his former girlfriend Claudia, in whose family's beach house the Sunlight Project was currently conducting operations. The family's patience with being denied access to their own vacation place, and with being billed for the Project's expenses, was wearing perilously thin, but Claudia's loyalty was still solid and cost him nothing but submission to her teasing. It was only midnight in Berlin. She was at a Spree-side club when he reached her and directed her to cover the photographer's medical expenses. "I'll text you the number," he said.

Claudia laughed. "Do you want me to hop on a plane and bring you a latte while I'm at it?"

"Low-fat milk, half caffeinated."

"It wasn't like I was sitting down to dinner with my friends or something."

Andreas knew very well that the only thing that could make her shine brighter in her friends' eyes than taking a midnight call from him was leaving the club to do important business for him. They knew she'd been his girl for six months, back in the middle of the sweet decade that now was over, the decade when fame was all good and no bad. He'd received interesting sex from Claudia, along with other considerations worth at least two hundred thousand euros, and yet she was the one who felt more grateful, because he was the famous outlaw hero. How sweet it all had been.

The photographer, whose name was Dan Tierney, emerged from the clinic an hour later. His shaved head made him seem older than he probably was. The bandages on his arm and leg didn't look too serious. "Somebody in Berlin seems to have taken care of my bill," he said.

"A friend of mine," Andreas said. "How are you feeling?"

"The benchmark for me is getting stung on the eyelid by a scorpion. I'm maybe at four out of ten on that scale."

"Can I buy you a drink?"

"No. I'm going back to my hotel room and taking a Percocet."

"Rum goes well with Percocet."

"So you're my friend now? I wonder where you were when Insane Person was pointing a gun at me."

"Hiding behind a sport-utility vehicle."

"Rain check on the rum drink. Sorry."

"Do you mind if I ask who you work for?"

Tierney limped toward his minivan. "It varies. The *Times* is doing another Milliken story. The macaw thing, the local police. Tech world's biggest creepizoid, et cetera. It's hard to see how my image of him pointing a gun at me changes anyone's opinion."

"I don't suppose I can persuade you to delete the images of me and not tell anyone you saw me at his place."

"Why would I do that?"

"To help the Sunlight Project."

Tierney laughed. "You want me not to shed sunlight on your being pals with Insane Person. Is this irony, hypocrisy, or a contradiction? I'm never sure which term is appropriate."

"Call it all three if you want," Andreas said.

"Chutzpah. That's a fourth term."

"The thing is, I'm not Tad's pal. You'd be shedding false light."

"Really. I didn't know there was such a thing."

"The Internet is radiant with it."

"I'm surprised to hear you say that." Tierney unlocked his vehicle and got in. "Or half surprised. It's not that I don't like what you do. Your batting average is pretty good in terms of going after the right people. But I have to admit I always sort of figured you for an asshole."

Hearing this, the Killer stirred again in Andreas. If Tierney had figured him for an asshole, it was likely that many other people had, too. He felt a sudden strong anxious need to get to a computer and find out who they were and what exactly they were saying.

"I have nothing to offer you," he said to Tierney, "except the truth. Can I buy you a drink and tell you the truth?"

It was his best line, the line he'd used over and over in the past decade. He used it even when he didn't have to, because even when a woman had already signaled availability he loved to see the effect the line had. Everybody wanted to hear the truth from him. He watched Tierney think it over.

"I admit you're not a man I ever expected to meet in person," Tierney said. "There's a bar at my hotel."

At the bar, Andreas began with his boilerplate TSP speech, the list of governments he'd embarrassed and the longer list of corporations and power-abusing individuals. He hurried through the latter because Tierney seemed impatient. "So the truth has two parts," he said. "The first is that the Project lives or dies on the public's perception of me personally. The reason we're still thriving and WikiLeaks is going under is that people think Assange is an autistic megalomaniac sex creep. His tech capabilities haven't changed. What's changed is that people with dirt won't go to someone dirty. People who expose dirt do it because they're hungering for clean. If you don't help me out, we're in danger of going the way of WikiLeaks."

"Oh, come on," Tierney said. "It's one picture of two Internet titans inside a gated compound. Unless you're telling me this is just the tip of an iceberg—"

"That's the second part of the truth. This is where you really have to believe me. There is no iceberg. I lead a clean life. I was wild in my twenties, but I was living in a sick country and I was young. Given the level of scrutiny I've been under since then, do you think that if anyone had any dirt on me it wouldn't be all over the Internet?"

"I think if someone did, your hackers would be especially good at getting it buried."

"Seriously?"

"OK, so you're clean. Whatever. It only proves my point. One photograph is not a big deal."

"My being seen with Milliken is a disaster for the Project. It's like having one red sock in a load of white laundry. One red sock, and nothing is ever white again."

Tierney shifted in his chair and grimaced. "I'm sure I don't have to tell you this. But you are one strange dude. Who cares if your sheets are a little pink? Everybody's sheets are a little pink. People still go to Hugh Grant movies. People like Bill Clinton more than ever."

"Their business isn't being clean. Mine is."

"What were you doing at Milliken's anyway?"

"I was begging for money."

"Then I really don't see how you have anyone but yourself to blame for this."

"You're right, I don't. I was desperate and I had shit luck. You have total power over me."

"Is this the point where you offer me money?"

"If I had money, I wouldn't have been at Milliken's. And I'm less hypocritical than you think. I wouldn't offer money even if I had it. That would be a true betrayal of Project principles."

Tierney shook his head as if confounded by Andreas's strangeness. "I can probably get a couple thousand dollars for a picture of you two. I was also attacked by Rottweilers."

"If it's a matter of simple compensation, not hush money, my friend in Berlin can pay you a fair market rate."

"Nice friend."

"She believes in the Project."

"No matter what you say, you want me to not do to you the thing you do to other people."

"That's the truth."

"So you are an asshole."

"Sure. But I'm not Tad Milliken. I own nothing. I live out of a suitcase. Repressive governments hate me. There are only about ten countries in the world I can safely travel to."

This sounded good, came out well, and Tierney sighed. "Get me five thousand dollars," he said. "I'd be suing your pal Tad if I thought I could win a lawsuit in Belize. I'm still going to report him to the police. They'll ask who else was there. Do you want me to lie?"

"Yes, please."

"Of course you do." Tierney turned on his camera and let Andreas watch while he deleted, one by one, the images in which his face was visible. Andreas was reminded of the day, in a different decade, a different life, when he'd scrubbed the porn from his computer, and of his favorite lines of Mephistopheles: *Over! A stupid word. How so over? Over and pure nothing: completely the same thing! "It's over now!" What's that supposed to mean? It's as good as if it never was.*

But it hadn't never been. All Tierney had to do was mention the incident somewhere online, and it would stay in the cloud forever. In the weeks following the incident, while Andreas was closing down the beach house and exchanging strongly encrypted emails with Tad Milliken, his paranoia spread roots and flourished. With every different keyword he entered with his name in every different search engine, he was no longer content to read the first page or two of results. He wondered what was on the next page, the one he hadn't read yet, and after he'd looked at the next page he found yet another page. Repeat, repeat. There seemed to be no limit to the reassurance he required. He was so immersed and implicated in the Internet, so enmeshed in its totalitarianism, that his online existence was coming to seem realer than his physical self. The eyes of the world, even the eyes of his followers, didn't matter for their own sake, in the physical world. Who even cared what a person's private thoughts about him were? Private thoughts didn't exist in the retrievable, disseminable, and readable way that data did. And since a person couldn't exist in two places at once, the more he existed as the Internet's image of him, the less he felt like he existed as a flesh-and-blood person. The Internet meant *death*, and, unlike Tad Milliken, he couldn't take refuge in the hope of a cloud-borne afterlife.

The aim of the Internet and its associated technologies

was to "liberate" humanity from the tasks—making things, learning things, remembering things—that had previously given meaning to life and thus had constituted life. Now it seemed as if the only task that meant anything was search-engine optimization. Once he was up and running in Bolivia, he created a small team of truest-believing hackers and female interns who performed SEO by means both fair and foul. Tad's dream of luxury reincarnation may have been technically unrealistic, but it was a metaphor for something real: if—and only if—you had enough money and/or tech capability, you could control your Internet persona and, thus, your destiny and your virtual afterlife. Optimize or die. Kill or be killed.

For a year, he searched "tierney andreas milliken" two and three times a day. He monitored Tierney on Facebook and Twitter no less compulsively. His paranoia was evidently a fixed quantity. If he suppressed it in one place, it popped out in a different place. When Tierney finally ceased to worry him so much—if the guy was going to blab, he would have done it by now, and Andreas would have known about it—he didn't become any less anxious. He worried, serially, about former girlfriends, about disgruntled former employees, about surviving Stasi functionaries, until he arrived at the mother of all worries: Tom Aberant.

For a long time, for twenty years, he'd assumed that the secret of his homicidal past was safe with Tom. By helping to move the body, Tom had committed a serious crime himself, and in the letter he'd sent Andreas some months later, from New York, he'd apologized for "bailing" on him, had assured him that nothing he'd said in Berlin would ever see the light of day, neither in *Harper's* nor anywhere else, and had expressed the wish that their "little adventure" would allow Andreas to have the life he wanted with his girl. Injured though Andreas had felt by the distant tone of Tom's later postcards, especially the one in reply to his confessional letter, he hadn't been *worried* by it. Even when he'd taken one last stab at reviving their friendship, in 2005, by calling Tom in Denver and offering a major leak to Denver Independent, and Tom had rebuffed him, he hadn't worried. At worst, he'd thought, Tom was in professional competition with him. It was the sort of thing that could happen in abortive friendships.

But then one morning, in the barn at Los Volcanes, reading the daily digest of news about himself, he came across an interview that a Denver Independent journalist, Leila Helou, had given to the *Columbia Journalism Review*.

> The leakers just spew. It takes a journalist to collate and condense and contextualize what they spew. We may not always have the best of motives, but at least we have some investment in civilization. We're adults trying to communicate with other adults. The leakers are more like savages. I don't mean the primary leakers, not Snowden or Manning, they're really just glorified sources. I mean the outlets like WikiLeaks and the Sunlight Project. They have this savage naïveté, like the kid who thinks adults are hypocrites for filtering what comes out of their mouths. Filtering isn't phoniness—it's civilization. Julian Assange is so blind and deaf to basic social functioning that he eats with his hands. Andreas Wolf is a man so full of his own dirty secrets that he sees the entire world as dirty secrets. Fling everything at the wall, like a four-year-old flinging poop, and see what sticks.

Dirty secrets? Andreas reread the offending passage with cold dread. Who the fuck was Leila Helou? A quick search

turned up photos of her and Tom Aberant together at professional functions, along with catty remarks, on bottom-
feeding blogs, to the effect that sleeping with Denver
Independent's publisher had done wonders for her talent.
Leila Helou was Tom's girlfriend.

Dirty secrets? Flinging poop? Where was the filtering
in *that?*

He thought of the call he'd made to Denver in 2005.
The Halliburton Papers had been the Sunlight Project's
most significant international leak to date. He could have
taken them straight to the *New York Times*, but he knew
that Tom had started up an online news service and would
probably jump at the chance for overnight notoriety.
Although his motive in calling Tom was less than fully
pure—he enjoyed the idea that Tom now needed something from the friend he'd abandoned, the friend who was
now more famous and powerful than he was—the old
yearning for his friendship was part of it. He'd imagined
that Denver Independent could be the Project's American
mouthpiece; that he and Tom could finally work together,
albeit from separate continents. And Tom, on the phone,
had sounded interested. Yes, almost gushing—it was
fifteen years since they'd heard each other's voice. He'd
asked Andreas for one hour to discuss the leak with a
"trusted adviser."

This had sounded like a mere formality. But when Tom
had called back, after an hour and fifteen minutes, his
tone of voice had changed. "Andreas," he'd said, "I really
appreciate the offer. It means a lot to me, and it's a tough
call. But I think I have to stick with my core mission,
which is to nurture investigative journalism. Boots-on-
the-ground journalism. I'm not saying there's no place
for what you're doing. But I'm afraid that place isn't here."

Hanging up the phone, Andreas had vowed never to let
himself be hurt by Tom again. But only now, eight years

later, when he read the Helou interview, did he understand that Tom wasn't merely indifferent to him. Tom was an existential threat.

What he saw all at once: that Tom had glimpsed the Killer. In the light of dawn, in the Oder valley. The monster stiffy that hugging Tom had given him was not, as he'd supposed, the natural unleashing of the libido he'd suppressed since the night of the murder. Nor was it a gay man's stiffy, not in any meaningful sense. But it was nonetheless a stiffy *for Tom*. He had it for the same reason he'd had it for the fifteen-year-old Annagret: because Tom had made himself part of the murder. Man, woman—the Killer didn't trouble with such distinctions. And what had he done then? He couldn't remember for sure, it might have been a dream. But if it was a dream it must have been a vivid one. Straddling the grave, his stiffy in hand: had this really happened? It must have happened, because how else to explain why Tom had thenceforth shut him out? Tom had witnessed the thing the Killer had made him do. Tom had promised to have dinner with him but instead had run home to New York, taken refuge in his woman. And Andreas had proceeded to pursue him with a totally uncharacteristic lack of pride, sending him postcards, writing him a self-exposing letter, and finally calling him on the phone, not because the two of them were destined to be friends but because the Killer never forgot what it wanted, once it wanted it. There was no such thing as love.

The "trusted adviser" Tom had mentioned on the phone: who else could it have been but Leila Helou? Tom had asked his new woman what to do about the Halliburton Papers, his new woman had nixed it, and now, eight years later, it was all too obvious why: because Tom had told her about the murder of Horst Kleinholz. What else could *dirty secrets* refer to? She'd practically accused Andreas of cold-blooded murder.

When he reread her words yet again, the Killer stepped right out into the open, in the form of a wish to crush Tom's cranium with a blunt object. If there had been a way to get past U.S. Immigration, he would have gone to Denver and murdered Tom. For having glimpsed the Killer. For rejecting the most authentic overtures of friendship Andreas had ever made. For spurning him again and again, for the shame of that. And for submitting to his wife and deferring to his girlfriend. For seducing Andreas and then betraying him to the girlfriend; for not keeping his pretty mouth shut. But above all for his American *sanctimony*: "I'm not saying there's no place for the loathsome, criminal, fame-chasing, poop-flinging, grave-defiling things you do. But I'm afraid that my clean house is not the place for them." He'd all but said that on the telephone.

"I can't believe you did this to me," Andreas muttered. "I can't believe you did this to me . . ."

He was rational enough to recognize that Tom still wasn't likely to incriminate himself by exposing Andreas's crime. What inflamed his paranoia was the thought that Tom had seen the Killer in him. The thought was like an electrode in his brain. He couldn't stop pushing the button, and it gave him, each time, an identical jolt of dread and hatred.

Pleading illness to his interns, he holed up in his bedroom and searched for dirt on Tom and Helou. Already the blogosphere and social media were a-crackle with outrage at her *CJR* interview. In the world of so-called adults, Helou was a respected journalist, but in the online world she was getting reamed as fiercely as Andreas was being defended. Somehow, instead of reassuring him, this made him hate the Aberant-Helou nexus all the more. They'd deliberately provoked the very bloggers and tweeters whom he was devoting more and more of his existence to appeasing. Again the pointed sanctimony, again the message: *We're what you can never be. We disdain not only you but the virtual world in which you increasingly exist. We're capable of the love you were incapable of having for Annagret . . .*

According to Google, Helou was married to a disabled novelist on whom she presumably was cheating. But if she was appearing in public with Tom, they must not have cared what people thought. A more promising question was what had happened to Tom's wife. After 1991, there were zero contemporaneous records for anyone with her name and birth date. Andreas was seized with the hope that Tom had murdered her and gotten away with it. This seemed fantastically improbable, but in a way it also didn't. Tom had spoken, after all, of being unable to live either with Laird or without her. And he had, after all, helped Andreas bury a body.

Following an instinct, he turned his attention to Laird and discovered that her billionaire father had set up a trust fund for her; the *Wichita Eagle* had reported on the tax filings. There was also evidence that Tom had founded Denver Independent with money from the father. But not a lot of money. Not the kind of money that Anabel would be worth if she was still alive. Was she alive? Or, better yet, a corpse? An instinct told Andreas that, dead or alive, she might be a way to inflict pain and chaos on Tom from a distance.

He went to his lead hacker, Chen, and asked how easily they could steal a lot of computer processing capacity.

"How much?" Chen said.

"I have two good photos of a twenty-four-year-old woman who's now in her late fifties. I want to run a facial-recognition match on every photo database we can access."

"Worldwide?"

"Start with the U.S."

"It's a lot. Try to do it fast, they'll catch us. So many of these farms, you can only grab a few minutes at a time. We got some really good farms, but we don't want to lose them."

"What would less than fast be?"

"Weeks, maybe more. And that's just for U.S."

"See what you can do. Be as safe as you can."

Their facial-recognition software was nearly NSA-grade but still didn't work very well. (The NSA's didn't either.) Every day for several weeks, Chen forwarded Andreas pictures of late-middle-aged women who didn't look much like Anabel Laird. But going through the images gave him something to do, made him feel as if a plot were being advanced, took the worst edge off his paranoia. And then, for neither the first time nor the last time, he got lucky.

He'd always considered good luck his birthright—his mother had said it herself: the world conformed to whatever he felt like doing—but his bad luck with Dan Tierney had shaken his faith in it. The resolution of the image of a gray-haired supermarket employee in Felton, California, was too low to show the scar visible on Laird's forehead in the older pictures, and because the employee wasn't smiling he couldn't confirm the gap between her front teeth. But when he saw the employee's name, Penelope Tyler, and connected it with her years at Tyler School of Art, he sensed that his good luck had returned. He walked out of the tech building and looked up at the Bolivian sun, spread his arms, and soaked up its hot light.

Penelope Tyler was clearly a person who'd tried to disappear. The employee photo was the only image of her anywhere, and her official footprint was impressively faint. It took Andreas nearly an hour to discover that she had a daughter. This daughter, Purity, was relatively richly documented, with profiles on Facebook and LinkedIn and a very shaky credit history. He studied the pictures of her and recent pictures of Tom, comparing her eyebrows with Tom's eyebrows, her mouth with Tom's mouth, and concluded that she had to be his daughter. But there was no sign of contact between them, not on social media, not in her college or health records, nothing anywhere. Given that she'd been born not long after Laird vanished, it could only be that Tom didn't know she existed. Why else would Laird have changed her identity?

The girl was indirectly worth a shitload of money, a billion-size sum, and almost certainly didn't know it. She was making student-loan payments, living in a house that looked semi-derelict in Street View, and working as an "outreach associate" for an alternative-energy start-up. The money interested Andreas to the extent that it might make his life easier if he could get his hands on some of it. But it wasn't the reason he kept clicking through the photographs he had of Purity Tyler. Nor were her looks, though pleasant enough, the reason he conceived such a murderous desire for her. What mattered was that she was Tom's.

He set up a secure connection and called Annagret. Over the years, he'd been careful not to fall completely out of touch with her. He remembered her birthday and occasionally forwarded her links pertaining to one of her causes. For all the energy she'd invested in the project of closeness, it was remarkable how unclose she felt to him. How random it was—apart from her beauty—that he'd ever had anything to do with her. Not only was she small in her ambitions, she seemed perfectly content to be small. She'd left Berlin and moved to *Düsseldorf.* But her emails to him were always cordial and admiring, with many exclamation marks.

On the phone, after making sure she was alone, he

explained what he needed her to do. "Consider this a free vacation in America," he said.

"I hate America," she said. "I thought Obama would change things, but it's still just guns, drones, Guantánamo."

"Guantánamo is unfortunate, I agree. I'm not asking you to like the country. I'm just asking you to go there. I'd do it myself if I could, but I can't."

"I'm not sure I can, either," she said. "I know you always thought I was a good liar, but I don't like doing that anymore."

"It doesn't mean you're not still good at it."

"And maybe . . . Well. Is it really so terrible if this person tells the world what we did? I still think about it almost every day. I can't watch movies with any violence in them. Twenty-five years later, it still gives me panic attacks."

"I'm sorry about that. But Aberant is threatening to discredit everything I've done."

"I understand. The Project is very important. And I've always wished there was some way to make up for what I did to you. But—how does bringing his daughter to Bolivia help you?"

"Leave that to me."

A silence fell. Worrisome.

"Andreas," she said finally. "Do you feel bad about what we did?"

"Of course I do."

"OK. I don't know what I'm thinking about. I guess our time together. Sometimes I feel really bad about it. I know I disappointed you. But that's not why I feel bad. There's something else—I can't explain it."

He was alarmed but spoke calmly. "What is it?"

"I don't know. I see your life now, all your girlfriends, and . . . Sometimes I wonder why you didn't have affairs when you were with me. It's OK if you did. You can tell me now."

"I never did. I was trying to be good to you."

"You *are* good. I know all the fantastic good things you've done. Sometimes I can't believe I used to live with you. But still . . . Do you really feel bad about the thing we did?"

"Yes!"

"OK. I don't know what I'm thinking about."

He sighed. So many years, and they still had to have *discussions*.

"I feel bad about the sex," she said suddenly. "I'm sorry, but that's what it is."

"What about it?" he managed to say.

"I don't know. But I have more experience now, more to compare it to. And hearing your voice—I don't know. It's bringing back something I don't like to think about. Some really bad feeling I can't describe. It's making me panic, a little bit. Right now. I'm feeling panic."

"It was all mixed up with the thing we did. Maybe it was why we couldn't stay together."

She took an audibly deep breath. "Andreas, this girl— why do you want me to bring her to you?"

"To make her believe in the Project. That's our best protection. If she's on our side, her father won't do anything."

"OK."

"Annagret, that's all it is."

"OK. OK. But can I at least take Martin with me?"

"Who is Martin?"

"A man I feel close with. Safe with."

"Certainly. All the better. Just, obviously"—he laughed creakily—"don't tell him anything."

Safe with: the words pushed the button connected to the electrode. All these years, and he was still thinking of killing her. How much of his subatomic life he must

have unwittingly betrayed in his ten years with her! He'd
been lucky that she was too young to make sense of it. But
she'd lived with it and become aware of it in hindsight.
The thought of her latter-day awareness, his hideous
exposure in the eyes of someone who wasn't him, was
almost as bad as the thought of what Tom had seen.

While he waited to hear from her in Oakland, he took
honest stock of himself and saw how much ground he'd
lost in his battle with the Killer. How laughably venial his
old preoccupation with online porn now seemed; how poignantly tempered with good intentions his plot to murder
Horst. His inner life now consisted of little but obsessing
about his image on an Internet that felt like death to him;
of hating Tom and conspiring to take revenge on him. At
the rate he was going, he might soon be all Killer. And
again he sensed that he would be a dead man, literally,
once the Killer was fully in command. That he was who
the Killer was actually intent on killing.

It therefore came as something of a relief to hear from
Annagret that she'd botched her sales pitch to Pip Tyler
and alienated the girl. With a sense of reprieve, he threw
himself into the less insane work of collaborating on the
film that the American auteur Jay Cotter was making of
his life, based in part on *The Crime of Love*. He holed up
at the Cortez for two weeks with Cotter and his production
designer; he had long phone talks with Toni Field, in-
structing her in the ways of Katya. When he returned to
Los Volcanes, another project, no less dear to his heart,
was coming to fruition—a splendid dump of emails and
under-the-table agreements between the Russian petro-
leum giant Gazprom and the Putin government. Although
the Project now ran substantially on autopilot, Andreas
had personally brokered the Gazprom leak and dictated
the terms of its release to the *Guardian* and the *Times*. The
leak's provenance had required intricate laundering, an

impenetrable maze of electronic red herrings to protect
the source. Andreas also particularly loathed Vladimir
Putin, for his youthful work with the Stasi, and he was
determined to inflict maximum embarrassment on Putin's
government, because it was harboring Edward Snowden,
about whose purity of motive far too much had been said
online. In the twelve-minute video he recorded for uploading the day before the *Times* and the *Guardian* ran their
stories, he was at his artful best in needling Putin and re-
buking, subtly, the online voices who'd allowed the one-hit
wonder Snowden to distract them from his own twenty-
five-year record. His continuing ability to rise to great occasions, coupled with the prospect of being the hero of a
medium-budget movie with global distribution, was a
welcome distraction from the problem of Tom Aberant.

The email that Pip Tyler then sent him, out of the blue,
intensified his sense of reprieve. In reality, she was nothing like the figure from his vengeful imaginings. She was
young-sounding, intelligent, amusingly reckless. The humor and hostility of her emails were a balm to his nerves.
How sick of sycophancy he'd become since he succumbed
to paranoia! How refreshing it was to be called out on his
dishonesty! As he found himself warming to Pip's emails,
he imagined an escape route that the Killer had failed to
foresee, a providential loophole: what if he could reveal
to a woman, piece by piece, the complete picture of his
depravity? And what if she liked him anyway?

Inconveniently, principal photography had commenced
in Buenos Aires, and Toni Field had fallen for him hard.
He appreciated, for the first time, the travails of male porn
stars and the utility of Viagra. As if it weren't bad enough
that Toni was nearly his age and was portraying his
mother, he couldn't stop mentally comparing her with Pip
Tyler. And yet, for any number of strategic reasons, not
least to keep the leading actress happy, it was vital that

he seem gratified by the affair. During his days in Argentina, and even more so after he'd returned to Bolivia and met Pip, he engaged in grueling Toni management. If it hadn't been so inconvenient, it would have been hilarious how much like his mother Toni became before he managed to be rid of her.

He fell in love with Pip. There was no other way to describe it. His motives initially were nothing if not vile, and the dark part of his brain never stopped whirring with calculation, but real love couldn't be willed. Yes, he did his manipulative best to create a bond of trust with her, he confessed to the murder, he persuaded her to spy for him. But when, at the Cortez, to his amazement and delight, she let him undress her, he wasn't thinking about her father; he was simply grateful for the sweet good girl she was. Grateful that she'd lured him into her room even though he'd confessed to the murder; grateful that she wasn't repelled when he told her what he wanted to do to her. And when she then chastely declined to go further, there was, to be sure, a moment when he felt like strangling her. But it was only a moment.

He began to think she was the woman he'd waited all his life for. The hope she gave him was sweeter than the hope Annagret had once given him, because he'd already showed Pip more of his real self than he ever showed Annagret, and because, twenty-five years earlier, when he'd hoped that Annagret could save him, he hadn't even been aware of the Killer he needed to be saved from. Now he knew what the stakes were. They had nothing to do with Tom Aberant. At stake was the possibility that he might not have to be alone with the Killer. That he could finally have what he'd sought, unrealistically, in Annagret. A life with a young, bright, kindhearted woman who had a sense of humor and accepted him as he was and was nothing like his mother. Might it be possible, now that he was well into his fifties, to settle down with a woman without becoming bored? All the good luck he'd ever had was like nothing compared to the luck of spontaneously loving the person he'd intended to abuse for sick reasons. He daydreamed of marrying her on a sunny morning in the goat pasture.

But then the providential loophole closed. Almost as soon as she seemed to have fallen for him, hardly a week after he'd received her *burning look*, he found himself in a room at the Cortez where, from the very first moment, nothing felt right. He couldn't understand why she didn't want to be there, but she obviously didn't. He tried this, he tried that. Clumsily, feelingly. Nothing worked. She didn't like him. She didn't want to be there. But the way it felt to him was that the Killer didn't like *her*, didn't want *her* to be there; that it was the Killer who'd made him make the mistake of rushing her back to a hotel room before she really loved him, because the Killer was afraid of her.

Left by himself, kneeling on the floor, he didn't weep with disappointed love. He didn't weep at all. Three months of love evaporated in an instant. He'd been struggling to climb out of an abyss on a rope that she was holding, and as soon as he'd climbed close enough for her to see his face, she'd recoiled in disgust and let go of the rope. What you felt for the woman who did that to you wasn't love.

He trashed the hotel room. For some minutes, many minutes, he was both the Killer and the person enraged with the Killer for depriving him of love. He hurled food against the wall, broke dishes, ripped the blanket and sheets off the bed, upended the mattress, and hammered a wooden chair on the floor until its legs broke. He'd clung to his hope until the moment she shut the door behind her. Only then had he seen that she was as bad as her father—too *pure* for the likes of Andreas Wolf. She was a sanctimonious little cunt of a nobody. He trashed the hotel room to vent his rage at having hoped better of her.

Hope was the cheat that had prevented him from ordering her to fuck him (she would have done it! she'd said so!) until it was too late. He'd risked all and got nothing.

That he didn't physically harm himself that day or night, beyond bruising his knuckles by punching a wall, was owing to an idea that came to him after his rage had passed. It occurred to him that he still possessed a piece of information known to no one else, and that he might use this datum to revenge himself on Pip and Tom simultaneously. Although he hadn't poked the girl himself, conceivably Tom still could. The possibility was no less delicious for being remote. And then let Tom try being sanctimonious with him. Then let Pip try to say she wasn't sorry she'd rejected him.

It was a relief to stop fighting the Killer and submit to the evil of his idea; it turned him on so much that he went to the spot on the floor where Pip had stood naked and used the panties she'd left behind to milk himself, three times, of the substance he hadn't spent in her; it got him through the long night. Early in the morning, he went to several ATMs and withdrew enough cash from the Project's account to cover the damage he'd done to the room. He showered and shaved and was waiting in the lobby when Pedro arrived to take him to the airport. Katya's plane was fifteen minutes early. She came through the customs gate wearing a Chanel or Chanel-like suit, wheeling a brocade-fabric suitcase and carrying an old-fashioned briefcase with a shoulder strap, moving more stiffly than she used to, looking older, definitely, and wearing a wig of less wonderful redness, but still lovely from a distance. Andreas pushed through the crowd to greet her. He put his arms around her, and she rested her head on his breast. The first thing he said was "I love you."

"You always have," she said.

* * *

It ought to have felt good to be walking up the road to meet Tom Aberant, stretching muscles stiff from a week of inactivity. Down in the meadow by the river rapids, by the tumble of wet boulders, a large woodpecker was drumming on a hollow tree. A buzzard eagle soared past the vertical face of a red pinnacle. Warm late-morning air currents were stirring the woods along the road, creating a tapestry of light and shadow so fine-grained and chaotic in its shiftings that no computer on earth could have modeled it. Nature even on the most local of scales made a mockery of information technology. Even augmented by tech, the human brain was paltry, infinitesimal, in comparison to the universe. And yet it ought to have felt good to have a brain and be walking on a sunny morning in Bolivia. The woods were unfathomably complex, but they didn't know it. Matter was information, information matter, and only in the brain did matter organize itself sufficiently to be aware of itself; only in the brain could the information of which the world consisted manipulate itself. The human brain was a very special case. He ought to have felt grateful for the privilege of having had one, of having played his small part in being's knowledge of itself. But something was very wrong with his particular brain. It now seemed able to know only the emptiness and pointlessness of being.

A week had passed since the spyware in Denver had stopped functioning. He could have had Chen uninstall it after Pip asked him to, and he might have escaped detection if he'd acted quickly, but Pip's final text to him had made him so anxious he could hardly breathe, let alone communicate with Chen. *I want to delete all that and have a life here*: somewhere inside him his love and hope for her had persisted, in fragmentary form, until he read those words of hers. Now he felt nothing but pain and fear. Didn't care if he ever saw her again, didn't care what she or anyone else thought of him. Nothing that anyone did anywhere made any difference to him now.

Or almost nothing. In London, his mother had survived her cancer treatments and was recovering well. If he could have done anything, during the days that he'd been lying in his room, he would have asked her to come and visit him again. She'd always liked everything about him. She, the world's shittiest mother, was the best mother in the world for him. Lying there in bed, he would have accepted love and care from her on whatever terms she offered. Indeed, this seemed almost to be the essence of his condition.

He was approaching the concrete bridge over the river, trudging in one of Pedro's tire tracks to avoid the mud from the previous night's rain, when he heard the Land Cruiser downshifting around the bend in front of him. The one good thing that could be said about his condition was that the Land Cruiser's approach wasn't making him more anxious. He was already at maximal anxiety. The worst Tom could do to him was kill him.

But this thought, the idea of being killed by Tom, was like the prospect of rain in a desert. Not a relief in itself but a reason to keep moving forward. Death by any means would put an end to his throttling fear of it; the precise means should have been a matter of indifference. But to be killer and killed was arguably the closest form of human intimacy. In a sense, he'd been more intimate with Horst Kleinholz than he'd been with any other person since he'd left his mother's womb. And to die knowing that Tom, too, was capable of killing—to exit the world feeling he hadn't been so alone in it after all—seemed like a kind of intimacy as well.

Food for thought. He picked up his pace a little; he raised his head and squared his shoulders. With every step he took, an increment of time passed. Knowing that the number of steps remaining to him was countably small made the pain of taking them more bearable. When the Land Cruiser came around the bend, he smiled at the sight of his old friend.

"Tom," he said warmly, extending a hand through the passenger-side window.

Tom frowned at the hand more in surprise, it seemed, than anger. He was wearing the khaki shirt of a gringo journalist. Andreas had seen recent pictures of him, but in person the fact of his physical alteration, his thickness, his baldness, brought home how many years had passed.

"Oh, come on. Shake it."

Tom shook it without looking at him.

"Why don't you get out and walk with me? Pedro can go ahead with your things."

Tom got out of the vehicle and put on sunglasses.

"It's great to see you," Andreas said. "Thanks for coming."

"I didn't do it as a favor."

"I'm sure not. And yet—shall we walk?"

They walked, and he decided to plunge right in. The abatement of his mental pain was so liberating that he had the sense of being on the losing side in the final minutes of extra time—throw every man forward, anything goes. "Belated congratulations," he said, "on having a daughter."

Tom still hadn't looked at him.

"I've known about her for more than a year," Andreas said. "I suppose the honorable thing would have been to inform you right away."

"And Brutus is an honorable man."

"Well, I apologize. She's impressive in many ways."

"How did you find her?"

"Photo recognition. The software is so primitive, it had no business working. But, as you know, things have a way of working out for me."

"You get away with murder."

"Exactly!" He felt out of his body, weirdly buoyant. Tom truly was the only person in the world he had no secrets from. "You've done pretty well for yourself, too. Great story on the missing nuke. Do you have it up yet?"

"It's been up for a week."

"I gave it to you as a present. We should have been collaborating all along."

On a giddy impulse, he punched Tom's arm. He prattled away, proudly explicating the features of Los Volcanes, as he led Tom across the pasture and around to the main building's veranda. His father, Katya's husband, hadn't lived to see what he'd built with the gift of freedom he'd given him, but if he'd lived, and had come to Los Volcanes, Andreas might have been similarly giddy with him, similarly performative, enumerating his achievements while knowing that nothing could change his father's damning judgment of him.

On the veranda, Teresa brought them beer. A few stingless bees were hovering. Tom had been paternally silent for some minutes.

"So, what brings you to Bolivia?" Andreas said.

"You mean, apart from you hacking into my computers?" Tom's voice sounded choked with self-control. "Apart from you messing with the head of a young woman who happens to be my daughter?"

"Admittedly a dark picture," Andreas said. "But am I allowed to point out that no harm has come of any of that, and that you were the one who started it?"

Tom turned to him in disbelief. "*I* started it?"

"We had a dinner date. Do you remember? In Berlin. You never showed up."

"That's why you did this to me?"

"I thought we were friends."

"Given what you're saying, can you blame me for not wanting to be?"

"Well, at any rate, the score is even now. I'm willing to start over, clean slate. I'm sure we have some new leaks that would interest you."

"That's not why I came here."

"No, I suppose not."

"I came here," Tom said, not looking at him, "to threaten you. I will do a story on you. I will write it myself. And I will take the police to the grave site."

The harshness in his voice was understandable, and yet it hurt Andreas. It seemed like a failure of Tom's imagination to be unmoved by what he'd implicitly confessed—that he'd liked Tom more than Tom had liked him, and that his mental health was less than tiptop.

"Fine, then," he said. "You came here to threaten me. I presume there's an *or else*?"

"It's simple," Tom said. "Two simple things. First, you never communicate with my daughter again, ever, under any circumstances. And second, you digitally shred everything you took from my computers. You keep no copies and you never speak of anything you saw there. If you do all that, I'll keep my mouth shut."

Andreas nodded. The Tom he remembered from Berlin had been softer and more forgiving, more motherly. His sternness now was making Andreas feel like a bad little boy.

"I'll do whatever you say," he said.

"Good. We're done, then."

"If that's all you wanted, you could have just called me."

"I believe this merited face time."

He wondered what it might be that Tom was so intent on having shredded. He hadn't actually looked at much of what he'd stolen. Once he'd ascertained that Leila Helou wasn't pursuing a vendetta against him, he'd lost interest in the spyware, and for the past few weeks he'd been too disabled by fear and pain to be curious about the dirt he might have found on Tom's home computer.

"I don't care what you know about me," Tom said, as if reading his thought. "But I do care what Pip knows. If she finds anything out from you, I will destroy you."

"I take it you haven't mentioned that you're her father."

"I'd rather she not know. I'd rather she not know about the money, either."

"You don't want your own daughter to know she has a billion dollars coming to her."

"You wouldn't understand."

"She's a sensible girl. I don't think the money would ruin her."

"I'm not going to interfere with Anabel. And you're not going to, either."

"So you care more about your ex-wife than you do about your daughter. I guess I shouldn't be surprised. You were the same way in Berlin."

"It's just the way it is."

"And where does that leave your girlfriend? If you don't mind my asking."

"It has nothing to do with Leila."

"Presumably you've told her who Pip is?"

"Yep."

"Quite a shock, I'd guess."

Tom turned and gave him a smile. It took Andreas a moment to recognize the cruelty in it. "You want to know something?" Tom said. "It's been good for me and Leila. This famous sunlight of yours. It's been good for us."

Andreas closed his eyes. Creating darkness was that simple. He mentally sank into it, wishing it were a deeper darkness. "Say more," he murmured.

"You sent us Pip."

"I see."

"It was hard on Leila. I finally had to tell her everything, including what you and I did in Berlin."

"But you told her that a long time ago."

"No. Only after I found out what you'd done to me."

"You told her."

"Don't worry. Your secret's safe as long as you leave Pip alone. Leila's a vault, the same as me. But, just so you know, you did us a favor."

"I helped you . . ."

"She and I were stuck in something. It wasn't such a bad thing. But we needed a push."

"I helped you . . ."

"Don't get me wrong—what you did to Pip is unforgivable. I didn't come here to thank you. I'm simply giving credit where credit is due."

The darkness into which Andreas was falling was so contourless that he had a sensation of spinning, and to spin was nauseating. Bad enough to have failed to ruin Tom's life. But to have inadvertently made it happier . . .

He opened his eyes and stood up.

"I have some pressing work," he said. "Why don't you eat lunch, take a nap. We'll go for a walk when it cools off. Say four o'clock?"

"Thanks, but no," Tom said. "I've said what I came to say."

"Stay the night at least. Your daughter liked to hike the trails here."

Tom looked at his watch. He was obviously calculating how soon he could get away from Andreas and back to his woman. In twenty-five years, nothing had changed.

"You've already missed the afternoon flights," Andreas said. "There's a lot to see here. There's nothing in the city."

"I'd need a ride very early in the morning."

"Of course. We'll arrange it."

Upstairs, alone in his room, he opened his copy of Tom's home hard drive. He searched "andreas" and "anabel" and got few matches, nothing interesting. Tom's security was lousy—his log-in password, recorded as keystrokes, was leonard1980, no caps, no special characters—and his desktop was punitively well organized, folder after folder of third-party PDFs and boring photographs and business letters that he hadn't bothered to password protect. There was, however, a subfolder labeled X, in his main documents folder. This subfolder contained a single file, a river of meat.doc, password protected. Andreas tried leonard1980 and was denied access.

The file was substantial, nearly half a meg. He entered obvious variations on leonard1980 before giving up and wading into the keystroke log, the shortness of which was both a plus (less to wade through) and a serious minus, since Tom might not have used all his passwords since the spyware was activated. There was a leonarD1980 and a leonard198019801980. Neither of them opened a river of meat.doc. He went through the keystroke log again, keeping his eyes less focused, the better to see patterns, and this time he noticed a le1o9n8a0rd, followed by numbers that suggested online banking. This slightly less crappy password opened the document.

It appeared to be a novel or a memoir. He searched for his own name and found it toward the end. Everything about the document argued for its being a memoir, an attempt at precise and honest recollection, but when he reached the point in the narrative where Tom spoke of loving him he didn't believe a word of it. The narrative didn't become true again until the narrator turned against him. Then it all made sense again. Then it was exactly as he'd always known it was: nobody who knew him could love him. And they were right, as he'd been right. There was something very wrong with him.

He clawed his face. Time was passing. He stared at the computer screen for what seemed like a millisecond but must have been half an hour, because the document file was closed and he knew how the story ended. He was typing le1o9n8a0rd as the subject header of an email. He selected andtylertoo@cruzio.com from his address book and attached a river of meat.doc. The reason he couldn't feel time passing was that his mind was moving faster than it ever had before, moving without him, leaving him behind. He hit Send.

Tom was waiting for him on the veranda. Andreas couldn't look at him, but friendly words were issuing from his mouth, the number of hectares that Los Volcanes comprised, the protection status of the national park to the north. They walked down to the river and across the plank bridge and up the first trail leading to a height, a lesser pinnacle. As the trail steepened, Tom began to huff.

He ought to have moderated his pace, for Tom's sake, but it seemed urgent to reach the top as soon as possible. It seemed to him he had an assignation with a woman who might leave. He had something most glorious to dedicate to her. It was urgent that she not leave. Or die—that was it. She might die before he made it to the top. She wasn't even there but she might die before he got there. Even though he hadn't asked her to come and visit him, he hated her for not coming. Hated her and needed her and hated her and needed her. Everything was effect now, nothing cause. He had a dim recollection of having been a lucky person. Surely it was lucky that she'd survived her cancer treatments. She could still receive his dedication, if only he could make it to the top in time.

At the summit was a mirador with a rough-hewn bench. The pinnacles on the far side of the valley were aflame with the setting sun, but already this side of the valley was in shadow. The edge of the cliff was rounded and slippery with sandstone gravel. Below was a drop of several hundred meters, vertical bare rock with a few hardy epiphytes clinging to it.

Tom came huffing up the trail, his face red, his shirt blotched with sweat. "You're a fitter man than I," he said, dropping onto the bench.

"The view is worth it, don't you think?"

Tom dutifully raised his head to take in the view. Multiple flocks of parakeets were screeching in the valley. But the beauty of the red rock and green foliage and blue sky was only an idea. The world, its being, every atom of it, was a horror.

When Tom had caught his breath, Andreas turned to him and opened his mouth. He would have liked to say *Everything is a horror to me. Won't you be my friend again?* But instead a voice said, "By the way? I saw your daughter naked."

Tom's eyes narrowed.

He would have liked to say *You won't believe this, but I loved her.* "I told her to strip, and she stripped for me. Her body is exquisite."

"Shut up," Tom said.

I hardly knew her, but I loved her. I loved you, too. "I had my tongue in her pussy. It was very nice. Very *lecker*, to use the apt German word. She liked it, too."

Tom lurched to his feet. "Shut the fuck up! What is wrong with you?"

Won't you please help me?

"She didn't do anything you didn't want to do yourself. The only difference is that she did it."

"What the fuck is wrong with you?"

Somebody please help me. Mother, please help me.

"Were you thinking of me when you butt-raped your Anabel?"

Tom grabbed him by the collar. He seemed very close to striking a blow.

"I thought Pip might enjoy that little scene. That's why I sent her your document. Just now, while you were taking your nap. I included the password."

Tom tightened his grip on the collar. Someone took hold of his wrists.

"Don't strangle me. There are better ways to do this. Ways you can get away with."

Tom let go of the collar. "What are you doing?"

Someone went closer to the edge of the pinnacle. "I'm saying you can push me."

Tom stared at him.

I'm unbearably sad about this.

"I polluted your daughter. Just because she was your daughter, just for the fun of it. She said it was the best ever. I'm not making this up. It's all factual truth—she'll admit it if you ask her. And then I sent her your document, to make sure she knows how filthy she is. Didn't you promise to destroy me if I did that? If I were you, I'd kill me."

Tom looked afraid now, not angry.

Please help me. Not that anyone ever did.

"Sit down on the ground, so you don't fall. And then give me a hard push with your feet. Doesn't that sound good to you? Especially if I—here." Someone took a pen out of his pocket. "I'll write a note absolving you of responsibility. I'll write it on my arm. Here, see, I'm writing it on my arm."

The writing, on sweat-dampened skin, and with hairs interfering, went slowly, but his hand was firm. The text was complete in his head without his having thought of it.

*YOU KNOW ME TO BE HONEST. NO THREAT COULD
COMPEL ME TO WRITE UNTRUTH. I CONFESS TO
THE MURDER OF HORST WERNER KLEINHOLZ IN
NOVEMBER 1987. I AM SOLELY RESPONSIBLE FOR
THE ACT I COMMITTED TODAY. ANDREAS WOLF*

Someone showed the words to Tom, who was sitting on the bench now, his head in his hands.

"This should suffice, don't you think? The confession itself provides the motive. If need be, you can corroborate the confession. But I don't think anyone will question it." Someone extended a hand to Tom. "Will you do it?"

"No."

"I'm asking you as a friend. Do I have to beg?"

Tom shook his head.

"Do I have to drag you along with me?"

"No."

"Don't lie to me, Tom. You know what it's like to want to kill someone."

"The difference is I didn't do it."

"But now you can. You want to. At least admit you want to."

"No. You're psychotic, and you can't see it because you're psychotic. You need to—"

The sound of Tom's voice stopped. It was curious and abrupt. Tom's mouth was still moving, and there was still the distant rush of water, the screeching of parakeets. Only human speech had ceased to be audible. It was very disorienting and had to be the Killer's work somehow. But someone was the Killer. Had the Killer always been deaf to speech?

In the mysterious selective silence, he wandered away from Tom, out to the edge of the cliff. He heard a scrabble of feet on gravel and looked back to see Tom standing up, gesturing to him, apparently shouting. He turned back to the precipice and looked down at the tropical treetops, the large shards of fallen rock, the green surf of undergrowth crashing against them. When they began to drift slowly closer, and then moved rapidly closer, and more rapidly yet, he kept his eyes open wide, because he was honest with himself. In the instant before it was over and pure nothing, he heard all the human voices in the world.

The Rain
Comes

Fog spilled from the heights of San Francisco like the liquid it almost was. On better days it spread across the bay and took over Oakland street by street, a thing you saw coming, a change you watched happening to you, a season on the move. Where it encountered redwoods, the most local of rains fell. Where it found open space, its weightless pale passage seemed both endless and like the end of all things. It was a temporary sadness, the more beautiful for being sad, the more precious for being temporary. It was the slow song in minor that the rock-and-roll sun then chased away.

Pip was feeling not so temporarily sad as she walked up the hill to work. Sunday morning, early, the streets were empty. Cars that in sunshine might have looked merely parked looked abandoned in the fog. From some direction and some distance, a raven was croaking. Fog subdued the other birds but made the ravens talkative.

At Peet's, she found the assistant manager, Navi, loading pastries into the display case. Navi had wooden disks the size of poker chips in his earlobes and was scarcely older than Pip, but he seemed completely at peace with corporations and retail. It was her first day of work post-training, and the way he oversaw her, as she booted up the register and filled receptacles with liquids, was all business and no indulgence. She felt almost weepingly grateful to have a boss who was nothing but a boss; who let her be.

Three customers were waiting in the fog when she unlocked the front door. After she'd served them, a lull came,
and into this lull walked a person she recognized. It was
Jason, the boy she'd tried and failed to sleep with a year
and a half ago, the boy whose texts she'd read. Jason
Whitaker with his Sunday *Times*. She'd thought of him,
their Sunday mornings, when she'd applied for the Peet's
job. But she'd figured that by now he'd found some other
coffee place to be enthusiastic about.

She waited, with the particular exposure of a barista,
while he claimed his preferred table with his paper and
came over to the pastry case. To herself, she was no longer
the person who'd left him waiting forever in her bedroom
and then rained abuse on him, but he had no way of knowing this, because, of course, she was also still that person.
When he stepped up to the cash register, he saw this person
and blushed.

She gave him an ironic little wave. "Hello."

"Wow. You work here."

"It's my first real day."

"It took me a second to recognize you. Your hair is
short."

"Yes."

"It looks nice. You look great."

"Thank you."

"Wow, so." He looked over his shoulder. No one was
behind him. His own hair was shorter, his body still
skinny but less skinny than before. She remembered why
she'd wanted him.

"What can I get you?" she said.

"You probably remember. Bear claw and a three-shot
cappuccino, tall."

She was relieved to turn away from him and work on
his drink. Navi was occupied at the back with a large plastic drum.

"So are you part-time here?" Jason said. "Do you still work for the alt-energy place?"

"No." She tonged a bear claw from the case. "I've been away. I just came back."

"Where were you?"

"Bolivia and then Denver."

"Bolivia? For real? What were you doing down there?"

She got the milk steamer squealing so she didn't have to answer.

"This is on me," she said when she was finished. "You don't have to pay."

"No, come on."

He pushed a ten-dollar bill at her. She pushed it back. It lay there on the counter. Keeping her eyes on it, she said, "I never apologized to you. I should have apologized."

"God, no, it's OK. I'm the one who should have apologized."

"You did. I got your texts. I was so ashamed of myself I couldn't write back to you."

"I'm sorry."

"Not as sorry as I am, I suspect."

"It was like a perfect storm of wrongness, that night."

"Yah."

"That guy I was texting? I'm not even friends with him anymore."

"Seriously, Jason, you are not the one to apologize."

He left the money on the counter when he went back to his table. She rang up his purchase and put the change in the tip jar. A year and a half ago she might have resented him for being cavalier about the money, but she was no longer that person. Somewhere she'd lost her capacity for resentment, and for hostility as well, and thus, to some extent, for being amusing. This was a real loss, but there was nothing she could do about it except be sad. She was pretty sure the loss predated the knowledge that her mother was a billionaire.

For a while the stream of customers was steady. Navi had to pull her out of the weeds more than once; accidental coffee and dairy wastages were running high. During another lull, Jason returned to the counter. "I'm taking off," he said.

"It was nice to see you again. I mean, discounting my excruciating embarrassment."

"I still come here every Sunday. But now you can think, 'Oh, that's just Jason.' I can think, 'Oh, that's just Pip.'"

"Is that something I said?"

"It's something you said. Will I see you next Sunday?"

"Probably. It's not a popular shift."

He started to leave and then turned back to her. "I'm sorry," he said. "That sounded like something I didn't mean. Asking if you'd be here next week."

"It just sounded friendly."

"Good. I mean—I'm kind of with someone else. I didn't want to send the wrong message."

She felt a small pang but no surprise. "Message of friendliness received."

He was walking away when she found herself laughing. He turned back. "What?"

"Nothing. Sorry. Unrelated."

When he was gone, more laughter escaped her. A stupid condom! Was anything funnier than a condom? If she hadn't left Jason and gone downstairs to get one, a year and a half ago, she might never have taken Annagret's questionnaire, and everything that had happened to her since then wouldn't have happened. If she'd had a boyfriend, she wouldn't have wanted to leave town. She would never have learned about the *other* condoms, the comedy of *that*. The comedy of her even existing. Navi was giving her a chiding look, but she couldn't stop laughing.

In the afternoon, when her shift ended, she walked back down the hill. The sky was as clear as if there'd never been such a thing as fog. In theory, she was now supposed to work on a piece the *Express* had commissioned, a first-hand account of life as a Sunlight Project intern. But no matter how long or good the piece was, she wouldn't get more than a couple of hundred dollars for it, and she still had her loan payments to make; hence the full-time job at Peet's. She also didn't know how to write about Andreas. It might be a year, or a decade, before she could sort out how she felt about his death, and she already had so much else to sort out, such a mountain of unsorted material, that all she'd been good for, after putting in her hours at Peet's, was whacking dead tennis balls against the door of Dreyfuss's garage.

Dreyfuss was supine on his living-room sofa, watching an A's game. He was recovering from treatment of an intestinal parasite for which the freeganism of his housemates Garth and Erik was probably responsible. Garth and Erik themselves were temporarily in the Alameda County jail. Three days ago, they'd "assaulted" a real-estate agent attempting to show Dreyfuss's house to prospective buyers, and crowdfunding by their anarchist friends had yet to raise enough bail for both of them.

"Someone smells like coffee," Dreyfuss said.

"I brought you scones," Pip said, unzipping her knapsack. "Do you want milk with them? I brought some milk home, too."

"The challenge of stale scone and a perpetually dry mouth may be insurmountable without it."

Dreyfuss put the bag of scones on his diminished but still convex belly and reached into it. Pip set the plastic bottle on the coffee table. "Yesterday was the use-by date, just so you know. Have you heard anything more from the bank?"

"Even Relentless Pursuit rests on the Sabbath."

"It's going to be fine. They can't do anything until you've had your hearing."

"Nothing I've learned about Judge Costa inclines me toward optimism. He appears to have an eighth-grade education and slavish respect for the rights of corporations. I've edited my presentation to the bone, but there are still a hundred twenty-two discrete narrative elements. I suspect that the judge's attention will wander after three or four of them."

Pip wasn't so afraid of Dreyfuss anymore, and unfortunately his bank wasn't either. She patted one of his heavy and nearly hairless hands. She didn't expect him to respond in any way, and he didn't.

Upstairs, in her old room, she changed into shorts and a T-shirt. Half the room was piled with Stephen's belongings and scavenged crap, which she'd rearranged in more vertical form to make room for her mattress and suitcase. Two weeks ago, from her friend Samantha's apartment, after emerging from the haze into which she'd put herself with Samantha's Ativan, she'd called Dreyfuss to say hi and tell him he'd been right about those Germans. Dreyfuss told her that Stephen was adventuring in Central America with a twenty-year-old girl who had parental money. Currently Garth and Erik were Dreyfuss's only housemates; she was welcome to her old room if she wanted it. The male filth of the house was even more disgusting than she'd imagined, but cleaning it had given her some direction for a while.

In Stephen's pile of junk she'd found an old Pro Kennex tennis racquet. Dreyfuss's garage door was loose in its frame and weakened by dry rot. Even the hardest-hit balls hopped back from it with a puppyish lack of aggression. Behind the garage was a wall of broadleaf evergreens that served as a backstop. Balls she bombed over it were

easily replaced by searching the bushes in Mosswood
Park. The deader the ball, the better it suited her purpose,
which was to whack the shit out of it until she was physically exhausted. She thought this was quite possibly the
most satisfying thing she'd ever done.

From some weeks of tennis in her high-school gym
class, she knew she needed to keep her eye on the ball and
address it sideways. Her backhand was still a flail, but the
forehand—oh, the forehand. Her natural stroke was top-
spin, a ripping upswing. She could pound forehands for
fifteen minutes, scurrying around the return caroms, re-
positioning herself like a cat with her mouseball, before
she had to catch her breath. Each *whack* was another small
bite taken out of a too-long late afternoon.

She'd still been in Denver, having crashed for some
nights with her former share-mates in Lakewood, when
the email headed le1o9n8a0rd came in. She'd sensed right
away that the document attached to it was from Tom's
computer, which she'd promised never to violate. But later
the same day, after a punishing bus ride to the Denver
airport, there had followed two short emails from Tom
himself.

> Andreas dead. Suicide. I'm in physical shock but thought
> you should know.

> PS: I'm in Bolivia, I saw him go. If he sent you something,
> please shred it without reading it. He was mentally ill.

More than shock, or dread, or pain, what punched her in
the stomach and sickened her was *guilt*. And this was
strange: why guilt? But she knew what she knew. The sick
feeling was definitely guilt. Mechanically, because her
group number had been called, she went ahead and boarded
her cheap Frontier Airlines flight to San Francisco. There

were soldiers on the plane. They'd been invited to board early, and her seat was next to one of them.

He was mentally ill. She'd both known this and not known it. Had seen it but also had done what he'd asked her not to do: had projected. Projected her own sanity onto him. If he really was dead now, she must have had it in her power to save him. This idea was obviously a form of self-flattery, but when she examined her memories of their times alone, it seemed to her that he'd been asking her to save him. She'd thought she was doing the morally right thing by rejecting him, but what if it had been morally the wrong thing? A failure of compassion? She scrunched herself down in her narrow airline seat and cried as inconspicuously as she could, keeping her eyes shut, as if this could make her invisible to the soldier in fatigues beside her.

By the time she got to Samantha's, she was aware of a conflict of loyalties. On one side was her promise to respect Tom's privacy, along with the pointedness of his warning that Andreas had been mentally ill; Tom seemed to have been implying that there was sickness in her very possession of a document. And yet: emailing her had been one of Andreas's last acts on earth. Only a few hours had elapsed between his email and Tom's. However sick he'd been, he'd been thinking of *her*. To imagine that this mattered was obviously another form of self-flattery—a failure of compassion for a suicidally tormented person, a failure to respect how little anything mattered to him but the pain he was in. And yet: it had to mean something that he'd sent her the email. She was afraid that it meant she was part of why he'd killed himself. If she was somehow responsible for his death, the least she could do to accept her guilt was to read the message he'd taken the trouble to send her. She reasoned that she could look at the document and still honor her promise to Tom by never telling him. It seemed like a thing she owed Andreas.

But the document was like a box she couldn't put the lid back on; like the secret of nuclear fission, the so-called Pandora's box. When she came to Tom's description of his ex-wife's forehead scar and reconstructed front teeth, the most terrible chill came over her. The chill had to do with Andreas and consisted of strange gratitude and redoubled guilt: in his last hour of life, he'd given her the thing she'd most wanted, the answer to her question. But now that she had it, she didn't want it. She saw that she'd done a very bad thing to both her mother and Tom by getting it. Both of them had known, and neither of them had wanted her to know.

Without reading farther, she lay down on Samantha's foldout bed. She wished that Andreas would appear and tell her what to do. The most deranged command of his would have been better than no command at all. She wondered if Tom might conceivably be mistaken about his death. She couldn't stand his being dead; she missed him unbearably. She pawed at her phone and saw that Denver Independent, not normally known for spot reporting, had already broken the story.

jumped from a height of at least five hundred feet

She turned off the phone and sobbed until upwelling anxiety overwhelmed her grief and she had to go and wake Samantha and beg for Ativan. She told Samantha that Andreas had killed himself. Samantha, who had difficulty making sense of anything that didn't refer to herself in some way, replied that she'd had a friend in high school who'd hanged himself, and that she hadn't gotten over it until she'd understood that suicide was the greatest of mysteries.

"It's not a mystery," Pip said.

"Yes it is," Samantha said. "I kept struggling to get over it. I kept thinking I could have prevented it, I could have saved him—"

"I could have saved him."

"I thought that too, but I was wrong. I had to learn to see it had nothing to do with me. I didn't need to feel guilty about something that had nothing to do with me. It pissed me off, knowing that. I wasn't anything to him. I couldn't have saved him because I didn't matter to him. I realized it's actually much healthier to be angry . . ."

Samantha went on like this, a fountain of declarative sentences about herself, until the Ativan kicked in and Pip had to lie down. In the morning, alone in Samantha's apartment, she slowly read the rest of Tom's document. She wanted the basic information, but she had to do a lot of skimming and backtracking to obtain it without reading too much about her parents' sex life. It wasn't that she was squeamish about sex per se; the problem, indeed, was that her parents' weirdness about sex was so foreign to her, so old-fashioned, so intolerably sad.

There were plenty of other things in the document to be disturbed by, but by the time she'd reached the end of it she could sense that the biggest problem was the money. Certainly it was interesting to imagine having Tom and Leila as second parents. But she couldn't call up Tom and say "Hey, *Dad*" without admitting that she'd broken her promise and read his document and betrayed him yet again. Realistically, unless her mother spontaneously volunteered his identity, there was going to be no Tom and Leila in her life. And she was willing to live with this, at least for now. But a *billion-dollar* trust fund? How many times had her mother said she loved nothing in the world more than Pip? If nobody and nothing was more important to her, how could she have so much money and still be letting Pip suffer with her student debt and her limited opportunities? Tom's document was a testimonial of frustration with her mother, and she was feeling infected by it. She saw why her mother had been afraid that Tom would take her away and turn her against her. She could feel herself turning against her right now.

She swallowed another Ativan and emailed Colleen once more. This time, in less than an hour, after eight months of silence, she got a reply.

> Fooled again. I'd thought there were no more ways for him to hurt me.

The reply had come through a 408 phone number, which Pip immediately called. Colleen turned out to be living in California, across the bay, in Cupertino, and working as chief legal officer for a newish tech company. She didn't hang up on Pip but simply resumed her complaint with the world's crappiness where she'd left off eight months ago.

"His women are all tweeting up a storm," she said. "Toni Field says he was the most honest human being to ever walk the earth—in other words, '*I* got to fuck him, nyah, nyah, nyah.' Sheila Taber says the Hegelian spirit of world history was alive in him—in other words, 'I fucked him before Toni did, and for longer.' You might want to get tweeting yourself. Stake your claim to the sainted hero."

"I didn't fuck him."

"Sorry, I forgot. Your broken tooth."

"Don't be mean to me. I'm really upset about this. I need to talk to someone who gets it."

"I'm afraid I'm pretty much a flaming ball of hurt and anger at the moment."

"Maybe you should stop reading tweets."

"I'm flying to Shenzhen tomorrow, that should help.

The Chinese never understood what all the fuss was about, God bless them."

"Can we get together when you're back?"

"I think you've always had the wrong idea about me. It kind of hurts, but it's also sweet. We can get together if you want."

Pip knew she should call her mother and tell her she was back in Oakland. She now saw why her mother had been suspicious of her motives in going to Denver: one glance at the DI website, on her neighbor Linda's computer, would have revealed her ex-husband's head shot and weekly commentary at the top of the page. It must have tortured her to think of Pip there with him. It explained her silences and recalcitrance since then: she believed that Pip had found her father and was lying about it. If nothing else, Pip wanted to reassure her that she hadn't lied about *that*. But she didn't see how she could do it without revealing what she'd learned in the meantime and how she'd learned it. Her mother would die of shame, might literally die of being too *visible*, if she knew what Pip had read about her. Pip could simply keep lying, of course; keep pretending that her job in Denver had just been a job. But the thought of having to lie forever, and never mention the money, and deprive herself of Tom and Leila, and generally indulge her mother's phobias and irrational prohibitions, made her angry. Although Andreas obviously wasn't the most honest person who'd ever walked the earth, she thought her mother might be the most difficult. Pip didn't know what to do about her, and so, for a while, she'd done Ativan.

Whacking a tennis ball was her poor-man's Ativan. The Sunday sun had sunk behind the elevated freeway in a sky still fogless. California had been in a drought emergency for months, but only now, after the solstice (she'd sent her mother a not-birthday card saying nothing more than "Love always, Pip"), was the weather feeling properly droughty. If the fog had come back, she might have felt safe to stop whacking and go inside, but it hadn't. She tried working on her backhand, sent two balls over the arboreal backstop and into the next yard, and reverted to her forehand. Could a more perfect manufactured object than a tennis ball be imagined? Fuzzy and spherical, squeezable and bouncy, its stitching a pair of matching tongues, its voice on impact a *pock* in the most pleasing of registers. Dogs knew a good thing, dogs loved tennis balls, and so did she.

When she finally went inside, all sweaty, Garth and Erik were at the kitchen table with two quarts of beer that a good Samaritan had bought them on their long walk home after bail had been made.

"Crowdfunding rocks," Garth said.

"Especially when it's effectively a loan," Erik said.

"Are they still pressing charges?" Pip said.

"For now," Garth said. "If Dreyfuss prevails at his hearing, the realtor becomes a trespasser that it was legitimate for us to repel."

"I don't think he's going to prevail." Pip picked up one of the half-empty bottles. "May I?" Garth and Erik hesitated just enough that she set down the bottle. "I can go buy some more."

"That would be great," Erik said.

"I'll come back with lots and lots."

"That would be great."

On her way out to get beer, she looked for Dreyfuss and found him sitting on his bed with his face in his hands. His situation was legitimately dire. He'd managed to revive his old mortgage, but tech-driven market pressure had pushed the value of his property up by thirty percent or more in the year Pip had been away. This had triggered a new round of shenanigans with his modified mortgage payments. He'd been given differing figures for these payments and had naturally chosen the lowest one, provided by a bank employee who then disappeared and who the bank claimed to have no record of, despite his having taken down her name and location. But without Marie's paychecks and Ramón's disability checks, he couldn't pay even the lowest figure every month. All he had going for him legally was his meticulous litany of the bank's noxious and probably felonious behavior. Pip had tried to read this litany, but it was nearly 300,000 words long.

"Hey, listen," she said, crouching at his feet. "I have a friend who's a lawyer for a tech company. She might know some firms that do pro bono work. Do you want me to ask her?"

"I appreciate your concern," Dreyfuss said. "But I've witnessed the effect that my case has on pro bono lawyers. At first there's an agreeable atmosphere of bonhomie, of this-is-an-injustice-and-we-will-definitely-fix-it, of why-didn't-you-come-to-us-sooner. A week later, they have their hands and faces pressed to the window. They're screaming, *Let me out of here!* I suppose—oh, never mind."

"What?"

"It occurred to me that if we could find a mentally ill lawyer, an already premedicated individual . . . It's a silly thought. Forget I mentioned it."

"It's actually not a bad idea."

"No. Better to pray that Judge Costa falls down a flight of stairs between now and a week from Tuesday. Do you believe in the efficacy of prayer, Pip?"

"Not really."

"Try to," Dreyfuss said.

The following Sunday, Jason was among the customers waiting when she unlocked the front door of Peet's. Knowing that he had a girlfriend, Pip resisted overinterpreting his early arrival, but he did seem to have hoped to talk to her. Lingering at the counter, he updated her on the progress of his new statistics textbook and the presentations he'd been giving to professors who refused to believe that a method could be so simple and intuitive. "They say, 'OK, the geometry works in that one special case.' So I show them other examples. I ask them to give me their own incredibly complicated examples. The method *always works*, and they still won't believe it. It's like their entire careers are invested in statistics being an impossibly nonintuitive subject."

"That's what I always heard," Pip said. "Do Not Take This Course."

"And what about you? You didn't tell me what you were doing in Bolivia."

"Oh, well. I was interning with the Sunlight Project. You know—Andreas Wolf."

It was amusing to see Jason's eyes widen. The deification of Andreas was in full swing now, with candlelight memorials in Berlin and Austin, in Prague and Melbourne, and online memorial sites stretching to terabytes with messages of gratitude and sorrow; it was like the Aaron Swartz phenomenon, only a hundred times larger.

"Are you kidding me?" Jason said.

"Um, no. I was there. Not when he died—I left at the end of January."

"That's incredible."

"I know—weird, right?"

"Did you actually spend time with him?"

"Sure. Everyone there did. He was always around."

"That's incredible."

"Don't say that too many times or you'll make me feel bad."

"That's not what I meant. I know you're really smart. I just didn't know you were interested in Web stuff."

"Yeah, I wasn't. Then I was. Then I wasn't again."

Although it would have disappointed her, by showing Jason to be as starstruck as most of the world seemed to be, she expected him not to let the subject drop. But he did. He asked her what her plans were now. She confessed that she couldn't see much farther than going home after work and whacking a tennis ball. He said he'd recently taken up tennis himself. He remarked that they should hit together sometime, but it was a vague remark, deflated by the known fact of his having a girlfriend, and he retreated to his favored table with his Sunday *Times*.

Whatever chemistry she and Jason had had was still there, if only in the form of regret about never really having acted on it. She realized, with additional regret, that he was probably the sweetest good-looking boy who'd ever shown strong interest in her. She felt chagrined that she'd failed to appreciate this when it might have mattered. She hoped that he was feeling some additional regret of his own, now that he knew that Andreas Wolf had esteemed her.

After a long hiatus, she was back on Facebook. It was a way of letting her old friends know she was in town without actually having to see them, but her main motive was defensive. Among her Facebook friends was her mother's neighbor Linda, who reassured her that nothing much had changed in her mother's life, and who seemed happy to convey Pip's substanceless greetings to her. It was Pip's hope that Linda might show her Facebook page to her mother or at least report on what was on it—i.e., almost nothing. Pip was living in her old house in Oakland and working at Peet's, end of story. She wanted to spare her mother the torment of imagining her still in

Denver, reunited with her father. Linda was gabbiness itself and could be counted on.

After her shift ended, and after she'd whacked the ball and showered and walked to the BART station, she couldn't resist checking out Jason on Facebook. His capacity for enthusiasm was everywhere in evidence. But of course what she wanted to know was how pretty his girlfriend was. The news on that score was mixed. The girlfriend had a great face and a scarily hipster look and a scarily French name, Sandrine, but she appeared to be a full foot shorter than Jason; they looked awkward together. With a shudder of revulsion at herself, and at Facebook, Pip turned off her device.

She was on her way to a Peruvian restaurant in Bernal Heights, maximally inconvenient to her, because Colleen apparently had foodie tendencies and wanted to try it. This after Colleen had twice bailed out of earlier dates at the last minute, pleading overwork. If her intention was to keep punishing Pip and make her feel small, it was working well.

The season of gray was on Bernal Heights. Shouting techies in their twenties filled the restaurant. Colleen was at a small table awkwardly situated by a wait station; she'd left Pip the chair that was in the waiters' way. Pip was struck by the unnecessary makeup Colleen was wearing and by the obvious priciness of her silk jacket and jewelry. She remembered that Colleen's stated ambition was to do boring, safe things.

"Sorry I'm late," she said. "It's quite the schlep from Oakland."

"I ordered some small plates," Colleen said. "I have to go back to the office later."

Already it was clear to Pip that Colleen had been a summer-camp friend, not a real friend, and that she shouldn't have kept sending her emails. But she had no one else to talk to about Andreas, and so she ordered a sangria and talked. She led with the big picture—that he'd killed a man in Germany and had brought her to Los Volcanes in some insane attempt at a cover-up—so that Colleen might see that what had happened at the Hotel Cortez wasn't personal.

"I think he was really sick," Pip said in conclusion. "Sicker than anybody knew."

"This is not exactly making me feel better about spending three years wanting him."

"I wanted him, too. But the side of himself he showed me was too scary."

"You really think he killed someone."

"He said so. I believed him."

"You know, I've been reading way more about him than is healthy. It's pure masochism. But I haven't seen anything about a murder."

"Even if he left a confession or something, I'm sure they covered it up. It's hard to see Willow or Flor not protecting the brand."

"You should tell the world," Colleen said. "Just to squish fucking Toni Field and all the others. 'Your sainted hero was a psychopath.' Would you do me that favor?"

Pip shook her head. "Even if I wanted to go public, who's going to believe me? I have other problems anyway. He told me who my mother is."

"You mean, besides being your mother?"

"She's a *billionaire*, Colleen. She has a trust fund worth, like, a billion dollars. She's like a renegade heiress. I can't begin to figure out how to deal with that."

Colleen frowned. "A billion dollars? You told me she was poor."

"She changed her identity. She ran away from it. Her father was president of McCaskill, the food company."

"That's your *mother*?" Colleen gave Pip a sidelong look, as if Pip herself were a pile of money and Colleen was deciding whether to believe her eyes. "That's what Dear Leader told you?"

"More or less."

"I guess it's obvious why he liked you."

"Thanks a lot. He didn't care about money."

"Nobody doesn't care about a billion dollars."

"Well, my mom didn't. I'm not sure it's even still there."

"You should try to find out."

"I just want everything to go away."

"You should definitely find out." Colleen reached across the table and touched Pip's hand. "Don't you think?"

By the time she got back to Dreyfuss's house, very late, there was a long email from Colleen in her in-box. It wasn't the email's content that was strange. Colleen apologized to Pip for making her come all the way to Bernal Heights; the next time they met, which she hoped would be soon, Colleen would come to Oakland; so great to see Pip again; really liked the new haircut . . . There followed several paragraphs of vintage Colleen on the crappiness of the legal profession, the crappiness of China, and the crappiness of the techie she'd dated for two months before discovering his passion for tax avoidance. What was strange about the email was its timing. For eight months Pip had waited for a few warm words from Colleen. Only now, within two hours of her saying the word *billionaire*, was she getting them.

Was Colleen aware of how obvious she was being? Pip thought not. Then again, maybe she herself was being paranoid. She remembered what Andreas had said about fame, the loneliness of it, the impossibility of trusting that people liked the famous person for himself. She suspected that being a billionaire would be even lonelier in that regard.

The next day, Monday, brought another long email from Colleen, plus two affectionate phone messages. On Tuesday, Dreyfuss had his injunction hearing with Judge Costa, who gave him ten minutes to present his case and then issued his judgment: fifteen days to vacate the house. On Wednesday, Jason left a Facebook message for Pip, asking if she wanted to hit with him. This wasn't a message that a boy with a serious girlfriend sent innocently to a girl he'd nearly slept with in the past. Pip might have felt glad of it, or at least flattered by it, had Colleen not suddenly become so friendly. Now all she could think was that her connection to Andreas had piqued Jason's interest. Was this going to be her new normal? She'd already had enough trouble trusting people; now she was facing a whole lifetime of not trusting them. She wrote back to Jason: To be discussed at Peet's. Then she did some research and made some phone calls. Early the next morning, Thursday, she flew to Wichita.

From the back of the cab from the airport, she saw the name McCaskill on Little League fields, on a big pavilion downtown, on a day-care center and a food-distribution depot on the city's slummy east side, on billboards affirming that MCCASKILL CARES. The midday heat was as intense as anything she'd experienced in Bolivia. Lawns were fried nearly white, and the trees looked ready to drop their leaves three months early.

Thanks to air-conditioning, the offices of James Navarre & Associates were chilly. Pip had barely opened her mouth when the receptionist led her back to a large, wood-paneled office where Mr. Navarre was waiting at the door. He was short and white-haired and apparently one of those men who weren't comfortable in clothes that weren't rumpled. "My God," he said, staring at Pip. "You really are her daughter."

She shook his hand and followed him into his office. The receptionist brought her a bottle of cold water and left them alone. Mr. Navarre continued to stare at her.

"So," she said. "Thank you for seeing me."

"Thank you for coming here."

"I have pictures of my mom, if you're interested."

"Of course I am. I'm also obligated to be."

Pip handed over her phone. She'd selected night pictures from inside her mother's cabin, so as not to betray her location. Mr. Navarre looked at them and shook his head as if confounded. On one wall of his office were photographs, Midwestern faces in exotically unstylish clothes and settings, somebody else's idea of America. Pip recognized David Laird, her grandfather, one of the objects of her research, on a golf cart with a rumpled and younger Mr. Navarre.

He handed the phone back to Pip. "She's alive?"

"Oh yeah."

"Where?"

"I can't tell you. She doesn't know I'm here, but she wouldn't be happy about it. She just wants to be left alone."

"We'd given up looking," Mr. Navarre said. "Her father tried to find her more than once, in the nineties. After he died, I was obligated to try again. He always thought she was still alive. Me, not so much. People die all the time. But unless I could prove that she was no longer among the living, and had left no heirs, I was barred from dissolving the trust."

"So it's still there. The trust."

"Absolutely. Administering it has made me a very wealthy man. I have every reason to insist that you tell me where your mother is. She won't have to do anything more than sign the receipt on a piece of registered mail. She can go on doing nothing, but she needs to know that she's the beneficiary."

"No. Sorry."

"Sandrine—"

"That's not my real name."

Mr. Navarre nodded. "I see."

"I don't want anything to change. I just came by to ask you a favor."

"Aha. I'll hazard a guess. You need money."

"Not even. I mean I do, but that's not what I'm here for. Can I talk?"

"I'm all ears."

"I've been living in Oakland, California. There's a house there that's in foreclosure, and the guy who owns it has to vacate it in less than two weeks. He's a good guy, and the bank is trying to steal his equity. So I was thinking, there's a lot of money in the trust, and you get to decide how it's invested. My impression is that you don't have to do much except write big checks to yourself."

"Well, now, in fact—"

"The money's mostly in McCaskill stock. You're required to leave it there. How much work can that be? And you get, whatever, a million dollars a year for that."

"How do you know that?"

"I just do."

"You've been in touch with your mother's ex-husband. He told you."

"Maybe."

"Sandrine. Work with me here."

"I'm the guy's granddaughter. David's. That makes me a Laird, and I'm asking you a small favor that doesn't personally cost you anything. The amount of money is nothing compared to what's in the trust. I want you to buy my friend's house, right away, and then charge him some rent he can afford. It won't be a lot of rent, so it won't be a great investment. But you can invest the money any way you want, right?"

Mr. Navarre made a tent of his fingers. "I have a fiduciary responsibility to invest the money wisely. I would need, at a minimum, your mother's written authorization. I admit that it doesn't seem likely she'll be challenging my decisions any time soon, but I need to be covered for that eventuality."

"Does the trust say that I'm the heir?"

"There is a per stirpes clause, yes."

"So let me sign."

"I can't knowingly let you sign under a false name. Even if I were inclined to make this particular investment."

Pip frowned. She'd thought of a lot, during the two flights it had taken her to get to Wichita, but she hadn't thought of this. "If I give you my real name, you're going to use it to try to find my mother, even if I ask you not to."

"Let's slow down here," Mr. Navarre said. "Look at this from my side. I do believe that Anabel is alive and you're her daughter. This is a highly unusual situation, but I believe you're telling me the truth. But if you come to me next month and say you want another investment, for some other reason—where does it end?"

"I won't do that."

"So you say now. But if all you have to do is ask?"

"Well, then we'll have this discussion again. But we won't. It's not going to happen again."

Mr. Navarre increased the steepness of his tented fingers. "I don't know what happened in that family. Your family. I never understood your mother or her father. But the decisions he made about his stake in McCaskill created a heck of a lot of ill will. Given the tax hit he took, leaving her a quarter of the estate, he had to put most of the rest in charitable trusts. I know you think I get money for nothing, but liquidating enough shares to pay the estate-tax bill wasn't nothing. And meanwhile Anabel's brothers only got about eighty million apiece fungible. The rest is in trusts they control but don't much profit from. All this to make sure the daughter who hated David got her money in a lump. To say I never understood it is an understatement. And now you won't even let me tell her the money is there?"

That is correct, Pip thought. *Everyone needs to keep conspiring to protect my mother from reality.*

"I can work on it," she said. "But it has to be me. I don't want her getting some registered letter from you. If I agree to work on it, will you buy this house in Oakland?"

"Why should I do that?"

"Because I'm the heir and I'm asking for it!"

"So you're crazy, too."

"No."

"You could speak to your mother and be a billionaire, but instead you're asking me to buy a house in foreclosure for some third party. This person wouldn't happen to be your boyfriend?"

"No. He's a well-medicated schizophrenic in his forties."

Mr. Navarre shook his head. "You don't want to eradicate malaria. You don't want to send poor kids to college. You don't want to take a private trip to outer space. You don't even want to be a cokehead."

"Aren't all the Lairds and McCaskills messed up from having too much money?"

"About half of them, yeah."

"Didn't one of my uncles try to buy an NBA team?"

"Better than that. He wanted the David M. Laird Jr. Charitable Trust to buy it."

"So it sounds like my weirdness is totally within normal parameters."

"Listen here." Mr. Navarre sat up straight and fixed Pip with a look. "I'm never going to have to report to you. I'm older than your mother, and I have a fondness for fatty red meats. It's not because I owe you any courtesies that I propose the following. You're going to tell me your real name and sign an authorization. After you leave here, you'll go to the Laird family doctor and leave a blood sample. Six months from today, if I don't hear from you sooner, I will hire a detective to locate your mother. In return, the trust will buy your friend's house. I give you that, you give me your mother."

"You have to buy the house right away, though. Like, today or tomorrow. Monday at the latest."

"Do you agree to the terms? You'll have six months to sort things out with your mother."

Pip was weighing her wish to help Dreyfuss against her aversion to having a conversation with her mother. She realized that even if she didn't have the conversation, her mother wouldn't know for sure it was her fault that Mr. Navarre had found her. Her mother could imagine it was Tom's fault, or Andreas's. She could sign the registered receipt, burn the letter without reading it, and go right on denying reality.

"My legal name is Purity Tyler."

It was four thirty by the time she'd signed the authorization, been phlebotomized at the doctor's office, and taken another cab to the airport. Jets on the tarmac shimmered in fumes and unabated sun, but something was happening to the sky, some premonition that its depthless blue would soon be a more local gray. Her connecting flight, to Denver, was showing a delay of forty-five minutes. She had to be at work the following afternoon, but it

occurred to her that she could miss her connection in
Denver and rebook for the morning. She'd boldly asked
Mr. Navarre to reimburse her for her flights and cabs; the
trip so far had cost her nothing.

She couldn't see Tom without admitting that she'd read
his memoir, and although she felt a craving for Leila's for-
giveness she worried that Leila still considered her a
threat and wouldn't be happy to see her. With her phone,
she searched instead for Cynthia Aberant and found her
listed as an associate professor in a community-studies
program. The only impeccably kind and well-behaved
person in Tom's entire memoir was his sister. Pip dialed
her office number and got her.

"This is Pip Tyler," she said. "Do you know who I am?"

"I'm sorry. Say your name again?"

"Pip Tyler. Purity Tyler."

There was a dead cellular silence. Then Cynthia said,
"You're my brother's daughter."

"Right. So, I was hoping I could talk to you?"

"You should talk to Tom, not me."

"I'm on my way to Denver right now. If you had, like,
even just an hour tonight. You're the only person I can
talk to."

After another silence, Cynthia assented.

The flight, in a too-small jet, dodging thunderstorms,
cured Pip of any desire for future air travel. She expected
death the whole way. What was interesting was how
quickly she then forgot about it, like a dog to whom death
was literally unimaginable, while she rode in a cab to
Cynthia's. Dogs again had it right. They didn't trouble
themselves with mysteries that could never be solved
anyway.

Cynthia's house was in the same neighborhood as
Leila's husband's. She came to the front door holding a
glass of red wine. She was a plus-size woman with long

gray-blond hair and a pleasant face. "I needed a head start," she said, raising the glass. "Do you drink?"

Her living room was an academic version of Drey-fuss's, her art and her books and even her furniture steeped in leftism. Pip sat down by a cabinet with Latino peasants depicted in bright primitive paint. Cynthia took an armchair whose cushions bore the imprint of her body's ample contours. "So, you're my niece," she said.

"You're my aunt."

"And why are you here and not at my brother's?"

Pip drank her wine and told her story. When she was done, Cynthia poured her more wine and said, "I always thought Tom had a novel in him."

"He says it in the memoir," Pip said. "He wanted to be a novelist, but my mom wouldn't let him."

Her aunt's expression hardened. "She was all about not letting."

"Did you not like her?"

"No, I did like her, at first. I wanted us to have a rela-tionship. But she was somehow not approachable."

"She's the same way now. She's really shy underneath."

"I didn't like how she treated my stepmother. But Clelia was a person of strong judgments herself, and so I cut your mother some slack. But then . . . this is probably in the memoir . . ."

"The spitting thing?"

"I was there in the room, I saw it happen. Tom ex-plained it to me afterward, and I sort of understood—I'm no friend of agribusiness and bare-knuckled capital. But I couldn't help thinking that Tom had made a mistake. I thought, 'This woman is *nuts*.' And then for years I hardly saw him and I never saw her—I was raising my own daughter. But even from afar I had the sense that he was in a toxic relationship. He was so loyal to her, I could never get anything out of him while they were together. Even afterward, he wouldn't really speak ill of her. I thought he should be way angrier than he was. But eventually things worked out well for him. He's outstanding at what he does, and Leila—well, you know. Everybody loves Leila. He should have been married to her all along."

"Right. Everyone can see she's more wonderful than my mom."

"She is pretty great. I don't see why you're talking to me and not her."

"She seemed to think I wanted to take Tom away from her."

"I wouldn't worry about that. They seem to be more of a unit than ever these days." Cynthia refilled her own glass. "But here you are. Tell me why again?"

"Because I don't know what to do."

"You want my advice."

"Yes, please."

"You might not like it."

"Give it to me anyway."

"I think you should be really, really angry."

Pip nodded. "It's hard, though. I feel like I betrayed Tom by reading his memoir, and now I'm betraying my mother by going to Wichita and knowing things behind her back."

"That's nonsense, if you'll pardon me."

"How is it nonsense?"

"I got very mad at Tom when he told me about you. You lived in his house for however long, for weeks, and he knew you were his daughter and didn't tell you. Don't you think you had a right to that information?"

"I guess he was respecting my mom's privacy."

"Really? Is that not the most infuriating bullshit? Why should he protect her? Why should he defer to his ex-wife at your expense? She got herself pregnant without telling him. She never told him that she had you. She used him—

she used *you*—to continue some never-ending fight she had with him. He could have had a daughter, you could have had a father, but she 'wouldn't let him.' On what planet does he owe her anything?"

"That's a helpful insight."

"On what planet do *you* owe her anything? From what Tom tells me, you spent your entire childhood below the poverty line. Your mother made you for her own selfish purposes—"

"No, that's harsh," Pip said. "Weren't you a single mom, too?"

"Not by choice. Gretchen's father knew about her, and she knew about him. They have a relationship now. And I did everything I could for Gretchen. I quit organizing and went back to school because of her, so she didn't have to suffer from *my* personal choices. What personal choice did your mother ever give up for you?"

Tears came to Pip's eyes. "She loved me."

"I'm sure. I'm sure she did. But by your own account, she doesn't have anyone else in her life. She created you to be what no one else can be for her. *I'm* angry at the self-ishness of that. I'm angry that she's the kind of 'feminist' who gives feminism a bad name. I feel like going over to Tom's right this minute and slapping him in the face. For enabling her fantasies. She had real gifts—it's such a waste. I don't see why you're not out of your mind with rage."

"I can't explain it. She's a really lost person."

"Well, fine. I can't make you be angry if you're not. But do me a favor and try to keep one thought in mind: you don't owe these people anything. They owe *you*, big-time. It's your turn to call the shots now. If they give you any resistance, you're within your rights to nuke them."

Pip nodded, but she was thinking about how terrible the world was, what an eternal struggle for power. Secrets were power. Money was power. Being needed was power. Power, power, power: how could the world be organized around the struggle for a thing so lonely and oppressive in the having of it?

Cynthia made them a simple dinner, opened a second bottle, and talked about the world as she saw it: the concentration of capital in the hands of a few, the calculated demolition of faith in government, the worldwide abdication of responsibility for climate change, the disappointments of Obama. She oscillated between anger and despair, and Pip both did and didn't share her anger. Certainly it seemed unfair that she'd been stuck with a shitty world of her parents' making. They'd put her in an impossible position personally, and they belonged to the generation that had done nothing about nuclear weapons and less than nothing about global warming; it wasn't her fault. And yet it was oddly comforting to know that even if she could identify the ethically correct thing to do with a billion dollars, and proceeded to do it, she could never alter the world's shitty course. She thought of her mother's spiritual Endeavor, her striving merely to be mindful. For better or worse, she was her mother's daughter.

She kept thinking about her mother after she went to bed, in Gretchen's bedroom. What Cynthia couldn't know was how she'd made her mother smile. The pure, spontaneous love in that smile, every time she'd caught sight of Pip. And the shyness of it, the visible worry that Pip might not love her as much as she loved Pip. Her mother had a childlike heart. From reading the memoir, Pip suspected that she'd never stopped loving Tom, even to this day. Oh, the heartbreak of that scene with the stuffed toy bull: Pip knew exactly the nuttily, childishly hopeful look that her mother must have had on her face. There had been stuffed animals on her own childhood bed, a small menagerie of them, and she and her mother had played with them for hours on end, giving them voices, inventing moral crises to resolve. The little child and the big child, the one whose hair was going gray, the one whose shy sidelong glances the little one sometimes caught. Her mother had needed to give love and receive it. This was why she'd had Pip. Was that so monstrous? Wasn't it more like miraculously resourceful?

On Sunday, Jason again was waiting when she unlocked the door of Peet's. He loitered at the counter, ignoring Navi's unfriendly looks, until Pip could speak to him.

"So stop me if I'm being too intrusive," she said. "But can I ask why you aren't with your girlfriend on a Sunday morning?"

"She's a late riser," Jason said. "Like, afternoon late. She stays up online until four in the morning."

"Do you guys live together?"

"It's not that kind of thing."

"But it's the kind of thing where it's OK to play tennis with a girl you used to date."

"Totally. I'm allowed to have friends."

"Jason. Listen." Pip lowered her voice. "Even if your girlfriend's OK with our being friends, I don't think it's a good idea."

He seemed innocently puzzled. "You don't even want to hit with me? I'm not as good as a brick wall. But I'm getting better."

"If you didn't have a girlfriend, I'd be happy to hit with you. But you do, so."

"You're telling me I have to *break up* with my girlfriend before you'll hit with me? It's a pretty substantial upfront investment for just hitting a tennis ball."

"The city's full of people you could hit with for no investment. I don't know why you're suddenly so interested in hitting with me. Why I suddenly stopped being the abnormal girl who does scary things."

He blushed. "Because I've had two weeks to sit and watch you behind the counter?"

"Hmm."

"No, you're right, you're right," he said, holding his hands up. "I shouldn't have asked."

She felt a little sick, seeing him back away from her, his implied compliment echoing in her ears. But she was even sicker of betraying people.

When she got home from work, under a mercilessly clear sky, she found that she had no appetite for whacking the ball. It was like the spaghetti with eggplant in Tom's memoir: all at once, her satisfaction was exhausted. She both wished that she could hit with an actual person, a kind person, with Jason, and was relieved that she couldn't. Another lesson of Tom's memoir was that there ought to be a law against boy-girl relationships before the age of thirty.

The TV was on in the living room, but Dreyfuss was absorbed in typing on the computer. "I'm filing a complaint of judicial misconduct," he explained to Pip. "There's a clear pattern of bias in Judge Costa's decisions. I've examined more than three hundred relevant cases, and I believe the evidence can safely be described as compelling."

"Dreyfuss," Pip said gently. "You can stop doing that."

"I've amassed a wealth of new information about Costa since Tuesday. I hesitate to use the word *conspiracy*, and yet—"

"Don't use it at all. It's a worrisome word, coming from you."

"Some conspiracies are real, Pip. You've seen that yourself."

She pulled up a chair next to him. "I should have told

you this sooner," she said. "Somebody is buying the house. Somebody I know. Somebody who's going to let us keep living here."

An actual emotion, worry or sadness, flickered in Dreyfuss's face. "I own this house," he said. "I have equity in this house. I bought it with my departed mother's money. I'm not letting go of it."

"The bank took it before the market rebounded. You lost it and you're not getting it back. I did the only thing I could think to do."

Dreyfuss narrowed his eyes. "You have money?"

"No. But someday I will. When I do, you can have the house back as a present from me. Can you trust me? Everything will be OK if you trust me. I promise."

He seemed to recede into himself, into a more familiar absence of affect. "Bitter experience," he said, "has forced on me a policy of never trusting anyone. You, for example. You've always struck me as a responsible and generous person, and yet who really knows what's in your head? Still less what will be in your head in the future?"

"Believe me, I know how hard it is."

He turned back to the computer. "I'm filing my complaint."

"Dreyfuss," she said. "You don't have any choice but to trust me. It's either that or wind up on the street."

"There will be further legal actions."

"Fine, but in the meantime let's work out a rent we all can pay."

"I fear estoppel of the fraud claim," Dreyfuss said, typing. "To pay the supposed owner rent concedes the legitimacy of the sale."

"So give the money to me. I'll write the checks. You don't have to concede anything. You can—"

She stopped. A tear had rolled down Dreyfuss's cheek.

* * *

Evening sunlight was in the trees of Mosswood Park when Pip coasted up to the tennis courts on her bike. Standing next to Jason was an absurdly proportioned brown dog, huge-headed, low-slung, extremely long. It was smiling as if proud of the nest of ratty tennis balls at its feet. Jason caught sight of Pip and waved to her needlessly, goofily. The dog swished its bushy and cumbersome tail.

"This is *your* dog?"

"As of last week," Jason said. "I inherited him from my sister. She's going to Japan for two years."

"What's his name?

"Choco. Like his color, chocolate."

The dog presented Pip with a drooly, dirty tennis ball and pushed his head between her bare knees. End to end, there was a whole lot of Choco.

"I wasn't sure I could handle having a dog," Jason said, "but he's got this thing for chewing lemons. He walks around with them in his mouth, sort of half bitten, lots of slobber. He looks like he's wearing this big idiotic yellow smile. My practical intelligence said no, but my heart said yes."

"The acid can't be good for his teeth."

"My sister had a lemon tree behind her apartment. I'm putting him on a reduced-citrus diet. As you can see, he still has his teeth."

"Excellent dog."

"And a champ at finding tennis balls."

"Next best thing to lemons."

"Right?"

Four nights earlier, Jason had sent Pip a one-line message on Facebook: check out my relationship status. This she had duly done and mostly been dismayed by. The last thing she wanted was to be in any way responsible for a breakup. Among other things, it seemed to oblige her to be worth breaking up for: to be available. And yet, of course, she'd literally asked for it. Of all the ways she could have said no to hitting a tennis ball, she'd chosen to make an issue of Jason's girlfriend. Not only could no one else be trusted—she herself couldn't be trusted! She'd wrapped herself in relationship ethics when her real motive was to take Jason away from Sandrine. And sleep with him herself? She was certainly hungry to sleep with someone; it was practically forever since she'd done it. But she liked Jason a little too much to think it was a good idea to sleep with *him*. What if she started liking him even more? Relationship pain and relationship horror seemed probable. She'd written back:

> Obviously saying this WAY too late, but . . . I'm going through a lot of stuff of my own right now and I can't really promise you anything but returning balls hit to my forehand. Should have been MUCH clearer about this on Sunday. I apologize (again, again, again). Please don't feel you have to follow through and hit with me.

To which Jason had replied, very quickly, just hitting works for me.

As soon as they were on a court, she discovered that he was bad at tennis, even worse than she was. He tried to crush every shot, sometimes missing the ball altogether, more often sending it into the net or over her head, and his good shots were unreturnable bullets. After ten minutes, she called a time-out. Choco, leashed to the outside of the fence, stood up hopefully.

"I'm no tennis pro," she said, "but I think you're swinging too hard."

"It feels *fantastic* when I connect."

"I know. But we're trying to hit together."

His face clouded. "I suck at this, don't I."

"That's why we're practicing."

He swung less hard after that, and the hitting was somewhat more satisfactory, but their longest rally in an hour was six hits. "I blame the brick wall," Jason said as they walked off the court. "I'm realizing I should have drawn a line representing the top of the net. And maybe a higher line to represent the baseline."

"I sort of do that mentally," Pip said.

"I don't suppose you'd like to hear how to calculate the probability of a six-hit rally, given an arbitrary error rate of fifty percent? Or, slightly more interesting, how to calculate our actual combined error rate, given the empirical frequency of four-hit rallies?"

"Sometime I would," Pip said. "But I should probably get home."

"Do I suck too much to do this again?"

"No. We had some fun rallies."

"I should have told you how much I suck."

"Whatever you didn't tell me is dwarfed by how much I haven't told you."

Jason bent down to unknot Choco's leash. There was something humble and patient about the dog's very low-slungness, the drooping of his heavy head. His grin was silly, possibly in a sly way, suggesting awareness of his more general silliness as a dog.

"I'm sorry if I freaked you out," Jason said. "By breaking up, I mean. It was already in the works. I just didn't want you to think I'm the kind of guy who, you know. Sees two people at once."

"I understand," Pip said. "Loyalty is good."

"I also don't want you to think you were the only reason."

"OK. I won't think that."

"Although you were definitely *a* reason."

"Got that, too."

They didn't speak of it again, not the next time they hit, three days later, nor any of the many times they hit in August and September. Jason was every bit as compulsive about whacking the ball as Pip was, and for a long time the intensity of their mutual concentration, on the court, was an adequate substitute for the kinds of off-court intensity from which she was still shying and for which Jason, his eager personality notwithstanding, was sensitive enough not to pressure her. But she liked him a lot and loved Choco. Whatever else happened, she wanted a dog in her life. In hindsight, now that she'd read Tom's memoir and knew the historical depth of her mother's concern for animals, she was surprised that her mother had never had a pet. She guessed that she herself had been that pet. There was also her mother's strange cosmology of animals, a simplified trinity consisting of birds (whose beady eyes frightened her), cats (which represented the Feminine but to which she was totally allergic), and dogs (which embodied the Masculine and therefore, whatever their charms, could not be allowed to disturb her cabin with their pushy male-principle energies). Pip was in any case so dog-starved that she would have fallen for one far less excellent than Choco. Choco was *weird*, very unneedy as dogs went, a kind of Zen dog, all about his lemons and sly acknowledgment of his ridiculousness.

Hitting two or three times a week, she and Jason got better—enough better to be depressed or enraged when they were suddenly worse again. They never played games, only rallied, working together to keep the ball in play. Week by week, the light began to change, their shadows at the baseline stretching, the autumn-scented dusk arriving earlier. It was the driest and least foggy season of the year in Oakland, but she minded it less now that it meant consistently ideal tennis conditions. All over the state, reservoirs and wells were going dry, the taste and clarity of tap water worsening, farmers suffering, Northern Californians conserving while Orange County set new records for monthly consumption, but none of this mattered for the hour and a half that she was on the court with Jason.

Finally there came a crisp blue afternoon, a Sunday, the day after Daylight Saving ended, when they met at the park at three o'clock and hit for so long that the light began to fail. Pip was in an absolute groove with her forehand, Jason was bounding around and achieving his own personal-best low error rate, and although her elbow had begun to ache she wanted never to stop. They had impossibly long rallies, back and forth, *whack* and *whack*, rallies so long that she was giggling with happiness by the end of them. The sun went down, the air was deliciously cool, and they kept hitting. The ball bouncing up in a low arc, her eyes latching on to it, being sure to see it, just see it, not think, and her body doing the rest without being asked to. That instant of connecting, the satisfaction of reversing the ball's inertia, the sweetness of the sweet spot. For the first time since her early days at Los Volcanes she was experiencing perfect contentment. Yes, a kind of heaven: long rallies on an autumn evening, the exercise of skill in light still good enough to hit by, the faithful *pock* of a tennis ball. It was enough.

In near-darkness afterward, outside the fence, she put her arms around Jason and her face to his chest. Choco stood by patiently, his mouth open, smiling.

"OK," she said, "OK."

"It's about time," he said.

"I've got some things I have to tell you."

The rain came three weeks later. Nothing made Pip more homesick for the San Lorenzo Valley than what passed for rain in the East Bay. Rain in Oakland was ordinary, seldom very heavy, always liable to yield to clear sky between the chaotic tentacles of Pacific storm cloud. Only up in the cloud-trapping Santa Cruz Mountains could the rain continue for days without a break, never less than moderately heavy and often coming down an inch per hour, all night, all day, the river rising to lap at the undersides of bridges, Highway 9 covered with sheets of muddy runoff and fallen boughs, power lines down everywhere, PG&E trucks flashing their lights in the torrential midday twilight. That was real rain. Back in the pre-drought years, six feet of it had fallen every winter.

"I might need to go home to Felton for a while," Pip said to Jason one evening while they were walking, under umbrellas, down the hill from the St. Agnes Home. She'd been visiting Ramón at the home every month or so, even though things had changed between them. He was wholly Marie's adoptee now, not Stephen's at all. He had new friends, including a "girlfriend," and he took very seriously the janitorial duties he'd learned to perform. Pip had wanted Jason to meet him before she drifted out of his life altogether.

"How long is a while?" Jason said.

"I don't know. Weeks maybe. Longer than I have days off for. I have a feeling my mom's going to be difficult. I may have to quit my job."

"Can I come down and see you?"

"No, I'll come up. It's a five-hundred-square-foot cabin. Plus I'm worried you'll run for your life when you meet my mom. You'll think I've been concealing the fact that I'm like her."

"Everybody's embarrassed by their parents."

"But I have actual reason to be."

Pip was Jason's newest enthusiasm but thankfully not his only one; she could get him off the subject of her virtues by mentioning math, tennis, TV shows, video games, writers. His life was much fuller than hers, and the breathing space this gave her was welcome. If she wanted his complete attention again, all she had to do was put his hands on her body; he was not undoglike himself in this regard. If she wanted something more, like visiting Ramón with her, he agreed to it enthusiastically. He had a way of making whatever they were doing the thing he most wanted to do. She'd watched him rapidly eat four generic vanilla-cream cookies and then stop and marvel at a fifth, holding it in front of his eyes and saying, "These are *fantastic*."

If she became a rich person—and she could already feel herself becoming one; was sensing the mentally deformative weight of the word *heir*—Jason would be the last boy who'd liked her when she was still nobody. He did admit that her interning with Andreas Wolf had "confirmed" his assessment of her intelligence, but he swore it hadn't had anything to do with his breakup. "It was just you," he said. "You behind the counter at Peet's." She trusted Jason in a way that might well prove to be unique, but she didn't want him to know this. She was aware of how easily she could blow things with him, and she was even more aware, thanks to Tom's memoir, of the hazards of love. She felt herself wanting to bury herself in Jason, to pour her trust into him, even though she had evidence that self-burial and crazy trust levels could result in toxicity. She was therefore allowing herself to be heedless in sex only. This was probably hazardous, too, but she couldn't help it.

They had more sex as soon as they got back to Jason's apartment. Starting to fall in love with a person made it bigger, almost metaphysical; a John Donne poem she'd studied in college and failed to appreciate, a poem about the Extasie and how it doth unperplex, was making sense to her now. But in the wake of the Extasie she became anxious again.

"I think I'd better call my mom," she said. "I can't postpone it any longer."

"Do it."

"Can you just keep lying there like that while I do? With your arm there? I need you to hold me in case I feel like I'm getting sucked in."

"I'm picturing somebody getting sucked out of a blown-open airplane," Jason said. "They say it's surprisingly hard to hold on to a person when that happens. Or maybe not so surprising when you consider the p.s.i. differential at forty thousand feet."

"Do your best," she said, reaching for her phone.

She loved having a body now that Jason loved her having it. She was clutching his arm when her mother answered.

"Hi, Mom." She braced herself for a *Pussycat!*

"Yes," her mother said.

"So, I'm sorry I haven't called in so long, but I'm thinking I might come down and see you."

"All right."

"Mom?"

"You come and go as you please. If you want to come, come. Obviously I can't stop you. Obviously I'll be here."

"Mom, I'm really sorry."

There was a click, a cessation.

"Holy shit," Pip said. "She hung up on me."

"Uh oh."

It hadn't occurred to her that her mother might be angry at her; that even their extreme case of moral hazard might have limits. But now that she thought about it, her mother's entire story, in Tom's memoir, was one of serial abandonment and betrayal, followed by scorching moral judgment. Pip had always been safe from this judgment, but she could tell, from the fact that Tom still seemed afraid of it, even after twenty-five years, that it was awful to experience. She felt afraid of it herself now, and closer to Tom.

The next day, she gave notice at Peet's and called Mr. Navarre to tell him she was going to have the conversation with her mother, and to ask him for five thousand dollars. Mr. Navarre could have been judgmental or teasing about the money, but apparently he was impressed that she'd waited four and a half months to ask for any. She enjoyed the feeling that she'd passed some test, exceeded some norm.

Microclimates of the San Lorenzo: the pavement at the Santa Cruz bus station was nearly dry, but just two miles away, at the top of Graham Hill Road, the driver had to put his wipers on. Winter night had fallen. Pip's mother's lane was spongy with redwood needles dislodged and sodden with the rain, the sound of which surrounded her polyrhythmically, a steady background patter, heavier drippings, hiccuping gurgles. The musty wood-soak smell of Valley wetness overwhelmed her with sense-memory.

The cabin was dark. Inside it was the sound of her childhood, the patter of rain on a roof that consisted only of shingle and bare boards, no insulation or ceiling. She associated the sound with her mother's love, which had been as reliable as the rain in its season. Waking up in the night and hearing the rain still pattering the same way it had when she'd fallen asleep, hearing it night after night, had felt so much like being loved that the rain might have been love itself. Rain pattering at dinner. Rain pattering while she did her homework. Rain pattering while her mother knitted. Rain pattering on Christmas with the sad little tree that you could get for free on Christmas Eve. Rain pattering while she opened presents that her mother had put aside money for all fall.

She sat in the cold and dark for a while, at the kitchen table, listening to the rain and feeling sentimental. Then she turned on a light and opened a bottle and made a fire in the woodstove. The rain fell and fell.

The person who was both her mother and Anabel Laird came home at nine fifteen with a canvas bag of groceries. She stood in the front doorway and looked at Pip without speaking. Underneath her rain parka she was wearing an old dress that Pip loved and, indeed, coveted. It was a snug and faded brown cotton dress with long sleeves and many buttons, a kind of Soviet worker-woman's dress. Back in the day, her mother would probably have given her the dress if she'd asked for it, but her mother had so few covetable possessions that depriving her of even one of them was unthinkable.

"So I came home," Pip said.

"I see that."

"I know you don't like to drink, but this might be a good night for an exception."

"No, thank you."

The person who was both her mother and Anabel left the parka and groceries by the door and went to the back of the cabin. Pip heard the bathroom door close. It was ten minutes before she realized that her mother was hiding in the bathroom, not intending to come out.

She went and knocked on the door, which was just boards held together with crossboards. "Mom?"

There was no answer, but her mother hadn't used the hook that served as a lock. Pip went in and found her mother sitting on the concrete floor of the tiny shower, staring straight ahead, her knees drawn up to her chin.

"Don't be sitting there," Pip said.

She crouched down and touched her mother's arm. Her mother jerked her arm away.

"You know what?" Pip said. "I'm mad at you, too. So

don't be thinking being mad at me is going to get you out of this."

Her mother was mouth-breathing, staring. "I'm not angry with you," she said. "I am . . ." She shook her head. "I knew this would happen. No matter how careful I was, I knew that someday this would happen."

"That *what* would happen? That I'd come home and want to talk to you, and be honest, and be part of the two of us again? Because that's what I'm doing."

"I knew it the way I know my own name."

"What is your name? Maybe let's start with that. Will you come sit in the kitchen with me?"

Her mother shook her head again. "I'm getting used to being alone. I'd forgotten how hard it is. It's very hard, even harder this time, much harder—you brought me so much joy. But it's not impossible to relinquish desire. I'm learning it again. I'm making progress."

"So, what, I'm supposed to leave now? That's what you want?"

"You already left."

"Yeah, well, hey, but I came back, too, didn't I?"

"Out of duty," her mother said. "Or out of pity. Or because you're angry. I'm not blaming you, Purity. I'm telling you that I will be all right without you. Everything we have is temporary, the joy, the suffering, everything. I had the joy of experiencing your goodness for a very long time. It was enough. I have no right to ask for more."

"*Mom*. Stop talking like that. I need you in my life. You're the most important person in the world to me. I need you to stop being Buddhist and try to have an adult conversation with me."

"Or else what?" Her mother smiled faintly. "You'll leave again?"

"Or else, I don't know, I'm going to pull your hair and scratch you."

Her mother's failure to be amused was nothing new. "I'm no longer so afraid of you leaving," she said. "For a long time, the prospect was like death to me. But it's not death. At a certain point, trying to hold on to you became the real death."

Pip sighed. "OK, frankly—you calling me pussycat, me not being able to end a phone call with you, I'd be happy to retire all that. I'm a lot older than I used to be. You wouldn't believe how much older. But don't you want to know what I'm like now? Don't you want to know the person I've turned into? It's the same old me but also not. I mean, aren't I interesting to you? You're still interesting to me."

Her mother turned her head and gave her an empty look. "What kind of person are you now?"

"I don't know. I have a real boyfriend—that's one thing. I'm kind of in love with him."

"That's nice."

"OK, another thing. A big thing. I know what your real name is."

"I'm sure you do."

"Will you say it for me?"

"No. Never."

"You have to say it. You have to tell me everything, because I'm your daughter and I can't be in the same room with you if all we do is lie."

Her mother stood up gracefully, with her Endeavor-perfected limberness, but her head hit the shampoo basket and knocked a bottle to the shower floor. She threw herself angrily out of the stall, stumbled on Pip, and ran from the bathroom.

"Mom!" Pip said, chasing her.

"I want nothing to do with that part of you."

"Which part of me?"

Her mother spun around. Her face was pure torment.

"Get out! Get out! Leave me alone! Both of you! For the love of God, please just leave me alone!"

Pip watched, horrified, as the person who now seemed entirely Anabel fell onto her bed and yanked the comforter over her head and lay there rocking herself, crying full-throatedly in pain. Pip had expected difficulty, but this was extreme by any measure. She went to the kitchen and knocked back a glass of wine. Then she returned to the bed and pulled the comforter away, lay down behind her mother and put her arms around her. She buried her face in her mother's thick hair and breathed in her smell, the most distinct of all smells, the smell that there was nothing like. The brown dress's cotton was soft from a hundred washings. Slowly her mother's crying subsided into whimpers. Rain pattered on the sleeping-porch roof.

"I'm sorry," Pip said. "I'm sorry I can't just leave, I know it's hard. But you created me and now you have to deal with me. That's my purpose. I'm your reality."

Her mother said nothing.

Both of you?

Pip lowered her voice to a whisper. "Do you still love him?"

She felt her mother stiffen.

"I think he still loves you."

Her mother took a sharp breath and didn't let it out.

"So there's got to be a way to move on," Pip said. "There's got to be a way to forgive and move on. I'm not leaving until you do."

How she got the story out of her mother, the next morning, was by letting her believe that Tom had told her his version of it; she figured, correctly, that her mother would find this intolerable. Her mother omitted the details of her conception, saying only that it had occurred the very last time she'd seen Tom, but she was surprisingly calm and articulate about other details. Pip's actual birthday was February 24, not July 11. She'd been delivered naturally, by a midwife, in a safe house in Riverside, California. Until she was two, she and her mother had lived in Bakersfield, where her mother cleaned hotel rooms for a living. Then, by bad luck (because Bakersfield was really nowhere), her mother ran into a college friend who asked too many questions. A new friend from the women's shelter knew of a cabin for rent in the Santa Cruz Mountains, and there they moved.

"I heard terrible stories in the shelters and safe houses," her mother said. "So many women who were punching bags. So many stories of men whose idea of love was stalking and stabbing their ex-wives. I should have felt guilty about misrepresenting myself, but I didn't. Men's emotional cruelty can be every bit as painful as physical abuse. My father was cruel and my husband was crueler."

"Really," Pip said.

"Yes, really. I told him it would kill me if he ever took money from my father, and he did it. Did it specifically to hurt me. He slept with my best friend to hurt me. He took my advice and encouragement and used it to make a career for himself, and then, when I was struggling with my own career, he abandoned me. You're only young once, and I gave him my youth because I believed his promises, and then, when I wasn't young anymore, he broke his promises. And I knew it all along. I knew he would betray me. I told him all along, but it didn't stop him from making promises to me, which I believed because I was weak. I really was like the other women in the shelters."

Pip crossed her arms prosecutorially. "And so it seemed OK to you to have his baby without telling him. That seemed like the morally right thing to do."

"He knew I wanted a baby."

"But why his? Why not some random sperm donor's?"

"Because I keep my promises. I promised him I'd be his forever. He could break his promise, but I wasn't going to break mine. We were meant to have a baby, and we did. And then, right away, you were everything to me. You have to believe me that I stopped caring who your father was."

"I don't believe you. You had some sort of a moral competition going. Who's better at keeping promises."

"Things had become so violent and dirty between us. I wanted something purely good to come of it. And something did. You did."

"I am far from purely good."

"No one's really perfect. But to me you were perfect."

This seemed to Pip the right moment to bring up the money, by way of demonstrating her imperfection. She told the story of her visit to Wichita and explained that her mother needed to be in touch with Mr. Navarre. The way her mother shook her head in response was more bewildered than adamant.

"What would I do with a billion dollars?" she said.

"You could start by getting Sonny out to pump the septic tank. I've been lying awake at night worrying about what's in there. Has it *ever* been pumped?"

"It's not a real septic tank. I think the owner made it out of boards and cement."

"That's reassuring."

"The money is meaningless to me, Purity. It's so meaningless that I'm beyond refusing it. It's just—nothing to me."

"My student debt isn't nothing to me. And you're the one who told me not to worry about the money."

"Fine, then. You can ask the lawyer to pay your debt. I won't stop you."

"But it's not my money. You have to be involved."

"I can't be. I never wanted it. It's dirty money. It ruined my family. It killed my mother, it turned my father into a monster. Why would I bring all of that into my life now?"

"Because it's real."

"Nothing is real."

"I'm real."

Her mother nodded. "That's true. You are real to me."

"So here's what I need." Pip ticked off her demands with her fingers. "Student loan paid off in full. Four thousand more to pay off my credit-card debt. Eight hundred thousand to buy Dreyfuss's house and give it back to him. Also, if you insist on staying here, we should buy the cabin and really fix it up. Grad-school tuition if I decide I want that. Monthly living expenses if you want to quit your job. And then maybe another fifty thousand in walking-around money while I try to start a career. The whole thing is less than three million. That's like five percent of one year's dividends."

"From McCaskill, though. McCaskill."

"Their business wasn't only animals. There's got to be at least three million you can take in good conscience."

Her mother was becoming distressed. "Oh, why don't you just take it? All of it! Just take it and leave me alone!"

"Because I'm not allowed to. It's not in my name. As long as you're alive, it's just going to be great expectations for me." Pip laughed. "Why did you start calling me Pip anyway? Was that something else you 'knew all along'?"

"Oh, no, it wasn't me," her mother said eagerly. Pip's childhood was her favorite topic. "It was in kindergarten. Mrs. Steinhauer must have given it to you. Some of the little kids had trouble pronouncing your real name. I guess she thought 'Pip' fit you. There's something happy about the name, and you were always such a happy girl. Or maybe she asked you, and you volunteered it."

"I don't remember that."

"I didn't even know it was your nickname until we had a parent-teacher conference."

"Well, anyway. Someday you'll be gone, and the problem will be mine. But right now it's your money."

Her mother looked at her like a child seeking guidance. "Can't I just give it all away?"

"No. The principal belongs to the trust, not you. You can only give away the dividends. We can find some good animal-welfare groups, responsible-farming groups, things you believe in."

"Yes, that sounds good. Whatever you want."

"Mom, it doesn't matter what I want. This is your problem."

"Oh, I don't care, I don't care," her mother wailed. "I just want it to go away!"

Pip saw that bringing her mother back into firm contact with reality was going to be a long and possibly hopeless project. Nevertheless, she felt that progress had been made, if only in her mother's willingness to take orders from her.

The rain went away, came back, and went away again. When Pip was alone in the cabin, she read books and texted Jason and talked to him on the phone. She liked to sit at the kitchen table so she could watch the pair of brown towhees in the side yard as they foraged in the wet tree litter or perched on fence posts for no apparent reason but to show off how splendid they were. To Pip, no bird could surpass the excellence of brown towhees; in their avian way, they were as excellent as Choco. They were a perfect medium size, more substantial than juncos, more modest than jays. They were neither too shy nor too forward. They liked to be around houses but retreated under shrubs if you disturbed them. They didn't frighten anything except little bugs and her mother. They preferred hopping to flying. They took long and vigorous baths. Except under the tail, where the feathers were peach-colored, and around the face, where there were subtle gray streakings, their plumage was similar in color to Pip's mother's faded brown dress. They had the beauty of the second glance, the beauty that only revealed itself with intimacy. All Pip had ever heard a brown towhee say was *Teek!* But this they said often. The call was sharp and cheerful, like the squeak of a sneaker on a basketball court. It couldn't have been simpler, and yet it seemed to express not only everything that a towhee would ever need to say but everything that really needed to be said by anyone. *Teek!* According to the Internet, brown towhees were rare outside California and unusual in being monogamous and mating for life. Supposedly (Pip had never witnessed this) the male and the female sang a more complicated song in breeding season, a duet that announced to other towhees that he and she were spoken for. Indeed, wherever you saw one towhee, you soon saw the other one. They stayed together in one spot year-round; were Californians. Pip could imagine a whole lot of worse ways of being to aspire to.

As the days went by and the reality of the money sank in, she began to catch glimmerings, in her mother, of the young woman she'd read about in Tom's memoir, the rich girl whose vestigial hauteur was expressing itself again. One night she found her mother scowling at the tired dresses in the tiny closet on the sleeping porch. "I suppose it wouldn't kill me to buy a few new clothes," she said. "You say not all of the money is in McCaskill stock?"

And one morning at the kitchen window, glaring at her neighbor's chicken coop: "Ha. Little does he know that I could not only buy his rooster, I could buy his whole house."

And again one evening, returning from her shift at New

Leaf: "They think I can't afford to quit. But if I catch Serena rolling her eyes at me one more time, I might just do it. Who is she to roll her eyes at me? I don't think she's bathed in a week."

But then, pensively, to Pip, at the dinner table: "How much of my father's money did Tom take? Do you know? That has to be our absolute limit. Not even for you will I ever take more than he took."

"I think it was twenty million dollars."

"Hm. Now that I say that, I'm having new thoughts. I'm afraid I may not be able to take anything, pussycat. Even one dollar is too much. One dollar, twenty million dollars, it's the same thing, morally."

"Mom, we've been through this."

"Maybe the lawyer can pay off your debt. He's certainly done very well for himself."

"You at least have to buy Dreyfuss's house. That was a moral crime, too. A worse one, in my opinion."

"I don't know. I don't know. There is no afterlife. And yet, my father . . . The idea that he might somehow *know* . . . I need to think some more about this."

"No, you don't. You just need to do what I tell you."

Her mother looked at her uncertainly. "You did always have good moral sense."

"I got it from you," Pip said. "So trust it."

Jason was begging her to come home, but there was the pleasure of the mountain rain and the related pleasure of being on new, more honest terms with her mother. To the loving that had always been in Pip was coming a new and unexpected sense of *liking*. Anabel had been likable, at least to Tom, at least in the beginning, and now that her mother was allowed to be Anabel again, to acknowledge her old privilege and dip a toe in her new privilege, to have a bit of an *edge*, Pip could imagine how the two of them might actually be friends.

She also still had a task so daunting that she kept finding fault with every moment when she could have performed it. It took her two weeks to admit to herself that, in fact, no time on no day was a good time to call Tom. She finally chose a Monday at five o'clock in Denver.

"Pip!" Tom said. "I was afraid you'd never call."

"Really. Why's that."

"Leila and I think about you all the time. We miss you."

"Leila misses me. Really. It's not a problem that I'm your daughter?"

"Sorry, hang on. I'm shutting the door."

There was a fumbling, a bonk, a rustle, a clunk.

"Pip, sorry," Tom said. "What are you telling me?"

"I'm telling you I know everything."

"Yikey. OK."

"It's not what you think. I didn't read your document."

"Ah, good. Good. Excellent." Tom's relief was audible.

"I deleted it," she said. "But Andreas told me who you were, before he died. That made the research easy, and then my mom told me everything."

"Jesus. *She* told you. It's amazing you're even speaking to me."

"You are my father."

"I shudder to imagine her version."

"It's better than no story, which is what you gave me."

"That's a fair point. Although sometime I hope you'll give me a chance to tell my side."

"You had your chance."

"True enough. I had my reasons, but it's a fair point. And I'm assuming this is why you called me? To tell me I blew it with you?"

"No. I called because I want you to come out here and see my mother."

Tom laughed. "I'd rather be dropped in the middle of the Congolese civil war."

"You cared enough about her to keep her secret for her."

"I suppose . . . in a sense . . ."

"She obviously still matters to you."

"Pip, listen, I'm very sorry I didn't tell you anything. Leila's been after me to call you. I should have listened to her."

"Well, now I'm telling you how you can make it up to me. You can get on a plane and come out here."

"Why, though? Why would I do that?"

"Because I won't have anything to do with you if you don't."

"I can tell you, from our side, that would be a loss."

"Wouldn't you like to see my mom again anyway? Just once, after all these years? All I'm asking is that you guys forgive each other. I want to be allowed to see both of you, but I can't do it if I feel like I'm betraying one of you whenever I see the other."

"You don't have to feel that way with me. I don't have any claim on you."

"But I have a claim on *you*. And you've never had to do anything for me. This is the one thing I'm asking."

Tom sighed heavily across the time zones. "I don't suppose there's any liquor in your mother's house?"

"I'll make sure there's liquor."

"And we're talking—when? Next month?"

"No. This week. Maybe Friday. The longer you guys think about it, the worse it will get."

Again Tom sighed. "I could do Thursday. My Friday nights are for Leila."

Pip felt a twinge of resentment and was tempted to insist on Friday. But the road back to friendship with Leila was looking long enough already.

"One other thing," she said.

"Yep," Tom said.

"I've been looking at DI every week. I keep thinking you'll do a big story about Andreas."

"He wasn't well, Pip. I saw him at the end, I saw him go over the cliff. The only thing I feel is sadness. Leila's annoyed by the postmortem adulation, but I find it hard to begrudge him. He was the most remarkable person I ever met."

"The *Express* is still waiting for me to write something about him. I feel the same thing you do, sadness. But I also feel like somebody should tell the real story."

"About the murder? It's your call. One of the costs would be the girl, the one who helped him. There could still be legal consequences for her."

"I hadn't thought of that."

"But he left a confession, which his people covered up. There's definitely a story if you want to pursue it."

Was Tom also worried about his own complicity in the murder coming to light? Probably not, if he believed that Pip hadn't read his memoir.

"OK," she said. "Thank you."

When her mother returned from work, Pip explained to her what had to happen. She was relieved that her mother didn't immediately have a meltdown. But the reason she didn't was that the entire concept made no sense to her.

"What on earth did *I* ever do that needs to be forgiven?"

"Um—had me and didn't tell him? That's pretty big."

"How can he blame me for that? He abandoned me. He never wanted to hear from me again. *And I gave him that.* Like everything else. He always got everything he wanted. Just like my father."

"Still, at some point, you should have let him know about me. On my eighteenth birthday, whatever. It was wrong of you not to. It was spiteful."

Her mother huffed and puffed at this, but finally she

nodded. "If you say so," she said. "And only because it's you saying it."

"Weak people hold grudges, Mom. Strong people forgive. You raised me all by yourself. You said no to the money that everyone else in your family couldn't resist. And you were stronger than Tom. You put an end to it—he couldn't do it. You got everything *you* wanted. You won! And that's why you can afford to forgive him. Because you won. Right?"

Her mother frowned.

"You're also a billionaire," Pip said. "That's a kind of winning, too."

The next morning they rode the bus into Santa Cruz. It was a clear cold morning between storms. Homeless people were wearing their sleeping bags like shawls, Christmas bows were shivering on lampposts, the sky was full of wheeling seagulls. A hairdresser at Jillz trimmed Pip's mother's hair in a flurry of split ends. Then Pip took her for a manicure, and it was Anabel, not her old mother, who instructed the Vietnamese manicurist not to cut her cuticles, Anabel who explained to Pip that cutting cuticles was a racket, because they grew back quickly and needed to be cut again. It was Anabel who briskly worked through racks of dresses, through store after store, and continued to reject things long after Pip's own patience was exhausted. The dress that she finally deemed "adequate" was vintage and full-skirted, sexy in a prairie-schoolteacher way, with twin lines of buttons on the bodice. Pip had to admit that it was the most suitable dress they'd seen all morning.

She'd asked Jason to get a Zipcar and fetch Tom from the San Jose airport, so that she could stand guard over her mother and try to keep her calm. "Bring Choco, too," she said.

"He'll just be in the way," Jason said.

"I want him in the way. Otherwise my mom's going to

focus on her freak-out. She'll meet you, she'll meet Choco, and, oh yeah, here's the ex she hasn't seen in twenty-five years."

On Thursday morning, another storm arrived. By late afternoon the rain was drumming so hard on the roof that Pip and her mother had to raise their voices. Darkness had fallen early, and the lights had flickered several times. Pip had prepared a bean soup and laid in other supplies, including ingredients for a Manhattan. After her mother had showered, Pip applied a blow-dryer to her hair, brushing it and fluffing it. "Let's give you some makeup, too."

Her mother muttered, "Why I'm dolling myself up like this . . ."

"You're putting on armor. You want to be strong."

"I can put on my own mascara."

"Let me do it. It was something I never got to do with you."

At five o'clock, while Pip was lighting a fire, Jason called to report that he and Tom were stuck in traffic near Los Gatos. Her mother, sitting on the sofa, was looking altogether very good in her vintage dress, like the older Anabel she was, but she was doing her rocking thing, her mildly autistic thing. "You should have a glass of wine," Pip said.

"I feel betrayed by my Endeavor. The time I most need it . . . where is it?"

"Endeavor to drink some wine."

"It will go straight to my head."

"Good."

When the Zipcar finally came up the lane, its wipers laboring hard, its headlights making a white fury of the downpour, Pip left the side porch where she'd been waiting and ran, under an umbrella, to greet Jason. He looked a little harrowed by the drive, but his first thought was her first thought, which was to lock lips. Then Choco barked, and Pip opened the car's rear door and let him lick her face.

Tom emerged from the car tentatively, umbrella first. Pip thanked him for coming and kissed his meaty cheek. Somehow in the fifteen feet between car and front door Choco managed to get not only soaked but covered with wet redwood needles. He squeezed past Pip and ran inside. Her mother raised her arms, as if to ward him off, and gazed with dismay at the needles and muddy paw prints on the floor.

"Sorry, sorry," Pip said.

She corralled Choco and led him back onto the side porch, where Tom was scuffing his feet. "That is the most hilarious dog I've seen in my entire life," he said.

"You like him?"

"Love him. Want him."

They went inside, followed by Jason. Her mother, by the woodstove, wringing her hands, shyly raised her eyes to look at Tom. It was clear to Pip that both of them were struggling not to smile. But they couldn't help smiling anyway; both of them, broadly.

" 'Hello, Anabel.' "

" 'Hello, Tom.' "

"So, Mom," Pip said, "this is Jason. Jason, my mom."

As if in a trance, her mother turned away from Tom and nodded to Jason. "Hello."

Jason gave her a kind of vaudevillian two-handed wave and said, "Hey."

"So, like I said," Pip said, "just a quick H and G here. We'll come back after dinner."

"You're sure you won't stay?" Tom said anxiously.

"No, you guys need to talk. If there's anything left to drink later, we'll help you drink it."

Before any entanglement could develop, Pip hurried Jason outside. Choco was so long and the side porch so narrow that he couldn't turn around to make way for them but had to skitter backward. "Can we leave him here?" she asked Jason.

"I brought his porta-bowl and lemons."

Pip had intended to give her parents two hours alone, but in the event it was closer to four. First she and Jason had to go to the state park and make love in the back seat. Then, when they'd managed to get their pants back on, they had to take them off and do it again. After that they had dinner at Don Quixote's, where a local cover band, Shady Characters, was playing. Just when it was time to be leaving, the band launched into a must-dance song, the soul-sister song.

"Hate the lyrics," Jason said, dancing. "Hate the cooptation for a car commercial. And yet—"

"Great song," Pip said, dancing.

They danced for half an hour while the rain came down and the San Lorenzo rose. Jason was a silly dancer, a thinking dancer, and Pip loved that he could do what he did and she could do what she did, which was not think, just move, just be happy in her body. When they finally went outside, the rain had paused and the roads were end-of-the-world empty. Driving up her mother's lane, they saw Choco standing on the cabin's side porch, a lemon in his mouth, his tail swishing in its complex way. Jason let the car roll to a stop in the driveway.

"So," Pip said. "Here goes."

"Are you sure I can't just stay in the car?"

"You're getting to know the parents. These are the parents."

But as soon as she opened her door, she heard the voices. The shouting. The sound of raw hatred. It was coming right through the cabin's thin walls.

I did not say that! If you're going to fucking quote me, quote me accurately! What I said was—

I'm telling you the DISGUSTING SUBTEXT of what you said. You hide behind what everyone agrees is normal, you get the whole world on your side that way, but you know in your heart that there's a deeper truth—

The deep truth that I'm wrong and you're right? That's the only deep truth you ever knew!

You know it yourself!

You just ADMITTED that you have no case! That there isn't another person on earth who thinks you have a case—

But I do and you know it! You know it!

Pip shut the door again, to block out the words, but even with the door closed she could hear the fighting. The people who'd bequeathed a broken world to her were shouting at each other viciously. Jason sighed and took her hand. She held it tightly. It had to be possible to do better than her parents, but she wasn't sure she would. Only when the skies opened again, the rain from the immense dark western ocean pounding on the car roof, the sound of love drowning out the other sound, did she believe that she might.